I could swear I heard trouble outside my door.

My hand slipped reflexively beneath my pillow to grip the *kwi* I always kept within reach. The *kwi* was a weapon I'd conned out of the Chahwyn, a relic they'd dug up from the days of the Shonkla-raa war. An elegantly nonlethal weapon, it was capable of delivering three levels of pain, or three levels of unconsciousness, to anyone within its somewhat limited range.

There was, unfortunately, one catch: the *kwi* was telepathically activated, which meant I needed Bayta or a Spider to turn the damn thing on for me.

Which meant that if there was trouble coming through my door, I would need to bellow Bayta awake through our dividing wall and hope she got the message before someone tried to strangle me in my bed—

"Frank?" Bayta's voice came out of the darkness, tense and hurried and scared. "Frank, there's trouble. The Spiders want us in third class right away."

"What is it?" I asked, feeling a flicker of relief as I swung my legs out from under the blanket and grabbed for my clothes.

"It's one of the Shorshians," she said. "He's come down sick."

I paused, shirt in hand. She'd barged in on me for *this*? "So have them call a doctor," I growled.

"The doctors are already there," she said, her voice shaking, "and they say he's not just sick.

"He's been poisoned."

Praise for *Odd Girl Out*

"[Zahn's] characters and settings are engaging, and he's comfortable enough with the genre's conventions to make Compton's return worth opening up on a night when the mean streets beckon in the mind."
—*Starlog*

the DOMINO PATTERN

TIMOTHY ZAHN

A TOM DOHERTY ASSOCIATES BOOK  NEW YORK

THE DOMINO PATTERN

Edited by James Frenkel

A Tor Book
Published by Tom Doherty Associates, LLC
175 Fifth Avenue
New York, NY 10010

www.tor-forge.com

Tor® is a registered trademark of Tom Doherty Associates, LLC.

ISBN 978-0-7653-6193-6

First Edition: January 2010
First Mass Market Edition: September 2010

Printed in the United States of America

0 9 8 7 6 5 4 3 2 1

For the Fedukowskis:
Readers, teachers, analysts, Scrabblers

the DOMINO pattern

ONE :

Space, as some twentieth-century philosopher succinctly put it, is big. Really big. So big that even a single medium-sized galaxy, such as our own Milky Way, has plenty of room to be pretty damn huge all by itself.

So huge that even at a Quadrail train's incredible speed of a light-year per minute, if you followed the curve of the spiral arms it would take well over three months to get from one end of the galaxy's populated regions to the other.

Three months is a long time for business moguls of the Twelve Empires, who can make or lose millions in a single day. It's even longer for the galaxy's politicians, who can gain or lose a lot more than that, including both their careers and their skins.

Thus it was that, a few hundred years ago, when the Spiders and their secretive Chahwyn masters began building their multiple light-years of Tube across the voids of interstellar space, they looked for a way to shorten the cross-galaxy trip.

And they found one.

In theory, the super-express lines weren't any different from the rest of the Spiders' vast interstellar travel network. Inside each Tube were several sets of the Spiders' signature four-rail tracks on which all Quadrail trains ran. Down the geometric center of the Tube ran the Coreline, a brightly coruscating inner cylinder that was the actual driving force behind the light-year-per-minute speeds the trains could make, though that fact was a closely guarded secret.

In practice, though, there was something especially impressive, and especially disturbing, about the super-express system. A typical Quadrail train made frequent stops as it journeyed among the stars, rolling into station after station to drop one set of passengers and pick up the next. Even the express trains, which blew straight through the smaller stations without stopping, still gave their passengers those brief views of new scenery, new places, and new people.

That wasn't the case with the super-express lines. There were no stations at all between the Jurian Homshil system and the Shorshian system of Venidra Carvo, some sixty-two thousand light-years away on the other side of the galaxy. That meant nothing to break the visual monotony of gray, Coreline-lit Tube wall for six long weeks, nothing to show that you and your fellow passengers weren't in fact the only people left in the universe.

And if trouble of any sort broke out, there would literally be no place for anyone to run.

All this flicked with unpleasant clarity through my mind as the Quadrail super-express train left the maintenance area at the far end of Homshil Station and rolled toward our platform. It was a long train, at fifty cars nearly twice the length of a normal Quadrail. From the data chip I'd read I knew that roughly a quarter of those cars were devoted to baggage and cargo, supplementing the usual cargo trains that traveled this route. There were also extra food-storage cars, entertainment and exercise cars for all three travel classes, and other cars devoted entirely to shower and laundry facilities.

In many ways, in fact, the whole thing was less like a normal Quadrail train than it was a long, segmented ocean cruise liner.

A cruise liner in which we were about to be stuck for six long weeks.

"It'll be all right," Bayta said quietly.

I looked at the young woman beside me. Her dark brown hair glinted in the Coreline's coruscating light show, and her equally dark eyes were steady on my face. Bayta had been my constant companion, fellow soldier, and friend for the many months since I'd been coopted into this quiet little war of ours. "Of course it will," I agreed, keeping my voice light. "Why, do I look worried or something?"

One of her eyebrows twitched. "Six weeks locked inside a Quadrail?" she countered pointedly.

I looked back at the incoming train, suppressing a grimace. I knew I didn't *look* worried—I had better control of my face than that. But Bayta had been with me long enough to be able to read beneath the surface.

"We don't have to do this," she went on quietly. "There are regular express trains that travel mostly through the inhabited regions. We could just stick to those."

"And double the transit time?" I shook my head. "No. Six weeks is bad enough as it is."

She didn't reply. But then, she didn't have to. I'd been with her long enough to know how to read *her,* too, and I knew we were thinking the same unpleasant thoughts.

Because our enemy in this war, the group mind that called

himself the Modhri, also liked to ride the Quadrail. He also typically targeted the galaxy's rich and powerful, which meant there was likely to be a Modhran mind segment in the first-class section of the train we were about to board.

And the Modhri very much wanted both Bayta and me dead.

I couldn't really blame him. The Modhri was, bottom line, nothing more or less than a sentient weapon, designed a millennium and a half ago to be the ultimate infiltrator/spy/saboteur/fifth-columnist by a slaver race called the Shonkla-raa, who had been in absolute control of the galaxy and its sentient inhabitants for nearly a thousand years.

Though at the time of the Modhri's creation, they hadn't been much in control of anything. In fact, they had been fighting for their survival against a carefully crafted rebellion being carried out by an alliance of their slaves.

Unfortunately for the Shonkla-raa, the revolt had ended in their destruction before the Modhri could be deployed. Unfortunately for the rest of us, the Modhri hadn't simply died off. He'd lived on, waiting patiently until the Halkas had stumbled on his homeworld a couple of hundred years ago and found the exotic coral in which lurked the polyps that comprised his physical structure.

Decorative coral being what it is, and economics being what *it* is, the Halkas had ended up selling, trading, and otherwise distributing the damn stuff across the whole galaxy. Unfortunately, one touch of unprotected skin against that coral was enough to pick up a few polyp hooks, which eventually grew into full polyps and then a polyp colony, settling in at the base of the victim's brain. Once there, the new Modhran mind segment could watch and listen through his new walker's senses, whispering suggestions to guide the person's actions in order to benefit whatever the Modhri's goals were at a given moment. Should the mood strike him, the Modhri could also take complete control of his unwitting host's body, blacking out the host's own consciousness and leaving him only a puzzling memory gap when it was all over.

The Modhri's ultimate goal was to fill the galaxy with himself, which meant filling the galaxy with walkers. And up to now, he'd been doing pretty well for himself.

Or he had until the Spiders had tumbled to his existence. There'd been some false starts and some false assumptions, on both sides, as to exactly what was going on. But that had all been sorted out, and as of right now we all pretty much knew where we stood.

On paper, at least, where we stood was pretty depressing. On one side were the Modhran coral outposts, thousands of them, and his coopted walker allies, thousands if not millions of them. On the other side were the Spiders and the Chahwyn, species which were both constitutionally incapable of actual fighting, plus a handful of individuals who didn't have any such psychological shortcomings.

Two of that handful were Bayta and me.

The odds were frankly ridiculous. But despite that, Bayta and I and our allies had done remarkably well. Our latest trick, pulling a young Human girl named Rebekah and her wild-card cargo out from under the Modhri's collective nose on the Human colony world of New Tigris, had been one of our greatest successes, and had no doubt irritated the Modhri no end.

Wherein lay the problem. There *would* be a Modhran mind segment on our train—that was pretty much guaranteed. And once Bayta and I stepped aboard that train there would be nowhere we could go for the next six weeks. Nowhere to run, nowhere to hide, and my Beretta 5mm pistol buried away in a lockbox somewhere underneath the train.

And six weeks was more than enough time for the Modhri, should he be so inclined, to plan and carry out a couple of murders. Such as, say, those of Bayta and me.

The train was nearly to the platform now, and I took a moment to look up and down the line of our fellow passengers. One would expect that a super-express heading toward Filiaelian and Shorshic territory would mostly draw Filiaelians and Shorshians, and indeed those two species comprised nearly half our passenger list. But there were quite a few other species represented, as well: bulldog-faced Halkas, iguana-like Juriani with hawk beaks and clawed fingers, a few pear-shaped Cimmaheem, and even a couple of groups of delicately featured Tra'ho'seej.

More surprisingly, there were quite a few Humans, as well. I spotted at least three groups of four or five each, plus several couples and a healthy scattering of unattached individuals. Either something particularly interesting was about to happen at the far end of the galaxy, or else the Filly and Shorshic tourist bureaus were running some kind of tourism special.

Most of the Humans were down the line to our left in the second- and third-class sections of the platform. But there was at least one other besides Bayta and me waiting here for the first-class cars. He was middle-aged, with thinning salt-and-pepper hair, standing with his back to us as he conferred quietly with a group of four Fillies. Some top-level business executive, I concluded from the cut of his suit, or possibly an academic on a sabbatical exchange program.

There was the screech of multiple sets of brakes, and the train rolled to a stop. Directly in front of us was the middle of the three first-class compartment cars, the one in which Bayta and I had booked our usual double room. All along the train the doors irised open, and a line of seven-legged conductor Spiders stepped onto the platform, settling into their standard Buckingham Palace guard stances.

[All aboard Trans-Galactic Quadrail 1077 to Venidra Carvo of the Shorshic Congregate,] they announced in Juric, as always using the local language. For the rest of us, a multilanguage holodisplay with the same information floated above the train. [Departure in thirty-three minutes.]

This was it. Squaring my shoulders, reminding myself that so far we'd been able to handle anything the Modhri threw at us, I started toward the door.

And stopped short as the back of a hand suddenly pressed imperiously against my right shoulder. "Excuse us," a voice said tartly. "Coming through. Excuse us, please."

I turned to look. The owner of the hand was the middle-aged Human I'd seen talking to the four Fillies. Along with his salt-and-pepper hair, I saw now that he had a slightly bushy mustache, cut in the style currently in vogue among middle-level corporate drones. He was about my height, running a little to fat beneath his traveling suit. Confidence and authority and calm arrogance wrapped around him like a rain cloak.

His eyes flicked to me, sized me up and dismissed me in that single glance, and moved on. The pressure of the back of his hand vanished as he passed me by, still warning the rest of our fellow passengers to give him room as he ushered his four Fillies toward the door.

A few meters down from me, one of the waiting Juriani muttered something about decorum and proper procedure. But no one else seemed inclined to raise any objections. In fact, I spotted several of the passengers moving aside of their own accord.

The deference didn't surprise me. Depending on who was doing the counting, the Filiaelian Assembly was either the biggest or second-biggest of the Twelve Empires, with an overall power, prestige, and influence to match. Individual Fillies, in my admittedly limited experience, didn't pull rank all that often. But when they did, you could bet that everyone else in the vicinity was ready, willing, and eager to cut them the necessary slack.

But it wasn't Filiaelian prestige or influence that was suddenly sending shivers up my back, but the fact that the Modhri's shock front for our most recent operation against him had been a group of these self-same Fillies.

I looked at Bayta, noting the tightness around her eyes as she watched the procession. Granted, all Fillies looked somewhat alike, as did all Bellidos and all Halkas and all Humans. And I certainly had no reason at the moment to suspect that this group had anything whatsoever to do with the Modhri.

On the other hand, up until a few weeks ago we'd been under the impression that the Modhri hadn't penetrated Filly society at all. Our main purpose for this trip, in fact, was to take a run out to the Ilat Dumar Covrey system, where those six Modhran-controlled Fillies had come from, to see if we could find out what was going on out there.

The first of the four Fillies reached the door; and just as he started aboard, I saw their Human escort's shoulders twitch. He paused there, gesturing the rest of the group forward.

And as he did so, he casually turned back around for another look at me.

He held the look no more than half a second before turning back to his charges. But it was more than enough. He had recognized me, and the recognition hadn't been friendly.

Problem was, I didn't recognize *him*.

"Interesting," Bayta murmured.

I looked at her, wondering if she'd caught the man's reaction. But her eyes were on the four Fillies. "You think they're associated with our friends?" I asked, keeping my voice low. No telling which of the other passengers waiting their turn to board might be Modhran walkers.

"I don't know," Bayta said. "I was just noticing that none of the other Filiaelians seemed to mind letting those four push their way aboard first."

I looked around. Focused first on the Fillies, and then on their Human associate, I'd completely missed the audience's reaction to the little drama.

Bayta was right. All six of the other Fillies waiting to board our car were silently standing by, with no hint of impatience or annoyance on their long, horse-like faces. That probably implied the other four Fillies were even more upper-crust than the rest of us, though what the clues to that status were I didn't know.

What I did know was that the Modhri worked especially hard to get into the Twelve Empires' upper-upper crusts.

Terrific.

The four Fillies disappeared into the train, their luggage obediently rolling through the door behind them, followed by the Human and his three bags. Only then did the rest of the waiting Fillies make an orderly surge for the door.

I hung back, partly out of respect, mostly so I could watch the order in which the Fillies sorted themselves out. But as with the first four, the pecking-order cues they were using were too subtle for me to figure out.

When we ran out of Fillies, I let the waiting Shorshians, Halkas, and Juriani board. Then, with our section of the platform finally empty, I nudged Bayta ahead of me and we headed in.

I'd rather expected our double compartment to be different from those on standard Quadrail trains: a bit larger, or at the very least a bit more plush. But it looked very much the same as every other first-class compartment we'd traveled in over the past months. The luggage rack above the bed was longer, and there was an extra underbed drawer, both clearly put there with the assumption that passengers here would be traveling with larger wardrobes. But aside from that, the layout was the same. Super-express trains might include a plethora of extra cars, but the basic passenger accommodations had largely been left alone.

But there was *something* about the compartment that seemed subtly different. I took a couple of turns around the small room, studying the bed, the lounge chair and swivel computer, the curve couch, and the half-bath as I tried to figure it out.

And then it hit me. The compartment smelled fresher. Fresher, cleaner, and somehow more sprightly.

I stepped to the display window and looked out. The tracks in the super-express Tube were arranged slightly differently from those in ordinary Tubes. There were only six main tracks, for one thing, with the Tube itself being correspondingly somewhat narrower. A set of auxiliary service tracks paralleled each of the main tracks about five meters to the right, which the official brochure said were for tenders and other emergency equipment. That made a certain amount of sense, given the thousands of light-years we were about to traverse without a single station along the way.

Still, I couldn't help feeling an ominous undertone to the emergency-vehicle idea. I'd never heard of a Quadrail engine failing during a run, but just because it never had didn't mean it never would, and with my luck it would probably happen on a train I happened to be aboard at the time. It would be bad enough riding for six weeks with a Modhran mind segment without throwing in an extra week sitting dead on the tracks waiting for a new engine to be brought up.

There was a subtle puff of displaced air, and I turned to see the wall separating my compartment from Bayta's sliding open. The curve couches on either side folded into the wall as it collapsed, the whole thing depositing itself neatly into the narrow space between our half-baths.

Bayta was standing by the computer chair in her compartment, gazing out the display window at the crowds milling around Homshil Station's platforms. "What do you think?" she asked.

"About the compartment?" I asked. "Very nice. Smells fresh off the assembly line. Do they just build these trains from scratch when they need one?"

"There are a few hours scheduled between cross-galactic arrivals and departures," she said, still looking out the window. "The Spiders need time to unload and reload the cargo cars and to restock the food and supply areas. Because of that, there's time for a complete cleaning of the passenger spaces instead of just making do with the regular self-cleaning systems."

She turned to look at me. "But that wasn't what I meant. I meant what do you think of this idea now?"

"What do you want me to say?" I asked. "That I suddenly feel happy to be aboard? I don't. But I still don't see any practical alternative."

"Not even with that man aboard?" she asked. "The one who recognized you?"

I grimaced. "I was hoping you'd missed that."

Her eyebrows went up. "You were *hoping* I'd missed it?"

"Only because I knew you'd worry, and that there was nothing we could do about it," I hastened to assure her.

"Except maybe find out from the Spiders who he is before we leave the station?" she countered tartly.

"Touché," I admitted. "Okay. Who is he?"

She took a deep breath, and I could see her forcing herself to calm down. Even that mild touch of annoyance was more of an emotional display than she usually seemed comfortable with. "His ticket's under the name Whitman Kennrick," she told me. "He boarded the Quadrail at Terra Station, ultimate destination the Filiaelian Assembly system of Rentis Tarlay Birim."

"What about his four Filly buddies?" I asked, pulling out my reader and plugging in the encyclopedia data chip. "Did they all come aboard together, or did he meet up with them somewhere between Terra and Homshil?"

Bayta's eyes went distant, and I took the opportunity to punch *Rentis Tarlay Birim* into my reader and give the resulting page a quick skim. Back in Western Alliance Intelligence, where I'd once worked, there had been people—mostly the pompous and control-freak ones—who'd felt it necessary to create permanent links to their phones or data feeds. The affectation had always irritated me, especially when they went blank in the middle of intense conversations, and I sometimes wondered why Bayta's version of the same thing wasn't equally irritating.

Probably because it was a completely different situation. Bayta hadn't chosen to be wired into the Spiders' telepathic network; it was just something that came with the fact that she was a Human/Chahwyn melding. She could no more shut off that link than she could stop breathing.

Besides, the ability not only provided us with useful information but had saved our lives more than once. When you had an ace up your sleeve, it was the epitome of pettiness to complain that it chafed a little against your skin.

"The Filiaelians also came aboard at Terra," Bayta reported, her eyes coming back to focus. "Though that doesn't necessarily mean all of them already knew each other."

"True," I agreed. First-class Quadrail cars were one of the galaxy's great social mixers. Kennrick and the Fillies could easily have struck up a conversation and ended up twenty-one hours later as best-friend traveling companions, especially once they'd discovered they were all going cross-galaxy together. "What's the Fillies' destination?"

"The same place," Bayta said. "The same system, anyway. They could be traveling to entirely different places inside that system once they leave the Tube."

"There are certainly enough for them to choose from," I commented, gesturing toward my reader. "Rentis Tarlay Birim is a major industrial and manufacturing system, with three in-habited planets, five orbiting space colonies, and a truckload of minable asteroids. No way to know what Kennrick might be looking for there."

"You know who he is, then?" Bayta asked.

"Not a clue," I admitted, shutting off the reader and putting it away.

"Someone from your past, maybe?"

"What's this, the old 'your past coming back to haunt you' routine?" I scoffed. "That works okay in old dit rec dramas, but not so much in real life. As long as you've got the stationmaster on the line, how about checking to see if any of the passengers are planning to change trains to the Ilat Dumar Covrey system like we are after we hit Venidra Carvo."

Bayta's eyes defocused again. "No, no one," she reported. "At least, no one's carrying a multiple-leg ticket for that station."

"Good enough," I said. Though with thousands of Filly systems to choose from, the odds that someone on our train would be matching our ultimate destination had been pretty slim in the first place. "Thanks."

"You're welcome," she said. "*Do* you think Mr. Kennrick could be someone from your past?"

"I suppose that's possible," I said. So much for trying to deflect her interest away from Kennrick. I should have known it wouldn't work. "I wouldn't worry about it, though."

"You really mean that?" Bayta asked pointedly. "Or are you saying that *I* shouldn't worry about it?"

"Neither of us should worry," I said firmly. "Besides, we'll know soon enough who he is and what he's doing here."

Bayta gave me a wary look. "What are you going to do?"

"Don't worry, I'm not going to kick in his door or crash his next dinner party," I assured her. "But hey, we're all here on the same train. Sooner or later, I'm sure an opportunity will present itself."

But for the first two weeks, it didn't.

That alone was surprising. Surprising, and more than a little ominous. Quadrail trains, while larger than their Terran counterparts, were hardly the size of Class AA torchliners. More significantly, they were laid out linearly, without the kind of multiple pathways that could allow a couple of torchliner passengers to endlessly chase each other in circles.

The lack of contact with Kennrick wasn't from lack of trying on my part, either. I spent hours at a time wandering through the first-class areas of the train, checking the restaurant and bar and the entertainment and exercise facilities, without ever catching so much as a glimpse of our mystery man.

Through Bayta, I tried instructing the conductor Spiders to keep an eye on Kennrick's door when they weren't busy with other duties. But the two times I got word that he'd left his compartment he managed to disappear again before I could get there.

At one point, I lost my temper and ordered the Spiders to search the entire damn train for him. But the conductors and servers were no better than any other Spiders at distinguishing between Humans, and all my demand did was waste their time and irritate Bayta.

Otherwise, Bayta and I occupied ourselves as best we could. We watched dit rec dramas and comedies on our computers, ate far too much good food, and did our best to work off those indulgences in the exercise room. Often we had the facility to ourselves, as most of the other first-class passengers were older than we were, light-years richer, and had apparently decided they were beyond anything as plebeian and vulgar as sweat and strain.

It was late at night at the beginning of our third week of travel, and I was lying awake in the dark trying to come up with a new strategy for cornering Kennrick, when I felt a subtle puff of air across my face.

My hand slipped reflexively beneath my pillow to grip the *kwi* I always kept within reach. The *kwi* was a weapon I'd conned out of the Chahwyn, a relic they'd dug up from the days of the Shonkla-raa war. An elegantly nonlethal weapon, it was capable of delivering three levels of pain, or three levels of unconsciousness, to anyone within its somewhat limited range.

There was, unfortunately, one catch: the *kwi* was telepathically activated, which meant I needed Bayta or a Spider to turn the damn thing on for me.

Which meant that if the puff of air I'd felt meant there was trouble coming through my door, I would need to bellow

Bayta awake through our dividing wall and hope she got the message before someone tried to strangle me in my bed—

"Frank?" Bayta's voice came out of the darkness, tense and hurried and scared. "Frank, there's trouble. The Spiders want us in third class right away."

"What is it?" I asked, feeling a flicker of relief as I swung my legs out from under the blanket and grabbed for my clothes.

"It's one of the Shorshians," she said. "He's come down sick."

I paused, shirt in hand. She'd barged in on me for *this*? "So have them call a doctor," I growled.

"The doctors are already there," she said, her voice shaking, "and they say he's not just sick.

"He's been poisoned."

TWO :

I'd been about to toss my shirt back onto my clothes stack. Now, instead, I started pulling it on.

Poisons couldn't be brought aboard Quadrail trains. They just *couldn't*. The same huge station-based sensor arrays that sniffed out weapons and weapon components did an equally efficient job of screening out poisons. All sorts of poisons, and all known varieties of poison-producing flora and fauna. The sensors also looked for every known type of dangerous bacteria, viruses, and other microorganisms. The Shorshian back there simply couldn't have been poisoned.

But some doctor apparently thought he had. Either we had an incompetent quack aboard, or there was a serious problem.

All Quadrail trains came equipped with a couple of small dispensaries, typically tucked in at one end of the first-class and second/third-class dining cars. The server Spider on duty there could do little except dole out an assortment of general-purpose medicines, but there was usually at least one doctor aboard any given train who could be brought on in a medical emergency. In exchange for putting their names on the on-call list, doctors got a sizable discount on their tickets.

Here, instead of being an add-on to the dining car, the second/third dispensary took up a section of the exercise car. Like everything else on the super-express, it was also larger than usual. The glass-fronted drug cabinet was over twice the size of an ordinary one, and in place of the usual examination chair was a Fibibib-designed diagnostic/treatment table.

Bayta and I arrived to find a small crowd already assembled. There were a pair of Shorshians, hovering nervously in the back of the small room, their dolphin snouts silently opening and closing, their smooth skin rippling with little crescent-shaped goose bumps. At the back of the room on the other side, a petite server Spider was silently watching the proceedings. Standing on opposite sides of the treatment table were a white-haired Human male and a Filiaelian female with a graying brown blaze down her long face. The Human was holding a biosensor with one hand while he thumbed ampoules from a dispenser with the other. The Filly was taking the ampoules from him and feeding them into a hypo.

And in the center of attention, lying unnaturally still on the table, was the patient.

A person who had somehow dropped out of the sky from an entirely different galaxy and who had never seen a Shorshian in his life would still have recognized instantly that this one wasn't well. Someone like me, who'd had the standard Western Alliance Intelligence course in Shorshic culture, psychology, and physiology could see just as instantly that he was in a seriously bad way.

In fact, unless the two doctors could pull a rabbit out of their hat, I was pretty sure he was dying.

I eased toward the table for a closer look. The Shorshian's

skin was mottled, its black/gray/off-white color scheme mixed together like tiny tiles that had been thrown randomly on the floor instead of forming the smooth, flowing patterns that were the Shorshic norm. His breathing was labored, and there was some kind of mucus seeping from his nostrils and the corners of his mouth. I took another step forward, trying for a closer look.

"Get back," the Human doctor ordered me brusquely, not looking up from his work.

"Sorry," I murmured, and retreated back to Bayta's side. I looked over at the other two Shorshians, hoping to catch their attention. But they only had eyes for their downed comrade. Behind me, I heard a set of rapid footsteps approaching.

And I turned just as the elusive Whitman Kennrick hurried into the dispensary, his hair wild and unkempt, his clothes looking like they'd been thrown on by a paint spreader, his eyes with the half-lidded look of someone not yet fully awake. His throat was tight, and he was breathing almost as heavily as the patient. His eyes flicked to the table, the doctors, and the other two Shorshians.

And then he spotted Bayta and me.

Back on the Homshil Station platform, it had taken him a couple of seconds to make a connection with my face. This time, there was no such delay. His puffy eyes widened, and he skidded to a halt, reversed direction, and vanished out into the corridor.

I nearly knocked Bayta over as I charged out of the dispensary after him. "Hold it!" I called softly at his retreating back. "Kennrick!"

For a half dozen steps I thought he was going to ignore me, and that I would have to literally run him down and tackle him. Then, reluctantly, he slowed to a halt and turned around. "What do you want?" he asked, his voice halfway between sullen and wary.

"For starters, a little decorum," I said as I strode up to him. "Second-class passengers may not be as coddled as we are up in first, but they get just as cranky if they're woken up by a foot-race through their car."

"What do you *want?*" he repeated.

"A couple of answers," I said. "Let's start with who exactly you are."

A frown creased his forehead. "Whitman Kennrick," he said. "You just *said* that, remember?"

"And it tells me nothing," I said. "Let's try again: who *are* you?"

He searched my face another couple of beats, as if looking for a trap he knew had to be in there somewhere. "Eleven years ago," he said at last. "Shotoko Associates."

"Okay," I said. Shotoko Associates I remembered: an international law firm that had more or less unknowingly ended up as the base of operations of one of the more brazen spies Westali had taken down during my years with the agency. "So?"

A flicker of genuine surprise replaced his frown. "What do you mean, *so?* You were there. In fact, you were running the raid."

"Hardly," I said. "Senior Investigator Hartwell was the agent in charge. I was just one of the people she pulled in for rabbit-hole duty."

"Really," he said, again searching my face. "Well, you and your people missed one."

"You?"

"Yes," Kennrick said. "Not that I was anyone you actually wanted, of course."

"Of course not," I said. "You were just one of the dupes DuNoeva was using as cover for his operation."

"Not exactly the way I would have put it," Kennrick said sourly. "But basically correct."

"So why did you run?" I asked. "I'm assuming here that you *did* run."

"Of course I ran," he growled. "I didn't want to spend six months and a mountain of attorneys' fees defending myself from false charges."

"Charges like assaulting a couple of federal officers?" I asked pointedly.

He seemed to draw back a little. "What are you talking about? I never assaulted anyone."

"*Somebody* did," I said. "The men we had watching the east door were taken out sometime during the raid. One of them was DOA, the other died a few hours later without regaining consciousness."

"Hey, that wasn't me," Kennrick protested. "That *was* the door I left by, but I swear there was no one there when I went through." His eyes flicked around us, as if he was suddenly remembering where we were. "But I don't have to care what you think, do I?" he said. "You don't have any jurisdiction here."

Which begged the question of why he'd been evading me for the past two weeks and why he'd beat such a hasty exit from the dispensary just now. Maybe fugitive habits simply die hard. "Actually, I don't have any jurisdiction anywhere," I said. "I left Westali quite a while ago. Who's your Shorshic friend?"

The sudden change of subject seemed to throw him off-track. A slightly confused expression rolled across his face before his brain caught up with him. "He's a business associate," he said. His eyes flicked over my shoulder, as if he was suddenly remembering why he'd dragged himself out of bed at this ungodly hour in the first place. "Part of a contract team my employer brought to Earth for some consultations. I need to get back to him and the others."

"Certainly," I said. Stepping aside, I gestured him back toward the dispensary.

Warily, he slid past me. I let him go, then fell into step beside him. "This employer being . . . ?" I asked.

He threw me a sideways look. "Pellorian Medical Systems," he said. "Not that it's any of your business."

"What kind of consultations?"

"We were discussing genetic manipulation equipment and technique," he said impatiently.

"Ah," I said. That explained the four Fillies he'd been shepherding back at Homshil, anyway. The Filiaelians were enthusiastic proponents of genetic engineering and manipulation of all sorts, on everything up to and including themselves. Especially including themselves. "And so now, like a good host, you're walking them home?"

He didn't answer, but merely picked up his pace. I sped up to match, wondering if he would try to get through the dispensary door before me.

We were nearly there when the question became moot. Bayta appeared in the doorway, her face grim. "No need to hurry," she said quietly. "He's dead."

The Human doctor's name was Witherspoon. "Well?" I asked as he scrubbed his hands in the dispensary's cleansing sink.

"Well, what?" he countered. His voice was tired and bitter, with the frustration of a professional healer who's just lost one.

But through the frustration I could also hear an uneasiness that I suspected had nothing to do with possible malpractice charges. "What did he die of?" I asked.

He looked up at me from under bushy eyebrows. "You a relative of the deceased?" he asked, an edge of challenge in his tone.

"My name is Compton," I said. "I do investigations for the Spiders."

"What kind of investigations?"

"Investigations they need me to do," I said. "Was he poisoned, or wasn't he?"

Witherspoon looked at the server still standing silently across the room, then back at me, then over at the other side of the room, where Kennrick and the other two Shorshians were consulting in low voices with the Filly doctor. "He was definitely poisoned," he said, lowering his own voice. "The problem is that Shorshians are highly susceptible to poisons, and there are a thousand different ones that can create symptoms like this. Without an autopsy, there's no way to know which one killed him."

I nodded and turned to Bayta. "Where can we set up for an autopsy?" I asked her.

"Wait a minute," Witherspoon protested before Bayta could answer. "Even if I was practiced at non-Human autopsies, we don't have the kind of equipment aboard to handle something like that."

"How about just a biochem autopsy?" I asked.

"That takes almost as much equipment as the regular version," he said. "Not to mention a truckload of specialized chemicals and reagents."

"A spectroscopic test, then?" I persisted.

"Mr. Compton, just how well equipped do you think Quadrail trains are?" he asked, his patience starting to crack at the edges.

"Obviously, not very," I conceded. "Luckily for us, I happen to have a spectroscopic analyzer in my compartment."

"Right," Witherspoon said with a sniff. He took another look at my face, his derision level slipping a notch. "You *are* joking, aren't you?"

The conversation between Kennrick, the Filly, and the two Shorshians had faded away into silence. "Not at all," I assured the whole group. "I trust you at least know which tissue samples would be the most useful?"

"Yes, I think so," Witherspoon said, still staring at me. "You have a *spectroscopic analyzer*? In your *compartment*?"

"I use it in my work," I explained. "Do you have the necessary equipment for taking the tissue samples, or will the Spiders need to scrounge something up?"

"The Spiders have sampling kits," Bayta put in.

"I also have a couple in my bag," Witherspoon said, gesturing to the cabinet where a traditional doctor's bag was sitting on one of the shelves. "May I ask what kind of investigations you do that you require a spectroscopic analyzer?"

"Show me the medical relevance of that information and I may share it with you," I said. "Otherwise, let's get on with it."

Witherspoon's lip twitched. "Of course." He looked over at the Shorshians. "But I'll need permission for the autopsy."

Kennrick, who'd been staring at me in much the same way Witherspoon had been, belatedly picked up on the cue. "Master Bofiv?" he asked, turning to the taller of the two Shorshians. "Can you advise me on Shorshic law and custom on such things?"

[It is not proper that such be done by strangers,] Master Bofiv said, his Shishish sounding harsher than usual here in the dead of night. Or maybe it was the presence of the recently deceased that was adding all the extra corners to the words.

"I understand your reluctance," Kennrick said, giving a respectful little duck of his head. "But in a case of such importance, surely an exception can be made."

"And indeed *must* be made," I put in.

[We cannot grant this permission,] Bofiv said. [We are not kin, nor of similar path.]

"What about *di*-Master Strinni?" Kennrick asked. "I believe he and Master Colix were of similar paths."

The two Shorshians looked at each other. [That may perhaps be proper,] Bofiv said, a little reluctantly. [But the approach is not mine to make.]

[Nor mine,] the other Shorshian added.

"I understand, Master Tririn," Kennrick said, nodding to him. He looked over at me. "It was Mr. Compton's idea. Mr. Compton can ask *di*-Master Strinni."

[That is acceptable,] Bofiv said before I could protest.

I grimaced. But there was no way out of it. Not if we wanted to find out what had killed the late Master Colix. "Where's *di*-Master Strinni now?" I asked.

"He has a seat in first class," Kennrick said. "I'll take you there."

"Thank you," I said. "Bayta, you might as well wait here."

"I could—" she began, then broke off. "All right," she said instead.

I gestured to Kennrick. "After you."

We left the dispensary and headed down the darkened, quiet corridor toward the front of the train. "Thanks so very much for this," I murmured to him as we walked.

"My pleasure," he said calmly. "I still have a business relationship with these people. If they end up being mortally offended at someone, I'd rather it be you than me."

"Can't fault the logic," I had to admit. "What exactly is this *similar path* thing Bofiv mentioned, and how come he and a *di*-Master are at the same place on it."

"It's a religious thing," Kennrick said. "The Path of

something unpronounceable and untranslatable. Very big among the professional classes at the moment."

"Really," I said, frowning. Major changes in alien religious alignments were one of the things Human intelligence agencies worked very hard to keep tabs on. "I don't remember any briefings on that."

"It really only took off in the past couple of years," Kennrick said. "A lot of Shorshians call it a cult and look down their bulbous snouts at it."

"What's *your* take?" I asked.

He shrugged. "I'm just a lowly Human. What do I know?"

Di-Master Strinni's seat was near the center of the rear first-class car. Unlike the seats in second and third, those in first could be folded completely flat for sleeping, with extendable canopies instead of the far less roomy cylindrical roll-over privacy shields that were standard in the lower classes. Strinni himself hadn't bothered with the canopy tonight, but was merely lying asleep with his inner eyelids closed against the soft glow of the car's night-lights and the scattered handful of reading lamps still operating.

I'd never had cause to try waking a Shorshian from a sound sleep, and it turned out to be harder than I'd expected. But with Kennrick's encouragement I persisted, and eventually the inner eyelids rolled back up and Strinni came fully conscious.

He wasn't at all happy at being woken up out of his sleep. But his annoyance disappeared as soon as he heard the grim news. [You believe this not merely a random tragedy?] he asked after I'd explained the situation.

"We're not sure," I said. "That's why we need to test some tissue samples."

[Might there be a Guidesman of the Path aboard?]

"No idea, *di*-Master Strinni," Kennrick said.

"I could ask one of the conductors," I offered.

The inner eyelids dipped down. I was just wondering if he'd gone back to sleep when they rolled up again. [No need,] he said. [If there was one, that truth would have been made known to me.]

Kennrick and I looked at each other. "So is that a yes?" I suggested.

[No,] he said flatly. [You may not cut into Master Colix's flesh.]

I braced myself. "*Di*-Master Strinni—"

[The subject is closed,] he cut me off. He settled back in his seat, and once again the inner eyelids came down.

This time, they stayed there. "What now?" Kennrick asked.

I frowned at the sleeping Shorshian. Without some idea of what had knocked Colix off his unpronounceable Path, our options were going to be severely limited. "Let's go talk to his traveling companions," I said. "Maybe they'll have some idea of who might have wanted him dead."

The crowd in the second/third dispensary had shrunk considerably by the time Kennrick and I returned. Only Bayta, Witherspoon, and Master Tririn were still there. And Colix's body, of course. "Where'd everyone go?" I asked as Kennrick and I joined them.

"Dr. Aronobal—she's the Filiaelian doctor—went off to work up her report on the death," Bayta said. "Master Bofiv wasn't feeling well and returned to his seat."

"Well?" Witherspoon asked. During our absence, he'd laid out a small sampling kit, complete with scalpel, hypo, and six sample vials.

"Sorry," I said. "*Di*-Master Strinni wouldn't give his permission."

[Did you explain the situation?] Tririn asked.

"In detail, Master Tririn," Kennrick assured him.

"Unless there's a Guidesman of the Path around to supervise, we aren't allowed to cut into Master Colix's body," I added.

"Are we sure there *isn't* someone like that aboard?" Witherspoon asked.

"We'd have to ask the Spiders," I said, looking at Bayta.

She gave me a microscopic shrug. "I suppose we could make inquiries," she said.

Translation: she'd already asked. Either there wasn't a Guidesman aboard or else it wasn't something the Spiders routinely kept track of.

"Speaking of Spiders," Kennrick said, "where's the one that was here earlier?"

"He's gone about other duties," Bayta said. "Did you want him for something?"

"As a matter of fact, I did." Kennrick pointed to the drug cabinet. "I notice that none of those bottles are labeled."

"Actually, they are," Bayta said. "The dot patterns along the sides are Spider notation."

"If a passenger needs something, the Spider prints out a label in his or her native language," Witherspoon explained. "Saves having to try to squeeze a lot of different notations onto something that small."

"I'm sure it does," Kennrick said. "But that also means none of the rest of us has any idea what's actually in any of them."

Bayta frowned. "What do you mean by that?"

"I mean we don't actually *know* that the drugs Dr.

Witherspoon and Dr. Aronobal injected into Master Colix were actually helpful," Kennrick said. "It could easily have been just the opposite."

"Are you accusing the Spiders of deliberately causing him harm?" Bayta asked, a not-so-subtle challenge in her tone.

"Maybe," Kennrick said. "Or else someone might have sneaked in here while the Spider was absent or distracted and changed some of the labels."

I stepped around the body on the table and went over to the drug cabinet. I'd noted earlier that the doors were glassed in; up close, I could see now that it wasn't glass, but some kind of grained polymer. Experimentally, I gave it a rap with my knuckles, then tried the latch.

The door didn't budge. "That would have to be one hell of a distracted Spider," I said, turning back to Kennrick. "Besides, wasn't Master Colix showing symptoms of poisoning before they even brought him in here?"

"Symptoms can be counterfeited," Kennrick said. He looked at the body on the table. "*Or* faked."

"You mean Master Colix might have faked his own poisoning so as to get brought in here so he could get pumped full of something lethal from the Spiders' private drugstore?" I asked.

"Well, yes, if you put it that way I suppose it sounds a little far-fetched," Kennrick admitted. "Still, we need to cover all possibilities."

I turned to Tririn. "Did Master Colix have any addictions or strange tastes?"

[I don't truly know,] Tririn said, a bit hesitantly. [I wasn't well acquainted with him.]

"You *were* business colleagues, correct?"

[True,] Tririn said. [But he had only recently joined our contract team.] He ducked his head to Kennrick. [I would say that Master Kennrick probably knew him as well as I did.]

"And I only met him a couple of months ago," Kennrick put in.

Mentally, I shook my head in disgust. Between *di*-Master Strinni, Kennrick, and Tririn, this was about as unhelpful a bunch as I'd run into for some time. "How about Master Bofiv, then?" I asked. "Did *he* know Master Colix?"

[I don't know,] Tririn said. [I believe *di*-Master Strinni knew him best.]

I looked at my watch. I'd already had to awaken Strinni once tonight, and I wasn't interested in trying it again. "We'll start with Master Bofiv," I decided. "Where is he?"

"Four cars back," Kennrick said. "I'll take you."

"Just tell me which seat," I said, taking Bayta's arm and steering her toward the door. "You should stay with Master Tririn."

"I'm going with you," Kennrick said firmly. "These people are my business colleagues. Whatever happened to Master Colix, we need to resolve it before it poisons relations between us." He winced. "Sorry. Poor choice of words."

"I'll stay here with Master Tririn," Witherspoon volunteered. "There may be a couple of tests I can do that don't involve cutting."

"I'll stay, too, then," Bayta said. "I'd like to watch."

I eyed her. Her face was its usual neutral mask, but there was something beneath the surface I couldn't quite read. Probably she didn't like the idea of the body being left alone with a couple of strangers with no Spider present. "Fine," I said. "Come on, Kennrick."

THREE :

Second-class seats weren't as mobile as those in first class, but they were movable enough to allow families and friends to arrange themselves into little conversation and game circles. Those circles usually remained into and through the nighttime hours, which gave a cozy sort of sleeping-bags-around-the-campfire look to those cars when everyone set up their privacy shields.

Not so in third. In third, where the seats were fixed in neat rows of three each on either side of the central aisle, the rows of cylindrical privacy shields always looked to me like the neatly arranged coffins from some horrible disaster.

"He's down there," Kennrick murmured, pointing.

I craned my neck. Master Bofiv was in one of the middle seats to my right, his seat reclined as far as it would go, his privacy shield open. "I see him," I confirmed. "Quietly, now."

We headed back, making as little noise as possible. Third-class seats weren't equipped with sonic neutralizers like those in first and second, leaving it up to the individual passenger to spring for his or her own earplugs or portable neutralizers or else to hope for quiet neighbors.

Bofiv was lying quietly when we reached his row. One of the passengers three rows up from him had his reading light on, which had the effect of throwing the Shorshian into even deeper shadow than he would have been in without it.

Still, I could see him well enough to tell that his inner eyelids were closed. "I woke up *di*-Master Strinni," I whispered to Kennrick. "It's your turn."

"But you're so good at it," Kennrick said, gesturing. "Please; go ahead."

"You're too kind," I said, frowning. On Bofiv's left, against the car's side wall, was an empty seat, presumably that of his compatriot Master Tririn.

But on Bofiv's right, where I would have expected to find the empty seat of the late Master Colix, was the smooth half-cylinder of a closed privacy shield. "Who's that?" I asked, pointing at it.

"A Nemut," Kennrick said. "He's not part of our group."

"Why isn't that Colix's seat?" I asked. "Didn't he want to sit with his buddies?"

"I don't know," Kennrick said, frowning. "Huh. I hadn't really thought about that. You think maybe the others didn't like him?"

"Or vice versa," I said, making a mental note to ask Bofiv and Tririn which of the party had come up with the seating arrangements. "So where *was* Colix sitting?"

"There," Kennrick said, pointing to an empty middle seat across the aisle and two rows forward of the sleeping Bofiv.

I backtracked for a closer look. The late Master Colix's seat was flanked by a pair of privacy shields. Irreverently, I won-

dered if one of the shields concealed an attractive female Shorshian. Maybe that was why he'd chosen to ditch his colleagues.

And then, as if on cue, the aisle shield retracted to reveal a
young Human female.

A *really* young female, in fact. She couldn't be more than
seventeen, and even that was pushing it. Her face was thin and
drawn, with the look of someone who'd just gone two rounds
with food that didn't agree with her.

Make that three rounds. Even before the privacy shield had
retracted completely into the armrest and leg-rest storage lip
she was on the move, heading toward the front of the car at the
quick-walk of the digestively desperate.

I eyed the remaining privacy shield in that particular three-
seat block. Maybe *that* was the knockout Shorshic female.

"Well?" Kennrick prompted.

"Well, what?" I countered, turning around to watch the
girl. She reached the front of the car and disappeared into one
of the restrooms.

"Are we going to ask Master Bofiv about Master Colix's
habits and appetites?" Kennrick elaborated.

"In a minute," I said, a sudden unpleasant tingling on the
back of my neck as I stared at the closed restroom door. Colix
had gotten sick and died . . . and now one of his seatmates had
suddenly made a mad dash for the facilities?

Kennrick caught the sudden change in my tone. "What is
it?" he asked.

"I don't know," I said. "Maybe nothing."

"Or?"

"Or maybe something," I said, glancing at my watch. Five
minutes, I decided. If the girl wasn't back in five minutes I
would grab a Spider and send him in to find her.

It was something of an anticlimax when, three minutes

later, the door opened and the girl reappeared. She started a little unsteadily back down the aisle toward her seat, looking even more drawn than she had before.

"Or nothing, I take it?" Kennrick murmured.

"So it would seem," I agreed. The girl's eyes were fixed on me as she came toward us, a wary and rather baleful expression on her pale face. I waited until she was about five steps from us and then tried my best concerned smile on her. "You all right, miss?" I asked softly.

"I'm fine," she said, clipping out each word like she was trimming a thorn hedge. If my concerned smile was having any effect, I sure couldn't detect it. "You mind?"

I wasn't even close to blocking her way, but I gave her a little more room anyway. "I just wondered if you were unwell."

"I'm fine," she said again, brushing past me and flopping down into her seat. She adjusted herself a bit and reached for the privacy shield control.

"Because your seatmate had a bad attack of something," I went on, kneeling down beside her. No point including any more eavesdroppers in this conversation than absolutely necessary. "You might have noticed when his friends took him to the dispensary?"

She slid the control forward, and the shield started to rotate into its closed position. "The dispensary, where he died?" I finished.

The shield closed. I counted off three seconds; and then, the shield opened again. "What did you just say?" the girl asked, her face suddenly tight.

"I said Master Colix is dead," I repeated.

For a long moment she just stared at me. Her eyes flicked up to Kennrick, then back to me. "How?" she whispered.

"He was poisoned," I said. "What's your name?"

She hesitated. "Terese," she said. "Terese German."

"Frank Compton," I introduced myself in return. "How well did you know Master Colix?"

"Hardly at all," Terese said, looking at Kennrick again.

"You didn't talk to him?" Kennrick asked.

Terese hunched her shoulders. "Mostly I read or listened to music."

"But you must have at least occasionally talked to him," Kennrick persisted. "You've been sitting together for the past two weeks, after all."

"He's the one who did all the talking," Terese growled. "Mostly about his job. Oh, and he showed me a few holos of his family, too."

"He was married?" I asked.

A shadow of something crossed her face. "No, they were pictures of his parents and brothers," she said.

"Are *you* married?" Kennrick asked.

"Is that any of your business?" she countered stiffly, giving him an icy look.

"I was just wondering if you were traveling alone," he said in a tone of slightly wounded innocence.

"Then *ask* that," the girl bit out.

"Our apologies," I said hastily. "*Are* you traveling alone?"

"Yes," she said.

"Do you remember Master Colix mentioning feeling ill prior to tonight?" I asked.

"Not to me," she said. She let her glare linger on Kennrick another couple of seconds, apparently making sure he got the message, then looked back at me. "As far as I could tell, he felt fine. At least, up to a couple of hours ago."

"What did he say?" I asked.

"Nothing," she said. "But he was shifting in his seat a lot and making these funny noises."

"What kind of noises? What did they sound like?"

"Mostly uncomfortable-sounding grunts," she said. "Like his stomach was bothering him."

I gestured toward her abdomen. "Like the way your stomach was bothering you a minute ago?"

"It's not the same thing," she said tartly.

"How do you know?" I countered.

"I've got some stomach trouble, that's all," she insisted. "Nothing I'm going to die from."

"Okay," I said, wondering if Colix had been thinking the same thing up to the point where the doctors started poking hypos into him. "What happened then?"

"I was just wondering if I should give up and go to the bar for a while to get away from the noise when he got out of his seat and headed back to his friends," she said.

"How long ago was this?" Kennrick asked.

"Like I said, a couple of hours," she told him.

"Any chance you can pin it down a little more closely?" he asked.

"No, I can't," she said. "I was trying to sleep. I wasn't exactly looking at my watch."

"That's all right," I assured her. "Did anything in particular happen just prior to that time? Had he just returned from the dining car, or had a snack?"

"Or had he been talking to anyone other than you and his other seatmate?" Kennrick asked.

"He hadn't been anywhere or done anything that I saw." Terese nodded at Kennrick. "And the only visitor I saw was you."

I frowned at Kennrick. "You were back here this evening?"

"Early afternoon," he corrected. "I was working on the plans for a traditional Shorshic halfway-celebration meal for next week and wanted Master Colix's advice on menu and procedure."

"How long was this before the uncomfortable grunts started?" I asked Terese.

"Oh, hours," she said. "He had dinner afterwards. And if he had any snacks, I didn't see them."

Dead end. "Did Master Colix go anywhere else this evening? Maybe back to talk with his colleagues a couple of rows back?"

"No." Terese hesitated. "Actually, I had the feeling he didn't get along too well with them."

"How so?"

"For one thing, he didn't want to sit with them," she said. "The Nemut in the aisle seat offered to trade with him right after we left Homshil, but he turned him down."

I looked at Kennrick. "And you didn't notice any of this undercurrent during your meetings on Earth?"

"No, but that doesn't necessarily mean anything," he said. "Shorshians are very good at social compartmentalization. They can all behave in a perfectly friendly way in a business setting even if they personally can't stand each other."

"Not even now that they're on their way home?" I asked. "Wouldn't one of them have at least mentioned it?"

"They wouldn't have mentioned it to me," Kennrick said. "I work for Pellorian Medical, so wherever I am is by definition a business setting. Ditto whenever the Shorshians are with any of the four Filiaelians in our group."

"Are any of the Filiaelians in this car?" I asked, glancing around.

"No, they're all up in first," he said. "And I doubt any of them has made the trek back here since the trip started." He cocked an eyebrow. "But the fact the Shorshians won't talk about their problems to *me* doesn't mean they won't open up to *you*."

I made a face. "In other words, it's time for me to nudge, shake, or otherwise drag Master Bofiv back to the land of the living?"

"Just be persistent," Kennrick advised. "As you saw, they *do* wake up eventually."

He headed back toward Bofiv's seat. "Nice guy," Terese muttered.

"He's all that," I agreed, getting back to my feet. "Thanks for your time."

I joined Kennrick at Bofiv's row. The Shorshian was still lying on his back, his inner eyelids closed. As far as I could tell, he hadn't moved at all since our arrival. "Master Bofiv?" I called softly, giving his arm a cautious shake.

There was no response. "Master Bofiv?" I called again, wiggling the arm a little harder.

Still nothing. I glanced toward the front of the car, wondering if there might be a Spider nearby who I could commandeer for this duty. There wasn't, but I did note that Terese was leaning around her seat watching us.

I turned back to Bofiv. "Master Bofiv, I need to talk to you," I said. I shook his arm again, still without effect, then reached up to try patting the side of his neck.

It was cold. Not cold in the way a sleeping person's skin might get if he forgot to tuck his blanket all the way up to his chin. Bofiv's skin was much colder.

I pulled out my flashlight and flicked it on. The deep shadows had hidden his skin earlier, but I could see now that it had the same mottling that Colix's skin had shown there at the end.

I gazed down at his empty face, a hard knot forming in my stomach. No one was going to be nudging, shaking, or otherwise dragging Bofiv back to the land of the living. Not anymore.

I looked back at Terese. She was still peering around the side of her seat, her curiosity starting to drift over into uncertainty. "What's the matter?" she stage-whispered.

"Do me a favor," I told her. "Go find a conductor and tell him that I need him and another Spider back here right away. And have them get Dr. Witherspoon out of the second/third dispensary and bring him along."

Terese got out of her seat, her eyes on Bofiv's still form. "Is he sick?" she asked.

"No," I told her. "He's dead."

"Without tests I can't be certain," Dr. Witherspoon said as he straightened up. "But in my opinion, he died from the same poison that killed Master Colix."

I looked down at the dispensary's treatment table, where the late Master Bofiv now lay side by side with the late Master Colix. It was a cozy fit. "Great," I said. "We've got a pattern going."

"God help us all," Kennrick muttered. "What are we talking about, Doc, some kind of plague?" He looked pointedly over at the server Spider again standing unobtrusive vigil on the other side of the dispensary. "Something new the Spiders' fancy sensor net let slip through?"

"If it is, it would have to be something both new and very

slippery," Witherspoon said. "I've seen lists of what those sensors catch. Nothing harmful gets through, I assure you."

"Then it has to be something they ate," Kennrick concluded. "If it's not airborne, that's all that's left."

I looked at Tririn, who was standing against the wall beside the Filly doctor. His skin wasn't mottled like the late Master Bofiv's, but it definitely looked paler than it had earlier.

Small wonder. Two of his companions had now bitten the dust, companions who had probably been eating the same food and had definitely been breathing the same air he had over the past two weeks. In his place, I'd have been pretty nervous, too.

"There was nothing dangerous in the food," the server said in his flat Spider voice.

Every head in the room turned at that one. Servers were usually quiet, unassuming little Spiders, with a normal conversational range that was limited to asking a dining car patron what he wanted for lunch or telling a barfly that, sadly, the train was completely out of Jack Daniel's. To have one of them volunteer information, especially information like this, was unheard of.

Kennrick recovered his voice first. "So *you* say," he countered. "I'd want some actual proof of that."

"What about something one of the group brought aboard?" I asked. "Some foodstuff that maybe wasn't packaged properly and went bad?"

"I suppose that's possible," Witherspoon said. "Bacteria-generated toxins can certainly be nasty enough. But it's hard to imagine Master Colix or Master Bofiv eating something that was obviously tainted."

"Which makes it all the more urgent that we get an analysis

of the victims' blood and tissue," I said. "Until we know which poison was responsible, there's no way to backtrack it and figure out where it came from."

"And how do you intend to do that?" Kennrick demanded. "*Di*-Master Strinni has already said no autopsies."

"No, *di*-Master Strinni said no autopsy on Master Colix," I corrected. "He hasn't said anything about Master Bofiv."

"And why would he—?" Kennrick broke off. "You're right," he said, sudden interest in his voice. "Master Bofiv wasn't on the same Path *di*-Master Strinni is."

"Which means he might be willing to let us work on Master Bofiv," I said.

"It's worth a try," Kennrick agreed. "Go ahead. We'll wait here."

"You're the one who knows him," I reminded him.

"You're the one who knows how to wake him up," he countered.

"I've already had to do this twice," I said.

"Once," Kennrick corrected. "You didn't actually wake up Master Bofiv."

"What is the *matter* with you two?" Witherspoon snapped "There are people lying *dead* here."

"And I don't want to be the one to break that news to a business associate," Kennrick said coolly. "It was Compton's idea. He can do it."

Witherspoon rumbled something under his breath. "Oh, for—never mind. *I'll* do it."

He stripped off his examination gloves, tossing them onto the dispensary counter. With a final glare at me, he strode toward the doorway.

He'd made it halfway there when the obvious problem

belatedly caught up with him. "Only I can't, can I?" he growled with frustration and embarrassment. "*Di*-Master Strinni is in first class."

"I think that in this case the conductors will be willing to pass you through," I said.

"You will be permitted," the server confirmed. "A conductor will meet you in the rearmost first-class car and accompany you to *di*-Master Strinni's seat."

"Thank you," Witherspoon said. He got two more steps, then once again hesitated. "Perhaps, Master Tririn, you would accompany me?" he asked, turning to the remaining Shorshian.

Tririn looked at Kennrick, then back at Witherspoon. [Very well,] he said. He murmured something to Aronobal that I couldn't catch; then he and Witherspoon left the room and headed forward.

That left Kennrick, Aronobal, Bayta, and me. Plus the Spider, of course. "Well, that went well," I commented.

"He'll learn," Kennrick said cynically, his gaze lingering on the empty doorway. "Dr. Witherspoon, I mean. Everyone thinks dealing with Shorshians is a walk down the escalator. But he'll learn."

He looked at Aronobal. "But I don't have to tell *you* that, do I?" he went on. "The Filiaelian Assembly has been dealing with them for at least six hundred years now."

"I have never had trouble with the Shorshic people," Aronobal said diplomatically.

"Then you're the exception," Kennrick said. "Half my job seems to consist of smoothing those waters." He turned back to me. "So what now? We wait until they get back?"

"Unless you want to risk Strinni's wrath by starting before the opening bell," I said.

He grimaced. "No, thanks." He started to say something

else, but instead gave a wide yawn. "Hell with this. I'll be in my compartment if you need me."

"On your way, you might consider briefing the Filiaelians in your party about the situation," I suggested as he headed for the door.

"Forget it," he said. "You think waking up Shorshians with this kind of news is a bad idea, you should try it with Filiaelians." His lip twitched and he looked back at Aronobal. "At least with *santra*-rank Filiaelians," he amended.

Aronobal inclined her head but said nothing. Kennrick held his pose for a moment, probably trying to think of some other way to apologize further without looking like either a boor or an idiot, then gave up and looked back at me instead. "Call me if you learn anything."

With that, he escaped into the corridor. I drifted to the doorway, arriving just in time to see the vestibule door leading into the next car close behind him.

"He is not very diplomatic," Aronobal said darkly. "I am surprised that someone chose him to manage dealings with more civilized beings."

The insult had clearly been directed at Kennrick, but I found myself wincing a little anyway. Things that smudged one Human had a tendency to smudge all of us. "He may be better when he's not woken up in the middle of the night to deal with multiple deaths," I suggested.

Aronobal gazed down her long face at me, her nose blaze darkening a little. "A well-trained manager should know how to deal with even the unexpected."

"Maybe he's not as well-trained as we all might like," I said, turning to Bayta. "The server said there wasn't anything in the Shorshians' food. How sure is he of that?"

"Very sure," Bayta said firmly. "The packaging was intact,

and there's nothing in the ingredients of any of the Shorshic-style foods aboard that could be a problem."

"Unless there was some unexpected contamination during the cooking or packaging process," I said. "Maybe we should check that out. If the Spiders don't mind, that is."

From the expression on Bayta's face, it was clear that the Spiders did, in fact, mind. But she knew better than to have this discussion in front of a stranger. "We can certainly ask," she said instead. "The third-class dining car is four cars back."

I nodded and looked at Aronobal. "Keep an eye on Masters Colix and Bofiv, will you?"

"I will," she said. "You will let me know if you find anything?"

"You'll be the first," I promised.

We headed out, turning in the direction of the third-class dining room. I glanced at Bayta's profile as we walked, noting the stiffness in her expression. "If it helps," I said quietly, "I don't actually think this was caused by any negligence on the Spiders' part."

"Neither do I," Bayta said, her voice as stiff as her face.

"But we still have to check it out," I continued. "If for no other reason than to clear them of any responsibility."

"That's not the point," Bayta said. "The Spiders don't want passengers getting into their sections of the train." She sent me a furtive glance. "Not even you."

"I guess you'll just have to go to bat for me on this one," I said.

She gave a soft snort. "I *do* go to bat for you, Frank," she said. "More often than you know."

I studied her profile again, noting the smooth line of her nose, the curve of her cheekbones, and the softness of her skin. That was all most people saw when they looked at her, and while it made for a pleasant enough treat for the eyes, it also effectively hid all the solid stuff below the surface, the character strengths the casual tourist never saw. Intelligence, determination, loyalty, courage—they were all in there, ready to come boiling out whenever they were needed.

And she was right. She'd put her butt on the line for me time and time again. And those were only the times I knew about. "You're right," I acknowledged. "Let's do it this way. I'll wait outside while you go in and look at the facility. I can tell you what to look for, and walk you through anything that needs follow-up."

I could tell she was tempted. It would make life simpler, and give her one fewer telepathic battles to fight. "What would I have to do?" she asked.

I shrugged. "No way to know for sure until we get there. But probably nothing complicated."

She hesitated, then shook her head. "I don't think we can risk it," she said with a sigh. "You're the expert. You really need to look for yourself."

"You sure?" I asked. "I wouldn't want to be stuck on a Quadrail for four more weeks with a whole trainful of Spiders mad at us."

She gave me a wry look, and as she did so some of the tension in her face went away. "Since when do you care what other people think?"

"Oh, I don't care about *me*," I said. "I was worried about *you*."

"Well, don't," she said. "I can take care of myself." She nodded ahead. "Come on—the server's expecting us."

FOUR :

The third-class dining room was deserted when Bayta and I arrived, with only a single server Spider standing a lonely vigil behind the counter along the room's back wall. The counter, in turn, was separated from the area behind him by a slat curtain.

"The door's over here," Bayta said, leading the way toward the side of the serving counter. As we approached, a concealed panel popped open in front of us. I nodded my thanks to the Spider, got the usual lack of reaction in return, and followed Bayta through the doorway.

One of the perennial topics of conversation aboard Quad-rails was exactly how the Spiders managed to prepare so many meals for so many travelers. Now, standing in the food preparation room, I finally had an answer to that question.

It was a definite letdown. The prep room was lined with shelves loaded to the gills with flat white boxes covered with Spider dot codes. "Prepackaged meals," I identified them.

"Of course," Bayta said, her tone making me feel a little

ridiculous. "You didn't really think we had full gourmet kitch-ens on each train, did you?"

"There were rumors," I said, looking around. Along with the food storage shelves, there were other racks containing bottles of water and other liquid refreshments, plus a dozen cook stations that included microwaves, flash-heaters, and re-hydrators. Tucked away in one of the back corners was a closed trapdoor with what looked like a wide conveyor belt set verti-cally against the wall. "For bringing in fresh stock from the storage car?" I asked, pointing at it.

"Yes," Bayta said. "It connects to a conveyor system that runs beneath the cars. We only have those on cross-galactic trains, of course."

I looked back at the food shelves. "I guess we might as well start with the obvious. Which ones are the Shorshic meals?"

"There," Bayta said, pointing to the third stack from the left. "Do you want a list of the meals Master Colix had in the past day? Dr. Aronobal got it from Master Bofiv and Master Tririn earlier while you were speaking with *di*-Master Strinni."

"Did Colix eat the same thing every day?" I asked.

"I don't think so," Bayta said.

"Then I can get the menu later." Stepping over to the Shorshic rack, I picked up the top box.

It was heavier than I'd expected, which probably meant it contained a complete meal instead of appetizers or desserts or something lighter. The box itself was made of a thin but sturdy plastic, sealed with a quick-release strip. Experimentally, I pulled the strip open a couple of centimeters and then tried to reseal it.

It didn't reseal. I tried it again, just to be sure, then tried lifting the corner of the lid, hoping to get a look at the food inside.

But there was a wide flap in the way, and pulling on the

corner merely gained me another couple of centimeters of open strip. "I presume the Spiders would have noticed if one of the meals had shown up unsealed?"

"Of course," Bayta said. "Aren't you going to open it?"

"No need," I said, looking closely at the box in search of punctures or small tears. "What happens to the boxes once the food's been served? Do they get flattened and stored somewhere for reuse?"

"No, they go directly into the recycling system," she said. "The fibers are designed to serve as a catalyst for some of the waste breakdown."

"When you say directly, you mean . . . ?"

"I mean directly," she said, frowning. "Yesterday's packages are already gone. What do you mean, *no need*? I thought you wanted to check the food for contamination."

"I do," I confirmed. "Or rather, I did. But it's clear now that if the food was tampered with, it didn't happen at the kitchen where these things were cooked and packaged. It happened right here aboard the train." I grimaced. "And it happened on purpose."

Her eyes went wide. "Are you saying they were *murdered*?"

"I don't see any way around it," I said. "One death might be an accident. But not two. Not like this."

"But Dr. Witherspoon said Shorshians are especially susceptible to poisoning."

"Exactly my point," I said. "Even small amounts of poisons typically generate obvious symptoms in that species. If Colix and Bofiv had ingested the stuff gradually, over the past few days, the symptoms would have shown up long ago. The only conclusion is that they were both nailed with large, lethal doses, all at once. That kind of dosage doesn't usually happen by accident."

For another few seconds Bayta remained silent. But I could see the shock fading from her face as she realized I was making sense. "All right," she said slowly. "But why would anyone want to kill them?"

"I haven't the faintest," I conceded. "Actually, it's worse than that. We don't even know yet that they were specifically targeted."

Her eyes did the widening thing again. "You mean the killings might have been random?"

"Or the killer was aiming at someone else and missed," I said. "But one thing at a time. The easiest method for delivering poison is by food or drink, since everybody eats and nine out of ten people don't pay that much attention to their food while they're eating it."

"Yes," Bayta said thoughtfully. "Shorshic meals usually include a common dipping dish, don't they?"

"That's what the cultural profiles say," I confirmed. "Which would certainly make surreptitious tampering easier. The downside is that the poisoner pretty much has to be in the same group as the victim—a stranger leaning in so he can sprinkle fairy dust into a dipping dish in the middle of the table would be a little obvious."

"But if the poisoner was also a Shorshian, wouldn't he run the risk of being poisoned himself?" Bayta asked.

"Absolutely," I said. "Which is one of several intriguing questions about this whole thing. Namely, were both Colix and Bofiv murdered by a third party? Or could Bofiv have murdered Colix and then gotten caught in his own backfire?"

"Or vice versa?" Bayta suggested. "Master Colix murdering Master Bofiv?"

"Possibly," I agreed. "Colix would have to be a particularly incompetent killer for that scenario to work, but I've known my share of inept criminals. Still, it's more likely that the killer was someone else at their table."

Bayta's eyes went distant for a moment as she communed silently with the Spiders. "The servers don't have that information."

"That's all right," I said. "We'll corner Tririn later and ask him for yesterday's guest list."

Bayta was silent a moment. "Do you think the Modhri might be involved in all this?"

"That's definitely my default reflex these days," I said. "But we need some kind of motive before we start trying to pin this on the Modhri or anyone else." I cocked an eyebrow. "Why? Is your spider-sense tingling?"

She frowned. "My what?"

"Skip it," I said, making a mental note to add those dit rec adventures to the list of cultural classics I'd been showing her. "Can you think of some reason why he might want to kill a couple of Shorshians?"

"Not really," she said. "But I've been thinking a lot about him lately. Trying to get into his mind, to understand what he wants."

"I thought he wanted to take over the galaxy."

"Yes, but to what end?" she asked. "The Shonkla-raa certainly had a purpose—they wanted him to infiltrate the rebel forces and destroy them from within. But he doesn't have that purpose anymore. He doesn't have *any* real purpose."

"I don't know," I said doubtfully. "To me, taking over the galaxy sounds like a pretty solid reason for living."

"You know what I mean," Bayta said. "The Modhri isn't conquering so that he can institute political or economic changes, or even just so he can loot his victims."

"Okay, so he's unfocused," I said. "So what?"

Bayta shook her head. "I keep thinking that he's like a weapon that's been left on a shelf," she said pensively. "A sword, maybe. He can fall off, and he can do a lot of damage on his way down, but he's still just flailing about without serving a genuine purpose. That has to be frustrating and frightening both."

"So you're thinking he might throw up his hands and quit in disgust?" I suggested dryly.

"I'm wondering if he might go insane."

Something with a lot of cold feet skittered down my spine. "Oh, now *there's* a cheerful thought," I muttered.

"I'm sorry," Bayta apologized. "I probably shouldn't even have brought it up. I just . . . it's been bothering me lately."

"No need to apologize," I assured her. Privately, I thought the whole idea a bit far-fetched—from what I'd seen of the Modhri, he didn't strike me as the neurotic type. But I also knew better than to dismiss anything Bayta said without at least considering it. "It's definitely worth thinking about. Only not right now. Any word from *di*-Master Strinni?"

Bayta's eyes went distant. "He's just given Dr. Witherspoon permission to take blood and tissue samples from Master Bofiv."

"Good," I said, setting the meal box back on its stack. "Let's go make sure he does it right."

"All right." Bayta hesitated. "*Di*-Master Strinni has also insisted that Master Colix's body be removed for storage."

"Removed for storage where?"

"He asked that it be put in one of the baggage cars," Bayta said. "The Spiders are taking it back there now."

"Where are they going to put it?" I asked. "They can't just leave it lying around the aisles. More importantly, how are they going to seal it away from the rest of the train? It's still four weeks to Venidra Carvo, and things are going to get pretty ripe back there if they don't do something."

"They're constructing an isolation tank where they can store the body," she said. "They're also looking into whether they can use the same preservation techniques they use for food."

I tried to visualize the Spiders freeze-drying Colix's body, but I'd had enough disturbing images for one night. "Did Strinni say why he wanted Colix's body moved?"

"Only that he wanted the body to be as much at rest as possible."

More likely he didn't want Witherspoon's scalpel slipping during Bofiv's autopsy and cutting into his fellow Pathmate by accident. "Whatever," I said. "Come on, let's go."

We left the dining car and headed forward. On the way we passed a pair of conductors carrying the late Master Colix, his body wrapped in one of the dispensary's thermal blankets. Briefly, I wondered how many people in third class might be awake, and how many of those might recognize the bundle for what it was. But there was nothing I could do about it, so I put the thought out of my mind.

We reached the dispensary to find Dr. Aronobal and the server Spider still standing their quiet vigil over the remaining body. "The Spiders came in a few minutes ago and removed Master Colix's body," Aronobal said.

"Yes, we passed them on the way," I said, peering at Bofiv's body. It didn't seem to have been touched in the time Bayta and I had been gone.

"You and your companion speak to the Spiders," Aronobal said.

It had been phrased as a statement, not a question. "Of course we do," I said. "Everyone does. We ask them for directions to the dining car, where we can stow our valuables—"

"Not everyone talks to them as you do," she cut me off, her eyes peering unblinkingly at me down her long nose. "You have a special relationship with them."

"We just travel a lot," I assured him. "We've gotten to know the Spiders pretty well."

"Many people travel a lot," Aronobal countered. "Moreover, Humans have only begun to ride the Quadrails, whereas we of the Filiaelian Assembly have traveled among the stars for centuries. How is it that—?"

She broke off abruptly, and in the fresh silence, I could hear the sound of approaching footsteps. "We will continue this later," Aronobal said quietly.

A moment later, Witherspoon and Tririn appeared. "*Di*-Master Strinni has given us permission to take samples from Master Bofiv's body," Witherspoon announced. He stopped short. "Where's Master Colix?"

"The Spiders have already taken care of him," I told him.

"But we only just agreed on that a few minutes ago," Witherspoon protested. He stepped up to the table, looking around as if expecting Colix's body to leap out of hiding and say boo.

"The Spiders are extremely efficient," I said.

"Obviously so." Witherspoon seemed to brace himself. "Very well. Dr. Aronobal, you undoubtedly have more experience with Shorshic physiology than I do. If you would take the samples, I would be honored to assist you."

"Your deference is noted," Aronobal said, inclining her head approvingly. Apparently, this was the sort of servile diplomacy she'd been expecting earlier from Kennrick. Maybe

Witherspoon's humility would redeem the entire Human race a little in her eyes. "In actual fact, I do not have any specialized knowledge in this matter. How often have you performed this type of examination?"

"Thirty or forty times, I suppose," Witherspoon said. "But I've only done it on Humans."

"Your expertise nevertheless surpasses mine," Aronobal said. "You may proceed. I will assist."

Witherspoon glanced at me, took a deep breath, and pulled a pair of gloves from a dispenser beneath the table. "All right," he said. "Let's do it."

I'd seen plenty of dead bodies in the course of my career. Some of them had been spectacularly mangled, and nearly all of them had been pretty bloody. But I'd done my level best to avoid autopsies whenever possible. There was something about the casual, clinical slicing up of a body that bothered me in a way that even the aftermath of thudwumper rounds didn't.

Fortunately, this one wasn't as bad as I'd feared it would be. Witherspoon did the job quickly and efficiently, mostly just nicking off small skin samples or using a hypo to draw blood and other fluids. Only twice did he dig deeper than skin level, and in those instances I was able to keep my focus on the samples as he slid them into the small vials Aronobal held open for him.

Five minutes later, it was over. "That's it," Witherspoon said as he set the last sealed vial into the sample case and handed the Spider the hypos and scalpels he'd been using. "Do you want to bring your spectroscopic analyzer here, or would it be easier if Dr. Aronobal and I accompany you to your compartment?"

"Neither, actually," I told him as I took the sample case. "Bayta and I can handle it."

Witherspoon threw a frown at Aronobal. "That's not proper procedure," he warned.

"Aboard a Quadrail, proper procedure is whatever the Spiders say it is," I reminded him.

[And how will we know if you speak the truth?] Tririn demanded.

"You'll know because I will speak it, and because I have no reason to lie," I told him. "I'm not involved with your group, Pellorian Medical Systems, or any branch of the Human, Filiaelian, or Shorshian governments. I have no ax to grind, no agenda to push, no itches to scratch. More importantly, I'm the one with the necessary equipment and the knowledge and training to use it."

Tririn looked at Dr. Witherspoon, who looked at Dr. Aronobal, who looked back at me. It didn't take a genius to see that none of them was very happy with my executive decision.

It also didn't take a genius to know they didn't have much choice in the matter. [How soon will you have the results?] Tririn asked.

"By midmorning at the latest," I said, taking Bayta's arm. "You might as well all go back to bed. You'll want to get some sleep before the rest of the train wakes up."

We left the dispensary and headed forward. Second class was still pretty quiet, but a few of the passengers were beginning to stir as the early risers mixed with the insomniacs and those hoping to get a head start on the bathroom and shower facilities. First class, in contrast, was still almost uniformly quiet. *Di*-Master Strinni was again sleeping without his canopy, his lidded eyes pointed sightlessly toward the ceiling.

Bayta didn't speak until we were back in my compartment with the door locked behind us. "The analysis won't really take that long, will it?" she asked as I dug out my lighter and multi-tool.

"Not at all," I assured her, flipping the lighter's thumb guard around and positioning it over the flame jet. "But one of the cardinal rules is that you never let people know how long things actually take."

"Why not?" she asked, watching in fascination as I selected the smallest of my multitool's blades and dipped the tip into the vial containing Bofiv's blood sample.

"Because you never know when you might have to do that same something a lot faster than they expect," I told her. Touching the blade to the thumb guard, I deposited a droplet directly above the flame jet. "Here—hold this a second. Keep it vertical."

Gingerly, she took the lighter, holding it at arm's length while I pulled out my reader and data chip collection. The chip labeled *Encyclopaedia Britannica* was one of the oversized ones, as befitted its status as the repository of all Human knowledge.

Or so a casual observer would assume. In actual fact, that particular chip plus my specially designed, one-of-a-kind reader added up to a very powerful sensor/analyzer, one of the finest gadgets the Terran Confederation had to offer. I activated the sensor, took the lighter back from Bayta, and set the reader and lighter at the proper positions relative to each other. "Here we go," I said, and ignited the lighter.

A blue-white flame hissed out, and there was a small puff of smoke as the blood droplet flash-burned to vapor. I shut off the lighter and handed it back to Bayta, then keyed the reader for analysis. "And that's it," I told her. "A few seconds, and we'll have a complete list of what was in Master Bofiv's blood when he died."

"Amazing," Bayta murmured, eyeing the reader. "And Mr. Hardin just let you *keep* it?"

"He was a little preoccupied with other matters at the time," I said, thinking back to my somewhat awkward final confrontation with Larry Cecil Hardin, multitrillionaire industrialist and erstwhile boss. "The trillion dollars I'd just extorted from him was probably weighing a bit on his mind."

"I hope someday he'll learn what his money did for the galaxy," Bayta murmured.

"Actually, I'm not sure he'd really care," I said. "Maybe if you gave him a medal at a big public ceremony."

"After all this time, you still dislike the man that much?"

"I don't dislike him," I told her. "I just see him as he is, not as some idealized person he might someday become if you showed him where the profit was in being noble. Until then, he'll con, finagle, bargain, or outright steal every last dollar he can."

Bayta eyed me thoughtfully. "You practice that speech often?"

"Couple of times a week," I told her. "Still needs a little work."

"Mm," she said noncommittally. "Still, you can't deny that some good did come out of Mr. Hardin's ambitions."

"The trillion dollars," I said. "I believe I mentioned that."

"I was thinking of something even more valuable than that." Bayta gave a little nod toward me. "You."

I felt a lump form in my throat. "Worth more even than a trillion dollars, huh?" I asked, trying to keep my tone light. "I'm honored. Remind me to ask you to speak on my behalf the next time the Chahwyn try quibbling with me over the job we're doing for them."

"I've already done that," she said simply. "One of the other times I went to bat for you."

"Oh," I said, a bit lamely. "Yes, I guess you have."

"You *do* miss a lot not being telepathic," she commented.

I peered at her, wondering if she was being serious or trying to be funny. But her face was its usual neutral, her eyes on the reader in my hand. "I know," I told her. "I've been meaning to work on that."

Her eyes flicked up, the hint of a frown touching her face. Probably wondering if *I* was trying to be funny. "What happens now?" she asked, looking back at the reader. "We test the rest of the samples and look for a common element?"

"Exactly." The sensor beeped, and I watched as the analysis scrolled across the display.

And felt my stomach tighten. "Or not."

"What do you mean?"

"I mean we probably don't really need to test any of the other samples." I turned the reader around to face her. "Second line just above the bottom of the display."

She peered at the line. "Cadmium?"

"A heavy metal," I told her. "Westali's standard course on Shorshians was rather cursory, but heavy-metal poisoning was definitely one of the topics that was covered, mainly because it was considered one of the better ways of quietly dispatching members of that particular species. For the record, it's pretty good against Humans, too."

Bayta's lips compressed briefly. "What exactly does that number mean?" she asked.

"That there's enough in his system to kill a good-sized moose," I said grimly. "Whoever wanted Master Bofiv dead wasn't taking any chances."

Bayta shivered. "Or whoever wanted whoever dead," she said. "You said that he might have missed his real target."

"If he did, that was one hell of a miss."

"Yes," she murmured. "What do we do now?"

"I suppose we might as well run the rest of the samples, just to make sure there aren't any surprises," I said. "After that, we'd better get to bed. Tomorrow's likely to be a busy day."

"Shouldn't we let Dr. Witherspoon and the others know the results?"

I shook my head. "They've all gone back to bed. Not much point in waking them up just to give them bad news. Besides, I want some time to think about this before we spring it on them."

"I thought you said you were going to sleep."

"I said I was going to bed." I looked at the cadmium listing on the analysis. "I never said I was going to get much sleep."

FIVE :

Sure enough, I'd been lying in bed for no more than five hours, and had been asleep for maybe three of those, when I was awakened by someone leaning on my door chime.

Sometimes I hated being right. Stumbling to the door, darkly promising to cripple someone if this wasn't damned important, I keyed it open.

Kennrick was standing there, looking way too fresh and alert for a man who'd been up almost as late as I had. "Compton," he greeted me shortly, taking a step forward as if expecting to be invited in.

"Kennrick," I greeted him in turn, not budging from the doorway and forcing him to stop short to keep from running into me. "Any news?"

"That was *my* question," he said, trying to peer past my shoulder into the compartment. "Dr. Witherspoon told me he and Dr. Aronobal gave you the samples from Master Bofiv's body for analysis."

"And I told *him* that I would let all of you know when I had the results," I said.

"That was over five hours ago," Kennrick countered. "What are you doing, framing the samples for an art-house display?"

"I've been working," I told him stiffly. "These things take time."

"Not *that* much time." He ran a critical eye over me. "And if you don't mind my saying so, you don't exactly look like you just hopped up from your portable lab bench, either."

Silently, I stepped aside. He strode in, his eyes flicking around the room and coming to rest on the reader I'd left on the curve couch. "So what did you find?" he asked as I closed the door again.

"More or less what we expected," I said, brushing past him and picking up the reader. I turned it on, called up the analysis file, and handed it to him.

He frowned, tapping the control to scroll the numbers up and down the display. "How do I read this?" he asked.

I lifted an eyebrow. "I thought you worked for a medical company."

"As an organizer and meeting facilitator," he said patiently. "Not as a doctor. Come on—tell me what this says."

"It says cadmium poisoning," I told him. "Lots of it."

He ran the scrolling again and found the cadmium line. "Terrific," he muttered. "Any chance it could have happened by accident?"

"In theory, pretty much any death could have happened by accident," I said. "But when the string of required coincidences gets long enough, I think you can safely call it murder."

He flinched at the word. "That's insane," he insisted. "Who would have wanted Master Bofiv dead?"

"Wrong question," I told him. "The right question is, who would have wanted Master Bofiv *and* Master Colix dead?"

Kennrick stared at me. "Are you telling me they were *both* murdered? By the same person?"

"Unless you plan to string a few more coincidences together," I said.

He looked back at the reader. "No," he said firmly. "No, this just can't be. It *has* to have been an accident."

"You mean like someone accidentally uncapped a bottle of cadmium powder over their dinner plates last night?" I suggested.

"Or they ingested it some other way," he said. "Cadmium is used in batteries, alloys—all sorts of things. Maybe it flaked off a bad battery in Master Colix's luggage, got on his fingers, and from there into one of their shared meals. Or it could even have come off someone else's stuff and gotten into the air system."

"And then carefully proceeded to target Colix and Bofiv, but not Tririn or any of the other Shorshians in the car?"

"People react differently to infections and toxins all the time," Kennrick said doggedly. "There are cases on record where a group of Humans have eaten the same salmonella-infested food. Some got sick, some died, some hardly even noticed. Why should Shorshic metabolism be any different?"

I could almost feel sorry for the man, straining this desperately to find an explanation that didn't include the word *murder*. But facts were facts, and the sooner we popped all the irrelevant soap bubbles, the sooner we could get down to the unpleasant business at hand. "Because this isn't some random bug running up against a whole range of different immune systems," I said. "For Bofiv to have swallowed that much cadmium, the stuff would have had to be raining down like volcanic ash. I guarantee *someone* at the table would have noticed that."

"You're right, you're right," he said heavily. "What do we do?"

"We let me get on with my investigation," I said. "You said last night that you only met him a couple of months ago?"

"Yes, when he and the contract team arrived on Earth," he said, taking a final look at my reader and then handing it back to me. "Pellorian had invited them in to discuss a proposed joint venture in genetic manipulation."

"Were you the one who organized the conference?"

"I handled the details once the plan was up and running," he said. "But only after the initial contacts had been made and the invitations sent out and accepted. I didn't choose any of the contract team, if that's what you're asking."

"Who did?"

"The corporation's CEO, Dr. Earl Messerly," he said. "I imagine the board probably had some input, too."

"You have their names?"

He eyed me as if I'd just turned a deep and fashionable purple. "Are you suggesting upstanding medical professionals would go to the trouble of bringing a couple of Shorshians all the way across the galaxy just to kill them?"

"You know for certain that none of your upstanding medical professionals is harboring a grudge against the Shorshians?" I countered.

He snorted. "You must be kidding," he said. "I've been to full board meetings maybe three times in the seven years I've been with the company. I barely know their names."

"In other words, you can't vouch for any of them." I keyed my reader for input. "So. Their names?"

Glaring at me, he ran through the list. There were twelve of them, plus CEO Messerly. I keyed in the names as he went, knowing full well that Kennrick was probably right about this being a waste of time.

Still, I had a few Who's Who lists among my data chips, both the straightforward cultural ones and a rather more private set that had been assembled by the Confederation's various law enforcement agencies. Running a check of Pellorian's people against the latter might prove interesting.

But regardless of what the comparison turned up, Pellorian's board was back on Earth, and we were here. "Thank you," I said when Kennrick had finished. "Next question: did either Colix or Bofiv bring aboard any of their own food? Special treats or secret indulgences?"

"You'll have to ask Master Tririn about that," Kennrick said. "He was the one sitting with them."

"He was the one sitting with *one* of them, anyway," I said. "I trust he's well this morning?"

"I actually haven't checked," Kennrick said. "You want me to go ask him if Master Bofiv had a private food supply?"

"Not until we can both be there," I said. "Can you go off and amuse yourself while I shower and get dressed?"

He made a face. "It doesn't qualify as amusement, but I do need to give *Usantra* Givvrac an update. He's the head of the contract team."

"At least you shouldn't have any trouble waking him up at this hour," I said. "Unless he's been dipping into Bofiv's secret stash, of course."

Kennrick's throat tightened. "You think this is funny, Compton?" he growled.

"Not at all," I assured him. "Which is *Usantra* Givvrac's compartment?"

"He hasn't got one," Kennrick said. "He's in the first coach car behind the compartment cars."

I frowned, thinking back to our embarkation at Homshil Station. "And yet you escorted them aboard into a compartment car?" I asked. "Even though they had coach car seats?"

"Into *my* compartment car, yes," Kennrick said. "*Usantra* Givvrac and a couple of the others had some documents they wanted stored in my compartment, and they wanted to drop them off on the way to their seats."

Which wasn't proper procedure, since passengers were supposed to enter a Quadrail only through the door of their assigned car. Apparently, Kennrick and his Fillies didn't have a problem with skirting the rules everyone else had to follow. "Whatever," I said. "I'll pick you up on my way back to talk to Tririn."

Silently, Kennrick left the compartment. As I closed the door behind him, I felt the movement of air that meant the connecting wall was opening. "You heard?" I asked, turning around.

"Most of it," Bayta said. She was dressed in her nightshirt and a thin robe, her dark hair tousled and unwashed. But her eyes were clear and awake. "He sounded upset."

"He looked upset, too," I agreed. I let my eyes drop once to the figure semi-hidden beneath her robe, then forced my gaze back above her neckline where it belonged. Bayta was my colleague and ally in this war, nothing more, and I had damn well better not forget that. "What did you think of his suggestion that the cadmium might have been airborne?"

She frowned. "Didn't you already tell him that was ridiculous?"

"In the way he was thinking about it, absolutely," I agreed. "But he was trying to make it a careless accident. I'm wondering about it as a somewhat more careful murder."

"That still leaves the problem of why only Master Colix and Master Bofiv were affected," she pointed out.

"True, unless someone managed to uncork a bottle of eau de cadmium under the victims' snouts," I said. "Or maybe it was in the form of some cadmium compound that only Shorshians can absorb."

"I don't know," she said doubtfully. "There are toxins that target specific species, but those also get absorbed by everyone else. And most cadmium compounds are as toxic as the element itself, and to nearly all species to one level or another."

I raised my eyebrows. "Impressive."

She shrugged slightly. "I couldn't sleep last night after I went to bed, so I did a little reading," she explained. "The other problem is that since cadmium compounds are inherently poisonous, anything in a liquid or gaseous form should have been screened out by the station sensors."

"Maybe the killer brought the stuff aboard in component form," I suggested. "The cadmium in, say, a battery or alloy, and the delivery chemical as something else."

"The sensors are supposed to watch for that sort of thing."

"*Supposed to* being the key phrase," I said. "Assuming something like that was done, could traces of it have gotten sucked into the car's air filters?"

"Certainly," she said. "All the air in a car eventually travels through those filters."

I nodded. "It's a long shot, but I think it's worth checking out. What would it take to get into one of the air filters in that car?"

"It's not that simple," Bayta said, her eyes unfocusing as she conferred with the Spiders. "There's a whole mechanism that will have to be disassembled. I've sent four mites to start the job, but it'll take a few hours."

"That's okay," I said. "Have them contact you when they're almost done."

"All right," she said. "Are we going to go talk to Master Tririn now?"

"Or we could stop and have some breakfast first," I said. "Your call."

She hesitated, and I had the odd impression that she was searching my face looking for the right answer. "I'm not that hungry," she said.

That was the answer, all right. "Me, neither," I agreed. "Go get ready. We head out in fifteen minutes."

Eighteen minutes later, we passed through the rear vestibule of the third compartment car and entered the first of the first-class coach cars.

I'd rather expected that Kennrick would still be deep in conversation with *Usantra* Givvrac, and I was right. The Human was sitting on the edge of a seat near the right-hand wall, talking earnestly with one of the four Fillies I'd seen him boarding with at Homshil Station.

And now that I was focusing on the Filly himself, I could see that he had the graying body hair of someone well advanced in years.

That alone was mildly surprising. Fillies of that age and rank usually stayed close to home and sent out their younger colleagues and subordinates on fact-finding and contract-making missions. I wondered what kind of lure Pellorian Medical had lobbed into the water to bring out someone of Givvrac's standing.

Kennrick was sitting where he could watch the vestibule door, and as Bayta and I entered the car he spoke a few last words to the Filly and stood up. The alien himself looked at me and nodded a silent acknowledgment as Kennrick maneuvered his way through the little clusters of seats the rest of the passengers had constructed. "That was fast," he commented as he reached us. His eyes flicked to Bayta, but he didn't comment on the fact that I'd brought a guest along.

"Bayta and I can do this alone if you weren't finished with your conversation," I offered.

"No, that's all right," he said. "*Usantra* Givvrac wants me present when you question Master Tririn. He wants to get to the bottom of this even more than you do."

"I'm sure he does," I said, returning Givvrac's acknowledging nod with one of my own. "After you."

The three of us headed aft, walking through the rest of the first- and second-class cars and on into third. As we passed the second/third dispensary I glanced inside, but there was no one there except the server Spider on duty. There were no dead bodies, either, Bofiv having apparently been taken back to the baggage car while Bayta and I slept.

We found Tririn hunched over in his seat, his eyes staring fixedly at the seat back in front of him as he ignored both the exotic alien travelscape playing on the display window to his left and Master Bofiv's empty seat to his right. In the aisle seat of his row was the Nemut Kennrick had mentioned, his rainbow-slashed eyes focused on a reader, his truncated-cone-shaped mouth making little motions like a pre-K child trying to sound out the words.

Two rows ahead of them, Terese German was sitting with her eyes closed, a set of headphones locked snugly around her ears, a silent but clear warning to all and sundry that she wanted to be left alone. Two seats to her right, next to the train's outer side, a young Juri with the unpolished scales of a commoner was gazing intently at the dit rec drama playing on the display window to his right.

We passed their row and came to a halt beside the Nemut. "Master Tririn?" Kennrick called softly. "Master Tririn?"

The Shorshian didn't answer, or even turn to face us. "I don't think he wants to talk," Kennrick concluded. "Maybe we should try again later."

"Or maybe we should try a little harder right now," I said, looking at the Nemut in the aisle seat. "Excuse me?"

"Yes?" the other asked, his deep voice sounding a little slurred. Small wonder; now that I was standing over him I could see that he had an open bag full of small, colorful snack cubes resting in his lap. Apparently, the mouth movements I'd noticed earlier had had nothing to do with the sounding out of words.

"I'd like to get past, if I may," I told him, gesturing toward the empty seat between him and Tririn. I actually didn't need him to move—even third-class Quadrail seats allowed the average passenger plenty of legroom—but it was always polite to ask.

"Certainly," the Nemut said. Getting a grip on his goodie bag, he drew in his knees.

"Thank you." I sidled past him and sat down beside Tririn. "Good day, Master Tririn," I said. "Frank Compton. You may remember me from last night."

[I remember you, Mr. Compton,] Tririn said, the normal harshness of the Shishish tempered by the listlessness in his voice. [And the day is not good. No days from now on will be good.]

"I understand," I said, glancing back at Kennrick. He was still standing in the aisle, glowering at my brazenness at barging in on Tririn's solitude this way. Bayta, for her part, was standing a little apart from him, up near Terese's row, where she wouldn't crowd us but would still be close enough to listen in on the conversation. "Were Master Colix and Master Bofiv close friends of yours?" I asked, turning back to Tririn.

[They were business associates,] he said.

"I understand," I said again, wondering briefly if he was correcting me or agreeing with me. "Tell me, did all three of you eat together yesterday?"

[We ate sundown together,] he said. [Sunrise and midday were eaten individually.]

According to my encyclopedia, that was indeed the standard practice for non-family Shorshians traveling together. Unfortunately, it didn't tell me whether or not the three had been friends or something more distant. "Do you remember what you all ate at sundown?" I asked.

[The common dish was *po krem*,] he said. [It's a shred, a mixture of meat and fruits.]

"Yes, I've heard of it," I said. "What reaches did all of you use?"

For the first time since I'd sat down he turned his face toward me. [My apologies, Mr. Compton,] he said, eyeing me curiously. [I took you to be as other Humans, ignorant of Shorshic custom and honor nodes. For that unspoken slight, I ask your forgiveness.]

"Freely and openly granted," I assured him, giving silent thanks that I'd had the sense to sacrifice an hour of sleep last night in favor of a crash course in Shorshic social customs and terminology.

[Thank you,] he said. [My reach was *galla* bread. Master Colix and Master Bofiv used baked *prinn* scoops.]

So the two dead Shorshians had eaten from the common bowl with the same type of edible scoops, while the Shorshian alive and breathing had used something else. I made a mental note to check with the server Spiders to see if those choices were standard for the three of them, or whether they'd been unique to the fatal evening. "And your individuals?"

[All different,] he said. [*Birrsh* for Master Colix, *valarrki* for Master Bofiv, *sorvidae* for me.] His eyes flicked briefly past my shoulder. [Yet the Spiders said the death was not in the food. Do you believe otherwise?]

"I don't believe there was any death in the food when it was served to you," I told him. "But possibly something happened after that. Do you remember anyone approaching your table while you ate? Perhaps to ask a question, or to engage one of you in conversation?"

Tririn cocked his head in thought. I watched him closely, wondering if he was searching his memory or just trying to think up a good lie. [I don't believe so,] he said at last. [There were servers, of course, but no one else approached.]

"Did you happen to notice who was sitting at the nearby tables?" I asked.

Tririn's brow wrinkled. [We sat at a corner table,] he said. [There was only one table near us. Unfortunately, my back was to the occupants.]

I grimaced. "I see," I said. "Well, then—"

"I saw them," the Nemut on my other side volunteered.

I turned to him in surprise. "*You* saw them?"

"They were Humans," he told me. "One female, one male."

One female . . . "Was it by any chance that female up there?" I asked, pointing two rows ahead toward Terese.

Or rather, toward Terese's empty seat. Terese herself had vanished.

So had Bayta.

"Kennrick?" I demanded, standing up for a better look. Neither of the women was anywhere to be seen.

"Take it easy—they're in the restroom," Kennrick said, nodding toward the front of the car. "The German girl headed off—kind of fast, actually—and your friend followed."

"Ah," I said, frowning as I sat back down. That was at least twice now that Terese had suddenly been taken ill. "Let me rephrase the question," I said to the Nemut. "Was the woman you saw the same one who usually sits there?"

"I believe so," he said. "Though Humans are difficult to distinguish between."

"I understand," I said. "Can you remember anything about the male Human?"

The Nemut's angled shoulder muscles quivered briefly in one of their equivalents of a shrug. "His hair was white," he said. "That is all I remember."

"That's fine—you've been very helpful," I assured him. "Thank you." I turned back to Tririn. "My apologies," I said. "For the interruption in our talk, I ask your forgiveness."

[Freely and openly granted,] he assured me. [Do you believe the death was in these Humans?]

"I don't know yet," I said. "Two further questions, if I may. First, do you know whether either Master Colix or Master Bofiv had a private food supply? Something they brought aboard, as opposed to something supplied by the servers aboard the train?"

[Master Bofiv had no such supply,] Tririn said. [I would surely have seen if he had.]

"And Master Colix?"

[I don't know,] Tririn said. [You would need to inquire of one of his seatmates.]

"I'll do that," I promised. "Final question, then. Whose

idea was it for Master Colix to sit away from you and Master Bofiv?"

[It was Master Colix's choice,] Tririn said. [He asked specifically for that seat.]

Which was more or less what Terese had implied earlier. "Was there some trouble between the three of you?" I asked.

[Not at all,] Tririn said. [Master Colix prided himself on his knowledge of alien languages. He hoped that seated between a Human and Juri he would have the opportunity to practice and improve his skill at both languages.]

"Really," I said. "I was under the impression that Shorshic vocal apparatus couldn't handle either of them."

Tririn seemed to draw back, as if suddenly realizing he had strayed onto forbidden territory. [There are ways,] he said, his tone guarded.

"Ah," I said, keeping my expression neutral. According to my reader's data files, that was an outright lie. Shorshians were completely incapable of speaking anything but Shishish and a smattering of Fili unless they'd had what was rather sarcastically referred to as the Gibber Operation.

Had Colix gone under the knife? I couldn't tell—Tririn's phrasing had left that ambiguous, possibly deliberately so. It *was* clear, though, that he didn't want to discuss it further.

But there were other ways to get the answer to that one. If Master Colix had been able to speak English or Juric, one of his seatmates would surely know it. "I thank you for your time and patience, Master Tririn," I said. "Especially on this day of sadness. I hope you'll be equally gracious should I need to discuss the matter with you further."

[I will be most pleased to do so, Mr. Compton,] he said. His eyes flicked to Kennrick. [*You* are welcome to approach at any time.]

"Thank you," I said. "Good day, Master Tririn."

I sidled past the Nemut with a nod of thanks, brushed by Kennrick, and headed up the aisle toward the front of the car. I was passing Terese's empty seat when Kennrick caught up with me. "Wait a minute," he said in a low voice. "Damn it, Compton—*wait*."

"Problem?" I asked, not breaking stride.

"Yes, *problem*," he gritted out. "You may be the hotshot detective, but even I know that basic investigative technique includes double-checking everyone's story."

"That's exactly what I'm doing," I told him. "Or had you forgotten that Ms. German is up here in the restroom?"

"I was thinking about the Juri in the other seat," he growled, jerking a thumb back at Terese's row. "The one Master Tririn claims Master Colix was speaking Juric to."

"And you think I should question the Juri about that?" I asked mildly.

"Absolutely," Kennrick said. "You were right—Shorshic vocal apparatus—"

"You think I should question the Juri about it while Master Tririn is within earshot of the conversation?"

"It wouldn't be—" He broke off. "Oh. Right. That wouldn't be very politic, would it?"

"Hardly politic at all," I agreed. "But if you want to try it, be my guest."

Kennrick grimaced. "I guess you've noticed that Master Tririn and I don't get along very well."

"It's a little hard to miss," I agreed. "What's the problem?"

"I just can't connect with him," he said. "I really don't know why."

"Did you have the same problem when you were on Earth?"

"If we did, I didn't notice it," he said. "It was only after we came aboard the Quadrail at Terra Station that things started to go downhill." He shrugged. "Of course, it could just be that he was on his best behavior during the discussions at Pellorian. Maybe even back then he didn't really like me. *Or* the others."

"He didn't get along with the others?"

"I had that impression," Kennrick said. "But it's just an impression. Like I said, if there was trouble between them they probably wouldn't confide in me. But it makes sense that if he had trouble with me, he might have had trouble with the others, too."

"Perhaps," I said. Though privately I could easily see how someone could love his fellow man and still not like Kennrick. "I'll try to sound him out about that later."

The outer restroom door was still closed when we reached it. I considered going inside and seeing if I could figure out which stall Terese was in, decided she would probably take violent offense if I tried, and found a place by the door where I could lean against the wall and cultivate patience. Taking his cue from me, Kennrick found a spot of his own a little farther up the car and did likewise.

Patience is always rewarded. A couple of minutes later the door opened and Terese stepped out. She looked a little pale, which meant that when she reddened with anger at seeing me standing there her color came out just about right. "Good morning, Ms. German," I said, stepping into her path.

I expected her to try to push her way around me. Instead, she fired a withering glare in my direction, spun a hundred eighty degrees, and headed forward at the fastest walk she could manage without actually breaking into a jog. By the time I recovered from my surprise at her sudden about-face, she was into the vestibule and out of sight.

"Well, *that's* inconvenient," Kennrick growled.

"Relax," I soothed him. "Where's she going to go on a Quadrail?" I looked back at the restroom door as Bayta emerged. "What's the verdict?" I asked her.

"She was throwing up," Bayta said. "I don't know how bad it was—she wouldn't let me help her."

Kennrick swore under his breath. "So she's definitely sick," he said. "Compton, this has gone way beyond serious."

"Relax," I advised him, eyeing the vestibule door and thinking back to that last view I'd had of Terese's face. In my experience, people with serious illnesses usually didn't have the mental and emotional strength to spare for that level of annoyance. At least not against relative strangers.

"Because if you were wrong about the cadmium, and the Shorshians had something contagious—"

"I said *relax*," I repeated, more firmly this time. "Let's not start a panic until it's absolutely necessary, all right?"

He made a face, but nodded. "So what do we do?"

"We go after her," I said. "Either she's on her way to the shower/laundry car, which is unlikely since she hasn't got a change of clothing with her, or else she's headed for the dining car for something to settle her stomach."

"Fine," Kennrick asked in a tone of overstrained patience. "So can we go?"

In answer, I took Bayta's arm and headed for the vestibule. Assuming Terese kept up the same pace that she'd left here with, by the time she reached the archway into the third-class dining car she would have quick-walked for most of three long Quadrail cars. All that exercise, plus her stomach trouble, should take some of the starch out of her and make her a little easier to question.

We walked through the shower/laundry car, then the storage car, and finally through the vestibule into the third-class dining car. As with all such cars, the aisle here veered all the way to the right side of the car so as to avoid cutting the dining area in half. There were large, slightly tinted windows in the wall that separated the dining room from the corridor, allowing the patrons to watch those passing by and vice versa. "Any sign of her?" I asked, slowing down as I peered in through the windows.

"Not yet," Kennrick said. "Maybe she went past and has gone to ground somewhere forward."

"There," Bayta said, pointing.

I followed her finger. Terese was standing at the bar at the forward end of the car, talking earnestly to a tall Filly I didn't recognize. "Anyone seen that Filly before?" I asked.

"No," Bayta said.

"Me, neither," Kennrick said. "Does he look a little drunk to you?"

"Not really," I said. "You two stay out here. Be ready to corral her if she makes another break for it." Squaring my shoulders, I walked through the archway into the dining area.

I was halfway through the maze of tables and chairs when the Filly detached himself from Terese and headed toward me. "May you be well," I said in greeting as he got within earshot.

"You will not bother the Human female," he said, his tone flat and unfriendly.

"I'm not bothering her," I assured him, coming to a halt. "I just want to ask her a few questions."

"You will not bother the Human female," he repeated, his hands bunching into fists as he continued toward me.

I sighed. Apparently, Terese hadn't come here for something to settle her stomach. She'd come here looking for a white knight to protect her.

And she had apparently found one.

SIX :

"Easy, now," I cautioned, holding my hands out toward the Filly as I reversed direction, backing toward the archway and the corridor beyond. The last thing I wanted was to get involved in a brawl with one of the other passengers. The *very* last thing I wanted was for that brawl to take place in a dining room.

But the Filly kept coming, the thought of broken tables, crockery, and bones apparently not bothering him in the least. I continued giving way, still making useless soothing noises. The carefully designed privacy acoustics of Quadrail dining cars meant that none of the other patrons could really make out what either of us was saying, but pretty much everyone facing our direction had spotted the gathering storm and had clued in their dining partners. If I'd ever wanted to get beaten to a pulp in front of an audience, I reflected sourly, this was my big chance.

Apparently, Bayta was thinking along the same lines. The *kwi* snugged away in my pocket tingled as she telepathically activated the weapon.

I could certainly see her point. The Filly probably outweighed me by ten kilos, and while his species wasn't known for their prowess at unarmed combat, they weren't complete slouches at it, either. The chance to drop him where he stood was a very tempting proposition.

Unfortunately, the presence of an audience put that option off the table. Using a weapon, even a nonlethal one, on a supposedly weapons-free Quadrail would draw way too much unwelcome attention.

Fortunately, the *kwi* wouldn't be necessary. I'd backed up nearly to the archway now, and had finally reached my goal: a small section of empty floor space.

Time to make my move.

"All right, this has gone far enough," I said firmly, coming to an abrupt halt with my hands still held out in front of me, my palms toward the Filly. "I'm going to question Ms. German, and that's all there is to it."

He took the bait. "You will not bother the Human female," he said, continuing forward and reaching for my left wrist. As he stretched out his arm, I smoothly withdrew mine, bringing it inward toward my chest. He picked up his pace, reaching even more insistently toward me.

And with his complete attention now focused on the wrist that was somehow managing to remain just out of his grasp, I reached across with my right hand, grabbed his hand and bent the wrist in on itself, then snaked my left hand behind his elbow.

An instant later he found himself pinned upright in place, his arm locked vertically at his side, his weight coming up on his toes as I pulled the bent wrist upward and inward. "Now," I said softly to the long face and startled eyes fifteen centimeters from my own. "I'm going to ask Ms. German a few questions, and then she can go about her business. Is that all right with you?"

For a couple of heartbeats he remained silent. "A few questions only," he replied at last.

"Thank you," I said.

Releasing his arm, I took a step backward. I was taking something of a risk, I knew—he was uninjured, he still had those ten kilos on me, and he was perfectly capable of backing out of his verbal agreement if he chose to do so.

But he didn't. Apparently, he was smart enough to realize that someone who had just showed my brand of restraint in round one was likely to have more painful options available for round two. Stepping to the side, he gestured me back into the dining area.

Terese was still standing by the bar, her mouth hanging slightly open. Apparently, she hadn't expected her white knight to be vanquished quite so easily.

Which meant she'd had some expectations to begin with, either about me or about the Filly. I tucked away that little bit of data for future consideration. "Hello, Ms. German," I said, nodding politely as I came up to her. "Remember me?"

She clamped her mouth closed. "What do you want?"

"The answers to a few questions," I said. "A *very* few questions." I gestured her to one of the bar stools. "Have a seat?"

Reluctantly, she plopped down on the stool. I took the next one and sat down facing her. Out of the corner of my eye I saw that Bayta and Kennrick had now come into the dining area and were watching us from across the room. "I heard a rumor that Master Colix might have brought along some private snacks," I said. "Did you notice him with anything like that?"

Terese shrugged. "He might have had something."

"Were they in a bag?" I asked. "A nice box? A tube dispenser?"

"It was a dark brown bag," she said. "Small, like a meal from a quick-food spot. But I don't know where it came from." She gave a flip of her fingertips that somehow managed to take in the entire room. "He could even have gotten it from here, for all I know."

"We can check on that," I said. "Did you notice anything specific about the bag or its contents, anything about how either looked? Or were there any strange aromas that might have caught your attention?"

She shook her head. "Like I said, I didn't really pay much attention to him."

"So who *should* I be talking to about this?"

"The Juri on his other side," she said. "The two of them were jabbering all the time." She wrinkled her nose. "It was like bad Chinese or something."

That was actually a pretty fair description of how Juric sounded. "You said he showed you holos of his family?"

"Once," she said. "Mostly, he just talked about his job."

I nodded. "How was Master Colix's English, by the way? I'm told he was trying to brush up on his language skills."

She wrinkled her nose again. "He still had a long way to go."

"But you *could* understand him?"

"As much as I wanted to. Look, can I go now?"

"Sure," I said, gesturing her toward the exit. "You know, you really ought to see a doctor about that stomach of yours."

That got me another glare as she slid off her stool. "I'm fine," she insisted. "It's not contagious, if that's what you're worried about."

"Not really," I said as she turned away and took a step toward the archway. "I'm sure Dr. Witherspoon would have said something to the Spiders if you were."

Even with her back to me, I could see her reaction to Witherspoon's name. "Who?" she asked, stopping but not turning around.

"Dr. Witherspoon," I repeated. "The man you had dinner with last night."

"I didn't have dinner with him," she said, still keeping her face away from me. "I was eating by myself and he came over and sat down."

"And you immediately told him to take a hike, right?"

She hesitated, and I could see the tension in her shoulders as she tried to guess how much I knew, and therefore how much bending of the truth she could get away with. "He might have stayed for a few minutes," she conceded. "He said he'd noticed my stomach problem and wanted to ask me about it."

"What did you tell him?"

She gave me an oblique look over her shoulder. "Can I leave now?"

"I already said you could," I said. "Thanks for your cooperation."

She might have expelled a sarcastic snort as she strode off, but with the dining car's acoustics I couldn't tell for sure. She glared at the Filly who she'd sent to stop me, strode past Bayta and Kennrick without a glance at either of them, and headed back down the corridor toward her car.

"Well, that was interesting," Kennrick commented as he and Bayta joined me at the bar. "What exactly did you say to her there at the end?"

"I take it there was a reaction?" I asked.

"Oh, a beaut," Kennrick assured me. "What did you say?"

For a moment I considered not telling him. But he'd already heard the Nemut mention that Terese had met a white-haired

Human over dinner, and it wouldn't take much of a deductive leap on his part to tag Witherspoon for the part. "I asked about her dinner with Dr. Witherspoon," I said.

"Really," Kennrick said. "And?"

"She denied it was an actual dinner," I said. "According to her, he just dropped by to see how she was feeling."

Kennrick grunted. "Did you get anything about her sickness?"

"Not a whisper," I said. "I wonder if you could do me a favor."

He cocked an eyebrow, possibly noting the irony of a former Westali agent asking a former fugitive for help. But if he was tempted to make a comment to that effect, he managed to resist it. "Shoot," he invited.

"I want you to track down Dr. Witherspoon," I said. "Find out what the symptoms are of heavy-metal poisoning in Humans."

Kennrick looked at the archway where Terese had just exited. "You think *she's* the one who poisoned them?"

"No idea," I said. "But she seems to be the only one who was in the victims' immediate vicinity who's also noticeably ill."

"Yes, but *her?*" Kennrick persisted. "She doesn't exactly have that icy killer look about her."

"Not very many icy killers do," I said. "Maybe her stomach trouble has nothing to do with this. But if it does, I'd like to find it out before someone else joins the choir invisible."

"Point," Kennrick said heavily. "Any idea where Witherspoon might be?"

I looked at Bayta. "His seat is two cars back from Ms. German's," she said. "I don't know if he's there, though."

"But there are only fifteen third-class cars," I added helpfully. "He has to be there somewhere."

"Thanks," Kennrick growled. "If and when I find him, where will you be?"

"In my bed," I said, yawning widely. "I'm still way too short on sleep."

"I know the feeling," Kennrick said. "Talk to you later." With a nod at Bayta, he left the dining area and headed toward the rear of the train.

"Do you want me to see if the Spiders can locate Dr. Witherspoon?" Bayta asked.

"Even if they could, I'd just as soon have Kennrick wander around on his own for awhile," I said. "I know he's worried about his precious contract team, but I don't especially like having him underfoot. How's the disassembly of the air filter system going?"

"Slowly," Bayta said. "I don't think one of these has ever been taken apart while the train was in motion, and the mites are having to figure it out as they go. Do you think Ms. German is the killer?"

"My first impression is no," I said. "But I'm not ready to write anyone off·the suspect list quite yet. She's certainly had enough access to the victims over the past two weeks. *And* she's definitely hiding something."

Bayta looked at the archway. "Do you suppose she could be running away from home?"

"Jumping a Quadrail is a pretty pricey way of escaping Mom and Dad," I reminded her. "On the other hand, without access to the Spiders' station-based records, there's no way to know the circumstances of her coming aboard."

"No, there's not," Bayta murmured thoughtfully. "Do you suppose that's why the killer chose a cross-galactic express? So that we wouldn't be able to get anyone's records?"

"Could be," I said. "Or so we wouldn't be able to call for

help, get quick and complete autopsies, or get out of his line of fire. Pick one."

Bayta shivered. "You think he's planning more killings, then?"

"I would hope that two dead bodies would be enough for anyone," I said soberly. "But I wouldn't bet the rent money on it."

"No." She took a deep breath, and for just a moment her mask dropped away to reveal something tired and anxious. It was a side of her that I didn't see very often, and there was something about it that made me want to take her hand and tell her, don't worry, it'll be all right.

But I didn't. I didn't dare. Among his other tricks, the Modhri employed something called thought viruses, suggestions that could be sent telepathically from a walker to an un-infected person. In one of the lowest ironies of this whole miserable business, thought viruses traveled best along the lines of trust between friends, close colleagues, or lovers.

Which meant that once the Modhri had established a col-ony in one person, the walker's entire circle of friends was usu-ally soon to follow, lemming-like, in the act of touching some Modhran coral and starting their own Modhran polyp colo-nies. The Modhri had used that technique to infiltrate business centers, industrial directorates, counterintelligence squads, and even whole governments.

Bayta and I were close. We had to be, working and fighting alongside each other the way we were. But at the same time, we had to struggle to maintain as much emotional distance be-tween us as we possibly could. Otherwise, if the Modhri ever got to one of us, he would inevitably get the other one, too.

Bayta knew that as well as I did. The moment of vulnera-bility passed, her mask came back up, and I once again forced my protective male instincts into the background. "So what's our next move?" she asked.

"Exactly what I told Kennrick." I yawned again. "I'm going to get some sleep. You coming?"

"I think I'll wander around a little longer," she said. "Maybe go watch the air system disassembly. I don't think I could sleep just now."

I eyed her, that brief flicker of vulnerability coming back to mind. But her professional self was back in charge, cool and confident and competent.

And it wasn't like she would be alone out here. Not with hundreds of people milling around and other hundreds of Spiders watching her every move. "Okay," I said, pushing myself off the bar stool. "Just be careful. And let me know if anything happens."

"What if what happens isn't especially interesting?" she asked.

"This is a murder investigation," I reminded her grimly. "*Everything* is interesting."

This time I got nearly four hours of sleep before I was awakened by a growling stomach, the realization that I hadn't eaten since last night, and the delectable aroma of onion rings.

"I thought you might be hungry," Bayta said as she carefully balanced the onion rings and a cup of iced tea on the edge of my computer desk's swivel table.

"Very," I confirmed, sniffing at the plate with mild surprise. Offhand, I couldn't think of any other time when Bayta had brought me something to eat purely on her own initiative. Either she was finally getting the hang of this girl-Friday stuff, or else I was looking even more old and decrepit and pitiable than usual lately. "Thanks. Have a bite?"

"No, thank you," she said, her cheek twitching. "My stomach's been bothering me a little today."

"You're probably just hungry," I suggested as I sat down and took a sip of the tea. It was strong and sweet, just the way I liked it.

"No, I had a vegetable roll a couple of hours ago," she said. "I'm just feeling a little odd today, that's all."

I frowned at her as I bit into one of the onion rings. "Odd enough to have you checked over by one of the doctors?"

"Oh, no, it's nothing like that," she assured me. "Like I said, my stomach's just a little sensitive."

"Okay," I said, making a mental note to keep tabs on her digestive rumblings. With two confirmed poisonings, and Terese German apparently heaving her guts on a regular basis, I wasn't ready yet to chalk up Bayta's oddness to normal travel indigestion. "Any news on the air filter?"

"It's almost ready," she said. "Another hour, maybe."

"Good," I said, biting a third out of the next onion ring in line and washing it down with a swig of tea. "You didn't happen to bump into either Kennrick or Dr. Witherspoon while you were wandering around, did you?"

"I didn't spot either of them," Bayta said. "But I wasn't really looking. I was mostly talking to *Tas* Krodo."

"Who?"

"Master Colix's other seatmate," she said. "The one Ms. German said he mostly talked to."

I frowned at her. "You talked to him? Alone?"

"Not alone, no," she said evenly. "There were other passengers in the car."

"That's not what I meant," I said, setting down a half-eaten onion ring. Was that what the unexpected tea service had been all about? Some kind of preemptive peace offering? "Interrogation is an art, Bayta."

"It wasn't an interrogation," she said, her voice stiff. "We were just two people having a conversation."

I took a careful breath, the old phrase *poisoning the well* flashing to mind. Putting potential witnesses on their guard—or worse, accidentally planting suggestions as to what you wanted to hear—could wreck an entire session. Especially when aliens and alien cultures were involved. "Bayta—"

"I'm not a child, Frank," she snapped. "Don't talk to me as if I were. I've watched you enough times to know the kinds of questions to ask."

"All right," I said as calmly as I could. A fight right now wouldn't help either of us, or the situation, in the slightest. "What kinds of questions did you ask?"

"I first confirmed that he did talk a great deal with Master Colix," she said. Her tone was a near-perfect copy of a junior Westali agent reporting to a superior. "I also confirmed that Master Colix was able to speak both English and Juric. Apparently, Master Colix spent a lot of time talking to *Tas* Krodo about the Path of Onagnalhni."

"The—? Oh, right." I nodded. "Kennrick's Path of the Unpronounceable and Untranslatable. Not entirely unpronounceable, I see."

"Pretty close, though," Bayta said, relaxing slightly. For all her stubbornly defiant talk about doing her own bit of investigating, she really *had* been worried about how mad I would be at her. "He also said that Master Colix had a dark brown bag of what he thought were some kind of fruit snacks."

"He tasted one?"

"No, Master Colix never offered to share," Bayta said. "But they had a fruity scent."

"Sounds harmless enough," I said.

"Yes, it does," Bayta said. "But when I went to look for them in the overhead and underseat storage compartments, I couldn't find them."

I frowned. "The *locked* overhead and underseat compartments?"

"Those compartments, yes," she said grimly. "Only by the time I got to them they weren't locked anymore."

"Well, now, that's very interesting," I murmured, picking up another onion ring and chewing thoughtfully at it. "Did you notice anything unusual about the locks? Any damage to the catches or scratch marks anywhere?"

"I didn't see anything." Bayta's lips compressed briefly. "But I probably don't know what to look for, do I?"

"You'd have noticed if the locks had been forced," I assured her. "That's usually pretty obvious. But the differences between key and keypick aren't nearly so blatant."

"Keypicks don't work on Quadrail locks," Bayta said.

"If something can be coded to be unlocked, somebody will eventually find a way to fake that code," I said, picking up the last two onion rings and cramming them into my mouth. "That, or they'll get hold of a copy of the actual key."

"The passenger's ticket is the only key."

"So I've heard," I said. "So unless the thief forced the locks, we arrive at the conclusion that he also absconded with Colix's key."

"Before he died?"

"Or afterward," I said. "Dead people are much less argumentative when you're going through their pockets."

Bayta shivered. "Sounds awful," she murmured.

"It isn't high on anyone's pleasant-activities list," I conceded as I stepped into the half-bath to wash the onion ring breading off my hands. "But there's still a chance that someone simply broke in. We'll need to go take a look to be sure."

"All right," Bayta said slowly. "But why would anyone want to steal Master Colix's fruit snacks? You can get things like that in the dining car."

"Maybe you can't get his specific brand," I said. "Or maybe there's some other reason entirely." I scratched my head as a sudden ferocious itch ran through my scalp. "But one question at a time. Let's figure out first how the compartments were opened. Then we can tackle the who and why of it."

My plan was to first check out the late Master Colix's storage compartments and then hunt down Kennrick to see what, if anything, he'd learned from Witherspoon about heavy-metal poisoning symptoms in Humans.

Like most of my plans these days, this one didn't survive very long.

We were passing through the last first-class coach when we spotted both Kennrick and Witherspoon. They had pulled up a pair of chairs to face *di*-Master Strinni. Witherspoon was examining the Shorshian, who was gesturing oddly as he talked in a low voice.

And from Witherspoon's expression, I could tell something was wrong.

The doctor glanced up as we approached. "Mr. Compton," he greeted me absently, his mind clearly elsewhere.

"Dr. Witherspoon," I nodded back. "We having a conference?"

"Not exactly," Witherspoon said as he peered closely into Strinni's eyes.

"*Di*-Master Strinni is feeling strangely stressed and nervous," Kennrick explained. "He asked the conductor to allow Dr. Witherspoon into first to administer a sedative."

I eyed Strinni. His muscles were trembling beneath his skin, his breath was coming in short bursts, and his eyes were darting back and forth between the four of us. He certainly looked stressed. "How long before it takes effect?" I asked.

"I haven't given it to him yet," Witherspoon said. "This is something more than simple stress."

I felt my throat tighten. "You mean like—?"

"No," Witherspoon interrupted, throwing me a warning look under his eyebrows. "The symptoms aren't right for that."

"What *are* they right for?" I countered. "No—never mind. Let's just get him to the dispensary and see if—"

[No,] Strinni cut me off. His voice was harsh and dark and as shaky as his musculature. [I will not be poisoned by Spider medicine. The Spiders seek to destroy us all. I will not be placed within their metal claws.]

I frowned. Granted that I hadn't spent more than a few minutes with him before now, such a rabidly anti-Spider attitude was still a surprise. "I'm just suggesting a visit to the diagnostic table," I said. "They're Fibibib design, actually—nothing Spider about them."

[On such a table is where my comrades expired,] Strinni countered. [I do not wish to join them in the silence of death.]

"I'm sure their deaths had nothing to do with the table," I said, deciding to skip over the fact that Master Bofiv, at least, had died long before he reached the table.

"And we won't take you there against your wishes," Kennrick added, his eyes on Witherspoon. "Doctor?"

"I don't know," Witherspoon murmured, touching the edge of Strinni's armpit where the most prominent Shorshic pulse was located. "His pulse is thready, his skin conductivity is bouncing around, and he's so weak he can barely walk. But what that all adds up to, I don't know."

"Seems to me that it's time for a full-press consultation," I said. "Let's get Dr. Aronobal up here and see if she's got any ideas."

[No!] Strinni spat before Witherspoon could answer. [I will not be treated by a Filiaelian!]

"I've already suggested that Dr. Aronobal be brought in," Witherspoon told me grimly. "But *di*-Master Strinni absolutely refuses to see anyone but me."

[I will not be debased so,] Strinni insisted, his arm flailings widening their range.

"No one will force that on you, *di*-Master Strinni," Witherspoon said, holding out his hands. "Please, try to stay calm."

"We're just trying to help you," I added, catching Kennrick's eye and giving him a questioning frown. Wordlessly, he gave me a helpless shrug. Apparently, Strinni's freshly exposed bigotry and paranoia was a new one on him, too.

But my attempt at soothing noises had come too late. [You're with them!] Strinni snarled abruptly, leveling two fingers at my chest. [You serve and obey them!]

And without warning he heaved himself to his feet, knocked Witherspoon sideways out of his chair with a sweep of his right arm, and lunged straight at me.

I did my best to get out of his way. But I was caught flat-footed, my attention still on Kennrick, and standing between Bayta and the next chair over with zero maneuvering room.

My only chance was to back up as fast as I could and hope I could get to a better position before he reached me.

But Strinni was already in motion, and my combat reflexes were sadly out of shape. I'd barely gotten a single step when he slammed into me like a Minneapolis snowplow, his momentum shoving the two of us backward toward whatever bone-wrenching obstacles might be lurking in our path. His big arms wrapped around my back and neck, squeezing my torso and crushing my face against his shoulder. I caught a whiff of something sickly sweet—

Abruptly the bear hug was lifted, and I found myself tottering backward alone. I blinked my eyes to clear them, and found that Strinni had gained two new attachments: Bayta and Kennrick, one of them hanging on to each of his arms like terriers on a bull.

A single sweep of Strinni's arm had sent Witherspoon to the floor. Assuming Strinni was thinking at all, he was undoubtedly thinking he could shake off his new attackers with similar ease. With a bellow, he bent at the waist, half turning and swinging his arms horizontally like massive windmill blades.

Kennrick managed to hang on for about a quarter turn before he lost his grip and flew two meters across the floor to pile himself against the back of one of the other chairs, eliciting a startled bark from the Fibibib seated there. With one of his arms freed, Strinni now shifted his attention to freeing the other one.

But Bayta was stronger than she looked. She held on stubbornly as Strinni swung his arm and torso ponderously back and forth. I got my balance back, grabbed a quick lungful of air, and headed back toward the melee.

Only to be brought up short as a Filly forearm appeared out of nowhere to bar my way. "That is no way to behave toward one who is ill," the alien chided as he glared down a distinctive rose-colored blaze at me. His skin was flushed, his pupils wide with too much alcohol or excitement or both. "He must be treated with respect and care."

"You want to try respect and care, be my guest," I bit out, trying to push his arm out of the way.

But Rose Nose was as determined as I was, and I still didn't have all my wind back. For a couple of seconds we struggled, him still spouting platitudes, me trying very hard not to simply haul off and slug him.

It was just as well that I didn't. The Filly's delay meant that Kennrick recovered his balance and got back to Strinni before I did.

Which meant that it was Kennrick, not me, who caught a swinging Shorshic forearm squarely across the left side of his rib cage.

There was too much noise for me to hear the crack of breaking ribs, if there actually was such a crack. But even over Strinni's paranoid gaspings and Rose Nose's admonitions I had no trouble hearing Kennrick's strangled grunt as the arm sent him flying across the room again. He slammed hard into the floor, and this time he didn't get up.

But his sacrifice hadn't been for nothing. The rest of the car's passengers had finally broken out of their stunned disbelief at Strinni's bizarre attack, and even as I continued to struggle with my self-appointed Filly protector a Juri and a Tra'ho moved in from opposite sides and tackled the berserk Shorshian.

Even then Strinni didn't give up. Still ranting, he continued to stomp around the floor, trying to throw off his attackers the way he'd disposed of Kennrick. But Bayta was still hanging on, and neither the Juri or Tra'ho was giving way, either, and Strinni began to stagger as he burned through his adrenaline-fueled energy reserves.

And then Witherspoon was on his feet again behind the clump of people, reaching past Bayta's head to jab a hypo into the back of Strinni's neck.

For another few seconds Strinni didn't react, but kept up his bizarre unchoreographed four-person waltz. I finally got past my guardian Filly and headed in, balling my hands into fists as I aimed for a couple of pressure points in the Shorshian's thighs that ought to drop him once and for all.

But even as I cocked my fists for a one-two punch, Witherspoon's concoction finally reached Strinni's motor control center. His legs wobbled and then collapsed beneath him, and he and the others fell into a tangled heap.

I looked at Witherspoon. "If this is so weak he can barely walk," I said, still panting, "I'd hate to see what frisky looks like."

"We need to get him to the dispensary," Witherspoon said grimly. He was breathing a little heavily himself. "Can I get some help in lifting?"

"No need," Bayta said, pushing herself out of the pile and getting carefully to her feet.

I looked toward the rear of the car. A pair of conductor Spiders had emerged from the vestibule and were hurriedly tapping their way toward us. "Everyone off and out of the way," I ordered. "The Spiders can carry him."

"He doesn't like Spiders," Rose Nose reminded me. With the excitement over, his eyes were starting to calm down.

"He's unconscious," I reminded him. "I won't tell if you don't."

From across the room came a rumbling groan. I looked in that direction to see Kennrick pulling himself carefully up from the floor, one hand on the nearest chair armrest, the other pressed against his side where Strinni's arm had slammed into him. "You okay?" I asked, stepping over to offer him a hand.

"Oh, sure—I do this every day," he gritted out. "What the hell was *that* all about?"

"You tell me," I said, looking back as the two Spiders picked up the unconscious Strinni, each of them using three of their seven legs to form a sort of wraparound hammock. "This sort of thing happen often?"

"If it does, it's been the galaxy's best-kept secret." He winced as I helped him the rest of the way to his feet. "I've never heard *di*-Master Strinni even raise his voice in an argument."

"Except maybe with Spiders or Filiaelians," I said, easing Kennrick to the side as the Spiders maneuvered their burden past us toward the forward vestibule and the dispensary four cars ahead.

"Well, that was just plain crazy," Kennrick said firmly. "We have four Filiaelians right here on his contract team. *Ow!*"

"Sorry," I apologized. "How bad is it?"

"Like I've been kicked by a cow." He smiled wanly. "And I worked summers on a dairy farm, so I know exactly what that feels like."

"You need help getting to the dispensary?" I asked. Bayta was disappearing through the vestibule door, and I could see Witherspoon's shock of white hair just in front of her. "I can get a Spider if you want."

"No, I can make it," he said. "Just give me a hand."

"Sure," I said, getting an arm around his shoulders. "Easy, now."

"You see?" Rose Nose said sagely as we passed him. "I said that was no way to behave toward one who is ill."

"Thanks," I said. "I'll try to remember that."

SEVEN :

Three of Kennrick's ribs had been slightly cracked in the fight, fortunately not badly enough to require a cast or even a wrap. His side apparently hurt like hell, though. Witherspoon gave him a bottle of QuixHeals and another bottle of painkillers and ordered a regimen of rest and sleep. Kennrick allowed that he could probably manage that and toddled off toward his compartment.

Strinni's case, unfortunately, wasn't nearly so easy to fix.

"I've run the blood scan twice," Witherspoon said as he gazed down at the Shorshian now securely strapped to the diagnostic table. "We've got not one, but *two* different poisons that have invaded his system. The first is a relative of printimpolivre-bioxene, which the analyzer lists as a sort of combination hallu-cinogen and paranoic."

"That certainly fits his performance just now," I agreed. "Is that the sickly-sweet odor I caught when he was trying to crush in my ribs?"

"Probably." Witherspoon's throat tightened. "The other

poison appears to be a heavy metal. Probably the same cadmium that killed his two colleagues."

"How surprising," I murmured. "Are we in time to do something about this one?"

"I don't know," Witherspoon said. "I've got him on a double dose of Castan's Binder, which should be able to bond to the metal still in his bloodstream. But if too much has already gotten into his deep tissues—" He shook his head.

I looked at Bayta. She was gazing down at Strinni's closed eyes, absently massaging her right wrist. "Bayta, is there anything the Spiders can do?" I asked.

"Nothing that Dr. Witherspoon isn't already doing," she said. "I was just wondering if we should wake him up. Maybe he knows who did this to him."

"That would definitely explain why they slipped him a Mickey," I agreed.

"A Mickey?" Witherspoon asked, frowning.

"A Mickey Finn," I explained. "Knockout drops, usually."

"Yes, I'm familiar with the term," Witherspoon growled. "But *I'm* the one who gave him the sedative."

"I was referring to the hallucinogen," I said. "Maybe the poisoner was afraid *di*-Master Strinni knew something important, so he made him go berserk in the hope that we'd go ahead and knock him out ourselves, thereby saving himself the trouble."

"I suppose that's possible," Witherspoon said. "One problem: I believe printimpolivre-bioxene is on the Spiders' prohibited list."

I looked at Bayta. "Is it?"

"All hallucinogenic chemicals are supposed to be there," she confirmed. "Unless it was already in *di*-Master Strinni's system, it shouldn't have gotten past the sensor screening."

"It definitely wasn't in his system," Witherspoon said. "Like the heavy-metal poisoning, printimpolivre-bioxene's effects would have shown up very quickly. Within hours, most likely. Certainly long before the two weeks we've been traveling."

"This is starting to sound like a locked-door murder mystery," I said. "So what about Bayta's suggestion that we wake him up?"

"I don't know," Witherspoon said, rubbing his shoulder where Strinni's first attack had landed. "I'd prefer to let him just sleep off the sedative instead of adding another chemical to the mix that his system's already dealing with. Besides, until his kidney-primes are able to oxidize the printimpolivre-bioxene and flush it from his system, he'd most likely just wake up into the same frenzied state he was in before."

Which would make anything we *did* get out of him fairly useless. "How long before that happens?"

Witherspoon shrugged. "Three hours. Maybe four."

"We'll come back then," I said, taking Bayta's arm. "If his condition changes, or you need anything, just tell the Spider."

"And the word will somehow magically get back to you," Witherspoon commented, glancing at the server standing silently by the drug cabinet. "Yes, Dr. Aronobal told me you two seem to have an interesting relationship with them."

"We travel a lot," I said, steering Bayta toward the dispensary door.

"I don't believe that any more than Aronobal does," Witherspoon said, peering closely at us. "But it's not really any of my business, I suppose."

"You suppose correctly," I agreed. "See you later."

We headed out into the corridor. "Where are we going?" Bayta asked as I turned us toward the front of the train. "I thought you wanted to look at Master Colix's storage compartments."

"I do," I said. "But first we both need to get something in our stomachs."

She looked sideways at me. "Yours bothering you, too?"

"Yes, but that could just be the onion rings," I said. "I gather you're still running at half speed?"

"It's not that bad," she assured me. "Besides, I already told you that I had something to eat."

"A whole vegetable roll," I said, nodding. "And that after having missed breakfast *and* lunch."

"The vegetable roll *was* lunch."

"I've had Quadrail vegetable rolls," I reminded her. "Those are appetizers, not meals. If you really don't want to eat anything, fine. But at least come keep me company."

"All right," she said reluctantly. Maybe she was wondering about the propriety of stuffing our faces while Strinni was in the dispensary dying of cadmium poisoning.

But my gut was rumbling something fierce, and I needed to get something down there to keep it busy. Whether she thought so or not, Bayta probably needed something, too.

The main section of the dining car was mostly empty when we arrived. That wasn't particularly surprising, since we were between the normal lunch and dinner hours and most of the passengers were elsewhere reading, chatting, playing games, or watching dit rec dramas and comedies.

The bar end of the car, in contrast, was packed with passengers, some having pre-dinner drinks, others possibly not yet finished with their lunchtime libations. I glanced in through the smoked plastic dividers as we entered the dining section, just as glad we weren't going to try to get a table in there.

With my digestive sensitivity in mind, I'd already decided

to steer clear of anything exotic or heavy on spices. Accordingly, I ordered a simple steak and vegetable combo, passing on the half-dozen optional sauces offered by the menu.

Bayta, ignoring my raised eyebrows, just ordered another vegetable roll and a glass of lemonade.

"People *do* get indigestion on trips, you know," I reminded her as the Spider headed away from the table. "Especially long trips like this one."

"Maybe," she said. Her eyes were on the center of our table, her attention clearly on her rumbling intestinal tract. "But I've never had indigestion. Not like this. Never."

Abruptly, she looked up at me. "Did you ever find out from Mr. Kennrick or Dr. Witherspoon what the Human symptoms of heavy-metal poisoning were?"

"You were there the whole time," I pointed out. "That part of the conversation got short-circuited by Strinni's one-and-a-half-gainer into the deep end."

"I just thought you might have asked Mr. Kennrick about it while you were helping him to the dispensary."

"Never even occurred to me to bring up the subject," I admitted. "We were a little preoccupied with his ribs at the time."

"So we don't know if"—she glanced down at her abdomen—"if this is a symptom or not."

"Not specifically, no," I said as soothingly as I could. "But we know that the train's food supply isn't contaminated, and no one's been leaning over our dinner plates sprinkling cadmium garnish on our salads."

"What if it's airborne?" Bayta asked. "We still don't know about that."

"We will as soon as we finish dinner," I said. "You said they'll have the filter disassembled in, what, another half hour?"

Her eyes unfocused briefly. "About that."

"So we'll eat and then head back and take some samples," I said. "Five minutes after that we'll know whether the stuff was in the air or not."

"Compton?" Kennrick's voice came from behind me.

I turned, wincing as the movement strained freshly tenderized joints. Kennrick was standing a couple of feet back, his expression that of a man who's just eaten a bad grape. "I thought you were heading back to your compartment," I said.

"I was," he said. "Other matters intervened. *Usantra* Givvrac would very much like a word with you."

"I'd be delighted to give him one," I said. "Just as soon as we finish our meal."

Kennrick's eyes flicked pointedly to the empty table in front of us. "Or possibly beforehand?" he suggested. "*Usantra* Givvrac is right here, over in the bar section." His lip twitched. "We were discussing the situation when he spotted you coming in."

"You're as well informed about this mess as anyone," I reminded him. "What does he think I can add to the discussion?"

Kennrick glanced at Bayta. "He feels you may have a better handle on what's happening than I do."

"And you resent the implications?"

"What I resent or don't resent is irrelevant," he said evenly. "I'm Pellorian Medical's representative to these people, and the head of the contract team has made a request of me. The rule is, if you can satisfy such requests, you do."

"True enough," I agreed, feeling a twinge of sympathy. In my early days in Westali, when most of my missions boiled down to VIP-babysitting duty, I'd often found myself in the same unenviable position. "Well, we can't have you ignoring your mandate, can we? Tell *Usantra* Givvrac I'd be honored to give him a few minutes of my time."

"Thanks," he said, and headed back toward the bar section. I waited until he was out of earshot, then turned to Bayta. "Anything you want me to ask him?" I asked her. "Upper-rank Fillies are notorious for speaking only to the senior person present."

"No, I don't think so," Bayta said. "We can always ask him later if I think of something."

"Careful," I warned. "In classic dit rec dramas, putting off a conversation usually means that person is the next one to die."

Bayta shivered. "I wish this *was* a dit rec drama," she murmured. "At least then there would be some sense to it."

"Oh, there's sense to it," I promised her grimly. "We just don't know what it is yet. But we will."

"I hope so." She looked up again, her eyes focusing somewhere over my shoulder. "Here he comes."

Earlier, when I'd seen Kennrick and Givvrac conferring in the latter's coach car, I'd noted that the Filly looked fairly elderly. Now, as I watched him crossing the dining car toward us, I was struck by not only how old he was, but also how fragile. He walked carefully, as if balance was a conscious decision instead of something his body automatically did on its own. His eyes continually scanned the tables and chairs alongside his path, with the air of someone who fears a casual bump might break delicate bones. Kennrick walked close beside him the whole way, his eyes alert, his hand poised for an instant assist should the other need it.

I stood up as they approached, swiveling my chair partway toward them. "I greet you, *Usantra* Givvrac," I said, gesturing to the seat. "Please take my chair."

"I thank you, Mr. Compton," Givvrac said, sinking gratefully onto his knees on it in the standard Filly sitting position. He waited for the chair to reconfigure for his body, and then gestured to the chair across the table beside Bayta. "Please—sit. You as well, Mr. Kennrick."

"Thank you," I said, stepping around the corner of the table and sitting down in the indicated chair as Kennrick took the other empty seat beside Givvrac. "If I may be so bold, *Usantra* Givvrac, I'm surprised to see someone of your age so far from home."

"With age comes experience, Mr. Compton," Givvrac replied. "With experience comes wisdom and perspective. Or so one hopes."

"Your people thought such wisdom and perspective would be necessary in this contract discussion?" I suggested.

"They did," Givvrac confirmed. "And so it was. But I came here to question you, not to be questioned by you."

"My apologies," I said, inclining my head. "Please state your questions."

"I'm told by Mr. Kennrick that you are an investigator," Givvrac said. "Let us begin with a list of your credentials."

"I'm a former agent of Earth's Western Alliance Intelligence service," I said. "During those years, I traveled over fairly large stretches of our end of the galaxy, and gained experience dealing with members of several of the Twelve Empires."

"And now?"

"Now I travel the galaxy with my associate Bayta," I said, nodding toward her. "We do odd jobs and assist with investigations for the Spiders."

"I see," Givvrac said, and I could see him wondering, just as Witherspoon had, what sort of investigations the Spiders might possibly need assistance with. Unlike the good doctor, though, Givvrac was too polite to ask. "Any other credentials?"

For a moment I was tempted to tell him about my brief employment with Larry Hardin, who had hired me to find a way to steal, bribe, or extort control of the Quadrail away from the Spiders. Givvrac's reaction to such a revelation might have been interesting. "Various odd jobs when I was in school," I said instead. "Nothing remarkable."

Givvrac nodded, a rather awkward looking motion for that head and neck combination. Clearly, it was a gesture he'd picked up solely to use with Humans and a couple of other species. "Tell me what you've learned of the present situation."

"Unfortunately, at this point I probably don't know much more than you do," I said. "Yesterday evening Master Colix came down with cadmium poisoning, source unknown, and quickly succumbed to it. Shortly thereafter, Master Bofiv died from the same cause. It appears now that *di*-Master Strinni has also been poisoned, plus he's been dosed with a drug called printimpolivre-bioxene."

Givvrac looked at Kennrick. "Are you familiar with this drug?"

"Dr. Witherspoon says it's a hallucinogen," Kennrick said. "It was apparently the reason for *di*-Master Strinni's violent behavior earlier in his car."

"I've not heard of this drug before," Givvrac said, looking back at me. "Is it common?"

"It's common enough," I said grimly. "In the illegal drug trade, its street name is *necrovri*."

Givvrac sat up a bit straighter. "Necrovri," he murmured. "Yes, I've heard of it. A blight among the Shorshic and Pirkarli lower classes." His nose blaze darkened. "But how could such a thing have drawn in one of *di*-Master ranking?"

"The upper ranks of any species aren't immune to the lure of the forbidden," I reminded him. "However, in this case, I don't think *di*-Master Strinni took the drug on his own. I believe it was given to him without his knowledge, possibly to prevent us from learning something from him about the other two murders."

"Murders," Givvrac murmured, his blaze darkening a little more. "Mr. Kennrick said he believed the deaths were not accidental. Now you add your same opinion to his?"

"Yes, I do," I said, diplomatically passing over the fact that Kennrick wouldn't have had any such insight if I hadn't taken the time to beat it into him. "Dr. Witherspoon is trying to reverse *di*-Master Strinni's cadmium poisoning. If he succeeds, we should be able to question *di*-Master Strinni and see what he knows. If anything."

"Do you know how this poisoning was accomplished?" Givvrac asked.

"Not yet," I said. "Part of the problem is that we don't have a motive for the attacks. Typically, motives for murder fall into one of three categories: passion, profit, or revenge. Passion is out—clearly, these killings were carefully planned and executed. That leaves us profit and revenge." I raised my eyebrows in silent question.

"Clever, Mr. Compton," Givvrac said, a touch of amusement in his voice. "So in order for you to answer my questions, I must first answer yours?"

"All investigations require questions and answers," I pointed out. "Can you think of how anyone would profit from the deaths of Masters Colix and Bofiv?"

"No," Givvrac said, his tone leaving no room for doubt.

"Leaving us with revenge," I said. "Can you think—?"

"Just a minute," Kennrick interrupted. "Your pardon, *Usantra* Givvrac, but there *are* reasons of profit that could explain these deaths."

"No, there are not," Givvrac repeated, giving Kennrick a warning glare. "Your next question, Mr. Compton?"

"Let me first rephrase my previous one," I said, eyeing Givvrac closely as I thought back to his answer. I'd seen this before, usually with suspects trying to beat a polyline test by finding loopholes in the interrogator's questions. Teenagers, I recalled from years gone by, were also adept at the technique, especially during parental cross-examinations. "Can you think of how anyone would profit from Master Colix's death?"

Givvrac hissed out a quiet sigh. "Perhaps," he said reluctantly. "There was some disagreement among us as to whether we would grant Pellorian Medical Systems the genetic-manipulation knowledge and equipment they seek."

"Let me guess," I said, watching Kennrick out of the corner of my eye. "Master Colix was against the deal?"

Kennrick's expression didn't even twitch. "In actual fact, Mr. Compton," Givvrac said, "Master Colix was one of the strongest proponents *for* the contract."

"Interesting," I said. "I gather, then, that Master Bofiv was *against* the contract."

"He was," Givvrac confirmed, frowning. "Did he tell you that before he died?"

"Unfortunately, he didn't speak to me at all," I said. "I deduced that from your earlier statement that no one would profit by *both* Master Colix's and Master Bofiv's deaths. Ergo, they must have been on opposite sides of the disagreement, with both deaths together thus returning the contract team to its original status quo."

"Hardly the exact status quo," Kennrick said. "There were no more than two or possibly three of the eight in opposition to our proposal. With the unfortunate deaths of Masters Colix and Bofiv, the percentage of members favorable to Pellorian has actually increased."

"Not precisely true, Mr. Kennrick," Givvrac said. "In actual fact, before these deaths the contract team was evenly split on the matter: four for, and four against."

Kennrick stared at him. "You never said—" He broke off, glancing sideways at me. "I was unaware the contract team's feelings were running so closely."

"It's not a matter of your company's expertise and learning," Givvrac assured him. "You've proved that beyond doubt. The question is solely whether or not your species in general has the wisdom to use these methods properly."

"I see," Kennrick said, and I could sense his reflexive desire to argue the point in Pellorian's and humanity's defense. But this wasn't the time or place to reopen the negotiations. "Forgive my intrusion. Please continue."

"Thank you," I said. "So what you're saying, *Usantra* Givvrac, is that the original four-to-four deadlock has been reduced to a three-to-three deadlock?"

"Deadlock implies the matter may end without resolution," Givvrac corrected me sternly. "That will not happen. The decision *will* be made before Mr. Kennrick leaves the Assembly for his return home."

"Understood," I said. "May I ask which members of your group are currently on which side?"

Givvrac hesitated. "That's privileged information," he said. "I'm not sure even the current situation justifies my telling you."

Kennrick, to his credit, picked up on the cue. "Excuse me a moment, *Usantra* Givvrac," he said, getting to his feet. "It just occurred to me that we never told the server that we would be over here instead of back in the bar. I'll go get our refreshments."

He headed across the dining car toward the bar. "Speaking of refreshments, *Usantra* Givvrac, I must again extend my apologies," I said. "I neglected to ask if you would care to join us in a meal."

"No, thank you," Givvrac said. "Food does not interest me at the moment."

I frowned. Fillies liked their food as well as anyone else in the galaxy. "Is something you ate bothering you?"

"Most likely," he said. "I have been feeling somewhat delicate over the past few hours."

"There seems to be a lot of that going around," I commented, my own gut rumbling in sympathy. "While Mr. Kennrick is gone, perhaps you'd be willing to tell me which members of your team are for this deal with Pellorian?"

"You will agree not to share my words with Mr. Kennrick?"

"Of course," I said. "I'll sign a contract to that effect if you wish."

Givvrac visibly relaxed. Written contracts were very important to Fillies. Even if he and I never actually signed anything, my willingness to do so would go a long way toward putting me in the trustworthy category. "No need," he said. "*Di*-Master Strinni was the next strongest proponent of the Pellorian contract."

"Really," I said. So that was two aye votes either dead or on the critical list. "What about Master Tririn?"

"He stands against the contract," Givvrac said. "Oddly enough, the four Shorshians were evenly split."

"And of course, all of them knew where all the others stood?"

"Indeed," Givvrac said. "The eight of us had several meetings together during the torchliner voyage from Earth to the Terran Tube Station."

"Without Mr. Kennrick present, I presume?"

"You presume correctly," Givvrac said. "Only in his absence

can we speak freely on the subject." He cocked his head in a Filly posture of consideration. "Though such opportunities were uncommon. He often joined one or another group of us for our meals."

"Taking care to talk up the benefits of dealing with Pellorian Medical, no doubt?"

"Correct," Givvrac agreed. "He is a tireless representative of his company."

"I'm sure he is," I said diplomatically. He'd probably been a tireless representative of Shotoko Associates, too, right up until the day Westali had swooped down and broken up DuNoeva's spy ring. "So Master Colix and *di*-Master Strinni were for the contract. Who else?"

"*Asantra* Muzzfor is also on their side of the discussion," Givvrac said. "He is one of my colleagues."

"Yes," I said, catching the subtle vowel difference. Colleagues they might be, but an *asantra* like Muzzfor was lower in rank than an *usantra* like Givvrac. "And the fourth?"

"I also lean in that direction," Givvrac said. "I therefore count myself among them, though I have not entirely made up my mind."

I nodded. "And the other opponents would then be the other two Filiaelians?"

"*Esantra* Worrbin and *Asantra* Dallilo are also against the contract," he confirmed.

"Where do they and *Asantra* Muzzfor sit aboard the train?"

"All three have seats in the second of the first-class coaches, the one directly back of the exercise/dispensary car."

"Do they sit together for the most part?"

"Yes," Givvrac said. "To anticipate your next question, the four of us have frequently discussed the contract during this trip. *Di*-Master Strinni often joined us, as he too has a seat in first class."

"And the other three Shorshians?"

"I presume they also held such conversations, though I cannot say for certain." A shadow seemed to pass across his face. "Or rather, I presume they did when there were still three of them."

"You haven't spoken to them about the matter?" I asked.

"We travel in first class," Givvrac said. "They travel in third."

"Yes, of course," I said. "I just thought that since Mr. Kennrick had gone back there on occasion to talk to them you might have done similarly."

"I have not, nor have my colleagues," Givvrac repeated firmly. "Those of first class do not mingle with those of third while aboard the train."

Bayta nudged me, and I looked over Givvrac's shoulder to see that Kennrick had reappeared on our side of the car, a pair of drinks in hand. "Thank you for your openness and honesty," I said to the Filly, inclining my head. "Perhaps we can speak now of the other possible motive for these horrific crimes, namely that of revenge. Can you think of any reason why someone would be carrying anger or hatred toward either Master Colix or Master Bofiv?"

"Here we go," Kennrick said as he came up to the table. He set the drinks down and then resumed his seat beside Givvrac. "My apologies for the delay."

"No apologies required," Givvrac said. "As to your question, Mr. Compton, I believe it would be inappropriate for me to speak of another's life after his voice is silenced."

"I understand," I said, suppressing a grimace. Was it inappropriate to gossip about the deceased at all, or was it only inappropriate because Kennrick was now back in the conversation? "In that case, I think that's all I need for the moment. I thank you deeply for your time and wisdom, *Usantra* Givvrac."

"You are welcome," Givvrac said. "Feel free to approach me with further questions if you have the need. Will you also wish to speak with *Esantra* Worrbin, *Asantra* Muzzfor, or *Asantra* Dallilo?"

"Perhaps later," I said. "If I do, I'll be sure to obtain your permission first."

"No need," he said. "I hereby grant you open access to all Filiaelians under my authority aboard this train."

"I appreciate that," I said, inclining my head again. Fillies weren't the obsessive sticklers for protocol that Juriani were, but they had definite ideas of rank and chain of command. Violating those rules would burn whatever goodwill I might have started with, and could conceivably get the whole crowd of them to clam up on me completely. With Givvrac's carte blanche in hand, at least I didn't have to worry about that.

"Then we take our leave," Givvrac said, placing both hands on the table and carefully getting to his feet. "Perhaps, Mr. Kennrick, you'll assist me back to the bar area?"

"Certainly," Kennrick said, scrambling quickly to his feet and holding out a hand where the Filly could grab it if necessary. "Compton, could you give me a hand with the drinks? I can't handle both of them and offer *Usantra* Givvrac assistance at the same time."

"Certainly," I said, standing up.

"No need," Givvrac said, waving me down again. "My drink has lost its taste, and Mr. Kennrick can easily handle his own."

"Are you sure?" I asked. "It's no trouble, I assure you."

"I'm sure," Givvrac said. "Thank you for your time, Mr. Compton. Mr. Kennrick?"

"Ready," Kennrick said, picking up his own drink. As I sat down again, they turned away and started across the dining room.

And then, two steps away, Givvrac paused and retraced his steps back to our table. "One other thing, Mr. Compton," he said. "If I may be so bold as to offer you advice in your area of expertise."

"In my area of expertise there's always more to learn," I assured him, gesturing to the chair he'd just vacated. "Please speak on."

"Thank you," he said, making no move to sit down. "You stated that the motives for murder were passion, profit, and revenge. In your place, I would consider two additional possibilities."

"Those being?" I asked.

"The first is honor," he said. "With Filiaelians and Shorshians alike, damage or endangerment to one's honor can be reason to eliminate the one who presents that threat. I don't know if Humans feel similar motivations."

"We do, though perhaps to a different degree," I told him.

"And to varying degrees within our species," Kennrick added. "Certainly there are Earth cultures that hold honor very important."

"True," I said. "And the second motive, *Usantra* Givvrac?"

His eyes burned into me. "Insanity."

For a moment the word hung in the air like a bubble of black in a dark gray silence. Then, Givvrac gave me a final nod. "Thank you for your time, Mr. Compton. Good day."

"Good day, *Usantra* Givvrac," I replied. "Good health to you."

"Perhaps," he said. "We shall see."

He headed back across the dining area, Kennrick at his side. "What do you think?" I asked Bayta.

"I was just wondering if Mr. Kennrick has figured out who was on which side of the contract discussion," she said, her voice thoughtful.

"If Mr. Kennrick is worth anywhere near his salt, one would certainly hope so," I said.

"Could he want the contract enough to kill to make sure it went through?"

"Possibly," I said. "The problem with that theory is that, at the moment, two-thirds of the poisoning victims were already on his side."

"Unless he misread their intentions."

"True," I said. "But if we're going down the profit side of the street, it would make more sense if the killer was on the other side of the deadlock."

"Master Tririn?"

"He certainly shows promise," I said. "He's opposed to the contract, and he had easy access to two of the victims."

"But not to the third," Bayta pointed out. "*Di*-Master Strinni was in first class, where Master Tririn wouldn't have been able to get to him."

"Unless Strinni liked to go back and visit the others like Kennrick did," I said. "Givvrac implied that he didn't, but Givvrac may not know for sure. Or Tririn might have come up here if someone in first asked for him."

Bayta frowned into space. "No one asked Master Tririn to come forward," she said.

I shrugged. "It was a long shot. It's not like Master Tririn's been in high demand around the train the way Dr. Aronobal and Dr. Witherspoon have."

"True," Bayta agreed. "It also occurs to me that we only have *Usantra* Givvrac's word that Master Tririn was actually opposed to the Pellorian contract."

"Very good," I said approvingly. "As I told Givvrac, investigations require questions and answers. But you don't necessarily believe those answers. Any other thoughts?"

"Just this." She pointed at Givvrac's abandoned drink. "Do you know what this is?"

I picked it up and gave the contents a sniff. The concoction had a tangy, exotic aroma, but with no scent of alcohol that I could detect. "Not a clue," I said.

"It's *miccrano*," she said. "A traditional Filiaelian remedy for serious stomach and digestive trouble."

"Is it, now," I said, eyeing the drink with new interest. "Sounds like he may be feeling more than just a bit delicate. Has he had a chat with either of our two doctors?"

Bayta's eyes defocused as she again consulted with the Spiders. As she did so, the server appeared from the rear of the dining area with the meals we'd ordered before Kennrick first came to our table. I'd actually expected the food to show up during our conversation, which could have been a little awkward since Givvrac would certainly have insisted on a polite departure. Knowing Bayta, she'd probably telepathically instructed the Spider to hold the meals until we'd finished and our visitors had left.

Bayta's eyes came back. "He had a conductor bring Dr. Aronobal up from third class about an hour ago," she reported. "Dr. Aronobal is the one who recommended the *miccrano* to him."

"Which also probably explains why Kennrick was here instead of in his compartment," I said as the Spider set our plates in front of us. "Givvrac would have been in the bar, working through his tummy-soothers, when Kennrick passed by on his way to lie down. Do we know how many of them he had?"

"This was his third," Bayta said, nodding at the glass.

"Which he never touched," I commented, rubbing my chin. "I wonder why he decided to abandon it."

"Maybe he was feeling better," Bayta suggested.

"Or decided that the first two hadn't done him any good anyway," I said, something prickly running up my back as I eyed the glass. If someone had poisoned the drink . . .

I snorted under my breath. No—that one *was* pure paranoia. Even if Kennrick was the killer, he'd have to be crazy to poison Givvrac at a time when we knew they were having a drink together.

Still, it couldn't do any harm to check. "Bayta, can you have the server in the dispensary bring me one of those little vials from the sampling kit?" I asked.

"Yes, of course," she said, her voice suddenly uncertain. "You think there's something in *Usantra* Givvrac's drink?"

"No, but we might as well be thorough about this." I picked up my fork. "Meanwhile, this isn't getting any warmer. Let's eat."

The meal was up to the usual Quadrail standards. Unfortunately, it was impossible for me to properly enjoy it with my gut rumbling the way it was. Halfway through, I gave up and pushed the plate away.

Bayta was either feeling better than I was or else was stubbornly committed to not wasting any of the food her Spider friends had hauled across the galaxy for our benefit. She made it all the way through her vegetable roll, chewing silently but determinedly.

She was just finishing off her lemonade when a server Spider appeared and set a sampling vial and a small hypo on the table beside my plate.

"Thank you," I said. Taking the hypo, I extracted a couple

of milliliters of Givvrac's drink and injected it into the vial. "I said thank you," I repeated, looking at the Spider.

"He's waiting for you to give back the hypo," Bayta explained.

"Ah," I said, reversing the instrument and holding it up. The Spider extended a leg and took it, then folded the leg up beneath his globe and tapped his way back out of the dining area. "Any news on the air filter?" I asked Bayta.

"It's nearly done," she said. "It should be ready by the time we get back there."

"Good," I said, standing up and slipping the sample vial into my pocket. "Let's go."

EIGHT :

It was getting toward train's evening, and the third-class passengers were starting to drift back to their seats after a busy day in the entertainment car, the exercise area, or the bar.

Which meant there was a large and curious audience already in place when Bayta and I moved toward the rear of the car and the disassembled air filter system waiting there for us.

I'd never asked Bayta what exactly the disassembly procedure entailed. Now, as we joined a group of knee-high mite Spiders and a pair of the larger conductors, I could see why the job had taken this long. A section of ceiling nearly a meter square had been taken down, probably with the help of the two conductors, and was currently hanging by thin support wires attached to its four corners at about throat level over the back row of seats. The occupants of those seats, not surprisingly, had found somewhere else to be for the moment.

"We couldn't bring in a couple of cameras so the whole train could watch?" I grumbled as we passed our third knot of rubberneckers.

"I thought you'd want to take the sample yourself," Bayta countered, a slight edge to her voice. Clearly, she didn't like having the Quadrail's innards exposed to the paying customers this way any more than I did, and she didn't appreciate me getting on her case about it. "There's no way you could have reached the filter while it was still in place."

And given the tight tolerances of Quadrail floor space, there was probably nowhere more private where they could have lugged the filter assembly for the procedure. "I suppose," I conceded.

We reached the hanging plate, and I took a moment to study its upper side. The filter assembly consisted of about a dozen boxes of various sizes and shapes scattered across the plate, all of them marked with incomprehensible dot codes. They were connected to each other by a bewildering and colorful spaghetti of tubes, ducts, cables, and wires. Other tubes and conduits, carefully sealed off, ran to the edges of the plate, where presumably they connected to equipment tucked away above the rest of the ceiling. The plate itself had sixteen connectors, four per side, for fastening it to the rest of the ceiling. The connectors, I noted, were accessible only from above. It was pretty clear that no one was going to tamper with the system without Spider help. "Which one do I want?" I asked Bayta.

"That one," she said, pointing to the largest of the boxes. "The Spiders will take off the cover for you."

"Thanks," I said, looking down at the mites grouped around us like shiny seven-legged lap dogs. "Do they need a boost?"

"No," Bayta said, and I quickly stepped back as a pair of fist-sized twitters appeared from inside the ceiling and deftly slid down the corner lines onto the exposed machinery. Picking their way across the miniature landscape, they reached the box Bayta had indicated and started removing one of its sides.

"Here," Bayta said, pressing a pair of sample vials into my hand. "Will you need a hypo or scraper?"

"Got one, thanks," I said, pulling out my multitool and selecting one of the blades. The twitters got the filter's side off, and I leaned in for a closer look.

I'd expected to find some sort of thin but tangible layer of fluffiness, the sort of thing you might find in an office building air filter that hadn't been replaced for a few weeks. But the dimpled white material sitting in front of me looked as clean and fresh as if it had come right out of the box.

It looked, in fact, like some industrious Spider had given it a thorough cleaning sometime in the past few hours. And if one of them had, this whole thing was going to be a complete waste of time. "You *did* warn the Spiders not to clean it, didn't you?"

"Of course," Bayta said. "It hasn't been touched since Homshil."

"Looks pretty clean to me," I pointed out.

"It's the third-stage filter," she said. "It always *looks* clean."

I suppressed a grimace. Of course it did. All the larger dust and lint particles would have been captured by a larger-mesh filter somewhere upstream in the system. But it was this filter that would have a shot at trapping impurities the size of cadmium atoms and compounds. "Just making sure," I said, trying to salvage a little dignity.

Experimentally, I gently scraped the multitool blade along one edge of the filter. A small cascade of fine white powder appeared and drifted slowly downward. Moving the blade to a different part of the filter, I held one of the vials in position and scraped more of the white powder into it. I waited until the dust had settled and then handed the vial to Bayta for sealing. I repeated the operation on a third section of the filter, again handing the vial to Bayta when I was done. "That should do it," I told her. Folding the blade back into the multitool, I turned around.

And stopped short. Standing three meters away, right in the center of the ring of gawkers, was the Filly I'd had the brief tussle with earlier that day in the third-class bar. He was staring at me with an intensity I didn't at all care for. "Can I help you?" I asked.

"What do you do here?" the Filly asked, his long nose pointing toward the filter assembly.

"Just a routine maintenance sampling," I said in my best authoritative-but-soothing voice. "Nothing you need to be concerned about."

I'd used that voice to good advantage many times over the years. Unfortunately, this particular Filly wasn't buying it. "Is there danger in the air?" he demanded. "Is there risk to us all?"

"There's no risk to anyone," I said firmly if not entirely truthfully. "As I said, this is just a routine maintenance check."

But it was no use. A low-level murmur was already rippling through the rest of the onlookers, some of whom had probably ridden this line before and knew that there was nothing routine about what we were doing. "If there is risk, we deserve to know the truth," the Filly said firmly, his volume rising to a level that would reach most of the car instead of just the group assembled here at the rear.

"There is no risk," I said again, letting my gaze drift over the crowd as I tried to think up an answer that would satisfy them. "But you're right, you deserve to know the truth. If you'll all be quiet a moment?"

I stopped, waiting for them to pick up on the cue. I could

feel Bayta's eyes on me, and her concern as she wondered what exactly I was doing.

I wondered what I was doing, too. Telling them there was a murderer aboard the train was definitely out—we could wind up with a riot on our hands, with nowhere anyone could escape to. But I'd had enough experience with rumor mills to know that if we didn't give them *something* the situation would only get worse, possibly leading to the same riot I was hoping so hard to avoid.

Ergo, I had to give them some truth. The trick, as always, would be to figure out how much.

Slowly, in bits and pieces, the mutterings faded away. "Thank you," I said. "I presume you're all aware that two of your fellow travelers died yesterday."

The last mutterings abruptly vanished. I had their full attention now, all right. I heard Bayta mutter something under her breath, but it wasn't like the rest of the passengers wouldn't have noticed the two newly empty seats. "What I'm doing here is checking for the presence of what are called *after-elements*," I went on. "Those are bits of nucleic acid residue, antibodies, mucousids—the sorts of things that might have been exhaled by a person in his last battle against a lethal congenital defect."

The Filly's nose blaze darkened a bit. "A congenital defect? In both victims?"

"I can see no other likely conclusion," I said, noting in passing his unusual use of the word *victims*. "No one else in the car has shown any signs of illness, which eliminates the possibility that they died from some contagious disease."

I gestured toward a pair of Shorshians near the rear of the crowd. "It can't even be something specific to Shorshians, since other Shorshians in the car haven't been affected."

"So you say it was a congenital disease," the Filly said, his tone a bit odd.

"As I said, there's no other likely conclusion," I repeated. "Nothing for any of you to be concerned about. So please, return to your seats and try to put these unfortunate events from your minds."

A fresh set of mutterings began to circulate through the onlookers. But the tone was definitely calmer, and at the rear of the group the passengers began obediently heading back toward their seats. Within a minute, the whole crowd had joined the mass migration.

Everyone, that is, except the Filly whose questions had gotten everyone riled up in the first place. He stayed right where he was, his eyes never leaving my face, as the rest of the passengers dispersed. "Was there something else?" I asked.

He took a step closer to me. "You are lying," he said quietly. "If you sought a congenital disease, a proper investigation would begin with samples taken from the bodies of the victims."

"I'd like nothing better," I said. "But there are questions of religious protocol, and the leader of their group has prohibited me from taking direct samples."

The Filly looked at Bayta, his blaze darkening a little more. "Perhaps that prohibition will yet be lifted," he said.

"Perhaps," I said.

He took another step toward me. "But should you discover a different cause of death," he went on, lowering his voice still more, "I would urge you to let me know at once."

"In such an unlikely event, I'm sure the Spiders will let everyone know at the same time," I assured him.

"I would appreciate it very much," he said, putting an emphasis on the last two words. "Even small bits of preliminary knowledge would be worth a great deal to me."

"I'll keep that in mind," I promised. "If I should happen to learn anything, whom shall I ask for?"

He studied me another couple of heartbeats. "I am *Logra* Emikai," he identified himself. "My seat is four coaches forward, in the car just to the front of the dining car."

"Understood," I said. "A pleasant evening to you, *Logra* Emikai."

"And to you." With a brief nod of his head, he turned and headed down the aisle toward the front of the car and his own seat four coaches away.

"Interesting," I murmured, catching Bayta's eye and nodding toward the departing Filly. "You catch all that?"

"You mean the fact that he just tried to bribe us?" Bayta asked, her voice stiff.

"Well, yes, that too," I said, turning back to watch Emikai's progress. He was moving briskly, adroitly dodging around the slower-moving passengers who weren't in nearly so much of a hurry. "I was mostly referring to the fact that he seemed to know we'd already taken samples from Master Bofiv's body."

"How do you know that?" Bayta asked, her moral outrage at the bribery attempt starting to fade into fresh interest.

"From his reaction to my comment that *di*-Master Strinni hadn't let us take samples," I said. "The question is, how did *he* know? Okay—let's see what he does."

"With what?" Bayta asked, craning her neck to see over the crowd.

"Not with *what*," I corrected. "With *whom*. Specifically, with Master Tririn. Or hadn't you noticed that Tririn didn't bother to come back here to see what we were doing?"

"Maybe he's just tired."

"Or he already knows what we will or won't find," I said.

"Or he didn't need to come himself because he already had a friend on the scene."

"*Logra* Emikai?"

"Could be," I said. "You have any idea what sort of rank *logra* is?"

"Not in that form," Bayta said. "It could be a dialectal variant of *lomagra*, one of the middle artisan classes."

"Or else it's something new, something private, or something he made up out of thin air," I said.

"And you think he and Master Tririn are working together?"

"We'll know in a second," I said. "Even if they just know each other, there ought to be some signal or at least recognition as Emikai passes him."

But to my disappointment, the Filly passed by Tririn's seat without so much as a sideways glance in the Shorshian's direction. "Or not," I said. "Well, that tells us something, too," I added, turning away.

"Wait a second," Bayta said, her voice suddenly urgent.

"What?" I asked, turning back.

"*Logra* Emikai's head dipped to his right just there," Bayta said. "Like he was saying something to—"

And right on cue, Terese German stood up and stepped into the aisle.

"To our young friend with the bad stomach?" I suggested.

"Exactly," Bayta said. Terese made a show of stretching as she casually but carefully looked around her, then headed after the departing Filly. *Logra* Emikai reached the vestibule and disappeared inside, heading for the next car. A few steps behind him, Terese did likewise. "Coincidence?" Bayta asked.

"I don't think so," I said. "I've been assuming that when we were in the bar earlier she just grabbed the first likely-looking lug to protect her from me. The whole incident makes a lot more sense if the choice wasn't nearly that spur-of-the-moment."

Bayta pondered that for a moment. "Thought it still could be perfectly innocent," she pointed out. "They've been passengers on the same train for the past two weeks. If they'd already gotten to know each other, she would naturally go to him for help."

"Maybe," I said. "But she's never struck me as the gregarious sort. Come on—time to go."

"Where?" Bayta asked as I took her arm and steered us forward down the aisle. "We're not going to follow them, are we?"

"We just happen to be going the same direction, that's all," I assured her as we wove our way around the other passengers wending their way to and fro down the aisle. "Tell the Spiders they can put the filter equipment back together again. We're done here."

My original plan—actually, at this point we were probably on my second or third original plan—had been to have a look at the late Master Colix's storage compartments while we were checking on the air filter. But again, things weren't working out the way I'd hoped. This time, it was the large number of passengers still watching our every move that persuaded me to put off the compartment exam a little longer. Convincing them that two deaths a few hours apart had been just an unhappy happenstance would be a much harder sell if I was seen rooting through the personal effects of one of the dearly departs. Hopefully, we could come back later tonight when things had quieted down.

As I'd promised Bayta, we did indeed follow Terese and

Emikai toward the front of the train, but only because we all happened to be going in the same direction. The girl and the Filly only made it as far as the bar end of the dining car, I noted as we passed, whereas Bayta and I were going four cars farther, to the second/third dispensary.

"What are we doing here?" Bayta asked as I ushered her into the small room.

"Finding a place where we can be alone," I said. "Is there a curtain or something we can close over this doorway?"

In response, the server Spider standing his post by the drug cabinet skittered over and slid a cleverly hidden pocket door over the opening. "Thank you," I said, stepping over to the treatment table and laying out my newly filled sample vials. "More importantly, I wanted someplace I could do a quick analysis without a lot of people looking over our shoulders."

"Why don't we just go back to our compartments?" Bayta asked as I pulled out my reader and lighter.

"Because our next real stop is the first-class dispensary to check on Strinni, and I don't want to go all the way forward and then have to backtrack," I told her. "I don't know about you, but I'm getting tired of all this walking."

I started with Givvrac's untouched drink. I hadn't really expected to find anything sinister lurking there, and for once I was right. "As I said, even if Kennrick *is* involved, he wouldn't be stupid enough to lace a drink only he had access to," I reminded Bayta as I set the vial aside. "These others may be more interesting."

They were. But not in the way I'd expected.

"What *is* all that?" Bayta asked, staring in bewilderment as the chemical list scrolled across my reader's display.

And scrolled some more, and then kept on scrolling, for another four pages. Whatever the Spiders' third-stage filter was collecting, it was collecting a lot of it. "Whatever it is, the good news is that the air isn't the source of the poisoning," I said. "You can see—right there—that there's barely a trace of cadmium in the whole mix."

"Not enough to kill them?"

"Not even enough to make them sick," I said. "As to the rest of this soup, be patient. The analyzer has a huge database, and it'll take some time for it to sort through everything."

I watched the reader as the first trace compound ID came up, a type of perfume used by Fibibibi to mask some of the pheromones that appeared in females at potentially awkward times. "We've got a make on Contestant Number Two," I said as the next part of the analysis came up. "Actually, make that Contestants Two through Eight. It's a cluster of digestive exhalation products. Pirkarli, mostly."

Bayta wrinkled her nose. "There *were* two Pirks back there."

"And I'm sure the rest of the car is grateful for the focused ventilation system you have by Pirk seats," I said, looking over at the locked drug cabinet. Neither Witherspoon's nor Aronobal's kits were there. "I thought doctors' kits were supposed to be kept locked up."

"They are," Bayta said. "Both kits are in the first-class dispensary right now."

I frowned. As third-class passengers, neither doctor had normal access to that part of the train. "Are their owners up there with them?"

"Dr. Witherspoon is," Bayta said. "He's monitoring *di*-Master Strinni. Dr. Aronobal left her bag in first so it would be available in case she was called on again to treat *Usantra* Givvrac's stomach trouble."

"Digestion has always been the Fillies' weak spot," I commented, looking down at my reader. "Our next mystery guest has now signed in. Looks like this one's actually a group, too."

"More Pirkarli emissions?"

"Not unless our Pirks are also hypochondriacs," I said. "These are three different antibacterial sprays, the kind people like to waft around themselves to protect against alien germs." I cocked an eyebrow. "I wonder if one of them might belong to our friend *Logra* Emikai. He certainly seemed concerned about the train's overall air quality."

"He's not seated in that car."

"But his friend Terese is," I reminded her. "Maybe he gave her some of his spray. Or maybe they're both hypochondriacs." I gestured to the reader. "One more to go. How's *di*-Master Strinni doing?"

"He's conscious," Bayta said slowly, her eyes unfocusing as she communicated with the server in the first-class dispensary. "He seems to have calmed down, too."

"Good," I said. "As soon as this is done—" I broke off, glaring at the display. "Oh, for—"

"What is it?" Bayta asked, craning her neck to see.

"Contestant Number Whatever turns out to be nothing but fragmented Juriani scale material," I said, pointing to the line. "Apparently fragmented small enough to sneak through the other filters."

"Is that a problem?" Bayta asked, frowning.

"Hardly," I said, shutting down the reader and putting it back into my pocket. "But I doubt Larry Hardin's high-end techs worked this hard to design and build this thing just so I could use it to identify Jurian dandruff."

I took the sample vials and dropped them into my pocket

beside the reader. "Come on—let's see if *di*-Master Strinni is up to answering some questions."

We arrived at the first-class dispensary to find Strinni lying quietly on the diagnostic table, his skin showing the same mottling that Master Colix and Master Bofiv had demonstrated just prior to their deaths. Not a good sign. The Shorshian's breathing was labored, his eyes dull and listless. But at least he no longer looked inclined to throw the furniture around. "Good evening, *di*-Master Strinni," I greeted him, glancing around. Aside from Strinni himself and the server standing by the drug cabinet there was no one else in the room. "How do you feel?"

[Like I'm dying,] he said grimly. [It's good of you to come, Mr. Compton. And you,] he added, giving Bayta a small acknowledging nod. [I very much wanted to apologize for my behavior earlier.]

"No problem," I assured him. "I'm sure that was just the necrovri talking. You use the stuff often?"

A bit of fire came into his eyes. [I do not *use* any such poisons,] he said, the words coming out as crisp and emphatic as individual thudwumper rounds. [I don't know how it came to be in my body. But I assure you it was none of *my* doing.]

"I believe you," I assured him. Actually, I only believed him about eighty percent, but I wasn't going to call him a liar to his face. "Any idea how it could have gotten into your system?"

His brief surge of passion faded away. [Perhaps it was placed within my food without my noticing,] he said.

"Perhaps," I agreed. "Who have you shared a meal or drink with over the past three or four days?

[Only the others of my contract team,] he said. [Those in first class, of course.]

"No one else?" I asked.

[Do you accuse me of lying?]

"Just double-checking," I soothed. "Do you happen to know where Dr. Witherspoon is, by the way?"

[He went for food,] Strinni said.

"For *food*?" I asked, frowning. Bayta and I had just come up from the rear of the train, and we hadn't passed Witherspoon along the way. "When did he leave?"

[A few minutes only before your arrival.]

"He didn't go back to third," Bayta spoke up. "The Spiders are letting him eat in first tonight."

"Ah," I said, nodding. Unlike the third-class dining car, which was half a train back, the first-class dining car was just three cars away toward the front. All the same, I found it damned odd that Witherspoon would just take off and leave a desperately ill patient all alone this way. "He didn't ask Dr. Aronobal to take over while he was gone?" I asked Strinni.

[I didn't *want* Dr. Aronobal to take over,] Strinni said, a flicker of life again peeking through the weariness. [*I* sent Dr. Witherspoon for his food, Mr. Compton. He didn't abandon me, as you so obviously think. He's already done all that he can for my broken body.]

"My apologies," I said, not feeling particularly apologetic. Hungry or not, ordered out or not, Witherspoon still shouldn't have deserted his patient. "If I may suggest, though, in a case like this two sets of eyes and minds are always preferable to one. I'm sure Dr. Aronobal would be happy—"

[I will not be treated by that Filiaelian,] Strinni cut me off. [I will not be so debased.]

He'd said the same thing earlier, during the drug-driven

fracas in his coach car. At the time, I'd assumed it was the necrovri talking. Apparently, it wasn't. "I understand your reluctance," I said. "But still—"

"Frank," Bayta said, touching my arm warningly.

Grimacing, I nodded and shut up. There was a lot of specism in the galaxy, lurking in the dark corners where supposedly civilized people didn't like to look. In general, Shorshians and Fillies got along reasonably well, but there were fringe elements in any group. "Fine," I said to Strinni. "I gather you don't have any such reservations about Dr. Witherspoon?"

[Why would I?] he asked. [Dr. Witherspoon is part of our group.]

I stared down at him. "He's *what*?"

[He's a physician with Pellorian Medical Systems,] Strinni said. [He sat in with the contract team during many of our meetings, and travels now with us to Rentis Tarlay Birim to examine our facilities.]

"I didn't know that," I said, giving Bayta a quick look. Judging by her expression, this was news to her, too. "How come no one ever mentioned this to me?"

[Why was it any of your concern?] Strinni countered. [You're not part of our group. Neither have you any official authority or investigative position—]

He broke off in a fit of loud, wet-sounding coughs. "Are you all right?" I asked as the coughing showed no sign of stopping.

And then, abruptly, the mottling of his skin dissolved into a chaotic flow of black, white, and gray as all semblance of a normal Shorshic color pattern disappeared. "Bayta!" I snapped, grabbing for Strinni's arm as his body began convulsing.

"One of the conductors is getting him," she said tightly. "Shall I have Dr. Aronobal brought up, too?"

"Yes," I said. The hell with Strinni's prejudices—his life was on the line here. "Where is she?"

"In her normal seat," Bayta said. "Eighteen cars back."

I swore under my breath. Eighteen cars was a long ways away. "Yes, get her here," I ordered. Maybe Strinni was in better shape than he looked.

I had barely completed that thought when the Shorshian gave a final convulsion and collapsed into an unmoving heap on the table.

Not breathing at all.

"Get Witherspoon here *now*," I snarled at Bayta as I grabbed the bright orange LifeGuard unit off the wall by the drug cabinet. I punched the selector for Shorshic configuration and hurried back to the table. "Here," I said, pulling the arm cuff free of its holder.

Bayta took the cuff and fastened it around Strinni's arm. "Ready," she said. I made a final check of the breather mask I'd set over Strinni's face and punched the start button.

The LifeGuard chugged to life. I gazed down at Strinni's face, knowing full well that this was almost certainly an exercise in futility. But I had to do *something*.

And then, to my astonishment, Strinni's eyes stirred and opened to slits. [Compton,] he murmured, his voice muffled by the mask.

I frowned at the LifeGuard. The device hadn't finished running its diagnosis, but red lights were already beginning to wink on all across the display. This had to be the most heroic effort at last words on the books. "I'm here," I said, leaning closer to him as I gazed into those half-closed eyes. "What is it?"

[Don't desecrate . . . my . . . body,] he said, his voice fading until it was almost too soft to hear. His eyes closed again, and the lights on the LifeGuard's display went solid red.

I looked at Bayta. "Don't desecrate my body?" I echoed. "What in the world does *that* mean?"

"Probably that he doesn't want an autopsy," she said, her eyes aching as she gazed at this, the third dead body she'd seen in two days. "He's a member of the Path of Onagnalhni, re-member?"

"Right," I murmured. "I'd forgotten."

There was the sound of racing footsteps out in the corridor, and I turned as Witherspoon burst panting into the dispensary. "Don't bother," I told him as I stepped aside to let him see the unmoving figure on the table. "He's dead."

NINE :

Witherspoon wasn't willing to take my word for it. Or the LifeGuard's electronic evidence, either. Silently, grimly, he set to work with analyzers and hypos and modern medicine's magic potions.

In the end, he accepted the inevitable.

"I shouldn't have left," he said wearily, stepping over to the side of the room and touching a switch. A seat folded out from the wall, and he sank heavily onto it. "I should have stayed here with him."

"He told us he'd ordered you to go get some food," I reminded him.

"So what?" he countered. "I'm a doctor, not a servant."

"No, but when your patient orders you away, there's not a lot you can do," I said.

"I could have ignored him," Witherspoon said, dropping his gaze to the floor. "Or I could have stayed just outside in the corridor where I would have been available when he needed me." He hissed between his teeth. "Instead, I was out feeding my face."

"For whatever it's worth, I don't think you could have done anything even if you'd been here," I said. "He already had too much cadmium in his tissues. We don't have the facilities aboard to have cleaned it out fast enough."

"I know," Witherspoon said. "I should have been here anyway."

For a minute the room was silent. I gave him another minute to mourn his companion, or to sandpaper his conscience, then got back to business. "*Di*-Master Strinni said you were part of his contract team."

"Yes," Witherspoon acknowledged without hesitation. "Though technically, Mr. Kennrick and I are with Pellorian Medical, not the contract team per se."

"It might have been nice to know this earlier," I commented.

He turned puzzled eyes on me. "Why?"

"Because in case you've forgotten, this is a murder investigation," I said. "High on the list of useful things to know are the relationships between victims and suspects."

A whole series of emotions chased each other across his face, with outrage bringing up the rear. "Are you saying I'm a *suspect*?" he demanded. "How *dare* you!"

"I dare because we now have three unexplained deaths aboard our cozy little Quadrail," I said calmly. "*And* because you were in recent contact with at least two of the three victims."

"That's a gross misstatement of the situation," Witherspoon insisted stiffly. But his expression was rapidly fading from righteous anger to cautious apprehension. He'd surely seen enough dit rec thrillers to know how high the victims' doctor usually ended up on the cops' suspect list. "Besides, all three victims were showing symptoms before I was brought in."

"True," I agreed. "Tell me about Terese German."

He blinked. "Who?"

"The young Human woman you had the consultation with over dinner last night."

A flicker of recognition crossed his face. "Oh," he said. "Her."

"Yes, her," I said. "What did you—?" I broke off as another set of hurrying footsteps sounded out in the corridor and Dr. Aronobal came charging into the dispensary, her chest heaving even more than Witherspoon's had been at his entrance. But then, Aronobal had had farther to jog. "Dr. Aronobal," I greeted her gravely. "My apologies for dragging you all the way up here—"

"How is he?" Aronobal asked, slowing to a fast walk as she headed toward the table.

"—especially as it turns out to have been unnecessary," I finished. "I'm afraid di-Master Strinni has passed on."

Aronobal shot me a look as she came to a halt by the body. "My bag," she said tartly, jabbing a finger at the Filiaelian medical kit locked in the drug cabinet.

Obediently, the Spider unlocked the cabinet and handed over the bag. For all the good it would do. "Where were we?" I asked, turning back to Witherspoon. "Oh, yes. Terese German."

Witherspoon's eyes flicked over my shoulder. "What about her?"

"Let's start with what you talked about," I suggested.

Witherspoon hunched his shoulders in a shrug that I was pretty sure was supposed to look casual. "Not much," he said. "I'd noticed that she seemed to be having stomach or digestive trouble—frequent trips to the restroom and all—and I asked if there was anything I could do."

"You noticed that all the way from two cars back?" I asked. "You must have eyes like a hawk."

"Well, no, I—I mean," he stammered. "I mean—"

"Your seat *is* two cars back from hers, right?" I asked.

"Yes, but—" He broke off, his eyes flicking over my shoulder again. "I mean I noticed at the times I was in that car. When I was visiting Master Colix, Master Bofiv, and Master Tririn."

"And was there?"

"Was there what?" he asked, thoroughly lost now.

"Was there anything you could do for her?"

Again, his eyes flicked over my shoulder. "I really can't say anything more. I'm sorry."

I looked over my shoulder, wondering what Witherspoon found so fascinating over there. Aronobal was standing squarely in Witherspoon's line of glance, hunched over the table with her back to us. "You *do* remember that this is a murder investigation, right?" I asked, turning back to Witherspoon.

"It would be hard to forget with you reminding me every two minutes," Witherspoon said acidly. With the brief break, he was on balance again. "I'm sorry, but this is a matter of doctor/patient privilege."

"Dr. Witherspoon?" Aronobal called, not turning around. "A word with you, if you please?"

"What is it?" Witherspoon asked, getting up and crossing to the table.

I crossed to the table, too, circling the foot and coming up on the other side from the two doctors. "Look at this," Aronobal said, pointing to Strinni's hands.

The forefinger of Strinni's right hand was curved around

to touch the tip of his thumb like an okay sign, the other fingers sticking stiffly straight out together. His left hand, in contrast, was curved like he'd been holding on to a thick pipe that had been subsequently removed. "What did you do that for?" I asked.

"I did nothing," Aronobal insisted. "They were like this when I first reached him."

"Were they, Frank?" Bayta murmured as she came to my side.

"I don't know," I had to admit. "I wasn't focusing on his hands at the time."

"Was he holding anything earlier?" Aronobal asked. "In either hand?"

"No," I said. That much I *was* sure of. "There was nothing within reach, either."

"Your arm, perhaps?" Aronobal suggested, reaching over the table and wrapping her hand experimentally around my wrist.

"No," I said again. "I have no idea why his hands would have curled—"

"It's sign language," Witherspoon said suddenly.

I studied Strinni's hands. Now that Witherspoon mentioned it, they *did* look like finger-spelling letters. The letters F and C, in fact.

My initials.

"Can you read them?" Aronobal asked.

"Just a second," Witherspoon said as he started contorting his own hand. "The left hand is the letter C," he said. "The right hand . . . that's an F."

"CF," Aronobal murmured thoughtfully.

"More likely FC," Witherspoon said. "That's the order they're in as you look down at them."

"Or even more likely pure coincidence," I said. Whatever

had happened with Strinni's hands, the last thing I wanted was for Witherspoon or Aronobal to think there was a connection there to me. "Some trick of that last set of convulsions. He had enough breath to warn us not to autopsy his body, after all—if he'd wanted to leave a dying clue, he could have just said something."

Witherspoon looked sharply at me. "FC," he said. "*Frank Compton.*"

I held his gaze, a sinking feeling running through me. Damn. "That's ridiculous," I insisted.

"Is it?" Witherspoon countered. "Of course he couldn't say anything, not with you and your friend the only ones in the room. What other clue could he leave?"

"Okay, fine," I said. "Let's say those really are F and C signs—"

"Oh, please," Witherspoon growled. "There must be a hundred encyclopedias aboard that can confirm *that.*"

"I meant as opposed to random hand configurations," I said patiently. "That still leaves the question of how *di*-Master Strinni learned Human sign language in the first place. Come to think of it, if we're going down that road, we ought to be looking into what those mean in *Shorshic* sign language."

"There is no such thing," Aronobal said. "Deafness is curable or treatable among Shorshians, and hence is essentially unknown. Any signing system would have been lost generations ago."

"Ditto for most other species," Witherspoon agreed. "If *di*-Master Strinni knew any sort of sign language, it would be the Human variety."

"Which still doesn't prove he actually did know it," I said. "Besides, I only met him yesterday. What possible motive would I have for killing him?"

"That *is* the question, isn't it?" Witherspoon said, his tone going all dark and ominous. He would have been great in a dit rec mystery. "Perhaps we should get Mr. Kennrick in here and see if he can shed some light on this."

"Mr. Kennrick isn't an investigator," I said.

"No, but he seems to know something about you," Witherspoon said. "Maybe there are some dark secrets in your past—"

"Just a minute," Bayta spoke up suddenly, her eyes unfocusing. "*Usantra* Givvrac is in great pain. He's asked a conductor to bring him a doctor."

"You sure it's *Usantra* Givvrac, and not one of the other Filiaelians?" Witherspoon asked, a sudden anxiety in his voice.

"I'm sure," Bayta said. "But one of the other Filiaelians in his car is also feeling ill."

"I'd better go," Witherspoon said, gesturing to the Spider to hand him his bag.

"I'll do it," Aronobal said calmly, laying a hand on Witherspoon's shoulder. "I have more experience with Filiaelian medicine than you."

"You both need to go," Bayta said. "A Filiaelian four cars back, *Osantra* Qiddicoj, is also calling for a doctor."

"Four back?" I repeated, mentally doing my own count of the cars. "*Di*-Master Strinni's car?"

"Yes," Bayta confirmed.

Where Strinni had been poisoned with both heavy metal and a hallucinogen. Interesting. "Sounds like we suddenly have plenty of patients to go around," I said, looking back and forth between Witherspoon and Aronobal. "How do you want to sort it out?"

"Dr. Witherspoon can treat *Osantra* Qiddicoj," Aronobal said, already halfway to the door. "I will treat *Usantra* Givvrac and the other in his car."

"And I'll go with Dr. Witherspoon," I volunteered, falling into step behind Witherspoon as he headed toward the door.

"That's not necessary," Witherspoon said.

"I don't mind," I assured him.

Witherspoon stopped dead in his tracks. "Let me make it clearer," he said coldly. "I don't want you along."

"Sorry to hear that," I said. "Let *me* make it clearer: I don't give a damn what you want. You've got a sick patient. We both want to see him. You want me to stay here, you're welcome to try and make me. Otherwise, stop complaining and get moving."

He pressed his lips tightly together. "Fine," he said. "You first."

I rolled my eyes and moved into the doorway in front of him. "Bayta, stay here and watch *di*-Master Strinni's body," I said. "We'll be back in a minute."

We headed out, Aronobal hitting the corridor and branching left, Witherspoon and I branching right. "What is it with all this Filly stomach trouble?" I whispered over my shoulder to Witherspoon as we reached the first coach car and passed through the sea of canopied seats and sleeping passengers. "More heavy-metal poisoning?"

"It's not acting like it," Witherspoon whispered back. "But with gleaner bacteria in their intestines doing the bulk of waste processing and removal, Filiaelians are highly susceptible to digestive trouble."

"Like Terese German?" I asked.

He didn't answer. "I said—"

"I heard you," he interrupted. "And I already told you my dealings with her are confidential. Quiet, now—we don't want to wake anyone."

We passed through the rear vestibule and entered the first-class entertainment car. From the faint reflections of flickering light I could see from the various dit rec cubicles as we passed, it was clear there were still a few night owls up and about. We finished with that car, passed through another coach car full of canopied seats and sleeping travelers, and arrived at last at *Osantra* Qiddicoj's car.

Most of the passengers here had deployed their canopies, though a few seats contained Shorshians who, like *di*-Master Strinni, apparently preferred sleeping in the open air. Near the rear of the car, I spotted the soft glow of a conductor call light on one of the uncanopied seats. The seat itself was turned away from us, hiding its occupant from view, but I doubted that the call light was marking someone who merely wanted to know when the dining car started serving breakfast. "There's our boy," I murmured, heading toward it.

We were halfway back when I heard a soft thud behind me. Frowning, I started to turn—

Something exploded against the side of my neck, and the darkened Quadrail car went completely black.

I woke up slowly, with the nagging but persistent feeling that I wasn't at all comfortable.

I tried to bring my hands up to my eyes to help rub them open. But the hands didn't want to move. In fact, I wasn't even sure where exactly my hands were. I tried turning my head to look for them, but my head wouldn't move either.

Was I paralyzed?

That delightful thought snapped me fully awake. With my heart pounding, I opened my eyes.

In front of me was an unrelieved curtain of dark gray, and for another horrible second I thought I'd gone blind as well as paralyzed. Then my eyes focused, and I realized that what I was staring at was exactly that: a curtain of dark gray. I was sitting in a first-class seat with the sleep canopy deployed around me.

And the reason I'd thought I was paralyzed was that my wrists, ankles, and forehead were taped to that selfsame seat.

I looked downward as far as I could. There were at least four windings of tape around each of my wrists, possibly as many as five or six. I couldn't see my ankles or, obviously, my forehead, but I had no reason to suspect my assailant had been any less generous there than he had with my wrists.

Experimentally, I tried twisting my arms, hoping I could break free. Nothing. I tried the same move with head and feet, with the same lack of results. At this rate, I'd be pinned here like a prize butterfly until lunchtime tomorrow.

My gut gave one of its now all-too-familiar rumbles. The thought of lunchtime, or of food in general, was almost painful. I listened to the fresh growling, trying to figure out if this was the same problem as before or if my assailant had decided to go ahead and poison me while he had the chance. It certainly felt like I was dying from the inside out.

I stiffened, the sudden tightening of my stomach muscles adding a fresh burst to the intestinal turmoil lower down. There it was, damn it—so obvious I should have fallen over it. *Dying from the inside out . . .*

And then, outside my canopy, I heard something. I strained my ears, and the sound resolved itself into a set of quiet footsteps and the equally quiet but very distinctive tap-tap-tap of a Spider.

It was Bayta. It had to be. Clearly, I'd been gone long enough to arouse her misgivings and she'd grabbed a Spider to come looking for me. Feeling a surge of relief, I opened my mouth to call to her.

Only to discover that my friend with the tape had thought-fully taken the time to gag me, too.

I heaved my shoulders back and forth to the sides, trying to shake the seat enough to catch Bayta's notice. But it was an-chored solidly in place, and I doubted I was getting up enough momentum to even disturb the canopy. I tried grunting through the tape over my mouth, but even to my own ears the muffled sound sounded pretty pathetic. Looking in all direc-tions, I searched for inspiration.

And then, my gaze fell on the music controls by my left hand.

It was a long shot, I knew. Quadrail audio systems were heavily focused, precisely to prevent everyone else in the car from being disturbed by someone else's music. I would have to crank it up to eardrum-damaging levels for anyone out there to even hear it.

But it was a risk I had to take. If I didn't get Bayta's atten-tion now, it could be hours before one of the other passengers wondered why this particular traveler was sleeping in so late, and got curious enough to investigate. There were already at least three Fillies out there in serious medical trouble, with possibly more to come. Unless I got out of here, and fast, we were going to have more deaths on our hands.

Cranking the volume all the way up, I set my teeth and touched the switch.

It was like sitting front-row-center at a live concert where each musician had made a bet with all the others that he could get the most sound out of his instrument. I left the music on maybe a quarter of a second before switching it off again, and even with that short an exposure it felt like the my ears were coming off at the lobes.

But I couldn't stop now. I fired it up another quarter second, and then another. Then, bracing myself, I turned it on for a full second.

This time, it felt like the top of my head was joining my ears in their attempt to vacate the premises. I gulped a breath, fired off another full second, and another, and then thankfully returned to three more of the shorter quarter-second bursts of agony.

Bayta had had a sheltered upbringing among the Chahwyn, and had been playing a determined game of intellectual catch-up since then. Still, somewhere along the line, surely even she had learned the significance of a classic SOS.

I was midway through the third repeat, and was wondering if my ears were starting to bleed yet, when the canopy was pulled open, and I saw Bayta's worried face looking down at me.

In the brief time I'd been away, the dispensary had become an emergency room.

Witherspoon was sitting on one of the fold-out seats along the side wall, pressing a cold pack against the back of his head, his posture that of a man who had just gone three rounds with a bulldozer. Two Fillies were twitching in obvious discomfort on fold-out slabs on the other side of the room. One of them turned his head as Bayta and I entered, and I saw it was my friend Rose Nose, the one who'd pulled me out of the scuffle with Strinni earlier in the afternoon, just long enough for Kennrick's ribs to get cracked instead of mine.

Strinni's body, which had been on the diagnostic table when I'd left, was nowhere to be seen. In its place, lying ominously still on the treatment table as Aronobal worked feverishly over him, was *Usantra* Givvrac.

"Whatever you're doing, stop it," I said, wincing as the sound of my words assaulted my sore ears. "It won't work."

"Compton!" Witherspoon exclaimed, looking up at the sound of my voice. "Are you all right? Someone hit me—"

"Save it," I cut him off. "You need to get a load of gleaner bacteria from somewhere and inject it into his intestines."

"What?" Aronobal asked, frowning down her long nose at me.

"Are you deaf?" I bit out. "Their gleaner bacteria's been wiped out. The unneutralized waste is backing up and flooding their systems—that's what's making them sick."

"Impossible," Aronobal insisted. "What could they possibly have eaten that could have done so much damage?"

"They didn't eat it, they inhaled it," I said, disengaging myself from Bayta's supporting arm and making my slightly unsteady way to the table. "I took a sample earlier from one of the train's air filters and found traces of antibacterial sprays."

"You can't kill a Filiaelian's gleaner bacteria that way," Witherspoon said. "Everything they inhale is filtered through the respiratory system—"

"So is everything Humans inhale," I interrupted him. "But Bayta and I are both feeling the effects of something on our own gut flora. Whatever this stuff was our killer was spraying around, it digs deep and packs one hell of a punch."

Witherspoon looked at Aronobal. "Is this reasonable? Or even possible?"

"Do you have any other treatment to suggest?" Aronobal countered. "Very well, Mr. Compton. If your companion will ask the Spiders to find some Filiaelian volunteers, we'll try your suggestion."

"No," a weak Filly voice said.

It took me a second to realize the voice had been Givvrac's. "No what?" I asked, looking down at him.

"No need to find volunteers," he said, his eyes nearly closed, his nose blaze gone so dark now as to be nearly black. "My contract team—*Esantra* Worrbin, *Asantra* Muzzfor, and *Asantra* Dallilo. They will provide what is necessary."

"Works for me," I said, looking over at Bayta. "Can you get the Spiders on it?"

She nodded. "Already done."

"Compton?" Givvrac murmured.

I looked back down at him. "Yes?"

"My final wish," he said softly. "Find this murderer."

"I will," I promised, wondering distantly if Filly law listed any penalties for failing to deliver on a deathbed promise. "But you're a long ways yet from any final wishes," I added. "Half an hour, and you'll be as good as new."

"Find the murderer, Mr. Compton," Givvrac repeated, his voice trailing off into a whisper. "And kill him."

I looked at Bayta, then at Witherspoon, then at Aronobal . . . and there was something in the Filly doctor's eyes that warned there were indeed penalties for reneging on such a promise. "If it's within my power," I said, looking back at Givvrac, "I will."

His eyes closed, and he gave a microscopic nod. "Then will honor and justice be served," he murmured.

Five minutes later, he was dead.

TEN :

"Hold still," Witherspoon ordered as he gently pulled on the back of my right ear and eased the tip of his viewer into the labyrinth within.

"You just watch where you're poking that thing," I warned, wincing as his touch sent my ears' background throbbing onto a new and more exciting rhythm.

"Courage, Compton," Kennrick admonished, glancing around the otherwise deserted first-class bar as he took a sip of his brandy.

Normally this sort of examination would have been held in the dispensary. But the dispensary was more than a little crowded at the moment. Besides, the dispensary didn't serve brandy, which Kennrick apparently liked a lot.

It also didn't serve yogurt, which I didn't like at all, but which my gut badly needed to help replenish its supply of helpful bacteria. "I'm saving my courage for when he pokes something in *your* ear," I told Kennrick, taking a last bite and setting my spoon on the table beside my empty bowl.

"In that case, feel free to yell in agony," Kennrick said agreeably.

"I never scream in front of the help," I said, gesturing toward the server standing a couple of paces behind Witherspoon. The Spider, I knew, was here to keep an eye on Witherspoon's medical bag.

Kennrick, I was pretty sure, was here to keep an eye on me.

Witherspoon let go of my ear. "Other side, please," he instructed.

I swiveled my chair around, putting my back to Kennrick and the table. "We have got to be the saddest lot of travelers in Quadrail history," Kennrick mused as Witherspoon dug his viewer into my other throbbing ear. "Give us a drum and a couple of fifes and we'd be right at home in a Western Alliance historical painting."

"It's worse back in the dispensary," I reminded him.

"They were included in my list," he said, his voice grim. "*Damn* it all. I still can't believe this is happening."

"You mean the fact that your contract team is falling over like dominoes?" I asked.

"*And* the fact that the Spiders haven't lifted a leg to stop it," he growled. "I thought they were supposed to keep weapons off their damn trains."

"What weapons?" I countered. "Like you said earlier, cadmium's found in any number of gadgets used all over the galaxy. And people bring antiseptic sprays onto Quadrails all the time."

"Sprays strong enough to penetrate all the way into Filiaelian intestines?"

"I'll admit that's a new one," I conceded. "The point remains that up to now nothing that's been used has qualified as a standard weapon."

"They're supposed to screen for nonstandard weapons, too," Kennrick growled. "You about done there, Doc?"

"Almost," Witherspoon said. "And I think our energies would be better spent in figuring out how we can prevent this from happening again instead of trying to assign blame."

"Hear, hear," I said. "Actually, that's the main reason I wanted the two of you here while Dr. Witherspoon checked me over. I thought it was about time we all had a nice quiet conversation together."

"*You* wanted me here?" Kennrick asked. "The conductor said it was Dr. Witherspoon who sent for me."

"It was," I agreed. "A quiet conversation is the reason I let him do it. Doc? What's the verdict?"

"No permanent damage that I can see," Witherspoon reported, putting the viewer back into his bag and pulling out a packet of QuixHeals. "But both your eardrums are going to be tender for a while." He grimaced, his fingers digging briefly beneath his shirt collar to gingerly touch the back of his neck. "As will your neck," he added. "A few days on QuixHeals and you should be mostly back to normal."

"So what did you want to talk about?" Kennrick asked.

"Obviously, what's been going on aboard this train," I said. "Dr. Witherspoon has a theory."

The sudden change in conversational direction caught Witherspoon by surprise. "I do?" he asked, sounding bewildered.

"Of course," I said. "You think I did it."

It was Kennrick's turn to be caught flatfooted. "*You?*" he demanded.

"That's right," I said, watching Witherspoon closely. Under our dual gaze, he was starting to look a little squirmy. "*Di*-Master Strinni may have died with his hands making the sign-language symbols for F and C. Dr. Witherspoon thinks they're my initials."

"Ridiculous," Kennrick said. "Sorry, Doc, but it's ridiculous."

"Why?" Witherspoon countered. "We know nothing about Mr. Compton. Who he is, who he's working for, or what he's doing on this train."

"He's annoyed that I pointed out he'd been with two of the victims before they died," I stage-whispered to Kennrick. "Actually, with Givvrac, we're now up to three out of four."

"And who knows how many of them *you* dealt with?" Witherspoon shot back. "You *or* your Spider friends."

"Easy, Doc," Kennrick soothed. "You've got the wrong end of the stick here. Whatever Mr. Compton is now, what he *was* was Western Alliance Intelligence."

Witherspoon drew back a little, his eyes narrowing. "*Westali?*"

"That's right," I confirmed.

"You know this for a fact?" Witherspoon asked.

"I do," Kennrick confirmed.

"How?"

A muscle twitched in Kennrick's cheek. "He was—"

"I was involved in an operation at the law office where he was working a few years ago," I jumped in.

Witherspoon's wary look shifted to Kennrick. "Was Mr. Kennrick the target?" he asked pointedly.

"No," I said. It was mostly true. "And to answer your next question, I left the service voluntarily." That was also mostly true, though I certainly wouldn't have volunteered to resign if I hadn't been pressured to do so. "I can give you references, if you still want to check up on me after we reach Venidra Carvo. Won't do you much good right now, though."

"I'll get the list from you later," Witherspoon said, visibly relaxing a bit. "Did *di*-Master Strinni know about your history? Is that why he left us your initials?"

"We don't even know that they *were* initials, let alone mine," I reminded him. "They could have stood for First Class, Fried Chicken, or even Feeling Crappy. *If* he knew Human sign language at all, which we still haven't established."

"It's not impossible," Kennrick said. "I've seen a number of non-Humans using Human sign language over the years. Business people especially—some companies like to have a way of communicating in private across crowded rooms. I don't know about *di*-Master Strinni specifically, though."

"Maybe Master Tririn will know," I said. "In the meantime, now that my pedigree's been established, I'd like to ask you a few questions."

"I've got one of my own first," Kennrick said. "Are you operating under the authority of the Spiders on this?"

"They've asked me to investigate the deaths, yes," I said.

"Is this a one-time thing, or does your association with them predate this particular trip?" he persisted. "The reason I ask is because Pellorian Medical's policy is to always cooperate with the authorities, even if that cooperation leads to the disclosure of confidential company information. But that only applies to authorities with genuine credentials, not some thrown-together posse of rent-a-cops."

"I could probably order the Spiders to throw you off the train," I offered. "Would that that qualify as adequate authority?"

"I'd say so," Kennrick said. "Sorry, but murders or not, Dr. Witherspoon and I still have to cover our own rear ends here. What do you want to know?"

"Let's start with the obvious," I said. "Do you know of anyone who might have had it in for your contract team?"

"Or Shorshians and Filiaelians in general," Witherspoon put in. "Don't forget, there are two other Filiaelians being treated back there."

I shook my head. "Collateral damage. The members of your team are clearly the targets."

"But that's ridiculous," Witherspoon objected. "We're a *medical* group. Why would anyone want to attack *us*?"

"Because you're a medical group whose decisions will affect the distribution of millions of dollars," I said.

"There's your proof of Westali training," Kennrick commented dryly. "First instinct of every government type is to assume it's about money."

I shrugged. "That's because nine times out of ten it is."

"Maybe this is the once out of ten that it isn't," Kennrick said. "Dr. Witherspoon's right—when you're dealing with Filiaelians and Shorshians, it's just as likely to be about avenged honor." He cocked an eyebrow. "Which, I'll point out, *Usantra* Givvrac also mentioned."

"Fine," I said, giving up. To me, it was obvious this wasn't a revenge killing. That kind of murderer usually wanted everyone to know that honor had been satisfied, which meant killing his victim in a very obvious way. Something else had to be at the root of this, though I still had no idea what.

But Kennrick and Witherspoon were clearly not yet ready to let go of the revenge straw. I might as well humor them and get it over with. "What do you know about the late members of your group?"

"Not much," Kennrick admitted. "Doc?"

"I know that Master Colix and *Asantra* Dallilo have worked together on other projects in the past," Witherspoon said. "So have *Usantra* Givvrac and *di*-Master Strinni. Maybe they managed to offend someone along the way."

"Except that *Asantra* Dallilo is still alive," I pointed out.

Kennrick grunted. "Give it a few hours."

"He could be right," Witherspoon rumbled. "Do you think we ought to put the rest of the contract team under guard?"

"Whose guard would you trust?" I asked. "Yours and Mr. Kennrick's?"

"Or yours," Witherspoon suggested.

"Or the Spiders'?" Kennrick countered.

"I doubt the Spiders have anyone to spare for escort duty," I said, passing over the fact that they wouldn't be much use as guards anyway. "As for me, I don't work for you."

"What if we hire you?" Kennrick asked.

"You couldn't afford me," I assured him. "Next question. I'd like your reading on where each of the recently deceased stood vis-à-vis this deal with Pellorian Medical."

"Didn't *Usantra* Givvrac give you all that earlier?" Kennrick asked, frowning.

"He gave me his take on the lineup," I confirmed. "I want to hear yours."

Kennrick shrugged, wincing as the movement shifted his injured ribs. "I've always assumed that all four Filiaelians were for the deal, along with *di*-Master Strinni and probably Master Colix."

"Leaving Master Tririn and the late Master Bofiv as the only two opposed?" I asked.

"Right." Kennrick grimaced. "But since *Usantra* Givvrac said it was actually four to four, I obviously miscounted some-where."

"So it would seem," I agreed. "Was that the way you saw things, too, Dr. Witherspoon?"

"More or less," he said. "I wasn't so sure *Usantra* Givvrac was on our side, but I was counting on the other three Filiaelians."

"So who else in the group is against us?" Kennrick asked.

"That's unimportant at the moment," I said. "So by your reckoning—"

"Why is it unimportant?" Witherspoon put in.

"Give me a minute and you'll see," I told him. "So by your reckoning, the victims were three for Pellorian and one against?"

"Compton—" Witherspoon began.

"Yes," Kennrick said, holding a quieting hand toward the doctor.

"Just making sure," I said. "Now, the important question: have either of you discussed any part of this with anyone outside Pellorian Medical since the contract team arrived on Earth?"

The light seemed to dawn in Kennrick's eyes. "I get it," he said, nodding. "Unfortunately, no, we haven't. Well, *I* haven't. I assume Dr. Witherspoon hasn't, either."

"What do you mean, unfortunately?" Witherspoon asked. "Why is it unfortunate?"

"Because if we'd told someone about the team, and that someone was relying on our count, it might show up in the pattern of killings," Kennrick told him.

"Exactly," I said. "It's important to get into a murderer's head, but sometimes it can be enough to get into his eyes. If we can figure out how he sees things, we may be able to backtrack him. So, Doctor: did you discuss the contract with anyone outside Pellorian's walls?"

"Absolutely not," Witherspoon said firmly.

"How about on the torchliner from Earth to Terra Station?"

"Again, no," Kennrick said. "Ethics aside, loose talk like that can get you fired on the spot."

"How about discussing the matter with the rest of the contract team when you thought you were in private, but where someone might possibly have been able to eavesdrop?"

"I—" Kennrick broke off, turning a suddenly uncertain look on Witherspoon. "Well, actually, I don't really know," he said slowly. "Torchliner acoustics aren't as well designed as a Quadrail's. And the four Shorshians and I *did* have several mealtime discussions together."

"Did you ever take straw votes at these discussions?" I asked.

"They never did while I was present," Kennrick said. "But they might have done so after I left. They never talked about things like that in front of me."

"Or me," Witherspoon seconded.

"Understandable," I said. "I'll try asking Master Tririn about it in the morning."

"I'm sorry, but this still doesn't make sense," Witherspoon said. "If it's about whether the contract succeeds or fails, shouldn't the killer be eliminating only the team members who are opposing him?"

"In theory, sure," I said. "In actual practice, focusing exclusively on his opponents would be about as clever as taking out a full-page ad announcing his intentions. He'll need to muddy the water by killing at least one of his own side."

"Which fits the current situation exactly," Kennrick murmured.

"So you think he wants to defeat the contract?" Witherspoon asked.

"Possibly," I said, eyeing Kennrick. He was gazing off into space, a thoughtful look on his face. "But we've got a long way to go before we start jumping at that kind of conclusion. Something else, Kennrick?"

"I don't know," Kennrick said slowly. "I was just wondering if Dr. Witherspoon might be right about this being a revenge thing, only the killer was only after *one* of the victims, not all four of them. Is it possible that he killed the others just to make his real target less apparent?"

Witherspoon hissed between his teeth. "Good *God*."

"It *has* been done before," I agreed. "But again, without knowing anything about the victims' backgrounds, that theory won't get us very far."

"Probably not," Kennrick conceded. "I just thought I should mention it."

"Consider it mentioned," I said. "Let's switch gears a minute. Dr. Witherspoon, can you tell me anything about what happened earlier back in *Osantra* Qiddicoj's coach car?"

"Not really," Witherspoon said, fingering his neck gingerly. "I was following you to his seat when something hit me. The next thing I knew, your friend Bayta and a conductor were standing over me, trying to get me to wake up."

"Did you hear anything before you were hit?" I asked. "The sound of the vestibule door opening behind you, stealthy footsteps, heavy breathing—anything?"

Witherspoon shook his head. "He could have materialized out of thin air for all I know."

"Did you see or hear anything odd after you woke up?"

"Again, no," Witherspoon said. "Bayta and the conductor helped me back to the dispensary—and took *Osantra* Qiddicoj in there, too, of course—then went back to look for you." He grimaced. "And before you ask, I have no idea why anyone would want to attack me."

"Maybe it wasn't you he was after, Doc," Kennrick suggested, eyeing me speculatively. "Maybe he wanted Compton, and you were just in his way."

"That *is* a thought," Witherspoon agreed, giving me a speculative look of his own. "After all, you were the one who figured out what was wrong with the Filiaelians. If he wanted *Usantra* Givvrac dead, you were the one he needed to shut up."

"Except that at the time no one knew I had the answer," I reminded him. "Including me."

"The attacker still might have thought you were getting close," Witherspoon said.

"Or maybe you had something he wanted," Kennrick said suddenly. "You still have those tissue samples from Master Colix and Master Bofiv?"

"I assume they're still in my room," I lied, shifting my elbow slightly against my chest to press reassuringly against the vials in my pocket. The samples from the air filter and Givvrac's drink were indeed an obvious target for the killer to go after, which is why they'd been the first thing I'd checked when Bayta and the Spider got me out of that chair. "Any of your stuff gone, Doc?"

Witherspoon shook his head. "If it is, it's nothing important."

"What do you mean, if it is?" Kennrick asked, frowning. "Haven't you checked your pockets and your bag?"

"Of course I have," Witherspoon said. "My pockets haven't been touched, and he made a mess of my bag when he was looking for tape to tie up Mr. Compton with."

I focused on the medical bag still sitting in the middle of our table. "What kind of mess?" I asked carefully.

"A mess kind of mess," Witherspoon said with a touch of impatience. "Everything got moved or shifted around, with vials and pill cartridges and all dumped in the bottom. That sort of thing."

"He dumped everything in the bottom while he was looking for *tape*?" I asked.

"Yes," Witherspoon said, frowning. "What's your point?"

I looked at Kennrick, saw the light starting to dawn there. "Doc, no one throws a bunch of vials around when they're looking for a roll of tape," I said. "He wanted something else in there."

"Kindly credit me with a *little* intelligence, Mr. Compton," Witherspoon growled. "I've checked on all my painkillers and other potentially dangerous drugs. They're all still there. I doubt anyone would go to this much effort just to steal a packet of QuixHeals."

"So let's find out what *was* worth this much effort." I reached over and opened the bag. "Inventory. Now."

Witherspoon grimaced. "Fine," he said. "But I can tell you right now that we're not going to find anything significant."

"Five bucks says I will," I said nudging the bag a little closer to him.

For possibly the first time that day, I was right.

Bayta was alone in the dispensary, sitting on one of the fold-out seats and gazing wearily at *Usantra* Givvrac's body, when the Spider and I finally returned. "You all right?" I asked, peering at her as the Spider crossed the room and put Witherspoon's bag back under lock and key.

"I was just thinking about this afternoon, in the bar," she said. "When you told me that putting off a conversation usually meant that person will be the next to die."

I winced. "I'm sorry I said that."

"I'm sorry he's dead." Bayta paused. "The killer's not finished yet, is he?"

"Doesn't look like it," I conceded. "You listened in on our inventory of Witherspoon's bag?"

She nodded again. "There's a hypo missing."

"Right," I said. "Inevitable, I suppose, in retrospect. The three basic ways of delivering poisons are inhalation, ingestion, and injection. With the first two mostly off the table, that leaves only the last."

"What do you mean, mostly?" Bayta asked.

"We still haven't totally eliminated the possibility that someone added the cadmium to the Shorshians' food after it was delivered," I said. "Did you check with the servers, by the way, on whether Colix and Bofiv always used the same reaches for the common dish?"

"They didn't," Bayta said. "All three Shorshians switched off between *galla* bread, *prinn* scoops, and *rokbi* sticks, with no particular pattern the servers noticed."

"So no one could have poisoned the reaches, at least not if he was targeting specific victims," I concluded. "That leaves our killer with a choice of poisoning the common dish—or, rather, half the common dish, since Tririn wasn't affected—or two separate individual dishes. *And* all that without anyone at the table noticing. Not impossible, but pretty damn difficult."

"Unless Master Tririn himself is the killer," Bayta said slowly. "According to *Usantra* Givvrac, he was one of the four members of the team opposed to the contract with Pellorian Medical. Three of the four victims were *for* the contract."

"True," I agreed. "But that runs us immediately into another problem. Two problems, actually. If he was trying to stack the vote in his favor, Master Colix's death already accomplishes that. So why keep killing? Especially since the second death, Bofiv's, evens up the vote again?"

"It doesn't make sense, does it?" Bayta admitted.

"Not yet," I conceded. "A bigger problem with Tririn is that you've already proved he hasn't been up to first class since we left Homshil, which means he had no access to Strinni or Givvrac."

Bayta winced. "Actually, that might not be true," she said reluctantly. "It occurred to me—a little late, I'm afraid—to ask the conductors about unlimited first-class passes. They tell me eight passes came aboard the train, but only seven of the holders are actually riding in first class."

I stared at her. "Oh, hell."

"I'm sorry," Bayta apologized. "I should have asked about that sooner."

"Not your fault," I told her. So someone else had the same ability we did to flit back and forth between classes without a single locked door or raised eyebrow. Terrific. "If Spiders were smart enough to volunteer this stuff on their own instead of having to be asked—" I broke off. "Never mind. Water under the bridge. Very interesting water, too."

"Because it shows that the killer had everything planned in advance?"

"*And* because it shows he has some serious financial backing," I said. "I don't suppose there's any way of finding out who has this eighth pass?"

Bayta shook her head. "If it wasn't used to board, the conductors won't have that information."

"Who *would* have it?" I persisted. "The stationmaster back at Homshil?"

"Yes, he would have been the one who informed the conductors about the eight passes in the first place," she said. "But there's no way to get a message back there until we reach Venidra Carvo."

"Why not?" I asked. "There must be a few of your secret little sidings scattered along the way. Can't you shoot the Spiders a telepathic message as we pass, like we did on our last trip back to Earth? They could then load the request onto a message cylinder and send it back to Homshil via one of their tenders."

"It won't be easy," Bayta said doubtfully. "We don't get very close to the Spiders when we pass a siding. That'll make the contact difficult. We're also going much faster then we do when we pass through a station, so we won't be able to send anything very long or detailed."

"Then we'll just have to be clever," I said, trying to kick a few of my comatose brain cells back to life. "What if we give all the conductors aboard the same message and have them line up along the length of the train? Hell, let's give it to the servers, mites, and twitters, too. Maybe between all of them we can get enough of it across to make sense."

For a moment Bayta was silent, either thinking it over or consulting with the Spiders. "It might work," she said at last. "No guarantees, but it might."

"No guarantees expected," I assured her. "When will we pass the next siding?"

"In about six hours," she said. "It'll still take a while for a message cylinder to get from there to Homshil Station, though. And of course the only way to get the information back to us will be though a tender, and depending on where they have to send it from—"

"Yes, yes, I get it," I cut her off. "But even limited information will be better than nothing. Let's figure out the shortest way to phrase the message and then start rehearsing the Spiders."

"All right," she said, running a critical eye over me. "But I can do that. You'd better get to bed."

"I'm on my way," I promised. "One other thing."

I hesitated, wondering if I really wanted to do this. During my last private conversation with a Chahwyn Elder I'd promised that I would hold on to their new secret as long as I could. Not just because he hadn't wanted Bayta to know about it, but also because I agreed with him that the truth would be a troubling shock for her. Besides, at the time I'd made the promise there wasn't any particular reason she needed to know.

But circumstances had changed. We were locked aboard a super-express Quadrail, four weeks from our destination, with a shadowy killer who'd made an art out of sneaking death past the Spiders' sensors. We needed reinforcements, and we needed them now. "Along with the unlimited-pass information," I said, "I want you to put in a request for a couple of the Chahwyn's newest class of Spider."

"There's a new class?" she asked, frowning. "When did you hear about this?"

"When we were delivering Rebekah to her friends," I told her. "There was a Chahwyn aboard the tender, and he and I had a little chat."

Bayta's face had gone very still. "You never told me about that," she said.

"I was asked not to," I said, wincing. The hurt in her eyes was radiating at me like a heat lamp on a bad sunburn. "There was some concern about your possible reaction to the new Spiders."

"But you're telling me about them now," she said slowly. "That means you think I need to know. Because we're in danger, or because the train's in danger. We're alone against a killer—"

She broke off, her face suddenly stricken. "Oh, no," she said. "The *defenders*?"

I blinked. "You know about them?"

She closed her eyes, a wave of pain crossing her face. "The

Chahwyn Elders have talked about the idea for years," she said, her voice tight. "Since long before you were brought in to help us."

"Really," I said, trying very hard not to be annoyed and not succeeding very well. Here I'd been walking around with tape over my mouth for a solid month, worried that I'd let something slip. And now I find out Bayta had known the essentials all along? "Why didn't you tell me about them?"

"Why didn't *you* tell *me*?" she shot back, opening her eyes again to shoot a glare squarely between my eyes. "As far as I knew, the Elders were still just talking about the idea. *You* knew they'd actually created some of them." The glare suddenly evaporated. "I thought you trusted me," she said in a suddenly quiet voice.

"I *do* trust you, Bayta," I said, once again wanting to reach out and take her hand. Once again, I resisted the impulse. *Thought viruses . . .* "I was told to keep it quiet, and I'm sure you were too. It's the Elders' fault, not yours or mine."

"I suppose," she said. But I could still hear the quiet hurt in her voice.

"But I'm glad it's out in the open," I continued, searching for a way to deflect her mind away from thoughts of distrust or betrayal. "I gather you don't think much of the project?"

"Of course not," she said. "It would change the character of the Spiders forever. I don't want that."

"Unless they only make a few of them."

"You really think they'll stop there?" she countered. "With the Modhri threat the way it is? I've read about arms races, Frank. They never stop. Ever."

"Not until one side or the other goes down, anyway," I conceded. "Maybe the Elders don't think they've got any other choice."

"Of course we have a choice," Bayta said, her voice suddenly the color of despair. "We can end it. We can retreat back to Viccai and end everything."

I winced, glancing at the open dispensary door. We really shouldn't be talking about things like this in the middle of a crowded train. But the Spider who'd dropped off Witherspoon's case was standing just outside in the corridor, clearly on guard against eavesdroppers.

As well he should be. The Quadrail was essentially a fraud, the reality of its magic a closely kept secret I'd stumbled across on my first mission for the Spiders. The Tube and trains were nothing more than window dressing for the exotic quantum thread that ran down the center of the Coreline. Traveling close to the Thread was what allowed a vehicle to travel at speeds of a light-year per minute or better, the actual speed depending on how close the closest part of the vehicle was to the Thread. Anything inside the vehicle, connected to it, or even just touching it ran at the same speed, with no tidal or other nasty effects to deal with.

The problem the Chahwyn had faced when hoping to restart interstellar travel after the defeat of the Shonkla-raa was that you didn't need a train for the Thread to do its magic. You could just cozy up to it with a torchliner or torchyacht or even a garbage scow, and you'd be off to the races.

Which would have been fine if the Chahwyn could have trusted everyone in the Twelve Empires to stick with torchliners and garbage scows. Unfortunately, they couldn't. That was how the Shonkla-raa had conquered the galaxy in the first place, sending their warships along the Thread to the galaxy's inhabited systems, destroying or enslaving everything in their path.

And if the Thread's secret became common knowledge,

there was no reason to believe someone else wouldn't take a crack at replicating that achievement. Hence, the Quadrail, with its limited points of entry, its massive station-based sensor arrays, and its strict no-weapons rules.

But if the galaxy ever got a whiff of the truth, it would be all over. "You can't be serious," I said to Bayta, lowering my voice despite the presence of our Spider watchdog. "You destroy the Tube and the Quadrails, and someone's bound to figure out the secret."

"I said we end everything, Frank," she repeated, her voice weary in a way I'd never heard it before. "*Everything*. Including the Thread."

I felt my jaw drop. "You can destroy the *Thread*?"

She nodded. "You already know we can ravel off pieces of it—that's how we create loops and spurs. It's thought that if we ravel the Thread too many times, its mass will drop below a critical level and it will simply evaporate."

I felt a chill run up my back. "And what about the people who would be trapped off their worlds? How would they get home?"

"They wouldn't," Bayta said. "But exile is better than becoming slaves to the Modhri."

Except that most of the worlds where the new exiles would find themselves already had a Modhran presence, and a lot of those worlds also had at least one Modhran coral outpost. The Quadrail would be gone, but the Modhri would go merrily on his way, making slaves of anyone who crossed his path. The only difference would be that he would have to settle for being a whole lot of small, isolated, local despots instead of a single, vast galaxy-wide despot. I couldn't really see what difference that would make for his thousands of small, isolated, local groups of slaves.

Clearly, the Chahwyn who favored this approach hadn't thought it through. Just as clearly, this wasn't the time for a discussion of that shortsightedness. "Fortunately, we're a long way from that kind of irrevocable decision," I said instead. "Let's focus on the here and now. We've got a plan. Let's get it started and see where we go from there."

"All right," Bayta said. Her voice was still tired, but maybe a couple of shades less dark than it had been. "You go ahead. I'll be in later."

"Not too much later," I warned. "You've been up as long as I have, and there's time for at least a few hours of sleep before we pass that siding."

"I won't be long," she promised. "Good night."

"Good night." I headed toward the doorway, stepping past the Spider into the corridor.

And paused. On any normal Quadrail, with a contingent of Spiders wandering around and the station sensors having successfully blocked out all weaponry, I wouldn't have thought twice about leaving Bayta to wander the train alone.

But this was hardly a normal Quadrail. Not anymore.

And she was too important to risk letting our unknown assailant get a crack at her. Too important to our survival aboard this damn train. Too important to our war against the Modhri.

Too important to me.

"On second thought, you can set up your Greek Chorus from inside your compartment," I said, gesturing to her. "Come on—we'll go together."

ELEVEN :

Whoever our murderer was, he'd apparently decided to clock out for the night. I got Bayta to her compartment, made sure both our doors were locked, and just managed to get myself undressed and take one final QuixHeal before collapsing comatose on my bed.

I slept for ten hours straight, and when I finally dragged myself conscious I found the QuixHeals had done their chemical magic and I felt nearly back to full speed again. I took a quick shower, then opened the connecting door between our compartments to check on Bayta.

Only to find that she wasn't there.

Muttering curses under my breath, I left the compartment and headed aft, fervently hoping that she was merely having breakfast and not off doing more solo sleuthing. I reached the dining car and went in.

To my relief, I spotted her sitting at a two-person table behind a plate of something Jurian-looking. "Good morning," I said as I sat down across from her.

"Good afternoon," she corrected, her eyes flicking measuringly across my face. "How do you feel?"

"Much better," I said. "How about you?"

"I'm fine," she said. "I got a few hours of sleep before we reached the siding, and was able to sleep a little more afterward."

"That all go okay?" I asked, lowering my voice.

"We think so," she said. "But we can't be completely sure."

"I guess we'll find out," I said. "What's good for breakfast today? Or brunch, or whatever?"

"The *vistren* is good," she said, gesturing toward her plate. "But I understand the servers may run out of livberries before we reach Venidra Carvo."

"Say no more," I said. Livberries were my absolute favorite Jurian fruit. "A Belgian waffle with livberries, if you would, and a glass of sweet iced tea."

Her eyes flattened briefly. No point in dragging a server all the way over to our table to get my order when Bayta had a direct line to the kitchen. "On its way," she said. "I've been thinking about Dr. Aronobal."

"What about her?" I asked.

"Mostly just wondering," she said. "We talked a lot last night about the missing first-class pass. But Dr. Aronobal's been moving fairly freely between third and first ever since Master Colix's death."

"So has Dr. Witherspoon," I reminded her.

"True," she said. "But Dr. Witherspoon wasn't alone with *Usantra* Givvrac for several minutes before she called a conductor to help get him to the dispensary. Dr. Aronobal was."

"You mean just before Givvrac's death?" I shook my head. "No. The damage to his gleaner bacteria was done long before then. The poisons were already backing up into his system when we spoke to him in the bar yesterday afternoon."

"But she could have done something to help the process along," Bayta persisted. "The other two Filiaelians who were affected seem to be recovering just fine."

"Givvrac was a lot older than either of them," I reminded her. "Besides, unless Aronobal's working with a partner, she's off the hook for the attack on Witherspoon and me."

"How do you know?" Bayta asked. "The only conductor in the area was waiting with *Usantra* Givvrac. Couldn't Dr. Aronobal have followed you and Dr. Witherspoon to the rear, attacked you there, and then gone back to *Usantra* Givvrac?"

"For one thing, wouldn't either you or the server in the dispensary have seen her double back?" I asked.

She grimaced. "Actually, probably not," she said. "We were concentrating on *di*-Master Strinni's body, preparing it for transport to the baggage car."

So anyone could have been wandering around without being seen. That was useful to know. "It still couldn't have been Aronobal," I said. "Neither Witherspoon nor I heard the vestibule door open behind us, which means our attacker was already in the car waiting for us."

"Because," Bayta said slowly, "he knew you would come to help *Osantra* Qiddicoj. So could *Osantra* Qiddicoj's poisoning have been a deliberate way of drawing you there so that he could get that hypo?"

"Possibly," I said. "It's not like the killer hadn't already used the same stuff on *Usantra* Givvrac and the others. And of course, with *di*-Master Strinni gone, he even had the perfect hiding place to wait for us."

Bayta's lip twitched. "*Di*-Master Strinni's empty seat."

"Exactly," I confirmed. "And since we saw Dr. Aronobal leave the dispensary heading the opposite direction, there's no way she could have doubled back and gotten to *Osantra* Qiddicoj's car ahead of us."

"All right," Bayta said. "But it still couldn't have been Master Tririn."

Privately, I'd already put Tririn low on my suspect list— poisoning your dinner companions without giving yourself so much as a stomach ache was a little too obvious for someone with our killer's brand of subtlety. But it would be interesting to hear Bayta's reasoning. "Why not?" I asked.

"Because even if he has the missing first-class pass, going up to *di*-Master Strinni and *Usantra* Givvrac would mean approaching people who knew he was supposed to be in third," Bayta said. "Surely someone would have thought to mention that to us."

"Good point," I agreed, leaning back a little as the server appeared at our table and set my breakfast in front of me.

"Besides which, with *di*-Master Strinni's death the team is back to an anti-Pellorian vote count," she continued. "Why then kill *Usantra* Givvrac, too?"

"Let's assume you're right," I said, spreading the berries across the waffle. "Here's what we've got. Opportunity and motive are only so-so for Tririn. Opportunity is good for Aronobal and Witherspoon, but we have no motive for either of them."

"And both doctors also have method, assuming the poison was injected."

"True," I said, taking a bite of my waffle. Now that I knew the meals were prepackaged, damned if they didn't *taste* prepackaged. Sometimes it didn't pay to know how the magician did the trick. "But if either of the doctors is involved, why go to all that effort to clobber Witherspoon and me to steal a hypo? They have plenty of their own. And unlike the rest of the passengers, they have a legitimate reason to carry them around."

"Except that most of the time their hypos are locked up and inaccessible, even to them," Bayta reminded me.

"Unless they're out using them," I said, thinking that one over. "What about people who have to self-medicate? Type Four diabetics, for instance? Do they get to carry their own hypos aboard?"

Bayta shook her head. "The Spiders store them in the drug cabinets along with the doctors' bags. The passenger has to go to his area's dispensary to use them, under a server's watch."

"Any chance someone could smuggle one out of the cabinet?" I asked. "Take one while palming a second, for instance?"

"It wouldn't be easy," Bayta said thoughtfully. "At the very least you'd have to distract the server."

"So he'd probably need an accomplice," I concluded. "You have a list of passengers who have hypos on file?"

"Let me get it." Her eyes unfocused as she consulted with the Spiders. I took advantage of the break to work some more on my waffle. "There are three in second and one in first," she reported. "Interesting."

"What is?"

"The first-class passenger is *Esantra* Worrbin," she said. "Isn't that one of the Filiaelians on the contract team?"

"Not only one of the team, but one of the team opposed to the contract," I confirmed. "Just like Master Tririn. Do we know what *Esantra* Worrbin's particular condition is?"

"It's listed as Tintial's Disease," she said. "It's a rare form of diabetes that only appeared a few decades ago."

"Of course it is," I said with a cynical smile. "Rare diseases are so convenient when you want to snow a doctor or investigator."

"You think *Esantra* Worrbin and Master Tririn could be working together?"

"It's something we'll want to look into," I said, stacking my two remaining bites of waffle onto the fork and stuffing them into my mouth. It was a stretch, but I managed it.

"So what do we do now?" Bayta asked as I chewed my way valiantly through the mouthful. "Go see if *Esantra* Worrbin can account for all his hypos?"

I swallowed the last of the waffle. "Not quite yet," I said. "Something else occurs to me as a possible reason why Witherspoon and I were jumped last night. Which of the baggage cars is serving as our temporary morgue?"

"The third one back," Bayta said. "There was enough room in there to set up the isolation tanks."

"Okay," I said, taking a last swallow of my tea. "Let's go take a look."

We set off on the long walk toward third class. Three cars behind the dining car we passed the dispensary, and I noted that for the first time in a bad couple of days the room was empty except for the server Spider on duty. I wondered if we would catch the killer before it started filling up again.

The next car back, Bayta informed me, was the one where *Esantra* Worrbin and the two remaining contract team members were seated. I spotted the group at once as we headed through the car: three Fillies with their chairs turned to face each other, a hand of push-pull cards dealt onto their extendable trays. For the moment, though, the game was being ignored, the aliens instead speaking together in low voices. One of them glanced up as Bayta and I passed, but turned back to the conversation without speaking to us. I thought about pausing to introduce ourselves, decided I wanted to check my hunch about the bodies first, and passed them by.

Three cars later we reached the coach car where the late *di*-Master Strinni had had his seat, and where Witherspoon and I had been attacked in the dark of night. My neck throbbed in memory and edgy anticipation as we made our way through the clumps of chairs, my senses alert for trouble.

But no one jumped out at us. We arrived at the rear of the car and I reached for the vestibule release—

"Mr. Compton," a hoarse voice said from somewhere behind me.

A surge of adrenaline shot through my body and straight through my still tender neck and ears. I turned, trying to make the movement look casual, my hands ready to snap up into fighting stance if necessary.

It wasn't. The speaker was merely Rose Nose, or rather *Osantra* Qiddicoj, the Filly Witherspoon and I had been on our way to examine when we were jumped. He was resting in his seat, a blanket spread out across his legs and tucked up around his torso. His face and blaze were still noticeably pale after his bout with the digestive trouble that had killed Givrac, but he was definitely on the mend. "Good afternoon, *Osantra* Qiddicoj," I greeted him, hoping I was remembering his name right. Fillies hated it when you called them something like Rose Nose to their long faces. "You're looking much improved."

"Thanks to you and your friends," Qiddicoj said, inclining his head. "I'm told I owe you my life. My deepest thanks."

"You're welcome," I said. "But your thanks should more properly be directed to Dr. Aronobal and Dr. Witherspoon.

They're the ones who actually cured you. All I did was point them in the right direction."

"Yet without that direction, their skills would have lain fallow and unused," he said. "Again, I stand in your debt."

"Again, I'm glad I could help in my small way," I said. "Rest now, and continue to heal."

I turned and touched the release, and Bayta and I stepped into the vestibule. "Is extra modesty one of the necessities for detective work?" she asked as we crossed toward the next car.

"It wasn't modesty," I insisted. "I really *didn't* say anything that Aronobal and Witherspoon wouldn't have caught on to eventually."

"Maybe," Bayta said. "But whether they would have or not, the fact is that you *did* save *Osantra* Qiddicoj's life."

"In a small way." I gave her a sideways look. "Besides, it never hurts to be overly modest, especially where potential sources of information are concerned. People who consider themselves in your debt are often amazingly eager to help you out."

"I thought so," Bayta murmured.

We passed through the thirteen second-class cars without talking to anyone and entered third. Dr. Aronobal was seated in the first of the third-class coach cars, dozing in her seat after her grueling night, and I made a mental note to get the Spiders to pass her to first later so that *Osantra* Qiddicoj could give her his thanks in person.

Two cars farther back, we reached the scene of the first two murders.

I found myself looking at Master Colix's seat as we approached, an empty spot between the Juri, whom Bayta had already talked to, and Terese German, whom I was frankly tired of talking to. The Juri looked up as we approached, nodding politely as he recognized us. Terese, her headphones firmly in place over her ears, ignored us completely.

I was starting to pass the row when Bayta nudged me in the side. "Master Colix's storage compartments?" she prompted.

I looked at the upper set of compartments, then at Terese. She had slid down in her seat with her legs stretched all the way out in front of her. Getting to Master Colix's storage compartments would mean stepping over her, and would probably earn me a withering glare at the least. "We'll do it later," I told Bayta.

"You said that yesterday," she reminded me. "Don't you care that someone stole Master Colix's fruit snacks?"

Actually, I didn't. Despite what the Spiders probably claimed, I was pretty sure this kind of petty theft went on all the time aboard Quadrails.

But if it came to facing someone's irritation, it would be safer to deal with Terese's than Bayta's. "Fine," I said, coming to a reluctant halt. "Excuse me," I said to Terese's headphoned ears. Not waiting for a response, or expecting one for that matter, I lifted one leg and stepped carefully over her outstretched body.

Her head snapped up with a quickness and preset glare that showed she hadn't been nearly as oblivious of our presence as she'd been pretending. "You have a problem?" she growled, slipping the headphones down around her neck.

"I just need to get through," I soothed, getting my first foot planted in front of Colix's seat and lifting my other foot over her legs.

"For frigg's sake," she grumbled. "How many times are you people going to do this?"

I frowned as I brought my other foot back to the floor. "I don't know," I said. "How many times *have* we done this?"

"How about just *talking* to each other for once?" she bit out. "They're gone, I didn't take them, and I don't know who did. Can you leave me alone now?"

"What didn't you take?" I asked, sitting down in Colix's seat.

For a second I could see Terese trying to decide whether or not she should just get up and make for the relative sanctuary of the restroom. But Bayta had moved up beside her, blocking easy access to the aisle. "The Shorshian's fruit snacks," she answered me. "Or whatever they were."

"You think they were something else?"

"I don't know *what* they were," Terese snapped back. "All I know is that he never offered to share them, and he kept them right there under his legs where he could watch them until he swapped them out for his special sleepy-time blankie. And *then* he made double damn sure they were locked up tight." Her lip twisted. "I also know that everyone and his dog Rolf seems to want them. You tell *me* what they were."

I leaned over and pulled out the drawer of Colix's underseat storage. There was an assortment of personal stuff under there—a reader and a set of data chips, some headphones, fancier than Terese's, a flexible water bottle, a compact toiletry bag, and the small keepsake box that a lot of Shorshians liked to travel with. All of it was neatly and precisely arranged.

And right at the front left of the drawer was a gap in the arrangement, about fifteen centimeters square. The perfect size for a bag of something.

"Who else has been looking for them?" Bayta asked.

"Well, there was *you* for a start," Terese growled, flicking her a disdainful look. "Then there was that other Human you hang out with. He came by yesterday morning to look for them."

"You mean Dr. Witherspoon?" I asked.

"*No*, not Dr. Witherspoon," Terese growled. "I *know* Dr. Witherspoon's name. It was the other one, the one you were with when you tried to ambush me outside the bathroom."

I frowned. "*Kennrick?*"

"I don't *know* his name," Terese said with exaggerated patience. "Balding, mustache, a little chubby."

"That's Kennrick," I confirmed. "And you're sure he was after Master Colix's fruit snacks?"

"Well, he was after *something*," Terese said. "And he didn't find anything, either. You about done here?"

"One more minute," I promised. Returning my attention to the drawer, I slid my fingers over the lock mechanism. There was no evidence I could find that it had been forced. I stood up and gave the overseat compartment the same check. Again, nothing. Popping the compartment door, I peered inside.

There were two small carrybags in there, plus another toiletry bag, plus a carefully folded blanket. "Did he have the blanket down with him that last night?" I asked Terese as I pulled out the first carrybag and set it onto the seat.

"I don't know," she said. "I went to sleep before he did." She grimaced. "I mean, before he . . . you know what I mean."

"Before he went off to the dispensary to die?" I suggested.

I had the minor satisfaction of watching an emotion other than anger or resentment flicker across her face. "Yes," she muttered.

I looked over at the Juri on my other side. He was half turned toward me, surreptitiously watching the whole operation. "What about you, *Tas* Krodo?" I asked as I opened the carrybag and started sorting through its contents. There was nothing there but changes of clothing. "Did *you* see him with his blanket that night?"

"Yes, he had it," the Juri confirmed. "I distinctly remember him holding it when I returned from my evening ablutions."

"Good—that helps," I said. "Do you have any idea who might have put it back up in his compartment?"

He hesitated. "I'm afraid it was I," he admitted. "The next morning."

"Can you tell me why?" I asked, closing the carrybag and swapping it out for the other one.

"I heard about his death, and I saw his blanket lying crumpled on his seat," he said. "It seemed wrong to leave it there. It had been a relic of his childhood, which he always traveled with as a reminder of home and family. I'm sorry if I did wrong."

"No, it's all right," I assured him, pausing in my search of the second carrybag and pulling the blanket out of the compartment. It was old, all right, with a pleasant scent of distant spices to it. Exactly the sort of keepsake a Shorshian would like. "One could say it was your final honoring for Master Colix. When you put it back, did you happen to see whether or not his bag of fruit snacks was there?"

"It was not," the Juri said firmly. "The blanket would not have fit otherwise."

"Of course," I said, returning the blanket to its place. "I should have realized that. Is there anything else about Master Colix that you can remember?"

"Nothing specific," he admitted. "But he was very kind to me, and kept me entertained with tales of his many interesting journeys."

"And about his precious Path of whatever," Terese muttered. If the moment of maudlin sentiment was affecting her, she was hiding it well. "He talked about that a lot."

I finished going through the second bag—again, there was

nothing there but clothing—and replaced it in the storage compartment. "One final question, *Tas* Krodo. You say that Master Colix was kind to you. Did he ever offer you any of his fruit snacks?"

"He did not," the Juri said. "And I certainly wouldn't have taken one without his permission."

"I'm sure you wouldn't," I assured him. "Thank you for your time."

"You are welcome," *Tas* Krodo said quietly. "I grieve Master Colix's loss to the universe. If I can do anything to help you solve his death, I stand at your disposal."

"Thank you," I said. "If I need you, I'll let you know."

He bowed his head to me. I bowed back, then stepped over Terese's legs out into the aisle again. Typically, she didn't bother to draw up her knees to make the procedure any easier. "And thank you for your cooperation as well, Ms. German," I added as I regained my balance.

She didn't answer, but merely put her headphones back on and closed her eyes.

"A helpful public makes this job so much more rewarding," I murmured. Tririn's seat, I noted, was empty, our lone surviving contract team Shorshian out and about somewhere. That was all right—I hadn't wanted to talk to him right now anyway.

"Do you believe him?" Bayta asked as we resumed our trip toward the rear of the train.

"Who, *Tas* Krodo?" I shrugged. "Assuming he has no connection to Pellorian Medical or the contract team, he shouldn't have any reason to lie." I nodded back over my shoulder. "Actually, I'm more intrigued by Witherspoon's relationship with our helpful Ms. German."

"What sort of relationship?"

"I don't know, but there's *something* going on under the table," I said. "Remember when I confronted him with the fact that he was two cars away when he allegedly noticed all her stomach trouble?"

"But he explained that," Bayta said, frowning. "He said he'd noticed her when he was visiting the three Shorshians."

"That's what he said," I agreed. "But if that was actually true, he should have said it without floundering and fumbling all over himself."

"Maybe he was just nervous," she suggested. "You *did* catch him a little off-guard with those questions."

"True," I said. "But then he should have been caught equally off-guard when I told Kennrick that the good doctor thought I was the killer. But he wasn't. He was quick, decisive, and in complete control of the English language. No, there's something about him and Terese that we still haven't got nailed down."

We walked through the last seven third-class cars in silence, and finally passed through the vestibule into the first baggage car.

The casual passenger wandering into a Quadrail baggage car for the first time might reasonably think he'd accidentally stumbled into a classic English garden maze, with the role of the hedges being played by tall stacks of safety-webbed crates. Add in the silence and dim lighting, and the overall ambience could easily drift from the disconcerting into the spooky. Bayta and I had spent so much time in places like this that I hardly noticed. "Third car, you said?" I confirmed as we made our way through the second car and into the vestibule connecting it with the third.

"Yes, near the back." She shivered. "I don't like looking at dead bodies."

"They tell me you get used to it," I said.

"Have *you* gotten used to it?"

"Not really."

We were halfway down the car when I caught a subtle shift in lighting and shadow somewhere ahead. "Hold it," I murmured, catching Bayta's arm and bringing us both to a halt.

"What is it?" she murmured back.

For a moment I didn't answer, wondering if I'd imagined it. I stood motionlessly, staring at the stacks of crates and the meandering aisles between them.

And then, I saw it again.

So did Bayta. "Frank?" she whispered.

"Yeah," I said grimly.

We'd come way back here to examine the victims' bodies. Apparently, someone else had beaten us to it.

TWELVE :

"What do we do?" Bayta whispered tensely.

I watched the shifting shadows, thinking hard. Chances were good that our intruder was unaware of our presence—the fact that he was still moving around argued that assumption. If we kept it quiet, we might be able to sneak the rest of the way to the bodies and catch him in the act. Whatever that act turned out to be.

On the other hand, sneaking up on a murderer carried its own set of risks. But standing here in nervous indecision would be to lose by default. "Let's take a look," I said, slipping the *kwi* out of my pocket. It was tingling with Bayta's activation command as I settled it into place around the knuckles of my right hand. Tucking Bayta close in behind my left side, where she'd be partially protected and out of my line of fire, I started forward.

We were nearly to the gap where I'd estimated the earlier movement had come from when I realized that the motion had ceased. In fact, as I thought about it, I realized it might have stopped up to a minute or even a minute and a half earlier.

I stopped, turning to put our backs against the nearest stack of crates as I searched for some clue as to where he might have gone. Nothing. Whoever this guy was, he was quick and smart.

But then, I was quick and smart, too. And I had a huge advantage he didn't know about: I had a weapon. Resting my thumb on the *kwi*'s activation button, I gestured Bayta to follow and headed in.

No one jumped us before we reached the gap. Pressing my shoulder against the side of the last stack, I eased a cautious eye around the corner.

Wedged into the narrow space between crate stacks were four coffin-sized tanks. The lid of the nearest was cracked open, while the other three appeared to still be sealed. The intruder himself was nowhere to be seen. Touching Bayta's arm, I slipped around the corner into the impromptu mortuary.

"What do you think he wanted?" Bayta asked quietly as I stopped beside the partially-open tank.

"For starters, not to be caught," I said, getting a grip on the lid and experimentally pushing it closed.

It latched with a loud click that could probably have been heard fifteen meters away. "Which is why he left it open instead of closing it and trying to pretend no one had been here," I went on, popping the lid open again. It made the same loud click as it had when I'd closed it.

And then, from somewhere near the front of the car, I heard an answering sound. Not another click, but the thud of someone bumping into one of the crate stacks. Our intruder, it appeared, was making a run for it.

"Stay close," I murmured to Bayta, and headed at a dead run back toward the vestibule.

Or at least, I tried to make it look and sound like a dead run. But I knew this trick, and I wasn't about to be taken in so easily. The suspicious-noise ploy was a classic way to get the hunter charging off in the wrong direction while the prey slipped away through the dark of night to freedom.

Here, with only a single exit from the baggage car, slipping away for more hide-and-seek was pretty much a waste of effort. Hence, the prey had opted for suspicious-noise variant number two: lure the hunter into ambush range and clobber him.

Which was why my dead run wasn't nearly as reckless as it looked. I was in fact carefully checking every side aisle as I ran toward and past it, my *kwi* ready to fire in whichever direction it was needed. Between aisles I kept a careful watch on the tops of the stacks in case the intruder had scaled one of them in hopes of pulling a Douglas Fairbanks on me.

And with my full attention shifting between right, left, and up, I completely missed the low trip wire that had been stretched out across the aisle in front of me.

I hit it hard, catching my right foot and launching myself into an unintended dive across the dim landscape. I barely managed to get my hands under me before I slammed chest-first into the floor. Even with my arms absorbing some of the impact I hit hard enough to see stars.

For a long, horrible second I couldn't move, my brain spinning, my lungs fighting to recover the air that had just been knocked out of them. Then, through the haze, I felt someone grab my upper arms. I tried to bring the *kwi* around to bear, but my arms weren't responding and my wrists burned with pain. The hands gripping me pulled me up and half over, and

I saw to my relief that it was Bayta. "Where is he?" I wheezed at her.

"He's gone," she said, fighting to drag me over toward the nearest crates. I got my legs working enough to help push, and a moment later was sitting more or less upright with her crouching beside me. It was, I reflected grimly, the perfect time for an ambusher to attack.

Only no one did. Apparently, he really *was* gone. "Are you all right?" I asked Bayta, still working on getting my wind back.

"I'm fine," she assured me, eyeing me warily. "The question is, are *you* all right?"

"Aside from feeling like an idiot, sure," I said sourly, experimentally flexing my wrists. They still hurt, but they were starting to recover. "No chance of catching him now, I guess."

"Do we need to actually catch him?" Bayta asked. "Or do we just need to know who he is?"

I peered up at her. "You have a plan, don't you?"

She nodded toward the front of the car. "I've moved a conductor into the last passenger car," she said. "He's watching to see who comes out of the baggage section."

"Nice," I complimented her. "I don't suppose you and the Spiders have figured out yet how to relay images back and forth."

"Our communication doesn't work that way," she said. "But he doesn't have to send me an image or even a description. The conductors know who's assigned to which seat. All we have to do is see where he lands, and we'll have him."

"Sounds like a plan," I agreed. "But warn him not to get too close. We don't want our friend to know he's being followed."

"He won't *be* followed," Bayta said. "The conductor in the

rear car will stay there and merely pass him off to a Spider who's already in place ahead. In the two cars after that, if they're needed, there will be some mites working inside the ceiling systems who will watch his movements. The next car after that has another conductor, and so on."

"Sounds good," I said. "All those dit rec mysteries I've been pushing on you have obviously done you a world of good." I nodded toward the trip wire behind her. "Let's have a look at our friend's handiwork."

Successful booby traps, in my fortunately limited personal experience, tended toward one of three main flavors: simple, elegant, or opportunistic. This one managed to be all three.

The intruder had cut a section of safety webbing from the base of one of the crates, picking a strand about ankle height, and had continued his cut all the way around the stack until he'd freed enough slack to reach twice across the most likely aisle for us to take when we came charging after him. He'd stretched the line straight across the aisle, looped it through the webbing on the stack on that side, then run it back to the original stack at about a thirty-degree angle.

The result had been a pair of trip wires with a continually varying distance between them, the sort of arrangement that would be perfect for use against two pursuers with different stride lengths. Odds were very good that at least one of us would hit at least one of the lines, which was precisely what had happened. "Nice work," I commented. "This guy's definitely a pro."

"But how did he set it up?" Bayta asked, frowning as she poked experimentally at the taut line. "He couldn't have had more than a couple of minutes once he knew we were here."

"Which means he *didn't* set it up then, at least not completely," I told her. "He must have done all the cutting as soon as he came back here, leaving the loose cord wadded up against the base of the crate where we wouldn't notice it. Once he spotted us and slipped away around the back of the crate stacks, all he had to do was loop the end through here and tie it down back here."

"And then lure us into running after him," Bayta said, grimacing. "We should have known better."

"We *did* know better," I assured her. "I was just expecting a different sort of trap, that's all."

"Wait a minute—there he goes," Bayta said, staring suddenly into space. "He's left the baggage car and is heading forward."

"What species is he?" I asked. I knew Spiders usually couldn't distinguish between individuals, but a species identification would at least get us started.

Bayta frowned in concentration. "He can't tell," she said, sounding rather nonplused. "He's wearing a sort of hooded cloak that's completely covering his head, arms, and torso."

"What about his height? His build? *Anything?*"

"He's tall enough to be a medium-sized Filiaelian, a tall Human, a slightly overweight Fibibib, or a slightly underweight Shorshian," Bayta said, sounding rather annoyed herself. This was *her* plan, after all, that he was outthinking us on. "All the Spider can tell for sure is that he's not a Pirk, Juri, Bellido, or Cimma."

I mouthed a foul word one of my French-born Westali colleagues had been overly fond of. "Fine," I growled. "He wants to play games? We can play games, too. Have the Spiders keep an eye on him. Sooner or later, he'll have to take off the party outfit."

"Do you want the conductor to try to pull aside his hood when he passes?" Bayta asked.

"No," I said. "If he doesn't already know about our close

association with the Spiders, I don't want to tip our hand. Just have them keep an eye on him."

"All right," Bayta said. "What now?"

"We go do what we actually came here for," I said. Pulling out my multitool, I cut the trip-wire cord and pushed the ends out of the way. Then, getting a grip on the safety webbing behind me, I pulled myself carefully to my feet. "Let's go look at some dead bodies."

I had hoped there would be a way of telling which and how many of the storage tanks our intruder had broken into. But no such luck. There were no locks on the tanks, nor were there any breakable—or broken—seals. The four bodies lay quietly and peacefully in their temporary coffins, each wrapped like a mummy in wide strips of plastic. "I guess we'll start here," I said, gesturing to the coffin which had been ajar when we'd arrived. Swiveling the lid all the way up, I started gingerly un-wrapping the corpse.

"What exactly are we looking for?" Bayta asked, her voice sounding a little queasy. "Needle marks?"

"Mostly," I said. "I'm thinking one of the needle marks may have something different about it."

The wrapping came free of the head, and I saw that it was Master Colix's rest I'd disturbed. "Here we go," I said, work-ing the plastic free of his shoulders. "You want to start on one of your own, or shall we both work on this one?"

"You go ahead," Bayta said, making no move toward the other coffins. "I'll just watch."

"Okay, but this is the really fun part of investigative work," I warned. Forcing my mind into clinical Westali mode, I leaned into the coffin and got to work.

I'd expected the job to take a while, with a lot more unwrapping necessary before I got anywhere. But as seemed to be happening more and more these days, I was wrong.

"There we go," I said, pulling Colix's tunic back to reveal the tiny needle mark a few centimeters below the top of his collar and just to the left of his corrugated spinal ridge. "One needle mark, comma, hypodermic. Definitely fresh."

"How can that be?" Bayta objected. "The Spiders have accounted for all the hypos the passengers brought aboard."

"Which means it was either Aronobal or Witherspoon, or else someone managed to smuggle a spare aboard," I said.

Bayta shook her head. "That shouldn't be possible."

"Possible or not, here it is," I said, gesturing to the body. "Take a look."

Bayta shuddered, but gamely leaned in a little closer. "Seems like an odd placement," she commented. "How could someone make an injection back there without him noticing?"

"Actually, it's a perfect spot," I said. "Generally speaking, in order for poison to be injected without the victim noticing, he or she has to be asleep, comatose, or drunk. Those third-class nighttime privacy shields have openings at the top for ventilation. All our killer needed to do was go up to Colix's seat, reach in with his hypo—"

"Did Master Colix use his privacy shield?" Bayta interjected. "A lot of Shorshians don't."

I stared at her, then down at the needle mark I'd felt so proud about finding ten seconds earlier. Damn it, but she was right. And if Colix's whole skin surface had been available, surely the murderer could have picked a more out-of-the-way spot for his injection.

Had it happened at dinner, then? The mark was also in the

right spot for someone who'd sneaked up behind him and sur-reptitiously poked a hypo into his back.

Only that brought us back to the question of how that little trick could have been performed without Colix noticing. A brief twinge of pain he'd passed off and immediately forgot-ten? A close encounter, moreover, that his dinner companions hadn't even noticed? "Good point," I told Bayta. "Let's think about it a minute."

Gingerly, I slid my hand down inside the plastic wrappings to Colix's chest and started feeling around the vicinity of his tunic's inner top pocket. "What are you doing?" Bayta asked.

"Looking for this," I said, pulling out Colix's Quadrail ticket. "I guess the murderer didn't steal it after all."

"Then how did he get into Master Colix's storage com-partment?" Bayta asked, frowning at the card.

"Two possibilities," I said. "One is that he didn't need the ticket because Colix's compartments were never locked that night." I wiggled the ticket between my fingers. "The other is that that's precisely what our intruder was doing back here just now. He'd taken the ticket, used it to open the compartment and steal Colix's goodies, and was hoping to return it to its rightful owner before we came looking for it."

"That has to be it," Bayta said. "Master Colix was very pos-sessive of those snacks. He wouldn't have left them unlocked where they could be stolen."

"Not so fast," I warned her. "We also know that the com-partment was unlocked the next morning, when *Tas* Krodo returned Colix's blanket."

"Which only means the killer must have left it unlocked after he stole the snacks," Bayta countered.

"Or else that Colix was already feeling too sick to bother locking it after he got out his blanket," I said. "But that brings us to another interesting point." Sliding Colix's ticket into my own pocket, I reached back down to the body, loosened the braidings tying up the front of his tunic, and pulled the collar all the way down. "As the French say, voilà," I said, pointing to the faint parallel scars running lengthwise along his throat on either side of his larynx. "Twenty to one those are the marks of the infamous Gibber Operation."

"The what?" Bayta asked, frowning as she leaned over for a closer look.

"It's an operation the Shorshians don't talk much about," I explained, resisting the temptation to point out how unusual it was for me to have found a gap in her otherwise encyclopedic knowledge of the galaxy. "It creates enough range in the Shorshic vocal apparatus to allow them to speak languages other than their own."

"Oh," she said, her face clearing. "You mean the *Kilfiriaso* Operation."

"Ah . . . right," I said, feeling slightly deflated. Not only did she know about the operation, she even knew its real name. "I don't know how fast Shorshians heal, but I *do* know that the Gibber Operation isn't supposed to leave any permanent scars. The fact that we can still see something implies the work must have been done fairly recently."

Bayta frowned at me. "You mean it was done on *Earth*?"

"So it would seem," I said. "And given the typical Shorshic view of aliens, I imagine there would be a hefty percentage of them who would find it offensive that Colix would let a bunch of primitive Humans cut into him that way." I gestured. "Which may explain both why he wouldn't share his fruit treats, *and* why they were stolen."

"Because they weren't treats, but fruit-flavored postoperative throat lozenges?" Bayta asked.

"That's the first part," I agreed. "The second is that the facility that issued him the lozenges undoubtedly had their name or logo on the bag. Best explanation for the theft is that the killer didn't want it known where Colix had his operation."

Bayta was gazing down at Colix's throat. "And since we know Mr. Kennrick also tried to find the bag," she said slowly, "that suggests Master Colix had the operation at Pellorian Medical."

"Exactly," I said.

"But the rest of the contract team surely also knew about it," Bayta objected. "Stealing the lozenges wouldn't have kept the secret from getting out—" She broke off. "Are you suggesting . . . ?"

"That that's why the team members are dropping like dominoes?" I shrugged. "It certainly fits. The problem is, it fits a little too neatly. Especially when we add in that spare first-class pass. It could just as easily be that our murderer latched on to Colix's operation as a convenient smokescreen."

I smoothed Colix's collar back into place. "But that's just grist for the hopper at the moment. Come on—let's check out the other bodies."

It was a few minutes' work to open the other three containers and unwrap their occupants to the shoulders. Both Bofiv and Strinni had the same suspicious needle marks as Colix, and in similar places. Givvrac, in contrast, seemed to be unmarked, at least down to his waist, which was as far as I was willing to take this particular exercise.

"But we already knew that *Usantra* Givvrac died because of the antibacterial spray," Bayta reminded me as I closed his coffin again.

"We assumed that, anyway," I said, moving back to Strinni's body. "It was still worth checking. Shine the light in here, will you? Right here, on the needle mark."

"What are we looking for?" she asked, taking the light and directing the beam onto Strinni's neck.

"You'll see." Pulling out my multitool's thinnest probe, I began peeling away the skin at the edge of the needle mark.

"You probably shouldn't be doing that," Bayta warned. "If someone from the Path of Onagnalhni finds out we disturbed his body they won't like it."

"They're welcome to file a grievance," I said. My probe hit something solid, and I teased a little harder at the edges of flesh until I exposed the end. Putting the probe away, I pulled out my most delicate set of tweezers and gave a gentle tug.

And with a brief moment of resistance, the two-millimeter-long hypo tip that had broken off in Strinni's skin slid out.

"And now we *really* know why the murderer jumped Witherspoon and me last night," I said, holding up the tip for Bayta's inspection. "He managed to smuggle a hypo aboard, but unfortunately ruined it when he broke off the tip. He already had his cadmium, so he didn't need anything from Witherspoon's collection of drugs, but he hoped he could make off with a new hypo without anyone noticing."

"Only we did," Bayta said, her voice odd. "Did Dr. Witherspoon have anything in his bag that could kill?"

"Probably," I said. "Painkillers in particular tend to be lethal if you overdo the dosages. But our friend obviously prefers more subtle ways of offing his targets."

"I was just thinking," Bayta said slowly, staring at Strinni's needle mark. "Why did he just tie you into the chair instead of killing you?"

"That's a cheery thought," I said, an unpleasant chill running through me. Normally, it didn't do a murderer much good to kill the cop who was after him, since there were always more cops where the first one had come from.

But at this immediate point in time and space, that comforting logic didn't apply. As far as cops aboard this train were concerned, I was it. "Luckily for me, he didn't."

"No," Bayta murmured. "Not this time."

"This time was all he had," I told her firmly. "He won't get another shot. Not at me."

She shivered. "I hope you're right."

"Trust me." Pulling out a handkerchief, I carefully wrapped the needle tip and put it in my pocket. "Come on, let's put everything back the way it was," I said as I started rewrapping Strinni's body. "I think it's time we sat Mr. Kennrick down in some nice first-class bar seat and found out what other little secrets he and Pellorian Medical are sitting on."

THIRTEEN :

As it turned out, we didn't have to go all the way to first to confront Kennrick. We found him sitting in the late Master Bofiv's seat, conversing earnestly with Master Tririn. "There you are," Kennrick said, standing up as Bayta and I stopped beside them. "I was looking for you earlier."

"And now you've found me," I said. "What can I do for you?"

Kennrick hesitated, then looked down at Tririn. "Master Tririn, with your permission, I'll get back to you later on this."

[As you wish, Mr. Kennrick,] the Shorshian said with a polite nod. [Mr. Compton, have you any further information on the tragic deaths of my colleagues?]

"We're making progress," I said. "As soon as we have anything solid, I'll let you and the rest of the contract team know."

[Those of us who remain, at least,] he said heavily.

"Yes," I conceded. "Regardless, you *will* be informed." I raised my eyebrows to Kennrick. "Mr. Kennrick?" I said, gesturing for him to step out.

Carefully, Kennrick stepped past the Nemut in the aisle seat and joined us. "Shall we try the bar?" he suggested. "I don't know how your head feels, but my ribs could use a drink."

I gestured. "Lead the way."

We walked past Terese German, who was playing her usual oblivious self behind the social barrier of her headphones, and continued forward. "You looked like a man in full fire-control mode," I commented to Kennrick as we walked through the next car.

"You have no idea," he said grimly. "*Esantra* Worrbin is calling for a binding vote on the contract, even though the terms explicitly state that such a vote can't be taken until we reach Rentis Tarlay Birim and the team presents its findings to the Maccai Corporation controllers. *Asantra* Muzzfor and *Asantra* Dallilo are insisting we follow the terms as written. *Esantra* Worrbin has countered by threatening to pull rank on them and possibly even revoke their *santra* status if they don't go along with him."

"Can he do that?"

"A simple *esantra*? Of course not. But that doesn't mean he wouldn't try."

"And you were back here trying to talk Master Tririn onto your side?" I suggested.

Kennrick exhaled loudly. "I'm not sure I even have a side anymore," he said ruefully. "Like you said, from here on it's pure fire control. I'd settle for calming things enough that the Filiaelians and Shorshians don't put Pellorian Medical on eternal blacklist."

"Not much of a payoff for all the time and money you've put into this thing," I sympathized.

"Hopefully, my bosses will understand," Kennrick said

grimly. "Frankly, I'm more worried about Dr. Witherspoon than I am about myself."

"Really?" I asked. "Why?"

Kennrick gave me a sideways look. "Nothing," he said. "I shouldn't even have mentioned it."

"Well, now that you have, you might as well give us the rest of it," I said.

He grimaced. "I suppose it doesn't really matter now. The fact of the matter is that Master Colix had some work done while the contract team was on Earth. Medical work."

"You mean the throat job?" I asked.

He stared at me. "You knew about that?"

"We were told he and his seatmates were chattering up a storm," I said. "What does Dr. Witherspoon have to do with it? He wasn't the surgeon, was he?"

"Good God no," Kennrick said. "But he was the one who talked Master Colix into having it at Pellorian instead of waiting until he got back home."

"Why did he do that?"

"Which he?" Kennrick asked. "Master Colix or Dr. Witherspoon?"

"Both," I said.

"Witherspoon wanted to show the contract team how competent Humans were at surgical work. Master Colix liked the idea of getting the work done for free." Kennrick grimaced. "Free. It only cost him his life."

"Those freebies will get you every time," I murmured. So Kennrick was also thinking that Colix's demise had to do with the dishonor of his Gibber Operation. Interesting. "Any of his colleagues in particular take offense at his decision?"

"None of the other three Shorshians liked it, I can tell you that," Kennrick said. "Master Bofiv, in particular, was quite vocal in his objections." He grunted. "But I suppose he doesn't qualify as a suspect anymore, does he?"

"Not unless his return ticket covers more options than the Spiders currently offer," I said.

Kennrick grunted again. "Yeah. The Spiders."

Beside me, I felt Bayta stir. This wasn't the first time that Kennrick had mentioned Spiders in a disparaging way. Bayta hadn't liked it then, either. "You have a problem with the Spiders?" I asked.

"That depends," he said. "But let's not discuss that until we have some more privacy."

"This'll do," I said, gesturing to the third-class dining car just ahead.

He frowned. "*Here?* First class has a better selection."

"First class is twenty-four cars away," I pointed out. "I'm thirsty right now."

He grimaced. "Fine."

The bar was reasonably crowded, but we were able to snag a two-person table and a spare chair. "So what exactly is your problem with the Spiders?" I asked after we'd ordered our drinks and the server had left.

Kennrick's eyes shifted to Bayta. "Actually, this particular conversation is probably more for Bayta than for you," he said. "She's the one who seems to have an in with the Spiders."

"I'm listening," Bayta said evenly.

"I want to ask them a favor." Kennrick seemed to brace himself. "I wondered if they'd be willing to accept some of the responsibility for the four deaths."

Bayta stiffened. "*What?*"

"Just as a formality," Kennrick hastened to assure her. "A

public relations thing. I just want something that'll deflect a little of the blame away from Pellorian."

"And onto the *Spiders*?"

"It's not a big deal," Kennrick insisted. "The victims' families or organizations aren't going to bring the Spiders to court or anything. I'm just trying to salvage something out of this mess."

"And why do you think the Spiders should be giving you that cover?" I asked. "What have they done to deserve taking that kind of PR hit?"

"What has Pellorian Medical done?" Kennrick retorted. "Nothing, that's what. But you can bet your pension someone's going to try to blame us anyway."

"Not if we catch the murderer first," I said.

He snorted. "If there even *is* a murderer," he growled. "As far as I can see, this whole mess can be explained by purely natural causes." He looked pointedly at Bayta. "Or rather, *unnatural* causes."

"Meaning?" I asked.

"Meaning food poisoning," he said bluntly.

"How do you explain someone poisoning their food without them noticing?" I asked.

"*I'm* not convinced anyone did," Kennrick said. "I'm thinking the cadmium was in the food to begin with."

"Quadrail food isn't contaminated," Bayta said flatly.

"Then it must have been in the air," Kennrick persisted. "Food and air are the only ways to get something into a person's system."

"Really?" Bayta said icily. "As it happens—"

"As it happens, we've already checked the food *and* the air," I interrupted, gripping Bayta's knee warningly under the table. "However the cadmium got into their systems, it wasn't because of anything the Spiders did wrong."

"Maybe, maybe not," Kennrick said. "But they can't tap-dance their way out from under liability for *Usantra* Givvrac's death. *They're* the ones who let in whatever that damn antibacterial spray was that ended up killing him."

"People carry antibacterial sprays aboard Quadrails all the time," I reminded him. "This is the first time in seven hundred years that it's caused a problem."

"Do we really know that?" he asked. "Or do we just have the Spiders' word for it?"

He looked at Bayta, clearly challenging her to respond. I gripped her knee a little harder, and she remained silent. "Right," Kennrick said, turning back to me. "So here's the deal. Either the Spiders voluntarily step up to the line and accept some of the responsibility, or I'll step them up to that line myself."

"By spreading rumors?" I asked.

"By spreading truth," he said. "Slanted a little, maybe. But truth just the same."

"You could start a panic," I warned. "With the train still over three weeks from Venidra Carvo, that would be a very bad idea."

"Like you walking around talking about murder isn't just as bad?" Kennrick countered.

"Yes, but I've got facts on my side," I pointed out. "All you've got is innuendo." I cocked an eyebrow. "*And* a fair chance of getting locked up somewhere if the Spiders decide you're scaring the passengers."

"They'd better not," Kennrick bit out. "If they even *think* about—" He broke off. "Look. I'm trying to be reasonable about this. I really am. But I'm between the rock and the grinder here, and my whole future is on the line. All I want is for the Spiders to acknowledge that they *might* maybe have a little responsibility for what's happened. Just enough to lift some of the weight off Pellorian. Come on—what can it hurt?"

"Okay, you've presented your case," I said. "Was there anything else?"

There was a flicker of something in Kennrick's eyes. Maybe he didn't like being talked to like he was my underling. "No, that's it," he said.

"Fine," I said. "We'll take your request under consideration. In the meantime, I trust you'll keep your private rumor mill shut down."

His lip twitched. "For now," he agreed. "But *only* for now. And only if there aren't more deaths."

"Fine," I said again. "Nice talking to you."

Bayta stirred as if preparing to get up. I again squeezed her knee, and she subsided. I also stayed put, and after a few seconds Kennrick got the message. "Right," he said. "See you later." He picked up his drink and strode out of the bar, heading forward toward the upper-class sections and their better selection of drinks.

I watched until he had disappeared from view. "Nice guy," I commented, letting go of Bayta's knee and taking a sip of my iced tea.

"If he thinks the Spiders are going to take any responsibility for this, he's crazy," Bayta said stiffly. "Why didn't you let me tell him about the hypo marks?"

"Partly because it wouldn't have done any good," I said. "He could claim those marks came from the medical treatments Witherspoon and Aronobal gave the Shorshians before they died."

"The doctors would say otherwise."

"They *could* say otherwise," I corrected her. "The question is, *would* they? Especially Witherspoon—don't forget that as a fellow Pellorian employee he's in the same leaky boat as Kennrick. But the more important reason not to mention the marks is that Kennrick doesn't need to know about them. Information is leverage in this game, Bayta. Never give people more of it than they need."

"Even if it means letting someone get away with murder?"

"A temporary situation only," I promised. "Patience is a virtue."

Her eyes were still burning, but she reluctantly nodded. "I know."

"Good," I said. "Meanwhile, what's happening with our mystery guest?"

She gazed off into space. "He's gone into a restroom," she said. "Three cars ahead, the car just behind the second/third dispensary."

A bad feeling began to rumble through me. "How long ago was that?" I asked.

"About ten minutes."

The bad feeling grew stronger. "Has anyone come out during that time?"

"Two Filiaelians and a Human," Bayta said, a dark edge starting to come into her voice. "Oh, no. You don't think—?"

"Yes, I think," I growled. "Can you get a mite into the ceiling over that restroom?"

"It won't help—he won't be able to get into the lighting or ventilation grilles," Bayta said tightly. "I could have a conductor go in and take a look."

"Don't bother," I said, trying not to sound as angry as I felt. Damn stupid non-initiative-taking Spiders. "If by some miracle he hasn't flown the coop, that would just tip him off. If he has, it's already too late, and having a conductor charge in there would just start all the rest of the passengers wondering."

"I suppose," Bayta said, sounding miserable. "I'm sorry, Frank. I should have told the Spiders to alert us at once if he went out of sight."

"Yes, you probably should have," I agreed, a little more sharply than I should have. "But even if they had, you could hardly have said anything. Not with Kennrick sitting right there listening."

"But I could at least have let you know something was wrong," Bayta said. "We could have made an excuse and gotten away." She grimaced. "I *did* warn them he might take off his cloak and hood and so to pay particular attention to everyone's shoes."

"And did they?"

"Yes," she said. "But they insist none of the passengers who came out were wearing the same style of shoes as our attacker."

"He was probably wearing oversilks," I said. "Very thin, very light covers you can wear over other clothing. A good quick-change artist can get them off in seconds, even faster if he's got them tear-threaded to a magician's pull. He can then either flush everything down the toilet or else drop the pull into his pocket and stroll innocently back to his seat. The cloak and hood were probably made of the same stuff."

"Sounds very neat," Bayta said sourly.

"Very neat, and very fancy," I agreed. "And it tells us something new about him."

"That he's a professional?"

"No, we knew that from the trip wire," I said. "What we know now is that he knows about our chummy connection with the Spiders."

She frowned. "We do? How?"

"Because the only reason to wear a disguise out of the baggage car is if he thought we might have a partner watching for him. But if he was assuming a *Human* partner, he should have pulled his quick-change as soon as he was out of sight inside the first vestibule."

"How is that better than changing in a restroom?"

"Because that way he could either have continued forward out of the vestibule and plopped down into the first available seat, or he could have reversed direction and headed back the way he'd come," I told her. "Either way would have given him a good look at our presumed partner, who would be hurrying after him. The restroom change, in contrast, gives a normal pursuer a chance to settle into an empty seat of his own, which makes that pursuer harder to identify when the quarry *does* emerge."

"Only he *did* change in the restroom," Bayta said slowly, tracking through the logic. "Because he knew the Spiders didn't have to actually follow him in order to keep track of him?"

"Exactly," I said. "The vestibule change is useless if your tracker has watchers on both sides of the gap who can instantly compare notes. Since comms don't work inside Quadrails, the only ones who can do such an instant comparison are Spiders."

"All right," Bayta said. "How does that help us?"

"Because it shortens the suspect list from the entire train down to seven individuals," I said. "Witherspoon, Kennrick, and Aronobal, plus by extension the three remaining Fillies and one remaining Shorshian of the contract team."

"Plus everyone in the car where we disassembled the air filter," Bayta reminded me. "They all saw us talking to the Spiders."

I shook my head. "People talk to Spiders all the time. The key here is that after I tripped over his little booby trap our friend knew we could still get a message ahead of him. That means your special relationship with the Spiders, and that means one of those seven people I mentioned."

"Along with any secret allies any of them might have," Bayta said. "You *did* say he might have an accomplice."

"I did say that, didn't I?" I admitted, grimacing. Seven suspects had been such a nice, neat, manageable number. "Still, there's a good chance the primary murderer's ally or allies will also be from our same suspect pool."

"But you can't promise that."

I snorted. "I can't even promise we'll make it to dinnertime before someone else snuffs it." I drained the last of my iced tea. "Come on. Break's over—time to get back to work."

"Where are we going?" Bayta asked as she took a last sip of her lemonade and stood up.

"It's time we got to know the rest of the suspect list," I said. "Let's go talk to some Fillies."

We found the three Fillies right where we'd left them, with their seats formed into a circle and a hand of cards dealt out in front of them. This time, though, they were actually playing. I was wondering if we dared interrupt them when one of them looked up at us. "You are Mr. Compton?" he asked.

"I am," I acknowledged. "And you?"

"*Asantra* Muzzfor," he said. "Fourth of the Maccai contract team." His eyes seemed to cloud over. "I correct: *second* of the contract team."

With the late *Usantra* Givvrac and *di*-Master Strinni having been the team's original first and second ranking members? Probably. "My condolences on your loss," I said. "May I inquire as to which is your new first?"

"I am he," one of the others spoke up, his voice dark and unfriendly. "*Esantra* Worrbin."

"I greet you, *Esantra* Worrbin," I said. I shifted my eyes to the third Filly. "And you must therefore be *Asantra* Dallilo."

"I am," Dallilo said.

"Do you wish something of us?" Worrbin asked in that same unfriendly tone.

"A moment of your time only," I assured him.

Worrbin tilted his head. "We are otherwise occupied," he said.

"I would speak with him," Muzzfor said, setting down his cards. "Perhaps he has further information on *Usantra* Givvrac's death." He rose to his feet. "If you would accompany me to the dining car, Mr. Compton?"

"Reseat yourself, *Asantra* Muzzfor," *Esantra* Worrbin growled, leaning a little on the *asantra* part as if to remind Muzzfor of his lower status in the group. "Very well, Mr. Compton. You may speak." He cocked his head in challenge. "Concisely."

"Of course," I said, letting my gaze drift across them as I took a moment to organize my thoughts. Like many upperclass Fillies, especially those of the *santra* classes, these three showed the subtle and not-so-subtle differences spawned by their species' penchant for genetic manipulation. Muzzfor in particular seemed to have been the recipient of a number of treatments, sporting an odd-shaped nose blaze, an interesting speckled eye coloration, and the kind of extra-large throat Filly high-opera singers often got to extend their vocal range. Dallilo's customized body had extra-thick hair, flatter ears, and a two-tone blaze that shaded a dark brown into a lighter tan.

Esantra Worrbin, in contrast, seemed to have skipped all external improvements except the long, slender fingers prized by the artist and surgeon classes. Judging from the extra-large glass of the god-awful Filly drink *dilivin* resting in his seat's cup holder, I guessed he'd also opted for a strengthened digestive system. Given Givvrac's fate, that might turn out to have been an especially wise use of his money.

"You of course know about the tragic deaths of *Usantra* Givvrac and three of the Shorshians on your contract team," I said. "My question for you is simple and twofold. First, do any of you know any reason, professional or personal, why anyone would wish any of those four people dead? And second, do you know any reason how anyone would profit, financially or in terms of honor, from any of their deaths?"

"Well and concisely stated," Worrbin said with somewhat grudging approval. "It appears Humans can be efficient, after all."

"We're individuals, just as are the members of the Filiaelian Assembly," I reminded him.

He snorted, his eyes pointedly flicking back and forth between Bayta and me. "With such minor genetic variants? You don't even approach *asantra* class."

"That's all right," I assured him. "We like ourselves just the way we are."

"Then why does Pellorian Medical seek Filiaelian genetic manipulation equipment?" Dallilo put in. "If you don't seek to improve yourselves, what *do* you seek?"

"You'd have to ask Mr. Kennrick or Dr. Witherspoon about that," I told him, ducking a question that I sensed could only get me into trouble. "I know too little about the contract to either support or oppose it. I seek merely to find the murderer and bring him to justice."

"Then look to Mr. Kennrick," Worrbin said. "If there was indeed murder, I have no doubt he is the one you seek."

"Nonsense," Muzzfor put in before I could respond. "Mr. Kennrick is a fine Human."

"Nonsense doubled and returned," Worrbin retorted. "I am convinced he seeks to destroy the contract from within for his own ends. That leaves him alone with a motivation for murder."

"That's very interesting," I said. "What are these private ends you speak of?"

"How would I know?" Worrbin retorted. "He is a Human, with motivations beyond the understanding of civilized beings."

"Then what makes you think he's trying to sabotage the contract?"

"Because he displays incompetence at every turn," Worrbin said with a contemptuous sniff. "He deliberately ignores the finer points of dealing with superior peoples."

"His slights are not deliberate," Muzzfor insisted. "He is merely ignorant of proper procedure."

"And yet you stand ready to defend him?" Worrbin challenged.

"Competent or not, he *is* only a Human." Muzzfor looked sideways at me. "No offense to you personally, Mr. Compton."

"No offense taken," I assured him. First we'd had Master Tririn back in third class, whose profession of surprise at my understanding of alien ways had carried an implied dig at Kennrick, and now we had *Esantra* Worrbin singing the same tune. Either Kennrick had an outstanding knack of rubbing people the wrong way, or he really *wasn't* very good at his job.

Which brought up a possibility I hadn't thought of before. "Do any of you happen to know whose idea it was for Mr. Kennrick to represent Pellorian Medical to the contract team?" I asked the Fillies.

"That is hardly information we would have been given," Worrbin pointed out.

"True," I said. "But there was a chance you might have been so informed."

"Then you agree with *Esantra* Worrbin?" Dallilo put in. "That Mr. Kennrick or someone in league with him seeks to destroy the contract?"

"It's a possibility that can't be ignored," I said. "Especially given that three of the four deceased were in favor of the contract."

"Mr. Kennrick would never be a party to such a conspiracy," Muzzfor said firmly. "I know and understand this Human. He truly seeks only what is best for his corporation."

"Yet he could be involved without his knowledge," I pointed out. "Perhaps someone put him into this situation knowing he wasn't properly equipped to handle it, in hopes that his bumbling would ruin the contract as *Esantra* Worrbin suggests. In such a case, Mr. Kennrick could be perfectly sincere about doing his best, yet nevertheless still be helping to bring down the contract."

"And when his fumblings failed to turn all members against the contract, the evil one turned to murder?" Dallilo suggested thoughtfully.

"Then the murderer must be Dr. Witherspoon," Muzzfor jumped in. "He's the only other Pellorian representative aboard."

"Or at least he's the only Pellorian representative that we know of," I said, my mind flashing to the spare first-class pass floating loose aboard our train. "Do any of you have any idea why someone would wish to sabotage the contract?"

"An irrelevant question," Worrbin said. "The contract is dead. As dead as *Usantra* Givvrac himself."

The other two Fillies stirred uncomfortably in their seats. It *was* a rather offensive comment. "As I said, I know too little about the contract to comment one way or the other," I said diplomatically, skipping over Kennrick's earlier claim that none of the team had the authority to make such a pronouncement.

"Yes, I'm quite certain of that," Worrbin said loftily. "Have you any further questions?"

It was obvious he was fully expecting the answer to be no. "You still haven't answered my first one," I said. "Do any of you know of a reason why someone would want *Usantra* Givvrac and the others dead?"

"No," Worrbin said shortly. "In that I speak for all."

I looked at Muzzfor and Dallilo. But if they had dissenting opinions, they were keeping them to themselves. "Then I have only one further question," I said. "*Esantra* Worrbin, if we checked with the Spider at the dispensary, would the number of your visits correspond to the number of hypos used?"

"Yes," Worrbin said without hesitation.

"You're certain of that?"

"I brought twenty aboard," he said stiffly. "I have visited the dispensary seven times this journey. You may confirm for yourself that there are thirteen remaining." His eyes bored into mine. "As I'm certain you already have."

I inclined my head to him. "Then we'll take our leave of you," I said. "Thank you for your time. And yours," I added, nodding to the other two.

We left them to their cards and headed forward. "What do you think?" I asked Bayta as we stepped into the vestibule.

"*Esantra* Worrbin doesn't seem to like Mr. Kennrick very much," Bayta said. "But I find it hard to believe someone in Pellorian Medical would deliberately try to sabotage his own contract."

"I've seen political moves that were equally crazy," I told her. "But usually when there's someone trying to pull down the barn, the rest of the power structure learns about it quickly enough to counter the maverick's moves. I suppose this could be an especially clever maverick, though."

"Do you think we should tell Mr. Kennrick about *Esantra* Worrbin's animosity?" Bayta asked, lowering her voice as we emerged from the vestibule into the next car.

"I would guess Mr. Kennrick is fully aware of *Esantra* Worrbin's opinion of him," I said. "Still, I suppose it's only fair to get his side of the story. Let's wander up to his compartment and see what kind of reaction we get out of him."

FOURTEEN :

Kennrick's reaction was pretty much what I'd expected.

"Ridiculous," he snapped. "Which one of them made a boneheaded suggestion like that?"

"I don't think we need to name names," I said, giving his compartment a quick glance. It was about what I'd expected given the occupant: neat and tidy, no messes, no surprises. A few hangers' worth of clothing hung together in the clothes rack/sonic cleaner, a reader sat on the computer desk, and the luggage rack held the three bags I'd seen him board with at Homshil Station. "Incidentally, if *bonehead* is your typical characterization of non-Humans, I can see why you don't get along very well with them."

"Don't start, Compton," he warned, glaring at me. "I'm not in the mood. You have *no* idea what I've been through with these people."

"I'm sure it's been difficult," I said, again cranking up my diplomacy level. "Still, at least one of the team is solidly on your side."

"*Asantra* Muzzfor," Kennrick said, nodding. "Yes, he's been the one bright spot in all this."

"He'd certainly make a good sidekick, if you're ever in the market for one," I said. "So how exactly *did* you get hired?"

He shrugged. "The usual way. A matcher put my résumé with an opening at Pellorian, and next thing I knew I was on the payroll."

"Any idea why you were chosen for this particular job?"

"Obviously, my legal background," he said. "I was at Shotoko Associates, remember, and we were heavily into Filiaelian and Shorshic contract law."

"I suppose that makes sense," I said. "Strange that Pellorian didn't also send along an expert on Filly and Shorshic cultures."

"Not when you consider the price of Quadrail tickets," Kennrick said. "But you see now what I was talking about earlier. These people are bound and determined to dump this whole mess squarely on Pellorian's shoulders. That's why I want—that's why I *need*—the Spiders to take a little of the heat."

"No."

The word was so flat, so cold, and so unexpected that it took me a second to realize it had come from Bayta. Apparently, it hit Kennrick that way, too. "What did you say?" he asked.

"I said no," she repeated. "The Spiders aren't to blame for any of this, and they're not going to take any of the responsibility. *Any* of it."

I looked at Bayta, then at Kennrick, then back at Bayta. Suddenly, my quiet, emotionless, self-effacing assistant had caught fire. A slow fire, maybe, volcano rather than cooking-surface deep. But it was fire nonetheless.

And it wasn't hard to figure out why. There was a murderer running loose on the Quadrail—*her* Quadrail—defying not only us but the Spiders who had made these trains the safest mode of transportation in the history of the galaxy. Kennrick was pushing for Spider admission of responsibility, and if he was thinking such things it was a safe bet other passengers were thinking them, too.

And anything that reflected badly on the Spiders also reflected badly on their Chahwyn masters, including the Chahwyn bonded to Bayta within her own body.

For Bayta, this had become personal.

"Fine," Kennrick said. "Whatever. I just thought—never mind. Fine."

"Then let's hear no more about it," Bayta said darkly, the fire in her eyes slowly fading into watchful embers. "Have you anything else to add about your appointment to this job?"

"No, I think that's been covered," Kennrick said. He was still trying to be contrary, but his heart didn't seem to be in it anymore.

"Then I believe we're finished here," Bayta said, her tone stiffly formal. She looked at me, and I could tell she was belatedly remembering that I was supposed to be the one in charge.

But I wasn't about to undercut her. Not after that performance. "Thanks for your time," I said to Kennrick as I took a step backward toward the door.

And as I did so, my eyes drifted again to the clothing hung neatly on the sonic rack. The clothing, and the considerably larger capacity of the three bags sitting on the luggage rack. "We may have more questions later, though," I added.

"Feel free," he said sarcastically. "My door's always open."

We left, Kennrick closing and undoubtedly locking his door behind us. "Where to now?" Bayta asked.

"Dining car," I told her. "I'm hungry. Did you happen to notice the clothing hanging on Kennrick's rack?"

"Not really," she said, her voice suddenly hesitant. "Frank—"

"Interesting thing is that there wasn't much of it," I said. "Not nearly enough to fill all three of those carrybags."

"Maybe the rest of his clothing is in the drawers," Bayta suggested.

"I doubt it," I said. "I've seen what sort of outfits he typically wears, and I'm guessing the drawers are no more than half full. But even if they were loaded to the gills, he should still be able to cram everything into the two larger bags." I cocked an eyebrow. "Which leads to the intriguing question of what he's got in the third one."

"You have a theory?"

"Of course," I said. I might be rotten at solving actual murders, but theories I had by the truckload. "Remember when we asked Kennrick why the contract-team Fillies had come aboard our compartment car even though they had regular coach seats?"

"He said they had documents they wanted to store in his compartment."

"And since at least some of those documents might have concerned the Pellorian contract, I'm guessing they wouldn't want Kennrick snooping through them any more than they would want random citizens doing so," I said. "Which suggests that one of Kennrick's bags may in fact be a portable lockbox."

"How does that explain why they came aboard in our car?" Bayta asked. "Shouldn't the documents have already been inside the lockbox?"

"They should indeed," I agreed. "The only logical explanation is that the Fillies came aboard with Kennrick because he couldn't heft the thing up onto the luggage rack by himself. Which immediately implies that it's not just a simple lockable file case, but a genuine monster of a metal or layered-ceramic safe."

"Kennrick could have asked a conductor to help."

"And yet he didn't," I said. "He didn't put the papers into a standard Spider lockbox, either. That tells me Kennrick and the papers' owners didn't want the Spiders knowing what they've got, or having access to them."

"Considering Mr. Kennrick's attitude toward the Spiders, I'm not really surprised," Bayta said stiffly. "Where does that leave us?"

"I'm not sure," I said. "But if there's something in Kennrick's safe that somebody wants, and if *Usantra* Givvrac was the one carrying the key—" I shrugged. "We might have yet another possible motive for our murders. Like we needed one."

"Yes." Bayta wrinkled her nose. "Are all murder cases this messy?"

"Hardly ever, actually," I said. "We're just lucky."

"I suppose." She hesitated. "Frank . . . about the way I talked to Mr. Kennrick back there. I'm sorry if I was out of place."

"You weren't out of place, and I'm not sorry at all that you slapped him down," I assured her. "The whole idea of trying to pin any part of this on the Spiders is ridiculous. It was about time he heard that in a format he could understand."

We reached the dining car and went in. "I suggest you eat well," I advised Bayta as we seated ourselves at one of the tables. "I have a feeling we're in for another long night."

"You think someone else is going to be murdered?"

"Our killer didn't clobber Witherspoon and me and take that hypo just for the exercise," I reminded her grimly. "One way or another, he's going to use it."

We had our dinner, discussed the case without making any discernible headway, and retired to our compartments for the night. I hit the sack immediately, hoping to get at least a couple of hours of sleep before the inevitable alarm sounded.

Only the inevitable alarm never came.

I hardly believed it when I woke up eight hours later and realized that my rest hadn't been interrupted by emergency calls from doctors, Spiders, or dying passengers. I checked with Bayta, confirmed that the Spiders hadn't spotted any problems during the night, and grabbed a quick shower before taking her back to the dining car for breakfast.

The car's acoustics prevented me from eavesdropping on my fellow passengers as we ate, but there was nothing to interfere with my eyesight. If there was any fresh tension out there, I couldn't read it in anyone's face. On the contrary, it was as if the rest of the travelers had also noted the passage of a quiet night, and were equally relieved by it.

After breakfast Bayta and I set off on a leisurely tour of the train. The three remaining contract team Fillies were back at their card game, giving the impression they'd never left it. Possibly they hadn't. *Asantra* Muzzfor, the sole team member still on Pellorian Medical's side, nodded gravely as we passed. *Esantra* Worrbin and *Asantra* Dallilo, in contrast, ignored us completely. Three cars beyond them, *Osantra* Qiddicoj also nodded in greeting as we passed. He was still a little pale after his brush with gastrointestinal death, but was definitely on the mend. A small victory, I noted cynically, floating bravely along amid a sea of defeats.

We passed through second class, where we didn't know anyone, and reached third. *Logra* Emikai, the white-knight Filly who'd come to Terese German's aid a couple of days ago, was enscounced in the bar, where I'd noticed he seemed to spend a lot of his time. He spotted us about the same time as I spotted him, and I could see his eyes following us as we passed by. Possibly he was thinking about his offer of a bribe for inside information on my air filter analysis and wondering if he should follow through on that. But I made a point of not slowing as we passed the bar, and he apparently thought better of it and returned to his half-finished drink.

Three cars farther back we passed Emikai's damsel in distress herself, who ignored us as usual. Terese's Jurian seatmate, *Tas* Krodo, had his hawk beak buried in his reader, while two rows back Master Tririn was again staring moodily at the display window beside him. Still in private mourning for his late contract-team companions, I guessed, or else quietly plotting his next victim's death. I didn't spot either Dr. Witherspoon or Dr. Aronobal during our journey, but with the dining and entertainment cars up and running, there were a lot of passengers away from their seats.

And with our casual tour of suspect and acquaintance completed, we slipped back into the baggage cars for another look at the victims.

"Why exactly are we here?" Bayta asked as I started undoing Master Colix's mummy wrappings.

"Trying to find something we might have missed," I told her.

"Like what?"

"I have no idea." I finished unwrapping Colix, this time going all the way down to his waist, and set off on a careful, square-centimeter-by-square-centimeter search of the body.

And in the end, after half an hour, I found nothing.

"Two hypo marks, exactly," I reported, wincing as I straightened my back out of the crouch it had been in for most of the examination. "The killer's, and the one Dr. Aronobal made while he and Witherspoon were trying to save his life."

"Are you sure?" Bayta asked.

I looked down at the body. "Did you see something I missed?"

"No, I meant are you sure they were trying to save his life," Bayta corrected. She was gazing at the hypo mark in Colix's arm, an intense look on her face.

"Meaning?"

"I was just thinking," she said slowly. "After Master Colix died, Mr. Kennrick suggested that neither Dr. Aronobal nor Dr. Witherspoon actually knew what was in the vials they were using."

"I assumed the Spider read the labels for them."

"Actually, the way it works is that the doctor asks for the drug he or she wants and the server pulls those ampoules from the cabinet," Bayta said. "But what if Dr. Witherspoon had another drug with him that he added to the hypo when no one was looking?"

I scratched my cheek and tried to pull up the memory of the scene as Bayta and I had come charging in. It would have been tricky, but not impossible, particularly if Witherspoon picked his moment carefully.

Witherspoon *or* Aronobal. Now that I thought about it, I realized I hadn't actually seen that injection take place, mainly because Kennrick had popped his face into and out of the dispensary and I'd gone charging off after him. "Did you see Aronobal give Colix the injection?" I asked Bayta.

"I saw her remove the needle from Master Colix's arm," she said. "But not the actual injection."

"Because you were watching me take off after Kennrick," I said thoughtfully. "Interesting timing."

"It could just be coincidence."

"True," I agreed. "Especially since we know that Colix was showing symptoms long before the doctors started working on him." I frowned at Colix's body. "But there *is* something else here, Bayta. Something significant. I just can't put my finger on it."

"Maybe when we reach Venidra Carvo and can have a proper autopsy done," Bayta suggested.

"If it's even still there," I growled. "I'm sure the Spiders did their best, but after three-plus weeks of less-than-perfect preservation some of the more subtle evidence will almost certainly be gone."

Bayta sighed. "And even if it hasn't, the killer himself will be long gone by then."

"With probably a new identity and maybe even a new face to go with it," I agreed. "Possibly new DNA, too. We *are* headed for Filly space, after all, land of the lunatic gene-manipulators."

"We'll get him," Bayta said firmly, an edge of fire creeping back into her eyes. "And then we'll prove—to *everyone*—that the Spiders had nothing to do with it."

"Absolutely," I said, wishing I believed that. The farther we got into the mess, the more elusive proof of any sort seemed to be. "Well, nothing more for us here," I added, starting to re-wrap Colix's body. "Give me a hand, will you?"

The next few days passed quietly. No one else even got sick, let alone died, and life aboard the train settled back a bit gingerly into its normal low-key routine.

We reached the three-week midway point without incident and passed on to the back half of our journey. Bayta told me the next morning that Kennrick and Tririn had gone ahead and held their halfway-celebration meal, the one Kennrick had been discussing with Colix the night of the first two deaths.

Under the circumstances, I suspected the event was somewhat more subdued than originally planned.

I spent most of those days in my compartment, coming out only for meals, exercise, and occasional flybys of my primary suspects. Most of the compartment time was devoted to reexamination of the spectroscopic data I'd taken from the air filters and the bodies. But it was all just wheels spinning in mud. If there was anything in there aside from the bald fact of the cadmium poisoning, I reluctantly concluded, it would take someone better trained than me to spot it. All I could do now was wait for the other shoe to drop.

Two nights after the journey's midpoint, it finally did.

I had just taken off my shoes in preparation for bedtime when the divider opened and Bayta hurried into my compartment. "The Spiders say Dr. Aronobal is calling for you," she said tautly.

"What's the problem?" I asked, grabbing my shoes and starting to put them on again.

"They don't know," she said. "They just say she needs to see you right away. She's in the second/third dispensary, staring at the medications in the drug cabinet."

"Maybe she's thought of something relating to the murders," I suggested, finishing with my shoes and standing up. "I'll be back soon. Feel free to eavesdrop via the dispensary's server."

"What are you talking about?" she asked, frowning as she started for the door. "I'm coming with you."

"No, you're staying here," I corrected, getting to the door first. "Aronobal asked for *me*, remember?"

Her face had gone very still. "You think it's a trap, don't you?"

That was, in fact, exactly what I was thinking. "I just think she might feel more comfortable talking to me alone," I lied.

I reached for the door control, paused, and instead dug into my pocket. "Here," I said, handing Bayta the *kwi*. "This won't do me any good out there."

She took it, her eyes going even darker. "Frank—"

"Besides, if there's a problem and I have to fight, I'd rather you be here and not right in the middle of things where I have to worry about you," I cut her off. "I'll be back soon."

I escaped into the corridor before she could come up with a suitable retort.

The corridors of the compartment cars were deserted, most of the other passengers probably having turned in for the night. The first-class coach car just beyond had the same settled feel about it, though there were still a few reading lights showing.

I went past the dining car and its usual contingent of late-night diners and drinkers, then trekked through the storage, shower, and exercise/dispensary cars into the next coach car. I walked through it and into the first-class entertainment car, where reflected flickers of light showed that a few viewers were still finishing up their dit rec dramas and comedies, and entered the next coach car. One more, and I would finally be finished with first class.

After which would come the long walk through second class and then finally to third. After all this, I told myself darkly, Aronobal had better have either one hell of a significant breakthrough to offer, or else have one hell of an innovative ambush to spring.

I was nearly to the end of the last first-class coach when I heard a quiet voice call my name.

I looked around. The only passenger anywhere nearby who should even know my name was *Osantra* Qiddicoj. He was slumped in his seat, his eyes closed, apparently sound asleep.

And then, as I watched, his eyes opened. "Go back," he said, his voice soft and raspy.

I felt a sudden tightness in my chest. Qiddicoj's open eyes were slightly unfocused, his long jaw slackened, and even in the dim light of the compartment I could see his rose-colored nose blaze had gone a little darker.

Which meant that it wasn't Qiddicoj who was speaking to me.

I took a deep breath. For the past three weeks I'd been wondering whether the Modhri had a presence aboard our train. Occasionally, way back in the back of my mind, I'd also wondered if he might have something to do with our rash of mysterious murders.

Now, at least the first of those two questions had been answered. "Hello, Modhri," I said. "I've been wondering when you would pop up."

"Go back, Compton," the Modhri said again. "He's in your compartment car."

"Who is?" I asked. "What are you talking about?"

"He was hiding in one of the shower stalls," Qiddicoj's voice rasped, a sense of urgency creeping into his voice. "He waited until you'd passed, then moved forward. He has a device with which he hopes to gain access to your compartment."

The tightness in my chest went a little tighter. The double compartment, where I'd left Bayta waiting all alone. "Who is he?" I demanded. "What does he look like?"

"I don't know," the Modhri said. "He's wearing a hooded robe that obscures his features and his build."

So our baggage car intruder hadn't flushed his disguise down the toilet after all. The thrifty type. "What does he want?" I asked.

"How should I know?" the Modhri retorted. "Perhaps the deaths of us all. Do you wish to stop him, or not?"

I cursed under my breath. If this was a trick to get me to miss my appointment with Aronobal, the doctor could likely be facing some death of her own.

But Aronobal wasn't my responsibility, and on a personal level I didn't really care what happened to her. Bayta was, and I did. "You have any walkers up there?" I asked.

"I have an Eye in the bar and one in the first coach car," the Modhri said. "That's how I saw the intruder making his way forward."

There were a dozen other questions I needed to ask, starting with how this intruder thought he could get though a Spider-designed lock and ending with why the Modhri was giving me this warning in the first place. But those questions could wait. "Let me know if he starts back or goes to ground somewhere," I said.

I was ten cars back from our compartment car. I retraced the first nine cars' worth of steps at a dead run, slowing to a quieter and more energy-conserving jog for the last one. A well-dressed Juri in that first coach car watched me as I came through, his eyes bright and preternaturally aware. Almost certainly he was the walker the Modhri had mentioned, and I raised my eyebrows in silent question as I passed him. He gestured toward the car ahead in silent response. I nodded, and slipped through the door into the vestibule.

I crossed the vestibule, taking in huge lungfuls of air as I did so to try to restore my blood oxygen level after my mini-marathon run. I got to the front and reached for the door control.

And paused, my memory flicking back to the trip wire the intruder had left for me in the baggage car. This guy was a professional, and professionals didn't set themselves up for key jobs in the middle of exposed corridors without taking precautions against unexpected company.

Which meant there was probably a booby trap waiting on the other side of the door.

It wouldn't be a trip wire. That was fairly certain. I was the unexpected company he would be most worried about, and he would assume I wouldn't fall for the same trick twice.

On the other hand, given the lengths he'd already gone to in order to keep anyone from seeing who he was . . .

It was a gamble, but I had no time to think it through any further. Squeezing my eyes tightly shut and holding my breath, I hit the door release.

And as I charged through, a burst of cold air threw a choking cloud of dust squarely into my face.

I bellowed with feigned surprise, the sharp exhalation serving to blow the powder away from my nose and mouth. A simple talcum powder, I gathered from the taste. Simultaneously, I threw up my left forearm over my face, hopefully hiding the fact that my closed eyelids had protected me from the blinding effects of the powder. I staggered a couple of steps forward, feeling wildly around with my right hand as I watched the floor in front of me beneath the concealment of my left arm.

He fell for it like an egg from a tall chicken. Three seconds later a pair of feet entered my truncated field of view as he hurried toward me, clearly intent on putting me down for the count.

Instantly, I shifted my hands and body into fighting stance. I caught a glimpse of a billowing cloak and a dark-filled hood, then caught one of his outstretched arms at the wrist, levered it at the elbow, and turned his forward motion into a backward arc to slam his back hard onto the corridor floor.

With the average opponent, that would have ended the fight right there. But this one was tougher than average. Even as his shoulders hit the floor he was twisting his torso around, swinging one leg in a horizontal sweep straight at my ankles.

I managed to get one leg out of his way, but I didn't have the time or the balance to get the other one clear, too. His leg caught me just above the ankle, and I toppled over, the move forcing me to let go of his wrist so that I could use both hands to break my fall. Luckily, he was similarly unable to get his sweeping leg completely out of my way, and I landed partially on top of it, hampering his effort to regain his feet.

We made it back to vertical at about the same time, with me making sure I ended up standing between him and the door to the rear of the train. "Had enough?" I asked, still panting a little.

The intruder didn't reply. His hood, which I could see now had been wired to stay firmly in place around his head, had nevertheless slipped enough during the tussle to reveal the tip of a Filly nose. "I didn't think so," I went on. "You know, you're taking this contract thing way too seriousl—"

Without warning, he leaped forward, his hands grabbing my left shoulder and shoving sideways in an attempt to push me far enough out of the way for him to get past. I was ready for something like that, and responded by grabbing one of the arms and trying a repeat of my earlier aikido move.

Unfortunately, this time he was waiting for it. He spun around on one foot as I made my grab, the movement twisting my arm instead of his and breaking my grip. With his escape path now open, he made a break for the door.

He got exactly one and a half steps before I slammed a kick hard into the back of his leg, once again sending him sprawling.

I leaped for him, hoping to pin him down long enough to

get a wrist lock on him. But he was too quick. He bounced up off the floor and spun around, and as I grabbed his left wrist he gave me a shove with his free hand that threatened to break my hold and send me to the floor in my turn.

But I wasn't giving up, either. I hung on grimly, overbalancing him and bringing him tumbling after me. With the alternative being to let him land on me full-weight, I brought my left leg up and planted it into his lower torso. As I hit the floor I straightened my leg, executing a stomach toss of the sort so beloved of early dit rec thrillers and so nearly impossible to pull off in the real world.

Apparently, my opponent had never heard of this one. The toss actually worked, and he went sailing over my head to once again slam onto his back on the floor. Rather surprised myself at the move's success, I nevertheless had the presence of mind to execute the proper follow-through, using the momentum of my backward roll to somersault over him into a position where I would be sitting on his chest with my knees pinning down his upper arms.

Then again, maybe he *had* heard of this one. I was still in mid-somersault when he rolled over onto his side, giving a hard sideways yank to the hand I still had on his wrist. Pulled off my planned trajectory, I landed off balance. He twisted my wrist as I hit the floor, breaking what was left of my grip. I grabbed for the arm again, missed, and he bounded to his feet, heading for the rear of the car. Still off-balance, I threw myself at his feet, and by sheer luck got one hand on his ankle. He stumbled, nearly fell, and half turned. As I tried to get a grip with my other hand, out of the corner of my eye I saw his arm windmill as if he was throwing something at me.

An instant later, a patch of something black slapped across my face.

I inhaled sharply from the sheer surprise of it. That was a mistake. The stuff was some kind of clingcloth, of the kind sported by teenaged show-offs, and inhaling against the thing merely sucked the last bit of remaining air from beneath it and plastered it that much tighter against my skin. I tried exhaling, but I didn't have enough air to do more than temporarily puff out the middle of the cloth.

And with that move I was now completely out of air. I let go of the intruder's ankle, scrabbling with both hands to try to get a grip on the edges of my new blindfold. Clingcloth was legally required to be porous enough to breathe through, but my current oxygen needs were far greater than any level the regulators had anticipated. If I didn't get the damn stuff off, and fast, I was probably going to pass out.

Someone grabbed my arm. I shrugged violently against the hand, my fingernails still trying to locate the edges of the cling-cloth. "Hold still," Kennrick's voice came in my ear. The grip on my arm vanished, and I felt another set of fingers pulling at the edges of my face. "Mm!" I grunted, jabbing a finger down the corridor. I could get the clingcloth off by myself—what I needed Kennrick to do was get to my assailant before he could escape from the car and melt back into the Quadrail's general populace.

Only with my mouth covered, I couldn't say that. "*Mm!*" I tried again.

"Relax, it's covered," he said. His fingernails worked their way under the cloth and pulled it away from my face.

I blinked, gasping for breath as I looked around. On both sides, compartment doors were beginning to open as other passengers looked to see what all the noise and commotion was about. Between me and the far end of the car I could see that Bayta had also emerged from her compartment. She was facing away from me, but as I refilled my lungs I saw she was backing toward where Kennrick and I still huddled on the floor. She glanced behind her to double-check my position, then veered a little to her left and dropped down on one knee beside me.

And as she moved out of my line of sight, I saw that my assailant had not, in fact, escaped. He was lying in the middle of the corridor, his hooded cloak flapping like a wounded bird as he writhed in agony.

"You all right?" Bayta asked anxiously, her eyes flicking to me and then back to the thrashing Filly. Gripped in her hand, I saw, was the *kwi* I'd left with her.

"I'm fine," I assured her, still breathing hard. "Nice work."

"And then some," Kennrick put in, his voice sounding stunned. "Special relationship with the Spiders, huh?"

I focused on him, to discover that he was gazing at the *kwi*. Terrific. "Nothing special about it," I said, putting an edge on my tone, acutely aware of all the other eyes and ears gathered around us. "She got in a good gut punch, that's all."

Kennrick tore his gaze from the *kwi* and locked eyes with me. A flicker of something went across his face— "Ah," he said. "Right."

I held his eyes a moment longer, just to make sure he'd gotten the entire message, then looked back at the Filly. "Want to make any bets as to which of your three Filly friends is inside that hood?" I asked as I levered myself back to my feet. "My guess is that it's *Esantra* Worrbin."

"No bet," Kennrick said grimly. "Let's find out."

We headed down the corridor, and I noticed in passing that there was a small gray box lying on the floor beside my compartment door. I reached the Filly and leaned over him. "You going to cooperate?" I asked politely. "Or do we need to make sure you'll hold still?"

The Filly didn't answer. But he was clearly in no position to give any serious resistance. Straddling his torso, I slipped my hands inside his hood, found and disengaged the stiffening wires that had held it in place, and threw it back.

It was a Filly, all right. But it wasn't any of the contract-team members, as I'd assumed. It was, instead, *Logra* Emikai: barstool warmer, protector of Human maidens in distress, and attempted briber of Spider agents.

"Huh," Kennrick grunted from my side. "I guess I *should* have taken that bet."

"Hilarious," I growled, grabbing one of Emikai's arms. "Come on—help me get him into my compartment. He has some explaining to do."

FIFTEEN :

Emikai was pretty heavy, and his legs still weren't functioning all that well. But between Kennrick, Bayta, and me we got him into my compartment and seated more or less comfortably on the curve couch. Our next task was to remove his cloak and search for any other goodies or semi-weapons he might have on him. We confiscated another patch of clingcloth, a squeeze bulb filled with talcum powder like the booby trap he'd set up on the vestibule door, and, for good measure, the extra unlimited first-class pass that we'd known was wandering loose on our train.

We also confiscated the gadget he'd left lying by my door.

"So what now?" Kennrick asked when we'd finished our frisking.

"We start by calling in a couple of Spiders," I said. "Bayta, I need a conductor and two mites. Have them wait out in the corridor until I need them."

She nodded, her eyes unfocusing as she sent the message.

I watched Emikai closely during the silent communication,

searching for signs of surprise or interest. But there was neither. Clearly, he already knew all about Bayta's special relationship with the Spiders.

"They'll be here in a few minutes," Bayta reported.

"Thank you," I said. "So, *Logra* Emikai. How are you feeling?"

"I have been worse," he said stiffly.

"I'm sure you have," I said, looking him over. His convulsions had mostly ceased, but he was still twitching occasionally
from the aftereffects of the *kwi*. I wondered which of the three
pain settings Bayta had used, but I wasn't about to ask that
question with Kennrick standing there listening. He knew
way too much already. "I suppose we should first offer you the
easy way. Would you care to make a statement as to what the
hell you've been up to lately?"

For a moment Emikai gazed at me, possibly trying to decide which lie would be the most believable. "Several days ago
I asked you for information about the air filter analysis you
claimed you would be performing," he said. "You never returned with that information."

"So you thought you'd stop by and help yourself to the
data?"

"I stopped by merely to inquire on your progress," he
corrected.

"Of course," I said. "You must have forgotten that I'd
already told you that if there was anything relevant the Spiders
would inform everyone at the same time."

"Perhaps," he said. His eyes drifted around the room, pausing on the two carrybags sitting together on their rack above
my bed. "But perhaps they fear to reveal the truth."

"Has anyone else dropped dead?" I asked, watching his
eyes. He was definitely interested in my carrybags. Probably

wondering which of them held my alleged spectroscopic analyzer. "Has anyone else even gotten sick?"

"Not to my knowledge," he admitted, shifting his gaze back to me. "But the two Shorshians were in equally good health for over two weeks before their sudden deaths."

"Why are you even interested about the air in that car?" Kennrick asked. "I spent a fair amount of time back there with my associates, and I never once saw you put in an appearance. Is that even your car?"

"Should not one be concerned about the welfare of others?" Emikai countered. "Especially if one has the ability to guard that welfare?" He looked back at me. "Or claims to have that ability."

"Are you suggesting I don't actually have the spectroscopic analysis equipment Dr. Aronobal told you about?" I asked mildly.

His nose blaze lightened noticeably in reaction at Aronobal's name. More aftereffects of the *kwi*—normally he probably would have tried to suppress such a giveaway. "The Filiaelian physician?" he hedged. "I have not spoken to her about any such equipment."

"Oh, please," I scoffed. "It's painfully obvious that Aronobal's midnight call just now was to get me out of the way so you could use your little first-class pass to come up here and burgle my room." I gestured to the carrybags. "By the way, if you were hoping for a look at my analysis equipment, forget it. It's not actually here at the moment."

Again, his nose blaze lightened briefly. He'd been scoping out my bags, all right. "That may be," he said, an edge of challenge in his voice. "In my view, until I have evidence of its existence, I also have no belief."

"Wait a second," Kennrick said, looking back and forth

between Emikai and me. "Wait just a damn second. This guy has a *first-class pass*? I thought he was riding in third."

"He is," I confirmed. "Apparently, he likes slumming."

"Why, you son of a—" He jabbed a finger at the Filly. "It's him. It has to be. *He's* the one who's been killing off our contract team."

"I have harmed no one," Emikai insisted, his blaze lightening again in reaction. "I give you my word."

"Like your word means camel spit," Kennrick snarled, taking a step toward him. "Compton, this is the guy. It all fits."

"Calm down," I soothed, putting a restraining hand on his arm. "We're a long way yet from accusing him of mass murder."

"Are we?" Kennrick countered. "Who else had access to both third *and* first?"

"Well, for starters, everyone in first," I reminded him.

He stopped in mid-tirade, his lip twisting. "Oh. Yes, I suppose . . ." He trailed off.

"But attempted breaking and entering is another story," I went on, hefting the flat gray box we'd found outside my door. On the outside, it looked like a standard bypass mimic, the sort used by locksmiths when people lock themselves out of their apartments or cars. But I was betting its guts were considerably more sophisticated than that. "You have a license for this, I assume?"

"That device is not mine," Emikai insisted. "I never saw it before."

"Of course not," I said. "And you attacked me why?"

"I did not attack you," he said. "I saw something on the door explode into a white powder in front of you, and I was coming to offer my aid."

"You mean this kind of white powder?" I asked, holding up the squeeze bulb.

"I do not know what kind of powder it was," Emikai said, an edge of wounded indignation in his tone. "My powder is for relief of a painful rash from which I suffer."

"Ah," I said, nodding. With the effects of the *kwi* wearing off, he was proving himself a decent actor and liar both. I would have expected nothing less from the professional who'd snookered me into that trip wire in the baggage car.

The question was, what had he been looking for back there? And what had he hoped to find in my compartment?

But whatever the answers, we weren't going to get them tonight. I'd seen Emikai's type enough times to know that he was going to require a lot more persuasion, or the right lever, before he would give anything up. "Whatever," I said. "You realize, of course, that you're going to have to be locked up pending a full investigation."

"Nonsense," he said stiffly. "You have not reached the required legal bar for such action."

"Maybe not by Filiaelian standards," I said. "But in case you haven't noticed, we're aboard a Quadrail. Quadrails run under Spider rules."

Emikai looked at Kennrick, then Bayta, then back at me, and I could see that the full nature of his situation was starting to sink in. "The Filiaelian Assembly will not tolerate the mistreatment of its citizens," he warned.

"Oh, I don't think they'll have too much of a problem with it," I said, waving him to his feet. "In general, Filiaelians dislike criminals every bit as much as Humans do."

Slowly, Emikai stood up. His eyes flicked again to Bayta, probably checking on her alertness. Having been shot from behind, he couldn't know what exactly she'd done to lay him out on the corridor floor that way. But from his expression and cautious movements it was clear that he wasn't interested in having another go at it. "Where do you intend to take me?" he asked.

"Well, we don't have a proper brig," I said consideringly. "So I guess we'll have to put you in the morgue."

"The *morgue*?"

"Yes," I said. "Unless you're ready to have a serious talk?"

He drew himself up. "There is nothing to talk about," he said. "Show me to my prison."

"As you wish," I said. "Bayta, let the mites in, will you?"

She crossed to the door and opened it, and a pair of the little Spiders came in. "What do you want with those?" Emikai asked, a hint of apprehension creeping into his voice as the mites skittered toward us on their seven slender legs.

"Unfortunately, wristcuffs aren't allowed on Quadrails," I said. "So we're going to have to improvise. Turn around, please, and cross your wrists behind your back."

I actually wasn't at all sure this was going to work. But Bayta had caught on to the plan, and with a little experimentation— and probably a lot of silent communication—we got the mites wrapped solidly around Emikai's arms, their slender legs interlocked to keep them in place. "I'll have to remember this one," I commented to Bayta as we headed out the door into the corridor.

Bayta nodded toward the waiting conductor. "What did you want him to do?" she asked.

"He's to keep an eye on our compartments while we're gone," I said. "Just in case *Logra* Emikai and Dr. Aronobal have another friend aboard."

"I am not associated with Dr. Aronobal," Emikai insisted.

"Right—I keep forgetting," I said. "By the way, Bayta, is the good doctor still waiting for me in the dispensary?"

"Yes," she confirmed.

"Have the server tell her that I'm not coming and to go back to her seat," I said. "He can tell her I'll come by in the morning and talk to her then."

"All right." Bayta said doubtfully. "You sure you don't want to deal with this tonight?"

"Positive," I said. "This way, by the time we get back there, she'll hopefully have her privacy shield up and won't see us march Emikai past her. She'll then have a few hours to miss her friend and wonder what went wrong before I go see her." I nudged Emikai in the side. "Get moving—we've got a long way to go."

It was a long, but fortunately quiet, walk back to the rear of the train. Emikai, probably still aching from the *kwi* blast, had apparently opted for the fight-another-day strategy and gave us no trouble along the way. I half expected him to stumble, cough, or otherwise try to signal Aronobal as we passed the doctor's privacy-shielded seat, but he didn't even try that.

I'd had Bayta send instructions on ahead, and by the time we reached the third baggage car I found the Spiders had set up everything just as I'd requested. There was a chair, a small table holding a box of emergency ration bars and bottled water, and a spare self-contained toilet the Spiders had scrounged from one of the storage cars, everything laid out neatly in front of one of the stacks of cargo boxes. We settled Emikai on the stool, and using the pieces of safety webbing he'd cut earlier, I tied his wrists to opposite ends of the crate stack. I adjusted the lengths carefully, leaving him enough slack to be able to reach his food tray and to shift himself over onto the toilet, but not enough for either hand to reach the other hand's rope. With Humans or Shorshians I would also have had to keep him from biting through his bonds, but Filly teeth weren't configured for that sort of thing.

"There we go," I said, stepping back to examine my handiwork. "Enjoy the quiet, *Logra* Emikai. We'll be checking on you every once in a while, in case you decide you want to tell us what you and Dr. Aronobal are up to."

"Dr. Aronobal and I have nothing to do with each other."

"Right," I said. "Well, pleasant dreams. I hope you can sleep sitting up."

Ushering Bayta and Kennrick in front of me, we left Emikai to his new home. "Aren't you going to leave a guard?" Kennrick asked as we reached the vestibule and crossed into the next car forward.

"No need," I assured him. "He's not going anywhere." I carefully avoided looking significantly at Bayta who, I was sure, was similarly smart enough not to look significantly at me. There *was* a guard team on duty, in fact: a pair of twitters, lurking in nearby shadows where they could watch for visitors or escape attempts.

"I suppose not," Kennrick muttered. "Anyway, even if he gets loose, it's not like he can jump from a moving train. You still going to wait until morning to brace Dr. Aronobal about this?"

"Why? You think I should do it now?"

"It might not be a bad idea," Kennrick said. "She has to know that something has gone wrong. If you wait until tomorrow, she'll have had all those extra hours to come up with a good story."

"She'll also have had those same hours to sweat about what's happened to her accomplice and wonder what went wrong," I pointed out.

"I still think it'd be better to do it now," Kennrick said. "If you're too tired, I could run the interrogation while you watched. I trained in law, remember—I know all the techniques for getting witnesses to say the wrong thing."

"I'll keep that in mind," I said. "It's still not happening tonight."

Kennrick hissed out a sigh. "Whatever." He sent me a sideways glare. "Just remember that it was *my* contract teammates who were killed. Whenever you're ready to try and get a confession—out of either of them—I want to be there."

"You'll be at the top of the visitors list," I promised.

"Fine," he said. "By the way, do you think I could have a look at that bypass mimic of his?"

"What for?"

"Just curious," he said. "Early on in my career I handled a high-level corporate espionage case, and I ended up learning a lot about gadgets like that. I might be able to figure out if his would actually work."

"So you can duplicate it?" I asked mildly.

"So I can find out whether I can sleep for the next three weeks," he retorted. "Once Emikai and his buddies have finished off the rest of the contract team, who's to say they won't come after Dr. Witherspoon and me, too?"

"An intriguing thought," I agreed. "Maybe after the Spiders have checked it out they'll let you take a look."

We walked the rest of the way in silence. When we reached our car, I sent Bayta through her compartment door, nodded a good-night to Kennrick as he and I reached mine, and opened my door as he continued forward to his.

I'd barely closed the door behind me when the divider opened and Bayta came in. "How long do we wait?" she asked briskly.

"How long do we wait for what?" I asked.

"To go back and confront Dr. Aronobal," she said, frowning. "We *were* just dropping off Mr. Kennrick so he wouldn't be there, weren't we?"

"No, we were dropping off Mr. Kennrick so that we could all go to bed and get some sleep," I said.

Her face fell a little. "Oh," she said. "I thought . . ." She trailed off.

"You thought I was blowing smoke," I said. "And under other circumstances, I might have been. But not this time."

"Oh," she said again. "Well, then . . . I'll see you in the morning. Good night."

"Good night," I replied. "Sleep well."

She disappeared back into her compartment, and the dividing wall between us again closed.

With a tired sigh, I checked my watch. Twenty minutes, I decided, would be enough for her to finish her bedtime preparations and fall asleep.

It wasn't like I'd just lied to her, I reminded myself firmly. I really *wasn't* going back to third to confront Aronobal.

The Modhri had clued me in on Emikai's attempt on my compartment. Why he'd done that I didn't know.

But twenty minutes from now I was going to find out.

My first plan was to go back to the rear first-class coach car, where the Modhri had spoken through Qiddicoj to warn me about the intruder. But the Modhri was a group mind, after all, which meant that talking to one walker was the same as talking to another. On a hunch, I stopped by the bar.

Sure enough, the Juri I'd seen earlier was still there. He'd collapsed onto his table, his head pillowed on his folded arms, obviously sound asleep.

Back when I'd traveled third-class for Westali I'd seen occasional passengers sleeping that way. Up to now I'd never seen a first-class traveler who hadn't managed to make it back to his or her much comfier seat. The implications, and the invitation, were obvious. Walking over to the sleeping figure, I sat down across the table from him. "Hello, Modhri," I said quietly.

"Hello, Compton," the Juri replied instantly. "I see you were able to stop him."

"Yes, thanks to your timely information," I confirmed. "Why did you do it?"

"I hoped to prove myself trustworthy." He hesitated. "I need your help."

I felt my eyebrows creeping up my forehead. The Modhri as someone trustworthy was novel enough. The idea that he needed—and wanted—help from me was right off the scale. "To do what?" I asked.

"To find the murderer aboard this train," he said. "*Is* the intruder you stopped that murderer?"

"It's possible," I said. "He's got a first-class pass, and those don't come cheap, which means this guy has some serious financial backing." I grimaced. "But my gut says no."

"Then the killer is still at large," the Modhri said grimly. "And may kill again."

"Fair chance of that, yes," I agreed. "Why do you care?"

Again, he hesitated. "Because as he kills those aboard this train, he is also killing me."

I stared down at the sleeping face. "He's *what*?"

"He has killed four and tried to kill two others," the Modhri said. "Two of the dead were my Eyes."

I looked over at the server Spider standing behind the counter, out of range of our conversation, my brain swirling as everything about this case tried to realign itself. Could the as-yet-unexplained motive for these murders be something as simple as an attempt to kill off this particular Modhran mind segment? "Which two?" I asked.

"The first and third to die," he said. "Master Colix and *di*-Master Strinni."

"And what makes you think you can trust me?" I asked. "I'm your enemy, remember?"

"But you have destroyed my Eyes and Arms only in battle," he said. "Never have you engaged in direct murder." The sleeping Juri's mouth twitched. "And you have already saved one Eye that would also have been lost without your intervention."

He was right on that one, anyway. Qiddicoj would almost certainly have died of the same intestinal ravages that had killed Givvrac if I hadn't come up with the solution. "Of course, I didn't know *Osantra* Qiddicoj was a walker at the time," I reminded him.

"Would that have made a difference?"

I thought it over. The worst thing about fighting the damn Modhri was that most of his pawns were both unwilling and innocent. You couldn't go around slaughtering them for crimes they didn't even know they'd committed. You couldn't stand by and let someone else knock them off, either. "Not really," I conceded.

"As I thought," the Modhri said. "At first I feared you might be the person responsible for the deaths. But I'm now convinced otherwise."

"Glad to hear that," I said. I was, too. About the only thing that could have made this situation worse would have been to have a paranoid Modhran mind segment also gunning for me. "But just because I'm not going to let people get murdered doesn't mean I'm ready to jump on board as your ally."

"Yet I may be of assistance in your investigation," the Modhri pointed out. "And recall that two others who were not associated with me have also been killed. Do you not seek justice for them?"

I chewed the inside of my cheek. After all I'd been through with the Modhri, the thought of cooperating with him had all the skin-crawling unpleasantness of being offered lunch by a high-ranking member of the Inquisition.

And yet, the detached Westali investigator in me could see the possibilities here. One of the most frustrating roadblocks of the investigation so far had been my inability to nail down the last few hours of Master Colix's life. But if he'd been a Modhran walker, all those details were suddenly available to me, as clear and precise as if his whole life had been copied onto off-site backup. Which, in a sense, it had. "Let me get this straight," I said. "You're suggesting that we work together—you and I— to catch the murderer aboard this train."

"Correct."

"And afterwards?"

"You will have my thanks," the Modhri said.

"That's not what I meant," I said. "What's the rest of the Modhri going to say when he finds out you joined forces with someone he'd like to see dead?"

For a moment the Modhri didn't answer. I looked at the server again, wondering if he was even now informing Bayta that I was having a heart-to-heart with a sleeping passenger. "As with all beings, my first duty is to survive," the Modhri said at last. "Clearly, this murderer has found a way to bring weapons of death aboard a Quadrail. If he is permitted to escape undetected and unpunished, then none of us will ever be safe. Not you, and not I."

That was something I'd also thought about lately. I'd

thought about it a lot. "Let's hope the rest of the mind will also see it that way," I said. "So the plan is that we team up, catch this joker, then go our separate ways?"

"Yes," he said, and there was no mistaking the relief in his voice. "Thank you."

"Hang on," I warned. "Before you go all grateful, there are a few ground rules. First of all, how many walkers do you have aboard?"

"Three remain," he said.

Three out of an original five, kicking the mind segment down by forty percent. No wonder he was panicked enough to ask me for help. "Their names and species?"

He hesitated. "Why do you ask?"

"Because I need to know who, what, and where you are," I told him. "Partly for operational purposes; mostly because I don't like having potential surprises at my back."

"I have sworn to cooperate with you."

"And I'm pleased to hear that," I said. "Their names and species?"

He sighed, exactly the sort of sound a sleeping person might make. "First is *Osantra* Qiddicoj, the Filiaelian you saved from death," he said reluctantly. "Second is Prapp, a Tra'ho government oathling. His seat is in the first coach car. This Eye's name is *Krel* Vevri. He sits in the second coach car, the one between the dispensary and the entertainment car."

The same car, I noted, that the rest of Kennrick's contract-team Fillies were in. That could be useful. "Good," I said. "Ground rule number one: I call the shots. All of them. You can report to me, and you can recommend action, but nothing happens unless I explicitly sign off on it. Understood?"

"Understood," he said.

"Ground rule number two: when we do catch him, I'm the

one who'll interrogate him," I continued. "This guy is smart and well funded, and there will be some fairly ugly layers we'll need to dig through to get where we're going. You can sit in on the conversation and offer suggestions, but I'm the one who'll handle all the actual questioning."

A shiver ran through the Juri's body. "I have heard stories of Human interrogations. I will not interfere."

"Good." I hadn't actually been talking about torture, but it probably wouldn't hurt to let the Modhri think that I had. It probably wouldn't hurt to remind the killer of humanity's bloody past, either, when the time came. "Ground rule number three: I decide what to do with him after we've finished putting him through the spin cycle. I doubt the Spiders are set up for either executions or long-term prisoner storage, and there are already two different governments that have legitimate claims on his scalp. Depending on who and what he turns out to be, we might end up with three. Based on the interrogation, I'll make the decision as to who gets him."

"Agreed," the Modhri said. "How do we begin?"

I yawned. "With some sleep," I said. "The rest of the train's already settled down for the night, so there's no point trying to find anyone to question. And I'm way too tired to think straight, anyway." I gestured to him. "Sleeping on the table that way isn't doing your walker any good, either."

"Very well," he said. "*Osantra* Qiddicoj practices meditation several times a day. During those times, he allows his mind to empty itself."

I felt my stomach tighten. "And you're conveniently there to refill it?"

"It will be an opportunity for us to discuss matters and formulate a plan," the Modhri said. Apparently, he'd missed the irony in my tone.

"Fine," I said. "I'll have a couple of other things to deal with first tomorrow—mainly following up on tonight's little adventure—but I should be able to touch base with you by early afternoon at the latest."

"And if the killer strikes again this night?"

"He's been lying pretty low since *Usantra* Givvrac's death," I reminded him. "There's no particular reason for him to come out tonight."

"No reason that you know of."

"True," I conceded. "If it's any consolation, I don't think he's specifically targeting you." I stood up. "But I've been wrong before. Pleasant dreams."

SIXTEEN :

I half expected Bayta to be waiting for me when I returned to my compartment, her eyes blazing, her arms folded across her chest, demanding to know what I'd been off doing. But she wasn't. Apparently, the server Spider at the bar hadn't sold me out. Yet. Five minutes later I was climbing into bed, sleep tugging at my eyelids and my brain.

But even as I adjusted the blankets around my shoulders, I had a nagging sense that something significant had happened this evening. Something so subtle that I hadn't picked up on it on a conscious level.

For a minute I fought against sleep, trying to get a handle on the feeling and whatever it was that had sparked it. But it was an uphill battle, and after that single minute I knew it was hopeless. Tomorrow, when I'd caught up on my sleep, I would make another effort to track it down.

* * *

Once again, tomorrow arrived earlier than I'd expected it to.

And yet, at the same time, it nearly didn't arrive at all. At least for me.

I'd been asleep barely two hours when I was jarred awake by something soft and vague; a distant, eerie whistling sort of sound that was as much felt as it was heard. For a handful of heartbeats I lay still, my eyes wide open in the darkness, my ears straining against the silence as I waited for the noise to come again.

But it didn't. I'd just about decided it had been an artifact of my sleeping brain when I heard another sound.

Only this one wasn't vague and ethereal the way the first had been. This one was real, solid, and very close at hand.

Someone was scratching on my door.

I rolled silently out of bed and into a crouch on the floor, fighting against the mental cobwebs as I tried to figure out just what in hell was going on. There was a perfectly good door chime out there, not to mention equally good hard surfaces all around that anyone with working knuckles could knock on. There was no reason why whoever was out there should be scratching away like a pet malamute who wanted back into the house.

Unless he was too weak or too sick to do anything else.

I slid my hand along the floor until I found my shoes. I picked up one of them, getting a good grip on the toe. Holding it over my head like a club, I walked silently to the door and keyed the release.

To find that no one was there.

Frowning, I stepped out into the corridor and looked both directions. No one was visible along the car's entire length.

But someone *had* been there. At the rear of the car, the vestibule was just closing.

My first thought was that whoever this was, he must have

exquisite timing to have been able to get out of sight just as I was opening my door. My second thought was that whatever game he was playing, it probably boiled down to being a trap.

My third was that there was no way in hell he was going to get away from me.

I ducked back into my compartment, grabbed my other shoe and my shirt and headed out after him, making sure my door closed and locked behind me. I got my shoes on as I jogged down the corridor, and by the time I reached the vestibule I had my shirt on as well. Bracing myself, I keyed the door release.

The vestibule was empty. I crossed it and opened the door to the next compartment car, again preparing myself for whatever lay beyond it. But again, the corridor was empty. Hurrying past the closed compartment doors, I went through the vestibule and into the first of the first-class coaches.

Compartment cars didn't really lend themselves to ambushes, given that the only place you could launch one from was one of the compartments themselves. But coach cars were another matter entirely, as I'd already learned the hard way on this trip. Most of the seats scattered around the car were canopied, their occupants long since in dreamland, though there were a couple of quiet conversations still going on in various corners. But none of the conversationalists were near my path, and in fact didn't seem to even notice my presence, and I continued on through and into the dining car.

And nearly ran into my old Modhran pal *Krel* Vevri as he staggered out into the corridor from the bar end. "Compton," he breathed as he stepped into my path.

"Did you just scratch on my door?" I demanded, coming to a halt in front of him.

For a moment he just stared at me in silence, his body weaving a little, his eyes apparently having a hard time focusing on me. To all appearances he was as drunk as a goat. "Compton," he said again. "There's trouble."

I felt a tingle go up my back. Drunk Juriani nearly always slurred their words. Vevri wasn't doing that. Stepping close to him, I leaned forward and sniffed his breath.

One whiff was all it took. Any alcohol he might have poured into his system earlier that evening had been burned away hours ago. Whatever had put Vevri into this state, it wasn't anything the Spiders had served him.

Our poisoner had struck again.

"Understood," I said, taking his arm and trying to turn him around toward the dispensary three cars back. "Come on—we'll get the Spiders to call a doctor—"

"No doctor," he interrupted, throwing off my grip with an unexpected burst of strength. "Hypnotic—dizzy, but not in danger."

"We should at least try to figure out what it was," I insisted, trying to get a grip on his arm again. "Or wasn't it you?" I added as it belatedly occurred to me that Vevri himself might be completely unscathed, that the hypnotic or whatever might have been administered to one of the other walkers and merely be affecting the Juri via their shared mind.

But once again, he pulled away from my grip. "Not in danger," he insisted. "The prisoner. He's the one in danger."

I stared at him. "Emikai? What does the killer want with him?"

"Don't know," Vevri said. He wobbled suddenly and had to grab the edge of the archway to regain his balance. "Don't call Spiders. Warn him—warn him off. Never find him then."

I looked over his shoulder down the corridor. "Did you see the killer?" I asked Vevri. "The killer, *Krel* Vevri. Did you see who he was?"

Vevri shook his head. "He's on his way. Already on his way. You must stop him."

"Yeah," I said, gazing hard into the Juri's face.

And not believing it for a second, because this whole thing stunk to high heaven. Even if I actually trusted the Modhri—which I damn well didn't—it would still smell like a setup.

But I had no choice but to play along. If the killer really did want Emikai silenced, for whatever reason, the Filly was a sitting duck back there. The two twitters on duty might get a glimpse of the killer, but that would be pretty small comfort to Emikai himself.

Besides, knowing it was a setup gave me certain advantages, especially if the killer didn't know I knew. "Okay, I'll go take a look," I said to Vevri. "You stay here and keep an eye out in case he doubles back."

Vevri nodded. "I will. Good luck."

Slipping past him, I continued on my way. Knowing you were walking into a trap could definitely be helpful in beating that trap.

But it never hurt to also hedge your bets.

I had covered another two cars and was passing the line of shower compartments before I finally ran into a conductor tapping his way along on some errand or another. "Hey—you," I said, catching up to him. "You—Spider."

"Yes?" he said.

"I want you to call Bayta," I said. "Tell her I've had word that *Logra* Emikai is in trouble, and I'm heading back to check on him—"

"Bayta is asleep."

"Then wake her up," I snarled. "Tell her I want her to do a running track on me—conductors, servers, mites, and anyone else who's available. You got that?"

"Yes," he said.

"Good." I started to go, then turned back. "And she's to stay put," I added firmly. "Whatever happens, she's to stay in her compartment and not open the door. For anyone."

"Yes," he said.

I gazed hard into his silvery globe for another moment, the way you might underline the seriousness of an order if you were talking to a real, actual person, then turned and resumed my jog. If Bayta could mobilize enough of the Spiders to monitor the action, we had a chance of bringing this thing to an end right here and now.

The baggage car seemed quiet enough as I slipped through the vestibule doorway into the gloom. Setting my back against the nearest stack of crates, I paused for a moment to take stock of the situation. No shadows seemed to be moving out there, at least none that I could see from my current vantage point, and I could hear nothing above the muted clickity-clack of Quadrail wheels.

Was the killer still here? Or had he been and gone, leaving a fresh corpse where I'd earlier tied up a prisoner?

Only one way to find out. Taking a deep breath, I headed off through the maze of stacked crates.

The attack came without any warning, in spite of all the care I had been taking with corners and crate tops. An arm suddenly appeared from behind me, snaking around my neck and yanking me backward. I tried to twist sideways, to get my throat turned into the crook of his elbow where there was a little extra space, but he was already on it, his other hand snapping up to link into his choking arm and simultaneously push the back of my head forward.

Reflexively, I kicked backward. But my foot hit only air, and before I could bring it back for another try a foot slapped into the back of my other knee, just hard enough to break my balance.

And barely a second after the attack had begun, I found myself kneeling on the floor, the tiny prickly hairs of a Filly snout pressed against my right cheek, his chokehold ready to squeeze the life out of me.

I tried to reach up toward his head, in hopes of reaching his eyes or ears. But the arms wrapped around my throat and head blocked any such path. I switched direction and jabbed backwards with my elbows, landing solid blows against his torso. He grunted with the impact, but his grip didn't loosen.

So this is how it ends, the thought flitted through my mind as I continued my futile efforts to break my attacker's grip. I wondered distantly what Bayta would do without me, and what the Chahwyn and Spiders would do after I was dead.

It was only then that it belatedly dawned on me that the arm pressed against my throat, which should have been squeezing ever tighter, cutting off my air and choking the life out of me, was doing no such thing. In fact, it wasn't all that tight even now, more of a controlling hold than a killing one.

Was he just waiting so that I would sweat some more? Or did he genuinely want to keep me alive, at least until he could get something else out of me?

Bracing myself, painfully aware that if I was wrong, it would be the last gamble I ever made, I brought my pummeling hands and elbows to a halt.

He didn't press his attack. But he didn't let go, either. He just stood there, towering silently and motionless behind me.

I cleared my throat, which turned out to be a lot harder in my present condition than I'd expected. "If you're trying to make a point," I croaked out, "consider it made."

"What point is that?" he asked.

I grimaced as I recognized his voice. My assailant was none other than *Logra* Emikai himself. "That you're the greatest escape artist since Houdini?" I suggested.

"That I could have killed you," he corrected. Abruptly, the pressure against my throat disappeared as he let go of me and stepped backward. "And that I did not," he added.

I turned my head, massaging my throat as I looked up at him. He was just standing there, his arms hanging loosely as his sides, gazing back at me. "Interesting demo," I commented, getting back to my feet. "Of course, as has already been noted, you're on a super-express Quadrail with nowhere to run. Killing me would be kind of stupid."

"Agreed," he said. "But he who freed me apparently was not concerned with such questions of logic." He paused. "He who freed me, then ordered me to kill you."

"Did he, now," I said as casually as I could. So our killer was starting to sharecrop his business. "Did this helpful passerby have a name or face?"

"I'm certain he had both," Emikai said grimly. "Unfortunately, I was asleep when he freed me."

"*And* when he gave you your marching orders?" I asked, frowning. "What did he do, leave a voice message in your dreams?"

"You are actually not far off," Emikai said, for the first time seeming a little uncertain. "The words came to me in . . . it's hard to describe. It was a distant, whistling sort of voice. I'm afraid I cannot explain it more clearly than that."

"That's okay," I assured him, a prickling sensation running up my back. A distant, eerie whistling sort of sound was the way I'd characterized my own recent wake-up call. "How long ago did all this happen?"

He shrugged. "An hour. Perhaps a bit more."

Just enough time, in other words, for someone to make his way back up to the front of the train, dose a sleeping Modhran walker with hypnotic so that he could play shill for me, and call me awake so he could send me to my death.

In fact, with this added bit of information, the late-night conversations I'd noticed as I passed through first class suddenly took on an entirely new aspect. Odds were that one of those conversations had been the killer talking to one of the Modhri's other walkers, getting ready to feed *Krel* Vevri's lines to him by remote control. That was a capability of the group mind that had never occurred to me. "So why didn't you kill me?" I asked.

Emikai snorted. "I do not murder on anyone's demand," he growled.

"Glad to hear it," I said, rubbing my throat again. "So what now? We let bygones be bygones and I let you go back to your nice comfy Quadrail seat?"

He cocked his head. "Do you think that would be wise?"

My estimate of his competence, which had already been pretty high, rose a couple more points. Most citizens would have leaped at the offer. But Emikai was either more thoughtful or more canny than that.

Which led directly to the bigger question of who or what this horse-faced enigma was, and whose side he was on. If anyone's. "Unfortunately—unfortunately for you, anyway—no, I don't," I said. "I'm thinking it could be highly interesting to see what kind of reaction we get when I not only don't turn up dead, but you turn up back in irons."

"I expected you would say that." Emikai looked around us. "I presume this time you will have watchers present in the event that he attempts this again?"

"Absolutely," I promised, keeping my voice even. "If you're ready, let's go ahead and reset the stage."

He eyed me another moment, then nodded. "Very well," he said.

Five minutes later, with Emikai once again tied to his perch, I was on my way back to the front of the train. And this time, I was moving with a lighter, quicker step.

Because though Emikai didn't know it, there *had* been watchers present during his abortive rescue: the two twitters Bayta had left on guard.

It was going to be highly interesting to find out what exactly they'd seen.

What they'd seen, it turned out, was exactly nothing.

"That's impossible," I growled, glaring at Bayta from my seat at her computer desk as she sat stiffly on the edge of her bed. "You left them there. You ordered them to watch. How can they not have seen something?"

"I don't know," Bayta said. Her voice was as stiff as her posture. "They just froze up, somehow."

"How does a Spider freeze up?" I asked.

"I don't *know*," Bayta repeated tartly. "Something happened to them. Something I've never heard of happening before."

I stared at her . . . and then my fatigue-numbed brain finally got it. Bayta hadn't gone all stiff and angry because she was mad at me.

She wasn't angry. She was scared.

"Okay," I said, forcing the frustration out of my voice. This was no time for emotion of any sort. "Let's start at the beginning. When did this blank spot happen?"

"As near as we can tell, just under two hours ago," Bayta said, her voice still stiff but sounding marginally calmer now that I was no longer yelling at her. "About the same time *Logra* Emikai says someone cut him free of his bonds."

"And it knocked out both Spiders so that they didn't see anything?"

"It didn't exactly knock them out," Bayta said hesitantly, frowning out into space as if looking for the right words. "It was more like they had been looking somewhere else and . . . is 'spaced out' a correct English term?"

"It is indeed," I assured her. "Did they notice anything unusual happening just before or during this brain freeze?"

"How could they notice anything *during* the brain freeze?" Bayta asked patiently. "They were incapacitated."

"I know *they* were," I said. "But they're telepathically linked to the rest of the Spiders, and I assume no one else was affected."

"No, no one else was affected," Bayta said, shaking her head. "But the two twitters were somehow disconnected from the rest of the Spiders during that time."

"And no one noticed that?"

She shrugged. "The Spiders aren't a group mind," she reminded me. "They're not connected that tightly."

I grimaced. And even if someone *had* noticed, they probably wouldn't have done anything. That wasn't the way Spiders did things. "Well, it's certainly not the first dead end we've hit in this case," I said. "At least we've proved now that *Logra* Emikai isn't our killer."

"Have we?" Bayta countered. "Couldn't this have just been an elaborate plan on his part to deflect suspicion away from him?"

"Hardly," I said. "The whole story about being ordered to kill me implies that his midnight visitor thought he would be willing to do the dastardly deed, which implies a relationship of some sort with said midnight visitor. That actually puts him closer to the center of this mess than he would have been if he'd just stayed put like a good little prisoner. It's more likely that the real killer was hoping this would muddy the waters by throwing some of the suspicion onto Emikai."

"Or hoped *Logra* Emikai *would* kill you," Bayta said quietly.

"There is that," I conceded. "Fortunately, he couldn't be present to either encourage or assist. He had to be up here pulling Vevri's strings."

"Yes," Bayta said, her voice chilling a bit. "Let's talk about *Krel* Vevri, shall we?"

I took a deep breath. For a while I'd considered keeping my deal with the Modhri private, knowing that Bayta probably wouldn't take the news very well. But down deep, I'd known all along I couldn't do that. Bayta was my ally and my friend, and it would be neither safe nor fair for me to cut her out of something this important.

Besides, I could still see the quiet pain that had flooded into her eyes when she'd learned I'd held out on her about the Chahwyn's new defender-class Spiders. I wasn't about to go through that twice in one trip.

So as she sat still and silent on her bed, I told her all about it.

I was prepared for her to be stunned, or aghast, or outraged. I wasn't prepared for her to be quietly unreadable. "So there *is* a mind segment aboard," she said when I'd finished. "I'd always thought there probably was."

"It seemed a reasonable deal to make," I said, still trying to figure out what was going on behind that emotionless face. "This may be our only chance of getting fresh information on this case."

"And you'd rather work with the Modhri than let a killer escape punishment?"

"This isn't an ordinary killer, Bayta," I reminded her. "He's figured out how to commit quiet, subtle murder on a Quadrail. Not just beat someone to death with his bare hands, which we've seen before, but real, genuine, untraceable murder." I waved a hand. "Not to mention that he's also got a technique for freezing or otherwise incapacitating Spiders. You think the Chahwyn will want him getting away with all that?"

"It doesn't really matter what the Chahwyn wants, does it?" she countered. "You've already made the decision." She eyed me. "But there's a possibility you haven't mentioned. What if it was the Modhri himself who was responsible for what happened with *Logra* Emikai and the twitters?"

"And, what, he committed all the murders, too?" I asked. "Two of the victims being his own walkers? Why would he do that?"

"To get us killed," Bayta said quietly. "To get *you* killed. Maybe the reason he volunteered to help us was to set you up for a thought virus that would make sure you went back to the baggage car after he freed *Logra* Emikai."

I grimaced. There was some sense in that theory, I had to admit. More sense than I liked. Especially when you tossed in Bayta's speculation earlier in the trip that the Modhri might slowly be going crazy. "If that's the case, his reaction tomorrow when I turn up alive ought to be interesting," I said. "His explanation for what happened tonight ought to be interesting, too."

Bayta seemed to draw back. "You're not going to go *on* with this whole thing, are you?"

"I don't see that I have a choice," I said. "No matter who's behind the murders, the Modhri or someone else, the fact remains that *someone* has figured out a way to get poison aboard a Quadrail. If it wasn't the Modhri, he may be able to help us figure out how it was done. If it *was* the Modhri, he might let something slip while he's pretending to assist us. Either way, I have to play it out."

Bayta's throat worked. "I suppose you're right," she said reluctantly. "You won't do anything more until morning, though, will you?"

I thought about pointing out that, technically, it *was* morning. But she didn't seem in the mood for that sort of whimsy. "No," I promised. "No matter who comes scratching on my door."

"And we'll be going together?"

I winced. She hadn't added *this time* to her question, but I could hear it anyway. "Of course," I assured her.

"All right." She took a deep breath. "Then we should probably get some sleep now."

Apparently, the conversation was over. "Agreed," I said, standing up and stepping past the folded-up divider into my own compartment. "I'll see you in the morning." I reached for the divider control.

"Maybe you should leave it partly open tonight," she said.

So that we could be better able to protect each other? Or so that I would have a harder time running off somewhere without her again?

Or had this whole thing so spooked her that she just wanted the sense of a little company close at hand?

"Sure," I said. Touching the control, I let the divider close to about half a meter, then tapped the control again to stop it. "Pleasant dreams," I called through the opening.

"Good night, Frank," she called back.

SEVENTEEN :

I woke up seven hours later, still tired, and with an aching throat where Emikai had delivered his object lesson. The elusive thought that had been nagging at my brain after my first midnight conversation with the Modhri still eluded me, but on the plus side the possibility that our new ally was trying to kill me was looking considerably less likely here in the light of day.

"I don't think the Modhri is the killer," I told Bayta over breakfast. "If he'd wanted me dead, he could have done it when he took me out after all the Fillies started coming down with digestive trouble. As you yourself pointed out, he had Witherspoon's medical bag right there, with hypos and any number of potential overdoses to choose from."

"Except that he wouldn't have had a built-in perpetrator to take the blame, the way he would have if *Logra* Emikai had killed you," Bayta pointed out.

"Right, but why would he care?" I countered. "It would have cost him at most one more walker, whichever one he picked to take the fall. After killing off two other walkers, that hardly seems like a consideration."

"Perhaps," Bayta said. She still didn't seem convinced, but with her professional mask back up I couldn't tell what she was thinking or feeling. "Are we starting with him, then?"

"Actually, I was thinking we'd start with Dr. Aronobal," I said. "She's had plenty of time now to wonder where her pal Emikai's gotten to. Worried people often blurt out things they would keep to themselves if they were calmer."

"That seems reasonable." She took a final bite of her breakfast, her other hand reaching under the table. "Here—you should probably carry this."

I reached under the table, and she pressed the *kwi* into my hand. "Thanks," I said, slipping it into my pocket. "And thanks for the assist last night, too, when Emikai was making a run for it. You were right on top of things."

She nodded, thanks or simple acknowledgment, I couldn't tell which. "You ready?" she asked.

I sighed to myself. This was going to be a very long day. "Sure," I said. "Let's go."

We left the dining car and headed once again on the long walk toward the rear of the train. As usual, *Asantra* Muzzfor nodded politely as we passed the apparently eternal card game he had going with his two contract-team companions, while the other two Fillies, also as usual, ignored us completely. I looked around at the other passengers as we walked through that car, wondering which of them was Prapp, the Tra'ho government oathling the Modhri had named last night as being the third of his walkers. Both Tra'ho'seej in evidence, unfortunately, had the distinctive oathling half-shaved heads and flowing topcuts, which I'd counted on identifying him with.

Neither Tra'ho gave us a significant look as we passed, either, which was the other way I might have recognized him.

Osantra Qiddicoj was similarly preoccupied with other matters as we passed him three cars later. Apparently, the Modhri was keeping to himself this morning. Maybe he was ashamed of his unwitting part in the murder attempt against me last night.

Maybe he was just sulking because it hadn't worked.

Aronobal's seat was in the first third-class coach. We reached her car, to find the doctor herself was nowhere to be seen. She was probably farther back in the train, in the dining car having breakfast, or possibly sneaking back to our makeshift brig for a hurried conference with *Logra* Emikai. That would be the most interesting possibility of all. Passing her seat, we continued on.

We were just entering Emikai's assigned car, two back from Aronobal's, when I began to notice a change in the atmosphere around us.

At first it was nothing I could put my finger on. The passengers seemed quieter than they'd been in either first or second, but not quiet in the sense of peace or comfort. This was the quiet of fresh tension simmering beneath the surface.

Behind Emikai's car was the third-class dining car. Bayta and I took a quick look inside, confirmed that Aronobal wasn't there, and kept going toward the entertainment car.

As we did so, I could feel the quiet tension continuing to grow. More and more, the passengers' eyes turned toward us as we came into sight, and continued to follow us as we passed.

And the expressions on their faces were running the unpleasant gamut from neutral to suspicious to downright hostile.

Bayta noticed it, too. "Something's not right here," she murmured as we passed through the shower car.

"And whatever it is, we seem to be getting the blame for it," I murmured back. "Is anything happening with Emikai?"

"The twitters say he hasn't had any visitors since you left, and that he's still secured," she said. "The conductors aren't reporting anything odd with the rest of the train, either."

"So it apparently is just us," I concluded.

"Do you think we should turn back?"

It was a tempting idea. But we had a job to do, and somehow I doubted the passengers were going to get any less hostile as the day wore on. "Let's at least go as far as the entertainment car," I said. "If we haven't located Aronobal by then, we'll backtrack and wait for her at her seat."

Actually, I wasn't expecting we'd have to go that far back. Just behind the shower car was Terese German's car, and if Emikai, Aronobal, and Terese were in cahoots, there was a fair chance we'd find the latter two members of the troika in urgent consultation together.

For once, I was right. As we exited the vestibule into the car, I saw a small group of passengers gathered around Terese's row, their heads hunched forward the way people do when having intense, semi-private conversations. Two of the group were Halkas, one was a Juri, and the fourth was Dr. Aronobal.

"There she is," Bayta said.

"I see her," I said, the back of my neck starting to tingle. The conversationalists had turned to face us, and their expressions weren't even bothering with the neutral or suspicious areas of today's third-class mood scale. All four were deeply into the hostile end of the spectrum, and every cubic centimeter of that hostility was aimed at Bayta and me. "Maybe you ought to hang back a bit while I go talk to them," I said quietly.

Bayta reached over and got a grip on my left arm. "No," she said in a voice that left no room for argument.

"Stay a step behind me, then," I told her, gently disengaging her grip. "You might want to fire up the *kwi*, just in case."

I started forward again, the *kwi* in my pocket tingling as Bayta activated it. "Good afternoon," I said, nodding to the group as I got within polite conversational range. "Dr. Aronobal, I wonder if I might have a few minutes of your time."

To my surprise, Terese bounded up from her seat, planting herself squarely between me and the rest of them. "What do you want her for?" she demanded, her face dark with emotion.

"I just want to ask her a few questions," I said soothingly.

"And then, what, make *her* disappear, too?" Terese shot back.

I took another look at the group standing silently behind her. "What in the world are you talking about?"

"She speaks of *Logra* Emikai," Aronobal said grimly. "He's disappeared, and no one can find him." She drew herself up. "We've heard reports that you were the one responsible."

"Reports," I said, letting my tone go flat. "You mean rumors."

"Yes, that's what I thought you'd say," Terese said scornfully.

"You protest too glibly," the Juri agreed in a precise, clipped voice. "Rumors always have a basis in fact, a touchpoint with reality. The reality here is that *Logra* Emikai *has* indeed vanished."

I really wanted to ask him how he could possibly know that, given that he and his fellow worriers were all confined back here in third class while their buddy Emikai had a pass that let him roam the entire train at will. But I kept my mouth shut. Those who didn't already know that almost certainly wouldn't believe it anyway. "Maybe he's taking a long shower," I suggested instead. "Maybe the Spiders asked him up to first or second for some kind of consultation."

"Oh, right," Terese bit out. "Far as *I* can see, the only people consulting with the Spiders are you two."

"Let us also not forget that *di*-Master Strinni's final act was to form his hands into the sign-language symbols of your initials," Aronobal added.

I *had* forgotten about that, actually, and I made a mental note to hit up the Modhri later and find out what the hell he'd thought he was doing with that.

Assuming there *was* a later. Most of the nearby passengers were listening intently to the conversation, and their expressions reminded me of sharks at feeding time. They were scared, they were frustrated, and, worse, after nearly four weeks on the road they were bored. If there was no justice in me getting my ears pounded, there might at least be some entertainment.

I came to a sudden decision. Aronobal wasn't going to talk now anyway, not surrounded by indignant supporters who clearly thought I was out to add her to some phantom body count. There would be plenty of other opportunities to hit her up about her relationship with Emikai before we reached Venidra Carvo. "I get the feeling you really don't want to talk right now," I said, taking a casual step backward. "Fine. We'll do this later."

"Don't let him go!" Terese snapped. "If he gets away, we'll never find out what he did with *Logra* Emikai."

She started toward me, and to my surprise I saw she had tears in her eyes. Either she was choking with rage or she really did feel something for the supposedly vanished Emikai. "I didn't do anything with *Logra* Emikai," I insisted.

But it was too late. Behind her, one of the two Halkas—the bigger one, naturally—shouldered her aside and strode toward me, the glow of righteous indignation in his eyes.

"Move it," I murmured to Bayta, crowding backwards

against her as I dipped my hand into my pocket. Unfortunately, while the *kwi* gave me the power to drop the Halka where he stood, I couldn't use it, at least not openly. Kennrick already knew I had brought a supposedly forbidden weapon aboard, and *Logra* Emikai probably suspected it, and the last thing I wanted was for the rest of the train to find out, too.

But if I couldn't use the *kwi* openly, maybe I could use it *not* openly.

The Halka was still lumbering forward as I pulled my hand out of my pocket, the *kwi* in position around my knuckles. The second Halka had fallen into step behind the first, with Terese now third in line. "Take it easy," I said soothingly as I keyed the *kwi* for its lowest unconsciousness setting. "I don't want any trouble here. Neither do you."

The two Halkas merely picked up their pace a little. Knowing Halkas, I'd expected that. I continued to back up, keeping my hands moving in little circles to prevent anyone from getting a clear look at the *kwi*. The lead Halka got to within grabbing distance and reached out a large hand toward my neck.

And I slammed my right fist into his gut.

It wasn't all that hard a slam, actually. In fact, the punch was over ninety percent pure noise, with as little genuine impact as I could get away with while still making it sound real. There didn't have to be any impact, because an instant before my fist hit his torso I thumbed the *kwi*'s firing button.

The weapon worked with its usual gratifying speed, instantly sending the Halka off to dreamland. As his knees started to buckle beneath him I brought my left hand up and made a show of chopping him at the base of the neck. After that, my only job was to get out of his way as he collapsed with an impressive thud onto the floor.

The second Halka came to an abrupt halt. So did the various mutterings and twitterings that had been going on among the onlookers. Our entire end of the car, in fact, went deathly quiet.

And from behind me I heard Bayta give a short, strangled gasp.

I spun around, *kwi* ready, both hands coming up into combat position. But it was only Kennrick, his hands on Bayta's shoulders as he moved her sideways out of his way. "What the hell are you doing back here?" he demanded, his voice taut, his eyes flicking to the line of potential attackers still facing me. "Come on—we've got to get out of here before you get lynched."

I was opening my mouth to tell him that we had every intention of doing exactly that when the second Halka made his move.

Unfortunately for him, the same relative silence that had allowed me to hear Kennrick's non-assault on Bayta also enabled me to hear him coming with his more genuine attack. I spun back around, evaded his pile-driver punch, and dropped him to the floor with a second *kwi* shot and some more martial-arts window dressing.

And then Kennrick's hand was on my shoulder, pulling me backward toward the vestibule. "Come *on,*" he repeated urgently. "Let's get the hell out of here."

I took one last look at Terese's stricken, disbelieving, anguished expression, and got the hell out of there.

We reached the next car and Kennrick slipped around past me, putting himself behind Bayta and me and between us and any potential follow-up trouble that Aronobal and Terese might choose to send in our direction. But no one came bursting through the vestibule in hot pursuit. The three of us retraced our steps back through third class, and again I could feel the eyes of the passengers on my back as we hurried forward. Fortunately, none of them did anything but look, and a few minutes later we made our escape from third class into second.

"Whew," Kennrick puffed as we slowed our pace back to a normal walk. The passengers here, I noted, seemed to have no interest whatsoever in us. "That was way too close."

"Close to *what*, I'm not sure," I said, eyeing him over my shoulder. "What was all that about, anyway?"

"What, they didn't tell you?" he asked. "There's a rumor racing through third that you killed *Logra* Emikai during the night."

"That much I gathered," I said. "I was mostly wondering if this rumor has anything more to it. Like why I would do something like that or, better yet, how I managed to dispose of a body from a sealed Quadrail."

"You really think anyone's paying attention to actual logic?" Kennrick said sourly. "Especially when it's a trusted member of the medical profession who's telling you all this?"

"Dr. Aronobal started the rumor?" Bayta asked, frowning over her shoulder.

"Who else?" Kennrick said. "I'm just glad I got back there in time." He grunted. "Not that you seemed to need me. That, uh, asset of yours is really something."

"We like it," I said. "Which isn't to say that reinforcements aren't always welcome. How did you happen to be there, any-way?"

"Pure luck," he said. "*Asantra* Muzzfor went back to third earlier this morning to discuss the contract situation with Master Tririn. While he was there he got wind of the rumor about Emikai's mysterious disappearance, though your name appar-ently wasn't yet connected to it. He mentioned it to me when I stopped by his seat half an hour ago, along with the fact that

he'd seen you heading that direction. I put two and two together and went charging back to try to stop you before you
walked into a hornets' nest."

"Why would Dr. Aronobal start such a rumor?" Bayta asked.

"Obviously, to keep you two at bay while she locates Emikai and finds out what we know," Kennrick said. "Or, failing
that, to come up with another plan."

"But that doesn't make any sense," Bayta insisted.

"Of course it does," Kennrick said. "Like I said, she needs
to find Emikai—"

"Why doesn't it make sense?" I interrupted.

"Because if Dr. Aronobal knows *Logra* Emikai well enough
to send him to break into your compartment, she should also
trust him not to tell us anything," she said. "Especially about
whether or not the two of them are working together."

Kennrick snorted. "I think the *working together* part was obvious as soon as Aronobal tried to lure Compton out of his
compartment so that Emikai could break in."

"Obvious, but not provable," Bayta insisted. "We might suspect, but we couldn't know for sure. Given that, wouldn't Dr.
Aronobal do better to pretend she was innocent, or had been
set up, and try to find out what we know?"

There was an answer for that, I knew. But I kept quiet.
Bayta was doing just fine without my help, and I was curious
to see how Kennrick would respond.

Not very well, as it turned out. "Look, I'm not here to defend her cleverness," Kennrick said stiffly. "All I know is that the
rumor is there, and that she's the only one who benefits from it."

"Or possibly Terese German," I suggested. "They seem to
have some kind of relationship going, too."

"And the rumor also keeps you away from her," Kennrick
said with an air of vindication. "Like I said."

"Yes, you're probably right," I agreed. Bayta frowned at me, and I gave her a small warning shake of my head. She grimaced, but turned back without another word. "So what are your plans for the day?" I added to Kennrick.

"First I need to find out from *Asantra* Muzzfor exactly what he and Master Tririn talked about," Kennrick said. "I was about to do that when I found out you two were in danger and cut the meeting short. After that, depending on what he says, I'll need to sit down with all three of the Filiaelians and discuss the contract status."

"You don't sound very hopeful," I said.

"I'm not," he admitted. "But I have to try."

We reached the rearmost of the first-class cars, and as we entered I casually glanced around. *Osantra* Qiddicoj was seated in a corner by himself, his eyes closed, his breathing slow, his mind presumably emptied.

The Modhri was open for business.

"You go on ahead," I told Kennrick, taking Bayta's arm and bringing the two of us to a halt. "I want to see how *Osantra* Qiddicoj's doing."

"Yes, poor guy," Kennrick said, peering over at Qiddicoj. "I hear those Filiaelian stomach things can drag you down for weeks. He's looking better, though."

"Hopefully, he'll be recovered by the time we reach Venidra Carvo," I said. "Thanks again for coming to our rescue."

"Any time." With a nod to Bayta, Kennrick continued on forward.

I could feel the taut muscles in Bayta's arm as I steered us toward Qiddicoj's seat. "You okay with this?" I asked her quietly.

"Would it matter if I wasn't?"

"Sure," I said. "I could take you back to your compartment and do it alone."

She straightened her shoulders. "I'm all right."

There were a pair of empty chairs nearby. I pulled them over to Qiddicoj and we sat down. "Hello, Modhri," I said.

"Good afternoon, Compton," the Modhri said, Qiddicoj's eyes remaining closed. "And to you, Bayta, agent of the Spiders."

Bayta didn't answer.

"Let's start with last night," I said. "I'd like your take on just what the hell happened."

For a long moment the Modhri was silent. "It was very strange," he said at last. "I was . . . I could hear and see what I was doing, and I knew it was a lie. And yet, I could not stop myself."

Which was, I knew, the hallmark of a good hypnotic drug. "At least you were able to slip in the clue about the hypnotic," I commented. "So who was feeding you your lines?"

"I don't know," the Modhri said, a hint of frustration edging into his otherwise emotionless voice. "The voice spoke to my Eye Prapp, but spoke from behind him. I never saw who it was, neither before, during, nor after."

"Did you recognize the voice?" I persisted. "Male, female, species—did you get *anything*?"

"Nothing," he said. "But I do remember that a faint whistling sound seemed to underlie my attacker's words."

I looked at Bayta. I'd heard a whistling sound that evening, and so had Emikai. Now the Modhri had joined the club.

Obviously, that was significant. I just wished I knew how. "I don't suppose you have any idea how the hypnotic got into your system. *Any* of your systems," I amended. "I assume what gets into one walker affects the whole mind."

"It does," he confirmed. "Unfortunately, I have no idea how that was done."

I sighed. If dead ends were money, Bayta and I could retire rich. "You really ought to try to be more alert," I told the Modhri.

"I will," the Modhri promised. "And may I say that I'm pleased you are still alive."

"I'm reasonably pleased about that myself," I said. "Okay, back to the business at hand. What can you tell me about Master Colix's last day?"

"I've been pondering that question since his death," the Modhri said. "Unfortunately, there's little I can tell you that you don't already know. He ate his sunrise and midday meals alone. No one approached his table during either time. Sundown was eaten with Master Bofiv and Master Tririn."

"Master Tririn told us Dr. Witherspoon and Terese German were seated nearby at that latter meal," I said. "Did Master Colix have a good view of them?"

"He did, and neither of them approached the table," the Modhri confirmed. "They seemed interested only in each other." Qiddicoj's nostrils flared briefly. "Perhaps *too* interested."

I felt my ears prick up. Terese, and *Witherspoon*? There was at least a forty-year age difference there. "What makes you say that?" I asked.

"He touched her in a very intimate way," the Modhri said, and I could hear the contempt in his voice for primitive Humans who didn't know any better than to display their affection in public.

"Where exactly did he touch her?" I asked.

A hand lifted limply from Qiddicoj's lap. "Here," he said, his fingertips touching his lower abdomen. "And here," he added, moving the fingers upward a short distance.

I frowned. There wasn't a single Human erogenous zone in either place. "Are you sure?" I asked, holding my hand a couple of centimeters above Bayta's abdomen. "He was touching her right here?"

Qiddicoj's eyes flicked briefly open, then closed again. "Yes," the Modhri confirmed.

"I see," I said, bringing my hand back. "Well, well."

"What is it?" Bayta asked.

"At least one corner of this mess is suddenly making sense," I said. "This dinnertime get-together wasn't a meeting. It was a medical consultation." I tapped my own abdomen. "Remember Terese's stomach trouble?"

Bayta's eyes widened a little. "Are you saying . . . ?"

I nodded. "Our young friend Terese German is pregnant."

Bayta shot a look at Qiddicoj. "What in the world is she doing alone on a Quadrail heading for the far end of the galaxy?"

"That's the question, isn't it?" I agreed. "And it's clear now that our Filly friends Aronobal and Emikai are definitely involved with her."

"Why do you say that?" the Modhri asked.

"Because if they are, a few more of the pieces fall into place," I told him. "Emikai's concern for the air in Terese's car, for starters—air quality would be especially important for a woman carrying a baby. And then there's Dr. Witherspoon's reaction after *di*-Master Strinni's death, when I asked him about his rendezvous with Terese."

"Yes," the Modhri murmured thoughtfully. "He was very reluctant to speak of her."

I frowned. "*You* remember that?"

"The polyp colony within an Eye lives for a short time after the Eye's own death," he explained.

"Ah," I said, a shiver running up my back. I'd always suspected that was the case, but to have it confirmed in such a coldly clinical manner was a little disconcerting. "What you *couldn't* see was that Witherspoon kept looking at Aronobal during that conversation, as if he wasn't sure how much he was allowed to say. Physician/patient privilege is pretty much a standard of Human law these days, but other species handle it in different ways. And Witherspoon was only brought in as a consultant, after all."

"You think Dr. Aronobal was concerned about Ms. German's stomach trouble?" Bayta asked.

"That's my guess," I said. "I'm sure she knows about morning sickness, but the duration and intensity of Terese's bouts may have thrown her enough to want a Human doctor to take a look."

I looked back at Qiddicoj. "Speaking of death and Modhran afterlife, why did you try to finger me—no pun intended—with Strinni's silly dying clue?"

"My apologies," the Modhri said, a touch of embarrassment in his tone. "At the time I believed you to be the one killing off my Eyes. I wanted to raise that same suspicion in others so that they would keep watch on your future actions."

"That makes sense, I guess," I said. "You have no such suspicions now?"

"None," the Modhri assured me. "To return to Master Colix's sundown meal. His individual was *birrsh*, and the common was *po krem*, which he ate with *prinn* scoops."

"Yes, Tririn's already given me the menu," I said. "Any chance either Bofiv or Tririn spiked any of the food?"

"None," the Modhri said firmly. "I've replayed the memory of the entire meal through my mind many times since then. Neither of the others could have done so."

I nodded. I'd already come to the same conclusion, but it was good to have it verified by a fresh source. "Let's move on to the rest of Colix's evening. He finished dinner and . . . ?"

"He returned immediately to his seat," the Modhri said. "His stomach was starting to bother him."

I frowned. "By the time he reached his seat?"

"Even sooner," the Modhri said. "He was feeling the first twinges before the end of the meal."

"Really," I said, tapping my fingertips on the arm of my borrowed chair. Heavy-metal poisoning hit Shorshians quickly, but not *that* quickly. "Let's back up a bit. Did anything unusual happen that afternoon?"

"And did he have his throat lozenges with him all afternoon?" Bayta added.

I threw a sideways look at her. As distasteful as it might be for her to have to deal with the Modhri, she was obviously intrigued by the chance to access one of the murder victims' memories. "Including during dinner," I added, looking back at Qiddicoj.

"Mr. Kennrick visited him briefly in the early afternoon," the Modhri said. "They discussed the halfway-celebration meal Mr. Kennrick was planning."

I nodded. Kennrick had already told me about that. "And the lozenges?"

"They were locked in his lower storage compartment the entire time, including during the sundown meal." The Modhri considered. "Though Mr. Kennrick *did* handle them later that evening, when he retrieved Master Colix's keepsake blanket for him."

I sat up a little straighter. *That* meeting Kennrick *hadn't* mentioned. "What exactly happened?"

"Mr. Kennrick stopped by to say good night," the Modhri said. "Master Colix was feeling too ill to rise, and asked Mr. Kennrick to obtain his blanket and transfer his lozenges to the upper storage compartment."

"Were either of Master Colix's seatmates there at the time?" I asked.

"The Juri was absent," the Modhri said. "The Human female was already beneath her privacy shield. I believe Master Tririn was absent as well."

Which would explain why neither Tririn, Terese, nor the Juri in the window seat had mentioned the incident. "Did he lock the upper storage compartment after he got the blanket?"

A slight frown creased Qiddicoj's face. "I'm not certain. Master Colix watched as he pulled out the blanket, placed the bag of lozenges in its place, then flipped the blanket open and draped it across Master Colix's torso. Master Colix was looking at the blanket, adjusting its position, when Mr. Kennrick returned Master Colix's ticket."

"Where did Master Colix put the ticket?" I asked.

"In his tunic's inside top pocket."

Which was where Bayta and I had found it when we'd later examined the body. "Did anyone else go pocket-diving in his tunic between then and the time he was brought to the dispensary?" I asked.

"I don't know," the Modhri said, sounding frustrated. "Master Colix was so focused on his internal condition that he wasn't really paying attention to his surroundings."

"And you weren't either?"

"I have only my Eye's senses to work with," the Modhri reminded me. "If those senses are impaired, I'm as helpless as the Eye itself."

"Let's try a different angle," I suggested. "Did Master Colix always keep the ticket in that pocket?"

"Yes."

"Did his seatmates know that?"

"Most likely. Master Colix didn't keep it a secret."

"Master Tririn know it, too?"

"Again, most likely."

I grimaced. In other words, whether Kennrick had locked the compartment or not, way too many people knew where to find the key.

"But *Logra* Emikai was the one we caught in the baggage car," Bayta pointed out. "How would he have known where the ticket was?"

"*Logra* Emikai had Master Colix's ticket?" the Modhri asked, sounding confused.

"Possibly," I said. "We ran into him poking around the bodies a couple of days after the first deaths. He may have been returning the ticket, or he may have been up to something else he didn't want to get caught at. No chance you were still hanging around the morgue, I suppose?"

Qiddicoj shook his head. "Both Master Colix's and *di*-Master Strinni's colonies were dead soon after their bodies were taken there," the Modhri said. "Yet you told me *Logra* Emikai was not connected to the murders."

"I said that was my gut feeling," I corrected. "But that was largely based on the fact that I didn't have a motive for him, barring some deep, dark connection with either the victims or Pellorian Medical that we didn't know about. Now that we know there's at least a tenuous connection between him and Witherspoon via Terese, I may have to put him back on the list."

"At least as an accomplice," Bayta murmured. "He couldn't have created last night's situation by himself."

"Agreed," I said. "All that having been said, he still doesn't feel right for the job."

"I had hoped for more from you than mere intuition," the Modhri said with a hint of disapproval.

"Don't worry, you'll get more," I said, standing up. "Thank you for your assistance. We'll be in touch."

Qiddicoj nodded. "If I can be of further assistance, merely ask."

"I will," I said. "One other thing. One of your walkers shares a car with the three Fillies on the contract team. Have you seen any of them disappear for long periods, or head back toward third class?"

"No," the Modhri said without hesitation. "They leave for meals and hygienic needs, but that's all. All other time is spent sleeping, reading, or playing games together."

"Thank you," I said. "Good afternoon, Modhri."

"Good afternoon, Compton." Qiddicoj took an extra-deep breath, and the skin of his face tightened subtly as the Modhri disappeared back under his rock.

Bayta and I returned our borrowed chairs to their original places, then headed forward toward our compartments. "There, now," I said as we passed through the vestibule into the next car. "That wasn't so bad, was it?"

"He's a monster," Bayta said shortly.

"That he is," I agreed. "But sometimes in investigative work you have to deal with one monster in order to bring down another."

She was silent another half coach length. "Did we at least learn anything useful?" she asked at last.

"Oh, yes," I said softly. "For starters, we learned that Kennrick lied to us. Let's go find out why."

EIGHTEEN :

Kennrick was right where I'd expected to find him: sitting in the bar in earnest conversation with *Asantra* Muzzfor. Both of them looked up as Bayta and I approached, and neither looked especially happy to see us. "Compton," Kennrick greeted me perfunctorily as we got within conversation distance. "Sorry, but this is a private meeting."

"This'll only take a minute," I promised. "I just want to know why you lied to me."

That got his full attention. "What?" he asked, frowning. "When?"

"Perhaps we should step out into the corridor for a moment?" I suggested, inclining my head microscopically toward Muzzfor.

"No," Muzzfor said firmly. "I wish to hear this. Bring a chair for yourself and your companion, Mr. Compton."

I raised my eyebrows at Kennrick. "Kennrick?"

"Go ahead," he said firmly. "Whatever you think you've

found, I can already tell you there's a perfectly reasonable explanation."

I pulled over a pair of chairs from an unoccupied table nearby. Kennrick shifted his seat toward Muzzfor to give us room, and Bayta and I crowded in across from them. "I've been told you had a meeting with Master Colix the night he died," I said without preamble. "I was wondering why you never mentioned that."

"I did," Kennrick said. "I told you I was there that afternoon to—"

"Not the afternoon meeting," I interrupted him. "Later, after dinner, when you swapped out his keepsake blanket and his lozenges."

A muscle in Kennrick's cheek tightened. "Oh," he said. "That meeting."

"Yes, *that* meeting," I said. "Why didn't you tell us about it?"

Kennrick seemed to wilt a little in his seat. "Because I'd been ordered to stay away from him and the other Shorshians."

I flicked a glance at Muzzfor. He was watching Kennrick, his expression set in that neutral mask so beloved by prosecutors eyeing potential witnesses, or lions checking out a herd of elk. "Ordered by whom?" I asked.

"*Usantra* Givvrac," Kennrick said. "He thought I was spending too much time back in third and told me to give it a rest."

"Were you?" I asked. "Spending too much time back there, I mean?"

Kennrick looked sideways at Muzzfor. "I didn't think so," he said. "Others obviously had different opinions."

"You also spent a great deal of time with them aboard the torchliner from Earth," Muzzfor said.

"But not because I was trying to influence their votes,"

Kennrick insisted. "I just happen to like Shorshians, that's all. And Shorshic food, too. It was just natural that the five of us liked to spend time together."

"Especially on the torchliner, where there aren't any travel-class barriers between passengers?" I asked.

"Exactly," Kennrick said, looking back at me. "I was just trying to keep up those friendships here, that's all."

"To the point of defying *Usantra* Givvrac's orders about staying away from them?"

Kennrick grimaced. "The only reason I went back there was to tell Master Colix why I wouldn't be able to share the halfway-celebration meal with them," he said. "It didn't seem right to just disappear without explanation."

"What did he say?"

"Nothing, because I didn't tell him," Kennrick said. "When I got there he wasn't feeling well, and I decided it wasn't the time to drop this on him, too." He winced. "If I'd realized he was dying . . . anyway, I got his blanket down for him and put his lozenge bag in its place, and said good night."

"Did you lock the upper compartment before you returned his ticket to him?" I asked.

"Of course." Abruptly, Kennrick's eyes widened. "I'll be damned. *Logra* Emikai!"

"What about him?" I asked.

"His locksmith's bypass mimic," Kennrick said, his eyes darkening with anger. "*He's* the one who sneaked in and stole Master Colix's lozenges."

"Interesting thought," I said. "Why would he do that?"

"How should I know?" Kennrick growled. "The point is that no one had to have Master Colix's ticket to get in there."

I looked at Bayta, eyebrows raised. "Bayta?" I said.

"*Logra* Emikai's device doesn't work on Quadrail locks,"

she said. "The Spiders have tried it on several, and it won't even read them, let alone duplicate the trip codes."

"Maybe, maybe not," Kennrick said. "Do you have it?"

"At the moment, yes," I told him. "Why?"

"I'd like to take a look at it," he said, holding out his hand.

"Why?" I repeated, making no move toward my pocket. "You heard her—the Spiders have already concluded it's useless here."

"That assumes the Spiders actually know the mimic's whole potential," Kennrick countered, his hand still outstretched. "But there could very well be another tech layer below the surface that you can't reach unless you punch in an access code."

"And you know what *Logra* Emikai's code might be?"

"I already told you, I know a little about these gadgets," Kennrick replied. "Give me an hour, and I'll bet I can find the next level down."

"Interesting thought," I said again. "I'll ask the Spiders to have another go at it."

For a moment Kennrick and I locked eyes. Then, reluctantly, he withdrew his hand. "Fine," he said. "Whatever. But if you want my opinion, you've got the thief *and* the killer already tied up."

"Let's hope you're right," I said. "Thanks for clearing that up. We'll let you get back to your meeting now. Good day, *Asantra* Muzzfor."

"And to you, Mr. Compton," Muzzfor said, inclining his head. His face, I noted, still had that lion/elk expression.

Bayta waited until we were out in the corridor before speaking again. "Do you believe him about *Usantra* Givvrac's order?"

I shrugged. "It's plausible enough, I suppose, especially if Givvrac thought Kennrick was trying to unduly influence the three Shorshians back there."

"I wonder if Mr. Kennrick really does like Shorshians and their food that much," Bayta murmured.

"That part does seem a little thin," I agreed. "And of course, with Givvrac now inconveniently dead, there's no way to confirm any of it."

"I also find it strange that he disobeyed *Usantra* Givvrac and then didn't even tell Master Colix what he'd supposedly gone back there to say." Bayta hunched her shoulders. "You think we should ask the Modhri what they actually *did* talk about?"

"I don't think that'll be necessary," I told her. "Besides, there's also the possibility Kennrick thought he might be able to change Givvrac's mind enough to at least let him host the halfway celebration they were planning. In that case, he also wouldn't mention his new marching orders." I glanced behind us to make sure no one was within earshot. "Personally, I'm more interested in Kennrick's ideas about Emikai's mimic. *Could* it have another programming layer to it?"

"I suppose that's possible," she said. "I'll have the twitters look into it."

"Thanks," I said. "By the way, it sounded earlier like you were having doubts about Aronobal starting that rumor about us clobbering Emikai and throwing him off the train. That still true?"

She looked suspiciously at me. "Why?"

"Because I agree with you," I said. "More intriguing is the fact that Kennrick's IQ seems to have dropped a few points today."

"What do you mean?"

"I mean he's being remarkably slow at picking up on the obvious," I said. "First there was your suggestion that Aronobal should be trying to find out what we know instead of starting a rumor to keep us away from her. The obvious counterargument is that Aronobal is the amateur part of the team—amateur in the skullduggery aspects, anyway—and hasn't got the chops to brazen out a role like that. That should also have occurred to Kennrick, only apparently it never did."

I nodded back over my shoulder. "And now it only just occurs to him, after a whole bunch of hours, that Emikai's mimic is the perfect solution to the mystery of Colix's vanishing lozenges."

"Maybe he's just not as good at this as you are," Bayta suggested.

"Or maybe there are other reasons," I said. "Such as hoping we'll think of the mimic ourselves so he doesn't have to look like he's grabbing on to the first diversion that comes along."

Bayta pursed her lips. "So if Dr. Aronobal didn't start the rumor, who did? And why?"

"Not sure about that," I admitted. "On the surface, I can't see what sense it makes."

"Maybe it doesn't make sense because there's no sense to be made," Bayta said hesitantly. "Maybe *Usantra* Givvrac was right, that the killer is just insane."

"He's not insane, and it does make sense," I said firmly. "We just have to find the right way to put the pieces together."

She sighed. "I'm sorry I'm not being more help," she said. "Putting people's motives and thoughts under a microscope— that's not something I'm good at."

I stared at her, my stomach tightening as a memory abruptly popped into my mind: Emikai, still twitching from the aftereffects of the *kwi*, studying my luggage as if he could see through it to the spectral analysis equipment he assumed was inside.

There it was, the nagging feeling I'd been wrestling with. And with it, the clue I hadn't even known I'd been missing. Not what had been done, but what *hadn't* been done.

And suddenly, I had it. I had it all.

"Too bad *Korak* Fayr isn't here—" Bayta broke off with a muffled gasp as I grabbed her arm and picked up my pace, dragging her forward. "Frank?"

"Come on," I told her grimly. "We've got work to do."

"You've figured it out?" she asked, a flicker of hope in her voice.

"I think so," I said, my mind flashing back to the very beginning of our journey. Bayta had called it, all the way back then. She'd called it exactly.

My past had indeed come back to haunt me.

"It's the Modhri?" she asked, her arm tensing inside my grip.

"No," I said. "Actually, it's worse."

We spent the rest of the afternoon discussing the case, and laying out the facts to test against my new theory. By the time we broke for dinner, I was ninety percent convinced I was right.

With luck, I would get that final ten percent tonight.

I waited until two in the morning by the train's clocks, when even the most dedicated night owls among the passengers were probably thinking about turning in. Bayta offered to come with me, but I told her to go back to bed. There was nothing that could put the damper on a heart-to-heart, off-the-record conversation like having a third party present.

And so I made my solitary way back through first, through second, and through third, until I was in the baggage car by the dead bodies, standing in front of *Logra* Emikai.

I'd left the Filly in a fairly awkward and uncomfortable position when I'd retied his bonds, mainly because with my limited resources I hadn't had a lot of alternatives. To my mild surprise, I found he'd risen to the challenge of his situation. With strategic repositioning of the chair, toilet, and table, he'd been able to stretch out instead of having to sleep sitting upright. His head was pillowed, hammock-style, on one of his pinioned arms, while the other hung free. It looked tolerable, even marginally comfortable.

Of course, if he turned over in his sleep he would instantly roll off his makeshift three-point bed and land on the floor, which would snap him fully awake as well as possibly giving one or both of his arms a nasty sprain. Still, it was an ingenious use of resources. One more indication, I reminded myself, of the kind of person I was dealing with.

"Are you here to watch me sleep?"

Mentally, I tipped him a salute. His eyes still appeared closed, but I could see now the small slits he was watching me through. Professional, indeed. "Sorry—just me," I said. "I gather you were hoping for someone else?"

"Indeed," he said, opening his eyes all the way and shifting back up to a sitting position on the chair. "Still, a clever perpetrator seldom tries the same trick twice on the same person."

"You know something about perpetrators, do you?" I suggested, pulling out my multitool and flicking out the small knife blade as I walked toward him. "I thought you probably did."

He drew back as he watched me approach, his eyes on the knife. "What do you do?" he asked cautiously.

"Not what you're thinking," I assured him. Setting the blade against the safety webbing tying his left wrist to the crate stack, I carefully sliced through it. "I think I know what's going on," I said as I stepped to his other side and cut his right arm free, too. "But I need your help and expertise to prove it."

"What expertise is that?" he asked suspiciously as he massaged his wrists.

"The kind I'd expect," I said, "from a fellow cop."

He stiffened, just enough to show I'd hit the mark. "You misread," he said. "I am not an enforcement officer."

"Former cop, then," I said. "Come on—we both know I'm right. Back in my compartment you talked about not believing something until you had evidence of its existence, and of needing to reach the required legal bar for action. Those are both phrases I've heard before from Filiaelian security officers."

"That hardly constitutes compelling evidence."

"We Humans are pretty good with hunches," I said. "And of course, your current evasiveness just adds weight to my conclusion."

For a moment he eyed me. "Very well," he said. "I was indeed once an enforcement officer. But no longer. I am retired, with no official authority from any Filiaelian governmental body."

"Close enough," I said. "Let me try another hunch on you. Before your retirement, you were a forensic investigator."

His nose blaze darkened with surprise. "That was indeed my specialty. Remarkable. May I ask how you reached that conclusion?"

"It was a combination of things," I said. "You seemed very interested in my technique as I was taking samples from the air filter in Terese German's car. You also didn't fall for that 'congenital disease after-elements' soap bubble I spun for the rest of the passengers, either. More interestingly, you knew roughly how big a standard spectroscopic analyzer was, which was why you were studying my luggage last night in my compartment. You were trying to figure out if I'd lied about that, too."

I gestured behind me. "But mostly because Bayta and I

nearly caught you snooping around back here a couple of days ago. My first thought was that you were returning Master Colix's ticket to him after having used it to steal the lozenges from his storage compartment."

"The tablets were medicine?" Emikai asked, looking surprised again. "Ms. German said they were foodstuffs."

"Ms. German is not the most observant person in the galaxy," I said dryly. "Though to be fair, Master Colix wasn't exactly advertising it, either. Speaking of Ms. German, what exactly is going on with her, anyway?"

He shook his head. "I cannot tell you."

"Come on, *Logra* Emikai," I cajoled. "This is just between two ex-cops, remember? By the way, what kind of title is *logra*? It obviously doesn't come from *lomagra*, as my partner thought."

"It is a new rank, a title given me by my current employers," he said. "It refers to the ancient Filiaelian name for a *bulwark*, or a protector of the people."

"Ancient Filiaelian, eh?" I commented. "We have people who like mining old languages, too. Anyway, the point is that I already know Ms. German is pregnant, which is why you were concerned enough about the air quality in her car to try to break into my compartment to see what I'd found out about that. I also know that you and Dr. Aronobal are escorting her from Earth to Filiaelian space. I just want to know why."

He gazed at me for a long moment. I waited, keeping my best encouraging expression in place. Finally, he shrugged. "I suppose it cannot hurt. Several weeks ago Ms. German was assaulted near her home in the Western Alliance and impregnated by her attacker. Dr. Aronobal and I were already on Earth, seeking Human subjects for genetic testing, and we received orders to offer her our assistance and invite her to accompany us back to the Filiaelian Assembly for medical treatment and study."

"Who exactly did these orders come from?" I asked.

"One of Dr. Aronobal's superiors, I presume," he said. "I was never shown the actual message. We offered Ms. German our assistance, which was accepted, and we are now returning to the Filiaelian Assembly with her."

"Interesting timing, you being right there in the vicinity of this attack and all," I commented. Actually, the timing struck me as more suspicious than interesting, but this wasn't the time to go into that. "Dr. Aronobal's part I understand, kindly physician and all that. Where exactly do you come into it?"

"To be honest, I am not entirely certain," he said hesitantly. "I was asked to come out of retirement and accompany Dr. Aronobal to Earth as assistant and protector."

"Someone thought she needed protecting?"

"Apparently so." Emikai smiled suddenly. "It was apparently thought that I had the necessary skills for the position."

"And correctly so," I assured him, rubbing my throat. "So what kind of genetic testing are they planning for Ms. German?"

"That I also do not know," he said. "But it must be highly urgent for us to have been hired to bring her all the way across the galaxy."

"So it would seem," I agreed. And that, I sensed, was all I was going to get out of him on this subject. Time to move on. "But as I was saying, my first assumption was that you were returning Master Colix's ticket. But I know now that you stole neither the ticket nor the lozenges. Ergo, you must have come here for some other purpose." I raised my eyebrows. "You were examining the bodies, weren't you?"

He inclined his head. "I was attempting to do so," he said. "You interrupted me before I could complete my investigation."

"I presume you got far enough to notice the needle marks

on the three Shorshians," I said, mentally crossing my fingers. *Ninety percent sure . . .* "Anything interesting about them?"

He smiled tightly. "You would not ask unless you already knew," he said. "Your unstated hunch is correct: the needle marks were made *after* the victims' deaths."

I felt my stomach tighten. "You're absolutely sure about that?"

"I am," he said. "I also suspect the tip of the needle is still buried within *di*-Master Strinni's skin."

"Not anymore, but it was," I said. There it was, the last ten percent of doubt. "Thank you, *Logra* Emikai. I believe you've just helped me identify a killer."

His eyes locked hard into mine. "Who?"

I reached into my pocket and tossed him his first-class pass. "Come to the first-class dining car tomorrow at ten o'clock," I told him. "I'll introduce you."

"Thank you," he said softly as he slid the pass into a pocket. "I will be there."

"Good." I gestured in the direction of the bodies. "In the meantime, I have a couple of final tests to run on the bodies. I was hoping you would assist me."

He inclined his head. "I would be honored."

An hour later, our tests completed, we left the baggage car. I dropped Emikai off at his seat among the sea of privacy-shielded sleepers and continued on forward. I hoped he would get a good night's rest.

I hoped I would, too. But I still had one more task to perform.

I found *Osantra* Qiddicoj sleeping in the open, without his sleep canopy deployed. Qiddicoj himself was sound asleep, but the Modhri inside him was awake and alert and obviously waiting up for me. Our conversation took another hour, and when I finally dragged myself back to my own bed I had the whole, bloody story.

Back when I worked for Westali, the hours leading up to a high-profile arrest were generally cluttered with a million last-minute details. There were warrants to get, backup to arrange, logistics to plan, loopholes to anticipate, and bolt-holes to plug. If you did everything right, the arrest itself was almost anticlimactic. If you did anything wrong, the whole event was likely to blow up in your face.

But here on the Quadrail, where Spider authority was absolute and bureaucratic red tape nonexistent, none of those details was relevant. As a result, I got to spend eight of those final hours asleep. A more restful sleep than I'd had since Bayta and I had first been summoned to the second/third dispensary to watch Master Colix die. It was finally almost over.

I really should have known better.

It was ten minutes to ten, and Bayta and I were just finishing a light breakfast, when Emikai arrived. "I trust I'm not overly early?" he asked, glancing around the dining car as if he expected the killer to be wearing a sign announcing his identity.

"Not at all," I told him, standing up and offering Bayta my hand. She didn't need my help, of course, but Filly cops were genetically engineered toward courtesy, and my show of politeness toward my partner might buy me a few points when it came time to shake him down for more information. "The rest of the group should be assembled," I added as I gestured to the entryway. "Shall we go?"

I led the way four cars to the rear. Kennrick and the three remaining contract-team Fillies were indeed there, sitting in a circle and talking earnestly. For once, there were no dealt cards sitting in front of the group. "Greetings to you, *Esantra* Worrbin," I greeted the head of the group. "And to you, *Asantra* Muzzfor, and you, *Asantra* Dallilo," I continued, nodding to each in turn. "I appreciate your giving me a few moments of your time."

"What's *he* doing here?" Kennrick growled, eyeing Emikai darkly.

"I asked him to join us," I said.

"And he got free how?"

"It was actually pretty easy once I'd cut his ropes," I said. "The reason I asked you all here—"

"Without consulting any of us first?" Kennrick interrupted. "Our opinions and concerns don't matter?"

"Actually, no, they don't," I said. "The reason I asked you all here was so that you could bear witness to the end of the ordeal. I finally know the identity of the murderer."

Muzzfor sat up a little straighter. "You've found him?" he asked, an edge to his voice. "Why did you not say so earlier?"

"Because until last night I wasn't a hundred percent sure," I told him. "I thought—"

"Last *night*?" Muzzfor echoed. "And yet you waited until now to speak? How many more of us might have died in the dark hours because of your lack of haste?"

"You aren't in any danger," I assured him. "Not anymore. The contract team was indeed the target, but not for the reasons we all thought."

"A moment," Worrbin spoke up. "If this matter concerns the contract team, all members should be present. Master Tririn and Dr. Witherspoon must be summoned."

"He's right," Kennrick seconded. "And as long as you're

going to get them passed up from third, you might as well go the whole dit réc mystery route and have the rest of the suspects join us, too."

"Which suspects are those?" I asked.

"All of *his* friends," Kennrick said, nodding toward Emikai. "Dr. Aronobal and that Human girl, Terese whatever."

"Terese German," I said. "Actually, she's not a suspect. Never was, really, if you think about it."

"Why not?" Dallilo asked, gazing down his long Filly nose at Emikai.

"Because *di*-Master Strinni and *Usantra* Givvrac were killed here in first class," I said. "Ms. German didn't have access to this part of the train."

"Dr. Aronobal did, though," Kennrick persisted. "She and Dr. Witherspoon were making the rounds between here and third all the time."

"True," I agreed. "Still, I think we can dispense with their company for the present." I raised my eyebrows at him. "So, Kennrick. You want to tell everyone why you killed them? Or shall I?"

NINETEEN :

I'd said it so casually that for the first couple of seconds no one seemed to get it. Then, almost in unison, Worrbin and the others turned to look at Kennrick. "You're not serious," Worrbin said, sounding stunned. "Mr. *Kennrick*?"

"Absolutely serious," I assured him, watching Kennrick closely. His eyes were just starting to widen with shock as the words sank in. Exactly the correct reaction, with exactly the correct timing. The man was good, all right. "Would you like to make a statement, Kennrick?"

"Yes," Kennrick said, coming out of his pretended paralysis. "I want to state that you're completely and certifiably insane. Where in *hell* do you get off making outrageous accusations like that?"

"Truth is never popular, is it?" I said regretfully. "Fine—if you don't want to tell them, I will. The point is—"

"Just a moment, Mr. Compton," Worrbin interrupted me. "I have no great personal affection for Mr. Kennrick, but you cannot simply make public statements like that without proof in hand. *Have* you such proof?"

"Let's take this one step at a time," I suggested. "The point is—"

"I knew it," Kennrick muttered under his breath. "I *knew* you didn't just quit Westali. Loose damn cannon—they fired your butt, didn't they?"

"The point is," I said, raising my voice a little, "and the point we all missed, was that the murders had nothing to do with the contract itself. They were, in fact, an experiment. A field test to see if a new kind of murder technique could be slipped through Spider security and used aboard a Quadrail."

Around us, the car was starting to quiet down as more and more passengers tuned in on our conversation. "What is this technique?" Muzzfor asked.

"Nothing I care to talk about in the open," I said. "But trust me, it works."

"And I presume you've got an explanation for how *Usantra* Givvrac and the three Shorshians died in entirely different ways?" Kennrick demanded. "Come on, Compton. Playing detective can be fun, but you're way over the line with this one."

"Actually, I believe *Usantra* Givvrac's death was mostly accidental," I said. "Collateral damage, as it were, from *di*-Master Strinni's murder."

Muzzfor stirred in his seat. "*Esantra* Worrbin, I submit that this is not the proper venue for such a sensitive discussion," he said, looking significantly around the car.

"Agreed," Worrbin said grimly. "We must find a place with more privacy."

"We can go to my compartment," Kennrick offered. "There's enough room there."

"Or you can just confess and surrender now," I suggested.

"Once you're properly secured, I can go over the details with the others at their convenience."

Kennrick snorted. "If you think I'm going to confess to something I didn't do, you're crazy."

"I further submit that if there is to be a medical discussion that Dr. Witherspoon be asked to join us," Muzzfor continued.

"And Dr. Aronobal, too," Kennrick added. "She and Witherspoon are the only ones with access to hypos."

I felt a surge of relieved affirmation. I'd hoped he would fall for that one. "And how exactly did you know the three Shorshic bodies had hypo marks in them?" I asked.

If this had been a proper dit rec mystery, Kennrick would have inhaled sharply as he belatedly realized the folly of his revelation. Unfortunately, here in the real world, he was right on top of it. "How else could the poison have gotten into their systems?" he retorted without hesitation. "Besides, whoever jumped you and Witherspoon wanted that replacement hypo for *something*."

"He's correct," Muzzfor said. "Such obvious deduction is hardly proof of any wrongdoing."

"No, the murderer wanted the hypo for something, all right," I confirmed. "But not as a replacement. Kennrick knew I was sniffing around the other possible methods for introducing poison into someone's system, and he decided he needed to send me off in the wrong direction."

Worrbin grunted. "You make no sense."

"Actually, I make perfect sense," I countered. Kennrick's expression, I noted, was still walking that realistic path between bewilderment and outrage.

But there should have been something else there, too, a hint of concern as I backed him slowly into a corner. Only there was no such concern that I could detect.

What did he know that I didn't?

"His best shot at a wrong direction was to make me think the cadmium that killed Master Colix and the others had been injected," I continued. "So the night I was attacked he hid under the sleep canopy in *di*-Master Strinni's vacant seat, knowing either Dr. Aronobal or Dr. Witherspoon would eventually show up in answer to *Osantra* Qiddicoj's call for medical help. It was just my bad luck I decided to stick with Dr. Witherspoon that night. Kennrick waited until we'd passed, clobbered both of us, and stole the hypo."

"I was in my compartment," Kennrick said in a tone of strained patience. "The Spider who came for me will testify to that."

"By *then* you were, sure," I said. "After you got the hypo, you slipped past the activity in the dispensary and beat it back to your compartment so you could pretend to be asleep when we sent for you."

I looked back at the three Fillies. "But later that night, once things had calmed down, he went back to the morgue and made needle marks in the bodies. He also made sure to break off the needle tip in *di*-Master Strinni to make us think that was the reason the murderer needed a replacement hypo. After that, he probably just dumped the rest of the hypo down the toilet into the reclamation system."

"You say he wanted you to think the poison had been injected," Muzzfor said. "What makes you think it wasn't?"

"Because I availed myself of the services of *Logra* Emikai," I told him. "He's a former law enforcement officer who specialized in forensic investigations, and he confirmed that the hypo marks had been made postmortem."

The three Fillies looked questioningly at each other. "Is that the sum of your evidence, Mr. Compton?" Worrbin asked.

"Isn't it enough?" I countered.

"No, it is not," Worrbin said flatly. "I'm not convinced."

I grimaced. That wasn't really surprising, I conceded, given that Kennrick had avoided all my guilty-reaction traps and I couldn't afford to give them my actual evidence. "I'm sorry to hear that," I told Worrbin. "But that's certainly your privilege. This was just a courtesy call anyway."

"What do you mean, a courtesy call?" Worrbin demanded, his blaze darkening ominously.

"I mean that I really don't have to convince any of you of Kennrick's guilt," I said. "Here inside the Tube, the Spiders are in charge. Thank you for your time—we'll take it from here."

"Like hell you will," Kennrick said, standing up.

"Don't try it, Kennrick," I warned, motioning Emikai to step in a bit closer. "It's two against one, and we're both former cops."

"This has gone far enough," Worrbin said, his voice suddenly gone lofty and imperious with the weight of thousands of years of Filiaelian history and thousands of planets of Filiaelian geography. "This Human is associated with us, and through us with the Filiaelian Assembly. I forbid you to imprison him without incontestable proof of guilt." He pointed to Emikai. "I further call upon this former enforcement officer to support my decision."

"*Logra* Emikai is with me," I reminded him.

"Not any more," Emikai said softly.

I turned to look at him, a sinking feeling in my stomach. "We're not in Filiaelian territory, *Logra* Emikai," I reminded him carefully. "You're not required to obey their orders."

"Unfortunately, I am," Emikai said. He looked decidedly unhappy about it, but there was no wavering in his voice. "He is an *esantra* of the Filiaelian Assembly. No matter where in the galaxy we find ourselves, I have no choice but to uphold his legal decisions." His eyes flicked to Worrbin, then back to me. "It is what I am," he added.

And so it was. Retired or not, he'd been genetically engineered to be a cop, and the absence of his badge and gun didn't change that.

I looked back at Kennrick. His arms were crossed over his chest, a righteously indignant expression plastered across his face, a hint of a smirk lurking behind his eyes. Was Worrbin's interference the back door he'd been counting on? "You want proof, *Esantra* Worrbin?" I asked. "Fine." I held out my hand toward Kennrick. "Your reader, please."

Kennrick's expression didn't change, but the subtle smirk was suddenly gone. "Why?" he asked.

"Give it to me and I'll show you," I said.

"Not a chance," he said flatly. "All my personal records are on it."

"Consider this a subpoena," I said. "Let's start by showing them who Whitman Kennrick really is."

Kennrick looked at the Fillies. "*Esantra* Worrbin?"

Worrbin looked at him, then at me, then back at Kennrick. "Give him your reader," he ordered.

Kennrick's lips puckered, but he nodded. "Fine," he said. "But let it be noted that this is under protest." He reached his right hand into his jacket, got a grip on something, and started to pull his hand back out.

And without warning, he leaped in front of Bayta, his left fist snapping in a short punch from the hip into her solar plexus.

She gasped and bent forward, grabbing for her stomach. Kennrick kept moving, sidestepping around behind her, and I saw now that he was holding a pair of small cylinders in his right hand. As he turned back to face me he flipped one of the cylinders to his left hand, his hands tracing a quick pattern over and around Bayta's head. As I belatedly started toward them, he jerked both hands back toward his face, Bayta's head snapping backward in perfect synchronization.

And as her hands grabbed at her neck, I saw the glint of the thin wire wrapped around her throat.

"Careful, Compton," Kennrick warned, his voice quiet and deadly, as I came to an abrupt halt. "That goes for the rest of you, too."

"Do as he says," I croaked out through a suddenly dry mouth, my heart pounding in my throat. Oh, no. God, no. "Take it easy, Kennrick."

"Take it *off* easy, did you say?" Kennrick asked. He twitched the cylindrical handles of his garrote a little, making Bayta twitch in response.

"*Damn* it—" I broke off, clenching my teeth, fury and terror bubbling in my throat. Bayta's face was tight and pale, a hint of pain in her eyes from Kennrick's gut punch, her fingers trying uselessly to force their way between the wire and her throat. "Don't hurt her."

Kennrick smiled, a cold, evil thing. "Say please."

I took a deep breath. "Please don't hurt her."

"Good," he said, his voice brisk and almost businesslike. "Well, this is awkward, I must say. Any suggestions as to how we should proceed?"

"You want trouble, I'm available," I said, holding my arms away from my sides. From the positioning of his hands, a detached part of my mind noted, the garrote wire had to cross itself behind Bayta's head, meaning the loop completely encircled her neck instead of just pulling against the front and sides. It also meant that all Kennrick had to do was pull his hands apart to kill her. "Let her go, and you can do whatever you want to me."

"Oh, I know," he said brightly. "That handy little gadget of yours, the one you used on *Logra* Emikai two nights ago. Where is it?"

"I have it," Bayta croaked.

"Where?"

"Here." She reached for her right front pocket.

And gasped, her hand darting back up to her throat as Kennrick twitched the garrote again. "No, you just hold still," he ordered. "I'll get it."

I felt a surge of adrenaline. In order to get into her pocket, he would either have to let go of one end of his garrote or else hold both handles in a single hand. Either way, it would mean a brief chance to get to him before he could use the wire against her. If I was quick, and lucky, I might be able to get to her in time.

But he was already ahead of me. Watching me closely, he slid the wire around Bayta's throat, adjusting the positions of the handles, until the one in his right hand was back by his own throat. A quick twitch of his fingers, and he'd clipped the handle to his jacket collar. With his left hand still applying pressure against Bayta's throat, he reached with his right around her hip and pulled the *kwi* from her pocket. "There we go," he said, deftly wrapping it in place around his knuckles before unclipping the other garrote handle. "I think that officially leaves me holding all the cards."

"What do you want?" I asked.

"For now, to go back to my compartment," he said. "The lady goes with me, of course."

"Take me instead," I offered again.

He smiled tightly. "I'd rather bed down with a Malayan pit viper," he said. "Don't worry, I won't hurt her. Not unless you force me to."

I focused on Bayta's face, searching desperately for inspiration. The last thing I wanted was to let him get Bayta behind locked doors, with access to whatever other tricks he might have smuggled aboard. But with the wire pressing against Bayta's throat, there was nothing I could do without risking her life.

"Patience is a virtue," Bayta murmured.

"She's right," Kennrick seconded. "Your move, Compton."

I took another deep breath. "Go," I said.

"We'll talk later," he promised. He glanced once over his shoulder, making sure the path was clear. Then, holding Bayta close, he started backing toward the front of the car. I watched them go, my hands curled into helpless fists at my sides, still trying to come up with something—anything—I could do.

They were halfway to the vestibule when *Krel* Vevri quietly detached himself from the wall where he'd been standing and began moving silently to intercept.

I felt my breath catch in my throat. Vevri's eyes were shining with determination, a slight but unmistakable sag in the scales around his hawk beak. It was the Modhri who was currently in command of that body, coming to Bayta's rescue.

And about to get her killed.

I watched the unfolding drama, my brain and muscles paralyzed by indecision. Should I warn Kennrick of the approaching Juri, thereby temporarily protecting Bayta's life but destroying any chance the Modhri might have of stopping him? Or should I keep quiet, cross my fingers, and hope the Modhri's million-to-one shot actually came through?

I was still frozen in uncertainty when the decision was taken out of my hands. Abruptly, Kennrick spun halfway around, swinging Bayta around with him like a full-body shield as he lifted his right hand over her shoulder. I saw his thumb shift its grip on the garrote handle and squeeze the *kwi*'s firing switch.

Without even a twitch, Vevri collapsed to the floor with a thud and lay still.

Before anyone else could react Kennrick swung himself and Bayta back around to face me. "I'll be charitable and assume that wasn't your idea, Compton," he said. "If it happens again, there'll be consequences." He lifted the *kwi* again slightly. "This really *is* a handy little gadget."

And abruptly my spinning mind caught the tracks again, my eyes shifting to the unconscious Juri Kennrick had just shot with the *kwi*. The *kwi* that could only be activated by Bayta or one of the Spiders.

How the hell had Kennrick gotten the damn thing to work?

If any of the other passengers had it in mind to intervene, Vevri's failure convinced them otherwise. No one else so much as blinked as the killer and his hostage backed into the vestibule and vanished from sight.

The door had barely closed before Emikai started toward the door, a glint of fire in his eyes. "No—let them go," I said quickly.

"We cannot let him get to his compartment," Emikai said.

"How are you going to stop him without getting Bayta killed?" I demanded.

"He will not harm her," Emikai insisted. "Without a hostage, he is dead."

"So he kills her and grabs someone else," I snarled, my legs literally shaking with the overwhelming urge to go after Kennrick myself. "Don't you understand? This man is a professional, and he's clearly thought this through. We can't just go charging in after him. We have to figure out what his plan is, and outthink him."

Emikai looked at the door where Kennrick and Bayta had vanished. "And if we cannot?"

"We can," I said grimly. "We will."

For a long moment Emikai and I just stared at each other. Then, his shoulders slumped a little and he nodded. "She is your assistant," he said. "He is of your people. I yield to your authority."

"Thank you," I said. I squeezed my hands into fists to force out some of the adrenaline flooding my system and tried to think. "Okay, here's what we do. First of all, we need to make sure not to spook Kennrick again. Go find a conductor and tell him to alert any Spiders between here and Kennrick's compartment to make sure none of the other passengers tries to play hero."

"What if the conductor won't listen to me?"

"He will," I said. If he didn't, he would surely check telepathically with Bayta, who would just as surely confirm the order. "Next, we need to isolate Kennrick from other potential hostages. Tell the Spider to start figuring out where we can temporarily put the rest of the passengers in that car."

"I will obey," he said. "What about you?"

"Someone needs to talk to Kennrick and find out exactly what he wants." I squared my shoulders. "I guess that's me."

I forced myself to take my time, not wanting to come within sight of Kennrick before he reached his goal lest he think I was crowding him. I passed through the exercise/dispensary, shower, and storage cars, bypassed the dining car with its mostly oblivious patrons, and reached the first coach car.

I'd made it barely five steps inside when a hand darted in from my right, grabbed my arm, and spun me around.

And I found myself staring into the angry eyes of a Tra'ho government oathling. "What did you do?" he demanded.

I took another look at his face, with its sagging jowls and the slight flatness of the eyes. "Later, Modhri," I said shortly, reaching over to pull his hand off my arm.

"Not later," he insisted. "Now. What did you do?"

"What did *you* do?" I countered. "That stunt could have gotten Bayta killed."

"And so you allow the weapon to work?" he shot back. "How does that benefit either of us?"

"What makes you think *I* control the weapon?" I growled, glancing surreptitiously around the car. Fortunately, the rest of the passengers were already gathered in small knots, talking quietly but nervously among themselves, with little attention to spare for us. Kennrick's passage must have made quite an impression.

"Do not lie," the Modhri bit out. "I know the weapon must be activated. There was no Spider present. The agent herself would not have done so. That leaves only you."

"And since when do I have—?" I broke off, a jolt of understanding abruptly hitting me. "No, you're wrong," I said. "Bayta *did* activate it."

"Why would she foil my attempt to rescue her?"

"Because your attempt didn't have a chance," I told him. "And because she was thinking ahead."

"To what?"

"To the next real chance we have, whenever that is," I said, smiling tightly. "Don't you get it? *Kennrick now thinks he has a functional weapon.*"

The other's face worked as he thought it through. Then, slowly, the anger faded from his eyes. "Indeed," the Modhri murmured. "So the next time he thinks to use the weapon, it will fail?"

"Or at least the next time he tries to use it when Bayta judges we have a real chance of success," I said. "That doesn't mean one of us won't get zapped if we try something stupid again."

"Understood," the Modhri said. "What's our next move?"

"I'm going to go talk to him," I said. "Try to find out what he wants, how he expects to get it, and hopefully find a chink in his armor that we can exploit."

"Dangerous," the Modhri rumbled. "But necessary. What do you wish me to do in your absence?"

"For the moment, just hang back and let me work," I said. "If the *kwi* was still on its lowest unconsciousness setting, your Jurian walker should recover in an hour or two." I leveled a finger at him. "But I mean that about letting me work. We *will* nail him, but we'll do it my way. Understand?"

"I'll await your instructions," the Modhri promised reluctantly. "Good hunting to you."

"Thanks." I nodded. "In the meantime, if you really want something to do, you could help soothe your fellow passengers. You might also start getting them mentally prepared for some changes in their traveling conditions. We're going to evacuate the rest of that car's compartments, which will mean an influx of displaced travelers settling down in here and the other coach cars."

"I can do that." The Tra'ho's eyes shifted to the front of the car. "What is this?"

I turned to look. Maneuvering his way awkwardly through the vestibule door was a pale, frail-looking Nemut in a Shorshic vectored-thrust-powered support chair. His truncated-cone-shaped mouth had a slight distortion in it, and one of his angled shoulder muscles seemed frozen in a permanent off-center hunch. I'd seen him a few times since we left Homshil, mostly eating solitary meals in the dining car. "Trouble?" I asked quietly.

"I don't know," the Modhri said. "His name is Minnario, journeying to a Filiaelian clinic in hopes of finding a genetic cure for his congenital difficulties. But I've never seen him leave his compartment except for meals, which he always takes alone."

Something pricked at the back of my neck. "Do you know which compartment he's got?" I asked.

"No," the Modhri said, his oathling topcut wobbling back and forth as the Tra'ho shook his head. "None of the conversations I've overheard has mentioned that."

Minnario finished getting through the door and started down the center of the car, his head turning slowly back and forth as he studied the passengers. His eyes passed me, then paused and came back. His fingers shifted on the chair's control box, and he altered course in our direction.

"Wait here," I told the Modhri, and moved ahead to intercept. "Are you looking for me?" I asked as we neared each other.

Minnario looked down at a plate that was fastened to the chair's control box by a slender stem. [Are you the Human who chases the other Humans?] he croaked in slightly lisping Nemuspee as he brought the chair to a halt.

"I am," I confirmed. "You have a message for me?"

There was another pause as he again studied the plate. I took a final couple of steps toward him and saw that it was running him a transcript of what I'd just said. Apparently, deafness was another of his congenital defects. [I was told to give you this,] he croaked. Reaching to a pouch in his lap, he carefully extracted a Quadrail ticket. [The key to my compartment.]

"Let me guess," I said grimly. "Your compartment connects to the male Human's?"

[I don't know where the male Human goes,] he said. [I was asked to give you my key, and told I could move into this one.] He held up another ticket, this one glittering with the diamond-dust edges of a first-class, unlimited-use pass. Bayta's ticket. [Is that all right?] he croaked. [Should I remain here instead?]

"No, that's all right," I said, taking his ticket from him. "Go ahead and make yourself comfortable. I may ask to come in later to collect some of the female's personal effects."

[Certainly,] he said when the transcript had finished scrolling across the plate. [Is there trouble? The female seemed frightened.]

"There is, but it doesn't concern you," I assured him. "Thank you for this." Stepping past him, I continued forward.

The corridor of the rear compartment car was empty. I made my way through it, then entered the equally deserted corridor of the middle car. I located Minnario's compartment and used his ticket to open the door. "Hello?" I called carefully.

"There you are," Kennrick's muffled voice came back. "Don't just stand there—come on in."

I stepped into the compartment, letting the door slide shut behind me. The room was a typical Quadrail compartment, to which strategically placed grips and bars had been added to assist Minnario with his physical challenges. At the front of the room, the dividing wall between compartments had been opened about ten centimeters and a soft light was showing through. "Okay, I'm in," I called.

"Come over to the divider and take a look," Kennrick's voice came through the gap. "But carefully, please. Very carefully."

I crossed the compartment, stepping past the curve couch frozen midway into its collapse into the divider. I reached the opening and eased an eye around the edge.

Kennrick was all the way across the room, sitting cross-legged on the bed and turning the *kwi* thoughtfully over in his hands. Between him and me, sitting with unnatural stillness in the computer desk chair, was Bayta, a pair of wire loops wrapped around her neck.

"Let me explain the situation," Kennrick said. "You'll note the usual control on the wall beside you that will open the divider the rest of the way. I'd strongly advise you not to bump it."

"Because if I do, one of those wire loops will strangle her?" I suggested.

"It might," Kennrick said. "These are actually thinner wires than the garrote I pulled on you a few minutes ago, so it's possible the loop would slice her head clean off instead of just strangling her. Me, I'm not all that anxious to find out for sure. But if you're curious, be my guest."

"No, that's all right," I said. "I suppose the other loop is fastened to the corridor door?"

"You suppose correctly," he said. "Rather clever, if I do say so myself."

"Oh, it's brilliant," I assured him. I'd wondered how he thought he would be able to hold out another two and a half weeks without falling asleep and thus leaving himself open to attack. With this setup, he could sleep until noon every day without worrying about anyone charging in on him. "Your boss will be proud."

"Thank you," he said. "Incidentally, what exactly gave me away? Assuming something *did* give me away, and that you weren't just blowing smoke out there."

"Oh, no, I'm on to you," I assured him. "You're my replacement, the man who's supposed to figure out how to take control of the Quadrail from the Spiders."

I cocked my head. "So tell me. How *is* our good friend Mr. Larry Cecil Hardin?"

TWENTY :

"I was right," Kennrick said, shaking his head in admiration. "The minute I saw you getting on my Quadrail I knew you were going to be trouble. So again: what gave me away?"

"Several things," I said. "Though it wasn't until I'd collected enough of them that I started to see the pattern. For starters, Colix wasn't even room temperature when you were blaming the Spiders for incompetence or worse. Given their seven-hundred-year spotless operational record, it was a strange attitude to take. In retrospect, I can see it was just part of the plan to undermine confidence in their ability to run the Quadrail."

"Yes, I thought you seemed surprised by that," Kennrick conceded. "I suppose it was a bit of a risk, but with Aronobal and a couple of Shorshians in the room I really couldn't afford to pass up the chance to start planting seeds."

"And it was a theme you kept coming back to the whole trip," I said, trying to visually backtrack the wires around Bayta's neck. But my field of view was too limited for me to see where and how either of them was attached at the far end. "You also were way too incompetent for the liaison job you'd supposedly been hired for. Quite a few members of your team agreed on that."

"I thought I already explained that," he reminded me.

"Yes, and rather badly, too," I said. "There must be hundreds of people on Earth who are competent at both the legal *and* the social aspects of Filly and Shorshic cultures. Surely Pellorian could have hired one of them in your place, if that was actually the job you were supposed to be doing."

"I'm starting to think Mr. Hardin could have hired someone better than me for the real job, too," Kennrick said calmly. "Fortunately, it's too late for him to reconsider."

"If I were you, I wouldn't make assumptions like that," I warned. "Not with Hardin. And of course, there was the near-riot you sparked by starting the rumor back in third class that I'd done away with *Logra* Emikai. That whole thing made no sense until I realized its purpose was to maneuver Bayta and me into a situation where you'd get to see the *kwi* in action again."

"Now, *that* one you shouldn't have caught," Kennrick commented. "Excellent. I can see why Mr. Hardin was so complimentary about you."

"He was complimentary about *me*?"

"Within the context of hating your guts, yes," Kennrick said. "Anything else? Come on—honest criticism is how we learn to do better the next time."

Only there wouldn't be a next time, I knew. The last thing the Spiders could afford—the last thing *any* of us could afford— was for him to make it to the next station and send a report back to Hardin on the success of his ghoulish little mission. One way or another, Kennrick was going to have to die aboard this train.

Even if Bayta had to die along with him.

"Compton?" Kennrick prompted. "You still there?"

"I'm still here," I assured him.

"Anything else?"

"Just one more," I said. "The bit that finally caught my attention. Remember when we hauled Emikai in here two nights ago and he was looking around trying to figure out if I really had a spectroscopic analyzer? He spent a lot of that time looking at my luggage, because obviously something like that would have to take up a lot of space."

"Obviously," Kennrick said. "So?"

"It got me thinking about the morning after Colix's death, when you barged into my compartment also wanting to see the results of my tissue analysis," I said. "Only unlike Emikai, you never even glanced at my luggage. Your eyes went instantly to my reader. My one-of-a-kind, high-tech, super-spy-loaded reader." I cocked my head. "Only it isn't one-of-a-kind anymore, is it?"

"Not anymore, no," he agreed. "You know, I never even thought about that. *Damn*, but you're good."

"You're too kind," I said. "Yours must be even more interesting than mine for you to have sacrificed your high-ground bluff to keep it out of my hands."

"Oh, it's probably no more advanced than yours," Kennrick said. "But I could hardly let you go poking around the encrypted files where my detailed report was hidden. Not with your familiarity with the thing."

"Interesting," I said. "Actually, my plan was just to show them that your reader was gimmicked like nothing they'd ever seen before. It never occurred to me that you'd be careless enough to actually have the data sitting in there where someone could find it."

"You're kidding," Kennrick said, looking chagrined. "Well, *damn* it all. I guess I should have stood my ground a little longer."

"It wouldn't have made a difference," I said. "We already knew enough about the killings to put you on ice, with or without Worrbin's approval."

"Speaking of which, what do you think of the method?" Kennrick asked. "Pretty clever, eh?"

"Hellishly clever," I agreed, my stomach tightening. Back in my Westali days, I reflected, I could actually sit back and dispassionately discuss techniques for murder and torture without qualms. Not anymore. Not with Bayta's life in this lunatic's hands. "Where did you come up with a bacterium that could pack away that much heavy metal, anyway?"

Kennrick barked a laugh. "You want the real irony? That strain was originally designed with an eye toward *curing* heavy-metal poisoning. You inject the bacteria into the patient and let the little bugs spread out through his system, gobbling up every heavy-metal atom they happen across. Since their own biochemistry actually needs the stuff for reproduction, they multiply like crazy, but only up to the point where the metal's all been found and locked up. All you do then is flush them out of the system, and voilà—patient's cured. Send him home and charge his account."

"Only here you reversed the process," I said. "You spent the torchliner trip from Earth feeding the Shorshians bacteria that were already loaded to the gills with cadmium. You gave it a couple of weeks on the Quadrail to settle into their deep tissues, then uncorked a bottle of that really high-power antiseptic spray we found in the air filter. The bacteria die, in the process dumping their supplies of cadmium into the Shorshians' bodies, and we've got three impossible murders."

"Beautiful, isn't it?" Kennrick said, a disturbing glint in his eyes. "There are no warning symptoms because the bacteria have the metal solidly locked up. The Spiders' sensors won't notice anything, because the bacteria themselves are perfectly benign and the detectors aren't keyed for anything as low-level as basic elements. You can pick your time and place—hell, you don't even have to be anywhere near your victim when he's supposedly poisoned. It's the perfect crime."

"Only if you make sure there aren't any Fillies around," I pointed out.

His lip twisted. "There is that," he conceded. "I didn't realize how potent that spray really was, or that it would go deep enough to kill off Filiaelian gleaner bacteria. Too bad about Givvrac, really. I kind of liked the old coot. He was so—I don't know. So old-world calcified, I guess. Wanting everything to be just like it had always been."

"As opposed to the new world order you and Hardin are trying to make?"

"Not *trying* to make, Compton," he corrected me softly. "*Going* to make."

"Right," I said. "So why let Tririn live? And why steal Colix's throat lozenges that last night, when he thought you were putting them away for him?"

"Oh, come now," Kennrick chided. "What's a good murder without a suspect or two? Tririn's annoyance over Colix's throat operation made him the perfect patsy. I figured all I had to do was make the lozenges mysteriously disappear, to make it seem like Tririn was trying to cover up what Colix had done, and you'd fall all over yourself burying him in circumstantial evidence."

"Without nailing down the method?" I shook my head. "Not a chance."

"It was still worth a try," Kennrick said. "Besides, this was an experiment, remember? I wanted to see what effect distance from the antiseptic spray had on the bacteria's demise. Apparently, Master Bofiv was right on the edge—that's why it took him longer to croak—and Master Tririn was just past it." He picked up his reader from beside him on the bed and held it up for me to see. "It's all in my report," he added, a mocking edge to his tone.

"What about Strinni?"

"What about him?" Kennrick asked. "Oh—you mean the extra necrovri-laden bacterial strain I put in his food?" He shrugged. "I thought that as long as I was at it I might as well test the bacteria that had been designed to carry more complex molecules. Strinni was the perfect candidate for that one, sitting isolated from the others up in first class and all." He snorted gently. "Also the perfect candidate because he didn't usually eat with the other Shorshians aboard the torchliner. Made it easy to feed him his special servings without getting it mixed in with the others' dosages."

"As well as making him look like a drug addict to his fellow Quadrail passengers?" I suggested.

Kennrick shrugged again. "I never liked him anyway."

"And the thing with *Logra* Emikai and *Osantra* Qiddicoj?"

He frowned. "What thing?"

"Cutting Emikai loose and pumping Qiddicoj full of hypnotic," I said. "How did you pull that one off?"

He frowned a little harder. "Sorry, but you've lost me," he said. "But enough reminiscing. You ready to take a few orders?"

"Not yet," I said, frowning in turn. If Kennrick hadn't been involved with Emikai's mysterious midnight visitor . . . but there was no time to worry about that now. "I want to know first what's going to happen to Bayta," I said. "She obviously can't sleep sitting up in that chair."

"Don't worry, I've got things rigged so that I can let her lie down on the floor later," Kennrick assured me. "It's going to be a little hard on her back, but there's only one bed in here. Unless she wants to share?"

"I don't think so," I said, sternly forcing back a sudden surge of rage. If he so much as touched her . . . "Let me go get her a pillow and blanket."

"From your compartment?" he countered. "Sorry. I'm not letting you go pick through whatever other goodies you've got back there and try to smuggle something in. Before you leave, you can grab a pillow and blanket from right there behind you and stuff them through the gap."

"Good enough," I said. Not that I had anything in my compartment that would help Bayta anyway. "What about food?"

"Not a problem," he said. "I have enough ration bars to last me to Venidra Carvo." He raised his eyebrows. "Sorry—did you mean food for *her*?"

I took a deep breath, again forcing down my anger. He was taunting me, I knew, trying to see how far he could push before I lost it.

He could just keep pushing. I wasn't going to give him the satisfaction. More to the point, I wasn't going to let anger crowd out brainpower that would be better used for tactical thinking. "We've got plenty of other ration bars aboard," I said. "Let me get her some."

"In a bit," Kennrick said. "My turn now?"

I swallowed. "Go ahead."

"Okay," he said. "First of all, obviously, no one is to attempt to come in here. Not you, not the Spiders, not anyone."

"Don't worry," I said, eyeing the glinting wires wrapped around Bayta's throat. "How the hell did you get all that wire past the Spiders' sensors, anyway?"

"Ah, ah—*my* turn," Kennrick said firmly. "When we get to Venidra Carvo, I get to walk free and clear without interference. Sorry—*we* get to walk free and clear."

I saw the muscles in Bayta's throat tighten, a sudden stricken look in her eyes. Apparently, she hadn't thought past our arrival at Venidra Carvo. "You planning to take her along all the way back to Earth?" I asked Kennrick.

"Why not?" Kennrick said blandly, letting his eyes run up and down Bayta's body. "I'm sure she's very pleasant company." He looked back at me and gave me a faint smile. "Relax, Compton. She stays with me only until I feel safe. At that point, I turn her loose. I promise."

As if the promise of a murderer was worth a damn. "Fine," I said. "Anything else?"

"Yes; the accommodations," he said. "Rather, everyone else's accommodations. I'm sure you've already made plans to isolate me by moving everyone else out of this car?"

"We thought it would help keep down the noise," I said. "You know how neighbors can be."

"Oh, there's no need to convince me," he said. "I agree completely. In fact, let's go whole hog and move everyone out of all three compartment cars."

I frowned. "*All* of them?"

"Like you said, peace and quiet. You've got two hours to get everyone out of here. Including you."

"I'd like to stay, if you don't mind," I offered. "You might realize there's something else you need."

"I do mind, and I won't need anything," he said coolly. "More to the point, I want to know that any noises I hear in the night aren't coming from some clumsy Shorshian falling out of bed. This way, anything I hear after the next two hours will be unauthorized." He shifted his gaze to Bayta. "And will be dealt with accordingly."

"I already said there wouldn't be any intrusions."

"This way, I'll know you mean it," he countered. "You'd better get going—you've got a lot to do in the next two hours."

"Look, Kennrick, I understand—"

"Just go, Frank," Bayta interrupted tautly. "You heard him. Go, and start getting it done."

I frowned at her. There was a tightness around her eyes that hadn't been there a minute ago. Was she suddenly worried about Kennrick's order to move everyone out?

I didn't know. But whatever the reason, I'd clearly run dry on hospitality here. "Okay, I'm going," I said. "First let me get your bedding for you."

I crossed the room and pulled the pillow and blankets off Minnario's bed, wincing at the thought of him about to be kicked out of his compartment for the second time today. I thought about asking Kennrick if he would make an exception, decided I might as well save my breath. A four-time murderer was hardly likely to have any residual compassion for children, puppies, or cripples.

The blankets slipped easily through the gap in the divider. The much thicker pillow was trickier, but I eventually managed it. "That's good," Kennrick said. "I'll take it from here."

"What about Bayta's food?" I asked. "And are you going to want anything in the way of liquid refreshment?"

"I think we can make do with water from the sink," Kennrick said. "That way, since you'll never know who's going to be drinking next, I know you won't try poisoning it or anything."

I sighed. "You know, Kennrick, paranoids don't really live any longer than other people. It just feels like it. What about her food?"

"Come back here in two hours," he said. "Bring enough to last her the rest of the trip."

"All right," I said. "If you change your mind and want anything else—"

"Good-bye, Frank," Bayta cut me off, the intensity in her voice matched by the look in her eyes.

"Yes, good-bye, Frank," Kennrick repeated sarcastically. "See you in two hours. Don't be late."

"I'll be here." I looked at Bayta, wondering if I should try to say something soothing. But she didn't look like she was in a soothable mood. Nodding to her, I headed back across the compartment. I had just reached the door when I felt a subtle puff of air behind me, and turned to see the divider seal itself against the wall.

I swore under my breath. But it wasn't a curse of anger or frustration or even fear. The conversation with Kennrick had burned all such emotions out of my system. All that remained was the cold, detached combat mentality Westali had worked so hard to beat into me. *We'll outthink him,* I'd told Emikai. It was time I got started on that. Punching the door release, I stepped out into the corridor.

And came to an abrupt halt. Standing motionlessly in the corridor between me and the car's rear door were two conductor Spiders. "What?" I demanded.

Neither of them answered. I opened my mouth to ask the question again . . . and then belatedly, my brain caught up with me, and I took a second, closer look.

Because they weren't conductors. They were larger, with the pattern of white dots that usually denoted a stationmaster.

I'd almost forgotten about the message we'd tried to send as we'd blown past the hidden siding a few days ago. Apparently, the gamble had paid off.

No wonder Bayta had been so anxious for me to cut short the conversation and get out here.

"Frank Compton?" one of the Spiders said in the flat voice all Spiders seemed to have.

"Yes." I took a deep breath, a cold chill shivering across my skin. "Welcome, defenders. And may I say, it's about damn time."

I'd expected to have to spend at least the first hour helping get all the compartment cars emptied of passengers. But either Bayta or the defenders had already given the orders, and I quickly discovered that the conductors had the procedure under way. Leaving that task to them, I took the defenders back to my compartment for a quick tactical session.

"Let's start with you," I said as I closed the door behind me. "How many of you are there, and where's your tender?"

"We are two," one of the defenders said. His particular white-dot pattern reminded me of a military chevron lying on its side; privately, I dubbed him Sarge. "Our tender currently travels behind this train."

"Which I assume means you came aboard from the rear through the baggage cars," I said. "Did you bring any specialized equipment?"

"What sort of equipment?"

"Anything besides standard Spider tools and replacement parts," I said. "Weapons, another *kwi*, burglar tools—anything?"

The Spiders were silent for a moment, probably discussing the matter between themselves. "No weapons or tools," Sarge said at last. "But the tender is equipped with a side-extendable sealable passageway."

I frowned. "You mean like a portable airlock?"

"Yes," Sarge confirmed.

"Good," I said. "Let's get whatever you do have within a bit easier reach. Can you bring the tender up the auxiliary service tracks alongside the right-hand side of the train?"

"We require a crosshatch to change tracks," Sarge said.

"Yes, I know," I said. A crosshatch was a section of spiral-laid tracks that allowed a Quadrail to quickly switch from one track to another without having to first get to a station. "Are there any coming up?"

Another pause as they again communed with each other. If defenders were the Chahwyn's attempt to create Spiders with quick minds and the ability to take the initiative, I reflected, they still had a long way to go. "The nearest is three hours away," Sarge reported.

"That should do," I said. "When we hit the crosshatch, bring the tender up alongside—let's see—alongside the door into the center compartment car. Kennrick's compartment is on the opposite side, so he won't spot it."

"Other passengers may notice its passage," Sarge warned.

"Not if they're all watching dit rec dramas at the time," I said. "But you're right. We'll have the conductors opaque any open display windows before you move the tender, just to be on the safe side." I braced myself. "Now we need an update from the inside. Can you get in contact with Bayta?"

Sarge seemed to straighten a little on his metallic legs. "Frank?" Bayta's voice came.

I jumped. I'd never even heard of Spiders being able to do *that*. Something new the Chahwyn had come up with for their defenders? "Bayta? Is that you?" I called.

"Yes," Sarge said, still in Bayta's voice. "I hope things look better out there than they do in here."

"I'm working on it," I assured her. "Can you see where the other ends of your nooses are connected?"

"One's attached to the door, the other to the curve couch," she reported. "Both are running through pulley systems, so that if the door opens or the couch collapses into the divider . . ." She left the sentence unfinished.

"Understood," I said quickly. I didn't want to dwell on the consequences, either. "Is there any way to get to the wires from outside the room? Maybe open the door or divider just far enough to send in a mite with wire cutters?"

"No," the response came immediately. "Opening the door at all will kill me. And the divider can only be opened about as far as it was earlier."

Which hadn't left enough of a gap for a mite to squeeze through. I wondered briefly about the even smaller twitters, but quickly abandoned the thought. Twitters were delicate creatures, designed for electronics repair and assembly, and I doubted they would have the strength to carry and operate something as big and heavy as wire cutters. "How about the ceiling?" I asked. "We've still got almost two hours' worth of Spiders and moving passengers thudding around. Could the mites disassemble their way through enough of the ceiling so that they could get the rest of the way through later tonight while Kennrick's asleep?"

"Two hours wouldn't be nearly enough time," Bayta said. "Besides, I think he's put sensors up there. There are six lumps of what looks like clay attached to parts of the ceiling and wired into his reader."

"Gray-colored clay?"

"Dark gray, yes."

"They're sensors, all right," I confirmed. "Certainly audio, possibly motion, too. There are six, you say?"

"Yes, with four more lined up by the door," Bayta said. "From the lengths of their wires, I'd guess he's planning to put them out into the corridor after everyone's left."

I grimaced. The man had definitely thought this through. "Anything else?"

"He's been stretching more wires like the ones around my neck over the floor," she said. "I think they're all just fastened to the walls, but I can't be completely sure."

"Probably just window dressing," I told her. "The more wires he loads the room with, the harder it'll be for us to know which ones we have to cut. Anything else?"

"I don't know what it means," Bayta said slowly, "but he's brought in the oxygen repressurization tank from our car."

I frowned. Every Quadrail car came equipped with a self-contained and self-controlled supply/scrubber/regulator system as an emergency backstop against a sudden loss of air pressure. Bayta and I had used them ourselves on occasion. "What's he thinking, that we're going to try to gas him?"

"I don't know," Bayta said. "He also spent a few minutes earlier cutting into the end of his ticket. Not the key end, but the other end—"

"You talking to Compton?" Sarge interrupted himself.

Only now his voice was Kennrick's.

A shiver ran up my back. I could understand why the Chahwyn might have thought it a good idea to design their new Spiders to channel voices as well as words. But reasonable or not, it was definitely on the north end of creepy.

"If you àre, be sure to tell him about the sensors on the ceiling," Kennrick's voice continued. "I don't think he'd be stupid enough to try to get those little mite Spiders digging in from that direction, but better to err on the cautious side. Oh, and ask him how the evacuation's going."

"Frank?" Bayta's voice came back anxiously. "What do I do?"

"Go ahead and tell him," I said. "He already knows you can communicate with the Spiders. *Don't* mention the defenders, though."

"All right."

Sarge's mimicry shifted tone, presumably indicating that his relay had changed from Bayta's thoughts to her verbal conversation with Kennrick. I listened with half an ear as she described how the passengers were being moved and listed how many were left to go.

"Sounds like it's under control," Kennrick said when she'd finished. "Just remind Compton that he needs to be back here in exactly—let's see—one hour and forty minutes. If he's not, the doors close and you're going to be mighty hungry by the time we get to Venidra Carvo."

"I'll tell him," Bayta's voice came back. "Frank?" she said, Sarge's tone again shifting as she switched back to telepathy. "Did you hear all that?"

"Yes, thanks," I told her. "Overconfident SOB, isn't he?"

"What do you want me to do?"

"For now, just try to relax," I said. "And keep me informed as to what he's doing."

"All right." There was a brief pause. "Frank . . . if it doesn't look like it's going to work out . . ."

"It's going to work out," I interrupted. "You just relax, okay? I'll come up with something."

"I'll try," she said. "Thank you."

Sarge fell silent. As he did so, the other defender stirred.

"One of the conductors has been asked how long the passengers will need to remain out of their compartments," he relayed.

I stared out my compartment's display window at the dull landscape of the Tube racing past, illuminated only by the coruscating glow of the Coreline above us and the faint light from our train's own windows. Over two weeks to go before we reached Venidra Carvo. Over two weeks for Bayta to be trapped with a murderer.

I looked back at the defenders. Their white-dotted silver globes didn't carry the faintest hint of an expression, but there was something about the way they were standing, something in their stance and stillness, that conveyed an unpleasant mixture of determination and ruthlessness.

The defenders weren't going to let Bayta spend two weeks as Kennrick's prisoner, either. The only question was whether I would come up with a plan to free her, or they would.

And which of our plans would get her through this alive.

"Compton?" Sarge prompted.

I took a deep breath. "Tell them six hours," I said. "One way or another, they'll be back in their compartments in six hours."

TWENTY-ONE :

Precisely two hours after being dismissed from Minnario's compartment, I was back.

"Right on time," Kennrick said approvingly as I came up to the narrow gap he'd again opened in the divider wall. "Excellent. All that Westali training, no doubt. You have your friend's rations?"

"Right here," I said, peering through the gap as I held up the package for him to see. He was back to his earlier cross-legged posture on the bed, this time with his reader propped up on the pillow beside him.

Bayta, in contrast, was now lying on her back on the floor with her feet toward me, the blanket covering her from neck to ankles, her head resting on the pillow. Her face was under control, but I could see the low-level nervousness beneath it. I also noted that there were now three loops of wire around her neck instead of two.

When Bayta had said Kennrick was stringing new lengths of wire around the room, she'd definitely been understating the case. The place was full of the damn stuff, most of it criss-crossing the room at shin height. Half a dozen of the wires ran over Bayta's torso and legs, while the rest were arranged in front of the door and divider. Even if none of them were actually attached to Bayta's neck loops, making a mad dash across the room to wring Kennrick's neck was now out of the question.

"You like the new arrangement?" Kennrick asked.

"Looks like the hobby room of a tall-ship model maker," I said. "Listen, the gap here is too small to fit the package through. Can you open it up a bit?"

"I could," he said consideringly. "But it would be a bit tricky for her to eat with a sliced throat, don't you think?"

I grimaced. "How about I open the package and send them through individually?"

"How about you do that," he agreed. "Only be careful where they land."

Tearing open the package, I started dropping the bars through the gap, making sure to miss all the wires. "I hope you're not going to try to tell me all of those are connected to Bayta."

"Some of them might be," he said. "Others might be holding back other lines, so that her throat only remains intact if you leave them alone. Just in case you were thinking about sending in some twitters with instructions to cut everything in sight."

"I wasn't," I assured him. "Look, Kennrick—"

"Hey, you have to see this," he interrupted, reaching down to the bed beside him and picking up a flat piece of dull gray metal. "Especially since you asked about it earlier. This is part of the stiffening frame for my larger carrybag. Watch."

Picking up his multitool, he used the needle-nosed pliers to get a grip on the corner of the plate. He pulled carefully to the side; and, to my amazement, a thin wire began to peel away from the metal. "Isn't that cool?" he asked, continuing to pull wire from the plate until he'd reached the full extension of his arm. "It's called knitted-metal something-or-other. The stuff's perfectly solid and perfectly innocent until you need to garrote someone." He smiled. "I'll bet Mr. Hardin didn't give *you* toys like this."

"I wouldn't have taken them if he had," I said. "Kennrick, we may have some trouble here. Another side has joined the game."

"What, *Esantra* Worrbin's making threatening noises again on behalf of the Assembly?" he asked contemptuously.

"This has nothing to do with the passengers," I said. "It has to do with the Spiders."

"The *Spiders* are making threatening noises?"

"I'm not joking," I growled. "There's a new class of Spider that's just come on line. They're called defenders, and they're like nothing you've ever seen before."

"I'll be sure to watch out for them," Kennrick promised solemnly. "Along with the ogres and hobgoblins that have also been hiding aboard since we left Homshil. Really, Compton. I was hoping for something a little more imaginative."

"Two of them came aboard an hour ago from a tender that's pulled up behind us," I went on doggedly. "Up to now, my experience with defenders has mostly consisted of being slammed up against a wall by one of them. They're strong, they're smart, they're aggressive, and they're not going to let you walk off this train. Not alive."

I shifted my eyes to Bayta. "And unlike me, they don't particularly care whether you die alone or with company."

For a long moment Kennrick studied my face. "Okay, I'll play along," he said. "Let's assume I'm sufficiently scared. What do you suggest I do next?"

"I suggest *we* get the hell off this train," I said. "I suggest you and Bayta and I get aboard that tender, turn it around, and head back toward Homshil."

"All three of us, you say?" Kennrick asked. "Interesting."

"You and I can't operate the tender," I explained. "Bayta can. But you'll need me as a hostage to guarantee her cooperation."

"As well as guaranteeing a much more exciting ride, I assume?"

"You can tie me up for the whole trip if you want," I said. "The point is that we have to get you off this train while we still can."

"I'll take it under advisement," Kennrick said. "You about done with those?"

I flipped through the last of the ration bars. "Yes."

"And the passengers are out of all three compartment cars?" he asked. "Except for you, of course."

"Yes, everyone's out."

"Good." Unfolding his legs, Kennrick got up from the bed. "See, here's what I'm more concerned about at the moment than imaginary attack Spiders: the question of what you're going to do when I close down that divider."

"I leave the car like you told me to," I said, frowning. "Why?"

"Don't be naive, Compton," he said, picking his way carefully between the wires as he walked toward me. "And don't assume I am, either."

"You can unfasten the wire from the door and watch me go," I suggested.

"You mean open the door and discover to my chagrin that you're standing right outside ready to punch me in the throat?" he countered. "No, thanks."

He came to a stop just out of arm's reach. "So let me explain how this is going to work." He held up a small object. "This is the electric motor from my shaver," he said. "I'm going to use it to rig up a device that'll automatically strangle Bayta after a preprogrammed number of seconds or minutes."

I felt my stomach tighten. "You don't need to do that," I said.

"Ah, but I do," he countered. "You see, once you've gone I'm going to go through all three cars with the infrared sensor in my reader, and it's a very *good* sensor. If I get even a hint that you or someone else is hiding in one of the compartments, I'll come straight back here and make sure Ms. Bayta regrets your stupidity."

"You kill her and you'll have lost your hostage," I warned.

"Oh, I wouldn't kill her," he assured me. "Not right away. I'd probably start by slicing off the end of a finger or two. I'm assuming she's strong enough not to succumb to shock, but of course I don't know that for sure."

I took a deep breath. "Anything else?"

"Two things." He dug into his pocket and pulled out his ticket, and I saw it was sliced about halfway through. "Point one: note the tear," he went on. "If you or anyone else tries to jump me while I'm outside my compartment, all I have to do is tear it the rest of the way through and it becomes useless as a key. You *might* be able to put it back together, but not before the automatic strangler kicks in."

"You don't have to belabor the point, Kennrick," I said. "I recognize that you've thought this whole thing through very carefully."

"Good," he said. "Point two . . ."

Without warning he turned halfway around, bringing the *kwi* on his right hand to bear on Bayta. His thumb pressed the switch, and Bayta's eyes rolled up and closed as her body went limp.

Before I could react, Kennrick had swung back to face me. "Point two is I don't want her giving you a running commentary on what I'm doing," he said conversationally. "Good-bye, Compton."

I lifted my gaze from Bayta to Kennrick's face. "Good-bye, Kennrick," I said. "Don't forget what I said about the defenders."

He was still smiling as he touched the control on the wall, closing the divider in front of me.

Sarge was waiting just inside the rear door of the last compartment car. "She is unconscious," he said in his flat Spider voice. "Why is she unconscious?"

So much for my hope that Bayta had been faking. But then, she could hardly have done anything else. There were ways of telling if someone was truly unconscious. "Because she still needs to maintain the illusion that the *kwi* works like a normal weapon," I told him. "Come on—we need to get out of here."

Reluctantly, I thought, he backed into the vestibule. "What now?" he asked as I followed him in.

"The groundwork's been laid," I told him. "Time to go to work."

We stepped into the first coach car. Many of the displaced passengers had opted to settle down there, I saw, instead of continuing on to coach cars farther back. No doubt they were hoping their proximity to the center of the action would give them a better chance of finding out what was going on.

They were going to be disappointed. "We need a base of operations," I told the defender. "Tell the conductors I need everyone cleared out of this car."

Considering the wealth and power of the travelers I was pushing around, they took the news remarkably well. Maybe the rumor mill had given a sufficiently dark cast to the situation to keep their indignation in check. Or maybe it was the look in my eyes. Either way, with a maximum of cooperation and a minimum of griping, they were soon gone. "What now?" Sarge asked when we were alone.

I checked my watch. Twenty minutes until we hit the cross-hatch section, if Sarge's earlier estimate had been correct. "Is your partner ready to move the tender alongside us?" I asked.

"He is," Sarge confirmed. "You still wish it to parallel the center compartment car?"

"No, we'd better hold it back here for now," I said. "I doubt Kennrick's sensors are good enough to spot movement or heat all the way through the compartments on that side of the train, but I don't want to risk it. Make sure the conductors know to opaque all the windows on that side of the train before the tender starts moving."

"It will be done," Sarge said. "What after that?"

"There's one more preliminary job you'll need to do," I told him. "After that, we'll just have to wait until Bayta's awake again so that we'll have a real-time tap into what Kennrick's doing."

"What is this preliminary job you wish me to do?"

Spiders, even defenders, didn't exhibit a whole lot of body language. Even so, as I told him what I wanted, I had no difficulty sensing his stunned outrage. "No," he said when I'd finished, his voice even flatter than usual. "Impossible."

"Why?" I countered. "Because it's against the rules? Trust me—we're going to be breaking a *lot* of rules before this is over."

"Which other rules?"

"Rules that you're going to break so that Bayta lives and Kennrick doesn't escape with information on how to kill people aboard Quadrails," I said bluntly. "Are we all on the same page? Or will I have to go back to the Chahwyn and tell them that one of their own died because you wouldn't cooperate with me?"

"But this is—" Abruptly, he stiffened. "Frank?" he said in Bayta's voice.

"Bayta?" I said, glancing at my watch. It had been only forty minutes since Kennrick had zapped her, though a low-level *kwi* shot was normally good for at least an hour. Her unique mix of Human and Chahwyn physiologies coming into play again, no doubt. "Are you all—?"

"Something's wrong," she interrupted urgently. "The oxygen repressurization tank is gone."

I frowned at Sarge. "What do you mean, it's gone? Gone where?"

"I don't know," she said. "He must have moved it while I was unconscious."

And then, suddenly, I understood. "Damn it," I muttered, heading for the forward vestibule and the compartment cars beyond it. "Come on," I called to Sarge over my shoulder.

The rearmost compartment car was deserted. Moving as quietly as I could, I headed along the corridor to the front. Bracing myself, I touched the control to open the door to the vestibule.

Nothing happened.

I tried twice more, but it was just going through the motions. "He's got us, Bayta," I said. "Damn him. Damn me, too, for not catching on sooner."

"He vented the tank into the vestibule?" Bayta asked.

"You got it," I said bitterly. Thereby increasing the air pressure in the vestibule's confined space, thereby engaging the automatic locks on both the vestibule's doors. Now, the only way to get through into Kennrick's car would be to drill, spike, or otherwise batter our way through.

Bayta and I had used the exact same trick against the Modhri not two months ago, and yet I'd never seen this coming. I must be slipping. "At least now we know why he's got audio sensors laid out in the corridor," I said, forcing back both the anger and the self-reproach. Now was not the time. "He knows we can't batter our way through the vestibule without making a lot of noise."

"That just means we'll have to come up with a different plan," Bayta said calmly. Or maybe the calm was just an artifact of Sarge's transmission. "You have any ideas?"

I stared at the vestibule door, thinking hard. All right. We couldn't get through without making a lot of noise. The noise would trigger the sensors, which would trigger the alarm, which would alert Kennrick to start lopping off Bayta's fingers.

But only if Kennrick was able to hear the alarm . . .

"Fine," I said slowly. "He wants to play cute? We can play cute, too. Here's the plan . . ."

Sarge wasn't thrilled by the plan, for at least three separate rule-breaking reasons. Bayta didn't seem particularly enthusiastic, either, for a whole other set of reasons.

But neither of them could think of anything better. In the end, I got my way.

Our preparations took another hour. We waited another hour after that, just to give Kennrick time to settle down comfortably in the center of his new fortress of solitude.

I spent most of that final hour staring at the walls, running the plan over and over in my brain, trying to think of any alternative actions Kennrick might take that I wouldn't be ready for.

There were, unfortunately, any number of things he *might* do, any one of which would wreck everything. But I knew the man now, hopefully well enough that I could anticipate his likely responses.

We would find out soon enough if I was right.

Finally, the hour was up. "He's stretched out on the bed reading," Sarge relayed Bayta's words and voice as he and I stood at the rear of the last compartment car. "He looks calm and very much at home."

"Good," I said. "Let me know right away when that changes."

"I will," she said.

I touched Sarge's leg. "Wait here," I told him, and passed through the vestibule into the first coach car, the one I'd made into my operations base.

Krel Vevri and *Osantra* Qiddicoj were waiting there for me, both of them standing straight and tall, Qiddicoj's long Filly face still a little pale from his earlier brush with death. "Well?" Vevri asked as I emerged from the vestibule.

Or rather, the Modhri within him said it. "It's time," I confirmed, looking back and forth between the flat eyes and sagging faces.

And it occurred to me, not for the first time, that this was the riskiest part of my plan. The Modhri had promised to co-operate, but if he decided he could do better by switching sides, this whole thing would collapse into disaster and death without warning.

The two aliens nodded in unison. "Let us get on with it," Vevri said.

I shook away the unpleasant thoughts. I couldn't make this work without the Modhri playing spotter for me, and that was that. I would just have to trust him, and watch my back. "Yes, let's," I agreed. "The Spider will take the *Krel* Vevri walker through the airlock into the tender. He'll ride him up to the first compartment car—"

"You've already explained the plan," the Modhri reminded me.

I grimaced. He was right, I had. Twice. "Just remember that once you're in the compartment you'll need to stay perfectly quiet if and when Kennrick passes by," I said. "If he hears you—"

"Bayta will die," Vevri interrupted again. "I understand. Again: let us get on with it."

"Right." I nodded to the defender. "Go."

The defender didn't speak as he led the way to the car's door, but I was pretty sure I could detect some residual reluctance in his body language. Letting a passenger actually go aboard one of their tenders was bad enough. Letting a passenger aboard who was also a Modhran walker was unthinkable. Distantly, I wondered what kind of report he and Sarge would be sending back after this was all over.

They reached the car's outer door and it irised open, revealing the extendable airlock leading to the tender. Vevri and the defender went inside, and the car door closed behind them. "You ready?" I asked Qiddicoj.

"Yes," he said. "Don't worry, Compton. I've agreed to help you, and will hold to that promise."

"That makes me feel so much better," I said, trying not to be too sarcastic. "Come on."

Sarge was waiting for us in the rear compartment car by the vestibule door Kennrick had sealed. "Anything?" I asked as Qiddicoj and I came up to him.

"No," he said.

I nodded. "Let me know when your buddy's in position."

He didn't bother to answer. But then, I'd already gone over this part of the plan twice, too.

The minutes ticked by. I found myself staring at the vestibule door, tracing its edge with my eyes, trying to estimate the strength of the metal. Sarge had assured me that even with the air-pressure seal locked down tight he would have no trouble opening the thing. If he was right, we had a chance.

If he was wrong . . .

"My *Krel* Vevri Eye has entered the first compartment car," Qiddicoj murmured suddenly. "He's found the proper compartment and is unlocking the door."

The compartment at the very front of the train, the one right beside that car's emergency oxygen repressurization tank. I'd had to talk long and earnestly to the compartment's proper occupant to get him to loan me that key. "Is he in yet?"

"Yes," the Modhri confirmed. "He's sealed the door behind him."

I nodded and turned to Sarge. "Your partner ready?"

"He is in place," Sarge said.

"Tell him to go, and then connect me to Bayta," I ordered. "Bayta?"

"I'm here, Frank," her voice came from Sarge's metallic sphere. "Nothing new is happening here."

"It's about to," I assured her. "Keep the relay open."

"All right."

I listened intently, but for the first thirty seconds nothing happened. "What's happening?" I demanded at last.

"I can hear scraping," Bayta reported, her voice tight. "Coming from the edge of the display window, I think. I can't tell for sure—Mr. Kennrick has it opaqued."

"Has he noticed the sound?"

"Yes, he's looking around," Bayta said. "He doesn't look happy—wait; he's figured it out. He's clearing the window—"

"What the *hell*?" Sarge gasped, his voice abruptly switching to Kennrick's. "What the *bloody*—get the hell off my window. You—Bayta—tell it to get off my window."

"I can't," Bayta said aloud. "He's a defender—Mr. Compton told you about them. He won't listen to me."

"Tell him to get off," Kennrick snarled again. "Or by God, I *swear*—"

"He has a loop of wire twisted around her wrist," Sarge reported.

Beside me, the Modhri hissed anger. "Coward," he said contemptuously.

"Shall I order him to leave?" Sarge asked.

I squeezed my hand into a fist, emotion and logic doing a vicious tug-of-war with my soul. If this was a bluff, and I blinked, our best opportunity to nail Kennrick would be gone.

But if it *wasn't* a bluff, Bayta was about to lose a hand.

"Compton?" Sarge asked again.

Abruptly, the decision was taken from me. "No," Bayta's voice came firmly from Sarge's metal sphere. "Keep going. It's our only chance."

"Compton?" Kennrick's voice demanded. "Compton? Call him off, damn you. You hear me?"

"Keep going," Bayta said again.

"Compton? *Compton?*"

"He can't do anything," Bayta told him, her voice frightened and pleading. "Please—he can't do any—"

Abruptly, her voice went silent. "Bayta!" I barked.

"She's unhurt," Sarge said. "He has shot her with the *kwi*."

I braced myself. "What about her hand?"

"Also unhurt," Sarge assured me. "The Human has opaqued the window again."

"And?" I demanded.

"A moment."

I rubbed a layer of sweat off my forehead, willing my heart-beat to slow down as the defender hanging on to the outside of the car did whatever changes were necessary to his sensor suite to let him see through an opaqued display window. "The Human has moved to the door and is working with some of the wires connected there," Sarge reported.

"Which ones?"

"They appear to be the ones connected to Bayta's neck," Sarge said.

"It's working," the Modhri said.

"So far," I agreed cautiously. It was still way too early for us to start congratulating ourselves. "What's he doing now?"

"He has attached his reader to the motor fastened near the door," Sarge said. "The wire from the motor reaches across the compartment to loop around Bayta's neck."

The automatic strangler Kennrick had warned me about. Our quarry was about to make a sortie out of his fortress.

"He is leaving the compartment," Sarge said. "The door is closing . . . I can see no more."

I took a deep breath. It was working. It was actually work-ing. "Tell your partner to stop scraping," I instructed Sarge. "Modhri, let me know the minute you hear movement outside Vevri's compartment."

"I will," the Modhri promised, a note of what sounded like genuine awe in his voice. "You amaze me, Compton. How did you know he would behave in precisely this manner?"

"Because I have a good idea how people like that think," I said. That, plus the fact that Kennrick had damn few options right now. If the Spider managed to break the seal around his window, his air would go rushing out into the near-vacuum of the Tube. Without keys to any of the other compartments, there was nowhere else he could relocate to, even if he was willing to leave his carefully laid defenses. Trying to camp out in the corridor wouldn't be any better.

Which left him only one real option: buy himself some time, and hope he could figure out how to get the Spider off his window. Time, in this particular case, being oxygen.

And since he'd already used the tank in his own car to block the vestibule, he was going to have to go to the next car forward and steal theirs.

"You understand him, indeed," the Modhri murmured. "My congratulations."

"Let's save the celebration until he actually gets to the tank," I warned, still refusing to allow my hopes to get too high. "He could still decide to hunker down in the corridor while he tries to think up a new—"

"There!" the Modhri cut me off. "He's outside the forward car stateroom, and has begun to unfasten the oxygen tank."

And with Kennrick a car and a half away from all his audio sensors and alarms, it was time to go. "Your turn," I said, gesturing Sarge toward the vestibule door.

The words were barely out of my mouth when two of the defender's legs lanced forward, their tips spearing hard into the edge of the door. Before my ears could recover from the sound he hit the door again, with an even harder double blow than before.

And then, through the ringing in my ears, I heard the angry hiss of escaping air. The Spider had dented the door just enough to break the seal, releasing the pressure that had kept it locked.

I stepped forward and hit the release. The door opened halfway, then faltered as the deformed metal hung up on its rollers. I grabbed the edge, and with the defender joining my effort we shoved it the rest of the way open. I crossed the vestibule, stepping over the spent oxygen cylinder Kennrick had put there earlier, and touched the control at the other end.

The door opened into a deserted corridor. I stepped inside the car and headed forward at a fast jog. "How's he doing?" I asked over my shoulder.

"The sounds of disassembly have just finished," the Modhri reported. "The sounds now are those of one hefting a large object . . . he's starting back along the corridor."

Which meant our grace period was nearly at an end. "Thanks," I said, picking up my pace. "Get back into the vestibule and make sure the door closes behind you."

I reached Minnario's compartment door, keyed it open, and slipped inside. Sarge was right behind me.

It wasn't until the door slid shut again that I discovered that Qiddicoj had followed us in. "I told you to go back," I snapped.

"You may need me," he said.

I cursed under my breath. But it was too late for him to go back now. "Just stay quiet and out of my way," I growled.

I crossed the room to where the divider sealed against the wall. Kennrick had undoubtedly locked it from his side after my last visit, and in theory I couldn't unlock it from here.

But Bayta and I had run into this problem once before, and we'd come up with an answer to it. "Ready," I said, nodding to Sarge. "Have the conductors cut power now."

For three heartbeats nothing happened. Then, the compartment around us went dark. I counted out two more heartbeats, and the light came back on.

And with that, the divider returned to its default position of being unlocked.

"The Human's footsteps have faded from my other Eye's hearing," the Modhri murmured. "Do we open the divider?"

"Not yet," I said, kneeling on the curve couch and pressing my ear against the divider. "We have to wait until Kennrick gets back and disarms the automatic strangler setup. Defender, better have your partner start his scratching again." I frowned as a sudden thought struck me. "He *can't* actually dig all the way through the seal, can he?"

"No," Sarge said. But I could hear the disapproval in his voice. Letting passengers aboard tenders was broken rule number one; even pretending to do damage to one of their own Quadrails was broken rule number two. In his place, I decided, I would probably be unhappy, too.

For almost two minutes nothing happened. I was starting to wonder if Kennrick had decided to make a camp out in the corridor after all when I half heard, half felt a faint thud. There was a short pause, another thud—

"He has returned," Sarge confirmed as he picked up the commentary from the defender hanging outside the opaqued window. "He carries the oxygen tank with him."

I started to breathe again. It was nearly over. Kennrick had jumped perfectly through every hoop I'd set in front of him. All he had to do now was disarm the automatic strangler, reconnect the door trip wires to guard against intrusion from that direction, and then take the oxygen tank to the bed and start rigging it for his use if and when the defender made it though his window seal. I pressed my ear a little harder against the divider, even though I knew I'd never pick up the subtle sound or vibration of Kennrick heaving the oxygen tank onto the bed.

Which meant I was completely unprepared for the sudden thump that bounced against the divider right beside my ear. "What was that?" I whispered urgently. "Defender? Where the hell—?"

"He has seated himself on the curve couch," Sarge reported. "He is working on the pressurization tank's valve."

I felt the blood freeze in my veins. Kennrick wasn't supposed to be on the curve couch. He was supposed to be on the bed, like he'd been every other time I'd come in here. He was supposed to be concentrating so hard on his new oxygen tank and the Spider hanging outside his window that he wouldn't notice the divider open the crucial few centimeters I needed.

But he wasn't on the bed. He was on the curve couch, which would start retracting into the divider the instant I touched the control. There was no way in hell he could possibly miss that.

The Modhri must have sensed my sudden turmoil. "What is it?" he murmured.

"I need to open the divider without him noticing," I said grimly. "*And* I need him in front of the gap where I can see him, not way off to the side the way he is now."

"I see," the Modhri said calmly. "Do you still have the bypass mimic you took from *Logra* Emikai?"

"Uh . . ." I floundered, caught off balance by the sudden change in subject. "Yes, I've got it. Why?"

"Give it to me," the Modhri said, holding out his hand.

I stared at him. What in the world was he up to? "It doesn't work on Spider locks," I said.

"I don't need it to," the Modhri said, his hand still outstretched. "You wish the Human Kennrick in front of the opening. I will make that happen."

Trusting the Modhri, the words whispered through my mind. But time was running out, and I didn't have anything better to suggest. Digging the flat gray box out of my pocket, I handed it over.

"Thank you," the Modhri said, fingering it thoughtfully.

"Stay quiet, and stand well clear." He looked at the defender. "You, too," he added.

The defender seemed to think it over. Then, with obvious reluctance, he stepped all the way back to the compartment door. I took advantage of the moment to climb off the curve couch and press myself against its end, a meter from the wall where the divider would be opening.

The Modhri waited until we were set, then stepped over to the divider control. "Stand ready," he told me, and touched the control.

The divider started sliding open. It had barely cleared the wall when I heard an explosive curse from the other side of the widening gap. "What the—? *Compton?* Compton, *damn* you—"

"Not Compton," the Modhri called hastily through to him. "I am *Osantra* Qiddicoj. I have come to make you a bargain."

"What the—how did you get in there?" Kennrick snarled, and I could hear the subtle shift in the sound of his voice as he moved away from the collapsing curve couch.

"With this," the Modhri said, poking the corner of the bypass mimic through the still-opening divider. I tensed, but almost before I could start to wonder if he'd forgotten about Bayta he touched the control again, stopping the divider at just the right position. "It's a duplicate of the locksmith's bypass mimic Compton took from *Logra* Emikai. I offer it to you as part of a—"

"What the hell are you talking about?" Kennrick demanded. "The damn thing doesn't work on Spider locks. Compton said so."

"Compton was wrong," the Modhri countered, wiggling the mimic as if to emphasize his words. "I bought this spare from *Logra* Emikai, who showed me its secret. I offer it to you now in exchange for *your* secret of bringing death aboard the Quadrail."

Abruptly, he snatched the mimic out of the gap, and I caught a glimpse of Kennrick's fingertips as he grabbed for the device. "Give it here," Kennrick snarled.

"Not until you swear to the bargain," the Modhri said firmly. "With this you can move to a different room, where the Spider attacking you cannot—"

And right in the middle of a sentence, he collapsed abruptly into a heap on the floor, the mimic clattering against the deck as it fell from suddenly nerveless fingers.

"Nice try, Compton," Kennrick called from the other side of the divider. "You really think I'm that stupid?"

I pressed harder against the divider, gesturing to Sarge to likewise keep silent and motionless. Kennrick had obviously used the *kwi* on Qiddicoj . . . but with Bayta still unconscious, I knew for a fact the *kwi* hadn't worked. Qiddicoj was faking, lying supposedly unconscious with the perfect bait lying millimeters from his hand.

"I know you're in there, Compton," Kennrick bit out, raising his voice over the scraping sound of the defender outside his window. "Come out right now, or I'm going to start cutting off your girlfriend's fingers."

I clenched my teeth, my eyes riveted on the mimic. Because it *was* the perfect bait, and Kennrick had to know that. If he could get it to work on Spider locks, then every compartment in these two cars would be open to him. He could move himself and his hostage back and forth between rooms, resetting his traps and strangle lines, keeping himself clear of whatever the defenders tried to do to pin him down or root him out.

"You hear me, Compton?" Kennrick called again. "Show yourself. *Now.*"

Only the Modhri had forgotten one crucial detail. The

rigged vestibule had been sealed by means of a purely mechanical pressure lock, with nothing that a key or bypass mimic could do anything about. If Kennrick paused long enough to wonder how Qiddicoj had gotten through that, this whole house of cards would collapse.

"Compton?" Kennrick called. The light coming through the gap shifted subtly, and I had the sense that he was now pressing his eye against the opening, trying to see as much of the room as he could. "Compton? Last chance before I start cutting her."

I took a careful breath. He was going for it, I realized with cautiously rekindled hope. He was still calling for me, but he was no longer sure I was really here. Either he hadn't thought about the vestibule question, or he didn't realize the pressure lock couldn't be triggered remotely, or he was desperate enough to take the risk.

I gathered my feet under me, ready to push off the partially collapsed curve couch the minute he made his move. I would have only one shot at this . . .

And then, without warning, Kennrick's left hand darted through the gap and grabbed the mimic.

I shoved off the couch toward him, knowing even as I did so I would be too late.

But as Kennrick had mistakenly written the Modhri out of his calculations, so had I. Even as Kennrick's fingers closed around the mimic, Qiddicoj's limp hand came suddenly to life, darting up to lock itself around Kennrick's wrist.

Kennrick gave a startled curse, twisting his arm against Qiddicoj's thumb to try to break the grip. Qiddicoj held on gamely, but Kennrick was stronger and had better leverage, and half a second later he was free.

But a half second was all I needed. I reached them as Kennrick started to pull the mimic back through the gap, locking my own fingers around the man's wrist with all the strength adrenaline-flooded muscles could manage.

Kennrick yelped in pain as I yanked his arm hard toward me, slamming his shoulder against the edge of the divider, his face contorted with rage as he glared through the gap at me. "I knew it," he spat. "Clever, Compton. Now go to hell!" Lifting his right arm over his head, he pointed the *kwi* at me and jammed his thumb against the trigger.

"Sorry, Kennrick," I gritted. "Afraid you're out of bullets."

His face twisted even more viciously as he thumbed the *kwi* again. "So now what?" he retorted as he lowered his arm. "You still can't come in here without killing her. What are you going to do, stand there holding my wrist all the way to Venidra Carvo?"

"No," I said as I reached with my left hand around to the small of my back. The worst rule-breaking of all, I reflected, a request which Sarge had nearly vetoed even with both Bayta and me pleading my case. "I'm going to dispense justice."

And with that, I brought my Beretta around to the front, the weapon that had been in a lockbox beneath the train until I'd talked Sarge into sending his partner to retrieve it. Pressing it against Kennrick's side beneath the arm I was holding, I pulled the trigger.

The blast was deafening in the enclosed space. For a second Kennrick just stared at me, his eyes wide and disbelieving. Then his legs collapsed, and he fell to the floor, landing with his torso twisted awkwardly against the wall as I continued to grip his wrist.

"It is over?" Sarge asked.

I took a deep breath and let go of Kennrick's arm. It dropped limply to his side, the impact sending a small ripple through the blood already spreading through the carpet. *Find the murderer,* Givvrac had appealed to me with his last breath. *And kill him.*

Sometimes people did indeed get what they wished for.

"Yes, it's over," I told Sarge quietly, gazing at the eyes now staring their residual astonishment at the compartment's ceiling. "Tell the mites to get busy—I want them through the ceiling as soon as possible, and never mind the mess. And you can tell the other defender he can come back inside."

I leaned forward and peered through the gap. Bayta was lying on the floor, her breathing slow and even, the loops of now useless strangling wire glittering around her neck. As I gazed at her, the scraping from the window stopped, replaced by a sort of mice-in-the-wall sound as the mites set to work on the ceiling.

Beneath my feet, I felt Qiddicoj stir. "May I?" the Modhri asked.

"Sorry," I apologized, stepping clear and offering my hand.

He ignored it, getting to his feet without assistance. "A straightforward yet effective plan," he commented, peering through the gap at Kennrick's body. "My congratulations."

"Thank you," I said. "Much as I hate to say this, I owe you."

"You know the repayment I desire," he said, his voice hardening as he gazed into my eyes. "The method of death used by the Human Kennrick must never be allowed to become public."

"It won't," I promised. "And now that we know how it was done, we should be able to tweak the Spiders' sensors to keep it from happening again."

"Good." Qiddicoj's long Filly face twitched in a wry smile. "After all, I hope someday to rule the galaxy. I can't achieve that goal if the Quadrail system is destroyed."

I felt my stomach tighten. "No, of course not," I agreed. "You'll forgive me if I don't wish you luck with that."

He inclined his head to me. "Then with your permission I'll return to my fellow passengers." He smiled again. "*Osantra* Qiddicoj will be chagrined to discover that he slept through these momentous events."

"As will *Krel* Vevri, no doubt," I agreed. "I presume he's on his way back, too?"

"Yes," Qiddicoj confirmed. "Farewell, Compton. I will most likely not speak to you again."

"Likewise," I said.

I watched as he crossed to the door and disappeared out into the corridor. "There will be repercussions from this," Sarge warned.

"There are repercussions from every action," I said. With the excitement over, I was suddenly very tired. "That's the way of things."

Sarge seemed to digest that. "I will take your weapon now."

I'd almost forgotten the Beretta still hanging loosely in my grip. "Yes, of course," I said, putting on the safety and handing it over. "Back to the lockbox, I presume?"

"Immediately," he said, taking the weapon with one leg and folding it up beneath his metal sphere. Tapping his way to the door, he left the compartment.

I turned again to the opening. Yes, there would be repercussions. Possibly very serious ones.

But we would deal with them as they arose. Right now, all I cared about was that Bayta was alive.

With one last look at Kennrick's frozen eyes, I settled down to listen to the mites working overhead, and to watch Bayta sleep.

TWENTY-TWO :

It took the mites three hours of banging, pounding, and unfastening to clear a corner of the ceiling enough for them to squeeze through. Bayta was awake for most of that time, and I spent a good deal of it bringing her up to speed on what had happened, as well as how the devil's bargain I'd made had worked out.

Even here at the payoff, I could tell she still wasn't happy about the deal. But at least she had the grace to simply thank me for my efforts, and to not argue any further about my methods.

Once the mites were through, the rest was easy. They traced all of the wires that Kennrick had laid out, confirmed that all but the obvious ones were dummies, carefully cut the ones that weren't, and Bayta was finally free.

We left the two defenders in the compartment with Kennrick's body and headed back through the deserted compartment car to announce that the crisis was over and that everyone could start heading back to their compartments. "I was only off by an hour," I commented to Bayta as we passed the jammed vestibule door that Sarge had wrecked. It wasn't going to stay wrecked long; a half-dozen mites were already working on it. "I said things would be back to normal in six hours, and it only took us seven."

"And you probably could have let them back while the mites were working on the ceiling," Bayta pointed out.

"I didn't want to risk any of them getting a look at Kennrick's body as it was dragged out dripping blood," I said. "Aside from the gruesomeness of the whole thing, I didn't want them wondering what I'd used to open up that size hole in his chest. You'll let me know when they've got him to the tender, right?"

"Yes," she said. "A shame it had to end this way. We might have learned more about Mr. Hardin's plan if we'd been able to question him."

I shook my head. "Kennrick would have been trained to hold out against all the more popular forms of interrogation," I said. "In retrospect, I'm guessing now that he *was* part of Du-Noeva's team, that spy Westali was after when we raided Shotoko Associates eleven years ago. In fact, he was probably the one who killed those Westali agents guarding the east door. How he hooked up with Hardin I can only guess."

"I imagine a man with Mr. Hardin's resources has many interesting contacts." Bayta paused. "Thank you for not arguing over the reader, by the way."

"You mean not arguing more than I did?"

"If you want to put it that way."

"No problem," I assured her, fudging the truth just a little. I'd really, really wanted a chance to go through Kennrick's reader before the defenders took it away. Larry Hardin wasn't the type to load all his oranges in one crate—the fact that he'd apparently had Kennrick already prepped and ready to take over my slot the minute I'd resigned from his payroll showed that much. I doubted this was the only plan he had in the works for taking over the Quadrail, and I wanted to see if Kennrick had taken any notes on possible future shenanigans.

But the defenders had been adamant about taking the reader and Kennrick together as a package, and I'd had enough fighting for one day. "So the plan is to load Kennrick aboard the tender, then take it back to the rear of the train and load in the other four bodies?" I asked.

Bayta nodded. "Officially, they'll be removing the bodies for direct transportation to their families. Along the way, though, they'll stop at a siding and take some tissue samples and readings."

"Sounds good," I said. Between the Spiders' readings, the samples Emikai and I had run though my analyzer the previous evening, and the data in Kennrick's reader, the Spiders and Chahwyn ought to have everything they needed to plug this new loophole in their security net.

We passed through the vestibule at the end of the third compartment car and entered the first coach car, the one I'd cleared out as my operations base.

Only it wasn't completely cleared out anymore. *Osantra* Qiddicoj, *Krel* Vevri, and Tra'ho Government Oathling Prapp, the three Modhran walkers, were standing silently a half-dozen steps in front of us, obviously waiting for us to make our appearance. Just behind them stood *Asantra* Muzzfor, the contract-team Filly who had been Kennrick's staunchest supporter and apologist. "It's over?" Muzzfor asked as Bayta and I stepped into the car. "He's dead?"

"Yes, he's dead," I confirmed, taking another, closer look at the walkers. All three were standing unnaturally stiff, their eyes looking odd in a way I'd never seen in a walker before.

And there was something else: a faint, high-pitched dog-whistle sound hovering right on the edge of my hearing. I glanced at Bayta, noting the sudden uncertainty and pain-edged tension in her face. Apparently, she could hear the sound too, possibly better even than I could.

"So then you know," Muzzfor said.

"I know lots of things," I said, frowning. Muzzfor's eyes were hard and cold, and I saw now that the oversized, gene-tically engineered throat tucked beneath his long Filly face seemed to be rapidly quivering. "Anything in particular you had in mind?"

"No matter," he said calmly. "If not now, soon enough." Without any word or signal that I could see, Prapp detached himself from the group and walked toward us. His eyes still looked odd, but as he approached I could see that there was a strangely bitter edge to his expression. "Forgive me," he said as he stepped up to us, and out of the corner of my eye I could see the other two walkers saying the same words in unison.

And then, abruptly, Prapp swung his arm at the shoulder, slapping his hand with vicious strength against the side of Bay-ta's head.

It was so unexpected that she never even had time to gasp as the blow sent her spinning to the floor. I had no time to do more than gape before Prapp turned his attack on me, his arms windmilling like a threshing machine gone berserk.

Reflexively, I gave ground, backing across the room as I blocked and deflected and dodged his blows, trying to get my brain on line. Treachery from the Modhri was nothing new, but treachery *now*? It made no sense.

Fortunately for me, Prapp was untrained and unskilled in

hand-to-hand combat. Now that I was ready for him, I was able to deflect or block most of his punches and kicks with ease, and the few that made it through were weak and ineffective. Another minute to let him wear out his reserves, I estimated, and I should be able to take him down.

But I wasn't going to get that minute. The other two walkers were moving in now, swinging wide in opposite directions to flank me. I shifted direction toward Vevri, hoping that after I took down Prapp I could similarly deal one-on-one with the Juri before Qiddicoj could reach me.

For a few seconds it looked like it was going to work. Then, over Prapp's gasping and my own somewhat less strained breathing I sensed the strange ultrasonic sound change pitch and intensity. A moment later Qiddicoj suddenly increased his pace toward me while Vevri slowed his, with the obvious mutual goal of reaching me simultaneously.

I changed direction again, ducking around behind a pair of chairs and then suddenly jumping up on one of them and kicking at Prapp's head. The blow I landed was only glancing, but it was enough to send him staggering backward out of the fight.

Just in time. I was hopping off the chair again when Vevri and Qiddicoj caught up with me.

Neither of them was any better trained than Prapp. But both were just as determined, and at two-to-one odds I found myself at a dangerous disadvantage. I kept backing and turning, using every bit of cover and blockage available, trying to work my way toward the end of the car where I could escape into the vestibule. At least there they could only come at me one at a time.

And then, out of the corner of my eye I saw the front vestibule door open. I backed a quarter circle, trying to bring the door into my direct view without having to take my eyes off my opponents. If this was another walker whom the Modhri had conveniently failed to mention, I was going to be in serious trouble.

It wasn't another walker. It was Sarge.

For the first couple of seconds no one seemed to notice his arrival. Then, abruptly, Vevri and Qiddicoj abandoned their attack on me. Turning, staggering with muscle fatigue and gasping for breath, they charged full-tilt toward the defender.

I'd seen defender Spiders in action, and Sarge should have counterattacked like a runaway freight. But to my surprise, he didn't. In fact, for those first crucial seconds he stood there, staring like a rookie at his first crime scene. By the time he stirred and lifted his three nearest legs into a sort of combat stance, it was too late. Vevri and Qiddicoj hit him like a matched pair of heat-seeking missiles, slamming into his remaining four legs and staggering him backward. Breathing hard, I shoved off the chair I had been pressed against and headed over to give him a hand.

And was suddenly shoved three meters to my left as Muzzfor slammed into my right side.

I hit the floor in a tangled mess, astonishment and exhaustion conspiring to throw off my usual hit-and-roll reflexes. I tried to get my legs under me, but before I could do so Muzzfor flung himself on top of me, nearly breaking my rib cage in the process.

And as I fought for breath, his hands closed firmly around my neck. "Foolish Human," he said, his voice abruptly deep and resonant and no longer even recognizable as Filiaelian. It made for an eerie contrast with the high-pitched background hum that seemed to be rattling even louder against the base of my skull. "I tried to avoid this," he continued. "I tried to turn you against Emikai, the Modhri—anyone except the Human Kennrick. But you would not be dissuaded." His grip tightened around my throat. "So now do you pay the cost of your cleverness."

My vision was starting to waver. But what most people didn't know, and Muzzfor almost certainly didn't, was that even with my breath cut off there was enough residual oxygen already in my muscle fibers for one good, solid, last-ditch punch.

And with his quivering, oversized throat hanging right over my face, there was only one logical target. Releasing my grip on his wrists, I curled my hands into fists and jabbed upward as hard as I could.

I had expected it to be like hitting a tube of slightly undercooked mostaccioli. To my dismay, it was more like slamming my fists into well-insulated plastic pipe. Whatever the Filly genetic engineers had done to Muzzfor's throat, they'd put some heavy-duty musculature around it.

And with that, my last reserve was gone. My hands dropped back to Muzzfor's wrists, but I had no strength left to try to tear them away from my throat. I couldn't hear the high-pitched whine anymore, and in the distance the clatter of bodies against metal as Vevri and Qiddicoj beat themselves against Sarge likewise faded into the roar of blood rushing in my ears. Muzzfor's face was an expressionless mask, the sort of face Bayta often wore. My thoughts drifted toward Bayta, wondering if Muzzfor and the others would leave her alive or if whatever I'd done to trigger the Modhri's wrath would bring her the same sentence of death.

And then, without warning, something shot into view around Muzzfor's arms and barreled full-tilt into the Filly's side, hurling him off me and ripping his hands away from my throat. Gripping my neck, gasping in great lungfuls of air, I rolled onto my side.

I found myself faced with an incredible sight. Prapp was straddling a prone Muzzfor, pounding his fists against the Filly's head and torso with the same determination he'd used in his earlier attack against me.

But even as I lay there trying to figure out what the hell was happening, Muzzfor seemed to get either his composure or his wind back. One hand slammed against Prapp's throat, snapping his head forward like the clapper of a bell. Prapp went limp, and with a surge of legs and arms Muzzfor sent the Tra'ho sailing helplessly to slam into the floor three meters away. An instant later Muzzfor was back on his feet, his cold, soulless eyes turning back to his unfinished business with me—

Just as Vevri and Qiddicoj slammed into him in a perfectly coordinated high/low double tackle.

Muzzfor gave a bellow as he hit the floor again, a deep, furious ululation that momentarily froze me where I knelt.

If Vevri and Qiddicoj were affected by the roar, it didn't show. They were all over their target, punching and clawing at him with an almost mindless fury.

I still didn't know what the hell was going on. All I knew was that Muzzfor had tried to kill me, the Modhri was no longer on his side, and I was damned if I was going to sit out the rest of this fight.

But even as I got to my feet, Vevri abruptly gave out a choked-off scream and rolled off the downed Filly. As I staggered forward Qiddicoj gave a similar scream and also fell backward, clutching at his stomach. He curled into a fetal position around himself, but not before I saw the blood spreading out across his clothing.

And then Muzzfor was on his feet again, his fingers dripping two different shades of red. He turned toward me, and as he did so his hands curved themselves into raptor talons. Something else the genetic engineers had no doubt graced him with.

For a moment we locked eyes. Then, lifting the talons to point at my stomach, he stalked toward me.

"At least tell me why you want me dead," I croaked, taking an angled step backward. He continued toward me, and I matched him step for step, walking us around in a slow circle that was taking me back toward the rear of the car. I was still breathing heavily; with luck, he would assume I was just trying to buy time. "What did I ever do to you? *Tell* me, damn it. What did I ever do to you?"

Muzzfor didn't answer, but just kept coming. I continued to back away, not daring to look behind me and see if I was about to back into a chair or some other obstacle. The Filly was getting closer, and I imagined I could see a fresh surge of bloodlust in those empty, empty eyes.

He was still coming when two of Sarge's legs stabbed like twin spears into his back.

For a moment Muzzfor just stood there, his gaze on the bloodied metal legs poking out of his chest, a disbelieving expression on his face. Very much the way Kennrick had reacted to his own unexpected defeat and death, a small, detached part of my mind noted. Then, without a sound, the Filly's eyes closed, and he sagged against the Spider legs still holding him mostly upright.

"He is dead?" Sarge asked into the silence.

"He'd damned well better be," I said. Angling in cautiously from the side, just in case, I went up to Muzzfor to check.

The examination didn't take long. Filly genetic engineers could do a lot of strange and interesting things to their clients, as Muzzfor himself had more than proved. But there were only so many places you could put the heart and lungs. "Yes, he's dead," I confirmed, stepping thankfully away from the dangling corpse. "Almost no thanks to you, I might add. What were you doing, waiting for scorecards to be passed out?"

"No," Sarge said, an odd tone to his voice. "I could not . . . it is difficult to explain. I could not think, nor could I properly react to the threat facing me."

"Compton," a voice whispered.

I swore as I stepped past Sarge and Muzzfor and hurried toward the three bodies lying crumpled on the floor. In those last tense minutes, I'd completely forgotten about the Modhri.

Prapp and Vevri weren't moving, but Qiddicoj was still breathing weakly. "Defender, get the doctors up here," I snapped as I dropped to my knees beside the wounded Filly. "*Now*. And get me that LifeGuard," I added, pointing to the orange case on the wall.

"No use," Qiddicoj murmured. Or rather, the Modhri within him murmured. "I'm sorry, Compton. Please believe this was not my doing."

"I know it wasn't," I assured him. "Lie still, now—the doctors are on their way."

The Modhri shook his head. "No use," he said again. "The other Eyes are already dead, and this one will soon join them. When that happens, I too will die."

He looked down at his blood-soaked midsection, then up at me again. "It was a call in my mind and my ears," he said. "The same as I heard two nights ago. Only this time, I was not ordered to lie, but to kill." He coughed, bringing specks of blood to his lips. The blaze on his long face, I noted, had gone deathly pale. "Even knowing it ordered me to evil, I had no power to resist."

Abruptly, a piece fell into place. "Was the compulsion tied to that high-pitched sound I kept hearing?" I asked.

"Yes," Qiddicoj confirmed. "When it ceased . . . the orders were still there, but I no longer had to obey."

And the sound had ceased right after I'd punched Muzzfor in his genetically modified throat. The damn thing hadn't been created so that he could sing high opera. It had been created as a weapon.

But a weapon against whom? The Spiders? The Modhri?

A metal leg appeared in my peripheral vision, and I looked up as Sarge handed me the LifeGuard. I set it down beside *Osantra* Qiddicoj, keying the selector for Filiaelian, and started connecting the arm cuff.

"Compton."

"Lie still," I said. I finished the cuff and leaned over him with the breather mask.

His hand lifted, brushing weakly against the mask. "No use," he said. "Compton. Remember our bargain."

"I will," I said, moving the mask around his flailing arm and pressing it over his nostrils.

"A shame it must end now," the Modhri said as I keyed the LifeGuard. His voice was so weak I could barely hear it. "We worked . . . well . . . together."

"Yes, we did," I agreed, an odd feeling trickling through me. The Modhri was my enemy . . . and yet, this particular mind segment and I had somehow been able to unite against a common threat.

There was a lesson in there somewhere, but at the moment I couldn't be bothered. The Modhri could have run away when I'd wrecked Muzzfor's Pied Piper whistle, but instead he'd sacrificed his life to protect mine. I was *not* going to just sit back and let him die.

I was still talking soothingly to him when the LifeGuard's lights went red. I punched the start button again, but it was pure, useless reflex. Qiddicoj was dead.

And then his eyelids fluttered. "Compton," he whispered.

"I'm here, Modhri," I said.

"A new bargain," he whispered. "In return for saving your life. Learn the truth of what happened here."

I nodded. "Bet on it," I said grimly.

The eyelids fluttered again and went still.

For a minute I continued to kneel over the body, until the LifeGuard's lights again went red. Taking a deep breath, wincing at the ache in my throat, I got tiredly to my feet. "You have made yet another bargain with the Modhri," Sarge said.

"Doesn't count as a bargain," I said, crossing to where Bayta was still lying unconscious. "I'd already promised that to myself."

I lowered myself to the floor beside Bayta, carefully touching the side of her neck. Her pulse was slow but strong, and her chest was moving up and down with steady breathing. There was an ugly handprint on the side of her face where Prapp had slapped her, but it didn't look like anything was broken.

"Shall I move her to one of the seats?" Sarge asked.

"I'll do it," I told him. Getting an arm under her neck, I carefully lifted her head and shoulders up off the floor.

For a long moment I gazed into her face, my eyes tracing all those familiar features. My partner, my ally, my friend . . . and I'd nearly lost her.

Thought virus, the warning whispered through my mind. Too close, and we would both be dangerously vulnerable if one of us was ever infected with a Modhran colony.

I felt my lip twist. The hell with thought viruses.

Leaning close, I kissed her.

Her lips were softer than I'd imagined they would be, probably because I'd so often seen them pursed or stiff with disapproval over something I'd said or done. Her scent was subtle and exotic, with an equally subtle taste to her lips. I got my arm around behind her and held her close, savoring the kiss even as I shivered with what had almost happened to take her away from me.

And then, suddenly, I felt a slight change in the feel of her muscles. I opened my eyes.

To find her eyes were also open. Looking straight back into mine.

I jerked back, a sudden flush of embarrassment and guilt heating my face and neck. "Uh . . ." I floundered.

"Yes," she said, and I could sense some of the same embarrassment in her own voice. "Uh . . . I think I'm all right."

"Are you sure?" I asked, trying to shift my hands to a more professional grip on her arms. This sort of thing wasn't supposed to happen. Especially since neither of us wanted it to.

"I think so," she said. For another moment, her eyes held mine. Then, she tore her gaze away.

And I felt her stiffen. "Frank," she gasped.

"Yeah," I said grimly, following her stricken eyes to the four bloodied bodies scattered around the car. "Not a pretty sight, is it?"

"What hap—?" She broke off, and I had the impression Sarge was feeding her the entire blow-by-blow.

I looked at the bodies again, perversely glad for the distraction they provided, and wondered if Bayta would want to talk later about that impulsive kiss. Part of me hoped she would. Most of me hoped she wouldn't.

"But it doesn't make sense," she said into my thoughts. "Why did *Asantra* Muzzfor do that? *How* did he do that?"

"I don't know," I said. "But I know where to start looking. You up to a little walk?"

"Of course," she said. She got a grip on my arms, which were somehow still wrapped around her, and together we got her to her feet. "Where are we going?"

"Kennrick's compartment," I said. "From the way Muzzfor was talking, I think there's something in there he assumed we'd already found. Something he thought was worth killing us for."

"Something in Mr. Kennrick's lockbox?" she suggested.

"That's the logical place to start," I agreed, tightening my grip on her arm as she wavered a bit. "Can you make it, or do you want to wait here?"

"I can make it," she said grimly. "You think we'll be able to open it?"

"Depends on how good Emikai's bypass mimic really is," I told her. "Easy, now—let's go."

Prapp's attack, plus the ordeal that had preceded it, had apparently taken more out of Bayta than she'd realized. Emikai's mimic was still only midway through its work on Kennrick's portable lockbox when she went over to the bed to lie down. By the time I pulled the lockbox lid open, she was fast asleep.

The box was well stocked, mostly with papers but also with a couple of collections of data chips. Some of the papers had belonged to Givvrac, the ones I skimmed consisting of notes and observations from the contract team's time on Earth. Other papers were Kennrick's, and I made a point of putting those aside for later study. Each of the other members of the contract team had also made donations to the stack, and I was nearly to the bottom before I found a small, sealed folder with Muzzfor's name on it.

I opened it up and carefully read through the contents. Twice. Then, sitting down on the curve couch, I stared at the bloodstained carpet and waited for Bayta to wake up.

And as I sat there, I thought distantly about the many phrases and similes and mental images we used every day without really thinking about them. Never again. Not me. I'd seen the contents of *Asantra* Muzzfor's folder.

I knew now what the Gates of Hell truly looked like.

I'd fallen into a light doze when I was jolted awake by a soft moan. I tensed; but it was only Bayta, stretching carefully on the bed across the compartment from me. "Sorry," she apologized, gingerly touching her face where Prapp had hit her. "I guess I was more tired—"

"We've got trouble," I interrupted her.

Her hand froze against her skin. "I'm listening," she said, her voice back to its usual calm.

I took a deep breath. "We were wrong," I said. "Or at least, I was. Tell me, what do the Chahwyn know about the Shonkla-raa?"

"You know most of it," Bayta said, frowning. "They were a slaver race who conquered most of the galaxy's sentient peoples almost three thousand years ago. They held that power for a thousand years, at which point their subjects staged a coordinated revolt and destroyed them."

"You're almost right," I said. "But there's one small detail you and everyone else has gotten wrong. *Shonkla-raa* isn't a race. It's a title. Specifically, an old *Filiaelian* title."

Her eyes widened. "The Shonkla-raa were *Filiaelians*? But then—?"

"But then why haven't they conquered everyone again?" I finished for her. "Simple. Because the Shonkla-raa was a specific Filly genetic line, and that line *was* destroyed in the revolt."

"The Filiaelian obsession with genetic engineering," Bayta said, nodding slowly. "They've been trying to re-create the Shonkla-raa."

"*Some* group of them has been, anyway," I agreed. "Only they're not trying anymore." I held up Muzzfor's folder. "They've done it."

Bayta stared at me, the blood draining from her face. "Oh, no."

"Oh, yes," I confirmed. "But it gets worse. Remember why the Modhri was created in the first place?"

"He was a weapon," Bayta said, the words coming out mechanically, her eyes staring out at a horrifying future. "A last-ditch infiltrator and saboteur."

"Which was also designed to be under Shonkla-raa control." I nodded back toward the coach car two cars behind us. "What did you think of the demo?"

She shivered. "All that because he couldn't get *Logra* Emikai to kill you earlier?"

"All that because he had to deflect me away from Kennrick," I corrected. "So that he and the others could get off the Quadrail without me ever seeing these papers." I shrugged. "And probably also because he'd figured out Kennrick was the killer and wanted to get the murder technique for himself and his buddies." I grimaced. "Remember, a few days ago, when you pointed out that the Modhri hasn't got any purpose? Well, he's got one now. The sword's on the shelf, and the swordsman's all set to pick it up again."

For a long minute neither of us spoke. "What are we going to do?" Bayta asked at last.

"I don't see that we've got much choice," I told her. "We have to take them down."

Bayta stared at me in disbelief. "Frank, it took the whole galaxy to stop the Shonkla-raa the last time. And they didn't have the Modhri to help them then."

"I didn't say it would be easy," I conceded. "But we have a couple of advantages they don't know about."

She barked out a sound that was midway between a chuckle and a sob. "Like what?"

"One: we don't have a whole galaxy's worth of them to deal with this time," I said. "With luck, they've only got a few thousand up and running."

"*Only* a few thousand?"

"*And* they don't have all the warships and weapons they had back then, either," I said. "Number two: they may be really good fighters—and they are," I added, rubbing my ribs. "But they don't know about the new defender-class Spiders. As much as you and I may disagree with the whole defender concept, it's a wild card we ultimately may be glad we've got."

Bayta shivered. "If they don't save the Quadrail only to destroy it," she murmured.

"We'll just have to make sure that doesn't happen, either," I said grimly. "And finally—" I lifted the folder again. "We know where they are."

Bayta sat up a little straighter. "Their location's in there?"

"I think so," I said. "It's clear now that it wasn't a coincidence that Aronobal and Emikai were on Earth at the same time that Givvrac's contract team was at Pellorian Medical. My guess is that the attack on Terese German and her subsequent pregnancy were already planned, and that whoever's in charge of the Shonkla-raa decided the Pellorian Medical thing would be good cover. They then maneuvered Muzzfor onto the team so that he could monitor the others while they brought Terese German to Filly space."

"But why?" Bayta asked. "What do they want with her?"

"Something disgusting, I have no doubt," I said. "But whatever the *why*, the *where* is a space station called Proteus."

Bayta frowned. "That doesn't sound like a Filiaelian name."

"It isn't," I agreed. "The station actually has thirty different names, one corresponding to each of the Twelve Empires' official languages. Apparently, it was designed to be the jewel of Filiaelian diplomatic glory and finesse." I tilted my head. "Want to take a guess as to where this multispecies crown jewel is?"

She frowned; and then, her face cleared. "The Ilat Dumar Covrey system," she said. "Where those six Modhran Filiaelians we ran into on New Tigris had come from."

"Bingo," I said. "Muzzfor had a new set of tickets and passes made out for himself, Aronobal, Emikai, and Terese. I assume he was planning to spring the package on them at Venidra Carvo."

"And we're going to follow them there?"

I turned the folder over in my hand. "Actually," I told her, "I had something a bit different in mind."

TWENTY-THREE :

We found Terese and the two Fillies waiting on the far edge of the Venidra Carvo Station, their luggage gathered in a pile around them. "Good day, Dr. Aronobal; *Logra* Emikai; Ms. German," I greeted them as Bayta and I came up. "If I may say so, you all look a little lost."

"Well, we're not," Terese spoke up, giving me one of those glares she did so well. "So go away."

"Actually, I think you are," I said. "I'm afraid the guide you're expecting won't be joining you."

"What do you mean?" Aronobal asked, frowning down her long nose at me.

"I'm sure you heard that there were four final victims of the murderer Kennrick shortly before he himself was killed a couple of weeks ago," I said.

"Yes, we heard," Aronobal said darkly. "A tragic occurrence."

"Very tragic," I agreed. "Even more so as it turns out that one of them was supposed to contact you here and give you the tickets to your final destination. Specifically, *Asantra* Muzzfor."

Aronobal jerked her head at that. "*Asantra* Muzzfor? Are you certain?"

"He told me so himself, before he died," I assured her. "Here are your tickets." I pulled out the tickets I'd gotten from Muzzfor's folder and passed them out.

Aronobal peered at the destination on her ticket. "These are for *Kuzyatru* Station."

"Never heard of it," Terese said, frowning at hers.

"In English, it's called Proteus," I told the girl. "You may have heard of it by that name."

"Well, I haven't," she growled. "No one said anything about going to a space station. I thought I was going to some big clinic on Dojussu Sefpra Major."

"That was my understanding, as well," Aronobal seconded.

"Maybe you'll be going there after you visit Proteus," I said. "All I know is that these tickets are made out in your names, and that I was asked to deliver them to you."

"You were asked by *Asantra* Muzzfor?" Emikai asked, an odd expression on his face.

"Yes," I confirmed, looking him straight in the eye. "I was with him when he died. He also asked me to accompany you to Proteus, to make sure you got there safely."

"There is no need for that," Emikai said firmly. "I will watch over them."

"I'm sure you will," I acknowledged. "And I certainly imply no slight on your capabilities. But I promised *Asantra* Muzzfor I would go with you, and I would ask that you permit me to honor that promise."

"Of course," Aronobal said distractedly, looking around. "Very well, then. Do you happen to know which track our new train will be taking?"

"Number Eighteen," I said, pointing across the station. "Just follow us."

With Bayta beside me, I started toward our new track. I'd gone only a couple of steps when I felt a soft but insistent grip on my upper arm. "Keep going," I told Bayta as I allowed the hand to slow me down. Terese and Aronobal passed me by, Aronobal giving me barely a glance, Terese ignoring me completely. As their trailing luggage rolled past me I came to a halt. "You have a question?" I asked quietly, turning to face Emikai.

For a moment he didn't speak, his hand still gripping my arm. "They will wish to know exactly how *Asantra* Muzzfor died," he said at last. "Those who now employ me."

"And I'll be glad to tell them," I assured him.

"Will you?" he countered. "Even if they assign a portion of the blame to you?"

"Why would they do that?" I asked, keeping my voice and expression calm. There was no way, after all, for Emikai to know the truth about what had happened to Muzzfor. "I had nothing to do with his death."

"You are the same species as the killer," Emikai pointed out. "That may be enough." His eyes flicked ahead to Bayta and his two companions. "There is no need for you to escort us. It would perhaps be better for you to go about your own business."

"My business is the protection of innocent people," I said. "I have an obligation to see Ms. German safely to Proteus."

Emikai's eyes bored into mine. "Very well," he said. "If you are truly determined, I will not forbid you to accompany us."

"Thank you," I said.

I started to turn away, turned back as his hand darted up again to grip my arm. "But remember," he added. "I too am a protector of my people."

"Indeed you are," I said softly. "Don't worry. I won't forget."

TOR

A handsome, rich
playboy qualifies as
a PARTY favor.

ALWAYS know the location
of the nearest exit.

Falling in the pool
is bad form; falling
in love is highly
RECOMMENDED.

PARTY Crashers

"You want to stay?" Jolie asked, unable to keep the surprise out of her voice.

Beck cleared his throat. "Considering everything that's happened, I thought it best if someone stayed with you."

He strode to the window and nodded at the two-foot cactus she'd set on the floor beneath the sill. "Nice touch," he said approvingly. He raised the blinds and ran his hands along the closure, then frowned. "Have you had this window open lately?"

Jolie shook her head and walked over, her heart jumping in her chest.

"This latch is open." He leaned down to peer at the windowsill. "Looks like someone has either come in or left by this window in the past few days."

She sagged onto the foot of her bed.

"You should report the entry to the police," he said, coming up behind her.

"I will," she said, then turned and smiled up at him. "Thank you for . . . thank you." His eyes were dark with concern and other emotions she didn't want to investigate as a wholly inappropriate pang of lust hit her.

She suspected the light of day would only reveal more and bigger dilemmas.

The dilemma sleeping on her couch notwithstanding.

By Stephanie Bond

PARTY CRASHERS
KILL THE COMPETITION
I THINK I LOVE YOU
GOT YOUR NUMBER
OUR HUSBAND

STEPHANIE BOND

PARTY
Crashers

AVON BOOKS
An Imprint of HarperCollinsPublishers

AVON BOOKS
An Imprint of HarperCollins*Publishers*
10 East 53rd Street
New York, New York 10022-5299

Copyright © 2004 by Stephanie Bond Hauck
Party Crashers copyright © 2004 by Stephanie Bond Hauck; *And the Bride Wore Plaid* copyright © 2004 by Karen Hawkins; *I'm No Angel* copyright © 2004 by Patti Berg; *A Perfect Bride* copyright © 2004 by Sandra Kleinschmit
ISBN: 0-06-053984-4
www.avonromance.com

First Avon Books paperback printing: May 2004

Avon Trademark Reg. U.S. Pat. Off. and in Other Countries, Marca Registrada, Hecho en U.S.A.
HarperCollins® is a registered trademark of HarperCollins Publishers Inc.

Printed in the U.S.A.

10 9 8 7 6 5 4 3 2 1

Acknowledgments

The opening, closing, and merging of various department stores in Atlanta caused me grief in writing my previous book, *Kill the Competition,* and again in *Party Crashers,* because some of the scenes reference or take place in department stores that were defunct by the time I turned in the manuscripts. But simply changing the names of the department stores can create other problems. In the store originally featured in *Party Crashers,* the men's and women's shoe departments were together. When that store announced it was closing, I changed the setting to Neiman Marcus. If you're a customer of Neiman Marcus, you know that the men's and women's shoe departments are in separate areas of the store, but I left the shoe departments in proximity to each other. I hope you don't mind the liberty I took for the sake of the story.

With every book there are people to whom I turn for answers to obscure questions. For *Party Crashers,* I'd like to thank Tim Logsdon, Steve Grantham, and Chris Hauck for their unblinking resourcefulness. Many thanks also to my wonderful agent, Kimberly Whalen of Trident Media Group. And there aren't words to thank my editor, Lyssa

Keusch, for allowing me to run with my ideas and providing insightful feedback to make my stories better. Lyssa, your trust is humbling.

Also, many thanks to my readers who send notes of encouragement just when I'm ready to throw my hands in the air—you help me to muddle through. I hope I'm keeping you entertained.

Stephanie Bond

One

"It's like, I can't decide between the Kate Spade slides and the Via Spiga T-straps, you know?"

Kneeling on the floor of the Neiman Marcus footwear department, Lenox Square, Atlanta, Georgia, Jolie Goodman peered at the tortured coed over a mountain of overflowing shoe boxes. Jolie's knees were raw and carpet burned. Her arms twitched from relaying stacks of shoe boxes to and from the stockroom. Her fingers ached from tying laces and finagling straps to ease shoes onto malodorous feet. Yet her considerable discomfort was apparently minuscule in comparison to the momentous decision weighing on the young woman's mind.

Jolie reached into her sales arsenal and pulled out a persuasive smile. "Why don't you take both and decide when you get home? You can always return a pair later."

The woman's shoulders fell in relief. "You're *right*. I'll take them both. Oh, and the Prada flats, too."

Jolie nodded with approval, scooped up the boxes, and trotted to the checkout counter before the girl could change her mind. Michael Lane, a senior sales consultant, waited for a receipt to print. He eyed the three boxes in her hands with an arched brow. "You're catching on," he murmured. "You just might last after all."

Only through the holiday sales season, Jolie promised herself. Eighty-one more days, if one were counting. The salary and commissions would tide her over until the housing market picked up after the first of the year and she could resume building her real-estate business. She had hoped the experience would sharpen her sales skills . . . She hadn't counted on the bonus of raising her threshold for pain.

Michael ripped off the long sales receipt and handed it to his customer with an ingratiating smile. "Thank you for shopping at Neiman Marcus." As he turned toward Jolie, he said, "Don't forget about the sales meeting tomorrow morning at nine. I know you're not on until noon, but everyone is expected to be there."

Jolie groaned inwardly. She'd been planning to assemble a mailing to her former customers the next morning—one day into her temporary job, and she was already neglecting her primary goal. She rang up the slightly enormous sale, swiped the young woman's credit card, then sent her on her way with a brimming Neiman Marcus shopping bag. The satisfaction over the big fat sale was short-lived, however, because she had to straighten and clear thirty-some boxes of discards before she could move on to the next customer.

Discards—that was a laugh. The boxes held some of the most exquisite designer shoes available, each stuffed and wrapped with form-holding stays, some swathed in cloth bags, some with registration cards. In her previous unenlightened world, she hadn't known that people actually registered their footwear, but she had since learned that when consumers forked over hundreds of dollars for a pair of shoes, they expected prestigious, if hollow, bonuses.

Jolie stooped, ignored the twinge in her lower back, and began repackaging the shoes. She reminded herself she should be thanking her lucky stars for landing this position. According to Michael, the shoe department ranked high in dollar sales per customer, and was always busy. She could do worse for a temporary job. While she repacked a pair of Anne Klein mules, she scanned the customers for the person who seemed most eager to be waited on. They were in the midst of a Columbus Day sale, and the temperatures had begun to dip in earnest, so Atlantans were rushing to the mall in droves to replace their sandals with more substantial fare. And six-hundred-dollar faux crocodile stiletto-heeled boots would definitely keep the chill at bay.

Her gaze skitted over the after-five crowd, then caught on a familiar dark orange ball cap. Her heart stalled. *Gary?* The man stood several yards away, his profile obscured by other shoppers. In a split second, her mind rationalized it could be him—he certainly had preferred shopping at the upscale stores in this mall. Her heart jumpstarted, thudding in her ears. What would she do first—confront him or call the police? Kiss him or kill him?

Jolie craned for a better look just as the man turned. Her pulse spiked, then a fusion of disappointment and relief shot through her. It wasn't Gary. Again. She dropped her gaze and stared at the box in her hand until her vital signs recovered. She felt like a fool all over again, just like a month ago when she explained to a dubious officer that her boyfriend—and her car—had simply disappeared. But

Gary drove a Mercedes—why would he want her Mercury? In her mind, her car being stolen and Gary dropping out of sight were mutually exclusive. The uniformed man hadn't been nearly so magnanimous when he'd told her flat out that she'd been royally scammed.

Squashing the train of thought, she gave herself a mental shake—she couldn't afford to be distracted, not now, when she needed to be on her sales game. She resumed scanning for ripe customers.

Her gaze landed on a tanned and rumpled sandy-haired man, strangely dressed in holey jeans and an expensive sport coat, hovering near a sleek blonde to whom Michael was showing a strappy shoe that Jolie hadn't yet memorized—Stuart Weitzman? Stubbs and Wootton? Her head swam with trendy monikers. From the restless look on the man's rugged face, he was a salesman's worst enemy—a "straggler," the person who accompanies the primary shopper and shifts from foot to foot until the shopper moves along. Interesting face or no, he wasn't useful to her.

Scan, scan—*stop*. Jolie cringed.

Ten feet away, Sammy "Sold" Sanders, real-estate agent extraordinaire and Jolie's ex-boss, scrutinized a Manolo Blahnik bootie with laser blue eyes. Jolie's pulse hammered as she imagined the belly laugh that Sammy would enjoy when she discovered that her employee who had quit in a puffed-up huff over the questionable ethics of a deal had been reduced to selling shoes. Jolie had hoped to see Sammy again, but not until the Jolie Goodman Real Estate Agency was well into the black . . . or at least had letterhead. She stacked boxes high in her arms and lifted them to obscure her face as she hurried toward the stockroom. Maybe she could hide out until Sammy left.

During the two hundred or so trips she'd made to and from the stockroom that day, Jolie thought she had the path and its obstacles memorized. *Apparently not,* she realized, as she collided with something solid and bounced back. She teetered on the heels of her sensible pumps, trying to stabilize the boxes that swayed one way and then the other. She failed spectacularly and acrobatically, falling hard on her tailbone while propelling the boxes into the air so high, she had time to envision the sound and sight of the merchandise crashing to the ground before it actually happened.

Except it was so much worse than she'd imagined.

The shoe boxes landed on and around Jolie in a thudding avalanche. Everyone within earshot turned to stare, including Sammy Sanders, which was bad enough on its own, but since Jolie sat on the floor with her legs spread and her skirt rucked up to her thighs, it was the stuff of which nightmares were made. In those first few seconds of stunned silence, she was afraid everyone was going to start clapping, like the time she dropped her tray in the school lunchroom in the seventh grade. But no one clapped: The customers of Neiman Marcus simply seemed annoyed that she'd interrupted their pristine environment.

"I beg your pardon," a deep voice said.

Jolie bent her head back to find the sandy-haired man with the holey jeans standing over her, his hand extended. A smile played on his mouth. "I wasn't looking where you were going."

Afraid that she might pull him down with her when she tried to stand, Jolie rolled over on her side and pushed herself to her knees before accepting his hand and being helped to her feet. His gentlemanly behavior, she noticed, didn't keep him from stealing a peek at the expanse of leg she had on display.

"Thank you," she chirped, yanking down her hem. She'd managed to lose one of her own shoes in the aftermath, and proceeded to toe it upright and stick her foot inside before anyone noticed it wasn't a brand that came with a registration card.

"Are you okay?" the man asked.

She nodded, cheeks flaming. "I should be asking *you*. I just clobbered you with five thousand dollars' worth of shoes."

One side of his mouth lifted. "I'll live."

But it was the smile in his brown eyes that made her tongue do a figure eight.

Michael Lane rushed up. "Are you all right, sir?"

"I'm fine."

"Please accept our deepest apologies. This is Jolie's first day on the job." Michael shot her a frown that indicated it might also be her *last* day on the job.

"No harm done," the man said smoothly.

"Jolie? Jolie Goodman, I *thought* that was you."

Jolie closed her eyes briefly, then turned to face the music. Sammy Sanders glided toward them in all her pink and white blonde glory.

"Hello, Sammy."

Sammy's gaze landed on Jolie's lapel badge, and her eyes rounded. "Are you *working* here?"

"Yes."

Sammy made a distressed noise, as if she were stepping over a homeless person, and touched the arm of Jolie's jacket with a manicured hand. "Jolie, it doesn't have to be like this. Come back to the Sanders Agency and we'll let bygones be bygones."

Jolie glanced down at Sammy's hand, then pulled away. "Excuse me while I clean up the mess I made."

Sammy's face reddened, then she tossed her pale hair. "While you're in the back, Jolie, fetch me this little number in a size seven, will you?"

Fetch . . . like a dog. Sammy had been having her fetch things for years—would she never be able to get one up on the woman?

The man she'd plowed into stepped in. "I believe the lady was helping me."

Sammy flicked her gaze over him, then conjured up an ingratiating smile. "I'll wait."

He looked around and picked up the nearest men's shoe, a lustrous Cole Haan loafer, quite a contrast to the battered tennis shoes he wore. "Do you have this in size eleven?"

Jolie gave him a grateful look. "I'll check." She stooped to grab an armful of shoes, lids, and boxes, and scrambled toward the stockroom.

Michael was on her heels with a second armload. "Do you know who that is?"

"My former boss, Sammy Sanders."

"I mean the *man*."

"No. Should I?"

"That's Beck *Under*wood."

She dropped her load on a table. "Of Underwood Broadcasting?"

"The same. His family owns more media outlets and production companies than anyone on the East Coast."

Egad—she subscribed to their movie channel. "I've seen his father and sister on the news," she said, suddenly realizing why the woman with him seemed familiar, "but I don't remember him."

"He's been away from Atlanta for a few years, living in Costa Rica, I believe."

Which explained the longish hair and the deep tan.

"Carlotta told me he was back in town."

"Carlotta?"

"Carlotta Wren—she works upstairs, usually in the Prada department. Hard-core celebrity groupie, knows everyone who's anyone in Atlanta. She'd wet her capris if she knew Beck Underwood was in the store."

Jolie held out the requested size-eleven loafer. "Maybe you should handle this sale."

"I'm handling the sister," Michael reminded her, pulling Jimmy Choo boxes from the shelf by twos. "I'm counting on you to keep *him* busy while I sell *her* the entire fall line."

"Will you cut me in on your commission?"

"No, but I won't fire you."

She swallowed. "Deal."

"Besides," Michael said with a wry grin, "the man probably owns nothing but jungle footwear—maybe you can sell him some civilized shoes." He gave her the once-over, then squinted. "You might want to . . . *fluff* or something." Then he walked out, laden with enough shoes to shod the Rockettes.

Jolie glanced into the mirror on the door of the employee bathroom and groaned. Her short dishwater-blonde hair, curly and fine textured, was unruly under the best of circumstances. But after a confrontation with the carpet, the stuff was a staticky, high-flying nest. Her dark jacket and skirt were lint covered, and the makeup she'd applied so carefully this morning had vanished. She resembled one of the mannequins in sportswear—prominent eyes and knees, with a chalk white pallor—and she felt as insubstantial as she looked. For someone who prided herself on her fortitude, she conceded that six hours on her feet, plus the false sighting of Gary, plus the scene she'd created, plus the run-in with Sammy Sanders . . . well, it was enough to wear a girl down.

Weighing her options, she glanced at the doorway leading back to the showroom, then to the fire-exit door leading to a loading dock. She had the most outrageous urge to walk out . . . and keep walking.

Is that what Gary had done? Reached some kind of personal crisis that he couldn't share with her, and simply walked away from everything—from his job, from his friends, from her? As bad as it sounded, she almost preferred to believe that he had suffered some kind of breakdown rather than consider other possible explanations—that he'd met with foul play, or that she had indeed been scammed by the man who'd professed to care about her.

The exit sign beckoned, but she glanced at the shoe box in her hands and decided that since the man had been kind enough to intercept Sammy, he deserved to be waited on, even if he didn't spend a cent.

Even if people with vulgar amounts of money did make her nervous.

She finger-combed her hair and tucked it behind her ears, then straightened her clothing as best she could. There was no helping the lack of makeup, so she pasted on her best smile—the one that she thought showed too much gum, but that Gary had assured her made her face light up—and returned to the showroom.

Her smile almost faltered, though, when Mr. Beck Underwood's bemused expression landed on her.

She walked toward him, trying to forget that the man could buy and sell her a thousand times over. "I'm sorry again about running into you. Did you really want to try on this shoe or were you just being nice?"

"Both," he said mildly. "My sister is going to be a while, and I need shoes, so this works for me."

At the twinkle in his eyes, her tongue lodged at the roof of her mouth. Like a mime, she gestured to a nearby chair, and made her feet follow him. As he sat, she scanned the area for signs of Sammy.

"She's behind the insoles rack," he whispered.

Jolie flushed and made herself not look. The man probably thought she was clumsy *and* paranoid. She busied herself unpacking the expensive shoes. "Will you be needing a dress sock, sir?"

He slipped off his tennis shoe and wiggled bare, brown toes. "I suppose so. I'm afraid I've gotten into the habit of not wearing socks." He smiled. "And my dad is 'sir'—I'm just Beck."

She suddenly felt small. And poor. "I . . . know who you are."

"Ah. Well, promise you won't hold it against me."

She smiled and retrieved a pair of tan-colored socks to match the loafers. When she started to slip one of the socks over his foot, he took it from her. "I can do it."

"I don't mind," she said quickly. Customers expected it—to be dressed and undressed and re-dressed if necessary. It was an unwritten rule: *No one leaves the store without being touched.*

"I don't have to be catered to," he said, his tone brittle.

Jolie blinked. "I'm sorry."

He looked contrite and exhaled, shaking his head. "Don't be. It's me." Then he grinned unexpectedly. "Besides, under more private circumstances, I might take you up on your offer."

Heat climbed her neck and cheeks. He was teasing her—his good deed for the day. Upon closer scrutiny, his face was even more interesting—his eyes a deep brown, bracketed by untanned lines created from squinting in the sun. Late thirties, she guessed. His skin was ruddy, his strong nose peeling from a recent burn. Despite the pale streaks in his hair, he was about as far from a beach boy as a man could be. When he leaned over to slip on the shoes, she caught a glimpse of his powerful torso beneath the sport coat.

She averted her gaze and concentrated on the stitched design on the vamp of the shoe he was trying on, handing him a shoe horn to protect the heel counter. (This morning Michael had given her an "anatomy of a shoe" lesson, complete with metal pointer and pop quiz.)

The man stood and hefted his weight from foot to foot, then took a couple of steps in one direction and came back. "I'll take them."

A salesperson's favorite words. She smiled. "That was fast."

He laughed. "Men don't have a complicated relationship with shoes."

She liked his easy laugh, it was a happy noise that drew attention—including Sammy's, Jolie noticed. Her former boss came over, her pale brows knit in frustration. "Jolie, were you able to find the shoe I wanted?"

Jolie glanced in Beck's direction. "Go ahead," he said. "I'll wait."

"Give me just a minute," Jolie murmured, then manufactured a smile for Sammy. "A size seven, wasn't it?"

"Yes. And please hurry—I have a big closing in thirty minutes."

Embarrassment flooded Jolie, setting her skin on fire. For the thousandth time, Jolie thought how attractive Sammy would be without her permanent smugness. "Yes, ma'am." She returned to the stockroom, her ego smarting.

Despite the fact that she'd worked for the Sanders Agency for over a decade, it had been inevitable that she and Sammy would part on bad terms. Edgar Sanders had hired her as a receptionist right out of high school, and from the beginning she had clashed with the man's daughter. Sammy was a few years older than Jolie and on the fast track to realty royalty. She'd hated Jolie at first sight. Mr. Sanders, on the other hand, had rewarded Jolie's hard work by moving her up through the company. The two women had developed an uneasy relationship based on avoidance. Jolie had managed to put herself through night school, to become an experienced agent, and three months ago, to obtain her broker's license with an eye toward commercial real estate. Unfortunately, it had coincided with Mr. Sanders' retirement, and suddenly, Jolie had found herself working for Sammy.

Remarkably, the woman's personality seemed to change overnight. She'd been downright helpful to Jolie . . . and two weeks ago, Jolie had discovered why. In order to close a big deal, Sammy wanted Jolie to pass information to the buyer that would breach the company's confidentiality agreement with the seller. Gary had been missing for a few days, and Jolie was already stressed. In fact, she had a feeling that Sammy had purposefully targeted her during a vulnerable time, thinking she would cave. Jolie didn't, and Sammy threatened to fire her. Instead, Jolie had quit.

Sammy said Jolie'd lost her mind—no one left the Sanders Agency voluntarily.

And now Jolie was selling shoes. Boy, she had really shown *her*.

She sighed and scanned for the pair that cost more than her week's salary selling shoes, then removed two boxes from the shelf. She carried them out to Sammy, who apparently had taken advantage of the opportunity to introduce herself to Beck Underwood. The oversize Barbie doll had extended her business card in his direction and he was accepting it, although somewhat reluctantly, Jolie noted.

"We only have a size six and a half and a size seven and a half," Jolie said to Sammy, holding up the boxes. "Would you like to try them?"

Sammy made a face and waved her hand. "No, that's okay. I really was only killing time until my big closing."

Jolie nodded. "It must be a really big closing, since you've already mentioned it twice."

Sammy's eyes narrowed. "Happy *shoeing*, Jolie."

Jolie watched Sammy sashay away, her stomach churning over the way she'd handled the situation. This was a bad time to be starting her own brokerage company, and she had very few resources to fall back on. Considering how many agencies were struggling, if she couldn't get enough business going in the next few months, she might have to go crawling back to Sammy or start at square one somewhere else.

She glanced down at the boxes in her hands. She didn't seem to have much of a future in shoes.

"I sense history between the two of you."

Jolie glanced at Beck Underwood, who sat patiently

with his new shoes on his lap. He had put his old tennis shoes back on, and Jolie wondered about the ground those battered shoes had covered, places she hoped to see someday.

"Former boss," Jolie murmured, then reached for his new shoes. "I'm sorry you had to wait. Do you need anything else?"

"Yeah." Then he smiled. "But it'll give me an excuse to come back—this is the most excitement I've had since I returned to Atlanta."

She managed a shaky smile, thinking she didn't know how much more excitement she could take today. She just wanted to go home and soak her feet, and maybe call her friend Leann to report on what had to be the world's worst first day on the job.

She set aside the shoes Sammy had passed on and carried Beck's loafers to the counter to ring up his sale.

A willowy black woman wearing chinos and a dark jacket walked up to the counter.

"I'll be right with you," Jolie said.

"Jolie Goodman?"

Jolie tensed. "Yes."

The woman opened her coat to reveal a silver badge. "I'm Detective Salyers with the Atlanta PD. I need to speak with you."

Two

Jolie stared at the detective and her stomach caved. "Is something wrong?"

"I just need to talk with you, ma'am."

"Is this about Gary?"

"Yes." The woman's expression gave away nothing.

Jolie's mind reeled. She looked up and saw that Beck Underwood had overheard everything and was watching her carefully. Across the sales floor, Michael Lane stared curiously in her direction. She glanced at her watch, then looked back to the detective. "My shift ends in fifteen minutes. Can you wait?"

The woman nodded. "How about meeting me at the Coffee Shack in the food court?"

Jolie swallowed hard. "Okay." She watched the policewoman walk away and wanted desperately to run after her. Her heart slammed against her breastbone, and her hands were shaking so badly, she could barely finish ringing up the sale.

She looked up and tried to fix her face in a natural expression. "Will you be using your Neiman Marcus card?"

Beck was staring at her. Slowly, he reached for his wallet and flipped through before removing a platinum bank credit card. "There isn't a Neiman Marcus where I've been living."

She ran the card and handed him a receipt to sign. While she bagged his purchase, her gaze drifted toward the mall entrance. The detective had to have some kind of news, didn't she? And if it were good news, the police would have called, wouldn't they? Or Gary himself?

"Jolie?"

She started, then took the signed receipt he extended. "Thank you."

He cleared his throat. "This is none of my business, but is everything okay?"

She nodded and held up his shopping bag. "Thank you for shopping at Neiman Marcus." Then she gave him the best smile she could manage. "Please come back and I'll try not to bulldoze you."

He hesitated, then took his bag. "Take care."

She maintained a cheery smile until he turned away. Then she grabbed the Sammy rejects and checked the floor for debris she might have overlooked from the crash. In the stockroom, she spent the last few minutes of her shift methodically returning the jumble of boxes, lids, and shoes to order.

Snippets of Gary Hagan kept popping into her head—his crooked smile, his curly black hair that he kept gelled in place or covered with an orange cap, the cell phone that was at his ear more often than it was in his pocket. He was wiry and athletic, with an electric personality, always moving. Gary had been the most thoughtful man she'd known—he'd never missed an opportunity to celebrate an occasion, and often had brought her flowers for no reason. But the police didn't understand any of those things.

She climbed onto a stool to reshelve the boxes, and unbidden tears clouded her vision. She swayed, then grabbed the edge of the shelf to keep from falling.

"Jolie?" Michael Lane was behind her, his hand against her back. "Are you okay?"

"Just a little light-headed," she said, allowing him to help her down.

"Who was that woman? She asked me to point you out to her."

Jolie hesitated, but if Michael was left to concoct his own answer, he might come up with something worse than the truth. "She's a detective from the police department. A guy I was dating disappeared a few weeks ago."

"Disappeared?"

She nodded. "The detective must have news, because she wants to talk to me. I asked her to meet me when my shift ended."

"Go," he said, pointing toward the door. "I'll put everything back. I hope she has good news."

She nodded gratefully, then retrieved her purse from a locker in the break room and walked out across the showroom toward the entrance to the mall. She resisted the urge to look for Beck Underwood. In the space of a few minutes, he had learned that she was a hopeless klutz, estranged from her former boss, and that the police wanted to talk to her. The man probably thought she was a total drama queen. He'd never know how much she'd appreciated his concern.

She nodded to the security guard at the doorway and hurried out into the mall, instantly assaulted with voices, music, and crowd noise reverberating between tile floors and glass ceilings. Because of Columbus Day, kids were off school and had been at the mall all day in full force, cruising for attention and trouble. The girls were squeezed into provocative clothes and looked old enough to do things they shouldn't. The boys looked overwhelmed.

A far cry from her own sheltered upbringing. She had been an only child, a change-of-life baby, and her frugal parents had harbored rather old-fashioned notions about child-rearing. But even if she hadn't worn the most fashionable clothes or obtained her driver's license until she was eighteen, she could thank her parents for loving her and for giving her a good value system. She'd lost them both to illness when she was in her early twenties. Work had been her solace, and night school had kept her plenty busy. Oh, there had been occasional dates and sporadic boyfriends, but Gary Hagan had been the first man who had made her think about sharing her future. He was an orphan too, having lost his parents to a car accident. She thought it had made them closer, their aloneness.

Would her parents have approved of Gary? She'd asked herself this question many times over the months they had dated. In the beginning they would have been uncomfortable with his exuberance, just as she'd been. But eventually, they would've been won over by his relentless cheerfulness.

At least she liked to think so.

Through gaps in the crowd, Jolie saw the lady detective up ahead, pacing in front of the coffee vendor.

Pacing . . . that couldn't be good.

Jolie drew in a shaky breath and strode forward, eager to get the meeting over with. Detective Salyers spotted her and stood still, waiting until she came close enough to speak.

"Would you like a cup of coffee?"

Jolie shook her head.

"I'm going to get a cup, why don't you grab us a table?"

Another delay. Jolie found a table for two away from the din and studied what looked to be cookie crumbs left from the previous occupant. It was a trick she'd learned: Focusing on mundane details allowed her to get through difficult times because they were reminders that life went on. No matter what the detective had to say, life would go on. Tomorrow someone else would be sitting here, maybe falling in love for the first time, or contemplating what to cook for dinner. And Gary would either be dead or alive.

"Here you go," Dectective Salyers said, sliding a cup of caramel-colored coffee in front of her. The woman smiled. "I thought you might change your mind."

Jolie thanked her.

The detective claimed the opposite seat. "Ms. Goodman, you're a difficult woman to track down. You weren't home, and we have your employer listed as the Sanders Agency."

"I left there a couple of weeks ago."

"We contacted the woman you had listed as your closest relative on the missing person's report you filed on Gary Hagan—a Leann Renaldi in Jacksonville?"

"Yes, she's a good friend." And she was probably frantic by now.

"She told us where we could find you."

Jolie sipped the coffee, flinching when the scalding liquid

hit her tongue. "Did you find Gary?" she blurted. "Is he alive?"

Detective Salyers sat forward, her long, dark fingers wrapped around the paper cup. "No. And we don't know."

Jolie heaved a sigh of relief and frustration. "What's this all about then?"

"We found your boyfriend's car."

"His Mercedes? Where?"

"In the Chattahoochee River."

Jolie's heart jerked. "In the river? Where?"

"Near Roswell." The detective wet her lips. "And we found a body inside."

Jolie inhaled against the sharp pain in her chest and covered her mouth with her hand. "I thought you said—"

"It's not Mr. Hagan. It's . . . a woman. Belted into the passenger seat."

Jolie's mind spun in confusion. "A woman? Who?"

"The body hasn't yet been identified. I was hoping you could give us some idea who it might be. She's Caucasian, dark hair."

Jolie shook her head, trying to make sense of what the woman was saying. "I don't . . . I can't . . . think . . ."

"His sister?"

"No. Gary was—*is* an only child."

"Mother?"

"She's deceased. As well as Gary's father."

"Business associate? Secretary, maybe."

Jolie shook her head. "Gary worked for himself and he worked alone."

Detective Salyers sipped from her coffee cup. "Perhaps an old girlfriend?"

Jolie bit her lip and closed her eyes briefly. Nothing

about this situation sounded sane. A woman was dead . . . in Gary's car . . . He was missing . . . *and so was her own car.* She hadn't wanted to believe that Gary had stolen her car, couldn't imagine why he would have needed it. But now . . .

"I don't know any of Gary's old girlfriends." She touched her temple. "Although he did mention once that he'd had problems with a girl he'd dated."

"Problems?"

She frowned, trying to remember. "It was an offhand comment about a fatal attraction."

Salyers looked interested. "Did he mention a name?"

"No. You'd have to talk to his friends."

"You're my first stop. Since you filed the missing persons report, I assumed you two were . . . close."

Jolie paused, wondering how she could best describe her relationship with Gary. Friendly lovers? Loverly friends? "We dated, but Gary kept company in . . . high circles. I never met any of his friends."

"You didn't find that to be suspicious?"

She could feel the older woman's censure. "I got the feeling that he wanted to keep that part of his life separate."

"You mean, that he was ashamed of you?"

Anger sparked in Jolie's stomach. "Actually, I thought he might be ashamed of *them.*"

Salyers put pen to paper. "I need names."

Jolie shook her head. "I'd tell you if I knew any, but I don't."

The detective pursed her mouth and withdrew a notebook. "Would you mind if we started from the beginning? I inherited this case, and I'd like to get some fresh notes now that we have a new lead."

Jolie shrugged, suddenly very glad for the coffee.

"Your boyfriend's name is Gary Hagan—H-A-G-A-N, right?"

"Yes."

"When was the last time you saw Mr. Hagan?"

"A month ago, September tenth."

"Do you remember what day of the week that was?"

"Friday."

"What was he doing the last time you saw him?"

"He dropped me off at my apartment around eight thirty."

"And was headed where? Do you know?"

"To Buckhead. We'd had an early dinner near my apartment. He said he had a few things to take care of and that he'd call me the next day. He wasn't specific."

"Was that typical, for him to go out after the two of you had had a date?"

Jolie frowned. "I wouldn't say it was typical, but it had happened a few times."

"Did he seem different to you that night?"

"What do you mean?"

Salyers shrugged. "Had he received a phone call that upset him? Was he overly tired? Had he been drinking?"

She had replayed her last conversation with Gary so many times, looking for clues as to his frame of mind. "He seemed a little . . . irritable."

"Had you argued?"

Jolie shrugged. "It was nothing, really. Gary was a bit of a slob, and I was picking up after him. He snapped at me."

"So he had a temper."

"I'd heard him raise his voice during phone calls, but he'd never lost his temper with me."

"Until that night?"

Jolie nodded.

"Did you break up?"

She bit her lip. "No."

"Did you get the feeling that he wanted to stop seeing you?"

Yes. "Maybe. He'd grown distant in the previous few days, and when he snapped at me for picking up after him . . . Well, I remember thinking it was the kind of nit-picking that couples go through when they're on the verge of breaking up."

"Was he wearing a hat when you last saw him?"

Jolie's heart jumped. "Why?"

"We found a man's hat in the car."

"H—he liked to wear an orange ball cap, one of those rounded ones that fit close to the head, with a gray bill. Is that the cap you found?"

"After that much time in the mud, it's hard to say what the original color was, but the shape is similar."

Jolie covered her mouth, the image of Gary's body submerged in the thick muddy water of the Chattahoochee too awful to imagine.

"Ms. Goodman, what exactly was Mr. Hagan's occupation?"

Jolie squirmed—it was the one point of contention between her and Gary. "He was vague about what he did, but he called himself a services broker."

"A services broker?"

"Gary had this incredible network of acquaintances. If a person wanted something special, they called Gary. He said he could arrange a ride in a traffic helicopter, or courtside seats for the Hawks, things like that."

Salyers nodded, making notes. "Did his services extend to supplying drugs or prostitutes?"

Jolie winced. "What? No, of course not."

"Are you certain? If he were deliberately vague about what he did, maybe he was covering up."

Jolie didn't know what to say, so she simply lifted a hand. "I suppose anything is possible."

"Did the two of you ever do drugs?"

"*No*."

"Were you aware that Mr. Hagan has a record for dealing coke?"

She felt nauseous. "No. When?"

"Eight years ago in Orlando."

"I didn't even know he'd lived in Orlando."

The look that Salyers gave her made her feel stupid and susceptible. "Did Mr. Hagan own a gun?"

Anxiety eddied in her chest. "If he did, he never mentioned it."

"You didn't see a gun at his apartment, in his car?"

"I only visited his apartment a couple of times, but no."

Salyers made more notes. "Okay, you said that Mr. Hagan left that night to go out—what happened next?"

"I watched TV, then I went to bed. I got up the next morning and when I went out to run errands around nine o'clock, my car was gone."

"Were there signs that the car had been broken into—glass on the ground, for instance?"

"No."

"Did Mr. Hagan have a key?"

"Yes. I had locked my keys in the car once, so we made a copy for the sake of convenience."

"Was that your idea or Mr. Hagan's?"

Jolie squinted. "Gary's, I believe—why?"

"Just asking." She consulted her notes. "You drove a 2001 gray Mercury Sable Sedan, is that right?"

"Yes."

"But you didn't make an immediate connection between your car missing and Mr. Hagan?"

"No. After I called the police to report my car stolen, I called Gary, but he didn't answer his phone. Several hours later, I began to suspect that something was wrong, except I was worried about Gary, not my car."

"You called his cell phone?"

Jolie nodded. "He was never without it. He didn't even have a land line at his apartment."

"And he lived in Buckhead?" The woman turned back a few pages in her notebook and read off the address.

Jolie nodded. "That's right. But there was a fire at his complex a few days after he . . . disappeared."

Salyers heaved a sigh. "It seems like we had an apartment fire every week this summer. We have two serial arsonists in custody. His unit was damaged?"

"And almost everything in it."

"Almost?"

"I called the manager to tell him that Gary was missing when I saw the news about the fire. The manager called me a couple of weeks ago, said he had salvaged a box of Gary's things and if I wanted them, I should stop by." She frowned. "When I got there, he tried to extort the overdue rent but wound up giving me a box of things that probably came from Gary's fireproof desk—photographs, piled-up mail."

"Did you keep them?"

"Yes, the box is at my place."

"The same address listed for you on the missing persons report?"

"Yes, near Roswell," she said, and she realized she had repeated the name of the area where Gary's car had been found.

"Would it be possible for you to bring the box by the midtown precinct tomorrow?"

Jolie nodded.

Salyers made a note of it. "Ms. Goodman, when did you report Mr. Hagan missing?"

"The following Wednesday, I believe."

"That seems like a long time to wait."

Jolie bristled at the woman's accusing tone. "Gary is an adult. I didn't keep tabs on him."

"But you still didn't believe he had anything to do with your missing car?"

"No. I thought it was a coincidence. Gary had a nice car—I couldn't imagine why he would have wanted mine." Then again, it hadn't occurred to her that he'd just rolled his own vehicle into the river and needed a getaway car.

"It didn't cross your mind that he might simply have sold your car for cash?"

Jolie shook her head. "He wouldn't have done something like that."

Salyers pursed her mouth. "How long had you been seeing Mr. Hagan when he disappeared?"

"About four months."

"How did you meet him?"

"I was working for the Sanders Agency. He came in one day to ask for directions."

Salyers smiled. "And he got your number instead?"

Jolie nodded, smiling for the first time. "Gary was very . . . persuasive."

"Were the two of you serious?"

"What do you mean?"

"Did you date other people?"

Jolie rolled one shoulder. "We never discussed it—I didn't date anyone else, and I guess I just assumed that he didn't either."

"In the box of personal effects that the manager gave you, do you remember seeing an address or schedule book?"

"No, but I didn't go through the box closely."

Salyers frowned. "Really? If my boyfriend was missing, I'd have gone through it with a fine-tooth comb."

Again, the censure. Jolie tried to ignore the prickly nervousness that gathered around her pulse points. "Gary had a Palm Pilot, but he kept it with him—it wouldn't be in that box."

The detective studied her as if she were trying to size her up. Her entire life, Jolie had felt as if people were sizing her up, trying to figure her out. It unnerved her because she wasn't nearly as complicated as people thought she was. She wanted the same things in life that other people wanted . . . except she hadn't yet figured out how to get them.

"Has your insurance company paid the claim for your stolen car?"

"Not yet." Jolie angled her head. "What are you getting at?"

Salyers sighed and pressed her hand against the table. "Ms. Goodman, this is no longer a missing persons case. This is now a homicide investigation."

"Homicide?"

"And your boyfriend is a fugitive."

"Fugitive?"

"And if you know more than you're telling, you could be charged as an accessory."

Alarm squeezed Jolie's chest. "Accessory? I don't know what you're talking about." Her voice escalated until people around them turned to stare.

Salyers adopted a calming expression. "All I'm saying is that if Mr. Hagan came and knocked on your door that night and asked for your car, now is the time to say so, before this gets any worse for you."

She knew her mouth was open—she could feel the air on her tongue. She snapped her jaw closed and pushed to her feet. "When I filed the report on my car and the missing persons report on Gary, you people made me feel like an idiot. I was patronized and told that I'd been conned." She was shaking. "I didn't see Gary later that night, or any time after he left my apartment Friday. Now, if you don't have anything else to tell me, I'd really like to go."

Salyers stood. "Ms. Goodman, I'm giving you this information for your own protection. If Gary Hagan is a dangerous man and he's still alive, you could be in danger yourself." She handed Jolie a card. "If he tries to contact you, call me."

Jolie stared at the card, seeing nothing. She just wanted to escape to a quiet place where she could think. She shouldered her purse and stalked away, blinking rapidly. Nausea ebbed and flowed in her stomach. After threading her way through the food court, she stepped into the main corridor of the mall, into a stream of shoppers heading toward the exit. Dozens of people passed her, going in the opposite direction, brushing her shoulder, bumping her purse.

She searched their faces, desperately hoping to see Gary in his orange ball cap, laughing, saying everything had been a huge misunderstanding. But they were all strangers to her, giving her a fleeting glance, if that. People staring past her and through her, shuffling toward their respective destinations. Life went on.

Then her gaze settled on one familiar face a few yards away, walking toward her: Beck Underwood. He was walking next to his sister, who was talking, her blonde head turned toward him. He was laden with Neiman Marcus shopping bags—apparently Michael had scored a fat sale. At that second, Beck's gaze landed on her, and recognition registered on his face. Recognition and concern.

Jolie quickly turned her head and walked faster, carrying herself past and away from the man with the perceptive brown eyes. Unreasonable resentment flickered through her body—people with as much money as the Underwoods didn't have to worry about things the way that normal people did. If they were wrongly implicated in a crime, they'd simply make a couple of phone calls and the problem would disappear. Gary had called it the "Buckhead Bubble"—a magic bubble, he said, that surrounded the country-club set that lived in the ritziest part of Atlanta.

For a few seconds, she fantasized what it would be like to walk in the designer shoes of the rich and famous . . . to have all doors and possibilities and pleasures at your fingertips. It was an attractive daydream when her own humdrum life seemed so precarious.

Swallowing past a lump in her throat, her mind jumped to who the dead woman could be, and why she had been in Gary's car. Where was Gary, and why had he implicated *her* by stealing her car? And could Detective Salyers be right? Could she herself be in danger?

She pushed open the door leading to the parking garage

and stepped out into the uncharacteristic chill of the evening. It wasn't quite 7 P.M. yet, but the days were getting shorter, and the sunlight was already fading. In the parking garage, the light was even more diffuse, and two flickering bulbs didn't help to dispel the darkness in the corners. She jumped when the heavy metal door slammed closed behind her.

The garage was full of cars, but empty of people, except a few who were unlocking trunks for their shopping bags. She walked down the ramp a half level to where she'd parked her car, her pumps clicking against the concrete, sending rhythmic echoes around her. Jolie pivoted her head right and left, telling herself it was good policy to be alert, that the detective's words hadn't spooked her. But when she spotted her rental car, she found herself walking faster and faster.

Footsteps sounded behind her, and a shadow fell upon hers. She walked faster and the footsteps kept coming. Her heart thrashed in her chest and she whipped around. A man walking a few yards behind her held up his arm, aiming something in his hand. A scream gathered at the back of her throat just as his thumb moved and the car next to hers bleated, the lights flashing in response to a keyless remote. Oblivious to the fact that she was on the verge of cardiac arrest, the man nodded briefly, then walked past her and opened his door and swung inside.

Jolie slumped against the door of her own car in abject relief, chiding herself for letting the detective's words get to her. No doubt that Gary, wherever he was, was in a lot of trouble, but she had no reason to be afraid.

Then she wet her lips and listened to the blood rushing in her ears. So why was she?

Three

Jolie scooted into the tan Chevy Cavalier rental and closed the door behind her. When she pulled the seat belt across her shoulder, she had a grisly vision of a faceless woman belted into the passenger seat of Gary's Mercedes, the clawing fear she must have felt when she realized the car was going into the muddy river, the car filling up with water—

Her cell phone rang, sending her pulse and imagination into overdrive. Gary? She pulled the phone out of her purse with a shaking hand and checked the screen: Leann. With a sigh of relief, she flipped up the receiver. "Hi."

"The police called me looking for you!"

"They found me."

"What's going on?"

"They found Gary's car."

"You're kidding. Where?"

"In the Chattahoochee River." She bit her lip, loath to say the words. "There was a body inside the car . . . a woman."

"What? Oh, my God, who?"

Jolie released a shaky sigh. "No one knows yet."

"Did . . . did they find Gary?"

"No, just his hat."

"So they think he's still alive?"

"I believe so. They seem to think that he stole my car after sending his into the river."

"Omigod."

"It gets worse. They think I know something about . . . what happened. That I gave him my car so he could get away." She swallowed a wad of tears, but her voice still wobbled. "A detective told me I could be charged with accessory."

"To *murder*?"

"To whatever they charge him with."

"I can't believe this. Are you going to get a lawyer?"

She felt faint. "With what?" Her laugh sounded hysterical to her own ears. "My savings is gone from trying to get my business off the ground. I'm already eating into my credit cards. Besides, wouldn't that make me look guilty?"

"Possibly." Leann sighed. "I should be there for you."

"Your sister needs you right now."

"I know, I'm just sorry about the timing of this visit."

"I'm fine. A little shell-shocked, but fine." Salyers' warning about her safety reverberated in her head, and she looked over her shoulder at the dim, deserted parking garage. "I just keep hoping that Gary will turn up and this will end."

"What are the police going to do next?"

"I didn't ask," Jolie admitted. "They're trying to identify the woman."

"Did they give you a description of her?"

"Only that she was Caucasian with dark hair."

"Hm. What kinds of questions did they ask about Gary?"

"It was just one detective, a woman, and she asked me a lot about Gary's job."

"What did you tell her?"

"Not much—like I told you before, Gary was vague about that part of his life." Jolie hesitated, then said, "Leann?"

"Yeah?"

"I know you only met Gary a few times, and I know you didn't exactly click with him, but did you ever get the feeling that he was capable of . . . murder?"

"He was a little manic maybe, but capable of murder? I just don't know." Leann made a rueful noise. "On the other hand, Jolie, you have to admit that you might be a little gullible where men are concerned."

She blinked and allowed that painful tidbit to sink in.

"I'm sorry, Jolie, I shouldn't have said that."

"No," Jolie said in a hoarse voice, "it's okay. But I should go. I'll call you soon."

She disconnected the call and turned off her phone, then focused on the designs on her windshield made from various bugs whose lives had ended suddenly simply because she'd been going in the opposite direction. The randomness of it all was mind-blowing. She was assailed with an overwhelming sense of "float," that her life seemed to be shifting out from under her.

Maybe Leann was right. Maybe she was gullible where men were concerned . . . where Gary was concerned. She'd taken his smiles and stories at face value, and when red flags had raised in her mind, she hadn't probed or pushed because . . . Why? Because she felt special that someone like him wanted to be with someone like her and she didn't want to risk breaking the spell?

Waves of shame rolled over her. Forget what Gary had gotten himself into. What had *she* gotten *herself* into?

She had obviously overestimated Gary's feelings for her—but had she also overestimated her feelings for him? Maybe she intentionally turned a blind eye to the problem areas of their relationship because he had been such a source of moral support for her, he had constantly encouraged her to break out of her shell, to take on the world. Her shyness and aversion to new people and new situations had confounded Gary. Over and over he had said she had the makings of a successful individual—she simply needed to crash through her self-imposed barriers. She had believed him, had started making changes in her life even after his disappearance . . . only now to discover that he'd left her saddled with this unbelievable debacle.

She inhaled a cleansing breath, then started her car and eased her way out of the parking garage and into traffic. The worst of the rush hour was over, but there were still plenty of cars to weave through from where the Lenox mall was located in Buckhead north to her apartment complex in Roswell. Her route took her over a section of the muddy Chattahoochee River, running high from recent rains. Her throat convulsed as she gazed over the broken, angry surface of the rushing water.

Shortly after she'd met Gary, Mr. Sanders had put together an outing for the employees of the agency and their families that included an afternoon of "tubing" down the 'Hooch. Single employees were allowed to invite two guests, so she'd asked Leann and after much hesitation, Gary, to sit in an inner tube and float, butt in water, down the river. Leann had taken an instant dislike to Gary, but Jolie had felt the first stirrings of something deeper as he made jokes and entertained them all afternoon.

A memory chord strummed . . . Gary teasing her about

her fear of the brown, frothy water, about not knowing what was beneath the surface.

"The 'Hooch would be the perfect place to dump some-thing you wanted to get rid of," he'd said. *"There's no telling how many cars and guns and bodies are just beneath us."* Then he'd reached over and grabbed her bare leg like a snake striking, howling with laughter when she'd let out a little scream.

Had he remembered his observation when he was look-ing for a place to dump his car and a body? Had the woman already been dead? The likelihood of him being near the river bank and accidentally driving into the water seemed remote, and if it had been an accident, why hadn't he contacted the police?

Fear took root in her stomach, slowly encompassing all of her internal organs. Denial warred with reality. Had she allowed a cold-blooded killer into her home and into her bed? Was it only happenstance that had kept *her* from being the woman strapped into his car and sent to a watery grave?

When the enormity of her gullibility hit home, tears threatened to engulf her. She gripped the steering wheel and gulped for air until she gave herself the hiccups. By the time she pulled into her assigned parking space in the apartment complex, the day sat on the precipice of dark-ness, and she was thoroughly spooked. She gathered her things and swung out of the car in one motion, slamming the door behind her. She trotted to her first-floor apartment door, warily looking for movement, shadows, anything.

Looking over her shoulder, she stuck her key in the lock and turned the deadbolt, then practically fell into the dark interior. A ringing phone pierced the silence. She fumbled for a light and scanned the kitchen and living room for intruders. Seeing none standing out in the open, she pulled the door closed behind her and clambered for the phone. She yanked up the cordless unit, her heart hammering. "Hello?"

"I'm sorry," Leann said.

Jolie's shoulders yielded to the pleading tone in her friend's voice and she dropped into her favorite chair, an overstuffed wingback, with a heavy sigh. "It's okay."

"No, it isn't. You've probably had a nightmarish day, and I go and say something stupid like that."

"It wasn't stupid," Jolie said miserably, kicking off her shoes. "It's true—I'm gullible when it comes to men, else how could this have happened?"

"We've all been fooled by men," Leann said, her voice wistful. "Let's just pray the police leave you out of this."

Jolie murmured her agreement.

"So . . . how was your first day as a shoe salesperson?"

"Exhausting. I never knew how much there was to know about shoes. Oh, and get this: Sammy Sanders stopped by."

"Ew. Was she terrible?"

"Oh, yeah."

"Well, between her and the police officer, were there any bright spots?"

Beck Underwood's interesting face flashed into her mind. "Well, I crashed into a guy while I was carrying an armload of shoes."

"That doesn't sound like a bright spot."

"The bright spot is I didn't get fired."

Leann laughed. "I admire you, Jolie—no matter what life hands you, you simply take it in stride."

"Give me an alternative," Jolie said lightly. "How's your sister?"

"Bloated, nauseous, and depressed."

Jolie hummed her sympathy. "Do you know how much longer you'll be there?"

"At least five more months, unless the baby comes early. This sounds selfish, but I keep thinking about all the clients I'm losing to other interior designers." Leann sighed. "And now this business with Gary. Listen, you probably just got home, so I'll let you go. But call me if you need to talk about it."

"I will," Jolie promised, said goodbye, then returned the phone to its cradle. She sighed, missing her neighbor friend. They had met only months ago at the apartment laundry room, but they had become fast friends, bonded by Leann's occupation in interior design and her own job in real estate. Even though she was seeing Gary, Jolie had made time to foster the new friendship because she appreciated the other woman's plain-talking wisdom. She sent good thoughts toward the ceiling for Leann's sister's problem pregnancy. As she pushed herself up from the chair, the phone rang again—classic Leann.

Jolie picked up the phone and smiled into the receiver. "What did you forget?"

Silence greeted her.

"Leann?"

Someone was there, she could hear the openness of the connected call, a faint rustle in the background. "Leann, is that you?" When there was no answer, her heart skipped a beat. "Gary?"

The rustling sound grew louder, then a click disconnected the call. Jolie swallowed and listened to the dial tone for a few seconds, then set down the phone and looked toward the darkened bedroom. Unbidden, a horror movie came to mind, the one about the cute coed receiving threatening calls all evening, only to have the police to call her later and tell her they'd traced the calls as coming from inside the house.

She wasn't a cute coed, and for the life of her she couldn't remember how the movie had ended. *For the life of her?* Bad choice of words, she conceded, moving toward the bedroom as quietly as possible. She had her cell phone in her right hand, ready to punch the speed dial button for 911. Remembering something on an airline safety report about shoes being a ready weapon, she scooped up one of her chunky-heel pumps and wielded it in the other hand, thinking that if Gary Hagan was crouching in the bedroom, he would be more likely to die from laughter than from any wound she might inflict.

Moisture gathered around her hairline as she pounced on the light switch. When she stepped into the doorway, though, the most dangerous-looking thing in her bedroom was the multi-outlet strip in the floor overloaded with a spaghetti knot of appliance cords. She scoffed at her foolishness and sat on the mossy-colored duvet to remove her pantyhose, thinking she had to get a grip on herself. Gary Hagan wasn't a murderer. It was more likely that he'd been drinking and somehow had driven into the river, then panicked when he couldn't get his companion out.

Except why would he have been near the river, so far from his apartment, so far from his neighborhood of Buckhead? And who was the dead woman?

Her gaze landed on the book that Gary had given her to read—the sales bible, he had called it. *The Magic of Thinking Big* by David J. Schwartz. She had gotten a couple of chapters into it, but had quit reading it when he disappeared, because she'd begun to feel patronized . . . not by the author, but by Gary. He was always pushing her to think about the future, to become her own boss. *"Don't spend the rest of your life working for someone else, Jolie. Why spend your energy making someone else rich?"*

It was one of the reasons she had quit the Sanders Agency; when Sammy had made a snide remark about Gary absconding with her car, quitting had seemed like both a way to defend Gary and a way to follow his advice.

Now who felt like a big, broke fool?

She rubbed her temples and decided there was no warding off the headache that had been coming on all day. Backtracking to the kitchen, she tossed down a couple of aspirin and peered into the freezer for dinner options. One chicken breast and a package of frozen whole-wheat waffles.

The waffles won. She dropped two in the toaster, then walked to her desk and flipped on her computer. She'd missed the early local news, but suspected she'd be able to find something online about the discovery reeled out of the Chattahoochee River. She glanced at the to-do list next to her computer and frowned.

> *Have business cards printed*
> *Photocopy flyers for customer list*
> *Pay E & O insurance premium*
> *Pay fees for MLS*

The errors and omissions insurance was a must to prevent an honest contractual mistake from wrecking her real-estate career, but thankfully, it was affordable. A lifetime membership to the Multiple Listing System to access home listings online would be less expensive in the long run, but five grand stood between her and that option. For now, she'd have to go the monthly subscription route. And advertising on a shoestring budget meant lots of postcards, flyers, and good old-fashioned cold-calling. She was tempted not to do anything until this bizarre situation with Gary was resolved, but when the holidays were over, the brokerage company had to be up and running. Life would go on, and she needed to be able to support herself.

Assuming she wasn't in jail, of course.

Jolie was halfway through the waffles when she found the story she was looking for on a local news web site:

CAR AND BODY PULLED FROM CHATTAHOOCHEE RIVER—A local fisherman alerted Roswell authorities that he'd found what appeared to be a late-model car just below the water's surface near the Morgan Falls Dam. A 2003 silver Mercedes sedan registered to Buckhead resident Gary Edward Hagan was pulled from the Chattahoochee River. Authorities found the decomposing body of an unidentified woman inside. A warrant has been issued for Hagan's arrest. The local and state police are asking that anyone who knows of his whereabouts contact them.

She clicked on the link to photos and inhaled sharply at the color picture of Gary's car being pulled from the water by a winch, yellow water gushing from the fender wells. The next photo showed a black body bag being loaded into a van. A lump clogged her throat at the graphic nature of the photo—from the way the body handlers held the bag, the body seemed especially unwieldy. But when Jolie hit the button for the next photo, the air fled her lungs. Gary's license photo. He was a handsome man, dark-headed with smooth brown skin, pale eyes, and a charming smile. But the DMV photo made him looked heavy-lidded and surly. Any person who saw that photo would think him capable of murder.

The waffles forgotten, Jolie stared at the photo for the longest time, her eyes watering and her doubts rearing.

Was he?

She returned to her bedroom and opened the closet door to stare down at the box of Gary's belongings that the apartment manager had given to her. She debated whether she should sort through everything or not before delivering the box to Detective Salyers—after all, if she didn't look, she could always plead ignorance.

On the other hand, Detective Salyers already believed she *had* looked.

She heaved the box to the bed and gingerly lifted the lid, releasing a smoky odor into the room. Her heart squeezed with the thought that, fugitive or no, Gary's life had been reduced to this cardboard box. She sorted through bills and junk mail and set them aside, unopened. A wire tray held more mail, but the envelopes appeared to have been opened, she assumed by Gary. A check of the postmarks confirmed that they were received the week he disappeared. She uncovered his cell-phone bill, and a half dozen credit-card invoices, all with overdue amounts that were breathtaking. Gary was either slothful about bill paying or was deeply in debt.

There was a cube of yellow note paper, on the top of which he'd scribbled, "extra door key for Gordon." She didn't remember him mentioning anyone named Gordon, but if Gary was giving him a key to his apartment, they must be close. A neighbor? A cleaning service?

There were various flyers and postcards advertising all

kinds of happenings in Buckhead, midtown, and downtown Atlanta. Concerts, art shows, restaurant openings, club events, open houses. It was how he kept up with everything, she presumed. He was on the mailing lists of the Museum of Contemporary Art, the Woodruff Arts Center, the High Museum of Art, the Fernbank Museum, the Falcons, the Braves, the Thrashers, the Hawks, and every college in the vicinity. She turned over each flyer, looking for highlighting or more hand-scribbled notes. On the back of the postcard for the High Museum, he had written—illegibly—what looked like "hardy manuals." The nonsensical words meant nothing to her.

There were sales papers, random coupons, and other irrelevant pieces of mail. She almost missed a small envelope the size of a gift card. The envelope was blank, but contained a tiny pink card. Outside it read, "Missing you," and inside it read "Missing me?" The card was signed, not with a signature, but with a lip imprint in pink lipstick. The imprint was smeared, badly . . . purposefully, but by the sender or by the receiver? Was it a message from his "troubled" ex? Since the envelope had no address or stamp, the sender had obviously delivered it in person, or left it where Gary would find it.

She returned the card to its envelope, then delved through the rest of the box's contents—a couple of baseball caps, although not the burnt-orange-colored one he wore most often. A couple of sports-themed paperweights, a Swiss Army knife, a handful of matchbooks from local restaurants, some bottles of over-the-counter painkillers, a few music CDs he'd burned and labeled himself—80s ROCK, 90s ROCK, DELTA BLUES. She winced when she thought of his extensive music and movie collection being melted down by the fire.

At the bottom of the box was a dusty framed photograph of his parents, a Midwestern-looking couple dressed in sensible clothes, smiling as if they were having an appropriate amount of fun. She thought of her own parents and how frantic they would be if they had lived to witness this. A wry smile curved her mouth as she wondered which would consume her mother the most—her proximity to a hideous crime, or utilizing her hard-won college degree to sell shoes.

There was a small photo album, which surprised her because Gary didn't seem like the sentimental type. The photos in the beginning were dated and yellowed—various shots of him growing up, labeled on the back in a neat, feminine script, and she guessed that Gary's mother had started the album and perhaps he had added to it after her death. The more recent pictures were mostly snapshots of him with various well-dressed people she didn't recognize. The women were numerous, but none of them seemed to have been singled out by the camera. As she turned pages, however, the faces of four *men* seemed to occur more often than others—and the men appeared to know each other. Could one of them be the Gordon who was to receive an extra key? She slipped out each photo, but none of the recent pictures was labeled on the back.

There were also a couple of photos of Gary by himself outdoors. In one he was sitting on a rock, dressed in hiking gear and mugging for the camera. The next was of the same location, but a closer shot. Fingers obscured the lower edge of the picture—a woman's fingers, with nice nails. The picture was dated a year ago by the film developer, but again not labeled. Was the photographer the mysterious pink-lipped ex?

She turned pages and scanned photos of holiday parties, then she smiled, surprised to see photos taken during their inner tube float down the river. She had felt awkward giving them to him, had been afraid he would think she was trying to force the issue of them being a couple, but had reasoned that the shots were group shots, not just of her and Gary. They were all smiling, everyone wet—even Sammy—having a good time. Jolie turned the page and stared at the last photo, then her smile evaporated.

This was another group photo from that summer day, except Gary's tube was bumped up next to hers. She remembered the moment, had reached out to playfully push him away. But the way her hand rested on his arm looked proprietary.

And it obviously had disturbed someone who had viewed the picture, because her face had been obliterated by a slashing red *X*.

Four

"Is Detective Salyers available?" Jolie asked, setting the box on the counter lip in front of a thick window that she assumed was bulletproof.

The cop behind the counter pulled on his chin. "She's out on a case. Can I help you?"

"My name is Jolie Goodman. She asked me to drop this off. It's related to a case she's working on."

"Hold on." The man rummaged for a pen and paper, then slid both underneath the half-inch gap at the bottom of the window. "Write her a note, will you?"

Jolie took the pen and scrawled, "From Jolie Goodman re: G. Hagan," and added her cell phone number. She stuffed the note down in the top of the box, and the man came through a side door to take it from her. "I'll make sure she gets it."

Jolie thanked him, then exited the bustling station and jogged toward her car. If traffic wasn't too bad, she *might* make the sales meeting on time. She slid into her seat and closed the car door, fighting the urge to skip the meeting, to skip her shift—hell, to skip the entire day.

But that would only make things worse. In fact, she really should be around people today, around crowds, to take her mind off the events of yesterday that were threatening to consume her. She started the car and turned it in the direction of Lenox Square, stifling a yawn, a result of the sleep she didn't get last night.

She'd placed a giant cactus beneath her bedroom window and slept with a fire extinguisher—the only thing she had that could remotely be considered a weapon. She might have to use her employee discount to buy something more threatening today, although at the moment the most dangerous thing she could think of that Neiman Marcus had to offer was the employee discount itself.

She maneuvered back roads to get to the mall and found a good parking place at this early hour. Ten minutes later she slipped into the room where, to her great relief, the sales meeting had just gotten under way. From the front, Michael Lane gave her an approving nod, then pointed to his name badge and back to her. All employees, she recalled, were supposed to wear their name badges while on duty and during company functions.

She retrieved her badge from her bag, and fastened it while the store manager, Lindy, a neurotic redhead with a high-frequency voice, recited numbers from the previous weekend's sale. She recognized individual departments that were performing well, including shoes (Michael beamed), housewares, and women's fine apparel, specifically Prada.

"Speaking of which," Lindy said, her gaze landing somewhere behind Jolie, "here's our star sales consultant for the week, Carlotta Wren. Carlotta just topped the former weekly sales record, which she also set, by the way. Congratulations, Carlotta."

Jolie joined in the smattering of applause and turned to see what a star sales consultant looked like. Carlotta Wren stood behind Jolie's chair, tall, with long, straight dark hair clasped in a low ponytail. Her slender, hour-glass figure was wrapped in a sport-stretch red dress complemented with red platform shoes and a dark denim leather-trimmed Prada tote. She had large, exotic features, including a wide smile with a gap between her front teeth, reminiscent of Lauren Bacall. She took a little bow, then said, "Thank you, thank you," and dropped into the seat next to Jolie, smelling of something musky and mysterious.

"What did I miss?" she whispered.

"Not much," Jolie whispered back, instantly edgy from the nervous energy rolling off the woman.

"You're new. I'm Carlotta." She stuck out her manicured hand.

"I'm Jolie," she murmured, giving the outstretched hand a shake, conscious of her own gnawed-down nails.

"Jolie? Do you work with Michael in shoes?"

Jolie nodded.

"Oh, *you're* the one."

"The one what?"

Carlotta waved her hand. "Oh, honey, we definitely have to talk after this waste-of-time meeting."

Jolie had hoped to spend the time between the meeting and the beginning of her shift at the copy store printing flyers, so she didn't encourage the woman's attention. But when the meeting ended thirty minutes later, Carlotta turned and said, "I'm starving—have breakfast with me."

"Well, I—"

"What time do you clock in?"

"Noon, but—"

"Good," Carlotta said with a gap-toothed grin. "We have plenty of time to get to know each other. I'm meeting my friend Hannah and you'll love, love, *love* her."

Joining them seemed like a foregone conclusion, and the decision was cinched by Jolie's howling stomach—the waffles had been forever ago. "Okay." Besides, she missed having Leann around to talk to. She could use a friend or two.

Carlotta walked liked royalty, her shoulders hyper-extended and her chest thrust forward. She was a head taller than Jolie, and she had the longest neck Jolie had ever seen.

"How do you like it in shoes?" Carlotta's voice was nasal and clipped.

"My first day was a little rough," Jolie said.

"You'll be great—you have the perfect look for selling shoes."

Jolie glanced down at her non-designer uniform of khaki-colored skirt, pale blue blouse, black blazer, and low-heeled sandals. "Okay."

"Relax, I meant that in a good way. You look . . . approachable. That's important for shoes. Now where *I* am, in designer wear, it's best to look *un*approachable. That scares off the riffraff who want to waste your time trying on things they can't afford. Only the people with serious money have the balls to come up to me."

Jolie was beginning to see why this woman was a star sales consultant. "How long have you worked retail?"

"For most of my adult life, and trust me, it doesn't get better than Neiman's. Are you working part-time?"

"Yes, through the holidays."

"Did your company downsize? We've gotten a lot of part-timers from the telecom layoffs."

"Um, no, actually, I'm in real estate."

"Ah. Say no more. Plenty of my good customers are realtors, and they're hurting, skipping trunk shows and buying clearance instead." She sighed and shook her head. "It's so sad."

Jolie could only nod.

"On the other hand, there are just as many women who can no longer afford their shrinks or their Zoloft, so they're practicing shopping therapy." Carlotta grinned. "It all evens out."

The mall wasn't as busy today and the food court was nearly empty. Jolie eyed the spot where she had met Detective Salyers and felt a stirring of anxiety.

"We're meeting Hannah at the Crepe Cafe," Carlotta said, nodding toward the end of the corridor.

Jolie groaned inwardly, wondering how big a dent breakfast would put in her wallet. She'd lain awake most of the night wondering what she could sell if she needed an attorney, but all she could come up with was a kidney. She was a frugal person—she could get by on one.

"Hannah knows the chef here," Carlotta said, "so we'll eat for free as long as we leave a nice tip."

The woman was either a mind reader or she thought Jolie looked poor. Regardless, Jolie was grateful.

Carlotta's friend hadn't yet arrived, but they were shown to a cloth-covered table in a sunny alcove. Carlotta flirted outrageously with the waiter and asked for Pellegrino bottled water. Jolie asked for hot water and lemon, and scanned the menu, which sported some rather alarming prices.

"So, Jolie," Carlotta said over the top of her menu, "I must hear all about your encounter with Beck Underwood."

Jolie lifted her eyebrows, and the man's face came into her mind. "My encounter? I sold him a pair of shoes."

"No, back up," Carlotta said, waving her hand. "I haven't seen a picture of him in ages. What does he look like these days?"

She recalled that Michael had said Carlotta was a bona fide celebrity groupie. "Um, he was sunburned, mostly."

"Come on, is he still gorgeous?"

Jolie shrugged and her cheeks warmed. "I wouldn't say 'gorgeous,' maybe . . . striking."

Carlotta grinned and her shoulders shook with a dramatic shudder. "You know he's one of the most eligible bachelors in Atlanta."

"Um, no, I didn't."

"Do you have a boyfriend?"

Jolie swallowed hard and shook her head.

"Really? You're so pretty. With the right makeup, you could pass for Charlize Theron. I met her once at a club— her skin is, like, perfect."

A little overwhelmed, Jolie simply nodded. "Where are you from?"

"Here. I grew up in Virginia-Highland."

"That's nice," Jolie said, referring to the area of Atlanta and to Carlotta's circumstances. The woman was obviously from money. Old money.

"You?" Carlotta asked.

"I grew up in Dalton," Jolie said.

North of Atlanta on Interstate 75, Dalton, Georgia was the carpet capital of the Southeast. Both of her parents had retired from flooring factories, and she wasn't the least bit ashamed, although she was prepared for the woman to wash her hands of her.

Instead, Carlotta's eyes lit up. "Do you know Deborah Norville?"

Jolie smiled. Newswoman Deborah Norville was Dalton's other claim to fame. "I met her once at a charity walk, she seemed really nice."

"Darn, I'd love to have her in my book."

"Your book?"

Carlotta reached into her bag and pulled out a small, pink, leather-bound book. "I started when I was a teenager—I met Jane Fonda at a Braves game, and it changed my life." She flipped through the book, showing Jolie the tabbed pages. "I record who I meet and where, and every category has its own alphabetized section: actors, athletes, singers and musicians, politicians, newspeople, businesspeople, and personalities."

"Personalities?"

"You know—people you recognize, but you're not really sure what they do . . . like Fergie, Duchess of York. Who, by the way, I would *kill* to meet."

This woman would have loved Gary, Jolie thought. He could have introduced her to all kinds of celebrities. Jolie nodded toward the well-worn book. "So who's the biggest celebrity you've met?"

"Hmm, it's a toss-up between Antonio Banderas and Elton John, but since Elton has a home here, I guess I'd have to say Antonio. And maybe Bill Gates."

"Wow. How did you meet Bill Gates?"

"At a party. Elton I saw at a restaurant. And I've met lots of celebrities at the Sunglass Hut right here in the mall."

"No kidding?"

"Yeah, everybody famous needs sunglasses. Atlanta is a fabulous place to spot celebrities because there aren't that many places for them to go, and they usually don't have a paparazzi guard with them because it's the South and most people don't really care who they are as long as they wipe their feet."

Jolie laughed, grateful for the woman's entertaining banter. The waiter brought Carlotta's Pellegrino and Jolie's hot water, and while Jolie squeezed the lemon wedge into the steaming cup, Carlotta looked up and waved at someone behind Jolie. "Oh, here's Hannah."

Jolie turned in her seat to see a woman with short black-and-white-striped hair coming their way. She wore a white culinary smock, jeans, and black combat boots. A plain canvas bag slung over her shoulder hung almost to her knees. She smiled and swung into the seat adjacent to Jolie. "Hiya."

Carlotta made introductions. Hannah Kizer was more reserved than Carlotta, but adventuresome, judging by her hair and the silver barbell through her tongue. Jolie was so fascinated, she could barely focus on what the woman was saying. When the waiter took her drink order, they placed their food orders, and Hannah excused herself to say hello to the chef.

"Is she a chef too?" Jolie asked, watching her walk through the swinging doors of the kitchen.

"She's still a culinary student," Carlotta said. "But she works for one of the best caterers in town, and she flat-out knows food."

A minute later, Hannah came back and settled into her chair. "Sorry I was late—MARTA is running slow this morning." She tapped short, neat nails on the table and Jolie caught a slight whiff of cigarette smoke.

"We were just getting to know each other," Carlotta said. "Jolie works in shoes, so when you're ready for a new pair of ugly boots, she can help you out."

Hannah smirked, and Jolie, a loner all of her life, admired their teasing relationship.

"Have you heard about the bash at the High Museum tomorrow night?" Hannah asked, her tone slightly mocking.

Carlotta leaned forward, her eyes shining. "No—what is it?"

"A wine tasting for the big contributors, eight o'clock. The guest list is hush-hush, so I'm guessing there are some important people attending."

"We have to go!" Carlotta said.

"I have to work it," Hannah said, sounding disappointed.

"Jolie will go with me," Carlotta said, then turned to Jolie. "Doesn't it sound like fun?"

Jolie felt sheepish. "I'm kind of on a tight budget."

Carlotta pshawed. "I got you covered. Do you know where the entrance ramp to the museum is?"

Jolie nodded.

"Meet me there, eight thirty sharp."

Her mind raced and it occurred to her that the kind of people that Gary had worked for could be found at such get-togethers. Who knew? She might be able to find out something about his "work," and maybe a clue to the identity of his scary ex.

When her practiced excuses not to socialize rose in her mind, Jolie reminded herself it meant she wouldn't be sitting at home alone, imagining herself with a big red X on her head. "Okay . . . but what should I wear?"

"A black dress and great jewelry. Oh, and bring a biggish purse."

Five

The next evening Jolie was lucky enough to find parking along Peachtree Street, a mere block from the High Museum of Art. When she climbed out of the car, her stomach fluttered with nerves. Had she worn the right dress? Would she say the right things? Would she stumble across someone who knew Gary? And more immediate, how much, if any, of the story of Gary should she share with Carlotta?

She had sidestepped Michael Lane's questions at work, thinking that even if he'd seen the news, he couldn't possibly connect a car and a woman being pulled out of the river with her comment that her boyfriend was missing. She'd simply told him they were checking in with her. In fact, in the light of day, it was easy to convince herself that everything would work out all right. In was only after the sun set, like now, that her imagination went into overdrive, projecting all kinds of atrocities onto the slightest sound or movement.

She had taken only a few steps down the sidewalk when

from the depths of her "biggish" purse, her cell phone
rang. She stopped under a streetlight to remove the phone.
She didn't recognize the local number, but she punched
the CALL button anyway.

"Hello?"

"Ms. Goodman, this is Detective Salyers. Is this a bad
time?"

"Um, no," she said, stepping back to allow a well-
dressed couple to walk by.

"I'm sorry I didn't get back to you sooner, I got
slammed yesterday and today. I did have a chance to go
through the box of items you dropped off. I assume you
looked through them, too."

"Yes, I did."

"Did anything jump out at you as being odd?"

"You mean other than the photo with my head crossed
out?" she asked wryly.

"So you *did* see the pictures?"

"Yes."

"Do you think that Mr. Hagan was the person who drew
that *X* over your picture?"

Jolie sighed. "I just don't know. I can't imagine why he
would do something like that. Unless . . ."

"Unless?"

"Unless he was getting ready to break off our relationship, and that mark was some kind of joke."

"Did you recognize anyone in the other pictures?"

"No."

"Did you send Mr. Hagan the note with the lipstick
print?"

"No."

"And you don't have any idea who might have?"

"That's right."

"Did you realize that Mr. Hagan was heavily in debt?"

"We didn't discuss our finances with each other."

"When you were out together, did he use cash or credit cards?"

She squinted, trying to remember. "Cash, mostly."

"His bank account is overdrawn. I ran a check on Mr. Hagan's credit cards, and they haven't been used since that Friday before his disappearance. Does he have access to any of your cards?"

Jolie frowned. "No, and I didn't give Gary one of my credit cards, if that's what you're asking."

"He might have stolen a card. Have you noticed unusual activity on any of your accounts?"

Jolie opened her mouth to say no, then realized she hadn't received this month's statement on her VISA and American Express. She'd been in such a hurry to get inside her apartment the last two nights, she hadn't even stopped to check the mail. "I . . . haven't noticed, no."

"Have you heard from Mr. Hagan?"

"No," Jolie said. "But . . . I had a hang-up on my home phone Monday night."

"What time?"

"Between seven thirty and eight."

"You don't have Caller ID?"

"Not on my home phone."

"Do you think it was Mr. Hagan?"

"I don't know," Jolie said. "I'm just trying to keep you informed."

Salyers sighed into the phone. "Ms. Goodman, I want to believe that you had nothing to do with this, but I talked to the woman who lives above you. She said she had her window open one night a few weeks ago and heard you and a man arguing on your doorstep."

Jolie frowned. "Mrs. Janklo? The woman has a hearing aid."

"Well, she must have had the volume turned up. She said the two of you were arguing about your car."

Jolie's mind spun, trying to recall what the woman might have overheard. A memory surfaced, and she gave a little laugh. "Oh, one night when Gary left, he was teasing me about how boring my car was, and I got a little indignant. That must have been what Mrs. Janklo heard."

Salyers made a little snort of disbelief. "Do you remember when that conversation took place?"

"Not really . . . maybe a week before he disappeared."

A voice sounded in the background and the detective covered the phone to say something to someone, then came back on the line. "I have to take another call. But we'll be talking again, Ms. Goodman." Then she hung up.

Jolie frowned at the phone, irritated that she was being cooperative and the woman still seemed intent on implicating her in this mess. In fact, the more information she shared, the more the detective seemed to misinterpret. Detective Salyers' response made her feel determined to find out more about Gary on her own. Maybe she could find him herself, encourage him to give himself up . . . and maybe return her car.

She stashed her phone and resumed walking toward the museum, which was lit up like a big luminaria adorning midtown. The building sat back from the street on a rise, and the long, sloping, ramped entrance was part of its architectural grandeur. A spectacularly dressed woman as tall as Carlotta Wren waited near the bottom of the ramp, but as Jolie drew closer and slowed her pace, she realized the woman was blonde.

"Thank God. I thought you had left me hanging," the woman said.

Jolie squinted and walked closer. "Carlotta?"

The woman laughed and touched her Marilyn Monroe-like hair. "Sorry—I should have told you that I might alter my appearance."

"Is that a wig?"

"Of course—don't you have wigs?"

"No," Jolie said, feeling rather stodgy.

Carlotta waved her hand. "Well then, let's get a look at you."

Jolie stood stock still while Carlotta walked around her, perusing her modest black swing dress, clucking like a hen. "Not bad—are those real pearls?"

Jolie nodded and touched her throat. "My mother's . . . mine now."

"Nice touch." Then Carlotta looked down and frowned. "But your first purchase with your employee discount really must be shoes—what *are* those?"

Jolie squirmed and looked down at her chunky-heeled slingbacks. "I don't know—I've had them for a while."

"Hmm. Remember, vintage is good. *Old* is not good. But your makeup is great, and your hair is fabulous—what did you do to it?"

"Washed and combed it."

"Hmm. If you tell me it's naturally curly, I'm going to kill you."

"Trust me, curly hair is much more trouble than it's worth."

Carlotta sighed in obvious disagreement. "Let's go in before all the booze is gone."

Jolie took a deep breath and followed the woman up the

ramp. Carlotta had not adhered to her own advice to wear
a black dress—her zebra-striped coatdress fairly glowed,
and would have been almost loud, except it was overshad-
owed by her strappy pink and rhinestone shoes.

Jolie gaped. "Those are the shoes kept under glass by
the register."

Carlotta looked down. "Oh, right—the Manolos. Limited edition. Aren't they amazing?"

"Yes," Jolie murmured, stunned that star sales consultant or no, the woman could afford a two-thousand-dollar
pair of shoes. Then she remembered that Carlotta had in-
ferred that she'd grown up with money. Maybe she had a
trust fund. Jolie trailed her to the entrance, where a woman
in a staid suit eyed Carlotta suspiciously. "Tickets?"

"Of course," Carlotta said, producing two long tickets
and extending them with a glib smile.

The woman frowned and lowered her reading glasses
from her forehead to her nose. "Those aren't the right
tickets."

Carlotta laughed, then took the tickets back and opened
her purse—which was quite "biggish," Jolie noticed. "I'm
so sorry," Carlotta said, reaching into her bag. "I simply
have too much on my calendar this week. Are the tickets
blue?"

"Yes," the woman said.

"Ah. Here they are." Carlotta withdrew another pair of
tickets, this time pale blue.

The woman glanced at them, then nodded and dropped
the tickets through a slit into a wooden box. "Have a nice
time, Ms. Holcomb," she said with a magnanimous smile.

"Oh, we will," Carlotta said, then clasped Jolie by the
arm and pulled her forward.

"Are the Holcombs friends of yours?" Jolie asked.

"Hmm? Oh . . . I guess you could say that."

They walked down the narrow foyer, which made an abrupt left turn and opened into an extensive atrium, open to the top story of the museum. Suited men and decked-out women mixed and mingled on a shiny white marble floor. The room whispered *money*. The hum of voices and low, sporadic laughter were background to a quartet playing cymbal-brushing jazz. Wine and perfume wafted on the air, tickling Jolie's nose. In the presence of so much privilege, her pulse picked up. Tanned, glowing skin abounded—as well as severe, highlighted hair, waxed and gelled into individual little works of art. Everyone was trying hard—trying to jockey for a good position to be seen while casting furtive glances over their wineglasses in search of better people. Jolie noticed that *she* didn't garner more than a glance, but almost everyone stopped to consider Carlotta in her outrageous designer outfit and platinum blonde wig, although more than one mouth twitched downward.

"All I see are stiffs," Carlotta murmured. "Let's get some wine and find out where the interesting people are hanging out."

Jolie started to take a step toward the bar when Carlotta ducked into an alcove next to a bronze sculpture. At a loss, Jolie followed.

"Isn't this a stunning piece?" Carlotta asked, stepping in front of the sculpture with her back to the corridor.

Jolie looked at the stack of cubes seemingly melting into one another. "I'm not an art connoisseur, but yes, it's interesting."

"Step closer," Carlotta urged, and Jolie obliged.

"Keep talking as if we're having a conversation," Carlotta said out of the corner of her mouth.

"I thought we *were* having a conversation," Jolie said, then noticed that Carlotta had opened her purse.

"Don't stare at my purse," Carlotta hissed. "Keep talking."

Bewildered, Jolie jerked her gaze back to the sculpture. "Y—you don't have a gun in there, do you?"

"What are you, crazy? Of course I don't. Talk, for heaven's sake."

Jolie swallowed. "As I was saying, my knowledge of art is pretty limited. I know some of the names, but I have a difficult time—"

"Here you go," Carlotta said, nodding and smiling while pressing something hard and cold against Jolie's hand. "You don't have to look down, it's a wineglass and a napkin."

Jolie curled her fingers around both items, now thoroughly confused. "What for?"

"It's a wine tasting," Carlotta said through clenched teeth.

"And we have to bring our own glasses?"

"Unless we want to pay a hundred dollars for one of theirs," Carlotta said, still smiling. "How do you think they make money at these events? Just come with me and do what I do."

Jolie watched as Carlotta casually peeled off, carrying her empty wineglass in her right hand, a cocktail napkin held beneath the stem with her pinky. Jolie made her feet move and she lifted her glass similarly, although it took her a few seconds to get the pinky thing down. She followed Carlotta past the table where a gloved waiter was handing wineglasses to patrons in return for one-hundred-dollar bills, then joined one of the lines behind a semicircle of tables where stewards poured an inch of wine from any of a dozen bottles before them.

Despite the encouraging glances from Carlotta, a sweat broke out along Jolie's hairline. What if someone had seen them? She looked around, fully expecting a security guard to bound over and oust them.

"It's just a little wine," Carlotta whispered. "They'll never miss it."

Jolie nodded and tried to smile, but her palms were slick against her glass as she watched Carlotta hand the steward the smuggled stemware. The young man seemed a little too dazzled by Carlotta's curves to pay much attention to the glass. Carlotta gestured to a bottle of chardonnay, and he nodded happily, pouring the requisite inch, then adding an extra splash. Carlotta twisted and smiled prettily, then winked at Jolie when she turned to walk away.

"What can I get for you, ma'am?" the young man asked.

Jolie jumped. "Oh . . . the merlot would be fine."

He smiled and gestured. "I need your glass."

She flushed. "Of course." She handed it over, her chest tight.

He held up the glass and frowned, sending her heart pounding. "You have a smudge," he said finally, then polished the glass with a cloth.

She exhaled in relief and silently willed him to hurry as he poured the berry-colored wine into her glass. "There you are," he said, nodding.

She thanked him, then joined Carlotta, who was walking back toward the crowd.

"See, that didn't hurt, did it?"

Jolie sipped the ill-gotten wine. "It wasn't exactly honest, but I suppose the tickets to get in were expensive."

"I suppose," Carlotta said with a secret little smile.

"Did your friends the Holcombs simply give them to you?"

Carlotta shook her head, her lips wet with wine. "Jolie, I don't know anyone named Holcomb. My brother printed those tickets for me on a laser printer."

Jolie blinked and almost choked on her wine. "You mean, we're . . . party crashers?"

Carlotta laughed. "You should see the look on your face. It's not a crime, you know."

"But it's . . . it's . . . dishonest."

"It doesn't hurt anyone," Carlotta said, then swept her arm toward the crowd. "Do you think anyone in this herd cares?"

Indeed, no one seemed to be paying them any mind.

"Then why do it?" Jolie asked.

Carlotta shrugged her lovely shoulders and pursed her mouth. "Because it's exciting to see what you can get away with."

"You do this a lot?"

"Yeah, usually Hannah and I hit a couple of gigs a week. She knows every catered event in town."

"But how do you know about the tickets?"

"Every place in town uses the same printer. This museum uses the same ticket format on either white or blue paper."

"That's why you had two sets of tickets."

Carlotta answered with an exaggerated nod.

"Do the Holcombs even exist?"

"Somewhere," Carlotta said. "I always use an old Atlanta last name. That way even if someone suspects me, they're usually too intimidated to ask questions." She grinned, revealing her gapped teeth. "Come on, let's mingle."

Jolie fell into stride beside her. "What if someone asks who I am?"

"Well, I never give out my real name, but that's up to you. Tonight, I'm Carly Holcomb."

"Do you always wear a wig?"

"No . . . sometimes I wear glasses or do other things to change my appearance if I feel like it. It's fun to pretend to be someone else for a few hours." She nodded to a food-laden table. "And tonight I feel like being someone who eats Beluga."

"Have you ever gotten caught?"

Carlotta shook her head. "It's all about the attitude. The trick to party crashing is to act as if you belong. Oh, there have been times when people suspected I'd crashed, but who's going to bounce someone who's entertaining the guests? I talk to people, work the room. When I go to someone's home, I fawn over pets, and I always take a hostess gift." She grinned again and lifted her glass to herself. "I'm so gracious, who wouldn't want me to crash their party?"

Jolie was in awe of the woman's chutzpah. Carlotta made her feel as if she'd been living her life in a very small way. While she was squirreled away in her apartment eating frozen waffles, Carlotta was cruising upscale soirees eating caviar.

They filled tiny saucers with bite-sized delicacies, and Jolie's stomach rejoiced. Carlotta had impeccable manners, she noticed, eating precisely and blotting with her napkin between bites. The woman knew how to behave in polite society.

"Do your parents still live around here?" Jolie asked.

Carlotta's expression changed. "No, just me and my brother. Will you be okay if I split to find Hannah and say hello?"

Jolie nodded and watched Carlotta disappear into the crowd, wondering if she'd hit a nerve. She downed one more stuffed mushroom, then handed her plate to a passing waiter, feeling like a heel that she was there under false pretenses and being waited on. She glanced around the room, suddenly antsy as she surveyed the expensive clothes and winking jewelry, watching everyone moving with regal restraint as they sipped and nipped and glad-handed people around them. Everyone seemed to know everyone else, and she had the feeling that she was observing carefully trained animals. It was morbidly fascinating to watch them interact—this was the interplay that Gary had hinted at, the ongoing drama of the rich and famous.

Remembering her initial reason for coming, she opened her purse and slipped out the one group photo from Gary's album that she'd kept. It showed the four men that seemed to dominate the photos, and three women, plus Gary. She scanned each face, memorizing features that wouldn't have changed, then returned the photo to her purse. After fixing her expression into one of faint concern, she worked her way around the room, methodically glancing at faces while craning her neck as if she were looking for a lost friend. Face by face, she eliminated most of the crowd, then something about one man standing a few yards away made her look again. Early thirties, receding hairline, dark slashes for eyebrows . . . one of the men in the photos, she was almost certain. Then he lifted his drink-holding arm to rest it on the shoulder of a man next to him and her mouth went dry—it was the same pose, except in the photo he'd been leaning on Gary's shoulder.

"Did you find the person you've been looking for?" a man said near her ear.

Jolie jumped and turned to see Beck Underwood standing there, holding a one-hundred-dollar wineglass full of what looked suspiciously like beer.

Six

"Jolie, right?" the man asked, then pointed to his shiny new loafers.

She looked down, and on the way back up noticed that he'd traded his holey jeans and sport coat for a dark gray suit and collarless cream shirt. His brown eyes danced, and a smile played on his mouth. Jolie had heard people described as breathtaking before, but she'd never actually had the mere sight of someone squeeze the air out of her lungs. She opened her mouth and dragged in a deep breath. "Yes. And you're Beck . . . Underwood."

He nodded, then tsked. "Except you're one up on me— I don't know your last name."

Carlotta's advice not to use her last name flitted through her mind, but Jolie decided there had been enough deceit for one night. "Goodman."

"Well, Jolie Goodman, what brings you to this roaring bore of a party?"

She glanced inadvertently at the man she recognized

from Gary's photographs, then back. "Actually, I came with a friend."

"Ah. A male friend?"

"No."

He gestured vaguely to the crowd with his wineglass. "Am I keeping you from finding her?"

"No, she'll find me. In fact, she's rather eager to meet you."

His eyebrows lifted. "Me?"

"She says you're a celebrity."

"And why would you be spending time with an outrageous liar?"

She laughed. "We work together."

"In retail or in real estate?"

Suspicion suffused her chest. "Retail . . . but how did you know that I'm in real estate?"

"Your former boss gave me her card."

She felt foolish. "Oh. Right." Remembering the events of that ghastly day, she sipped her wine and glanced back to the man from Gary's photograph.

"Is Roger a friend of yours?" Beck nodded toward the man who had caught her attention.

"Um, no . . . but he looks familiar. Do you know him?"

"Roger LeMon. He and my sister Della dated years ago."

Jolie wet her lips, feeling like a gumshoe. "Do you know anything about him?"

"Old family, made their money in banking—I think Roger is a venture capitalist, but I've been away for a while." He grinned. "I've also lost my touch, if I'm standing here answering questions about another guy."

Her cheeks blazed. "I'm . . . just trying to place how I might know him."

He looked philosophical. "He's not available anyway—

the poor guy is married." Then he frowned. "At least he used to be. I've been gone too long to know for sure."

"Someone said Costa Rica, is that right?"

"Yeah. Wonderful place."

"What did you do there?"

"I went there to facilitate an agreement to broadcast in San Juan, but that didn't pan out, and I . . . stayed."

She took in his tanned skin, his sun-bleached hair, and felt a tickle of resentment—or was it envy?—that he had the means and the guts to simply pick up and live in a foreign country for a few years. She wondered idly if Costa Rica was by chance experiencing a shortage of real-estate brokers. Or shoe salespersons. "Why did you come back?"

He lifted his shoulders in a shrug. "I missed my family. My sister was going through some things I wanted to be here for." He lifted his glass, topped with a two-inch head of foam. "And I missed the cold beer."

Jolie laughed. "I thought this was a wine tasting."

"I found a sympathetic bartender." His smile dimmed a little, then he leaned forward. "Listen . . . I've been worried about you."

He was close enough for the earthy undertones of his cologne to reach her nostrils. Her skin tingled with awareness and she resisted the urge to take a step backward . . . or forward.

"Are you in some kind of trouble?" he asked.

She was struck by his protective stance and the sincerity of his gaze. The man emanated power and money and . . . security. She pressed her toes against the soles of her shoes to counter the inclination to lean into him. The urge to trust him was overwhelming. She wet her lips. "What if I am?"

"Well," he said slowly, "depending on what kind of trouble it is, I might be able to help."

Her breathing sped up, her chest moving up and down as she mulled the ramifications of taking Beck Underwood into her confidence. His accessibility to the people Gary knew would be helpful, but would he close ranks when he found out why she was asking questions?

"There you are," Carlotta said, gliding up to stand next to Jolie. Her wineglass was newly filled and she only had eyes for Beck. "Aren't you going to introduce me to your friend, Jolie?"

Jolie couldn't decide if she was happy or irritated to see her friend, but she splayed her hand. "Beck Underwood, this is Carlot—"

"Carly," Carlotta cut in, extending her hand. "I'm Carly."

If Beck was taken aback by Carlotta's flamboyant appearance, he didn't let on. "Nice to meet you, Carly."

"It's nice to meet you too," she said, batting her eyelashes. "Are you glad to be back in Atlanta?"

His eyebrows went up, but he nodded. "Yes."

"The city has changed so much in the last few years. Have you decided what part of town you'll be living in?"

He glanced at Jolie and said, "Actually, I'm in the market for a place. Do you think you could help me out?"

Jolie froze. Yes, she needed the business, but she wasn't sure she wanted to spend that much time alone with Beck Underwood. "I, um . . ."

"Of course she can help you," Carlotta oozed, then gave Jolie the evil eye before turning back. "Jolie is a real-estate whiz. She's only selling shoes at Neiman's for the holiday discount. Isn't that right, Jolie?"

Jolie stared. It was scary how the woman ad-libbed. "I,

um . . ." She looked up at Beck, drawn in by his eyes . . . and the dollar signs in her own eyes. "Sure, I can help you . . . find a place."

"Great." He smiled, then pointed over his shoulder. "I have to leave, but do you have a card?"

"No, but—"

"But I do," Carlotta cut in, flashing a toothy smile. "Jolie can write her contact information on the back." She dug in her purse and came up with a card and a pen. The card was pale yellow and read simply "Carly" with an e-mail address and cell phone number. Jolie turned the card over and wrote her own name and cell phone number, then handed it to Beck, feeling flushed and a little unwell. "Mornings and evenings are better for me. And I'm available on Sundays."

"I'll call you," he said, then lifted his hand in a wave.

Jolie nodded and watched him walk away until she realized that Carlotta was watching her watch him. She glanced over and Carlotta grinned triumphantly. "Well done. You managed to snag the attention of the most eligible pair of pants here."

Jolie shook her head. "I'm only interested in selling him a house. People like that make me nervous."

"You mean people with money?"

Had she just put her foot in her mouth? "Well, I—"

"Don't ever let people with money make you nervous," Carlotta said, her voice suddenly level. "But always be suspicious." She scanned the crowd. "Did you know the governor is here? And Arthur Blank? All the carats and the cash in this room would be easy pickings for a thief."

Her eyes were serious and her voice was tinged with a mixture of resentment and excitement that made Jolie wonder how much of a thrill seeker Carlotta was. She had a feeling the woman was more complicated than she pretended to be.

Jolie spotted Roger LeMon. "Carlotta, do you know that man in the yellow shirt?"

Carlotta squinted. "Yeah—Roger something or another. I see him out all the time. He's a big Buckhead muckety-muck. He's hit on me a couple of times. Why?"

"I think he and I have a mutual friend."

"Well, let's go see."

Carlotta barreled toward the knot of people where the man stood talking, and Jolie followed, her heart thudding in her ears. The man was in a mixed group, but was seemingly alone and disengaged, standing a half step back and constantly surveying the room.

"Excuse me," Carlotta said, touching his arm.

He pivoted his head and when he saw Carlotta, turned away from the group all together. "Hel-*lo*."

"Hi," Carlotta said with a flirty smile. "My name is Carly, and this is my friend, Jolie."

He glanced at Jolie and nodded. "Hi there." But his attention snapped back to Carlotta. "I'm Roger LeMon." He put the twirl of a French pronunciation on the last name, and he might as well have said, *"I'm* zee big cheeze." He wasn't wearing a wedding ring, she noticed.

"So, Roger *LeMon*," Carlotta said, mimicking the pronunciation and improving upon it, "my friend Jolie thinks you two have a mutual acquaintance."

He looked back at Jolie, his thick eyebrows raised high on his forehead. "Who would that be?"

Jolie tried to affect a casual tone. "Gary Hagan?"

He drew back slightly, his eyes narrowing, then he recovered and shook his head. "Hagan, did you say?"

"Yes, Gary Hagan."

He made a noise in his throat. "No, the name doesn't ring a bell. Why would you think I would know this Hagan fellow?"

Unprepared for his flat denial, Jolie chose her words carefully. "It was a photo I saw—you look like one of the men in it with Gary."

He gave a little laugh. "Well, they say everyone has a twin somewhere. Who *is* this Hagan guy?"

"Just a friend," she said, her breathing shallow.

He squinted. "What did you say your name was again?"

Fine hairs rose on the nape of her neck. "Jolie Goodman."

He nodded, then drained his wineglass. "Ladies, it was nice meeting you," he said, edging away. "But this is, after all, a wine tasting, and I need another taste." He lifted his glass, turned and strode away.

Carlotta gave her a wry smile. "I guess you were mistaken." Then she frowned. "It's weird, but the name Gary Hagan sounds familiar to *me*."

Jolie's heart rate picked up, but she tried to maintain a steady voice. "You know Gary?"

A furrow formed on Carlotta's forehead, then she shook her head. "No, I'm thinking of another guy I used to know, Gary Haggardy." She shrugged and looked around, already bored.

Jolie watched Roger LeMon moving through the crowd. His pace seemed more hurried than someone who was chasing a drink refill. Indeed, instead of stopping at the bar, he strode past and veered off down a hallway. Curious.

"I'm going to the ladies' room," she murmured to Carlotta.

"I'll meet you at the food table," Carlotta said. "Hannah said they were getting ready to put out lobster cakes."

Jolie barely heard her as she walked away. Keeping an eye out for Roger LeMon, she traced his steps through the crowd and down the side hallway. A twin bank of pay phones sat at the end of the hall, just before the entrance to the restrooms. Roger LeMon stood with his back to her, a black phone receiver pressed to his ear. From the angry, chopping gestures he made with his other hand, she gathered he wasn't talking to his mother.

Thankful for the carpet, she walked quietly toward him. As she drew closer, she could hear his agitated, lowered voice.

"—recognized me from a photograph . . . Hell, I don't know . . . She said she was a friend . . . Goodman, Jolie Goodman . . ."

At the sound of her own name, Jolie's feet faltered and her knees threatened to give way. She spun around to make a silent retreat, but as she rounded the corner, the wineglass slipped out of her hand. She clawed the air, but the glass tumbled and bounced on the carpet, spilling wine in a red arc. Jolie stared at the glass, knowing if she retrieved it, she'd be in LeMon's line of vision—and if he'd heard the noise, he would most likely be looking. Instead she turned and racewalked back through the crowd until she reached the food table.

Carlotta, in her look-at-me ensemble, was hard to miss. She grinned. "Jolie, try the quiche—"

"I have to go."

Carlotta frowned. "Is something wrong?"

"I'm . . . not feeling well," Jolie said. Which was true. "I'll s–see you tomorrow—thanks for the ticket."

She turned and practically trotted toward the exit, sending panicked glances over her shoulder for Roger LeMon. She flew by the ticket taker and stumbled down the entrance ramp, walking as fast as her shoes would allow along the dimly lit sidewalk to her car. She gulped air as she fumbled to get her key in the lock, then realized she'd forgotten to lock the door. She grabbed at the handle and opened the door, then practically flung herself inside and slammed it shut.

She gripped the wheel, inhaling and exhaling slowly to calm her vital signs, trying to figure out what to do next. Call Detective Salyers? The woman's suspicion resounded in her head. Would she accuse Jolie of grasping at straws, or maybe lying altogether? Jolie hesitated, then reached for her purse.

"Jolie," a man said. *From the back seat.*

She froze, and terror bolted through her body at the realization that someone had been lying in wait for her. The muscles in her legs bunched and her arm flew to the door handle.

"Jolie, it's me—*Gary.*"

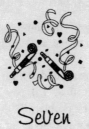

Seven

"Gary?" she whispered on a breath that seemed to be pulled out of her.

"*Don't* turn around, Jolie."

She stopped, mid-turn, her heart thudding in her ears. "Wh–why not?"

"So that when the police ask if you've seen me, you can say no." His voice sounded reedy and unfamiliar. Terrifying.

Her fingers curled around the metal door handle. "W–what happened to you?"

"I don't have time to explain now, but I want you to know that I didn't do what the police are accusing me of. I was set up." His voice ended on a choke.

Think, think, keep him talking. "Who . . . who was the woman in your car, Gary?"

"I can't tell you. The less you know, the better."

"But . . . where have you been?"

"Staying out of sight. They think I'm dead, and I want them to keep thinking it."

She frowned. "Who is 'they'?"

"Like I said, the less you know, the better." He sounded more agitated. "If anyone asks you about me, I simply disappeared."

"With my car," she reminded him.

"I'm sorry about that. I'll pay you back, I swear. Money, at least, isn't a problem."

She pulled the door release as far as it would go, without making noise. "How did you know I was here?"

"I followed you from your apartment. It was too dangerous to talk to you there. They would expect it."

Her skin crawled and her mind raced with questions. "Gary . . . if you were set up, why don't *you* go to the police? The detective I've been talking to—"

"Jolie, if anyone knows I'm alive, you could be in danger. That's why I had to do this—to warn you."

She swallowed. "Why would I be in danger?"

"Because of the envelope."

"What envelope?"

Silence, then . . . "Oh, God, maybe they intercepted it." He sounded desperate, making mewling noises.

"Gary," she said carefully, "what was in the envelope?"

A scrambling noise sounded from the back. "I have to go, Jolie. I'm sorry that I got you involved. I'm sorry for a lot of things." He sounded almost philosophical, as if he were talking about something in the very distant past.

"Wait, Gary—don't go. Let me drive you to a police station."

"*No.*"

"If you're in danger, they'll put you in protective custody."

He scoffed. "That only means I'll be alone when they come to kill me."

"*Who* is 'they'?"

"Bye, Jolie. Promise me you won't say anything to the police. Both of our lives depend on it."

She pressed her lips together and shook her head, fighting tears.

Suddenly he came up over the seat and put his arms around her, pressing his cheek against hers so she couldn't move her head. She screamed, but the sound was lost against the hand he cupped over her mouth. She sucked air through her nose, jerking in her attempt to fill her lungs. His hands smelled grimy, his rough beard pricking her skin. He had her arms pinned to her sides. He had never behaved aggressively toward her, and the possibility of him being high on cocaine blipped into her panicked mind. She struggled and tried to bite his fingers.

His grip tightened like a vise. "Jolie, for God's sake, I'm not going to hurt you, but you have to promise me you won't go to the police. *Please*," he begged, his voice tearful. "I need time to get my ducks in a row, then I'll go to the police."

His despair reverberated in the small car. Real or imagined, he was indeed afraid for his life. She nodded against his hand.

"Thank you," he breathed, then slowly released her mouth. "I'll be around, keeping an eye on you, but be careful, Jolie."

She gasped for fresh air and glanced in the rearview mirror, but she saw only the outline of his head and shoulders. The door slammed, sending a vibration through the small car. She clawed at the controls on the door panel until she heard the comforting *thwack* of all four doors locking, then she laid her head on the steering wheel, giving in to shuddering breaths and waves of relief . . . frustration . . . confusion. Nothing remotely like this had ever happened to her before. How had she, a normal, hard-working, *good* girl, suddenly become enmeshed in a murder investigation?

She massaged her temples, trying to chase away the fear, to clear her head enough to think. Gary was obviously terrified, but was it possible that he'd become mentally unstable—sometime before or after he'd driven his car into the river and killed that woman? And was he doing coke? With all the talk about what "they" would do to him, he'd sounded clinically paranoid. She'd promised him she wouldn't go to the police, but that went against her every gut instinct.

And what if he was telling the truth? What if he *had* been set up by some kind of drug ring and the police couldn't protect him? Roger LeMon had seemed intent on hiding his relationship to Gary, although the man didn't strike her as a criminal mastermind. If he were a successful investment broker, he might simply be worried about his reputation if the media tied him personally to a murderer.

Common sense itself kept pulling her away from Gary's fantastic tale of being set up. Wouldn't denial be a likely first line of defense? On the other hand, if he were guilty of murdering the woman in his car, why would he stay in Atlanta? Why not flee to another state, or to Mexico? He'd made it sound as if he were going to try to resolve the situation himself and go to the police afterward. What if he was right—what if she went to the police and their interference only made things worse . . . or cost him his life?

A knock sounded on the window. Jolie gripped the steering wheel and screamed until her tonsils quivered, then turned her head.

Beck Underwood stood there with his hands up, his eyes wide. "Didn't mean to scare you," he shouted, his voice muffled by the window.

Her shoulders fell in relief, but she'd had enough of men sneaking up on her for one night. She rolled down the window and demanded, "Are you following me?"

He looked perplexed. "What? No." He gestured in the direction Gary had gone. "I was coming back from walking my sister to her car and I saw you sitting here. Are you having car trouble?"

She looked up at him and burst into tears—a first for her, ever. And she wasn't sure who was more horrified, her or the man standing outside her car. While she tried to pull herself together, he squatted down to her level and placed his hand on the car door. He had big, strong hands that matched his physique . . . capable hands . . . capable of harm? She retreated a few inches, suddenly suspicious of everyone.

He sighed. "Look, Jolie, I don't know what kind of trouble you're in, but it's clear to me that you're scared of something. Does this have anything to do with that police officer coming to see you the other day?"

His voice pulled at her with a promise of comfort. Once again she had the overwhelming urge to confide in this stranger. But as the seconds ticked by, the desire to spill her guts was overridden by the fear that Gary might still be watching her, might even be within hearing distance. "I'm fine," she said, dragging a tissue from her purse. "I'm not feeling well, that's all." Now accustomed to the man seeing her at her worst, she blew her nose noisily.

"Let me drive you home," he said.

"No." She stuck the key into the ignition and turned

over the car engine. "I'll be fine. I just need a good night's sleep."

"I'll follow you home," he said.

"*No*," she said, more vehemently than she'd intended. What kind of mess was she that in the space of a minute she could find him suspicious, then trustworthy, then suspicious again?

"Good night," she said quietly, then buzzed up the window, displacing his hand.

As she pulled away from the curb, she glanced in the side mirror and watched him standing with his hands on his hips, staring after her. He had to be thinking she was the most bizarre woman he'd ever met.

Considering her current predicament, she would have to concur. In the past couple of days, she felt as if she'd entered the Twilight Zone. As she proceeded north on Peachtree Street, she scanned the sidewalks for any sign of Gary on foot, while keeping an eye on her rearview mirror for headlights. She wiped the corners of her eyes and exhaled heartily, then turned on the air conditioner full blast to dispel the faint smell of cigarettes and body odor Gary had left behind. How long had he been following her, waiting for her? She shivered, remembering the desperate edge to his voice.

What had been in the envelope he'd sent her—money? Drugs? And was this "they" he was talking about intercepting her mail? If so, "they" had already made a connection between her and Gary. Who were "they" . . . friends of his? People who knew about the missing person's report she'd filed? Police officers? Was that why Gary was afraid for her to go to the police, because they were involved somehow? Of course, the missing persons report was a matter of public record, for anyone to access.

She shook her aching head, realizing she was buying

into Gary's thin explanation of a conspiracy. Because, despite evidence to the contrary, she wanted to believe him, needed to believe him. Because she needed to justify her decision to become involved with him? Otherwise, what kind of a woman would she be if she could be conned by a con man?

Gullible? Or, in this case, *criminal*?

She reached for her purse and rummaged with one hand until she came up with her cell phone, her heart hammering against her ribs. Her thumb hovered over the number pad as she tried to decide whether to call Detective Salyers.

But what information could she provide really—other than the fact that Gary was alive, which the police already suspected? He'd given her no names, no specifics at all, to support his contention that he was set up. Salyers would probably dismiss his ramblings as those of a strung-out fugitive, then have him hunted down. And maybe haul Jolie in for good measure.

If he *was* guilty and she didn't call Salyers, he would eventually be found and brought to justice. If he was innocent and she didn't call Salyers, he might be able to gather more information in his defense before the police closed in.

So in reality, there was nothing tangible to be gained from telling Salyers about Gary's sudden reappearance. And if she implicated herself further, the police would pester her to no end. Gary's warning to be careful rang in her ears . . . The police couldn't help her there, either, other than to reiterate his warning . . . and maybe make things worse if "they" thought she was cooperating with the police.

She glanced down at the phone, wavering. When she

stopped at the next intersection, she punched in a number and waited while the phone rang one, two, three, four times.

"Hello," Leann said, sounding out of breath.

At the sound of a familiar voice, Jolie's blood pressure instantly eased. "Hey, it's me. Did I catch you at a bad time?"

"Just dealing with some throw-up," Leann said with a tired sigh.

Jolie cringed. "Your sister sounds miserable."

"Almost as miserable as I am," Leann murmured. "I thought you were going to a party tonight."

"I just left." She flipped on her signal, then merged onto Roswell Road.

"Wow, it must have been a bomb."

"No, it was fine," Jolie said. "A little ritzy for me, but . . . okay."

"Your new friend must be ritzy, too."

Was that a touch of jealousy in her voice? Jolie gave a little laugh. "Carlotta? Get this. She had fake tickets to get us in, and smuggled in wineglasses so we wouldn't have to buy them for the wine tasting."

"You *crashed* the party?"

"Yes."

Leann howled laughing. "I don't believe it! *You* crashed a shindig at the High Museum?"

Jolie frowned. "Yes." At this point, she didn't want to admit she'd been bamboozled into being bad. "Apparently, Carlotta and her friend are both serial party crashers."

"Sounds fun. So why did you leave early?"

She didn't feel like recounting the story of Roger LeMon, especially when there were more important things to report. "I was tired. But when I walked back to my car . . . Gary was waiting for me."

Leann gasped. "Gary? Are you shitting me?"

"No. He was in the backseat, hiding."

"Omigod, omigod, omigod. Are you all right? Did he hurt you?"

"No, he didn't hurt me, but he nearly frightened me to death."

Leann sputtered. "Tell me everything! Where has he been?"

"He didn't say, only that he's been hiding out. He said he's innocent, that he was set up for the woman's murder."

"Who set him up? And who was the woman?"

"He wouldn't tell me anything. He said the less I knew, the better. And he begged me not to tell the police that I'd talked to him."

"So why did he come to you at all?"

"He said he wanted to warn me that both our lives will be in danger if I go to the police."

"Gee, Jolie, he's either crazy or crazy in love if he'd risk his life just to talk to you. Do you believe him?"

"I don't know . . . maybe. He was definitely scared."

"*Tell* me you're going to the police."

Jolie bit into her lip. "I've been going back and forth trying to decide . . . but I don't think so, not yet anyway. Gary didn't tell me anything useful, and he said he needed some time to get his ducks in a row."

"You mean, like to get away?" Leann asked dryly.

"If he wanted to get away, he's had plenty of time to do that. I think he's trying to gather evidence against the people who set him up. He said then he'd go to the police himself."

"Jolie . . ." Leann's voice petered out.

"I know—you think I'm being gullible."

"Jolie, for God's sake, he's a fugitive. You could get into big trouble."

"Leann, I'm not harboring him."

"Do you know where he's staying?"

"No—if I did, I would definitely call the police. But they're already accusing me of knowing more than I do. If I told them I talked to Gary and that he didn't tell me anything, do you think they would believe me?"

"That actually makes sense. Either that or I'm sleep deprived. Do you think you'll see him again?"

"I don't know. He said he'd be keeping an eye on me, to make sure I'm safe."

Leann made a choking sound. "Doesn't that creep you out?"

"A little," she admitted. "But he actually sounded . . . protective."

"I didn't realize you cared so much for this guy."

Jolie sighed. "It's not a matter of how much I care for Gary. When that detective accused me of being an accessory, I felt helpless. If Gary is innocent, I don't want to be the person to make things worse. You had to be there, Leann, to hear his voice."

Leann made a rueful noise. "I'll support you if you're sure."

"I'm not sure of anything these days."

"I just don't want to see you wreck your life over someone like Gary Hagan."

Jolie gave a wry laugh as she wheeled into her parking place. "That would imply I had a life to wreck. I just pulled into the complex. Thanks for keeping me company on the way home."

"No problem. Look, Jolie, I know you're not big on guns, but think about getting a dog or something." She sighed. "I hate not being there—is there someone you can call if you're in real trouble? Your party-crasher friend, maybe?"

The thought of Carlotta coming to her rescue was so absurd, she almost laughed. Then, unbidden, the face of Beck Underwood popped into her mind. That protective air, the note of concern in his voice.

She swallowed. "There's . . . someone. But only if I'm in real trouble."

"Good," Leann said. "Look, I hate to run, but I think I hear my sister calling. Stay in touch, okay?"

"Okay." Jolie disconnected the call and exhaled a shaky breath. She looked all around the parking lot until she was satisfied that no one was lurking in the shadows. After gathering her purse, she opened the car door and pushed herself to her feet. She slammed the door with all her strength to warn any would-be attackers that if assaulted, she could at least make a lot of noise, then trotted to the bay of metal mailboxes next to the sidewalk. Her neglected six-by-six-inch box was stuffed full. She yanked the envelopes and catalogs out by handfuls, shoving them into her purse until she could scrutinize them in the light.

A noise behind her sent her heart to her throat, but it was only a neighbor's air-conditioning unit kicking on. Even so, she galloped to her door and unlocked it as if the devil were on her heels. Then she walked from room to room, slapping on lights and checking windows and lifting the dust ruffle on her bed. Satisfied that no one was lying in wait, she walked back into the living area and flipped on the television for comforting noise. Then she dropped into her favorite chair to sort through the mail.

Junk mail, catalogs, flyers, bills. A reminder from her doctor for her annual checkup, a schedule of adult education classes from a local university, a copy of the *Atlanta Business Chronicle*. She flipped through and sorted everything twice, but there was nothing from Gary. And while her credit card statements showed disquieting balances, there was no unusual activity.

But then hadn't Gary said that money was no problem?

She squeezed her eyes closed, trying to remember everything he'd said, and wondering if she should have handled things differently. So many questions orbited in her head, she could barely separate one from another. Was Gary involved with drugs? Who was the woman in his car? Had he been set up? And was she truly in danger?

She sat back in the chair and pulled her knees up to her chin. She'd been alone most of her life—an only child, a solitary student, an introverted teenager, a reserved adult. And she'd never minded, not really. Loneliness had a comfortable, insular quality that could lull a person into feeling secure in a distorted kind of way . . . secure in the knowledge that she'd never have to expose herself to another person's failings. If she didn't trust, she'd never be betrayed, and if she didn't love, she'd never be rejected. In fact, she had counted herself lucky, because while women around her seemed to be drowning in melodrama with their parents and their roommates and their boyfriends, she was immersing herself in school and work, positive she'd come out ahead on the other end.

Except here she was at thirty-one, losing ground.

Leann had once called her fatalistic, which was laughable now, considering the circumstances. But she'd preferred to think of herself as vigilant. She favored list-making, slow transitions, and backup plans. Then Gary had come along, with his winning smile and irresistible spontaneity and just enough detachment to make her believe that they had something in common. Except the side she concealed was emotional; and the side he concealed might be criminal.

Jolie hugged her knees to her chest and fought the swell of tears that pushed at her throat. Crying wouldn't help anything. Her lapse in front of Beck Underwood had been so humiliating, she wasn't sure she could face him again. It wasn't like her to lose control, and certainly not in front of a virtual stranger. And of all the virtual strangers in the world, why did he keep popping up when she needed someone the most—and the *least*?

Eight

Jolie tried to hide a yawn behind a shoe box lid as she repacked a pair of Christian Dior "padlock" sandals. The right shoe sported a tiny silver-tone padlock, and the left shoe, the miniature keys. After a gander at the price tag, she understood the gimmick—if someone paid that much for shoes, they needed to keep them under lock and key.

Fifteen minutes until her break, then she'd find a display to crawl under for a nap if she had to. She bugged her eyes, trying to shake herself awake, thinking that if she made it until the end of her shift, she was likely to fall asleep at the wheel on the way home. The lack of sleep was wearing on her—that and the strain of looking over her shoulder all day, after Gary's impromptu appearance last night. Her nerves were shot. Her neck ached and her eyes burned from constantly scanning the crowd for Gary, or anyone matching his build. If he had grown a beard, he might have done other things to change his appearance. Suddenly she felt a finger peck on her shoulder. Jolie stiffened and whirled around, her pulse skyrocketing.

"Remember me?" a young woman asked, holding up a Neiman Marcus shopping bag. "Kate Spade slides, Via Spiga T-straps? My dad made me bring back the Prada flats."

Jolie's memory stirred, then surfaced as her muscles relaxed. The coed from Monday who couldn't make up her mind. Jolie tried to maintain her cheerful smile. A return. The last time she'd handled a return, she'd accidentally processed a refund for over a million dollars. "Just a moment, I need to get a supervisor."

She signaled Michael, who was helping an elderly woman find shoes that would work with her orthopedic inserts. He excused himself, then walked over and spotted the bag. "Will you be exchanging these today?" he asked the young woman. Always the salesman, trying to salvage the sale.

"No, I'd like a refund," she said, then pointed to Jolie. "When she sold me the shoes, she said I could bring them back if I changed my mind."

Jolie squirmed, but Michael gave the woman a tight smile. "Yes, if the shoes haven't been worn outside, you may have a full refund."

"Oh, they haven't been worn outside," the girl said cheerfully. "Just in my house, trying to convince my dad how cute they looked with my outfit." Then her face fell. "But he didn't go for it."

Michael removed the shoes from the box and inspected the soles carefully, then, apparently satisfied, nodded and talked Jolie through the refund as she punched the appropriate buttons on the computer terminal/cash register. When the woman's refund had been processed, she flitted on her way.

"You have to be careful," Michael said. "Some customers buy a pair of shoes they can't afford, wear them once, then try to return them."

"Really?"

"Happens all the time—people buy an outfit for a big occasion, wear it, then bring it back the next day for a refund."

"What do you do?"

He sighed. "We handle it case by case. If they truly bought the wrong size and simply want an exchange, of course we'll do that because it's partly our job to make sure the shoes fit properly before the customer leaves. But if the shoe clearly has been worn and the person wants a refund, we have to apologize and explain the refund policy. If they're a good customer, we'll usually give them a store credit. It's only the ones that are out to cheat us that get upset." He looked past Jolie's shoulder and angled his head. "Well, look who's slumming."

Jolie turned to see Carlotta striding toward them wearing her normal smug smile, stunningly swathed head to toe in pea green—a color, Jolie noted, that would make *her* look like a zombie. Carlotta was carrying a shoe box and an inventory slip. She gestured toward the nearly vacant sales floor. "I see it's dead down here, too."

Michael nodded. "Everyone's holding out for the Blahnik appearance on Saturday."

"That's right," Carlotta said. "It'll be a zoo." She held up the box, marked SIZE 7. "You'll want to put these back right away."

Michael frowned. "Your customer didn't want them after all?"

"No," Carlotta said ruefully. "Pity, too—they looked great with the dress she picked out."

Michael opened the box and peeled back the tissue paper. Jolie swallowed her gasp—the limited edition pink and rhinestone shoes that Carlotta had worn the night before. She lifted her gaze to Carlotta, who was staring back with one eyebrow raised ever so slightly.

Michael removed the shoes lovingly and set them on the counter. Indeed, they looked pristine. "They'll sell Saturday after Manolo signs them." He removed a key from the cash drawer and unlocked the glass case next to the counter, then situated the sandals next to a pair of alligator slingbacks, and relocked the case. "Carlotta, we're going to need some extra help down here Saturday. Would you like to pitch in?"

"Sure. I could bring a dozen pairs of my own shoes for him to sign."

Michael wagged his finger. "No carry-ins for the autographing. Only shoes purchased during the event, and *maybe* a pair you're wearing, at Manolo's discretion."

Jolie looked back and forth between them. "The man is going to sign shoes?"

Michael grinned. "Hundreds of pairs, hopefully. And I need for you to come in as early as you can to help me set up ropes to control the lines."

Jolie balked. "There's going to be crowd control?"

"Oh, there will be lots of extra security, and Manolo will have his own crew, too. But it's always better if we try to maintain as much order as possible, set up a separate area for the media, that kind of thing." He glanced across the showroom. "I'd better get back to my customer. Jolie, you look exhausted. Aren't you due a break?"

She nodded gratefully, and stifled another yawn.

He winked. "I hope you were out doing something fun last night."

"She was with me," Carlotta said.

He scowled. "Don't corrupt Jolie—she's a good girl."

Carlotta stuck her tongue out at him, and he returned to his customer. She glanced at Jolie and frowned. "You look ghastly."

"Thanks."

"Are you still sick from last night?"

"I . . . haven't been sleeping well," she said evasively.

"Well, you left too soon. Guess who I saw!"

"Who?"

"Michael Stipe!"

Jolie squinted.

"Michael *Stipe*—the lead singer for R.E.M.?"

"Oh. Right."

Carlotta sighed and leaned on the counter. "You're slightly hopeless, you know."

Jolie blinked back sudden moisture in her eyes, then looked away, mortified.

"Hey, I didn't mean that," Carlotta said, her voice low and soft.

Jolie waved her hand. "Trust me, it isn't you. It's . . ." She looked back to see real concern on the woman's face. "I'm exhausted, that's all."

Carlotta made a cooing sound. "Come upstairs with me to the lounge—you can take a catnap. And something just arrived that I think will look sensational on you."

Jolie managed a laugh and followed her across the showroom. "Right."

"You should perk up your wardrobe a little, wear bright colors."

"I'm more comfortable in dark colors."

"Comfortable isn't fun," Carlotta fussed, stepping onto the up escalator. "You're too young to be comfortable."

Jolie pursed her mouth. "Those shoes you gave to Michael—were they the same shoes you were wearing last night?"

Carlotta's mouth twitched, then she nodded. "You're not going to tell on me, are you?"

"No. But why risk it?"

"It's *fun*," Carlotta said. "You're going to have to add that word to your vocabulary. F-U-N, fun."

"Fun, like the party crashing?"

"Exactly. I get to wear fabulous shoes, the shoes get exposure—a dozen women asked me where I got them. I bring the shoes back, someone comes in to buy them, everybody wins." She lifted her arms to underscore the brilliance of her logic.

"How do you keep them looking so new?"

A sly smile curved her wide mouth. "I have my little tricks—I tape the bottoms so they don't get scarred up, and I leave in the cardboard stays so the leather doesn't crease."

"That can't be comfortable."

"Like I said, comfortable isn't fun."

Jolie marveled at the woman's aplomb. As she followed her to the cool, hushed area of the fitting rooms, she observed that Carlotta's entire bearing was stamped with self-assurance. People turned to look at her, stepped aside so she wouldn't have to. Her hair was loose and flowing today, a dark curtain down her back. Far from classically beautiful, she had more presence than a roomful of models . . . yet she was enigmatically single, irresistibly aloof.

Carlotta led her to a spacious dressing room with lush carpet, and pointed to an upholstered chaise. "There. Lie down and take a nap. I'll come back in thirty minutes."

"Are you sure I won't get you into trouble?" Jolie asked, looking at the chaise with longing.

"I'm sure," Carlotta said with a laugh. "Besides, you're no good to Michael if you're dead on your feet. There's the light switch—get some rest."

She closed the door and Jolie hesitated only a few seconds before extinguishing the light and feeling her way toward the chaise. She removed her jacket and stepped out of her shoes, then eased onto the plump surface, reveling in the coolness of the smooth fabric against her skin. She turned on her back and exhaled slowly, flexing her feet to stretch her twitching leg muscles, then relaxed into the softness. Heaven. She closed her eyes to allow the haze of exhaustion to lull her into semiconsciousness, but her mind fought her body's need for rest.

The events of the past few days rose to haunt her, racing through her brain, merging and morphing until Gary had turned into a monster. He was taunting her, laughing at her fear of what lay beneath the surface of the brown, foamy Chattahoochee River, strapping her into the passenger seat of his car, then sending her rolling downhill into the water. First she was floating, then the water rose higher and higher, pulling at her clothes. She tried to free herself, but her arms were pinned to her sides. She was going to drown. A tremendous hatred for Gary seized her . . . until she turned her head to see him strapped in the driver's seat, also trapped. His eyes were big, apologetic, innocent . . .

Jolie jerked awake, the sheen of perspiration cool on her brow and neck. She inhaled deeply to relieve her squeezed lungs and to slow her elevated heartbeat. Closing her eyes, she wondered how long she'd been asleep—

five minutes? An hour? She didn't care, she just wanted to lie there for a few more minutes in the blessed dark.

Voices came to her, agitated and low . . . threatening. Slowly she recognized one of the voices as Carlotta's. She was arguing . . . with a man.

"—ever come here again, I'll call the police."

"Do that, *Lottie*. I'm sure the people you work with would be interested . . ."

Jolie sat up and scooted closer to the wall, where their voices were being funneled through an air vent.

"—*dare* threaten me," Carlotta said in a hoarse whisper.

A man's harsh laugh sounded. "You know that I don't make idle threats. Two grand by next Friday."

The stone-cold tone of the man's voice sent a chill down Jolie's neck. The silence stretched on, then Carlotta murmured, "H–how will I find you?"

"Don't worry, Lottie," he said. "I'll find *you*."

Footsteps sounded against the tile floor, then receded. Jolie held her breath, wondering what kind of trouble Carlotta was in, and what was going through the woman's mind right now. A couple of sniffles sounded, then a thump, as if Carlotta had brought her hand down on the counter in frustration. Jolie felt an instant kinship, then shook her head at the absurdity of suddenly feeling aligned with the woman because they both were in dire straits.

A light knock at the dressing-room door sent Jolie scooting away from the wall.

"Jolie, it's me," Carlotta said, then opened the door and stuck her head inside. "Are you awake?"

"Yes," Jolie said, then stood and flipped on the light. She blinked against the glare and glanced at her watch. She'd been asleep for twenty-five minutes.

"Were you able to get some rest?" Carlotta asked, showing no signs of being threatened only a moment ago.

"Yes, thank you so much," Jolie said, then slid her feet into her shoes and reached for the jacket she'd shed.

"Wait, I want you to try on something."

Jolie gave her a wry smile. "I don't have the time or the money."

"Oh, shush, Michael can spare you for five more minutes. Get a load of this." She held up a sleeveless butternut-colored Ultrasuede jumpsuit with wide legs and a silver-tone belt that hung low on the hips.

Jolie's lips parted and she felt an irrational gush of appreciation for the designer. "Oh, my."

"It's perfect for you; try it on."

"No, I couldn't."

"Sure you can," Carlotta said, stepping in and closing the door behind her. "Just *try* it."

Jolie wavered, then reached forward to touch the fabric and was lost in the exquisite liquidity of the cloth. "Okay, but I'm *only* trying it on."

Carlotta eased the jumpsuit off the hanger while Jolie undressed a bit self-consciously. Carlotta hummed and eyed her figure critically. "Wow, if you were a few inches taller, you could be a model."

"I've lost weight recently," Jolie said, glad that at least her Wal-Mart white underwear matched, but knowing it made her look bluishly pale. "I guess I haven't adjusted to my new schedule."

"How's your real-estate business coming along? Have you called that hunky Beck Underwood yet?"

Jolie stepped into the jumpsuit, nervous at the mere sound of his name. "He's supposed to call me." She didn't add that she'd left her cell phone turned off all day. She wasn't sure who she wanted to hear from less: him or Detective Salyers.

"Are you kidding me?" Carlotta gaped. "Do you know how many realtors in this city would sell their soul to be Beck Underwood's agent? We're talking a multimillion-dollar home. The commission would set you up for a year!"

She'd told herself the same thing a thousand times. "I know."

"You act as if you're afraid of him," Carlotta said. "Or is it men in general?" She wet her lips. "Um . . . Michael told me that your boyfriend is . . . missing."

Jolie glanced up from shrugging into the top of the jumpsuit.

Carlotta winced. "Don't be angry with Michael—he thought you could use a little moral support."

So that was why Carlotta was being nice to her. Jolie wondered if everyone would be as supportive if they knew all the details of her "missing" boyfriend.

"You don't have to talk about it if you don't want to," Carlotta murmured.

In answer, Jolie dropped her gaze and allowed Carlotta to fasten the silver-tone buttons running up the front from waist to breastbone. In light of the conversation she'd overheard, the woman had her own problems.

"There," Carlotta said, then stood back. Her face lit up, then she turned Jolie around to look in the wall mirror. "You," she said over Jolie's shoulder, "look like a goddess."

Okay, "goddess" was stretching it a bit, Jolie thought, studying her reflection with wide-eyed wonder. But "good" was not inappropriate. She slid her hands into the hidden side pockets and drank in the sight of herself in the luxe designer outfit. The style, the color and drape of the fabric—everything about the jumpsuit was perfect for her figure type and skin tone. She didn't look like herself. The woman staring back looked . . . accomplished. Situated. As if she knew who she was, and other people be damned.

With the impact of a thunderbolt, Jolie suddenly realized the attraction of haute couture: it wasn't how high fashion made a woman look, it was how high fashion made a woman *feel*.

"Well, was I right?"

She glanced at Carlotta in the mirror and nodded miserably. "It's incredible, but I couldn't possibly afford something like this. How much is it?"

Carlotta fidgeted. "Well . . ."

Jolie picked up the dangling tag and her heart dropped. "Oh. My. God. This is more than the Blue Book value on my car." A car that she didn't even have. She began fumbling with the buttons. "Carlotta, I shouldn't even be trying this on."

"Relax, Jolie . . . relax. I'll help you work out the financials. You simply must have this outfit."

"Even with my employee discount, it's an impossibility."

Carlotta put her hands on Jolie's shoulders. "I have a system."

Jolie was instantly wary. "What do you mean?"

"Buy the outfit at your discount, wear it to a big bash tomorrow night that you simply *must* attend with me, then return it." She lifted her arms in a happy "see?" shrug.

"I can't do that," Jolie said, shaking her head. "It wouldn't be honest." Then she squinted. "What bash?"

"It's a big reception for journalists—some kind of award nominations are being announced. I'm going, and you have to go with me."

Jolie gave her a wry smile. "You mean *crash* with you?"

Carlotta grinned. "All the best people will be there."

She thought of Roger LeMon. "Some of the same people that we saw the other night?"

"Sure, that pack runs together."

She'd like the chance to get close to Roger LeMon to find out more about his relationship to Gary, and why he cared that she had connected them. But how could she do that when he already knew who she was?

Jolie looked back at her reflection . . . *She didn't look like herself.* "Carlotta, do you think I could borrow one of your wigs for tomorrow night?"

Nine

Jolie sat slumped in her car, questioning her judgment for agreeing to meet Carlotta in the parking garage of the hotel. Sitting in the dimly lit structure, she was an easy target for anyone who might have followed her. Not that she'd noticed anyone following her, but between Gary's stealth, Roger LeMon's secrecy, and Detective Salyers' perseverance, she couldn't be certain.

Except surely Gary wouldn't have the kahonas to tail her in her own car.

She glanced at her cell phone display: 2 MISSED CALLS. Salyers had called twice yesterday, twice today. Jolie wondered if she were breaking some kind of law by not answering and not returning the detective's calls, but she'd promised herself that she'd call Salyers tomorrow about Roger LeMon, regardless if she learned something solid tonight. She picked up the folded sheets of paper she'd printed last night after researching her subject on the Internet.

Roger LeMon was thirty-four years old, graduated from

Vanderbilt University with a degree in finance, worked in the Buckhead office of LeMon and Pride, Ltd., the investment company his late father had founded. By all appearances, the man was a success in his professional and in his personal life. Recipient of various humanitarian awards for philanthropic contributions, winning member of an Atlanta tennis club, on the board of a local business college, on the vestry of his church. Married Janet Chisholm in 1995, lived in a gated neighborhood in Buckhead, no children that Jolie could find a record of. And no direct link to Gary that she could pinpoint, other than the photograph.

On the opposite end of the parking garage, headlights appeared, then a dark sedan . . . slowly climbing the ramp . . . turning into the aisle where she had parked. Carlotta had told her to look for a white Miata convertible, so she slumped lower and watched in her side mirror for the sedan to pass by.

Instead, it stopped . . . directly behind her car, trapping her. Tinted windows hid the face of the occupant. Realization of her stupidity hit Jolie full force, and she scrambled for her cell phone. The hypocrisy of calling the police now was not lost on her, but she didn't care. And how petty was it that she was thinking if she were shot wearing the jumpsuit, she wouldn't be able to return it?

The tinted window started to buzz down just as she punched in 9-1-1. Oh, God . . . "they" were going to get her. Her heart pounded in her ears so loudly, she could barely hear the phone ringing.

"Nine-one-one. Where is the emergency?"

Jolie opened her mouth to unload on the answerer, her eyes riveted on the car window as the top of Carlotta's head appeared, then her gapped grin. Jolie sighed in relief. "Operator, I'm so sorry, I made a mistake."

She disconnected the call, then climbed out of the car, irritated with herself. "I thought you were driving a white convertible!"

Carlotta frowned. "My battery was dead. I had to borrow my brother's car."

"Oh." Jolie gave herself a mental shake. She was either going to have to go to the police or calm the heck down.

Carlotta handed a Mui Mui shoe box out of the window. "I have your shoes, but put the box in your car so you'll have it to make your return tomorrow."

Jolie put the empty box in the trunk, already dreading the return tomorrow. Would Michael know she'd worn them tonight?

"Get in," Carlotta said, "and I'll find a place to park."

She locked her car doors, then shouldered her "biggish" purse and checked to make sure the shocking price tag of the jumpsuit was still secure, tucked down inside the bodice beneath her armpit, held in place with a tiny safety pin.

She climbed into the sedan and closed the door. The interior was luxurious and clean, but reeked of cigarette smoke. "What does your brother do?"

"He's a hacker," Carlottta declared. "Mostly he plays computer games, but sometimes he'll get in the mood to work, help companies with their security, things like that."

"He must be smart."

"Yeah, especially for a nineteen-year-old."

Jolie's eyebrows went up.

Carlotta sighed as she turned into a parking place. "Yes, there's a big age difference. Mother thought another baby would help their marriage."

Jolie could tell by the tone of her voice that it hadn't. "Sounds like you're close to your brother."

She shrugged. "He lives with me." Then she turned off the ignition and smiled with approval. "You look great."

"Thanks. So do you."

Carlotta preened in her "borrowed" red bugle bead jacket over a silvery three-quarter-length dress. Her lustrous dark hair was skimmed back and twisted into a chignon. Against her black, black hair and her olive skin tone, her blue eyes were captivating.

Jolie leaned in. "I thought your eyes were brown."

"Tonight they're blue."

"Contact lenses?"

"Yeah, I have green ones, too, and a pair that looks like cat eyes—those freak everyone out a little. Are you ready for your shoes and new hair?" Carlotta had already turned to retrieve a bag from the backseat. "Here are the shoes."

When Jolie opened the bag to find the soles of the silver-colored cut-out leather pumps covered with several layers of tape, she worked her mouth from side to side. "I feel like a thief."

"Let's don't go through that again. Come on, we're going to be late. Remember to leave in the cardboard stays."

Jolie removed the low heeled sandals she'd worn and pushed her feet into the yummy shoes.

"Put your other shoes in your bag, just in case you have to . . . leave in a hurry."

"You mean in case we get caught crashing and are chased out?"

"It's rare, but it happens," Carlotta said with a sniff. "It's just best to be prepared. Here's your wig." She hoisted a medium-brown pageboy wig, then angled her head. "But your hair looks great—are you sure you want to do this?"

Jolie nodded, then, using the visor mirror, tucked her

curls into a hairnet that Carlotta handed her and stretched the wig over her scalp. She tugged at the ends until all was even. The transformation was startling. She touched her face to prove to her brain that she truly was looking at herself.

"Let me see," Carlotta said, then gasped when Jolie turned her head. "You look . . . completely different. Your boyfriend wouldn't even recognize—" She stopped. "I'm sorry, Jolie, I didn't mean to upset you . . . Wait a minute." She gestured vaguely toward Jolie's getup. "Does *this* have something to do with *that*?"

Jolie's throat constricted. "Maybe."

Carlotta squinted. "At the museum the other night when you were talking to Roger what's-his-name, was the mutual friend you mentioned your boyfriend?"

"Yes."

"But Roger denied knowing him."

"He lied." Jolie hesitated, then pulled from her purse the photo she'd saved from Gary's album. "Gary is the one standing next to Roger. They look chummy to me."

Carlotta hummed her agreement. "But why would the man lie?"

Jolie was silent, knowing she could use an ally, but not sure if she could trust a woman who "borrowed" merchandise from the store and was having money problems. Then she glanced at herself—bewigged and wearing her own "borrowed" outfit—and realized that she was in no position to cast stones.

Carlotta looked up. "What's your boyfriend's name again?"

"Gary . . . Hagan."

"He's cute. I don't recognize him, but wow, that name still sounds so familiar."

Jolie took a deep breath. "You've probably heard it on the news. His car was pulled out of the Chattahoochee River earlier this week."

Carlotta's big blue eyes got even bigger. "He's dead?"

"His body wasn't found," Jolie said carefully. "But there was . . . a woman's body . . . in the car."

Carlotta gasped. "Who?"

"The police don't know yet."

"*Christ.* Oh, you poor thing." Carlotta reached out to touch her arm. "You must be going crazy."

Jolie sighed. "I'm muddling through."

"Do you think he's alive?"

"The police do. My car was stolen the same night Gary disappeared."

"*Christ.* He killed somebody, then he stole your car?"

Jolie wet her lips. "Actually . . . I don't believe he killed anyone."

"You think it was an accident?"

"I don't know," she said, weighing her words. "Gary had friends in high places. I'm thinking maybe he got in the middle of something, maybe he was . . . set up."

Carlotta's jaw dropped. "Christ, this is like something on TV. Are you on a mission to clear the name of the man you love?"

Jolie squirmed. "Well—"

"Christ, the police don't think *you're* involved, do they?"

"Well—"

"They do?"

"Not directly. But . . . the detective who questioned me practically accused me of giving Gary my car to get away."

"Christ, Christ, Christ." Carlotta bounced in her seat. "Your life is so much more exciting than mine!"

The woman's exuberance alarmed her. Jolie looked all around and lifted a quieting hand. "Carlotta, please . . . I need the job at Neiman's. If Michael or anyone else there thought I was somehow linked to a murder—"

"Say no more," Carlotta said, suddenly sober. "I hear what you're saying about the people you work with knowing your personal business."

Jolie remembered the quiver of fear in Carlotta's voice yesterday in the conversation she'd overheard from the dressing room, and wondered if she should tell Carlotta that she'd inadvertently overheard. But since she wasn't in a position to help the woman monetarily, she felt sure that Carlotta would rather not know that she knew.

"Thank you for understanding," was all Jolie said.

"So are you hoping to run into Roger LeMon again tonight, ergo the disguise?"

"Right. I shouldn't have given him my name. If I do see him, I'm hoping he won't realize I'm the same person he talked to the other night."

Carlotta tilted her head, and the tip of her tongue appeared. "Hmm . . . I know!" She pulled out a small case. "Wear my green contact lenses. They don't have a prescription, and they've just been cleaned."

Jolie hesitated. "I don't know . . . having something in my eye."

"It's like a tampon, you won't even know it's there."

Although the imagery did not soothe her qualms, Jolie agreed to try them. Carlotta coached and after much poking and blinking and tearing, they were in. She stared in the mirror, marveling how much the color did change her appearance. "My mascara is a wreck, though," she said, pulling her makeup kit from her purse.

"Do you have an eyebrow pencil?"

Jolie checked. "I have mascara, powder and lip gloss."

"Lip gloss? What are you, in the sixth grade? Here." Carlotta removed a makeup case the size of a loaf of bread from her purse and unzipped it. She rummaged, then withdrew a gold-tone case and twisted up a lipstick the color of cinnamon. "Try this."

Jolie eyed her bag. "That's some arsenal."

"Don't underestimate the power of the right shade of lipstick."

After smoothing on the color, Jolie had to admit Carlotta was right.

"Now, about your eyebrows . . ."

Jolie frowned. "What about my eyebrows?" They were pale, practically nonexistent.

"Eyebrows are the most distinctive feature you have— did you know that your eyebrows keep their basic shape from the time you're born unless you pluck them?"

"No."

She held up a brown pencil. "Give me a couple of minutes, and I promise, no one will recognize you."

Jolie acquiesced and a few pencil strokes later, sported darker, fuller eyebrows with an artful arch. That did it— she did indeed look like a different person.

Carlotta clapped her hands. "What else can I do to help?"

"Do you recognize anyone else in the picture?"

Carlotta turned on the overhead light and studied the photograph again. "No . . . wait, this woman looks familiar," she said, tapping the face of a smiling brunette standing on the end. Pretty, with a mod haircut.

"You don't know her name?"

"No, but she might be a customer. That's a seven-hundred-dollar Ralph Lauren Black Label sweater."

Jolie peered at the woman's yellow sweater—beautiful, but brand-unrecognizable to her untrained eye.

Carlotta drew the picture closer to her blue, blue eyes. "Hmm."

"What?"

"That picture on the wall behind them—I've seen it before."

Jolie studied the picture, which appeared to be an illustration of a pig wearing a suit—a page from a children's book? "Do you remember where? Was it a bar, or someone's house?"

Carlotta frowned, then shook her head and handed back the photo. "I can't remember."

"Okay," Jolie said on an exhale. "Well, I've held us up long enough. I have no idea what I'll say to Roger LeMon if I see him, but I guess I'll just play it by ear."

"Wait—a name, you need a name!"

"Right. How about . . . Linda?"

"Okay, and I'll be Betty." Carlotta grinned. "I've always loved that name." She opened her purse and removed a small white container. "I have a little disguise of my own."

Jolie watched her withdraw what looked like a retainer, then insert it into her mouth. When Carlotta turned and grinned, the gap between her front teeth was gone, replaced by perfect, sparkling white incisors. A slight adjustment, a remarkable change.

"Wow," Jolie murmured.

Carlotta shrugged. "My dentist is always after me to get caps, but I kind of like my smile. My father always said it gave me character." Her voice dropped an octave when she mentioned her father.

"Are your parents still living?" Jolie asked quietly.

"Yeah," Carlotta said with a stark laugh, opening her door. "If you can call it that. Ready?"

Jolie sensed more to Carlotta's story, but nodded and opened her own door, reminding herself that she had a reason for attending tonight's party besides bonding with Carlotta—although that idea suddenly held more appeal than dogging Roger LeMon. She stood, adjusted her clothes, and took a few tentative steps in the stiff shoes. "I hope I don't fall."

"You'll get used to them," Carlotta said.

But by the time they made it to the elevator and rode down to the ground floor, her feet were already chafed from the cardboard stays. The guilt of wearing the pricey outfit and the unfamiliar snugness of the wig seemed to weigh her down, making each footstep more difficult.

"You look like you're in pain," Carlotta chastised.

"I *am* in pain."

"Just think of how good you look and that'll make you feel better."

"At least we don't have far to go," Jolie said, turning toward the glass door that led from the garage into the hotel.

"We're going this way," Carlotta said, pointing in the opposite direction.

Jolie frowned. "What are you up to?"

Carlotta gave her a secret smile. "You'll see."

Jolie followed her to a side exit of the garage and out onto the sidewalk, then looked around to get her bearings. They were past the hotel and around the corner. In fact, most of the cars turning down the side street were taxis and limousines presumably circling back around to Peachtree Street after dropping guests at the hotel. Carlotta turned to the right and headed toward the street corner, farther still from their destination.

Clutching her bag closer to her body, Jolie was besieged by a sudden case of nerves, wondering how she'd made the leap from nice and predictable to . . . here.

Maybe Sammy Sanders had been right. Maybe she *was* out of her mind to leave her comfy job. What did it say about her that she could let Gary's disappearance throw her life into chaos? She wasn't even sure how she still felt about him, but his disappearance had been a catalyst in her life. Carlotta's earlier words resonated in her memory, in her heart. *"Your life is so much more exciting than mine."*

A few steps ahead of her, Carlotta stepped to the curb and flagged down a shiny black limo, then leaned in a lowered window and spoke to the driver. The woman's body language was pure flirtation. Suddenly she turned and beckoned Jolie forward. "Come on, we're going to arrive in style."

Jolie blinked the swimmy contact lenses into place, scooted forward in her stiff shoes and murmured, "Suddenly, *my* life is so much more exciting than mine."

Ten

Jolie slid in next to Carlotta on the long, black bench seat of the limousine. "We're taking a limo around the block?"

"It's all about perception," Carlotta said. "People will assume we're somebody important if we arrive in a service."

Jolie wasn't about to argue, because her feet were screaming for relief. And although the ride was over before her tootsies could get a break, Jolie conceded a little thrill of excitement when a gloved hotel doorman opened the door and helped her out onto the carpet under the canopied entrance, and people turned to look. "Are you ladies here for the broadcasters reception?"

"Yes," Carlotta said in a clipped voice, ringing with unmistaken authority. "Could you point us in the right direction, please?"

"Straight ahead to the lobby, then left," the doorman said, beaming at the women.

Carlotta folded a tip into his hand. "Thank you indeed."

Jolie was conscious of other people's heads pivoting

with interest as they walked toward the open double doors. The women seemed intrigued; the men were more blatant with their admiring looks. For a few minutes she forgot how much her feet hurt.

Out of the corner of her eye, a car on Peachtree Street caught her attention—a gray Mercury Sable sedan . . . Hers? Her breath caught in her chest at the thought of Gary following her. She craned for a better look, but the contact lenses moved on her eyes, obscuring her vision for a few seconds. She blinked furiously, but by the time she had focused, the car had already slid into traffic and out of sight. She exhaled a long breath, telling herself there were hundreds of cars like hers in the metro area. Surely Gary wouldn't risk being caught driving a stolen car along the Peachtree-Street corridor at night when the police patrols were in full force.

She wondered if he would be waiting for her when she returned to her car tonight, or if, as Leann had suggested, he had used the bought time to get the hell out of Dodge.

Was she being a colossal, gullible fool by believing him?

"Are you okay?" Carlotta asked.

"Fine," she murmured, and resumed walking.

They were directed down a lavishly tiled hallway that opened up into a spacious foyer with a small, tasteful sign that welcomed guests to the reception for the Broadcasters and Journalists Association of Georgia. Jolie's palms were moist when they chained onto a line of beautifully dressed guests waiting to give their tickets to a rather stern-looking middle-aged gentleman. She grew even more nervous when Carlotta, casting inconspicuous glances at the tickets people around them were holding, turned a little gray around the gills.

"What's wrong?" Jolie whispered.

"I was misinformed," Carlotta whispered back. "I had my brother print up the wrong tickets."

Jolie felt a full-fledged sweat coming on, and out of fear of staining the rented jumpsuit, concentrated on trying to contract her pores. "What are we going to do?"

"Follow my lead," Carlotta said just as the couple in front of them moved on and the ticket taker held out his hand.

"Tickets please."

"Forgive my ignorance, sir," Carlotta said in a distinct British accent. "This is the first time I have attended such an event, and I wasn't aware that I was supposed to bring the vouchers."

Jolie stared. The woman was a chameleon.

A wrinkle formed in the man's brow. "I'm not supposed to let you in without a ticket, ma'am."

"Oh," Carlotta murmured, fluttering her hands. "I'm quite embarrassed, still adjusting to American protocol and all of that." She turned to bestow a beatific smile on the people behind them. Then she turned back to the ticket holder. "Isn't there something you can do, sir? Check my name on a list, perhaps? Betty Halverson, CNN. And guest."

Jolie did her part, nodding as if she were indeed the guest of British-born Betty Halverson, CNN, although her neck itched and the contact in her left eye was beginning to feel like a tampon all right—a tampon in her eye.

The ticket taker leaned in to speak to Carlotta conspiratorially. "I asked for a list, ma'am, but they didn't give me one."

Carlotta made a rueful noise in her throat. "This isn't your fault, good sir, it's mine, all mine." *Flap, flap* went her false eyelashes.

Jolie could practically hear the man's resolve crumbling. "I think it would be all right this once," he murmured.

"You are a true gentleman," Carlotta crooned, and floated through the opening.

Jolie followed with a grateful American nod. When they had moved out of earshot, she looked at Carlotta. "What was that?"

"Accents will open doors," Carlotta said with a lovely shrug. "People with a British accent sound smart and trustworthy."

"You're scary," Jolie said.

"We're in, aren't we?" Carlotta said, then scanned the room full of milling guests. She stopped and inhaled sharply. "Oh, my God."

Jolie froze and tried to blink her contact lens into place. "Do you see Roger LeMon?"

"No, it's Thomas Roberts—CNN anchor." She sighed. "That man puts the 'ooh' in news."

"Maybe you should go introduce yourself to your coworker," Jolie said wryly.

Carlotta made a face and continued to survey the room. "I'm going to be able to add to my book tonight. Without moving, I see Paul Ossman, Monica Kauffman, and Clark Howard."

"The consumer reports guy?"

"Yeah." Carlotta frowned. "Someone should tell him that his advice to shop discount stores is not only bad for the economy, but bad for the Atlanta fashion scene."

"Oh, no," Jolie said with a laugh. "It's better to buy something and wear it, then return it."

Carlotta frowned harder. "I told you, this is good advertising. Do you know how many people are looking at you right now?"

"They're looking through me to get to you," Jolie said, then nodded toward the bar. "Since you hired the limousine for our long journey, I'll get us drink tickets."

"Wait," Carlotta said, clasping Jolie's arm. She stared at the table where tickets were being sold and murmured, "Yellow." Then she angled her body toward Jolie, opened her purse, and pulled out six yellow generic tear-off tickets. "Three for you, three for me."

Jolie's eyes widened, and her errant lens popped back into place. "You brought your own drink tickets?"

"You can buy them in rolls at any office supply store."

"How did you know the tickets would be yellow?"

"I didn't—I brought red, blue, *and* yellow, just in case."

"You really have this down to a science, don't you?"

"I prefer to think of it as an art," she said with a smile, as they walked toward the bar. "By the way, don't get red wine or anything to eat with red sauce—you know the old saying, 'If you break it, you buy it'?"

"Yes."

"Well," Carlotta said, gesturing at the jumpsuit. "If you stain it, you've just obtained it."

Jolie swallowed. "Got it." They joined the line at the bar and Jolie glanced around the ballroom. Even to her unsophisticated eye, this crowd seemed more affluent compared to the crowd of two nights ago. "What's the biggest event you've ever crashed?" she whispered to Carlotta.

"The governor's inaugural ball."

Jolie's eyes bugged. "How did you manage that?"

"Hannah loaned me a chef's coat to wear over my outfit. I walked in through the kitchen, picked up a tray and carried it to a table, detoured through the bathroom to remove the coat, stuffed the coat into my bag, and joined the party."

Jolie shook her head in amazement.

"By the way, Hannah will be here in an hour," Carlotta said, looking around, "so I need to find a side door to let her in."

"Oh . . . kay," Jolie said, moving up in the bar line.

"But the most *fun* I had," Carlotta said, on a roll now, "was watching the Hawks. I printed up a press pass, borrowed my brother's camera with a big honking lens, and parked myself courtside."

"When was that?"

"The entire 2000–2001 season."

Jolie gaped. "No one ever questioned you?"

"Nope. Of course, now, security at the big venues is too strict for someone like me to get in."

"Don't you think that's probably a good thing?"

"I suppose so," Carlotta agreed, then stepped up and handed the bartender one of the generic drink tickets in exchange for a gin and tonic.

Jolie got white wine, tipped well to assuage her conscience and then began to scout the room for Roger LeMon or one of the others in the photograph.

"I'll check out the other side of the room," Carlotta murmured. Jolie nodded and watched the men watch her friend as she glided across the room. When she realized she was getting a few looks of her own, she reached up to touch her hair and encountered the unfamiliar texture of the straight wig. The knowledge that tonight she didn't have to be mousy little Jolie Goodman shot through her. Tonight she could be anybody she wanted to be.

"Beautiful outfit," a woman next to her said.

Jolie smiled, then wet her lips. "Why thank yaw," she said, but her British accent came out sounding like Scarlett O'Hara with her mouth full of peanut butter. She cleared her throat. "I mean, thank you," she said in her normal voice, then felt compelled to add, "Neiman's."

The woman pursed her mouth and nodded, then turned back to her group. Jolie sipped her wine and moved around the room, forcing herself to join knots of people and make small talk about the weather and traffic, and to congratulate the people who wore colored badges, designating a nomination for broadcasting and journalism awards.

She introduced herself as Linda, an attorney—why not? She'd wondered what it was like to walk in the shoes of the rich and famous, and now she was getting a taste of it. Her feet had progressed beyond painful; they were anesthetized, allowing her to accept compliments graciously, plugging Neiman's at every opportunity. A couple of men tried to latch on, buy her a drink, and while she enjoyed the attention, she made excuses to keep moving.

For some reason, Beck Underwood's face kept popping into her mind, and she wondered if she'd see him tonight. Mixed feelings danced in her chest over the fact that if he did put in an appearance, she wouldn't be able to talk to him and not blow her cover. Which was probably for the best, she told herself. The last thing she needed was to develop a crush on Beck Underwood simply because he had a hero complex and was bored with being back home.

Blaming that disturbing mind tangent on the fact that her brain was trying to pump blood to her numb feet, she wiggled her toes (at least she thought she did) and forced herself to move on.

Everywhere she turned, she was drawn into light conversation. She attributed the warm reception she received to the clothes and the shoes, although she couldn't blame people for treating her differently. She *felt* different.

Taller, sexier, wittier. She was well-read and had observed local politics for years, but had never put herself in situations to engage in clever party dialogue. The wine and the new persona she'd adopted made her brave. In one crowd she ventured a joke that garnered bursts of laughter, to her great surprise. The attention was absolutely heady, more powerful than the wine. She caught a glimpse of herself in a mirrored column and was stunned at the woman who was reflected—self-assured, poised, polished. Was this the person she might have become, under different circumstances?

Jolie turned away and sipped from her glass, unnerved at her train of thought since arriving. She'd never wanted to be anyone other than herself until this mess had landed in her lap. In fact, people with money and power had always made her uneasy, and she'd do well to remember that the same people who had laughed at her jokes wouldn't give her a second glance if she were wearing her normal discount-store clothing and selling them shoes.

And that some people in this social echelon—perhaps in this very room—might be responsible for what had happened to Gary . . . and the woman in his car. Bolstered by a second glass of wine, she canvassed the room with new resolve. And then she spotted Roger LeMon, wearing a tuxedo, one hand wrapped around a drink, the other in his pocket. He was talking to a man who was wearing an award nomination badge, and they seemed to be deep in conversation. But what sent a stone to her stomach was the fact that the second man, a stout, round-faced fellow who looked prematurely gray, was also familiar. He too was in the photo in her purse.

"Do you see what I see?"

Jolie jumped and turned her head to see Carlotta, her intense blue eyes wide with excitement. "You mean Roger LeMon? I just saw him. Do you know the man he's talking to? He's in the photo too."

"I've seen him around, but I don't know who he is."

"He's wearing a nominee badge."

"Then by all means, let's go congratulate him."

Jolie touched Carlotta's arm. "Wait. What if LeMon recognizes us?"

"He's not going to recognize us," Carlotta said, then wet her lips. "Especially not *this* English rose," she said in her perfect British accent.

"How did you learn to do that?" Jolie asked as they made their way through the crowd.

"I had an English nanny."

More clues to her blueblood upbringing. Jolie followed her friend through the crowd, sensing the master party crasher had had a troubled life. Why else would she delight in mocking the class of people that would probably welcome her with open arms? Only a powerful resentment could drive a person to go to so much trouble to pull one over on a group of people who would never realize they'd been had.

The closer they got to Roger LeMon, the harder Jolie's heart pounded. His voice and his words from the other night reverberated in her head. *"She said she was a friend . . . Goodman, Jolie Goodman."*

She had to force herself to walk closer, terrified that he would recognize her, that he might even have found her dropped wineglass the other night and know that his conversation had been overheard. By the time they were near enough to the men to strike up a conversation, her tongue was immobile. Part by part, her body was becoming paralyzed. Not that she had to worry, with Carlotta in the vicinity.

"Hallo," the woman purred, stepping between the men. They stopped mid-conversation. LeMon seemed perturbed by the interruption, and took the opportunity to drink deeply from his cocktail. Carlotta directed her attention—and accent—to the unknown man. "I'm Betty, and this is my friend Linda, and we wanted to say congratulations on your nomination."

The plump man raked his gaze over Betty and interest flared in his eyes. He switched his drink to his left hand—the one with the wedding ring—and shook Carlotta's hand with his right. "Thank you. I'm Kyle Coffee. This here is Roger LeMon." His speech was slightly slurred, and he seemed to be well on his way to being toasted.

"How do you do, Roger?" Carlotta said. "Do both of you gentlemen work in the industry?"

"I'm in television production," Kyle offered. "My buddy Roger is a money man."

Carlotta smiled. "Ah. Sounds like a most fortuitous friendship. You work together?"

"No," Kyle Coffee said with an exaggerated wink. "I guess you could say we *play* together, wouldn't you, Roger?"

LeMon hesitated, then gave a little laugh and turned to look at Jolie.

She fought the clawing urge to run. The relief that he didn't seem to recognize her gave way to the heebie-jeebies from his lascivious stare. He wet his thin lips, then said to Carlotta, "So, does your friend have that same cute accent?"

Carlotta gave Jolie a questioning look. "Who, Linda? Well—"

"No," Jolie said softly, but emphasized the Georgia drawl she'd been raised with and had worked hard to dispel. "That is, I have a cute accent, but it's closer to home."

They all laughed and Roger moved a few inches closer. The hand in his pocket began to jingle change and his neck loosened with what she assumed was his "hey, chickie baby" stance. "Nice outfit," he said, looking at her boobs.

"Thanks." Her mind raced, searching for a line of questioning that might lead somewhere helpful. "Where do you live . . . Roger?"

He took another drink, as if he were debating on what—or perhaps whether—to tell her. "In Buckhead," he said finally. "You?"

"Vinings," she said, glad that her real-estate training had made her so familiar with the metro area. "I just moved to town. What did your friend mean when he said you were a money man?" She managed a flirtatious smile. "You don't *launder* money, do you?"

Kyle Coffee belly-laughed, blowing his flammable breath all over them. Roger joined in, slightly less amused, a half beat later. "No. I'm an investment broker. What do you do . . . um—"

"Linda," she supplied. "I'm an attorney."

Kyle elbowed Roger. "Maybe she's a divorce attorney." He laughed again, scorching the air.

Roger's thick, dark eyebrows came together. "Maybe you've had a little too much to drink, Kyle."

When the silence began to grow tense, Jolie asked, "So, Roger, do you come to these events to network for clients?"

He shook his head. "No, I come for the same reason that most everyone else is here: to kill time." He lifted his glass for another drink and winced as he swallowed. "Besides, almost everyone here is already a client of mine."

She glanced around to humor him. "I guess that means you deal only with high rollers."

He shrugged. "Well, not to brag, but my minimum investment for new clients is seven figures."

The man was so bragging. But with those requirements and Gary's wrecked finances, Gary certainly wasn't a *client* of LeMon's. "Do you have a business card?" she asked.

He extended his drink for her to hold, and she took it, feeling a little smarmy just by association. She had the feeling that Roger LeMon was used to people doing what he wanted, especially women. And while some women might find his arrogance attractive, she was repulsed. She watched as unobtrusively as she could as he removed his wallet. On his left ring finger was a gold band—a band he hadn't been wearing two nights ago. He made a show of opening his wallet, which boasted a thick stack of bills, then withdrew a business card and tucked the wallet back into his pocket.

Jolie glanced at Carlotta, who had noticed the wad of money and seemed to be deep in thought as she sipped her gin and tonic. Unease tickled Jolie's spine, but she cut back to Roger and offered him a beguiling smile as he handed her his business card.

Feeling bold, she asked, "Is there a private number on your card?"

He pursed his mouth and stared at her cleavage again, then pulled a pen out of his jacket and clicked the end with purpose . . . and a gleam in his eye. He turned over the card and wrote something on it, then reached forward to tuck the card in a small breast pocket on her jumpsuit (proportioned, she presumed, especially for small breasts). "Call me soon."

He stroked her breast as he pulled out his finger and she swallowed against the revulsion that rose in her throat. His hands were long and slender, his nails manicured. The edge of a small black tattoo on his wrist peeked out from beneath his shirt cuff. His smile was cocky as he returned his pen to an inside pocket. Her hands itched to throw the two drinks she held in his face.

"Don't look now, Roger," Kyle Coffee said with an elbow nudge. "Here comes history."

Both men looked over Jolie's shoulder and fixed smiles on their faces at whoever was approaching.

Jolie turned around to greet the arrivals, and nearly choked. Beck Underwood and his sister stood there, both of them giving Roger wary glances. It suddenly hit her that Beck had mentioned his sister had once dated Roger. Jolie ducked her head and frantically glanced around for an escape route, but found herself hemmed in between Roger and a gigantic sago palm tree. Desperate, she held up her wineglass to obscure her face.

"Hi, Della," LeMon said, dipping his chin.

"Hello, Roger," Della replied, her voice surprisingly tentative for an heiress, although based on the dark circles beneath her eyes, the woman looked a little under the weather.

"Hey, Beck," LeMon said a little too loudly. "Long time, no see. I hear you've been living with natives, or something like that."

"Or something like that," Beck said coolly.

Out of the corner of her eye, Jolie saw Roger's hand twitch as he suddenly realized he didn't have a drink— Jolie was still holding his glass. When he reached for it, Jolie felt all eyes land on her, and she dreaded looking up. When she did, newly shorn Beck Underwood, exquisite in a black suit, white shirt, and silvery tie, was studying her, then "Betty." Jolie averted her gaze and hoped like heck he didn't put two and two together and get two—namely, her and Carlotta.

"We came over to congratulate Kyle," his sister said, extending her hand and a smile to the inebriated man. "Dad couldn't be here tonight, but he can't say enough about your work on the *Yesterdays* series."

Kyle Coffee must have realized the significance of the Underwoods' presence because he visibly tried to gather himself. "Thank you," he said, shaking hands with Della, then Beck. "Good to see you b–back, B–Beck," he ventured, but the alliteration was too much for his sloshy tongue to handle and he giggled nervously. "Uh . . . meet our new friends," he said to cover his gaffe.

Jolie was caught.

"Della and Beck Underwood, this is Betty and . . . and . . . *Linda*!" Kyle said, proud of himself for remembering.

Carlotta nodded graciously. "Hallo."

"Oh, you're from England," Della Underwood said. "What part?"

"London," Carlotta said without missing a beat.

"What part of London?" Beck Underwood asked mildly.

Jolie's heart began to trip overtime. He was on to them.

"Liverpool Street," Carlotta said triumphantly.

"Ah. Near the station, or in the city?"

Carlotta's smile faltered for a split second. "Er, near the station . . . of course."

He nodded, then he looked at Jolie and his eyes danced with mischief. "Linda—it *is* Linda, right?"

She nodded, feeling like an idiot.

"Are you from London also?"

"N–no," she stammered in her resurrected Southern accent.

"Linda is an attorney from Vinings," Carlotta offered, trying to be helpful.

"*Is* she?" Beck asked, his eyebrows lifted.

"Beck Underwood," a woman's voice said behind them. "I *knew* our paths would cross again."

They all turned, and Jolie's intestines twisted at the sight of the blonde gliding their way dressed in shocking pink. Sammy "Sold" Sanders.

This night just kept getting better.

Eleven

Watching Sammy Sanders introduce herself around the circle was painful because the woman personified every stereotype that had plagued the real-estate business for decades: cheesy smile, fake boobs, and an elbow-wagging handshake straight out of Realty 101. Jolie decided to take her chances climbing over the palm tree, but came up short when Roger LeMon hooked his arm in hers.

"You're not *leaving* . . . ?" It was more of a statement than a question. He glanced toward Della Underwood for a split second, and it hit Jolie like a thunderbolt that he wanted to make the woman jealous. Her flash of anger dissipated when she considered the ramifications—and complications—of unresolved feelings between Roger and Della. A memory stirred . . . something Beck had said when she'd asked about his return to Atlanta. *"My sister was going through some things I wanted to be here for."*

A love affair gone bad?

By the time Jolie had processed the new possibilities,

Sammy was standing in front of her. "I'm Sammy," she said, grabbing Jolie's hand for a pump that would have brought up water from the Sahara.

"Linda," Jolie murmured.

"Hey, Linda just moved here," Kyle Coffee boomed. "Maybe *she* needs a house."

Sammy went from seven hundred and fifty watts to one thousand. "Really?"

"No . . . no," Jolie said as quickly as her acquired drawl would allow. "I don't need a house."

Sammy's face fell, then she squinted. "Have we met before?"

Jolie's heart skipped a beat, then resumed. "No. Like he said, I'm new in town."

"Linda is an attorney," Carlotta and Beck said in unison.

Everyone stared. Carlotta cleared her throat and added, "She lives in Vinings."

Sammy turned back to Jolie. "It's just that . . . you remind me of somebody . . . I can't put my finger on it."

Carlotta couldn't know that Sammy was her former boss, but Jolie suspected that her friend could see the panic on her face.

"Oh, you know what they say," Carlotta said with a laugh. "Everyone has a twin somewhere."

Next to her, Roger LeMon's head jerked toward Carlotta. Jolie winced inwardly when she realized that Carlotta had inadvertently echoed LeMon's response from two nights ago when she'd said she recognized him from a photo with Gary. Had he just made the connection?

His head pivoted back to her and Jolie saw suspicion flash through his eyes. She maintained a wide-eyed expression for his sake and for Sammy's. Then Sammy glanced down at Jolie's shoes and she snapped her fingers. "Did you get those shoes at Neiman's?"

Jolie felt her smile waver, but she managed a nod.

"Were you shopping there this week? Monday maybe?"

Jolie managed another nod.

"I'll bet that's it," Sammy said with a big smile. "I probably saw you in the shoe department."

Beck's burst of dry laughter got everyone's attention. He lifted his big shoulders in a casual shrug. "Eventually, you see everyone in Atlanta in the shoe department at Neiman's."

"So true," Carlotta said, jumping on the "save Jolie" bandwagon. Everyone laughed politely, but Roger LeMon kept staring at her. Jolie squirmed and her mind raced for a reason to excuse herself as the sudden lull in the conversation dragged on.

"Linda," Carlotta sang, "I hate to be a damp rag, but we did promise Hannah that we would meet her."

"Right," Jolie agreed in relief.

"It was nice to meet everyone," Carlotta said, backing away and bowing, leaving Jolie to wonder if bowing was still in vogue in England.

Afraid that Sammy would recognize her voice, Jolie nodded her agreement, sending a smile all around. Kyle Coffee waved good-naturedly and Sammy had refocused her fawning self on Beck Underwood, pressing a cream-colored postcard into his hand. Roger LeMon continued to watch Jolie through narrowed eyes with such dark intensity that if he were somehow involved in this mess, she could understand why Gary had sounded so terrified. She tried to smile, but LeMon's face remained immobile.

Her numb feet weren't responding well—she stumbled

past Beck Underwood and he reached out to steady her with his arm. The warmth and strength of his fingers against her bare skin sent a jolt of awareness through her. When she looked into his brown eyes, she saw questions there. She was grateful that despite his obvious bewilderment, he hadn't given them away.

"Thank you," she murmured.

"You're welcome," he said, holding her arm a few seconds longer than necessary before releasing her.

She blamed her heightened senses on the constant stream of adrenaline her body had been pumping throughout the evening, and turned to walk away as fast as her deadened feet would take her. Next to her, she could sense that Carlotta was ready to burst out of her skin. They had barely gotten out of earshot when Carlotta squealed. "Oh, my God, that was so exciting!"

Jolie exhaled. "That isn't a word I would've used."

"Did you find out anything from Roger LeMon?"

"Maybe . . . I don't know." She touched her thumping head. "This entire thing could be a dead end. Maybe I'm looking for a bigger connection than what's there."

"Are you going to call him?"

"I don't know. I'm not sure, but I think he recognized us toward the end."

Carlotta touched her temple. "Because of what I said about having a twin? I'm *so* sorry. That just popped out." She winced. "If I've blown our cover, I'll never forgive myself."

Jolie decided not to make her feel worse by telling her about the phone conversation she'd overheard the other night, and that if LeMon thought they were trying to pull one over on him, he might be incensed . . . to the point of being dangerous.

"It's okay," Jolie said. "I could be wrong about him recognizing us."

"Beck Underwood saw right through us." Carlotta elbowed Jolie. "But then again, the man seems to have radar where you're concerned."

Jolie's cheeks warmed. "I don't know what you're talking about."

"He has a *thing* for you."

"No, he doesn't, and if he did, I'm not interested." Not interested in being a novelty for a man who moved easily in circles she had to crash.

Carlotta pressed her lips together. "Are you still hung up on your boyfriend?" She made a rueful noise. "Of course you are, I didn't mean to be crass. You don't even know for sure if the man is dead or alive."

"R–right." Jolie drained the remaining inch of white wine in her glass. "Did you find out anything about Kyle Coffee?"

"Other than he can't hold his liquor? The only thing I noticed that was odd was that he and LeMon have the same tattoo."

Jolie frowned. "The one on LeMon's wrist? I noticed it, but I couldn't make out what it was."

"Kyle had one in the same place, but I could see his because the slob had lost a cuff link. It was some kind of crest . . . Maybe a college fraternity thing?"

Jolie splayed her hand. "It could mean nothing."

"Did your boyfriend have one?"

"No."

"Hmm. Well, you're right—it could be nothing. I gathered that you knew Realtor Barbie from somewhere?"

Jolie rolled her eyes. "Sammy is my ex-boss."

Carlotta made a face. "Did she fire you?"

"No. I quit."

Carlotta raised her eyebrows, then grinned, revealing her retouched smile. "I like you, Jolie Goodman. You've got chutzpah."

Warm surprise suffused Jolie's chest, and she conceded a little thrill to be accepted by someone like Carlotta, who was such an interesting character herself.

They climbed a short set of carpeted stairs to another bar area where they swapped two more tickets for fresh drinks. "This is my limit," Jolie murmured, already feeling a little light-headed. On the other hand, the guilt of consuming free drinks seemed to dissipate with each one, Jolie noted, sipping the crisp chardonnay.

Carlotta stopped a waiter and whipped out her British accent. "Pardon me, could you direct me to the smoking area?"

"There's smoking outside only," he said apologetically, and pointed. "Down this hall and to the right, out the doors onto a covered patio."

She thanked the man, then pulled out her neon-yellow cell phone. "I'll tell Hannah where to meet us."

While Carlotta talked on the tiny phone, Jolie realized the raised floor gave her a good vantage for spying. She slid a glance in the direction where they'd been standing earlier. Only Kyle Coffee remained, talking to a new group of people, none of whom she recognized. She picked out Beck and Della Underwood a few yards away, shaking hands with more nominees. Beck was hard to miss because he was at least a half head taller than most of the men in the room. His hand hovered at his sister's waist protectively and Jolie experienced a stab of envy over their closeness. If she ever became a mother, she would want more than one child to make sure they had siblings to grow up with and comfort and companionship after she and their father had passed on.

Why those domestic thoughts were whirling through her head now, she couldn't fathom. She had to get through this chaos surrounding Gary before she could move on with her life. But as she watched Beck move, undeniable attraction curled in her stomach. She liked the way he carried his body—with the grace of a natural athlete. It was, she realized, easier to observe him from a distance. When the man was in her proximity, in her personal space, his presence played havoc with her senses.

She wondered if he'd stepped in tonight for his powerful father, and if he'd minded. Was he the prodigal son returning home to pull his weight in the family conglomerate after whiling away a few years in paradise? Had he been summoned home?

His noise about finding a house notwithstanding, would he stay in Atlanta, or be off on another adventure when things became too staid? That kind of freedom frightened Jolie, it was too . . . uncertain. She needed boundaries to be able to organize and guide her life, a measuring stick against which to gauge her progress—a by-product of her blue-collar parents, she was sure. She supposed it would be different if one were raised without financial limitations, which probably explained why money married money . . . being rich was as much a state of mind as it was a state of bank account.

As she watched, a beautiful redhead engaged Beck in conversation. The woman was perfect in every way: perfect hair, perfect smile, perfect figure, perfect clothes, perfect carriage. She angled her body toward Beck in an unmistakable invitation, and he didn't turn away. He was, after all, a man. A rich man who was accustomed to having beautiful women throw themselves at him. Jolie's cheeks flamed that she had even briefly entertained the idea that he might be interested in her.

He laughed at something the woman said, revealing even white teeth, then he glanced around the room and before she could look away, looked up and caught her staring at him. Great. He lifted his chin slightly and a smile played on his mouth before he turned his head to respond to something else the redhead said.

Jolie looked away before she could make an even bigger fool out of herself. Undoubtedly, the man already thought she was certifiable—why not behave like a stalker too?

Keeping an eye peeled for Roger LeMon, she scanned the crowd methodically, thinking she should have watched where he'd gone. A few seconds later, she chastised herself. Just because LeMon gave her the creeps and lied—possibly—about knowing Gary didn't mean he was a criminal monster. He simply could be a run-of-the-mill chauvinistic jerk.

The wisecrack that Kyle Coffee had made about a divorce attorney—had he been hinting that he himself could use one, or Roger? Neither man, in her opinion, presented himself as being prime husband material. Is that what Della Underwood had decided, or had Roger LeMon ended their relationship?

Carlotta snapped her phone closed and stashed it in her bag. "Hannah will meet us outside in a few minutes. Want to come?"

"Sure. Carlotta . . . what do you know about Della Underwood?"

Carlotta pursed her mouth. "Actually, Della and I went to the same private high school for a while."

"Were you friends?"

"No. She was a year ahead of me, and she hung with a very exclusive crowd. Her mother has always been sickly, so she began making appearances with her old man when she was still in high school." Carlotta laughed. "I was wildly jealous of her, we all were."

It was hard to imagine that Carlotta would be jealous of anyone.

"After high school, Della was a social diva—a real party girl, but she had a lot of style, you know? Classy. Dated senators' sons, professional athletes, was always in the social column." She paused and lifted her shoulders in a slow shrug. "Then . . . I don't know, she just sort of dropped off the scene. There were rumors that she was in drug rehab, that she'd had a nervous breakdown, that she'd had a baby—but none of those things were ever verified. She started making appearances again, but she was like this scared little animal, like . . . like she'd been wounded."

"What year was that?"

Carlotta squinted. "Ninety-four, ninety-five."

"What do you think happened?"

Carlotta spoke behind her hand. "Personally, I always wondered if maybe Mrs. Underwood was a mental case, and if maybe Della inherited something." She shrugged. "But that's only speculation on my part."

"She's never been married?"

"No."

"Beck mentioned at the museum the other night that she used to date Roger LeMon."

Carlotta frowned. "Really? I don't remember that. Not that I'm an expert on the Underwoods."

Jolie wet her lips. "Has Beck?"

"Has Beck what?"

Her cheeks tingled. "Ever been married?"

A sly smile curved Carlotta's mouth. "Not unless he got married while he was in exile."

"What do you mean, 'in exile'?"

"Beck worked for his dad, but it was well known that they didn't always get along. Beck was a rebel, a real champion of the working man," she said, her voice heavy with sarcasm. "If you ask me, leading pickets against his dad's companies had more to do with making his old man crazy than with sympathy for the lowly masses, but regardless, Daddy Underwood sent him packing."

Admiration bloomed in Jolie's chest. Despite her best intentions, she stole another glance in Beck's direction and saw that he had been cornered by a reporter and camera crew. Of course anyone covering award nominations for broadcasters and journalists would want to talk to the successor to the largest broadcasting company in the Southeast. A spotlight haloed his wide torso as he spoke into the extended microphone. His body language didn't read like a rebel . . . He looked thoughtful and distinguished, like someone on the verge of taking over the reins of a company he would most likely inherit. A crowd had gathered around him, and from the expressions on their faces, it was apparent that men wanted to be him, and women wanted to be with him.

"He's something, isn't he?" Carlotta whispered with a sigh.

Jolie jerked her head around, then flushed. "He's . . . perplexing."

Carlotta linked her arm in Jolie's and pulled her in the opposite direction. "He's a man, Jolie—trust me, he's not that complicated."

Jolie closed her eyes briefly, trying to sort her jumbled

thoughts. With so many other matters pressing on her mind and her heart, she had no business wasting a brain cell on Beck Underwood.

They followed the waiter's directions through a set of glass doors to a covered patio. A chilly October wind had blown in, raising goose bumps over Jolie's bare arms. She shivered, thinking she should have worn a coat, although she didn't own anything nearly nice enough to wear over the jumpsuit.

Pedestals holding bowls of white sand had been situated around the perimeter of the patio for the smokers. They were a forlorn bunch: social outcasts relegated to a covered concrete pad to practice their vice. The lighting was dim and depressing, and the strident whine of nearby electrical boxes filled the night air. Everyone huddled in their jackets, their backs to the wind, huffing and puffing.

"And to think," Carlotta muttered, "smoking used to be popular." She handed her gin and tonic to Jolie to hold, then opened her purse and pulled out a box of menthol cigarettes. "Want one?"

Jolie started to shake her head, then decided she could use something to calm her nerves and warm her up. "Okay."

Carlotta opened the box and slid out two cigarettes, stuck them both in her mouth and pulled out a slender mother-of-pearl lighter. She lit both cigarettes, then traded one to Jolie for the drink she'd been holding.

Jolie drew on the cigarette until her adenoids stung, then coughed smoke into her hand. "I've never been much of a smoker."

Carlotta exhaled figure eights into the air. "I've quit twenty-seven times. I hate the way it makes my clothes smell." She gestured to Jolie's jumpsuit. "You'll have to turn it inside out and run it on air-only in the clothes dryer for at least an hour. Make sure you tape cardboard around the tags so they don't curl."

Jolie nodded obediently and attempted a more shallow inhale on the cigarette. She glanced over her shoulder, uneasy about the pitch-blackness surrounding the patio. A person could be standing a mere foot off the edge and no one would know it. Gary could be out there, watching her as he'd said. She shivered and took a step toward the center of the patio.

Carlotta looked toward the door, then emitted a little laugh. "Well, if his liver doesn't give out, his lungs will."

Jolie turned to see Kyle Coffee stumbling through the door, holding an unlit cigar that was at least nine inches long. He stopped next to a bowl of sand and set down his drink, then used both hands to search various pockets. Finally he pulled out what looked like one of the postcards that Sammy was handing out, rolled it lengthwise and used it to borrow a flame from the cigarette of the guy next to him. Jolie watched, poised to run in case Coffee set something—or himself—on fire, but he lit the tip of the cigar from the paper, then jammed the card into the sand without incident. He retrieved his drink, drew on the cigar until his face turned scarlet, and exhaled with a happy sigh. He didn't notice them, didn't notice much of anything, Jolie suspected. He seemed to be in a fog, shuffling around the edge of the concrete pad, tapping ashes into the grass.

Jolie looked at Carlotta. "Do you suppose that Coffee is even more chatty when LeMon isn't around?"

"Let's go see, shall we?"

When they approached him, his glassy eyes made it clear that he didn't remember them. They reintroduced themselves as Betty and Linda, and Carlotta congratulated him again on his nomination. He was loud and barely coherent. The cigar smelled like singed hair.

"That's an interesting tattoo," Carlotta said in her perfectly clipped accent, pointing to his wrist.

He frowned and leaned in. "Huh?"

"Your tattoo, what does it mean?"

Her words registered and he clamped the odorous cigar between his small teeth, then yanked back his sleeve to reveal a black tattoo the size and shape of a postage stamp. Jolie leaned in for a good look, and saw a border of what looked like four arms, one melding into another counterclockwise, the tiny hands on the corners. The center of the image was a filigree pattern that she couldn't make out.

"This," he slurred around his cigar, "was the biggest mistake I ever made."

"You don't like having a tattoo?" Jolie asked, enunciating clearly for his benefit.

"Hell, I got a half dozen tattoos," he said. "But this one has ruined my life."

Jolie's skin prickled. "What makes you say that?"

"His wife doesn't like it," Roger LeMon said behind them.

Twelve

Jolie jerked her head around and her heart slammed in her chest at the sight of LeMon's thin mouth pressed into a flat line as he considered their threesome. He walked up and put his arm around Kyle Coffee's shoulder, then pulled the man's head close to his. "Isn't that right, Kyle?" he asked in a tone that might have been good-natured except for his precise enunciation. "Your wife doesn't like that tattoo because it's in a more visible place than the others."

Kyle blinked at Roger dumbly, then nodded. "That'z right, Roger," he lisped around the cigar in his mouth.

Roger slapped him on the back. "I called you a cab, man. It's time for you to say good night."

"Okay," the man mumbled.

"I'll walk you out," LeMon said, and guided his big friend toward the doors. LeMon turned his head to give Jolie a suspicious glare, then herded Coffee inside.

Jolie exhaled.

"Coffee was getting ready to tell us something," Carlotta said. "I just know it!"

"Maybe. I wanted to ask him if he knew Gary."

"So call him. Make up a story."

"Right," Jolie murmured, except she doubted that Kyle Coffee would be as forthcoming when he was sober. And she was starting to feel as if this whole situation was getting out of hand. She didn't know which details might be relevant and which details might take her on a tangent. Plus she was feeling antsy that she hadn't heard from Gary again. She needed to talk to Detective Salyers, try to convince the woman to consider the possibility that Gary had been set up without revealing that she'd seen him. She gazed out into the inky darkness, and nearly swallowed her cigarette when she saw a figure move . . . and approach the patio.

"Hiya," Hannah said, stepping up onto the concrete.

Jolie's shoulders fell and a shiver overtook her. She needed food . . . and her life back.

Even Carlotta looked a little spooked, but recovered quickly. "Oh, hey. You startled me."

Hannah wore skinny black pants and a long flowing jacket that looked a bit vampire-ish. Her hair was slicked back from her slender face and gelled into place. Her makeup was dark and dramatic, and her chandelier-style earrings looked like little swords strung together. Retro Gothica. A fetish, or a lifestyle? Jolie had the sudden sensation that she wouldn't want to encounter Hannah Kizer on a dark street during the witching hour.

Hannah looked at Jolie's ensemble, wig to shoes. "Wow, I wouldn't have recognized you."

"Carlotta helped."

"Yeah, I've told Carlotta if she ever wanted to go underground, she could pull it off."

Carlotta drew on her cigarette. Jolie wondered if she were thinking about the money she'd have to come up with by next Friday.

Hannah looked back and forth between them. "Why are you two so jumpy?"

Jolie sent a warning glance to Carlotta. She didn't want to tell anyone about Gary who didn't need to know.

"This party was a tough nut to crack," Carlotta said, passing her half-smoked cigarette to Hannah, indicating she could finish it. "I'm Betty and she's Linda. If I break into a British accent, just go along."

Hannah shrugged. "Okay."

On the way back inside, Jolie stopped to grind her cigarette into the bowl of white sand and noticed the postcard that Kyle Coffee had used to light his cigar. On impulse, she pulled the stiff, cream-colored card out of the sand and unrolled it, flicking off the charred ends.

A party invitation . . . to Sammy Sanders' house the following evening—the same invitation Jolie had seen her press into Beck Underwood's hand.

You're invited to a champagne pajama party.

Jolie lifted an eyebrow. She'd heard rumors at the agency about the parties that Sammy hosted at her posh Buckhead residence, but of course she'd never been invited. According to the postcard, the attire was sleepwear, the guest list was exclusive, and invitations had to be presented at the door. Apparently Sammy had moved through the crowd tonight, picking and choosing her guests.

Jolie smiled wryly. Even disguised, she wasn't good enough for Sammy.

Tucking the creased invitation inside her purse, she followed Carlotta and Hannah back inside, where no one questioned Hannah's entry. They headed for the food tables as Hannah told them which items to avoid and which items to sample. Jolie filled a small plate with non–red-sauce foods and ate enough to dispel the slight buzz she'd gotten from the wine—she needed to be clear-headed for the drive home.

Beneath the wig, her scalp itched like crazy. The contact lenses felt gritty in her dry eyes. Her feet . . . Well, her feet might never be the same. She longed for a hot soak and a soft pillow and a positive balance in her savings account. She glanced around, expecting to see Roger LeMon lurking in the shadows, watching her. And God help her, she had hoped to catch another glimpse of Beck Underwood. She was sure the man would never work with her now, but she did want to thank him for being discreet, and try to offer some rationalization for her bizarre behavior . . . except she couldn't think of an explanation other than the truth. And she wasn't going to drag Beck into her drama, especially since he had an indirect connection to Roger LeMon through his sister Della.

Jolie pulled herself out of her dismal thought loop and turned toward Hannah and Carlotta.

"The bastard isn't here, is he?" Hannah turned her head for a quick sweep of the room.

"I didn't see him," Carlotta assured her.

"Who?" Jolie asked.

"Her boyfriend Russell," Carlotta said.

"Today I'd had it," Hannah said. "I found out where he

was having lunch and confronted him while he was eating with his boss."

Carlotta gasped. "You didn't."

Hannah nodded emphatically, her knife-earrings jingling. "Sure did. If he thinks he can simply ignore me after all I've put up with, he's insane."

Hearing the bitterness in the woman's voice, Jolie wondered briefly who, exactly, was the sane one. Hannah the Huntress was a tad intense.

"What happened?" Carlotta asked.

Hannah sighed. "He promised he was going to ask his wife for a divorce this weekend."

Jolie choked on a scallop.

Carlotta turned her head and muttered, "He's been promising to leave his wife for a year."

"I heard that," Hannah declared. "Carlotta thinks I'm throwing my life away." She scoffed. "As if her life is going somewhere."

Carlotta cocked her hip. "I'm not the one who spent my lunch hour accosting my married boyfriend."

Hannah leaned in. "When was the last time you *had* a boyfriend?"

"Stalker."

"Prune."

Jolie set down her drink. "*Look* at the time. I guess I'd better be going. I have to go in early tomorrow to help Michael with the Manolo Blahnik appearance."

Carlotta looked disappointed. "Okay. Well, I guess I'll see you tomorrow."

Jolie hesitated, then said, "I was wondering . . . would the two of you like to go to a pajama party tomorrow night? My ex-boss is giving it, so it should be nice, but . . .

we'd have to crash." She had no legitimate reason to go other than it was something fun she could offer up to the girls. Plus she could get one over on Sammy, and the woman wouldn't even know it.

Was that how Carlotta felt when she crashed upscale soirees? That it was enough for *her* to know?

Jolie withdrew the mangled invitation from her purse and handed it to Carlotta, who read it and looked up. "Realtor Barbie is giving a bash?"

Jolie nodded.

"And we're not invited?"

Jolie shook her head.

Carlotta grinned. "Sounds like fun."

"Can you reproduce the invitation?"

"Are you kidding?" Carlotta tapped her finger on the card. "Without raised lettering this won't even be a challenge."

Jolie felt a tiny stab of guilt over planning to crash a private party, but she remembered just a handful of the times that Sammy had dismissed her and the feeling passed rather quickly. "Do you have plans, Hannah?"

Hannah pursed her vampy mouth, then sighed. "No, I'll come."

"Unless her boyfriend calls," Carlotta muttered.

"I heard that."

"I'll see you tomorrow," Jolie said before she could get caught in another round of crossfire.

"Jolie," Carlotta said, "will you be okay walking to your car?"

Hannah gave her a strange look. "Why wouldn't she be?"

"She's worried about my feet in these shoes," Jolie said with a laugh. "Thanks, but I'll be fine. Good night. Oh, and . . . thanks."

Carlotta gave her a secretive nod, then Jolie threaded her way back through the crowd. She kept an eye out for LeMon and other persons of interest, but saw neither. When she walked back through the reception entrance, the ticket taker was still manning his gate and gave her a friendly nod. She waved, once again having misgivings about manipulating their way into the party.

But she did have more information to give Salyers when they talked—Jolie looked at her watch—tomorrow. She'd call the detective tomorrow. After the hoopla at the store, she'd have a few hours before the party. Enough time to put together that mailing to her former customers she'd been putting off. And to discuss a murder investigation concerning her boyfriend.

As she retraced her steps back through the lobby, her thoughts turned to the dead woman in Gary's car. Had she been identified? Did her family know she was missing? Did she even have family? Jolie chewed the tip of a polished nail, wondering if she were to disappear how long it would be before someone missed her. When her rent came due? When the IRS missed her tax return?

She asked for directions to the parking garage and was sent down a hallway and a short flight of stairs to the glass door that she remembered before Carlotta had taken them the roundabout way. She pushed open the door, then walked through another, more industrial door into the parking garage. The cool night air sent shivers through her body. She rubbed her hands over her arms as she waited for the elevator. Halfway up the ramp, a family of four approached their car, their boisterous noisiness a comforting sound in the gloomy concrete structure.

Car doors slammed, then the car with the family backed up and exited the garage. Jolie tapped her foot in the echoing silence, partly to pass time, and partly to send feeling to her toes. The elevator was on its way down, but moving slowly. Fifth floor, fourth. The glass door opened behind her, and a suited man stepped up next to her to wait for the elevator. He looked all around, including at the security camera above them, then stared straight ahead. Tiny red flags raised in her mind. Something wasn't right. His suit was ill fitting, his fingernails were grubby, and—she glanced down—his shoes were scuffed and soiled. Her heart lurched in her chest, stealing her breath. The elevator dinged and the door slid open. He boarded first, then held the door for her.

She stood rooted to the ground.

"Are you comin'?" he asked.

"No," she murmured, then took a step toward the door leading back into the hotel. "I . . . forgot something."

He pursed his mouth, then shrugged. "Suit yourself."

She shot a glance toward the security camera and stayed within its range until the elevator doors closed. According to the lights above the elevator, he rode to the third floor . . . where she had parked. She stood and waited for the man to drive down and exit the garage, but minutes ticked by and no man, no car. Jolie swallowed hard. Was he waiting for her by her car? *In* her car? If he and Gary were both there, the backseat could be crowded.

A foursome came through the glass door and waited for the elevator. She waved them on, and a few minutes later when they drove their car down the ramp and out the exit, the hair stood up on the back of her neck. When she realized the elevator was headed back down, she turned on her heel and jogged back toward the lobby of the hotel, trying to decide between calling the police or hotel security. She stumbled through the door and up the stairs into the lobby, frantically searching for someone who looked official. A guest walked off, freeing one of the women behind the long concierge desk. Jolie headed in that direction, and the panic must have been written on her face, because when the woman looked up, she said, "May I help you?" with a look of concern.

"There's a m–man," she stammered, "in the garage."

"Do you mean the man who's having car trouble?"

"Excuse me?"

"We called an auto service, it should be here shortly."

Jolie touched her temple. "No . . . I mean . . ." She turned and the man from the elevator was striding up behind her.

"I called from the garage," he said. "About the auto service?"

"It's on the way, sir," the woman said. "Third floor, right?"

He nodded. "Thanks."

Jolie watched him walk away and felt like a fool.

"Ma'am, did you need anything else?"

She turned back to the desk. "Um, no. Thanks."

"That's a lovely outfit," the woman said.

"Thanks," she murmured. "Neiman's."

The woman smiled at someone behind Jolie. "Hello, Mr. Underwood."

Jolie winced.

"Hello," he said good-naturedly, then added, "Hi, again . . . *Linda*."

Jolie turned slowly, and looked up into Beck's amused expression. Her cheeks flamed. "Hi. I, um, suppose you're wondering why I'm, um, dressed like this."

"And going by a fake name?"

"And going by a f–fake name," she parroted.

He crossed his arms, still smiling. "I admit I'm slightly curious."

She swallowed and touched her throat. "Well, my girlfriend and I were just having a little fun."

"You crashed," he said with a grin.

She nodded, thinking how childish it sounded, but willing to let him think she was childish rather than . . . childish and paranoid.

He covered his mouth with his hand. "The other night at the High Museum too?"

She nodded and flushed to her knees. "You must think that's terrible."

He uncovered his mouth and was laughing. "No, just . . . interesting I hate these events—I can't imagine crashing one for the fun of it."

Said the prince to the peasant girl. Cheeks burning, she straightened and walked past him. "I was just leaving."

"Wait—did you drive?"

She nodded.

"Valet?"

She shook her head, thinking he probably valeted his car at the mall. "I'm in the parking garage." The cheap seats.

"May I walk you to your car?"

She remembered her earlier experience and swallowed her pride. "Yes."

He seemed surprised, but fell into step next to her. His stride was one and a half times hers, but he paced himself, then held open the door. He had loosened his tie and unbuttoned the top button of his snowy shirt. He was so handsome that she couldn't look at him, and she couldn't *not* look at him, which only made her feel more like a groupie.

"Am I taking you away from your sister?" she asked.

"No, I was just seeing Della off. I'm living at the hotel for now."

"Oh." Her mind spun at the thought of that bill.

"You can see why I need to find a place to live," he said.

She looked up. "You still want to work with me?"

He grinned and pushed open the industrial door leading into the garage. "Are you a good realtor?"

"Yes," she said as she passed under his arm. "Actually, I'm a broker."

"So you work for yourself."

"Yes. I'm hoping to open an office after the first of the year. For now, I'm working out of my apartment. I can give you a client reference list." She stopped at the elevator and pushed the up button.

"No need," he said. "Anyone who is willing to work two jobs must be trustworthy."

In response, she fidgeted with the blunt ends of her wig. The man made her forget things, like how chaotic her life had become. And how numb her feet were.

The elevator doors opened and she walked inside, thinking when he followed how strange that since Monday, their paths had crossed so many times. She could say it was kismet, and Leann would chastise her for being gullible.

"I assumed your family already had a broker that you worked with." She punched the button for the third floor.

"We do," he said simply.

"Oh." So he was going out of his way to give her his business. Hmm.

"Did you have a good time tonight?" he asked.

Strangely, she had—before the run-in with Roger LeMon, of course. She nodded. "Actually, I did, earlier in the evening. It's obviously rote to you, but I thought it was fascinating to see all those important people in one room and to mingle as if I were one of them." She stopped, suddenly embarrassed at what she had revealed about herself—as if Beck Underwood would be interested in her private inadequacies.

A frown flickered across his face. "As far as I'm concerned, you're just as important as anyone in that room."

She tried to joke her way past her lapse. "You probably say that to all the girls."

But he didn't laugh. "No . . . I don't. But then again, I find myself saying things to you that I'd never say to other . . . women. And I'm not quite sure why that is."

He seemed to be studying her, his eyes filled with a curiosity she'd seen before. He was trying to figure her out. Silently she willed him to see what no one else could see—that she was a common woman looking for an uncommon connection, for a sign that life was more than random physical interactions. She waited, her breath coming in little spurts.

His lips parted, and just when he seemed on the verge of saying something, the elevator chimed its arrival at the third floor.

The elevator door opened and she walked toward her car, embarrassed that the Chevy was so . . . unremarkable, and irritated with herself that she cared what he thought. Their footsteps echoed against the concrete, and for some reason she liked the sound of it—their own pattern.

She closed her eyes briefly, reminding herself that there was no "their" anything. A "their" necessitated a "they," and there was no "they."

She walked up to the car and glanced in the backseat before unlocking the door. Empty. She turned back and smiled. "Thank you . . . for everything."

"I only walked you to your car," he said mildly. In the glare of the fluorescent lights, he looked tired. Which meant she must look like something from a crypt. In a wig.

"I mean thanks for . . . earlier," she said. "Covering for me when Sammy was on the verge of recognizing me."

"No problem," he said, hands in the pockets of his dark slacks. "I got the feeling that it was important to you to hide your identity." He wet his lips. "That there was more at stake than simply being able to crash a stodgy old party."

He looked at her as if she were transparent. She couldn't break away from his gaze.

"Are you interested in Roger LeMon?" he asked quietly.

Her throat convulsed. "Not in the way you think." Again, the urge to confide . . . but again, the overriding urge to protect him, and herself. To protect him from association with a terrible crime. To protect herself from making Beck Underwood a confidante.

"In what way, then?"

Her mind raced. "It's . . . business. Did things end badly between Roger LeMon and your sister?"

"I have no idea what she saw in the man, but I believe he broke her heart."

Was LeMon the source of Della Underwood's withdrawal from society years ago?

"What about you?" he asked.

She looked up. "What about me?"

"Did someone break your heart?"

Her lips parted. Gary's disappearance had left her wary, but heartbroken? On the other hand, it was best to let Beck know that her heart wasn't available, largely because of Gary. "There is a man," she said softly.

He gave a little laugh. "There always is. Is he in trouble?"

She nodded.

"Ah. And does this party-crashing have something to do with it?"

She nodded again.

He averted his gaze, then looked back. "So . . . when can you and I get together? To talk about what I'm looking for. In a house, that is."

Despite her best efforts to be immune to him, her tongue felt gluey. "H–how about here, Sunday afternoon?"

"One o'clock?"

"One o'clock is fine," she said, her heart thumping erratically.

He grinned. "How will I know you?"

She grinned. "Look for Jolie Goodman."

His grin faltered for a second. "I will."

Something happened then . . . an exchange of ions between them. She felt the charge of her body drawing energy from his, and the accompanying carnal tug. From his eyes, she knew he felt it too. She was old enough to know that to Beck, a tug was a tug; but in her confused state, a tug was open to wide misinterpretation, and she couldn't risk giving in to the temptation of his attention.

Jolie hastily opened the car door and lowered herself into the seat, closing the door with more force than necessary. Then she started the engine, backed up, and drove away with a wave. Capturing a glimpse of Beck Underwood in her side mirror, she mulled over the written warning. *Objects in mirror are closer than they appear.*

Hmm.

Thirteen

"Jolie, thank God. I thought you'd never get here." Michael Lane's anxiety was evident in his voice and in his hand-ruffled hair. "Customers are already starting to arrive."

Jolie stepped back to keep from being mowed down by a salesclerk who had jogged into the stockroom to grab more Manolo Blahnik shoe boxes. She looked at her watch. "Three hours early?"

"These people are rabid."

Jolie held up the box of Mui Mui shoes. "I had to bring these back."

He frowned and lifted the box lid. "Wrong size?"

She swallowed and tried not to fidget. "Just wrong for my feet."

He glanced at the pristine soles, then shrugged and tucked her receipt in his pocket. "I'll process your refund as soon as I get a minute. Meanwhile, I'll put them back in inventory."

Jolie nodded, relieved and a little remorseful for taking advantage of Michael's trust.

He handed her two silver poles with a fat black velvet rope strung between them. "Chain these on where I left off, then start waiting on customers."

Eager to assuage her guilt, she took the hardware, then emerged from the stockroom. Sure enough, a small crowd of people had already gathered on the edge of the shoe department, where signs had been posted to advertise the appearance. The women were tall and leggy, dressed in black so the eye was drawn to their Manolo Blahnik shoes. Both sides of the checkout counter were three-deep with shoppers holding MB boxes, and the floor was a flurry of activity. Jolie groaned inwardly, thinking this did not bode well for her blistered feet. She looked down to make sure none of the dozen or so adhesive bandages she'd applied this morning to toes and heels had crept over the sides of her sensible pumps, then shuffled forward, dragging the poles with her.

The women in line gave her superior looks—ironic, considering she was putting up gates to confine *them*. She pasted on her best sales smile and thanked them for coming, then limped back to the sales floor and waited on women who at the eleventh hour had succumbed to the temptation to own a pair of the infamous shoes so that they could have them signed by the creator. For two hours she sold shoes as fast as she could tote them from the showroom. She kept her mind off her aching feet by concentrating on the commission she was earning. She had just slid off one of her pumps to massage her heel when Sammy Sanders walked up wearing a tight black dress and a pained smile.

"Jolie, do you work on Saturdays *too*?"

Jolie bit the end of her tongue, then nodded.

"Wow, that doesn't leave you much time to sell real estate, does it?"

Jolie tasted blood.

"And, oh, you poor dear . . . I heard about Gary's car being pulled out of the river—with a woman inside!"

Jolie nodded.

Sammy's eyes were large and shocked. "Do you know who it is?"

Jolie shook her head.

"Do they think Gary is dead, too?"

Jolie pursed her mouth. "Did you need some help, Sammy?"

Sammy sniffed. "I understand—you can't talk about it while you're on the clock." She released a musically sympathetic sigh. "Well, I closed a big, big deal this week, and decided to splurge and buy myself another pair of Manolos, something really special. I figured the least I could do was to let you have the commission."

Jolie's cheeks burned, but Sammy seemed ready to spend a lot of money. Being in no position to turn away business, she suddenly had a bright idea. She smiled and removed the glass case key from the cash register. "I know just the thing—we have only a couple of pairs left, and the size seven is on display."

As Jolie expected, Sammy fell in love with the pink-and-rhinestone shoes that Carlotta had worn to the High Museum party a few nights ago.

"I'll take them," Sammy announced, then looked up. "I saw another pair of shoes while I was here the other day . . . silver-colored pumps with cutouts?"

Jolie's mouth twitched—the shoes she herself had worn

last night. "I believe I know which ones you're talking about. Just a minute." She went to the stockroom and returned with the box she'd given to Michael earlier. "These?"

"Yes, those are lovely."

Jolie removed the cardboard stays that had so distressed her feet, then knelt and eased them onto Sammy's perfectly pedicured puppies. Sammy stood and beamed her satisfaction. "I'll take these, too." She lifted her hands. "Gee, Jolie, you seem to have a real gift for retail sales."

Jolie wanted to kick her, but sucked up the backhanded compliment and repacked the pricey shoes. She was, after all, using Sammy to dispose of the shoes that she and Carlotta had "borrowed." "Thanks . . . Sammy."

When they reached the counter, the woman tossed her hair, then said, "The Singer deal fell through."

Jolie looked up. The deal she'd quit over. "Oh?"

"You didn't know?"

Jolie frowned. "How would I have known?"

Sammy shrugged. "I just wondered if anyone had . . . contacted you, asking questions."

Her mind raced—questions meaning someone had suspected Sammy was playing both sides against the middle? "No," she said evenly, and began ringing up the sale, sending inconspicuous glances in the direction of the woman for whom she used to work. Sammy seemed agitated, touching her face a lot, stroking her hair. Jolie had never before seen Sammy rattled. It was kind of . . . leveling.

Jolie announced the total of the sale—over twenty-four hundred dollars, thankyouverymuch. When Sammy opened her small, green Kate Spade bag, Jolie caught a glimpse of metal and remembered with a jolt that Sammy had a permit to carry a concealed handgun. Jolie conceded that being a female real-estate agent could land a woman in remote locations with strangers, but she'd always wondered if Sammy had ulterior motives for being armed, such as protecting herself from anyone she might have double-crossed.

Sammy withdrew a pink lizard-skin wallet and removed a wad of hundreds. Jolie wasn't completely surprised—it would be just like Sammy to keep some of the agency's business off the books and pocket the cash.

Jolie counted the hundreds carefully, then said, "You gave me five hundred too much," and slid the extra bills back toward Sammy.

"That's for you," Sammy said, her expression completely still.

Jolie blinked. "Excuse me?"

Sammy pushed the money back toward Jolie. "Call it severance."

Astonishment bled through her limbs even as her mind was screaming, *Take it! Take it!* She could buy a copier, stationery, a ticket to Cancun. "I . . . can't take that money, Sammy."

"Sure you can."

A bribe in case someone came around asking questions about Sammy's business practices. Jolie hardened her jaw and pushed the money back with finality. "But I *won't*."

Sammy gave a little laugh and folded the extra cash back into her wallet. "That's always been your problem, Jolie—you can't see that sometimes the right thing to do is the easy thing to do."

Swallowing the words that jumped to her throat, Jolie finished ringing up the sale and passed Sammy her change. She reached for the boxes to bag them, and Carlotta materialized by her side.

"I'll do that," she said, then smiled at Sammy. "Nice shoes."

Sammy tilted her head. "Aren't they?"

"Yes," Carlotta said, handing her the shopping bag. "Thank you for shopping at Neiman Marcus. Enjoy the event."

"I will, thank you." Sammy glared at Jolie. "I hope they catch your boyfriend." Then she whipped around and stalked off.

"Brrr," Carlotta said. She was dressed in a black jacket that was longer than her black miniskirt, dark tights, and a pair of black-satin-and-embroidered stiletto demi-boots with tassels around the top. Vintage Manolo. She offered a gapped grin. "I can't *wait* to crash her party tonight. Did I see her trying to give you *money*?"

Jolie nodded. "Hush money."

"You didn't take it?"

"Nope."

Carlotta emitted a dry laugh. "Well, tell me whatever it is and she can pay *me* hush money."

Jolie bit into her lip, knowing her friend was thinking about the money she owed in a few days' time to the man who'd come to see her at work.

"I see you sold our shoes," Carlotta said, changing the subject. "I take it Michael didn't give you any problems?"

"No," Jolie said. "But I feel terrible."

"It'll pass. Christ, this place is a zoo."

Jolie looked up to see Michael directing the placement of enormous bouquets of white helium balloons. Thumping music played over the speakers at a volume that Jolie had never heard in the store. Nervous energy crackled in the air as the conversation level rose from a hum to a dull roar. Black suits abounded as senior management arrived and store security multiplied. The press had been funneled into an area near the front of the line so cameras could capture the frenzy. Reporters interviewed the women standing in line. She saw Sammy put on her Sanders Realty badge and mug for a camera.

"Where's the jumpsuit?" Carlotta murmured.

"In my locker in the break room."

"Let me have it, and I'll process your return while no one is around."

Carlotta followed her into the stock room, quizzing her.

"No stains, right?"

"Right."

"Did you run it through the dryer on air to get out the cigarette smoke?"

"Yes."

"How are the tags?"

"Perfect."

She unlocked the locker and withdrew the black dress bag. "Thanks, Carlotta. I felt like Cinderella last night."

Carlotta pshawed, but Jolie could tell she was pleased. "You didn't leave anything in the pockets, did you?"

Jolie covered her mouth. "Oh my God—his business card. I can't believe I forgot about the card."

"LeMon's?"

Jolie nodded and unzipped the bag. "It might have fallen out in the dryer—no, here it is." She pulled out the card and turned it over to see if the "private" number he'd written was still legible. It was . . . and so was the note he'd scribbled.

I know what you want.

She inhaled sharply, then showed Carlotta the card. "He must have recognized me."

Carlotta squinted. "Wait . . . He gave you the card just as the Underwoods walked up. If he knew who you were, he hadn't figured it out at that point . . . had he?"

"I don't know." Jolie touched her temple, trying to remember the series of conversations and events.

"Maybe the jerk meant it as a come-on, as in 'I know what you want: me.' "

Jolie's shoulders dropped. "You're probably right," she said, trying to convince herself. "Else, why would he have written his number?"

"Right."

"Right." Jolie tucked the card inside her jacket pocket and zipped the garment bag with a shaking hand.

"Jolie," Carlotta said, her voice tinged with concern. "Have you told the police about LeMon?"

"I'm going to call the detective on the case this afternoon." She checked her cell phone—Salyers had called again.

"Jolie!" Michael yelled into the stockroom. "A totem-beaded mule in size six, and a Carmine ankle-tie pump in size nine! Hurry!"

Carlotta hooked her fingers into the hanger and slung the garment bag over her shoulder. "I'll catch up with you later."

Jolie nodded, then scrambled to get the shoes that Michael needed, trying to put Roger LeMon out of her head. When she emerged with the shoes, she was confronted with a crowd that had grown exponentially—the sales floor was a solid mass of bodies, and the line to meet Manolo Blahnik snaked out of the department and through the belly of the store. Jolie handed the requested shoes to Michael, then glanced around to see what she could do to help in the confusion. A bearded face in the crowd caught her attention. Gary?

Her pulse spiked as she stepped to the side to get a better look. But the crowd shifted too, and the face was lost in a sea of shuffling bodies. A droning noise sounded, like a swarm of killer bees, as a murmur moved through the crowd. The mob of shoppers turned collectively to see Manolo Blahnik stride in, flanked by security and his "people." A cheer went up and the older gentleman raised his hand and smiled in greeting. He was a striking figure dressed in a dark suit, his thinning white hair combed back, his jet-black eyebrows setting off inquisitive eyes.

Jolie's first thought was that he looked like a banker. But when the crowd pressed forward and his security inched closer, her next thought was that anything could happen in a crowd like this—shoplifting, pick-pocketing . . . or worse. She scanned the crowd frantically, looking for the face she thought was Gary's. Manolo Blahnik began to speak to the press, and someone jostled her from behind as everyone surged forward for a better spot. She jerked around, jittery now and a little claustrophobic. The air conditioner hadn't caught up with the crush of bodies, and her underarms and neck were moist. She fanned the neckline of her blouse and decided to move toward the front to get more air.

With whispered apologies, she elbowed and sidled through bodies until she was standing a few feet behind the shoe designer. Lights glared on him and cameras rolled, reminding her of last night when Beck Underwood had been interviewed at the reception. She'd sat up like a groupie to catch the fifteen-second spot on the local news.

"Beckham Underwood, son of Lawrence Underwood and heir to the Underwood Broadcasting empire, was on hand to honor the award nominees of the Broadcasters and Journalists of Georgia. Mr. Underwood, who has been living in Costa Rica for the last few years, says he's glad to be home, but is cagey about whether or not he'll stay to take over his father's company."

"I love Atlanta," Beck had said. "But I enjoyed the work I did in Costa Rica, helping to build the infrastructure to support a broadcasting venture there. I haven't ruled out going back. It's important that we support communications growth in developing countries."

He had looked so handsome, she was sure hearts were breaking all over Atlanta at the news that he might not stick around for long.

Not my heart, of course, she thought while easing around the perimeter of the crowd. Her heart was perfectly intact and beating wildly at the thought of Gary being close by. Was he watching her, worried about her? Did he have a message for her?

Or was her mind playing tricks on her?

She kept her eyes peeled, but when Manolo launched into the history of his involvement with shoes, her pulse had begun to settle down. And then she saw Roger LeMon.

His head was turned and he wore sunglasses, but she recognized his profile. He was about ten yards away. The reporters and the guest of honor stood between her and him.

The breath froze in her lungs. It couldn't be a coincidence that she thought she'd seen Gary, and now LeMon was standing right in front of her. Before Jolie could decide what to do, LeMon turned his head and appeared to look directly at her. In fact, he took a half step forward before he seemed to remember where he was and stopped.

At that moment, the speech ended. Applause sounded and chaos reigned as Manolo Blahnik headed toward the line of shoppers waiting to meet him. In the confusion, Jolie lost sight of LeMon, and hoped he'd lost sight of her. Panic rose up in her stomach. Had Gary followed LeMon, or had LeMon followed Gary? She made a beeline for cosmetics and was almost in the clear when a shot rang out, then another, then three more in rapid succession. Startled screams sounded and Jolie dove under a hosiery display, covering her head and waiting for something to bleed.

She peeked through her fingers and saw people gathered around, gaping at her. It must be bad, she thought, because she couldn't feel any pain.

Suddenly Michael's face appeared above hers. "Jolie," he hissed. "You're causing a scene."

She patted various parts of her body. "But the gunshots . . ."

"They weren't *gunshots*, for God's sake—a few balloons broke free and hit the lights. Come out from under there."

She closed her eyes briefly and considered telling Michael to roll her out of the way. Instead she allowed him to help her to her feet, and gave a tentative smile to those standing around. Their guest of honor had paused, but Michael signaled that he should resume, then put his hand on Jolie's elbow and shepherded her toward the stockroom.

"What was that all about?" he asked when they were out of earshot.

Jolie glanced behind her, looking for Gary or Roger LeMon, but saw neither. She looked back and lifted her hands. "I . . . I've been jumpy . . . lately."

"Does this have anything to do with your boyfriend?"

"Indirectly," she murmured. "I'm sorry."

He sighed. "Why don't you call it a day? I'll see you Monday."

She nodded and went to gather her things from her locker. Michael must think she was a lunatic. Which wouldn't be surprising, considering she was starting to have her own doubts about her sanity.

"Hey."

She looked up and saw Carlotta standing at the door of the break room. "Hey."

"I heard."

Jolie inhaled and touched her forehead. "I thought I saw Gary, and I'm sure I saw Roger LeMon, and when the balloons burst—"

"You saw your boyfriend? Are you sure?"

"Not positively. But I did see Roger LeMon, and why would he be here?"

Carlotta shrugged. "He's married, isn't he? Maybe he's here with his wife." She bit into her lip. "Look . . . Jolie. I don't like Roger LeMon any more than you do, but . . ."

"But you think I'm being paranoid?"

The woman touched Jolie's arm. "You're in a bad place," she said softly. "Your boyfriend is missing, a woman is dead—no one would want to believe that someone they care about is capable of that kind of thing. You're starting a new job . . . Maybe the stress is just too much for you. Even if the two men knew each other, that doesn't mean that Roger LeMon had anything to do with what happened to your boyfriend . . . does it?"

Jolie looked into Carlotta's clear eyes and wondered how far out a limb her own imagination had taken her. She had thought the man with the car trouble was stalking her, and just a few minutes ago she had thought she was being shot at. The only true threat was Gary. He was the one who'd stolen her car, who had lain in wait to threaten her. She needed to talk to Salyers, to tell her everything.

Jolie exhaled. "You're right . . . You're right."

Carlotta looked relieved. "Now go home and get some rest." She grinned. "You're going to need it for the party tonight."

Jolie shook her head. "I don't think I should go."

"Of course you should go. It won't be fun for me and Hannah to crash without you. Besides, I'm going shopping for us later in sleepwear."

Jolie's eyes widened. "Carlotta, I don't want to do that again. I feel like it's stealing."

Carlotta dismissed her concerns with a wave. "How often do you get a chance to wear fabulous loungewear?" She grinned. "Come on, let's have some fun tonight—at your ex-boss's expense."

It *would* be nice to get one up on Sammy for once. Jolie mulled over that thought. And she was dying to see the woman's home. "Do you have another wig?"

Carlotta nodded emphatically. "Tell me where you live. Hannah and I will come to your place to get ready."

Jolie gave in to a smile and supplied Carlotta with the address and directions, then said goodbye and left by the back hallway that emptied into the men's department. She skirted behind the crowd, feeling a little better. She would let the police take care of everything where Gary was concerned, so she could concentrate on getting her brokerage company off the ground. Finding Beck Underwood a place to live would give her a tidy nest egg to draw from.

The fact that he might live there only temporarily was his business.

She left the store and walked to her rental car feeling closer to normal than she had in ages. She used her cell phone to call Detective Salyers.

The woman answered on the first ring. "Salyers here."

"Detective Salyers, this is Jolie Goodman."

"Goodman . . . You're the girlfriend in the Hagan case."

"Yes."

"Nice of you to return my call, Ms. Goodman. Finally."

Jolie ignored her sarcasm. "Do you have some information about Gary?"

"Maybe. We traced the hang-up call to your apartment on Monday to a pay phone three blocks away from your apartment complex. Have you had any more hang-ups?"

Jolie's pulse kicked higher and she spoke carefully. "No."

"Has Mr. Hagan called you?"

"No," she said, grateful she could answer truthfully. Crawling into the backseat of her car wasn't calling. "Has the woman in the car been identified?"

"No. We're still waiting on the medical examiner's report."

At the abrupt answers, Jolie swallowed. "Is there something else?"

Papers rattled in the background. "Ms. Goodman, do you know a Mr. Roger LeMon?"

Her heart jumped in her chest. "Yes. How do you know about him?"

"He came by this morning, said you've been harassing him."

Her eyes bugged. "*What*?"

"According to Mr. LeMon, you've been following him, asking him questions about Gary Hagan, whom he denies knowing."

Jolie clenched the phone tighter. "He's lying."

"You haven't been following him?"

"I . . . I mean he's lying about knowing Gary. He's one of the men in Gary's photos."

"Is he?" Salyers asked mildly. "You said you didn't know any of Mr. Hagan's friends."

"I d–don't."

"Then how did you find Mr. LeMon?"

"I went to a party in midtown Wednesday night and recognized him. I asked him if he knew Gary and he said he didn't."

"What made you think he was lying?"

"His body language. And when he excused himself, I . . ."

"Yes?"

Jolie sighed. "I followed him."

"Oh, you want my job, do you?"

Jolie frowned at her sarcasm. "I followed him because he said he was going to get a drink, but he walked right past the bar. When I found him, he was talking on a pay phone and I heard him tell the person my name, and that I'd recognized him."

She assumed the silence meant that the detective had perked up. "Do you know who he was talking to?"

"No."

"Did he see you?"

"I don't know. I left immediately, but he might have seen me."

"Hmm. Is that the only incident?"

Jolie squirmed. "I saw LeMon last night, and he was talking to another guy from the photos. Kyle Coffee."

"Where was this?"

"At another party."

"Another party, huh? You're really torn up over your boyfriend's disappearance, aren't you, Ms. Goodman?"

Jolie's stomach clenched.

"In fact, one might think that you aren't worried because you know he's alive."

Her inclination to tell the detective about Gary's late-night appearance in her car or her possible sighting of him in the store vanished. No way the woman would believe she hadn't helped him.

"I saw Roger LeMon again today," Jolie said, diverting the conversation. "He came to Neiman's."

"Did he approach you? Threaten you?"

"No," she admitted.

"What exactly did he do?"

Jolie bit into her lip. "He didn't do anything, I guess. He was just . . . there."

"Did you tell him where you worked?"

"No."

"I don't understand—was he shopping?"

"No. There was an event taking place in the store, a big crowd."

"So he was just standing in the crowd at a public event?"

Coming from someone else, it sounded harmless. "Yes, but . . ." But what?

The detective sighed. "Ms. Goodman, do you think maybe you're overreacting? Isn't it possible that Mr. LeMon, a wealthy man who probably shops in upscale stores, just happened into Neiman's to buy something?"

"Yes," Jolie admitted.

"Ms. Goodman, let me a give you some friendly advice. I don't know Roger LeMon, but I'm told that he's a wealthy man with a long reach." She lowered her voice. "He even donated money to buy bulletproof vests for the police department—do you get my drift?"

The woman's "drift" was unmistakable. "Yes," Jolie murmured, trying hard not to feel like a fool. "Was there anything else you wanted to tell me, Detective?"

"No, except to stay away from Roger LeMon before he slaps a restraining order on you."

Jolie disconnected the call with shaking fingers and acknowledged an instant headache. She touched her temples, trying to slow her thinking, to make some sense of things.

If Roger LeMon was up to no good, surely he wouldn't go to the police. She'd been hoping to talk to Salyers about the possibility that Gary had been framed, but the woman wasn't going to listen to a shoe clerk who stalked a pillar of the community.

She sighed, wishing for divine inspiration. Maybe she should just forget about Gary, forget about her car, and forget about the dead woman, whoever she was. Cut her losses and walk away. Before things got . . . worse.

The idea of going out with the girls tonight and crashing Sammy's party was starting to sound more appealing. What was it that Carlotta had said? That Jolie needed to add the word "fun" to her vocabulary.

"*Fuunnnnn,*" Jolie said aloud, testing the word on her tongue. Then she tested a smile, suddenly anticipating the well-heeled pajama party.

At least she could wear house shoes.

Fourteen

"Are you sure it was Gary you saw in the crowd?" Leann asked.

Jolie sighed into the phone receiver and dropped into her favorite chair. "I thought so at the time, but now . . . I just don't know."

"Did he look as if he was trying to make contact with you?"

"I only got a glimpse of him, but he seemed to be looking at me."

"And who is this other guy you said was there?"

"Roger LeMon? Well, long story short, I recognized him from a picture in a photo album of Gary's."

"What? How did you get Gary's photo albums?" From Leann's tone it was clear she didn't approve of the kind of intimacy that having his personal items implied.

"The apartment manager gave me a box of things he salvaged from Gary's apartment after the fire. The album didn't have much in it, some childhood pictures, group photos from parties." She decided not to mention the *X*'d-out picture of herself.

"And this guy LeMon was in some of the photos?"

"Yeah." She told Leann about recognizing LeMon and following him to the pay phone, and the snippet of conversation she'd overheard.

"Maybe Gary is mixed up in something dangerous," Leann said, her voice solemn. "Drugs, maybe."

"That what's the detective insinuated. In fact . . ." She winced. "Gary has a record for selling cocaine."

"*What*? You're kidding, right?"

"No."

"And he never told you?"

"No, but then again, I never asked," she said dryly.

"What a slimeball," Leann seethed. "I can't believe he would deceive you like that, and now . . . *this*."

Jolie could tell she was pacing, and she was touched by her friend's concern. "Please don't worry about me—you have enough on your hands with your sister."

Leann sighed. "Jolie, I just wish you had taken my advice and stayed away from Gary Hagan. I told you he was trouble."

"You were right." Jolie laid her head back and stared at the water stain on her ceiling. "Why could you see that and I couldn't?"

Leann sighed. "Just a matter of experience, I guess. Gary seemed . . . too good to be true."

The water stain looked like a misshapen heart. "I'm gullible."

"You just haven't dated enough jerks to make you cynical."

She frowned wryly—linking up with a possible murderer had made her a quick study.

"Jolie, do you think Gary is still following you?"

"Yes," Jolie admitted. "I thought I saw my car drive by last night as I went into the hotel for the reception. I think he'll contact me again. For some reason, I think he feels that he can trust me. I can't decide if that's a good thing, or a bad thing."

"What will you do if he does contact you again?"

"Try to get him to go to the police."

"And if he won't?"

"I'll call them myself," Jolie said. "Stall him until the police get there . . . something." She pushed to her feet and walked to the desk to re-sort the mail, keeping an eye out for the alleged envelope Gary said he'd sent, but the only thing unusual was Mrs. Janklo's *AARP* magazine that the mail carrier had put in Jolie's box by mistake. "I just want this to be over."

"Me too," Leann said.

Jolie tried to smile. "I'm trying to forget about Gary, at least for one night. I wish you could drive up and crash the party with us." She glanced at her watch. "If you left now, you could make it."

"Yeah, right. Besides, you don't need me there, not with your new friends."

Jolie wasn't sure if the envious tone made her feel needed or crowded. She'd never before had multiple female friendships to maintain. She missed Leann, but she was grateful for Carlotta's companionship, especially since Leann would be in Florida for a few more months. Torn, she said, "Hopefully, by the time you get back to Atlanta, this mess will have blown over and *all* of us can be friends."

"Okay," Leann said, but she still sounded forlorn. "Hey, aren't you afraid that Sammy will throw you out of her party?"

"Carlotta is a master of disguise. Sammy won't recognize me." Jolie frowned suddenly, thinking she was getting way too blasé about deceiving others. This would be the last party she would crash, she promised herself.

"Is it a costume party?"

"No, actually, it's a pajama party. I think it's Sammy's version of a costume party."

"Sounds decadent."

Why the word "decadent" conjured up the face of Beck Underwood, Jolie wasn't sure, but she pushed him out of her mind. When she met with him tomorrow to try to sell him an expensive house, she would be all business. If the man had decided that she was his cause for the week, she would take it, but she wasn't going to risk more than her time. If there was such a thing as too good to be true, it was Beck Underwood. If nothing else, Gary had taught her a lesson about keeping her heart under wraps until her head caught up with it.

"With Sammy, I don't know what to expect," Jolie said. "I forgot to mention that she came by today, too. Tried to give me a bribe."

"For what?"

"I think she's in trouble for a deal that went bad and she's afraid I'll be questioned."

"Did you take the money?"

"Of course not!"

"You should have taken the cash and told the truth anyway. What's she going to do—fire you?"

"I don't want to have anything to do with the woman's money . . . unless I have to go back and beg for a job. And after the spectacle I made of myself today, I might get fired from Neiman's."

"So how is your brokerage business?"

She flipped on her computer so it could boot up while they talked. "Anonymous. But I'm sending out a mailing today to some of my former customers. And I'm meeting with a guy tomorrow who's looking for a house."

"That sounds promising."

"Uh-hm," she murmured casually.

"Anyone I would know?"

Because of her interior design connections, Leann knew almost everyone. "Er, possibly. Beck Underwood?"

"Of Underwood Broadcasting?"

"Yup."

"Oh, my God. How on earth did you meet him?"

"Remember I told you about running into a guy when I was carrying that armload of shoes my first day on the job?"

"Yeah . . . it was *him*?"

"It was him."

"Wow, what a coup. I can't imagine what kind of a house he's going to buy."

"Well, I don't have his business yet." She'd seen plenty of customers—especially wealthy ones—drop agents at the last minute to give their business to a buddy or to a buddy's wife, son, daughter, hairdresser.

"Oh, Jolie, I hate to go, but I have to get ready for a doctor's appointment."

"Sure," Jolie said. "Thanks for listening. Tell your sister that I hope everything is okay."

"I will. Good luck with Beck Underwood, and have fun tonight."

"Bye." Jolie hung up the phone reluctantly, conceding that she dreaded spending the afternoon alone. She leaned against the desk and surveyed her surroundings with an eye toward what Carlotta and Hannah would think when they arrived. The living room-slash-office, galley kitchen, breakfast area, all visible from where she stood. A sad collection of odd-lot furniture she had accumulated situated on gray builder-grade carpet. The layer of dust on every flat surface seemed to sum up her general mindset over the past few weeks—since Gary's . . . departure. Well, enough of that.

She unearthed the feather duster and gave everything a good going over. In the bedroom, though, she paused at the sight of finger marks in the dust on the top of the bookcase that was built into the headboard. She swiped her own fingers in a dusty patch, and the marks were much smaller. Her neck prickled with unease. Had someone been in her apartment, in her bedroom, or had she somehow made the marks herself when she'd reshelved the books strewn around the apartment? She experimented again, this time putting her weight on her hand, and, to her relief, the impressions were more similar. She wiped away the marks, telling herself that she truly was becoming paranoid.

After dusting and running her ancient vacuum cleaner, she looked around the small apartment where she'd lived for four years and tried not to feel depressed. Having worked in real estate for most of her adult life, she knew that the sooner she invested in a home, the better. Yet some small part of her resisted the idea of buying a home to live in alone. She had always envisioned that she and her husband would shop for a first home together. Between school loans and living expenses, she had managed to squirrel away a few thousand dollars, but when she'd opted to invest in her own brokerage firm, she had postponed owning a home for a while longer.

Now she wondered if that had been some kind of unconscious decision to wait for Gary—or someone else—before buying a home.

She shivered. The outside temperature had plummeted to an unseasonable low, and the apartment had acquired a distinct chill. Rebelling against turning on the heat in the middle of October, she donned jeans and a sweatshirt to work at her desk. To the tune of a smooth jazz station, she assembled a postcard mailing to a list of former clients, giving her new e-mail address and cell phone number if they had referrals. Sammy would probably shoot her if she caught her poaching clients, but Jolie reasoned that she had developed a relationship with the clients and had a right to ask for their future business. She welcomed the mindlessness of labeling and stamping the postcards. It was, she realized, the most normal thing she'd done in days and took her mind off the disturbing tangents her life had taken lately.

She was actually humming under her breath as she bundled the postcards into a bag and left to drive to the post office. A surprisingly cool wind gusted around her, tossing her hair into her eyes. Two young girls skipped along the sidewalk, holding hands, pigtails bouncing. Their pink cheeks and exuberant feet made Jolie smile. Had she ever been so carefree? At what point in life had she begun to accumulate baggage, to make poor decisions that had led her to this moment?

She dropped off the postcards, purchased more stamps, and on the way back to her apartment, pulled into a drive-through to pick up dinner. While she waited for her order, she leaned forward and peered through the windshield, squinting into the sun. The day was so luminous, it was difficult to imagine that anything was wrong with the world, much less the horrible mess that Gary had gotten himself into. When her order came through the window, she snagged a French fry from the bag and glanced in the side mirror in preparation for pulling away.

A gray Mercury Sable sedan sat behind her. With one occupant. A man whose build resembled Gary's. Was he following her?

She choked down the fry and looked harder, but the man wore a ball cap pulled low over his face. Coincidence or intentional? She kept her foot on the brake and reached for her cell phone. After retrieving Detective Salyers' number, she waited for the call to connect while her pulse climbed. Another car had pulled in behind the Sable, so as long as she stayed put, he would be trapped by a curb and some rugged landscaping. The young man in the drive-through window frowned at her.

At last the woman answered. "Salyers."

"Detective Salyers, this is Jolie Goodman. I think Gary Hagan is in the car behind me."

"What makes you think so?"

"It looks like my car, and a man is driving it."

"Are you sure it's Mr. Hagan?"

"No, I'm not positive."

"Is there some way you can get behind the car to check the license plate?"

"No. I'm sitting at a Wendy's drive-through."

"Where?"

"Holcomb Bridge Road."

"What's the cross street?"

She glanced around frantically, trying to remember. "East of Old Alabama Road."

"I'll dispatch a cruiser there. Can you sit tight?"

A horn blared a couple of cars back. "I'll try."

"Stay on the line."

More horns blared. She shut off the car engine, put on the hazard lights and locked her doors, all the while keeping the phone to her ear and her eye on her driver's side mirror.

The young man at the window waved to get her attention. She rolled down the window and said, "I'm so sorry—my engine light flashed, then it went dead."

From the look on the young man's face, it was clear the training manual hadn't prepared him for this. "I need to get the manager." Then he disappeared.

The horns kept blowing, although the man in the car behind her seemed calm enough.

"Ms. Goodman, are you still there?"

"Yes," she said into the phone. "But I have a bunch of angry, hungry people behind me."

"An officer is on the way, ETA less than five minutes."

Which sounded like an eternity to Jolie. Sweat gathered on her hairline and she felt nauseated.

"Can you still see him?" Salyers asked.

"Yes."

"What is he doing?"

"Just sitting there."

No sooner had she spoken than the door of the Sable swung open as far as the narrow driveway would allow. A jean-clad leg emerged.

"He's getting out," she said.

"Don't risk it," Salyers said. "Drive away."

She dropped the phone and fumbled to turn the ignition key. As the engine roared to life, she gunned the gas and vaulted out of the drive-through, tires squealing. When she looked in the rear view mirror, the man took off his hat to scratch his bald head. Definitely not Gary.

Relief flooded her limbs and she pulled into the next shopping center to retrieve her phone. "Detective?"

"I'm still here—what happened?"

"It wasn't him. Sorry."

"No problem," the detective said. "Hang on—let me cancel the call."

Jolie alternately berated and calmed herself until Salyers came back on the line.

"Ms. Goodman, are you okay?"

"Yes. I apologize for the false alarm."

"Don't worry about it. Gary Hagan is a fugitive. Even if you *think* you see him, I want you to call me, is that clear?"

"Yes."

"Because we both know he's still alive, don't we, Ms. Goodman?"

Jolie caught herself, then murmured, "Like you, I'm assuming that Gary stole my car."

"Ms. Goodman, when we spoke before, you neglected to mention the condo that Mr. Hagan owned."

Jolie frowned. "Condo? Here in Atlanta?"

"In midtown, on West Peachtree—ring a bell?"

"No. I don't know anything about it."

"Hm, that's interesting, since you're listed as the buying agent."

Jolie's mind raced. "That's . . . impossible. It had to be someone else named Goodman. I never handled a property for Gary."

Salyers sighed. "It won't do you any good to cover up business dealings that you had with Mr. Hagan."

"I'm not," Jolie said hotly. "Why would I lie about something like that?"

"Because when we raided the condo this morning, it showed signs of someone having been there recently. Plus, the freezer was full of coke—and not the cola kind."

Jolie's stomach roiled. "I . . . don't know . . . anything . . . about . . . anything."

"Of course you don't," Salyers said, and Jolie couldn't tell if the woman was serious, or if she was mocking her. "Will you agree to come down to the precinct to be fingerprinted?"

Her skin crawled just thinking about it. "What for?"

"Well, if you don't know anything about the condo, your prints won't be there, will they?"

Jolie swallowed. "No. I mean, yes—I'll be f—fingerprinted. I don't have anything to hide."

"In that case, you wouldn't mind submitting to a polygraph as well?"

Her breath caught in her chest. "A lie detector test?"

"Right."

Could she unwittingly incriminate herself? "I . . . this is a little overwhelming."

"It's nothing to worry about, unless of course you're keeping something from me."

Jolie closed her eyes, her heart hammering.

"There's my other line. I tell you what, Ms. Goodman— why don't you come by the precinct Monday morning at ten o'clock? We'll have another cup of coffee and discuss the new developments in the case, and I can take your prints, just for everyone's peace of mind."

She hesitated, already dreading the meeting. "What about the polygraph?"

"That will have to be scheduled—we'll talk more about it Monday."

"Okay."

"Meanwhile, Ms. Goodman, try to stay out of trouble."

Jolie disconnected the call and puffed her cheeks out in a sigh, thinking at least she would be safe crashing Sammy's pajama party tonight. The most trouble she and the girls were likely to encounter was unbridled pretentiousness in Realtor Barbie's funhouse.

Fifteen

"This is cozy," Carlotta said as she and Hannah walked into Jolie's apartment. The women's hands were full of shopping bags. "How long have you lived here?"

Jolie smiled. "Too long."

Hannah studied her shabby collection of furnishings as if Jolie were an oddity to the stripe-haired woman. She picked up a coaster that Jolie's mother had crocheted from orange yarn and scrutinized it. As a distraction, Jolie offered them something to drink, and Hannah helped herself in the refrigerator, emerging with a bottle of water each for Carlotta and Jolie, and a bottle of beer for herself.

With a start, Jolie stared at the bottle that Hannah lifted to her mouth. It was the premium label that Gary preferred. Hannah stopped. "Is it all right if I drink this?"

"Of course," Jolie said, recovering. She had bought a few to keep on hand and he hadn't had the chance to drink one before he . . . disappeared. She remembered thinking

•

later that she had cursed the blossoming relationship with that casual act of intimacy—stocking his favorite beer.

"Wait until you see what I brought," Carlotta said with a grin, lifting a shopping bag. "We're going to knock 'em dead." From a bag she withdrew a burgundy-colored velvet robe with bishop sleeves. "I thought this would be perfect for you, Jolie."

Jolie petted the thick pile and began to salivate. "I hope you shopped the clearance rack."

Carlotta looked perplexed. "Why would I shop the clearance rack if we're going to be returning everything?"

"Will they let you return nightclothes?" Hannah asked, peeking into the bags.

"Robes they'll take back," Carlotta said. "And pajamas if they haven't been worn." She made a face. "Doris in Intimates actually sniffs things. It's disgusting."

"Uh, actually, I think it's a health code," Hannah said, pulling out a black high-necked satiny robe. "This is wicked."

"That one's yours," Carlotta said, then pulled out a teal-colored raw silk robe with a ruffled shawl collar. "This one's mine." She dug in a different bag and removed handfuls of colorful silk. "Pajamas for all of us: a cream chemise for Jolie, pink tap pants for me, a red gown for Hannah."

Jolie balked at the sight of the knee-length chemise. "Er, I was thinking more along the lines of cotton pajamas."

Carlotta looked horrified. "What? No!" She handed Jolie the chemise as if she were dressing a child who didn't know better.

Jolie rubbed the pale, thin fabric between her fingers with awe. "What if I ruin it?"

"You're not going to ruin it." Carlotta whipped out packages of what looked like shoulder pads. "Dress shields, so we don't sweat on the silk. And be careful what you eat and drink."

Jolie turned over the dangling price tag on the chemise and gasped. "Eight hundred dollars? You can't be serious."

"Your robe is twelve hundred."

Jolie looked at that tag, then dropped it as if it were dangerous. "You don't expect me to wear two thousand dollars' worth of pajamas to this party?"

"Of course not," Carlotta said, then reached into another bag, withdrew a shoebox, and flung off the lid. "Don't forget the two hundred dollar mules!"

Jolie gawked at the delicate burgundy shoes trimmed with feathers. "Two hundred dollars for house shoes?"

"*Designer* house shoes. The kind that Garbo and Hepburn used to wear." She sighed and angled her head. "It's one night—you'll look so fabulous."

Jolie chewed on her lower lip. "I promised myself I wasn't going to do this again."

Carlotta rolled her eyes. "Okay, just this last time. Think of how much *fun* it will be to pull one over on your ex-boss." She raised her eyebrows. "Who knows? Beck Underwood might even put in an appearance."

A ridiculous flush burned her face. "This sounds petty, but I really just want to see the inside of Sammy's house. When I worked at the agency, she talked about it nonstop. I actually drove by it once, but this could be my only chance to cross the threshold."

"All the more reason for you to look like a million bucks," Carlotta urged, then leaned in. "I brought you a long red wig. We'll do your eyebrows, and with the contact lenses, she'll never know who you are."

"Are you wearing a wig too?" Jolie asked.

She nodded. "I'm going as Marilyn tonight, and Hannah is going to wear the brown page-boy that you wore a few nights ago." Carlotta looked at her watch, then shrieked. "We only have two hours. Where's your bathroom?"

Jolie felt more than a little absurd leaving her apartment wearing a nightgown, robe, and feathered mules, but thankfully, the dipping temperatures necessitated a coat, so her long, navy all-weather coat covered most of her garb. Her new auburn tresses were stiff against her neck, the green contacts, swimmy in her eyes. Thank goodness it was close enough to Halloween so that anyone who spied them might realize they were headed to a costume party. Still, she already regretted not wearing a bra—the slippery silk slid over her breasts like a constant caress, with predictable results.

"Where did this cold weather come from?" Carlotta demanded, belting her own long coat—except hers was black cashmere, and stunning against her blonde wig.

"It's called winter," Hannah snapped. With her blunt page-boy wig, severe makeup and long black leather duster, she looked every inch the dominatrix.

Carlotta frowned. "If you're going to be in a bad mood all evening, don't come."

"Sorry," Hannah mumbled. "I expected Russell to call before now."

Carlotta sniffed and looked like she wanted to say something, but didn't. Jolie remembered that Hannah's married boyfriend was supposed to tell his wife that he wanted a divorce sometime this weekend. It appeared he was leaning toward the "end" of the weekend.

She locked the apartment door behind them and, out of habit now, looked left and right as they made their way down the sidewalk to the parking lot by lamplight. "Do you want to ride with me?" she asked. "Or are we driving separately?"

"I'm driving," Carlotta said, stopping next to a mirror-shiny dark Monte Carlo SuperSport parked in the handicap spot. "Like my new car?"

Remembering the woman's imminent rendezvous with the man who'd demanded two thousand dollars, Jolie's eyebrows went up. "What happened to the Miata?"

"I thought it was time to get a new ride."

Jolie opened the back door of the spanking-new sedan and inhaled the new-car smell. "Nice."

They were settled inside and fastening seat belts when Hannah, who sat in the front passenger seat, looked over at Carlotta. "Aren't you going to tell Jolie the truth?"

Carlotta started the engine. "She won't approve."

Jolie frowned and leaned forward as far as her seatbelt would allow. "What do you mean, I won't approve?"

Carlotta twisted in her seat and backed out of the parking place, then pulled toward the entrance of the apartment complex. "Well . . . some dealers are allowing customers to keep a vehicle for twenty-four hours before they actually buy the car, so . . . I'm trying it out." She grinned.

Jolie gave her a wry look. "You have no intention of buying this car, do you?"

"None whatsoever."

She couldn't be too self-righteous, Jolie reminded herself, not while she wore over two thousand dollars' worth of jammies that she planned to return. She sat back in her seat, marveling over the way Carlotta connived to get what she wanted. On the surface, it didn't seem right . . . yet she wasn't doing anything illegal. Besides, was it really so different from bending the rules on tax returns?

A small part of her admired Carlotta's cheekiness. The woman's obituary was bound to be more interesting than her own.

From the backseat, Jolie gave directions to a north Buckhead neighborhood where the streets were narrow and the homes were enormous. Old money had built the McMansions, and new money had upgraded them. Sammy Sanders' house was an expansive two-story white home with yellow light blazing from the multitude of windows. The structure sported a dozen different roof angles, various verandas and offshoots of smaller buildings (the servants' quarters?) connected by breezeways, testimony to at least a half dozen additions.

"It's a freaking compound," Hannah murmured.

Jolie nodded her agreement. She remembered it being impressive in the daylight, but at night it was downright imposing. With its circular drive lit by dozens of lights, it resembled a country club more than a residence. "Looks like things are in full swing."

"One of the party-crashing rules," Carlotta said. "Never be the first person to arrive . . ."

"Or the last person to leave," Hannah said.

"She has a valet," Carlotta said, her voice ringing with approval. She pulled up behind two other cars from which coated people were alighting. Jolie felt a tiny surge of relief that she wasn't the only person who felt compelled to cover her sleepwear in public, but she was starting to get nervous about crashing a private party . . . especially Sammy's party. She shifted, hoping the dress shields were protecting the expensive silk chemise from her nervousness.

A coated and gloved man was leaning down to address the drivers, then taking their invitations. The people two cars ahead appeared to have everything in order and were assisted from their car. The occupants of the Jaguar in front of them, however, after much head-shaking and shrugged apologies from the ticket-taker, were sent away. Jolie swallowed. "How did the invitations turn out?"

"My brother had to tinker with it some," Carlotta admitted. "The first pass looked better than Sammy's original, so he had to downgrade the print resolution."

Jolie bit back a smile as they pulled up and Carlotta zoomed down her window. "Hello," she said in a perfect imitation of the Buckhead bourgeois.

"Good evening, ma'am," the man said. "Invitations, please—one for each guest."

"Of course," she cooed, handing over the cards.

The man glanced at them, then nodded and smiled. "Leave your key in the ignition and the valet will park your car." He opened Carlotta's door, then tore off a ticket and handed it to her when she stepped out.

The man stepped back and opened Jolie's door. She gave him her hand and stepped out into the night air, which fell around her like a cold sheet, raising chill bumps . . . and concern. Suddenly spooked, she turned to look at the car behind them, half expecting to see Gary following her. But the driver was female . . . and wearing a fur coat, she noted wryly.

Because the winters in Atlanta were so short-lived, women who could afford fur broke them out at the first frost, without fear of the paint-throwing PETA people who targeted soirees in New York and Los Angeles. Jolie suspected the animal rights activists subscribed to the belief that everyone south of the Mason-Dixon Line was armed and that their red paint parties might get them shot down here.

Which probably wasn't too far off the mark, she thought, remembering the handgun tucked into Sammy's designer purse. She smoothed her hand over her trusty all-weather coat—so old, it bordered on retro. Unless there was a group of polyester activists that she wasn't aware of, she was safe from paint slinging—a bonus of belonging to the lower middle class. Then she frowned—since leaving Sammy's employ, she might have dropped into the upper lower class.

When they started up the steps to the glowing manor house, Jolie's nerve faltered. On the other side of the tall windows, people mingled, holding glasses and moving in that "let me slip through here" way that people use to sidle through parties.

"Come on," Carlotta hissed, waving her forward.

"I have a bad feeling about this," Jolie murmured, stepping up. Assailed again by the feeling that she was being watched, she turned to look back to the driveway, but no other guests had arrived. Then headlights from the street caught her eye. A car sat at the end of the sloping driveway, its nose jutting out past the brick pillars that flanked the entrance. In the darkness, she couldn't tell the model or the color. Gary? A lost driver, perhaps? A guest fumbling for their invitation? Or simply someone who had pulled to the side of the street to make a phone call? A dozen harmless possibilities, and one that unsettled her, yet seemed highly unlikely . . . especially in light of her paranoid scene at the drive-through today.

"What's wrong?" Carlotta asked. She turned her head

in the same direction, then frowned and reached for Jolie's arm. "Come on, let's go inside."

The woman's fingers bit into the back of her upper arm through the multiple layers of fabric. Carlotta herded her toward the door, on the heels of Hannah, and Jolie picked up on her unease. Had she recognized the car? Was it the man to whom Carlotta owed money, or perhaps someone else?

Carlotta released her hold on Jolie's arm, the gargantuan door opened, and Jolie watched as she morphed into a gracious guest, her smile wide and ready. A finger of disquiet nudged Jolie: If the woman could transform herself so quickly, who was the real Carlotta Wren?

Her thoughts were cut short by the haunting music and the sporadic blasts of voices and laughter. And blessed heat. Jolie looked up to see Sammy standing in the doorway, wearing a revealing leopard-print teddy topped by a long, transparent robe. Long, tanned legs ended at five-inch-high leopard-print satin mules. Her cleavage was precarious, and she looked perplexed as she glanced over the trio. "Hello," she said with a little squint. "I'm Sammy Sanders."

Carlotta laughed gaily. "I'm Carly, and these are my friends, Hallie and . . . Gwen." Sammy's gaze flitted over the other two women. Jolie nodded, but Sammy had already looked away. With a start, Jolie realized that she needn't have worried about Sammy recognizing her. The female bulldozer had never given Jolie credit, had never seen her for who she truly was. To recognize someone, you had to first know them.

Her former boss wavered, stealing a helpless glance toward the valet stand as another group of guests alighted from their car. Although it was clear Sammy had no idea who they were, Jolie suspected that neither did she want to create a scene. She knew they couldn't have gotten in without an invitation, so she was trapped.

Carlotta whipped a wrapped gift from her bag—the essential hostess gift. "Candles," she said sweetly.

After a brief pause, Sammy rearranged her face into a polite expression, stepped back and swept her arm toward the cavernous foyer. "Welcome, ladies. I hope this is a night you won't soon forget."

Jolie walked by Sammy and into the black-and-white checkerboard tile foyer of the palatial home. Her gaze traveled upward to the enormous chandelier, which looked as if it might have once belonged in a theater. She tried not to gape at the contemporary paintings on the soaring walls. Secretly, she'd hoped that Sammy would have tacky taste, and although her style was a little ostentatious, it was spectacular, in quality and in scale.

Meanwhile, her entire apartment would fit nicely within this entryway.

"May I take your coats?" a tuxedoed man asked a few feet inside.

Jolie unbuttoned the inexpensive navy coat and relinquished it self-consciously in return for a ticket. She turned the corner and glanced into a colossal great room where guests stood in happy clumps, clinging to champagne glasses and to each other. From this spot she could see the entrance to what appeared to be a French Country dining room, and across the great room, a wall of glass doors was open, leading to an indoor pool. Chlorine and perfume stung her nose.

She recognized a few faces from the night before, but she couldn't place them. The two attractive blondes standing next to the fireplace were sisters, she remembered, al-

though she couldn't recall if their name was York, or if
they were *from* New York.

The woman who had complimented her on the jumpsuit
was talking to a man half her age, the man who had
laughed at her joke talking to a woman half *his* age. Of
course, they'd never recognize her in this getup.

Everyone, it appeared, had adhered to the suggested
dress code. Most of the men wore silky pajamas—striped
or paisley—and short robes or smoking jackets. The
women, on the other hand, put a tad more skin on display.
Teddies, tap pants and camisoles, shortie nightshirts, long
gowns with high slits, gossamer robes. Breasts and Botox
abounded. There were a few elaborate caftans (adult one-
sies), but for the most part, Jolie felt overdressed. Still,
when the lower part of her robe gapped and air rushed
over her bare legs, she shivered and pulled the robe closer
around her.

"Please, don't obstruct the view," a man said next to her.

Her nipples knew that voice.

Jolie turned to find Beck Underwood smiling down at
her legs. He wore a plain black cotton robe a la Target that
hit him mid-shin, and flip-flops that looked to be on their
last flop. In one hand, he held a champagne flute that
looked diminutive between his big fingers; in the other he
held a bottle of champagne by the neck. The *V* of his
belted robe revealed dark chest hair with golden ends.
She'd bet her last dollar that the man had never worn a
robe in his life. Obviously, he wasn't a pajama man.
Jolie's gaze dropped lower and she couldn't help but wonder what, if anything, was underneath the robe.

When she looked up, Beck was staring at her as if she
were his personal party favor.

Sixteen

Beck Underwood walked closer, his mouth pursed in an ironic smile. "I had a feeling you might be here."

Jolie glanced around. Carlotta and Hannah were standing a few feet away, their heads close in conversation. Sammy was greeting more guests. Jolie looked back to him and shook her bewigged head. "How do you always recognize me?"

He shrugged, then leaned in. "Did you crash?"

She crossed her arms, then nodded sheepishly.

He threw his head back and laughed. "That's great. Someday you're going to have to tell me how you do it."

Jolie bristled at the thought of being the man's entertainment.

"Who are you tonight?" he whispered.

Feeling more foolish by the minute, she mumbled, "Gwen."

"Ah. Well, Gwen," he said, picking up a lock of her long fake, red hair, "I've always had a thing for blondes, but in your case, I might make an exception."

Her heart fluttered irrationally until she realized that he was probably well on his way to emptying the bottle of champagne that he held. "You really shouldn't flirt with the person who might become your real-estate agent."

His teeth flashed white against his tan. "Why not?"

Jolie managed a watery smile that she hoped passed for coy. "B—because she might take advantage of you."

He lifted one eyebrow. "Careful, Gwen, you give a man hope."

Her heart skipped a beat, and she told herself he was teasing her, maybe looking for a rendezvous after the party . . . or *during* the party. And while she couldn't deny that she was incredibly attracted to the man, she wasn't about to put herself in the position of being one of Beck Underwood's groupies. She'd had casual sex before, but this situation was different. Besides the fact that she needed the man's business, she was dangerously close to caring what he thought of her. A caution flag was raised in her mind, warning her that there might be more at stake here than a missed commission.

"Is your sister here?" she asked, to change the subject.

He nodded. "Della's by the pool."

"Ah, yes, the pool."

"I suppose you've been here before."

"No, but Sammy talked about the pool, um . . . *occasionally* at the office."

"Ah. Then allow me to take you on a tour. It's quite the place." He winked. "Sammy gave me the full treatment earlier."

Jolie hesitated, then glanced over his shoulder and saw Sammy watching them with a proprietary eye on Beck, a warning eye on her. Revenge sparked in Jolie's chest and she looked back to Beck. "A tour would be nice. Maybe you can point out some things you do and don't like."

His gaze raked over her. "I like short, silky nightgowns and silly house shoes."

It was as if she weren't wearing a ten-pound velvet robe. "I meant what you like in a house," she added quickly, then nervously licked her lips. "Do you think I could have some of that champagne?"

His mouth curved into a grin and he flagged a passing waiter. "You, interesting lady, can have anything I've got. But," he added in a conspiratorial tone, "we need to work on getting rid of that troublesome boyfriend of yours." He juggled his own bottle and glass to snag a clean champagne flute from the waiter's tray, then held it out to her as if he were laying a kingdom at her feet.

Jolie swallowed. Why had she told him she had a boyfriend who was in trouble? She stared into his shining brown eyes and her knees felt loose, and then she remembered why she'd told him she had a boyfriend who was in trouble: To create enough distance to circumvent any possibility of developing a crush on him.

Giving herself a mental shake, she took the glass and held it with amazingly steady hands while he filled it with pinkish-gold liquid from his personal bottle.

"Why don't we start upstairs?" he suggested, and gestured toward the wide staircase—red carpet on white marble made the staircase itself a work of art. Other guests were walking down the stairs, returning from their own tours, she presumed, so she agreed. But she felt Sammy's stare when they moved away from the crowd.

As she climbed the stairs, Jolie sipped the champagne, cool and fizzy against her tongue, and studied the gold foil wall treatment on the massive curved wall. Despite the fact that she and Beck were in their bedclothes and drinking bubbly, Jolie was determined to be professional. "Is this the size home you'll be looking for?"

He lifted his big shoulders, straining the cotton fabric of his inexpensive robe. "I really hadn't thought about it—that's why I need you."

She refused to read anything into that statement. "I, um, saw you on the news last night. You didn't sound as if you were going to stay in Atlanta long enough to buy a home."

A pink stain crawled over his tanned cheeks. "Slow news night. Besides, if I buy a house and decide not to stay in Atlanta, I'll lease it out."

Hearing him say that he might not stay in Atlanta shouldn't have bothered her, but it did. Yet it was even more reason, she told herself, not to buy into his flirtation. Beck Underwood was looking for something to pass the time until he moved along, and she didn't want to be another short-term project.

At the second-floor landing, they stopped for a bird's-eye view of the magnificent chandelier and the grand entryway. Sammy was welcoming a male guest who was dressed in a red velvet smoking jacket reminiscent of the Rat Pack era, all the way down to the arrogant way he held himself. Jolie froze—she knew that pose. While she stood staring down, Roger LeMon looked up, directly at her and Beck. She gasped and stepped back.

"Is something wrong?" Beck asked, turning.

She couldn't very well tell him that Roger LeMon had reported her to the police, especially since Beck himself was aware of her tendency to stalk the man. "Um . . . the height," she lied with a laugh. "I had a sudden bout of vertigo." Her mind spun. Would LeMon recognize her tonight and accuse her of following him? Tell Sammy who she was? Call the police again? She looked around her. On the other hand, this house was enormous—maybe she could simply avoid him all evening.

"Feeling better?" Beck asked.

She nodded and tried to act normal. "Lead the way."

From the landing, two ten-foot-wide hallways split off in opposite directions. Honey-colored hardwood was covered with plush oriental-style carpet runners. Down the hallway to the right, a man and woman walked away from them, peering into rooms, apparently also enjoying a self-guided tour. The man who had collected her coat walked by, his face obscured under a mountain of coats—mostly furs. He disappeared into a room that she assumed had been set aside for a coat check. In the distance, doors opened and closed, voices oohing and aahing. The house appeared to go on forever, an astonishing amount of square footage for one resident.

She followed Beck down the hall to the left and glanced into a room that was perhaps an office or a den, although it was ornate to the point of distraction.

"The décor is too busy for my tastes," he murmured, "but I like the lines of the ceiling."

Jolie nodded. She'd learned to withhold her own opinion when working with a potential client, to listen as their likes and dislikes were revealed. Sometimes clients were unaware of their own tastes, although Beck Underwood did not strike her as a person who waffled. About architecture, anyway.

The next room was a feminine guest room with a daybed and overstuffed upholstered chairs. The textured wallpaper was perfectly coordinated to the comforter. "Why do people do that?" he whispered, his mouth close to her ear. "You have my permission to shoot me if I ever wallpaper a room to match a bedspread."

As if she would be around to witness his hypothetical case of hyper-decorating.

He walked to the next doorway and peered inside. "I believe Sammy said this was her spa room."

Tiled floor, ambient lighting, double massage tables, a whirlpool tub, ceiling fans and an abundance of plants. "Is this something you would be interested in having?" Jolie asked.

"Me? No way. The plants are nice though."

All told, on the hallway were four bedrooms and three den-ish rooms of ambiguous purpose but crammed with oversized furniture and electronic toys. One room was lined with glass display cases for Sammy's collection of crystal houses, most of them reproductions of famous buildings or antebellum homes. Jolie did some mental arithmetic and estimated the woman had tens of thousands of dollars invested in the fragile knickknacks. The outrageousness of it bordered on vulgarity, but before righteous indignation could set in, Jolie looked down at the twelve-hundred-dollar robe she was wearing and flushed with shame.

No more borrowing clothes, she vowed, and no more party crashing, no matter what.

The next room was a decidedly masculine guest bedroom stocked with beautiful hardwood furniture and expensive bed linens and curtains in muted animal prints. The walls were cocoa brown. She followed Beck into the room, although there was something distinctly intimate about being in this bedroom with him while they were both wearing pj's. She surveyed the windows, carpet, the faux finish on the walls—anything to keep from looking at the giant four-poster bed that sat in the room like a big pink elephant.

"Nice," he said vaguely, then turned and gestured toward the bed. "It's a little tall, don't you think?"

She glanced at the bed sideways. "It's tall," she agreed.

He stared at the bed. "I prefer sort of falling into bed versus having to climb up."

She took a drink from her glass. "Do you already have furniture that you'll need to fit into your home?"

"Such as?"

"Family heirlooms? A bed, perhaps?"

"A few things—a chest of my grandfather's, a bookcase I built when I was a teenager, but nothing big."

"You didn't bring things back from Costa Rica?"

"What little I accumulated there, I left there. It's a much simpler place to live."

"It sounds nice."

He nodded. "It is. I miss it. I felt like I was doing some good there."

She angled her head. "And what exactly was that?"

He drained his glass and refilled it from the bottle. "I was a teacher."

She couldn't keep the surprise from her face. "Really? What did you teach?"

"English, economics, math."

She pursed her mouth. "Is that your background?"

"No. My diploma from Duke says I'm an environmental engineer. But since Costa Rica has a greater need for teachers than for environmental engineers, I thought I'd give it a try."

"And?"

He shrugged. "And I'm pretty good at it."

She smiled, trying to visualize him in front of a chalkboard, pounding home an idea. "I'm sure you are. Will you teach here?"

He shook his head. "No, it's time to make amends with my father and step into the family business. My dad's going to retire soon, and I've left Della to carry the burden for too long." His laugh was dry. "Cry me a river, right?"

Bolstered by the champagne and his openness, she shrugged. "I guess most people would think that being heir to a family fortune isn't such a bad thing."

He nodded. "But what do you think?"

Her tongue stalled. "I . . . don't have an opinion. Besides, I have a vested interest in seeing you remain in Atlanta."

His eyes lit up. "You do?"

"My commission, remember?"

"Oh. Right."

"Shall we continue?" Jolie asked, eager to return to a larger group. She wasn't afraid of Beck, but she *was* afraid that the little twinges in her chest when she looked at him were bubbles warning her of emotional quicksand.

A little-boy smile climbed his face and he nodded toward the bed. "We could hang out in here."

Her thighs twinged, and her heart jumped with the optimism that every woman feels when she tries to justify the urge to let a man have his way with her: If the physical attraction is so strong, there must be feeling behind it. For him to be looking at her with such longing, he had to be feeling the same, overwhelming sense that he'd never been so attracted to another person, and never would be again. That sex with this person would be different. A religious experience. Lasting.

That with Roger LeMon afoot, she had a good reason to kill a few hours in Beck's arms.

Jolie came back to earth with a thud. The man was half drunk, after all. And it was up to her to protect her heart from a man who was undoubtedly just passing through—literally and figuratively. "We could," she said carefully, "but we won't."

His shoulders fell. "Okay. Can't blame a man for trying. I've been in the jungle for a few years."

She angled her head. "Something tells me you weren't lonely."

He gave a little laugh. "I've been lonely my entire life."

Jolie looked up, surprised to see the seriousness on his handsome face. She panicked—his teasing banter was so much easier to dismiss. In an effort to restore the light mood, she smiled. "Is that a pick-up line?"

He straightened, his solemnity gone. "Of course. Is it working?"

She smiled. "No, I don't feel the least bit sorry for you."

He made a rueful noise, then asked, "So, *Gwen*, where did you grow up?"

If he had planned to catch her off guard, he'd succeeded. She instantly missed the sexual tension. "Dalton."

"Really? On a farm?"

"No, although we did raise a small vegetable garden. Lots of green beans."

He smiled. "I like green beans."

"That's probably because you've never had to pick and string them."

"You could be right. Do you get back there often?"

She shook her head. "My parents are both gone, and I don't have any siblings."

His mouth parted slightly. "I'm sorry."

"It's not your fault," she said with a wry smile.

But he looked stricken. "You don't have *any* family?"

"There are a couple of great-aunts, and a few stray cousins," she said, trying to sound cheerful.

Concern clouded his eyes. "It's strange, but I can't remember having a conversation with my father that didn't end in an argument, yet I can't imagine him not being around."

Was she supposed to offer commentary on his family dynamics? "Arguing is a form of communication, I suppose."

He scowled, then lifted his glass. "I suppose you're right."

She walked to a window and looked out over the circular driveway. From this view she could see the rows of cars parked farther down the road, and distant lights from neighboring houses. "Are you like your father?" she asked, feeling brave.

He joined her at the window. "Everyone says so, but I don't see it." Then he looked contrite. "Don't get me wrong: My dad is a brilliant businessman, but he was a terrible father and—" He stopped, as if he realized he was revealing too much. "Well, no family is perfect, is it?"

She shook her head. "What's your mother like?"

"Oblivious," he said, his voice wistful. "Mother has been in her own little world for some time now. We all sort of move around her."

"I'm sorry," Jolie said.

One side of his mouth lifted. "It's not your fault."

"You and Della seem close," she ventured, feeling guilty that she was embarking on a fishing expedition.

"We are."

"What does she do for your father's company?"

"Besides sitting on the board, she's very good with the publicity department, which basically means she does public appearances, shmoozes advertisers, that kind of thing."

"And that doesn't interest you?"

"Not in the least."

"What *does* interest you?" She regretted the words before the vibration of them left her tongue.

His eyes trained on her, pulled at her. "*You* do, Jolie Goodman. You interest me, with your full-time dreams and your part-time job and your costumes and disguises and the little wrinkle of problems between your eyes that are normally hazel." He shook his head. "I can't figure you out, but I have a feeling there's a lot about you that you don't reveal to just anyone."

She glanced up and felt her heart opening to him, beckoning. *Look at me. Look at me and* see *me.* Her chest rose and fell, wondering if this man had any idea how uncomplicated she was, how remote she felt most of the time, how much and how little she needed from him at this precise moment.

"Yes," he murmured, as if she'd spoken aloud.

Even he seemed confused at his response as he leaned close, then closer. She had time to dodge the kiss, to step back or turn her head . . . but she didn't. Tonight she didn't have to be herself—and she decided to be the woman who was going to be kissed by Beck Underwood.

He lowered his lips to hers and she had the simultaneous impressions of champagne and warmth and firmness and desire. His hands were full, and she held her own glass out to keep from spilling champagne on Sammy's rug. With just their lips touching, the kiss seemed to grow in intensity as they strained toward each other. He stopped suddenly and pulled back, and before disappointment could settle in, she realized from the look in his eyes that he was surprised . . . but at her response or his own, she couldn't tell. Regardless, a split second later he was kissing her again, this time with hands-on features and sound effects.

And then slowly she began to grasp the fact that the sounds were coming from someone other than the two of them. They parted and Jolie looked up to see their hostess, Sammy, standing in the doorway of the bedroom with her arms crossed, looking, frankly, somewhat inhospitable.

Seventeen

"Why, Beck, I see you're having a good time."

"Great party, Sammy." Either Jolie was imagining things, or Beck inched even closer to her side. Was he afraid Sammy was going to recognize her?

She was afraid enough for the both of them, Jolie decided. At that exact moment, her left contact lens decided to revolt, folding onto itself and obscuring her vision. Jolie blinked liked mad and the thing finally righted itself, to bring Sammy back into view.

With her low- and high-cut (respectively) leopard-print teddy, severe makeup, and killer high-heeled mules, the woman looked ready to bare her fangs and pounce. "I'm sorry, what did you say your name was again?"

"Gwen," Jolie murmured, trying to disguise her voice.

"I didn't get your last name, Gwen."

Jolie's mind raced and came up with, "Yarborough."

"Gwen Yarborough," Sammy said, then shook her head. "When did we meet?"

"Gwen was at the media reception last night," Beck broke in. "The two of you must have met there."

"That's right," Jolie said. "You were wearing the most lovely pink dress."

Sammy's expression eased a smidgen. "Gwen, dear, you spilled champagne on my rug."

Jolie looked down in horror to see a wet spot next to the tip of her burgundy satin mule. In truth, though, she was relieved she hadn't spoiled the expensive shoes.

"I did that," Beck said quickly. "My apologies, Sammy."

The woman gave a dismissive wave. "I'll send someone to soak it up. That's why I don't serve red wine at my parties. Things tend to get a little . . . out of hand."

She stared at Jolie and she took a half step forward. "Are your eyes two different colors?"

Jolie's palm felt sweaty against the glass she held. "Uh—"

"Yes," Beck said. "Isn't that something? I'd heard of people having different-colored eyes, but I'd never met anyone who did, until Gwen."

Sammy was still staring at her and Jolie couldn't look away, like prey prior to being caught and eaten. Sammy's mouth parted slightly and something flickered in her eyes, then vanished. Suddenly, she smiled, then straightened. "Enjoy the tour, then come down and join the rest of the party around the pool. The games will begin soon."

"Games?" Beck asked.

"What's a party without games?" Sammy wet her lips, then turned on her five-inch heels and strode out, her sheer robe floating out behind her like a cape.

Jolie shivered, and the bad feeling she'd had when they'd first arrived descended over her again.

"Whew," Beck muttered. "That was close."

Jolie nodded absently, then glanced down. "I don't suppose you could help me find my contact lens?"

"Don't move. It's probably on that fuzzy robe that's covering practically every inch of you," he teased, setting down his glass and bottle. "This might require a little hands-on search." He lifted his eyebrows, waiting for her permission.

She pressed her lips together, then gave a curt nod. *Why* hadn't she worn a bra?

He took her glass of champagne and set it next to his. Then he gave her a sexy grin and skimmed his hands over her neck and shoulders in a slow sensual caress that made her wish the heavy garment wasn't between her skin and his hands. She swallowed hard against the pull of him, the memory of his kiss still on her lips. Longing pooled in her stomach, thighs. He must have felt it too, because his grin faded when he brought his hands down over her breasts, and his breathing increased.

Her nipples budded and she closed her eyes briefly. He continued to stroke his hands down the robe, spanning her waist and smoothing his hands over her hips, then down her thighs. When he crouched to lift the flowing hem of the garment for a closer inspection, cool air hit her exposed legs.

He took advantage of the opportunity to peek, grunting in satisfaction. She gave into a little thrill of pleasure, thanking God that she'd shaved. "Did you find it?" she asked.

"Find what?" he said, still peeking.

Exasperated, she reached down to close the bottom of her robe. "My contact lens, did you find it?"

"No," he said sadly, then stood and reached for her champagne glass. "Oh, but what do you know—there it is, floating in your bubbly." He grinned. "You would've thought I'd have seen that before I patted you down."

"Ooh!" She swatted at him and he clasped her hand, pulling her against his chest, stealing her breath. Beneath her palm, the hair in the opening of his robe felt coarse, and his heart thudded his intention. She looked into his eyes and realized miserably that Beck Underwood would be so easy for her injured heart to fall for. He was just the man to take her mind off her problems, to sweep her into his world, where his name opened doors and no material thing was out of reach. It would be so easy . . . and so dangerous, heaping heartache upon heartache when he tired of her or resumed his adventures.

Before he could kiss her again, she stepped back and inhaled deeply. "We should see the rest of the upstairs, then join the other guests."

He pursed his mouth, then nodded and handed her the glass with a wink. She retrieved the contact lens and stored it in the case in her bag. Beck disappeared into the connecting bathroom and emerged with her glass, empty and rinsed, which he replenished from the bottle. He didn't press her about what had happened between them, and she felt torn about the foregone chance to explore the chemistry. The irony was that Beck Underwood was intrigued by her aloof and bizarre behavior, but her aloof and bizarre behavior had been precipitated by Gary's disappearance, and it was Gary's disappearance that had left her in such emotional disarray.

But Beck was nothing if not resilient. Two minutes later, when they resumed the tour, he was whistling tunelessly under his breath, his gait easy, his smile ready. Jolie couldn't help feeling a little put out that one minute he was kissing her and the next he seemed unaffected. His behavior made her feel better about her decision to nip their budding attraction . . . but only a tad.

They crossed the landing to reach the second hallway. Laughter, music, and the occasional popped cork sounded from downstairs. Sammy had to be spending a fortune on champagne, Jolie decided. On this new corridor, they passed the converted coat check room and two additional opulent rooms before they reached the open French doors leading into Sammy's bedroom, a suite as large as a cottage.

White carpet, white walls, white linens, white built-in cabinetry, white leather upholstered furniture, a white-light chandelier. To the left, a doorway into a bathroom hinted at more of the same. A red ribbon had been secured across the opening as a polite reminder to guests that they could look, but not touch—or use—the facilities. To the right, a white door leading to yet another room was closed.

"I feel really creepy about being in her bedroom," Jolie whispered, although it was clear the woman intended for people to look—and to be in awe.

"I know what you mean," Beck said, then wagged his eyebrows. "Let's go look in her medicine cabinet."

"What? No."

"I'm kidding. But there is one thing I wanted to show you, the sitting room off to the right. I like the fireplace."

Apparently, he'd gotten the behind-the-scenes tour. She wondered perversely if he were the least bit interested in Sammy—beyond said fireplace. Especially now that Jolie had given him a bit of a brush-off.

Which, in hindsight, was starting to feel like a foolish decision.

Jolie followed him, but practically tiptoed across the snowy carpet.

Beck opened the door leading into the room that appeared to be another office—this one more functional by the looks of the complicated phone system. Most real-estate agents had home offices, and Sammy was no different—hers was just nicer than most. A massive, gleaming white desk and two white wood file cabinets to match, a white leather executive chair on rollers, 20-inch flat-screen monitor, with an impressive CPU tower on the floor. And the fireplace was indeed incredible—floor-to-ceiling gray stone facing with white masonry grout. Beck set down his glass and the bottle to inspect the hearth. No surprise, he also admired the on-wall plasma television and speaker system.

A five-by-seven picture frame on the desk caught Jolie's eye, and she circled behind it, curious as to whom Sammy would think enough of to display on her workstation. Her parents? Mrs. Sanders had died when Sammy was young, which was why Sammy was so close to her father. When Jolie saw the photo, though, she laughed to herself—only Sammy would have a picture of *herself* on her desk. The only surprise was that it wasn't a Miss America shot—instead Sammy was outdoors, dressed in a turtleneck, jeans, and sturdy boots, her hair pulled back into a ponytail, and she was sitting on a rock.

A familiar-looking rock.

Jolie picked up the frame and jammed her face closer. She studied the photo and tried to conjure up in her mind the photo of Gary sitting on a rock, mugging for the camera. Was it the same place, the same day? Was it possible that *Sammy* had been the woman who'd taken the photo of him? Her mouth went dry—did Sammy and Gary have a romantic history, or was this photo a mere coincidence?

She recalled introducing them at the agency and hadn't noticed anything more than a polite exchange. Ditto on the tube-float down the river. In fact, she'd gotten the feeling that Sammy thought he was unsavory because she'd commented once that someone who drove a nice car with no apparent signs of employment was either a trust-fund kid or a criminal.

Jolie scoured the photo, looking for any details that might help prove or disprove her wild theory, but in truth, the photo could have been taken anywhere, on any rock. She couldn't check the back for photo finishing details unless she took the whole thing apart . . . and that would take some privacy. She glanced at Beck, who was still mesmerized by a beautifully sculpted chrome remote control. Feeling like a bona fide crook, she slid the photo into her standard "biggish" party-crashing purse.

"We probably should go," she said abruptly.

He turned and nodded. "You're right—Sammy might think we're snooping."

A shamefaced flush climbed her cheeks as she left the office and strode across the bedroom. Amidst all the white, the edge of Sammy's green Kate Spade bag was especially noticeable sticking out from under the bed's dust ruffle. She detoured from her straight path to push the purse beneath the bed, thinking that would help assuage her guilt. She nudged the green bag with her shoe, but it wouldn't budge. She lifted the bed skirt, saw the bag was caught against a leg of the bed frame and reached down to push it out of sight. Just in case there were unscrupulous people about.

Party crashers, for instance.

"Something wrong?" Beck asked from the door.

"Nothing," she murmured, standing. Then she spied the bathroom. "Um, actually, I need to powder my nose. Do you think it would be okay to—"

"I'll be your lookout," he cut in, his tone as grave as a spy's.

The "keep out" ribbon had been affixed with tape. She unfastened one end, then entered the bathroom and closed the door behind her. The expansive whiteness was blinding—tiled floor, floating sink, slick cabinets, shiny garden tub, long, white sheers at the windows. Leann had once told her that white was a prestigious color among her clients because of the implication that one had to have money to maintain anything white. So true.

Jolie pulled the picture frame from her bag and studied the photo again. Hopefully she would find some innocuous description on the back like "Me and Dad at Yosemite," then she'd feel foolish and return it to Sammy's desk.

She turned over the frame to find the back held together with small screws. Cursing under her breath, she rummaged in her purse to find anything that would suffice as a tool. The screw heads were too small to be turned with a coin, and a paperclip wouldn't work. She needed a metal nail file or tweezers or something similar. She pulled out cabinet drawers, aware of the time ticking away. Lots of beauty products, combs, curlers, hair appliances, but nothing she could use as a screwdriver.

Jolie glanced toward the wide mirrored cabinet over the floating sink, remembering Beck's suggestion that they snoop in Sammy's medicine cabinet. She sighed and gingerly pulled open the mirrored door.

A second later, a shelf in the cabinet collapsed, sending its contents toppling and setting off a horrific, crashing chain reaction as bottles and jars and other personal toiletries landed in the sink. She cringed and counted to ten.

A quiet knock sounded. "Everything okay in there?" Beck asked, his voice muffled . . . and concerned.

"Fine," she returned shakily. "Just a little . . . accident. I'll be right out."

She slipped the shelf back into place with shaking hands, then scooped up the items and situated them back onto the shelves wherever they would fit. Men's toiletries were mixed in with the feminine items (a diaphragm, ew) and Jolie told herself that more men than Gary used Zirh brand premium shave gel. And old-fashioned razor blades. She fingered the packet and realized suddenly that a blade was thin enough and strong enough to loosen the screws on the picture frame.

Carefully, she removed a blade from the package and was successful in loosening one screw before the blade slipped and slashed the fatty pad of her left palm. She dropped the blade, instinctively pressed her hand to her chest, and puffed out her cheeks, knowing before she looked that the cut was deep . . . and bloody.

When she pulled it away, not only did the bleeding resume exuberantly, but the pain lit up her entire arm. She sucked air through her teeth, and looked for something to wrap around her hand. A stack of white fingertip towels sat on a cabinet. She grabbed one and held it against her hand until the bleeding slowed. Upon closer observation, the cut was only an inch long, but it throbbed unmercifully. Remembering the package of adhesive bandages she'd seen in a drawer, she appropriated three to cover the wound. Luckily, the damage was to her left hand, so she was able to restore order to the medicine cabinet, although

Sammy would have to be in a stupor not to realize that things had been rearranged.

She returned the picture frame to her purse, deciding it would go home with her. If it turned out to be unrelated to Gary's photo, she would return the picture to Sammy anonymously.

Now, what to do with the mess she'd made? A bloody towel, Band-Aid debris. The paper went into the step waste-can. She used the towel to wipe down the white counter and the white sink, then wrapped it inside another small towel and stuffed the whole kit-and-caboodle into her purse. Only then did she get a look at herself in the mirror and saw the big, bloody stain on the silk cream-colored gown where her robe gapped open. She shrieked, which elicited another knock on the door.

"Do I need to call someone for you?"

"No!" she called, then gulped a calming breath. She was no textile expert, but she had a feeling that the only way to get blood out of silk was to cut it out. She closed her eyes, chastising herself. Her amateur sleuthing had led to ruining an eight-hundred-dollar nightshirt. She whimpered, thinking how many shoes she'd have to sell. Served her right for stealing clothes, crashing this party.

She pulled herself up, thinking at least she had her commission from Beck Underwood's home to look forward to. If she hadn't completely blown it with him, of course. He didn't seem like the type of man who would take his business elsewhere because she wouldn't sleep with him, but then again, he didn't seem like the type of man who would do business with a nobody. So if this night was to be salvaged, she needed to leave feeling good about getting his business.

She pulled her robe together and tightened the belt, relieved to see the bloodstain was covered as long as she didn't flash anyone. She stuffed her aching hand into her pocket, retrieved her champagne glass, took a deep breath, and emerged with as big a smile as she could muster.

Beck straightened, his expression opening in relief. "If you ever want to make a man go crazy, go into the bathroom and start making a lot of loud, dangerous-sounding noises."

"Sorry," she murmured. "I was looking for an aspirin, and her medicine cabinet exploded."

That made him smile, and thankfully, he didn't notice her hand, or the fact that she kept glancing at her own chest every few seconds.

"I guess we'd better go," she said, "before Sammy sends out a search party."

He shuddered dramatically and she laughed as they walked into the hall.

"Thanks for the tour. Do you have an idea of where you'd like to live?"

"Maybe midtown," he said. "Or downtown." Then he grinned. "Or maybe a farm in Dalton."

Her heart flooded with intense like. "That really narrows it down."

He looked around and lifted his arms as they reached the landing that overlooked the enormous entryway on the first floor. Guests' voices carried up, bursts of laughter and clinking glasses. "Do you like this house?" he asked.

She took in the grandeur around her. "It's a beautiful house."

"Yes, but would you live here?"

Her cheeks warmed. "That's something I'll probably never have to worry about."

"Humor me. If you had the money, is this the kind of house you would choose to live in?"

"I . . . probably not. I have to admit that large houses seem . . . daunting to me. All that space demanding to be used." She blushed, thinking she'd probably offended him since the Underwood family home was near the governor's mansion in Buckhead, but was twice the size. She rushed to explain. "But what I think is missing most in this house is personality. Yes, it's beautiful, but it feels more like a showcase than a home. Anyone might live here. As a broker, I'm probably not supposed to say this, but owning a home is more than buying an address and filling it up with nice stuff. It should be personal, unique, symbolic even." She flushed because she thought she'd overstepped her bounds. After all, the man was probably looking for a tax shelter.

But instead of laughing at her, he looked at her in that dangerous fall-for-me way. "Do you have your own home?"

"Not yet," she said. "But someday."

"You're hired."

She grinned, but her pleasure over a potentially huge commission was cut short by a commotion on the first floor—Carlotta, flailing her arms, asking guests, "Have you seen a woman with long red hair?"

"Carlot—" Jolie stopped and cleared her throat. "Carly, I'm up here."

Carlotta looked up, then disappeared, apparently coming up after her. When she reached the landing, she was out of breath.

"What's wrong?" Jolie asked.

"There's been a little . . . complication."

Jolie frowned. "What?"

"Russell is here."

"Who?"

"Hannah's boyfriend."

"Oh."

"With his wife."

"Oh."

"Right," Carlotta said, her voice grim. "I tried to get Hannah to leave, but she wouldn't. She said she was going to make a scene. She was headed to the pool where they were, and I'm afraid someone's going to get hurt."

"What can I do?" Jolie asked.

"Find our coats, and meet me down there." Carlotta looked at Beck. "Would it be too much to ask you to run interference?"

"Who are we talking about?" he asked, scratching his head.

"Our friend Hannah, who came with us," Jolie explained. "She's been dating a married man, and apparently he's here—with his wife."

Beck winced. "Who's the stupid guy?"

"Russell Island," Carlotta supplied.

"I know him," Beck said. "And his wife. This won't be pretty." They started down the stairway and Jolie jogged toward the coat check room, thinking Hannah was likely to blow their cover and Sammy would toss them all out on their party-crashing behinds. Maybe even have them arrested for trespassing.

The attendant was gone, so Jolie undid the familiar and ineffective ribbon across the doorway and started her own search. The nicer coats—the furs, the leathers, the brocades—were hanging on portable racks. The jackets, hats, shawls, and assorted cheap coats had been draped over the bed—ten dollars said that's where her all-weather standby had been relegated. It was difficult to maneuver with her injured hand, but after searching three racks, she spotted Carlotta's black cashmere coat and pulled it off the rack. Hannah's leather duster was more elusive, but she finally found it. Then she turned to the bed to dig for her Montgomery Ward special.

She displaced a dozen hats and wraps and pulled three navy coats out of the tangle that weren't hers. She was starting to become frustrated when she touched something unexpectedly solid. Jolie frowned and pushed aside a pile of coats, then was struck mute with shock . . . terror . . . disbelief.

It was Gary. And from the hole in his chest, he appeared to be . . . checked out.

Eighteen

There are times in every person's life when they find out what they're made of. Looking down on Gary Hagan's body—lifeless eyes, gray pallor, unnatural position—Jolie discovered that she was made of soft, gooey, blubbery stuff. The only thing that kept her from collapsing entirely was the knowledge that if she did, she'd fall on a dead person.

She tried to scream, but no sound came out of her constricted throat. She stumbled backward on her high-heeled house shoes, twisting her ankle and ricocheting off the doorframe and out into the hall. Her mind reeled, rejecting what her eyes had just seen, and she was distantly aware that she was keening like a small animal.

She half staggered, half fell down the vacated stairs, grateful to the red carpet for sparing her knees from the marble beneath, and at one point thinking it would be faster if she just rolled down. Her hand felt wet and sticky and she registered the fact that she might be smearing blood down the handrail. By the time she'd reached the first floor, she was minus a shoe, and she still hadn't encountered a live person.

Judging from the empty great room, everyone had migrated to the pool. She lumbered forward, heedless of anything except getting to Beck or Carlotta . . . or even Sammy. The good news was that Beck and Carlotta were standing together by the edge of the pool with their backs to her. The bad news was they were restraining Hannah, who was kicking at a cowering man as if they were in a Ninja movie. The guests were crowded around, fascinated.

At last the scream that had been caught in Jolie's throat erupted like a volcano, echoing off the surface of the aqua-colored water dotted with floating candles, reverberating around the glass-enclosed room. Every head pivoted her way. Beck took a half step in her direction.

"Help!" she bellowed, running toward them as fast as she could considering she was wearing one shoe.

The one shoe betrayed her. She hit a slick spot and skidded, flailing. A bewildered-looking Carlotta, who was closest, reached for her, and Hannah reached for Carlotta, and the next thing Jolie knew, she had entered the pool by way of a belly-flop chain.

The good news was the bracing water cleared the fog from her head. The bad news was she'd fallen into the deep end and the heavy robe instantly soaked up ten times its weight in water. She struggled with the tie belt, but only managed to pull it tighter around her ribs. Meanwhile, Carlotta floated by, her eyes wide, her mouth open—not exactly the safest expression for being underwater. She was in trouble. Jolie grabbed Carlotta's leg and shoved her toward the side of the pool while trying to kick her own way to the surface.

She yanked at the tie around her waist again and miraculously it loosened. She pushed her way out of the robe but it wrapped around her legs, immobilizing her, dragging her down. Red ribbons of blood colored the water around her—the wound on her hand had reopened. Panic clawed at her chest as she sank, and Jolie understood how Gary must have felt when he knew he was going to die. Petrified, helpless . . . remorseful. What had she done with her life, really? Would anyone care that she wasn't around? Drowning at a party that she'd crashed wasn't the way she'd hoped to make headlines. Her body jerked in preparation for taking a death breath.

Suddenly two big arms came around her from behind and jerked her upward. She inhaled water to satisfy her lungs, but her body rebelled, bucking. The robe fell away, brushing her feet. Air bubbles rushed past her face, then her head broke the surface of the water. She coughed and sputtered, thrashing her arms like a windmill.

"Relax," Beck said into her ear. "Don't fight me."

He eased her over to the side of the pool. Wheezing, she blinked the ceiling of glass into view, acknowledged the hard muscle of his torso and legs pressing against hers. Her brain must have been deprived of oxygen for a tad longer than was healthy, because the thought struck her that if she hadn't just seen the dead body of her boyfriend and hadn't almost drowned, this might have been a nice moment.

He boosted her up over the pool edge as if she weighed nothing and set her down next to Carlotta and Hannah, who were huddled miserably on the side of the pool like wet cats dressed in upmarket lingerie.

"Are you okay?" Beck asked, looking up at her from the water, his hand on her knee. His breathing was labored, his wet hair falling over his dark eyes.

She nodded, hugging herself in her transparent chemise. "Th–thank you."

"You're bleeding," he said, pulling her hand toward him for a look.

"It's not bad," she said between coughs. "Considering I could be dead right now."

A full-body shiver seized her.

"I'll get some blankets," he said, then hoisted himself up out of the pool. Once again she was struck by the inappropriateness of noticing the man's physique, but he was mesmerizing in blue cotton boxers molded by the water. She had wondered what he was wearing underneath the robe, but she hadn't planned on going to these lengths to find out.

They had managed to turn the pool into an ocean— their splashing had extinguished most of the floating candles. Their robes and purses littered the bottom. Their wigs bobbed on the surface like dead animals. Speaking of dead, she needed to tell someone—everyone—about Gary. She suddenly felt light-headed, and she couldn't stop shaking.

"My book," Carlotta whispered, gazing into the water.

"Your celebrity book was in your purse?" Jolie asked.

Carlotta nodded miserably.

"I'm so sorry," Jolie murmured. "Can you forgive me?"

"*Jolie Goodman.*"

Jolie looked up to see Sammy staring down at her. Unhappily.

The woman walked closer, hands on hips. "I *thought* that was you earlier, but I told myself that you wouldn't *dare* put on a disguise and *crash* my party! That was you last night at the media reception, too, wasn't it?"

Jolie could only wince.

"And you had the nerve to bring these two troublemakers with you!"

"I brought you a hostess gift," Carlotta muttered.

"Candles?" Sammy shrieked. "I ought to call the police."

"They're from Neiman's," Carlotta retorted.

"I mean to have you arrested for trespassing!" Sammy screeched, her volume off the chart in decibels. She jabbed her finger at Hannah. "And you, for assaulting one of my guests!"

Hannah glowered at a man across the pool touching his swollen eye. The woman next to him, presumably his wife, appeared ready to black his other eye. Russell Island seemed dazed . . . and vaguely familiar.

But enough stalling.

"Sammy," Jolie said, pushing herself to her wobbly feet. Water ran off her, splashing onto Sammy's shoes. "You do need to call the police."

"You're bleeding," Sammy said, looking disgusted, as if something might get stained.

"Yes," Jolie said, feeling bout of nausea coming on. "But it actually gets worse."

Re-dressed in his black robe, Beck walked up and settled a chenille throw that Jolie had seen on a couch around her shoulders. The warmth was heavenly, but having Beck behind her made her even more nervous—his desire to help her was about to change.

Sammy flinched at the sight of the expensive throw soaking up pool water. "Jolie, *what* are you talking about?"

"G–Gary Hagan is upstairs in the coat check room."

"Gary Hagan?" Sammy's expression turned lethal.

"What on earth is that criminal boyfriend of yours doing in my coat check room?"

"He's dead," Jolie murmured, seeing starbursts. She was going to faint. And God help her, she aimed herself at Beck for one last favor.

Jolie sat at a table in a holding room wearing an oversized gray "Property of Fulton County, Georgia" sweat suit and flip-flops since the police had confiscated her "borrowed" clothing. How she was going to pay for those nightclothes, she didn't know.

Of course, at the moment, paying for outrageously expensive clothes wasn't the biggest worry on her plate, but concentrating on the more mundane details helped her not to dwell on the fact that Gary was dead.

And that the police seemed to think that she and Carlotta and Hannah had something to do with it. The girls were elsewhere, in similar rooms, she assumed. Just like on television, the police had split them up so they couldn't devise a story. As if they would even try to come up with a better one.

Fatigue weighted her limbs, and her lungs felt raw. Her hair was a crusty nest. She had chewed her fingernails to the quick. She touched a goose egg on her forehead—Beck had caught her when she'd fainted, but she'd cracked her head when she'd gotten into the police car for the ride to the clink. The threesome was instructed by Salyers and her partner not to talk to each other, so Carlotta had cried the entire trip, and Hannah had conjugated her boyfriend's name with every expletive ever conceived. Jolie had concentrated on counting the squares in the metal grate between the front seat and the back, trying to forget the look on Beck's face as she was being stuffed into the cruiser. Condescension? Disappointment? He had turned away to put a comforting arm around Della's shoulder, and Jolie imagined they were saying how glad they were that Beck hadn't become involved with the poor-white-trash shoe salesperson-slash-real-estate-agent-slash-murderer.

The clincher was that she wasn't particularly good at any of those things.

The door to the holding room opened and Detective Salyers walked in, looking none-too-pleased to be awake at three in the morning. By the time she and other officers had been summoned to the scene and guests had been questioned, Carlotta's car impounded, and the three of them transported to jail, a few hours had slipped by.

"Hi, again," Jolie ventured.

"Alone at last," Salyers said, tossing a pad of paper on the table. "Ms. Goodman, I thought I told you to stay out of trouble."

"Trust me, this wasn't intentional."

Salyers blinked. "Was that a confession?"

Alarm blipped in Jolie's chest. "*No*. I meant that I was just going to a party. I had no idea Gary—alive or dead—would be there."

Salyers emitted a long sigh. "Why don't we start from the beginning. Want some coffee?"

Jolie nodded.

Salyers exited and Jolie glanced at the notepad—the first several pages were waffled with handwritten notes. Even upside down, she could make out "Goodmans" all over the page. She covered her mouth with her hand in an attempt to knock back the panic. This could be bad.

Salyers walked back in carrying two large cups of coffee. Jolie sipped with gratitude. It wasn't Starbucks, but it was hot.

The detective dropped in the seat opposite her. "Okay, Ms. Goodman, tell me everything that happened since you called me today—er, yesterday."

"Am I under arrest?"

"No."

Jolie swallowed another mouthful of coffee. "Do I need a lawyer?"

"That's up to you. If you want to call a lawyer, I can get you a phone."

"I don't know any criminal lawyers."

"Then I can get you the phone book."

Jolie shook her head. "I just want to get this over with and go home."

Salyers gave a curt nod, then removed a pen from her jacket pocket and clicked the end. "Ms. Goodman, what did you do after you left the drive-through yesterday?"

"I went back to my apartment."

"Did you talk to anyone on the phone—cellular or otherwise?"

"No."

"E-mail?"

"No."

"Did you go anywhere?"

"No."

"Then?"

"Then Carlotta and Hannah came over, and we got ready for the party."

"You were aware that the party was being given by your former boss?"

"Yes."

"And you were intending to crash the party?"

Jolie squirmed. "Yes."

"You didn't know Mr. Hagan would be there?"

"Absolutely not."

"Did Ms. Wren or Ms. Kizer know Mr. Hagan?"

"No."

"Do you have any idea why Mr. Hagan was at the party?"

She lifted her hands. "No . . . unless he followed me there. As we walked into the house, Carlotta and I both saw a car sitting at the end of the driveway."

"Could you tell what kind of car it was?"

Jolie shook her head.

"Were you and your friends wearing disguises?"

Jolie hesitated. "We were wearing wigs."

"And very expensive garments with the tags still attached—can you explain that?"

She swallowed. "We . . . were planning to return them."

"I see. Are you in the habit of buying expensive clothes, wearing them, then returning them?"

Jolie pursed her mouth. "I wouldn't say it was a habit, per se."

"But you've done it before."

Jolie nodded.

Salyers gave a little "the nerve" snort, then looked back to her notes. "Ms. Sanders said you were also wearing colored contact lenses."

"That's right."

"And Ms. Wren said she altered your features with makeup."

"It's true that I didn't want Sammy to recognize me."

"Because she wouldn't have wanted you at her party?"

Jolie flushed. "That's right."

"The two of you have a history. She said she fired you from her agency."

"That's a lie—I quit."

"When was that?"

"About three weeks ago."

"Why did you quit?"

"Because . . . Sammy asked me to do something un-ethical."

"What was that?"

Jolie sighed. "We were representing the seller in a com-mercial real-estate deal. She asked me to reveal to the buyer the amount the seller would settle for, which was much less than the asking price and confidential between the agency and the seller."

"And you refused?"

"Yes. And I quit."

Salyers leaned back, tipping her chair on two legs. "Ms. Sanders said that you came to her party to rob her."

Jolie gasped. "What? That's absurd!"

"Is it? Ms. Sanders said that some items are missing, in-cluding one thousand dollars in cash from her purse. She also said that her medicine cabinet had been ransacked, and a sterling picture frame was taken."

And the picture frame had been found in her biggish purse at the bottom of the pool. Jolie closed her eyes and when she opened them, Salyers was still there, unfortu-nately.

"Is there something you'd like to say, Ms. Goodman?"

Jolie steepled her hands over her nose. "I put the picture frame in my purse because of the photo, not the frame."

Salyers arched an eyebrow. "I understood it was a photo of Ms. Sanders."

Jolie frowned at the implication. "It *was* a picture of Sammy, but the rock she was sitting on and the back-ground reminded me of a photo in Gary's album." She lifted her hands. "I thought maybe Sammy was with him the day it was taken."

"Meaning you think Mr. Hagan and Ms. Sanders were romantically involved?"

Jolie shrugged. "I don't know, but it seemed like too big of a coincidence to ignore. I thought if I could take the photo out of the frame, I'd be able to compare the film processing date and the paper. I went into Sammy's bathroom to remove the photo, but I couldn't find anything to use as a screwdriver."

"So you were the one who ransacked the medicine cabinet?"

Jolie nodded. "And the only thing I could find was a razor blade. It didn't work and I cut myself." She held up her re-bandaged hand.

"You said that's where the blood came from."

"The blood on my gown? Yes. Where is the photo now?"

"Taken into evidence, I would assume."

"Then you can look into my theory?"

Salyers gave her a skeptical look. "Sure. Okay, let's back up. What about the money that's missing?"

"I don't know anything about that."

"Ms. Sanders said you were aware that she normally carried a lot of cash."

"Anyone who knew Sammy well knew she carried cash."

"Did your friend Ms. Wren know?"

Jolie remembered the conversation she'd had with Carlotta about the hush money Sammy was trying to give her. Her heart sank when she realized that lifting cash from Sammy's purse would solve her friend's financial dilemma. "I might have mentioned it."

"The money was found in the pool filter. You, Ms. Wren, Ms. Kizer, and Mr. Underwood were the only ones who took a swim."

"We fell in," Jolie said.

"Are you sure you didn't jump in?"

She frowned. "Why would I have jumped in?"

Salyers shrugged. "Maybe you couldn't live with yourself."

Jolie's breath stuck in her throat. "You think I was trying to kill myself? That's crazy!"

"Or maybe you were trying to destroy evidence."

"I wasn't," Jolie said evenly.

Salyers leaned forward, settling her chair on the floor. "Ms. Goodman, how well do you know Carlotta Wren and Hannah Kizer?"

"Carlotta and I work together at Neiman's. Hannah is a friend of Carlotta's. I've known them for less than a week."

"So you really don't know them that well, do you?'

Jolie splayed her hands. "No, but they seem nice."

"Nice? They trespass for kicks. And the one with the pierced tongue, besides fooling around with a married man, looks like she's into some pretty kinky stuff."

"You'd have to ask her."

"Have either of them ever mentioned owning a gun?"

"No." Then a memory surfaced, and she snapped her fingers. "But Sammy owns a gun. She was at Neiman's yesterday and she paid for her purchase in cash." Jolie decided not to mention the five-hundred-dollar tip that Sammy had offered on the chance it might lead to questions she'd rather not answer. "When she opened her purse, I saw a gun."

But Salyers seemed unfazed. "Ms. Sanders informed us that she has a permit to carry a concealed weapon, that she kept a nine-millimeter handgun in her purse, and that it's missing. Do you know if the weapon you saw was a nine-millimeter?"

"I couldn't say—I'm not familiar with guns. Was that the kind of gun used to kill Gary?"

"Officers are still on the scene searching for the murder weapon."

"Everyone at the party had access to Sammy's gun," Jolie said. "I saw the green purse sticking out from underneath her bed. I pushed it back."

"Does that mean we'll find your fingerprints on the purse?"

Jolie closed her eyes briefly, then nodded.

"Did anyone see you push the purse underneath the bed?"

Loath to implicate Beck, she hesitated, but she'd seen the police officers on the scene talking to him. "Beck Underwood was in the room."

Salyers' eyebrow arched. "You and Mr. Underwood were in Ms. Sanders' bedroom?"

Her cheeks warmed. "We were taking a tour. Mr. Underwood had asked me to help him find a house—he was pointing out his likes and dislikes."

"Are you and Mr. Underwood friends?"

"Acquaintances," she said.

"No offense, Ms. Goodman, but how did you become acquainted with one of the richest men in Atlanta?"

So it was obvious to everyone that they didn't exactly move in the same circles. "I sold him a pair of shoes at Neiman's, and our paths crossed again at a couple of parties."

"Parties that you and your friends crashed?"

Jolie bit the end of her tongue, then nodded. "But I went to the parties looking for people who might know—have known—Gary." Her voice caught and she inhaled deeply. "That's when I ran into Roger LeMon."

"I see."

"*He* was at the party tonight," Jolie said, sitting forward on the hard chair. "LeMon's the one you should be questioning—he was probably the one who killed Gary."

Salyers nodded, but Jolie could tell the woman was only humoring her. "Why do you think that Mr. LeMon killed Mr. Hagan?"

"Because Gary was set up. He didn't kill that woman who was in his car."

The detective leaned forward on her elbows. "And how would you know that?"

She swallowed. If she told the detective about talking to Gary Wednesday night in her car, she could be in even more trouble for not coming forward sooner.

There was a rap on the door, then Salyers' dark-haired partner stuck his head into the room. "Got a minute?" he asked Salyers.

"Sure, Alexander."

He darted a worried look at Jolie that made her pulse pick up and handed a note to Salyers. After she read it, they had a murmured conversation, then he closed the door and left.

Salyers walked back to the table, note in hand, working her mouth from side to side. "Ms. Goodman, you were wearing a long, blue all-weather coat, Montgomery Ward brand, size six, is that correct?"

She nodded. "Did you find it?"

"Sure did. And guess what was in the pocket?"

Exhaustion was closing in. Jolie dragged her hands down her face. "Breath mints? Ticket stubs?"

"Try the murder weapon."

Jolie's mouth fell open. Tiny lights appeared behind her eyelids. A whining noise sounded in her ears.

Salyers crossed her arms. "Ms. Goodman, what do you have to say for yourself?"

That I'm gullible. "I . . . I m–might be needing that phone b–book after all."

Nineteen

Detective Salyers slid two three-inch-thick volumes of the Atlanta Yellow Pages across the table, then handed Jolie a cordless phone. Jolie stared at it and wondered if they were afraid jailbirds would hang themselves with a phone cord. Which, under the circumstances, seemed a preferable way to meet one's Maker than a needle in a vein.

"I'll be back in a few minutes," Salyers said, then left the room.

Jolie choked down her panic and gripped the phone so hard it made a popping sound. She had no idea how to go about choosing a criminal attorney—all the attorneys she knew represented irate buyers and sellers at mortgage closings. Generating enough paperwork to kill someone probably didn't qualify as the kind of experience she needed.

The L–Z volume had telltale curled pages near the beginning—countless other inmates had rifled through the "Legal Services" listings, which were handily categorized under "Attorneys, by Practice Area." She ran her finger down the page: Bankruptcy (she'd probably need an attorney for that later), Corporate, Criminal. She scanned the listings and the ads. Names (singular and multi-partnered), pictures (from stern to smiling), and slogans ("If you're in a jam, call Pam!") ran together after a while. Jolie was secretly hoping to find an ad offering representation for the wrongly accused, but conceded that in this situation that had to be just about everybody.

On the other hand, how many truly innocent people accumulated enough circumstantial evidence to incriminate themselves in a murder? Jolie had to admit that if she were the detective, *she* would arrest her.

Knowing that time was running out, she narrowed the choices to office addresses that sounded affluent (Buckhead, downtown, anywhere on Peachtree Street), and had launched into the scientific elimination process of eenie, meenie, miney, moe when the door opened suddenly and Salyers stepped in. "That was quick," she said to Jolie.

Jolie frowned in confusion as a woman who looked amazingly like Barbara Bush, except she was wearing a nylon running suit instead of a blue dress and pearls, strode into the room. She set a big, black briefcase on the table, and turned to Salyers. "I'd like a few minutes alone with my client before questioning resumes." Salyers nodded, then left.

Still holding the phone, Jolie looked up at the woman. "I'm sorry—who are you?"

"Pam Vanderpool."

Jolie squinted. " 'When you're in a jam, call Pam' Vanderpool?"

The woman grinned. "That's right. I'm your attorney, Ms. Goodman."

At a loss, Jolie shook her head. "How?"

"We have a mutual friend—Beck Underwood."

Jolie's eyes widened. "Beck called you?"

The woman nodded and pulled out a steno pad. "We go way back, Beck and I." With a rustle of nylon, she sat down in the seat Salyers had vacated. "Now, bring me up to speed. Tell me everything you told the police, and everything you didn't."

Jolie tingled with wonder, gratitude, and concern that Beck would take it upon himself to help her. Pam Vanderpool had a stern, motherly quality that comforted.

"I don't know where to start," Jolie stammered.

The woman shrugged. "Start at the beginning. How are you acquainted with the deceased?"

The deceased. Jolie's chest ached and her eyes blurred with unexpected tears. "I didn't kill Gary," she murmured. "I'm innocent."

The woman reached across the table and patted Jolie's arm. "I wish I could say that's going to make my job easier, sweetheart, but it's too early to tell." She sighed. "You're exhausted, so let's get through this real quicklike, so you can go home."

Jolie gave her a brief background and repeated the conversations she'd had with the police, startling with when she'd first filed the missing persons report to her most recent tête-à-tête with Salyers. Vanderpool wrote furiously, asking questions here and there. Jolie ended with Salyers' announcement that they'd found the murder weapon in her coat pocket.

"Do you know how the gun might have gotten there?" the woman asked, looking eerily calm for someone defending a murder suspect.

Jolie shook her head.

"Have you ever fired a gun?"

"No."

"And you have no inkling as to the identity of the woman found in Mr. Hagan's car?"

"That's right."

Pam Vanderpool played with her pen, turning it end over end. "Ms. Goodman, if there's anything you haven't been truthful about with the police, I need to know now, so there aren't any surprises."

Jolie swallowed hard and clasped her hands together. "Well, there's this one little thing."

Vanderpool squinted. "What?"

"Wednesday night when I left the party at the High Museum, Gary was waiting in my rental car."

The woman wet her lips. "And?"

"And he told me not to go to the police, that if I did, both of our lives would be in danger."

"Did he say why?"

"He said that he hadn't killed the woman found in his car, that he'd been set up, but he wouldn't tell me anything other than 'they' were out to get him, and if I went to the police, 'they' might come after me."

"Why would 'they' come after you?"

"He said because of an envelope that he'd sent to me. When I told him I hadn't received an envelope, he grew frantic and said 'they' must have intercepted it."

"Did he say what was in the envelope?"

"No. He wouldn't answer any of my questions about the dead woman or who he was afraid of. He said the less I knew, the better. He wouldn't even let me see his face."

"And you didn't report this to the police?"

She shook her head. "I convinced myself that he hadn't

said anything that would help them in their investigation and that I might actually make things worse."

The woman pursed her lips. "You still haven't received this alleged envelope?"

"No."

"Did you see Mr. Hagan again after that?"

"No, not until . . . tonight."

"You didn't see him at the party alive?"

"N–no."

"Okay, well, since you withheld information, no polygraph for you, young lady, but I'm going to try to convince the police that arresting you right now wouldn't be in anyone's best interests."

Jolie swallowed. "Okay."

"Is there anything else you'd like to tell me before I call Detective Salyers back in?"

"I . . . don't have much money . . . to pay you."

The woman winked. "But Beck does."

Jolie sat in stunned silence while her prepaid attorney summoned Detective Salyers. "My client wishes to go home."

Salyers smiled, tapping a rolled sheath of papers against her palm. "We all *wish* to go home, Ms. Vanderpool, but there's the little matter of a murder."

Vanderpool crossed her arms. "A man is shot at a party with dozens of people around—no one hears a thing. You're not even sure that the victim was actually shot at the party, are you, Detective?"

At Salyers' hesitation, hope bloomed in Jolie's chest.

"We're still waiting for the M.E.'s report," Salyers said. "Meanwhile, we want Ms. Goodman to take a polygraph test."

"No," Vanderpool said bluntly. "But my client is willing to submit to a gunpowder residue test."

Jolie's eyes widened. She was?

Salyers' mouth quirked to the side. "Your client took a swim in a pool. Any gun powder residue on her person or her clothes was washed away."

Vanderpool lifted her arms. "Then you got nothing."

"We have the murder weapon in Ms. Goodman's coat pocket."

"Which anyone could have placed there. Besides, if my client were guilty, why wouldn't she simply have left the party rather than raising an alarm?"

"Maybe she panicked."

"Detective," Vanderpool cooed. "Does Ms. Goodman strike you as a cold-blooded murderer?"

They both swung their heads toward Jolie. Her entire left arm throbbed from the cut in her palm. Her head felt as if it were in a vise. Every cell in her body sagged. If she looked half as pitiful as she felt, Salyers would give her a cookie and send her home.

Salyers frowned. "Looks can be deceiving. Case in point," she said, withdrawing a sheet of paper from the stack she held. "Ms. Goodman, you've just been served with a harassment restraining order, filed by Mr. Roger LeMon."

Jolie pushed to her feet. "What?"

"This is the man you told me about?" Vanderpool asked her.

Jolie nodded, fury burning in her empty stomach.

"What's this all about?" her attorney asked, taking the form.

"Mr. LeMon said he came to the party, but was forced

to leave because he was afraid Ms. Goodman would accost him."

"Accost him?" Jolie said. "That's ridiculous!"

Salyers shrugged. "Ridiculous or not, if you knowingly come within fifty yards of the man, you will be arrested."

"Don't you see?" Jolie asked, flailing her good arm. "He's giving himself an alibi! Roger LeMon killed Gary and is trying to pin it on me!"

"Another conspiracy theory?" Salyers asked, her eyebrow arched.

Jolie inhaled sharply and hiccupped.

Salyers considered her, then jerked her head toward the door. "You're free to go, Ms. Goodman. But I'll be keeping tabs on you—and your friends. Don't even think about leaving the city."

"Where are Carlotta and Hannah?"

"Ms. Wren and Ms. Kizer were released . . . with similar warnings." The detective hesitated, then said, "I think you should know that both of your friends have had run-ins with the law before."

Jolie blinked.

"Until this investigation is over, Ms. Goodman, you might want to steer clear of questionable company. And trust me, this investigation is only beginning."

On that ominous note, Jolie skedaddled before the woman could change her mind. She walked out of the room one step ahead of her attorney. They stopped at a counter to retrieve Jolie's personal effects which, since everything she'd been wearing and her purse had been confiscated as evidence, consisted of her keys and water-logged wallet. As they rode down one floor on the elevator, she asked, "Now what?"

"Now you sit tight," Vanderpool said. "Remember, the police and the district attorney have to build a case—let them do all the work." She handed Jolie a carbon copy of the restraining order. "And steer clear of Roger LeMon—I know the man, and he's formidable. Plus he's a friend of the police department, even lobbied the city council for raises for the force."

"Salyers told me as much," Jolie said.

"Don't fret. LeMon might be able to pull in a few favors, but that doesn't mean he can get away with murder."

"You think he might have killed Gary?" Jolie asked.

"I have no idea," the woman said, her expression stern. "But something has Mr. LeMon spooked enough for him to take out a restraining order on a girl half his size and half his means."

"*Less* than half his means," Jolie assured her.

As they walked off the elevator, Pam Vanderpool stopped. "Ms. Goodman, do you live alone?"

"Yes."

The older woman pressed her lips together. "Do you have a way to protect yourself?"

"What do you mean?"

"I mean there are already two people dead, and no one seems to know why. Maybe you should stay with a friend in town until this blows over."

Jolie nodded solemnly, embarrassed to admit she didn't have a friend in town with whom she was close enough to ask to hole her up. "I will."

"And here's my card. I sleep with my cell phone, so call if you need me, no matter what time it is."

Jolie gripped the business card in her hand as if it were a lifeline. "I don't know how to thank you for your help."

"Don't thank me," Vanderpool said as she resumed walking. "Thank Beck."

Beck. At the sound of his name, her nerve endings stirred. "How do you know Beck?"

"I've known Beck for years," she said, smiling fondly. "We've worked on many charitable causes together."

Jolie balked. She was a *cause*? She'd had similar thoughts herself concerning Beck's motivation, but to hear someone else say it was like a punch to the spleen.

"I will thank him," Jolie murmured, her cheeks flaming. "When I see him."

"Speak of the devil," the woman said as they entered the narrow lobby, which was deserted except for a security guard and Beck Underwood. Beck tossed aside a newspaper and stood. Jolie's heart beat wildly, and she had the crazy urge to run so she wouldn't have to face him. Since she'd last seen him, he had found jeans and a sweatshirt. His dark blond hair had dried at funny angles. Jolie suspected that she looked less cute after her own dip in the pool and subsequent air-dry.

"Hi," he said.

"Hi," she squeaked.

"She's free to go," Vanderpool said, all business.

He reached out to clasp her hand. "Thanks, Pam."

"You betcha," she said, then marched toward the exit as if she were accustomed to being summoned in the wee hours of the morning.

Jolie listened to the sound of the woman's retreating footsteps as if they were a ticking clock . . . counting down the time until she was alone with Beck. When the door closed with a resounding echo, Jolie finally found the nerve to meet his gaze. Abject mortification bled through her that she had allowed herself to become involved in such a mess . . . and had involved her friends and Beck Underwood by association. She was speechless with humiliation and weak from exhaustion.

He scanned her outfit with serious brown eyes. "How did they treat you in there?"

"Okay," she said, then pressed her lips together. "Ms. Vanderpool arrived just in time—I don't know how to thank you."

He winked. "We'll think of something. For now, let's get you home and in bed."

Since she looked like a ghoul and reeked of chlorine and now had this little murder rap hanging over her head, she was relatively sure that there was no innuendo intended. Still, that didn't keep her sleep-deprived mind from conjuring up a wonderful fantasy of crawling into bed with Beck Underwood and curling up next to his big body, reveling in the protection his presence and his name afforded.

The Buckhead Bubble, as Gary had always called it. The working-class girl in her railed against the double standard, but the nearly indicted girl in her longed to be included. She followed him to a side door, which he held open.

"How do you know Pam Vanderpool?" she asked.

But his answer was thwarted by the flash of a camera. "Mr. Underwood, over here!"

Flash! Flash!

Jolie blinked at the huddle of reporters and cameras gathered, her mouth opening and closing like a guppy's.

"Are you Jolie Goodman?" someone yelled.

"Are you under arrest for murder?"

"Mr. Underwood, is this woman your lover?"

"Come on," Beck growled, wrapping his arm around her shoulder, putting himself between her and the cameras. Frozen with shock, she stumbled to keep up with him, blindly walking forward to the parking lot until they stopped next to a dark-colored SUV. He swung open the door and helped her up into the seat. She didn't miss the concern on his face as he closed her door and glanced over his shoulder. The security guard had stopped the reporters at the mouth of the parking lot, but they were still shooting footage, and Beck would have to drive past them to get out of the lot. Dismay hit her like a slap when she realized how juicy a story it was for the media to cover one of their own. Rival networks of Underwood Broadcasting would be rubbing their hands with glee.

She covered her mouth with her hand, choking back a sob. The man had gone above and beyond the call of duty to help her for no legitimate reason and at great professional risk to himself.

He opened the driver's side door, climbed in, then slammed it shut.

"I'm so sorry," she said. "I'm sorry I got you involved."

"*I* got me involved," he said, his voice brusque. And regretful? "Put on your seat belt," he said, doing the same. "And look away from the cameras when we drive by."

Sensing that talking would only make matters worse, she nodded and stared at her shaking hands. By the time they drove to the exit, reporters were on both sides, so Jolie looked down and shielded her face with her hands. Beck slowed enough to take the curve, then they were speeding away. At the street, he slowed and gave her a wry little smile. "Where do you live?"

"Roswell," she said, pointing left, then gave him the street address and name of her apartment complex. She idly wondered how Carlotta and Hannah had gotten home, feeling yet another gush of remorse for involving them . . . and for trusting them. Their actions—and police records—made her look more guilty.

Beck pulled into the sparse pre-predawn traffic, slowing to allow an indigent pedestrian to cross illegally. "Hope he makes it until morning," Beck said ruefully.

With a start, Jolie wondered if that was how he saw her—as a poor person who needed a break? A handout? She gulped air. Pity? Waves of shame washed over her as they drove down the street. She didn't want the man's charity, but she was in no position to turn it down.

"I assume this will make the news," she said quietly. "You . . . with me, I mean."

He shook his head. "Don't worry about it. I'll make a couple of phone calls, pull in some favors. With any luck, it won't hit the air."

She leaned her head back on the headrest. "Is that how things are done?"

"What do you mean?"

"Favors are owed, favors are exchanged."

He shrugged. "I suppose that's life, isn't it?"

"I wouldn't want you to waste a favor on . . . me."

She felt his gaze on her, but she couldn't look him in the eye. "Oh," he said finally. "Well . . . there's my family name to think of, too."

Jolie wasn't sure if that made her feel better or worse. "I owe you an explanation—I . . . I didn't kill Gary Hagan."

"I suspected as much," he said. "And we can discuss everything later, after you've had a chance to recover."

Although she was grateful for the reprieve, Jolie had never been so thoroughly miserable in her life. Gary was dead, and the people who should believe in her innocence didn't, and the one person who shouldn't did. She felt like a glove that a hand had been ripped from—her right side turned in, her insides exposed. Her body ached with the intensity of a profound wound laid open, but she didn't have the energy to cry.

She concentrated on the rhythm of the engine and tires, the sound of her own breath entering and leaving her body. She closed her eyes, yielding to the hazy sense of nonbeing that sleep promised. Tension drained from her spine, sending the dead weight of her body into the seat.

Her next conscious thought was that the vehicle had stopped. A distant, dark feeling of dread came zooming back, jolting her upright. Moonlit hedges hemmed the nose of the SUV. Slowly Jolie became aware of streetlamps, sidewalks, connected two-story buildings. Her apartment complex.

"We're here," Beck said. "I think."

She nodded.

"You didn't say what your apartment number was."

She looked around to get her bearings, trying to shake the cobwebs from her brain, then pointed. "I'm in that building over there. We can walk."

She undid her seat belt and ran her tongue over her dry lips, moving gingerly to allow her sleep-laden limbs a chance to catch up. Before she realized what was happening, Beck was at the passenger door, helping her down in the dewy darkness. His hand against her waist, her back, sent a perilous feeling spiraling through her chest—she wasn't afraid of him, but she was afraid of how good his touch felt. She couldn't remember the last time a man had touched her just to comfort her instead of as a prelude to a sexual encounter. She leaned on Beck liberally while walking to her apartment door. She unlocked the door and pushed it open, overwhelmed with a sense of relief at being home.

Flipping on lights, she stumbled inside, not caring what Beck thought of her crocheted coasters and shabby furniture. He looked around, hands on hips, his expression unreadable, then he finally nodded toward her ancient sofa draped with a camouflaging throw. "Looks like a comfortable couch," he said, and from the tone of his voice she realized with a start that he was looking for a spot to crash.

"You want to stay?" she asked, unable to keep the surprise out of her voice.

He turned over his wrist to consult his watch. "Well, it *is* four in the morning." Beck cleared his throat. "And considering everything that's happened, I thought it best if someone stayed with you."

Was he afraid she would do something to hurt herself, or like Vanderpool, that someone else might? At the moment, Jolie didn't care. "That would be nice."

He returned to the door to check its security, then walked over to the picture window above the couch, pulled up the blinds, and tested the closing mechanisms. "Do you have any other windows?" he asked.

"Only in the bedroom," she said, pointing. "Come on, I'll get you a pillow and a blanket."

"Just a pillow will be fine," he said, following her into the bedroom.

He scrutinized the room where she slept, but his expression was devoid of personal interest in her intimate space—he seemed more concerned about the layout of the room. He strode to the window and nodded at the two-foot cactus she'd set on the floor beneath the sill.

"Nice touch," he said approvingly. He raised the blinds

and ran his hands along the closure, then frowned. "Have you had this window open lately?"

Jolie shook her head and walked over, her heart jumping in her chest.

"This latch is open." He leaned down to peer at the window sill, then indicated the clean scrape in the dust. "Looks like someone has either come in or left by this window in the past few days."

Her lungs squeezed as she remembered the finger swipe in the dust on her bookshelf headboard. She really needed to dust more often.

"Have you noticed anything missing?"

"No." Although she hadn't looked. She gasped and hurried to her hand-me-down dresser, lifting the lid of her jewelry box with trepidation. Her shoulders fell in relief when she removed the little felt bag holding her pearl choker. "Everything's here," she said.

She turned to find him studying her, and she flushed when she realized how meager her "everything" must seem to him. "They were my mother's," she murmured.

He nodded, then gestured vaguely toward the other rooms. "Any stereo equipment missing? Computer? Cash?"

She shook her head. "There's only the computer on my desk, and it's almost as outdated as my television. And . . . I don't keep cash here."

Nor in her bank account, but that was off topic.

He scratched his head, then spotted the fire extinguisher on her nightstand. "Have you had a fire recently?"

She flushed to the roots of her gritty hair. "That's the closest thing I had to a weapon."

He looked incredulous. "You've been sleeping here alone and afraid, with a fire extinguisher to protect you?"

She sagged onto the foot of her bed. "I didn't feel as if

I was in imminent danger." She nodded toward the window. "If someone was in my apartment, they obviously didn't mean me harm."

"This time," he added, his mouth drawn downward. "I've probably obliterated any prints," he said, but used the hem of his sweatshirt to refasten the window. The movement gave her a glimpse of the planes of his brown stomach, and she remembered the way he'd looked climbing out of Sammy's pool, his boxers clamped to his body, water streaming off his powerful shoulders. A wholly inappropriate pang of lust hit her, and she stood abruptly to distract herself, turning her back to remove one of the two pillows from her bed.

"You should report the entry to the police," he said, coming up behind her.

"I will," she said, then turned and smiled up at him. "Thank you for . . . thank you." She handed him the pillow and their fingers brushed. His eyes were dark with concern and other emotions she didn't want to investigate—regret? The most eligible bachelor in Atlanta probably could have found a more entertaining way to spend his evening, and with a less complicated partner. Or two.

"Try to get some sleep," he said. "But yell if you suspect that anything is wrong."

Everything was wrong, but Jolie nodded. He walked out, leaving the bedroom door ajar and a warm feeling of assurance in the cool air. She flipped off the light and crawled on top of the bed covers fully clothed. Hugging her remaining pillow, she willed her body to indulge in as much rest as possible, because she suspected the light of day would only reveal more and bigger dilemmas.

The dilemma sleeping on her couch notwithstanding.

Twenty

Jolie awoke to a sound alien to a single person—the shower running. Adrenaline shot through her, bringing her upright. Then she saw the "Property of Fulton County, Georgia" sweats she was still wearing, and the horrific events of the previous evening came crashing back down on her. Her first instinct was to pull the covers over her head, but her mother had once told her that the only thing that went away faster if a person ignored it was time.

The clock read 11:47 A.M. The day was already almost half gone.

She pushed herself up and took stock of her physical condition, running her finger over the knot on her forehead—better, but tender. The bandage on her hand seemed a little tighter, but the absence of dried blood indicated that the wound had not reopened during the night. Her throat and adenoids felt raw from the pool water she'd ingested and expelled violently.

She dared a glance in the mirror and cringed. Her fine, frizzy hair had exploded to new heights, and there wasn't enough concealer in Neiman's makeup department to neutralize the circles under her eyes. The sweat suit hung off her like a feed sack on a scarecrow.

She had never been a woman who rolled out of bed looking particularly good, and this morning was especially unkind.

She straightened the covers on her bed and ventured into the hall. The shower was still going full blast and she hurried past so as not to dwell on the fact that Beck Underwood was standing naked in her shower, using her soap and her towels. Her face burned when she thought about the relative inelegance of her bath accoutrements, but at least he would have found everything clean—it was only dusting that she abhorred.

She scanned the couch where he'd slept and wondered if the big, lumpy sofa had afforded him any rest at all. Her extra feather pillow was still indented from his head. She returned it to her bedroom, thinking Gary had been the last person to share her bed or her pillow, although he had spent the entire night on only one or two occasions.

Tears filled her eyes when the breathtaking sadness of him not being alive hit her anew. Maybe Gary Hagan wouldn't have saved the world, and maybe he'd been in his share of trouble, but he didn't deserve to be shot in the chest and abandoned under a pile of outerwear.

The cordless phone rang, jangling her nerves. She couldn't think of anyone she wanted to talk to at the moment—unless it was Detective Salyers saying the murder had been solved and she was off the hook. But without caller ID, she had to take her chances and hit the button to receive the call. "Hello?"

"Jolie?" a man asked.

"Yes."

"This is Michael Lane. I just opened my paper—I called to see if you were okay."

"I'm fine," she said breezily, wondering if she should ask what the paper said. "A little shaken up, but fine."

"Yes, well, under the circumstances, I was thinking it might be better for you to take some time off from Neiman's."

She gripped the phone. "Michael, please—I *need* this job."

He sighed. "After the incident at the Manolo event yesterday—"

"Give me another chance," she pleaded. "Michael, to be blunt, I need the money." Else, how would she pay off the nightclothes?

He sighed again. "Okay, but only because I'm a wonderful person."

"Yes, you are," she said. "I'll see you tomorrow." She disconnected the call before he could change his mind, but the phone rang again almost instantly. She punched the TALK button. "Hello?"

"Jolie? This is Trini Janklo, upstairs."

Jolie rolled her eyes upward. "Hello, Mrs. Janklo. How are you?"

"Shocked, frankly. I opened the *Atlanta Journal-Constitution* this morning to find your name connected with the murder of a young man. Is that the same man I heard you arguing with?"

Her heart fluttered and she closed her eyes briefly. "We weren't arguing, Mrs. Janklo. This is all a big misunderstanding. You can't believe everything you hear . . . or read."

"It says you were so distraught that you tried to drown yourself."

Her eyes widened—no wonder Michael had been concerned. "That's simply not true—"

"I want you to know that I've already contacted management about having you evicted."

Her jaw dropped. "What? Why?"

"How am I supposed to sleep at night knowing there's a murderer living right underneath me?"

She pinched the bridge of her nose. "Mrs. Janklo, I'm *not* a murderer."

But the woman had already hung up, leaving an angry dial tone in her wake.

Jolie stabbed the DISCONNECT button and exhaled, dragging her hand down her face. She went to the door and unlocked it in search of her own Sunday paper. She opened the door and retrieved the paper, but when she straightened, a reporter was sprinting down the sidewalk toward her, his cameraman running behind him. "Ms. Goodman! Will you answer a few questions? Is there a love triangle between you, Gary Hagan, and Beckham Underwood?"

She was stupefied. "No!"

"Didn't Mr. Underwood spend the night here?"

She spun and scrambled back inside the door, slamming it hard. The door to the bathroom opened and Beck came out dressed in his jeans, pulling the sweatshirt over his head. He was frowning. "What was that?"

"A TV reporter," she said, distracted and comforted by his appearance . . . and self-conscious about her own.

He picked up his cell phone from a side table and began punching in a number. "What station are they from?"

"I didn't notice."

"Man or woman?"

"Man."

"What did he say?"

She wet her lips. "I don't think you want to know, but they're aware that you spent the night here."

He put down the phone before he finished dialing, then jammed his feet into his sneakers and strode toward the door. "I'll take care of this."

She wanted to watch, but decided she'd better take a peek at the paper. There she was, bottom half of page two: PARTY CRASHERS TERRORIZE BUCKHEAD HOME—BODY DISCOVERED.

Her heart dropped. Peppered with appropriate amounts of "allegeds" and "unnamed sources," the article mentioned her name ("questioned for the murder of the boyfriend for whom she filed a missing persons report a month ago"), Carlotta's name ("questioned in connection to widespread looting in the host's home during the party"), and Hannah's name ("reportedly assaulted a guest and held other guests hostage"). The article stipulated that no charges had been filed and hinted that it was due in part to "Goodman's unexplained association with Atlanta socialite, Beckham Underwood."

She closed the paper with a crunch just as Beck walked back in the front door. "That guy won't be bothering you anymore," he said.

"What did you do?" she asked, biting into her lip.

"Smashed his camera."

She held out the paper. "You might want to read this before you . . . do anything else on my behalf." She jerked a thumb toward the bathroom. "I'm going to take a shower. If you're gone when I come out, I'll understand."

He gave her a pointed look. "I thought we were going to talk."

"Oh." She tried to smile. "Right. I'll hurry."

She closed the door behind her and stripped off the offensive sweat suit, tossing it into a heap in the floor. Beck's towel was draped neatly over the shower-curtain rod. She withdrew a fresh towel from a tiny closet, then stepped under the shower spray and adjusted the head back down to her level. Her skin tingled at the intimacy of sharing a bathroom with Beck, and her mind reeled at the series of events that had brought them together in this—how had the newspaper worded it?—"unexplained association."

Protecting her bandaged hand from the water as much as possible, she scrubbed her hair and skin, then toweled off and shrugged into a long terry robe to make the dash to her bedroom to dress. When she opened the door, the smell of strong coffee reached her, as well as the sounds of cooking. She poked her head around the corner to see Beck, his back to her, tending to something on the stove that smelled wonderful. At least the article hadn't scared him off. He caught sight of her and waved her forward. "I made grilled cheese and tomato sandwiches—hope that's okay."

Jolie's stomach growled and she nodded. "Let me change."

"You're okay," he said. "Let's eat while the food is hot."

If he was so nonchalant about her being in a state of near undress, she didn't want to overreact. She joined him in the kitchen nook and withdrew plates and napkins from the cabinets, maneuvering around him with an ease that belied their impending discussion. A few minutes later they were settled at the rectangular plain maple table that doubled as her desk, sharing the space with her desktop computer. The chairs were mismatched, a collection of odds and ends from her parents' home that she'd painted white. Beck claimed a chair, seemingly unaware that he looked out of place in the quaint domestic scene.

Jolie sipped the coffee, murmuring in appreciation

when the warm liquid spread through her. She waited until she had eaten one sandwich and Beck had eaten two before she said, "I guess you read the article."

He nodded. "Want to fill in the holes?"

She set down her cup and retold the story, starting from when Gary had first disappeared.

"So the day I first met you, the detective had come to tell you about Hagan's car being recovered."

"Right." Then she told him about agreeing to attend the party with Carlotta on the chance she'd meet someone who had known Gary. "I didn't know we had crashed until we were already there," she felt compelled to explain, then realized the ridiculousness of minding that she'd been labeled a party-crasher in the larger scheme of things.

"I recognized Roger LeMon from a picture I found in one of Gary's photo albums. And later, Kyle Coffee."

"Do you have the photo?" Beck asked.

She nodded and rifled through papers next to her computer until she found it. "That's Gary next to LeMon, and Coffee is in the middle."

When Beck looked at the photo, he blinked.

"Do you recognize someone?" she asked.

He glanced up. "Besides Russell Island?"

She frowned. "Hannah's boyfriend? Let me see."

He pointed. "Different hair and he was heavier, but that's him. And that's his wife next to him."

She gasped. "So there were two more people at the party who knew Gary. Is the woman next to LeMon his wife?"

He lifted his shoulders in a shrug. "I never met his wife."

"How about the woman standing next to Kyle Coffee?"

"I don't know her either."

"Do you know the fifth man?"

He studied the picture, then rubbed his hand over his mouth. "I've seen him before. I want to say his name is Gordon something."

Jolie's head whipped around. "Gordon?" Gary's scribbled note on the pad rose in her mind: *Extra door key for Gordon.* It was too pat to be a coincidence. "Beck, please—can you remember his last name?"

He scratched his head. "I want to say it was a German name—something like 'bear,' but an unusual spelling." Then he shook his head. "I can't say for sure, but I can find out." He held up the picture. "May I borrow this?"

She hesitated, then felt foolish—Beck had done nothing but help her. "Sure. Do you know how these men are connected?"

He splayed his hand. "Movers and shakers, second-generation family businessmen. Like me," he added wryly. "They might belong to the same country club, or live in the same neighborhood."

"Have you ever heard of them doing anything illegal?"

Beck cleared his throat and sat back. "Like what?"

Surprised by his retreating body language, she spoke carefully. "Detective Salyers told me that Gary had a record for dealing cocaine in Orlando."

"And you think he might have gotten back into the business?"

"I don't know." She wet her lips. "Do you remember last Wednesday when you found me sitting in my car outside the High Museum?"

"Yeah, you were spooked."

"I was spooked because when I got in the car, Gary was waiting for me. He had just gotten out of the car before you walked up."

His head jutted forward. "Did he hurt you?"

"No. He told me he'd been set up, that he hadn't murdered the woman who was found in his car."

"I take it he didn't say *who* had set him up?"

"No. But I wondered if drugs might be involved."

Beck pulled on his chin. "I guess it's possible."

There was that hesitation again, that reluctance. Beck had a lot of money at his disposal—perhaps he had dabbled in drugs himself. Unease invaded her chest and she decided to change the subject. She pulled a sheet of paper and a pen from the office clutter on her table and did a rudimentary sketch of the tattoo on Roger LeMon's wrist. "Does this symbol mean anything to you?"

He squinted at the paper, then shook his head. "What is it?"

"A tattoo that LeMon and Coffee both have."

"Fraternity?"

"Friday night at the media reception, Carlotta and I cornered Coffee and asked him about the tattoo. He said it had ruined his life."

"What did he mean?"

"I don't know—Roger LeMon interrupted us, made some joke about Coffee's wife not liking the tattoo, then put Coffee in a cab. I think by that time LeMon had recognized me." She took a long drink from her mug. "Last night LeMon filed a restraining order against me."

"*What?*"

"He told the police that I've been harassing him, that he came to Sammy's party but had to leave because he was afraid I would 'accost' him."

"I was there, and it was clear you were trying to avoid him. Do you think he had something to do with the murder?"

She nodded. "I think he did it and set me up, then filed the restraining order to prove he left the party."

"To give himself an alibi."

"Right." Jolie stood and began clearing their impromptu meal.

He joined her, his expression thoughtful . . . and bemused. "So your theory is that LeMon killed the woman in your boyfriend's car and set him up for it, then killed your boyfriend and set you up for it?"

Jolie's hands stilled. When he put it that way, the story did sound too fantastic to believe. She flushed and leaned against the kitchen counter, her energy suddenly zapped. She was focusing on the puzzle pieces to detach herself from the fact that Gary was dead. She covered her mouth with her hand. "You're right. It's probably much simpler than I'm making it out to be—a debt owed, a drug deal gone bad. Roger LeMon might have nothing to do with it."

"Didn't you say that your boyfriend's apartment burned a few days after he disappeared?"

She nodded.

"Was the cause ever determined?"

"I don't know."

"Have you considered that the fire might have been directed toward Hagan as a warning? Or maybe to destroy evidence of, say, a drug deal?"

She shook her head, then sighed. "The thought hadn't occurred to me. I guess I didn't want to think that Gary could be involved in something that . . . sordid."

"So . . . were you in love with this guy?"

Startled, she looked up, and the air sizzled without the benefit of a fried sandwich.

Beck lifted his hand. "Never mind—that's none of my business."

Before she could agree or disagree, his cell phone rang. He stepped to the doorway to take the call, and Jolie decided to take advantage of the time to dress. She walked to the bedroom and closed the door, her mind racing with conflicting emotions—how *did* she feel about Gary . . . before, and now that he was gone?

Betrayed, mostly, on so many levels. She had genuinely believed that he cared for her, although she had sensed that Gary himself had been surprised by his feelings for her. It was almost as if he'd gone out with her on a lark—the handsome, eligible man about town who dates a quiet, spindly girl—with no pedigree or particular promise as a socialite—and becomes enchanted by her lack of pretense. At times she wondered if her conservative sensibility had attracted him because it helped to keep him grounded, or if he simply liked the idea that she would never compete with him. Regardless, she was beginning to think she loved the idea of Gary loving *her* more than she actually loved *him*. Had she mistaken flattery on her part for love?

And on those occasions when he'd looked at her with contrite eyes—when she'd thought that he was silently apologizing for underestimating her—had he instead been trying to think of a way to reveal the underhanded side of his life? She had sensed that he was struggling with something, but she hadn't asked.

Hadn't cared enough to ask. If she had, maybe he would've confessed the truth and she could have persuaded him to go to the police.

She pursed her mouth. On the other hand, she could have wound up as fish food in the Chattahoochee River.

She dressed quickly and opted for a few makeup basics to perk up her complexion while pondering Beck's interest in her feelings for Gary. Maybe he was feeling guilty over kissing her at Sammy's party. Or maybe if she admitted that Gary had been the love of her life, he could bow out with no pressure, no strings.

Jolie opened the bedroom door and walked into the living room quietly because Beck was still on the phone, his back to her.

". . . Jolie doesn't know," he said.

Her stomach plunged—at his words and at the guarded tone of his voice. She stepped back out of sight and strained to hear him, her heart hammering.

". . . You should be thinking of a story. Yes, I got it from her and I have it with me . . . I shouldn't be here much longer."

She tried to make sense of the words—a story, the photo he'd gotten from her . . .

The answer hit her so clearly that she almost laughed out loud at her stupidity—she'd just given an exclusive interview to a man who had his own news organization! Of course he was going to use it to his advantage. A part of her didn't even mind. Beck had saved her life, after all, and provided her with an attorney. But she felt so damn foolish, thinking he was helping her for altruistic reasons or maybe simply because he liked her.

She shook her head, blinking back tears. Then, it was as if something inside of her switched to "on." She straightened and inhaled deeply, filling her chest with resolve. She was almost relieved Beck was using the information she'd given him; it put their relationship on a professional plane. Neither of them would have emotional ties to the situation. She would no longer feel guilty about involving him, and she would no longer entertain fantasies about the man. Her head would be clear to navigate through the mess that Gary had left behind.

"Right," he said. "I'll take care of everything."

Jolie fumbled with her bedroom door to make noise, then acted as if she were just walking out.

Beck looked up and had the grace to blush. "Yeah," he said into the phone, his voice louder. "I'll be there as soon as I can. Okay." He closed the phone and looked apologetic. "I assumed you weren't exactly in the mood to take me house hunting today as we'd planned."

She nodded carefully, surprised that he'd remembered, then gestured to the computer. "How about if I print some listings to take with you? It'll only take a few minutes."

He glanced toward the door as if he were eager to leave, but nodded. "Sure."

She booted up the machine, trying to school her emotions as he walked over to stand behind her chair. She sensed the invisible barrier between them in the physical distance he maintained and in the rigid posture she maintained.

In her most professional tone, Jolie explained the search criteria—address, price range, amenities—then fed the program several scenarios of his responses and printed the results.

"See?" she said cheerfully, handing him the printouts. "That didn't take long."

He took the papers, but he averted his gaze. "Thanks."

"Beck," she said softly, "I will certainly understand if you decide to continue your house search without me."

He pursed his lips and nodded. "We both have other things going on right now."

"Right."

"Right." He pushed his hand through his hair. "Well, I'd better be going. Thanks for the sofa."

It was hard to smile, knowing the things that were going

through his mind, but she tried. "Thanks for the cheese sandwiches."

"You have Pam's number?"

She nodded.

He started to leave, then turned back. "Listen . . . I have a suite at the hotel. You're welcome to the extra bed."

She had to give him credit for trying to keep his source close by, and God help her, he was difficult to refuse. "Thanks, but I'll be fine."

He looked unconvinced. "I'll call you."

She followed him to the door, smiling until it was closed. Jolie leaned against the door and allowed herself a few seconds of quiet heartbreak, of wishing things could have been different, before forcing her thoughts to how to most constructively spend the afternoon. What was it Leann had said about her—that she always took things in stride? This was no time to break stride. Or to break down.

She gasped, realizing that Leann didn't even know about Gary, or that she'd almost been arrested. She called her friend's cell phone, relieved when Leann answered.

"Hello?"

"Hey, it's Jolie. Can you talk?"

"Just for a little while," Leann said quietly. "My sister . . . lost the baby early this morning."

"Oh *no*," Jolie said, her heart squeezing. "What happened?"

"Well, the doctors said all along that miscarriage was a possibility. I guess her body just couldn't handle the stress."

"You sound exhausted," Jolie said.

"I am," she said tearfully.

"How's your sister taking it?"

"Not well. You know at first she didn't want the baby,

couldn't bear the thought of raising it by herself, then she came around, and now . . . well, she feels so guilty."

The word of the day, Jolie decided. "Leann, I'm so sorry. Is there anything I can do?"

Leann released a shaky sigh. "No, but thanks for offering. What's up with you?"

Jolie couldn't bring herself to heap more bad news on her friend's personal tragedy. "I hate to ask, but I was wondering if you'd mind if I stayed in your apartment for a while."

"Of course not. Mrs. Janklo making you crazy?"

"Right," she said with a little laugh, although she suspected her friend sensed that other reasons were afoot.

"Sure, stay as long you need to. I probably won't be back for at least another couple of weeks, maybe longer."

"Thanks. Get some rest. Tell your sister how sorry I am. I'll call you later in the week."

"Okay. Bye."

Jolie hung up the phone feeling horribly self-centered. People all over the world were suffering through tragedies. She couldn't imagine the toll it would take on a person's mind to lose a baby at four months. And all this time she'd been selfishly thinking how Leann's sister's crisis had taken her friend from her, forcing her to make new friends.

Carlotta and Hannah. A knot formed in Jolie's stomach just thinking about her two party-crashing cohorts. They were all in a heap of trouble. She wanted to call Carlotta, but Salyers' warning to steer clear of the women's company reverberated in her head.

The phone rang again, and she picked it up with trepidation.

"Hello?"

"Jolie Goodman?" a woman asked.

"Yes."

"This is the Atlanta city morgue. A Detective Salyers gave me your name and number to contact for a next of kin for G. Hagar."

A lump formed in her throat. "Hagan," she corrected hoarsely.

"Hagan," the woman repeated. "The autopsy is done; the body needs to be claimed."

Jolie bit her tongue to keep from retorting that the woman needed to get a bedside manner. "There is no next of kin that I know of. What do I do?"

The woman sighed, mightily put out. "Somebody needs to let us know where to send the body to be embalmed. Two more days, and the state will start making decisions for you."

"Okay. What do I do?" she repeated calmly.

"Come down, identify the body, and fill out a form," the woman said in a bored voice.

Jolie swallowed hard. "I'll be there within the hour." She took down some directions and disconnected the call with a shaking hand. She didn't think she could do this alone, but who could she call? She hesitated, then found her purse and rummaged for a card. Working her mouth from side to side, she picked up the phone and dialed, nearly hanging up twice before the phone was answered with a groggy "Hell . . . o?"

"Carlotta . . . It's me, Jolie."

The woman moaned. "Christ, this had better not have anything to do with dead bodies."

"Well, actually . . ."

Twenty-one

"I don't believe I'm doing this," Carlotta muttered as they walked through the doors of the morgue. She wore dark sunglasses and looked like a movie star.

"I can't tell you how much I appreciate your coming," Jolie said. She wore a Band-Aid on her forehead and looked like a movie star's "person."

"If I so much as see a dead fly, I'm out of here."

"What can I do to make it up to you?"

"Get my car out of the police impound lot on a frigging Sunday afternoon."

Jolie winced. "They won't release your new car?"

"Not until tomorrow, *after* the twenty-four-hour trial period has expired."

"You're going to have to *buy* the car?"

Carlotta sighed. "Technically, I've already bought it. If I had taken it back this morning as planned, they would've ripped up the contract. Now I'm stuck, big time."

Jolie winced again. "If it's any consolation, the police have my car, too."

"The one that Gary stole?"

She nodded. "The police found it about a half mile from Sammy's house, but they're still 'processing' it." She tried to smile. "At least the car you got stuck with is a nice car."

"Yeah, well I've learned my lesson about borrowing things—I just wish I hadn't learned it all in one weekend."

Jolie had money concerns, too, but she knew the ruined clothes and now the car only heaped fuel onto the fire of Carlotta's financial problems. She felt responsible . . . sort of, but her hands were tied. "Have you talked to Hannah?"

"Briefly—she's prostrate with grief over her beloved Russell." Carlotta rolled her eyes.

"Remember the photograph I showed you with Gary and LeMon and Kyle Coffee? Russell is in it."

"He is?"

"Beck said he'd changed his looks, but it was definitely him."

"*Beck* said?"

Jolie flushed. "He took me home last night—er, this morning and . . . stayed. On the couch."

"Sure he did."

Ignoring the sarcasm, Jolie said, "And he said the fifth guy in the picture was named Gordon something, maybe Gordon Bear, with a German spelling?"

Carlotta shook her head. "Doesn't ring a bell. But I need to remember to ask Hannah if Russell has the same tattoo as LeMon and Coffee."

"May I help you?" a security guard asked in a funereal tone as they approached his desk.

Jolie swallowed twice before she found her voice. "I'm here . . . to identify a . . . person."

"Are they expecting you?"

"Yes."

"Third floor."

They moved toward the elevator in tandem and boarded the empty car. "Your boyfriend didn't have *any* family?" Carlotta asked.

Jolie pushed the button for the third floor and the door slid closed. "None that I know of, and none the police could find."

"Wow, that's kind of sad," Carlotta said as they were carried up.

Nodding, Jolie seconded her friend's observation. There was being alone in the world, and then there was being *alone* in the world. The door slid open and they walked out onto yet more tiled floor. The temperature here, though, brought to mind the phrase "meat locker." Jolie shivered at the implication alone.

"I mean, my family aren't the Cleavers," Carlotta whispered, "but at least someone in my tribe would claim my body if I got offed."

Jolie's eyes burned and she sniffed.

Carlotta looked over. "Ah, Jolie, I'm sorry. This has to be tough for you, seeing him again like this."

She nodded, terrified. Plus the chemicals in the air were killing her eyes. They walked toward a rounded counter reminiscent of a nurses' station. Two women in green scrubs were filling out paperwork and eating stromboli sandwiches—the source of the "chemicals."

"May I help you?" one of the women asked, then took a bite out of her sandwich.

Jolie rubbed her nose. "Yes, my name is Jolie Goodman. I received a call about an hour ago regarding . . . Gary Hagan."

The chewing woman frowned, then looked at the other woman, who was eating potato chips and licking her fingers. "Hagan?"

"Last night's gunshot," the licker said.

The chewer nodded. "Oh, yeah." She pointed down the hall with a tomato-sauce stained pinkie. "Ward Two."

"Gawd," Carlotta muttered when they started off in search of Ward II, "I may never eat again."

Jolie tried to smile through the panic that was beginning to build in her stomach. Since last night, every time she pictured Gary dead, she had forced the image from her mind. Now she not only had to relive it, but she would have brand-new images with which to torment herself.

They walked past Ward I, then located the stainless-steel double doors of Ward II. Jolie lifted her hand to knock, felt foolish and pushed one door open. Just inside, a young man in a white orderly uniform looked up from a computer. "May I help you?"

"I'm Jolie Goodman, here regarding Gary Hagan."

He looked over the top of his glasses. "Spell that, please."

She did, and while he tapped on his keyboard she looked around the room. The temperature was at least ten degrees cooler in here than in the hallway. Two opposing walls were lined with enormous stainless-steel file drawers . . . for cadavers. Her knees started to feel a little slack.

"Sign here," the man said, pointing to a line on a sheet of paper attached to a clipboard. "And I need to see a picture ID."

She signed her name, then removed her still-damp wallet and flashed her driver's license.

"Follow me."

She did, and Carlotta lagged a few steps behind. Carrying the clipboard, he consulted numbers on the sheet and the cabinets, finally reaching down to grab the handle of a drawer on the second row, about knee height. At the last second, he looked up.

"You should prepare yourself to see your loved one in what might seem like an unnatural state," he said in a rehearsed monotone. "Your loved one will be nude, but modestly covered with a cloth. In the event the person suffered wounds to the head, arms, or torso before they passed away, please know that those wounds will be visible."

Next to her, Carlotta grunted. "I'm not looking."

"Let me know when you're ready," he said.

Jolie nodded and steeled herself as the young man slid the drawer out from the wall. She stared at the still face of the dead man, her heart thumping against her breastbone.

Carlotta looked over Jolie's shoulder. "I thought Gary was white."

Jolie sagged. "He is—that's not Gary."

The young orderly's eyes widened behind his glasses, then he consulted his clipboard again. "Oh, you're right. Sorry 'bout that."

"Christ," Carlotta muttered.

He slid the first man back into the wall, then pulled open the next drawer over. A nauseating medicinal odor filled the air. As awful as it was to see Gary's ashen face, at least his eyes were closed and he looked peaceful, Jolie decided. If one's gaze didn't stray to the two-inch round black hole in the middle of his chest. Her own chest constricted painfully.

"Yes," she said, nodding. "That's Gary Hagan." Carlotta grabbed her hand for a surprising squeeze and Jolie was grateful.

"Okeydoke," the orderly said, closing the drawer with a metallic click. He pointed to the clipboard. "Sign here and here and I'll get the personal effects."

She did, blinking away the tears gathered in the corners of her eyes, then followed the young man back to the front. He consulted another computer screen and gave an exasperated sigh. "The personal effects are in police custody—sorry. But I need to know where you want the body to be sent."

"Leed Funeral Home." Jolie extended a card for the small funeral chapel on the northern side of Buckhead that she'd found in the Yellow Pages ("In your hour of need, lean on Leed.") When she got her broker business off the ground, she was definitely going to come up with a catchy slogan and take out an ad. "They're expecting the . . . Gary."

"Okay, you're all set." The orderly smiled. "Just go back out these doors the way you came. And have a nice day."

They exited into the hall and Jolie stopped to gulp fresh air.

Carlotta jammed her hands on her hips. "Ugh. I complain about my job way too much. Are you okay?"

Jolie nodded, trying to dispel the thought of Gary being warehoused like an auto part. They made their way past Ward I, where two uniformed police officers stood by and mournful cries were audible from inside the room. Jolie's heart went out to the family. The door opened suddenly and Detective Salyers emerged to speak to the officers. They nodded obediently, then left.

Salyers turned and her face registered surprise and recognition. "Ms. Goodman." Her gaze darted to Carlotta. "Ms. Wren."

"Hello, Detective," Jolie said.

"I suppose you're here to make arrangements for Mr. Hagan."

"That's right."

Salyers' face looked grave. "Well, this is opportune—I have news."

"What?"

"The woman found in Mr. Hagan's car has been identified."

Jolie glanced at the closed doors, her heart welling for the unknown family. "Who . . . who is she?"

"Janet Chisolm LeMon, wife of Roger LeMon."

Jolie gasped and covered her mouth.

"The man didn't know his own wife was missing?" Carlotta asked.

"According to Mr. LeMon, his wife was supposed to be on a spiritual retreat in upstate New York. She wasn't allowed to contact anyone and no one was allowed to contact her."

Jolie scoffed. "Who loses track of their spouse for a month?"

"Two of Mrs. LeMon's friends confirmed his story, and I have to say that he seems pretty torn up about her death."

"If he didn't know she was missing, how was she identified?"

"Her suitcase and purse were pulled out of three feet of mud at the bottom of the river. Ms. Goodman, you should know that Mr. LeMon has admitted that his wife was having an affair with Mr. Hagan."

Jolie gaped. "He told me he didn't even know Gary."

"He said he lied for his wife's sake because she had ended the affair."

"But doesn't that give him a motive for killing Gary?" Carlotta said.

Salyers crossed her arms. "Actually, Mr. LeMon seems to think that Mr. Hagan killed Mrs. LeMon because she ended the affair, then you, Ms. Goodman, killed Mr. Hagan in a jealous rage."

Jolie fumed, shaking her head. "That's insane."

"But it would explain your preoccupation with Mr. LeMon."

"I'm not preoccupied with Roger LeMon! Don't you think it's strange that his name keeps popping up in the investigation?"

"So does yours, Ms. Goodman."

Jolie frowned. "How did she die?"

"Gunshot. The weapon was also pulled from the mud, registered to Mr. Hagan."

Jolie was still digesting that troubling detail when the door to Ward I opened and Roger LeMon came staggering out, wiping his eyes. He immediately zeroed in on Jolie, pointing at her. "What's *she* doing here?"

"Ms. Goodman is here on a personal matter," Salyers said in a calming voice.

"Seeing about that killer boyfriend of yours?" he shouted. "You ought to see what he did to my wife!"

Jolie shrank back while Salyers put her hand on his arm.

"I should thank you for killing Gary Hagan! You saved me from killing the bastard myself!"

"That's enough, Mr. LeMon," Salyers said. "Come on, I'll walk you to your car."

She gave Jolie a look that said to stay put until they were out of sight, then she led him to the elevator.

"He seems upset all right," Carlotta murmured as the elevator door closed. "But is he upset about his wife being dead, or about her being identified?"

Jolie bit into her lip. "Good question. The thing is, for all

I know, Gary *could* have had an affair with Janet LeMon."

"Did he ever talk about his old girlfriends?"

"No, although he did refer to one simply as a fatal attraction, and I found a card in his things that looked as if it might have come from someone . . . clingy."

"Do you still have the card and the envelope?"

"The police do."

"Then they should be able to do DNA tests to see if Janet LeMon was his fatal attraction."

"Even if she was, that doesn't mean that Gary killed her."

"True."

Jolie mulled over the new information as they walked past Licker and Chewer.

"Talk about a bad day," Chewer said. "The man lost his best friend, then his *wife*."

"Death comes in threes," Licker said emphatically.

"Excuse me," Jolie said leaning over. "Did you say that Roger LeMon had also lost his best friend?"

Licker nodded and flipped through a stack of papers. "Here it is—killed in a car accident in Vegas just this morning. The body should be here any time now. Name was Coffee. Kyle Coffee."

Twenty-two

Jolie was a bona fide basket case on the drive home. She'd done her best to keep her panic at bay around Carlotta, but after they'd picked at a salad and she'd dropped her friend at her townhouse, Jolie had yielded to the shakes. Her mind ran in circles, shifting bits and pieces of the puzzle around to see if one detail would fall unexpectedly in place next to another. Only she kept coming up with the same scenario: Gary had killed Janet LeMon, and Roger LeMon had killed Gary in retaliation. It was a classic lovers' triangle, except LeMon was trying to position *her* as the third party.

The news of Coffee's death had shaken her. A car accident seemed too pat, too coincidental. Coffee was a loose cannon whose range was extended with each cocktail. Whatever he had been on the verge of telling them at that party had probably gotten him killed.

She flipped on her turn signal and veered right onto Roswell Road from Peachtree in the waning light, eager to arrive home . . . or rather, at Leann's apartment, located in another building in the complex. She had arranged to have her land-line calls forwarded to Leann's number, then packed a duffel bag of clothes and toiletries and tossed it in the trunk before leaving, so she wouldn't have to go back to her own place when she returned.

Last night's irregular sleep was catching up to her, along with the day's events. And her palm was throbbing again beneath the bandage. Being tired *and* nervous was a dangerous combination on any roadway, but in Atlanta traffic, the mixture was almost guaranteed deadly. She fought to stay awake.

Suddenly a pair of headlights came zooming up behind her. Adrenaline flooded her limbs at the reminder that something could go wrong so quickly. She tapped the brake and gripped the steering wheel tighter. The car moved into the left lane, presumably to pass her, but when the car came abreast of hers, it cut into her lane, scraping metal against metal.

Jolie screamed and glanced over at the other driver. The man sneered at her and recognition hit: the man from the parking garage who had been having "car trouble." He cut his wheel right again. He was trying to kill her. She hit the brakes, sending her car into a skid onto the grassy shoulder. She fought to regain control, then guided the car to a safe stop while the other car roared away, lost in the sea of taillights heading north. Her pulse pounded in her ears, and the bandage on her hand was bloody from gripping the wheel so hard.

She put on her hazard lights and checked to make sure that everything was in working order (on the car and on her person) before pulling back into traffic. This was perfect timing too—just when she was on the verge of returning her rental car and retrieving her violated Mercury, she had another insurance claim on her hands. Then there were the clothes, of course.

Top that with a funeral bill for Gary, and she was pretty much going to be in debt the rest of her life unless she could sell Beck Underwood a palace and get her brokerage business under way. Oh, and stay out of prison.

At the next traffic light, she made a U-turn into the southbound lanes. No way was she going back to the apartment complex tonight. And Carlotta's place was already crowded with her brother. She would simply have to get a hotel room. Then another solution presented itself.

She removed her cell phone and punched in a number with her thumb. After a couple of rings, a voice came on the line. "This is Beck."

"Beck . . . this is Jolie."

"Hi. I saw the news about Janet LeMon come over the wire. Are you okay?"

At least he sounded genuinely interested. "Um, not really. Kyle Coffee is dead, too."

"The guy I spoke to at the media reception?"

"Yeah, the one who was buddies with LeMon. Supposedly, he was in a car accident in Vegas, but—"

"But the timing seems pretty coincidental."

"Right. Anyway, I was wondering if that offer of your extra bed is still good?"

"Absolutely. Do you want me to come and get you?"

"No. I'm in my car—I can be there in a few minutes."

"Valet your car. I'll be waiting in the lobby."

"Do you think Ms. Vanderpool could join us?"

He hesitated, then said, "I'll call her," in a strained tone.

Jolie disconnected the call, feeling torn about using Beck for protection, but rationalized that they were using each other. During the drive, she dialed Salyers' cell phone.

"Salyers here."

"Detective Salyers, this is Jolie Goodman."

"Ms. Goodman, I apologize for the scene at the morgue. Mr. LeMon, as you can understand, is very upset."

"I could see that," Jolie said. "Detective, did you know that Kyle Coffee is dead?"

"Mr. LeMon told me that he was killed in a car accident this morning in Vegas."

"Right. Don't you find that suspicious since he's involved in this case?"

Salyers sighed. "The only reason Mr. Coffee's name came up in association with this case, Ms. Goodman, is because you mentioned it. People die in car crashes every day—it's a horrible coincidence." Papers rattled in the background.

"Did you check into the photo of Sammy Sanders I told you about?"

"Yes, but as it turns out, only the frame was taken into evidence. The photo was returned to Ms. Sanders, who said she threw it away because it was ruined."

Jolie grunted. "Great."

"But I did question Ms. Sanders, and she denied being romantically involved with Mr. Hagan."

And Sammy never lied, Jolie noted wryly. "Okay, here's something else—Russell Island, the man my friend Hannah, um, assaulted at the party is in the photos with Gary, Roger LeMon, and Kyle Coffee. The other man's name is Gordon Bear, possibly with a German spelling."

"Where did you get that information?"

"Beck Underwood identified them from the photo I kept."

"Hmm. While we're on the subject, Ms. Goodman, I have a waiter from the Sanders party who says he overheard you and Mr. Underwood say something about getting rid of your boyfriend."

Jolie swallowed past a dry throat. "That was a joke—I'd told Beck that I had a boyfriend who was in trouble. He had no idea who Gary was, or that he was missing."

"So are you and Mr. Underwood romantically involved?"

"No."

"Really? Because Ms. Sanders said she walked in on the two of you kissing in a bedroom at her party."

"I . . . trust me, that is irrelevant to this investigation."

"I'd say the fact that you have a new boyfriend could be damned relevant to your former boyfriend being dead."

She gripped the wheel tighter, sending pain shooting through her bad hand. "I didn't kill Gary, and I think you know that, Detective."

"Give me a better alternative."

She sighed. "*Roger LeMon.*"

"He has an alibi—a guest saw him leave the party a few minutes after he arrived."

"He could have returned. Have you questioned LeMon about his tattoo?"

"No."

"Why not?"

Salyers covered the mouthpiece and made a brusque comment to someone in the background, then came back on the line. "I'm sorry, where were we?"

"Roger LeMon's tattoo. And have you looked into the cause of the fire at Gary's apartment complex?"

Salyers emitted a long-suffering sigh. "Look, Ms. Goodman, I don't mean to be rude, but I have a file folder full of murders to investigate and limited resources to do it with. I can't chase down every tangent, especially when it's given to me by the prime suspect in the case."

Jolie fumed. "Well, here's another tangent: I was just run off the road—purposefully."

"Where?"

"Roswell Road, heading north just past Peachtree. The driver was a man I'd seen before, in the parking garage of the hotel where the media reception took place Friday night."

"Were there any witnesses?"

"To me being run off the road? Scores of them, but in Atlanta this kind of thing barely warrants a horn blow. Maybe the scratches and dents down the side of my rental car will convince you?"

"Are you injured?"

"No."

"Can you give me a description of the other car and the driver?"

Jolie squinted. "Dark-colored two-door . . . boxy . . ." Her voice petered out when she realized how little information she was giving the woman to act on. "The driver was dark-headed, maybe forty, possibly Hispanic . . . or not," she finished weakly.

"Okay, Ms. Goodman, I made a note of it, and I'll have units notified to keep an eye out for an errant driver of that er, description."

Frustration welled in Jolie's chest. "I don't blame you for not believing me, Detective, but I think there's something bigger going on, and Janet LeMon, Gary, and Kyle Coffee all died because they knew about it. Make a note of *that*." She disconnected the call, wondering too late if it was a crime to hang up on a cop. If so, maybe they would allow her to serve concurrent terms for murder and impoliteness.

Jolie flexed her aching hand and glanced in her rearview mirror. She might not have managed to spook Detective Salyers, but she'd managed to spook herself. Especially since she was returning to the same hotel where she'd first seen the driver of the car that had run her off the road. She took as winding a route as possible when traveling into the heart of Buckhead, exhaling a sigh of relief when she saw the canopy for the hotel.

The valet seemed slightly less happy to see her—or rather, her tin-can rental car, degraded even more by the freshly ruined paint job on the driver's side. She emerged with an apologetic look, then withdrew her decidedly inelegant duffel bag from the trunk. Beck came striding out, dressed in jeans and a different sweatshirt than he'd left wearing that morning. The sight of him was so comforting she felt a rush of sadness, although she took solace in the knowledge that he probably had the same effect on women everywhere.

She looked around. At various bellhops.

"What happened?" he said, inspecting the car.

She opened her mouth and burst into tears—God, that was the second time she'd done that around him.

"Hey, hey," he said, taking her bag and drawing her against his chest. He walked her toward the lobby. "You're safe now. Let's go in. Pam will be here as soon as she can."

She blubbered her story to him, letting the day's stress ooze down her cheeks. He wiped her tears with his thumbs, his expression troubled. "Did you call the police?"

She nodded. "But I think Detective Salyers is ready to lock me up just so I'll leave her alone."

"And you're sure it was the same guy you saw here?"

"I'm sure. He gave me the heebie-jeebies, so I didn't get into the parking garage elevator with him. I was going to wait until I saw him drive away before going to my car, but he came back down and supposedly was having car trouble. The concierge called an auto service for him."

"But you think that might have been a ploy?"

She shrugged.

"Come with me."

He walked across the hotel lobby to the concierge desk. Jolie recognized the attractive woman behind the counter. Her instant perkiness when she caught sight of Beck was familiar . . . Jolie'd seen that same look in her own mirror.

"Hello, Mr. Underwood. How can I assist you?"

"Can you help me track down some information about a man for whom you called an auto service Friday evening?"

She frowned. "That was at the end of the reception, wasn't it?"

He nodded.

She opened a log and ran her finger down a list of entries. "I don't have the gentleman's name, but here's the service I called—want me to write it down for you?"

"Please."

She gave him the information, then glanced at Jolie's duffel. "Will you be needing extra linens for your guest?" she asked slyly.

Jolie's face flamed.

"I'll let you know," Beck said easily, then guided Jolie toward the elevator bay. "Sorry about that."

"No problem," she murmured, following him into a mahogany-lined elevator.

When the doors closed, he lifted her hand in his. "You're bleeding again."

"I broke it open during the car-chase scene," she said with a little smile. His warm touch sent little thrills up her arm that made her forget the itchy pain.

He winked. "We'll get you fixed up."

They rode to a floor that was exclusive enough to require guests to insert their room key just to gain access. Jolie followed him down a plushly carpeted hallway and into a suite that was twice as big as her apartment, and decorated in a style that was at least two decades more current. Cocoas and creams and beiges and black, very masculine, very posh. His bed was enormous . . . she tingled with embarrassment over the thought of him bunking down on her lumpy sofa.

"Wow," she said, feeling a tad out of place standing there with her shabby duffel bag.

"The place is a little much," he said sheepishly, "but it's one of the company's corporate apartments, and since it sits empty most of the time, I thought I'd hang out here until I . . . decide what to do."

She looked up at him. "You mean until you decide if you're going to stay in Atlanta?"

He nodded, then pointed toward a door off the entryway. "There's a first-aid kit in this bathroom, let's take a look at your hand."

She followed him into a high-ceilinged, lavish cream-and-gold room. He found the first-aid kit and spread the items he needed on the vanity, then sat on a low stool and pulled her hand toward the sink. She stood and pivoted her head like a tourist while he carefully removed the blood-stained bandage from her hand.

"It looks puffy," he said. "It might be a little infected."

She sucked air through her teeth when he held her hand under a gentle stream of cold water from the faucet.

"Maybe you should go to the emergency room and get stitches."

"It'll be okay," she said. "I'll just be more careful."

"I'll put antibiotic cream on it," he said, then dabbed it on so carefully, she could barely feel it. The man was a paradox, raised in luxury but plainly uncomfortable with the idea of having so much. He could probably live the rest of his life off his trust fund, but his hands were calloused from physical work. And by right, no man so masculine should be so gentle. He wrapped her hand with a fresh bandage and taped it into place.

"There," he said, sandwiching her mended hand between his.

"Thank you," she murmured. "I feel like I'm always saying thank you to you."

He gave her a little smile. "You're welcome. You don't like asking for help, do you?"

"I don't like to take advantage."

"Asking for help when you need it isn't taking advantage."

She pursed her mouth. "That's easy to say if you've never had to ask someone for help."

He looked down at their hands. "Everyone needs some kind of help at one time or another."

She gave him a wry smile that belied the desire that coursed through her body. "This has been the neediest week of my life—you caught me at a bad time."

"Or a good time," he said, reaching for her other hand and pulling her between his knees. He curved his arm around her lower back and drew her closer. She wanted so badly to be kissed by him, but things were different now . . . Gary was gone . . . She was in real trouble . . .

Nothing good could come of an affair with this man. Well, nothing that would last longer than a few minutes . . .

When their mouths were a mere inch apart, he whispered, "Jolie Goodman, what am I going to do about you?"

Her lips parted involuntarily, and she leaned into his kiss. Their mouths met in a gentle exploration that grew in intensity as he slid his hands down her back. All she could think of was . . . nothing, actually . . . and it was nirvana to be lost in the moment. The fear, the sadness, the confusion she'd felt over the past few weeks and for most of her adult life, all of it channeled into pure passion for a man who was so compelling to her, she felt a little desperate around the edges.

He moaned into her mouth and stood, lifting her. She wrapped her legs around his waist and her arms around his neck, pressing her chest against his. He carried her to the bed as effortlessly as if she were a hat that just happened to be folded around him. Somewhere along the way, her shoes slipped off her feet. When he lowered her to the massive white bed, she'd never felt so reckless, her senses never so keen. His face was pained with desire, his dark eyes hooded as he pulled his sweatshirt over his head and slid onto the bed next to her.

She skimmed her fingertips over his collarbone and shoulder, captivated by the smooth muscle of his powerful torso, the mat of light brown hair over his chest that narrowed to a dark furrow over his stomach.

He unbuttoned her blouse, celebrating every liberated square of skin with his tongue. Jolie had always been modest, but with Beck she wasn't revealing her body—she was revealing everything she wanted to be and might never have the chance. Gone was any awkwardness, any hesitation. Beck controlled his body with athletic grace, every movement intentional and effective. Anticipation coiled tighter between her thighs as each piece of their clothing was cast aside. At the sight of him nude, Jolie felt the shudder of Eve inside her, breathless with the necessity of him. This was the essence of life: a magnificent man, and hormones run amok.

But time was ticking, so when he parted her knees and kissed the heart of her, the frugal girl in her arched in appreciation of his attention to detail and economy of motion. Determined to be more participatory than a hat, Jolie returned the favor with equal consideration, then after a few mental calculations regarding expansion, contraction, and overage, she straddled him in what proved to be a gradual yet successful maneuver. They found a natural glide, urging each other to higher heights. She came first, and second, and he arrived a gentlemanly third, breathing her name with an urgency that resounded in her defeated, gullible heart. She lowered her head to his chest, but his heart gave no indication of a similar distress.

He stroked her hair and made satisfied noises. She closed her eyes tightly, knowing that remorse was looking for her and would find her soon enough.

A knock sounded on the door, and her eyes flew open.

Beck lifted his head. "That will be Pam."

Remorse, remorse, remorse. Jolie disengaged herself from him as elegantly as possible, scooped up her clothes, and sprinted toward the bathroom.

"Jolie."

She turned back and raked her hair out of her eyes.

His head popped through the neck of his sweatshirt. "That was great."

That was inappropriate sprang to her lips, but it wouldn't be fair to drag Beck into her guilt event: *Goodman, party of one.*

Instead she nodded, then dove into the bathroom. After running a damp washcloth over key areas, she jumped into her clothes and gave herself a good mental shake. What was she thinking, entertaining the idea of having feelings for Beck Underwood? As if she didn't have enough to worry about right now—her reputation, her career, money, freedom. And how much more clear could he make it that he was a temporary . . . *benefactor?*

She opened the bathroom door just as the attorney he'd bought for her walked in wearing slacks and a black corduroy blazer, her phone to her ear, speaking in staccato phrases to the person on the other end. If-you're-in-a-jam-call-Pam Vanderpool was rattled.

"Okay . . . okay . . . *okay.* Keep me posted." She snapped her phone closed and sighed. "Not good news, I'm afraid."

Jolie hugged herself. What now?

Beck's hand brushed her waist. "Why don't we sit down?"

She saw Pam's gaze dart to the intimate gesture and a little wrinkle form between her dark eyebrows that contrasted so drastically with her white hair. "Good idea."

Jolie crossed the room, ignoring the blaring white bed, and purposefully sat in a chair, resisting the temptation to sit next to Beck on the loveseat. She looked down and saw, to her horror, one of her knee-highs rolled up in a little taupe-colored ball on the floor a few inches in front of her foot. How had she missed it when she re-dressed . . . and where was the other one? She extended her leg and flattened the ball beneath her loafer before Pam could notice.

"Okay," Pam said, sitting in a chair opposite Jolie. "I've been talking to the assistant D.A. Janet LeMon's death has a lot of influential voters upset. They've been lighting up the phone lines, clamoring for an arrest."

Jolie's mouth went dry. "They're going to arrest me?"

Pam sat back in her chair. "Not yet . . . but maybe soon. For the murder of Gary Hagan and possibly as an accessory to the murder of Janet LeMon."

The room tilted. Jolie grabbed the arms of the chair until the room righted itself, then expelled a shaky breath. "They can arrest me on circumstantial evidence?"

Pam nodded. "But remember—an arrest is one thing, a conviction is something else entirely."

Beck leaned forward, his handsome face wreathed in concern. "But they might make an arrest even if they know they can't get a conviction, just to quiet the public."

"And the media," Pam added pointedly.

Beck pulled his hand down his face. Jolie was distracted for the split second it took to register the fact that the great sex aside, she could fall in love with him based on this conversation alone. The one thing that kept this predicament from being even worse was the fact that Beck Underwood was in her corner.

"The one bit of luck," Pam continued, "is that the D.A. is on vacation and won't be back in her office until Wednesday. No one is willing to make a move without her go-ahead."

Jolie closed her eyes briefly and decided to throw up a quick prayer while she was in the proper position, then said, "There's nothing we can do?"

"Keep cooperating with the police, keep trying to remember details you might have forgotten."

"Do you happen to know what Janet LeMon looks— looked—like?"

Pam nodded. "I met her a couple of times. Seemed like a nice enough person to me."

"Beck," Jolie said, "do you have that picture? I'd like to see if Pam can identify one of the women as LeMon's wife."

He hesitated, then looked toward the desk. "I . . . put it in the glove box of my SUV. Sorry."

She nodded and looked back to Pam. "Okay . . . I'll try to remember details to tell the police. But short of a witness coming forward or someone making a full confession, the police will come to get me Wednesday?"

"There's a chance the D.A. will disagree with the charges," Pam said. "But if she doesn't, then I'll try to arrange for you to surrender yourself into police custody."

Bile backed up in Jolie's throat.

"I'll offer a reward for information," Beck said, standing. He reached for his cell phone. "Maybe that will shake something loose."

Pam Vanderpool studied him warily, then stood. "I have to go. Ms. Goodman, would you mind walking me out?"

Jolie pushed herself up and moved somewhat unsteadily toward the door. As they stepped into the hallway, Pam Vanderpool looked past Jolie's shoulder into the room, then leaned closer. "Ms. Goodman, do you know that Beck has been calling in favors all over town to keep your name and picture off the television and out of the papers?"

Her heart swelled. "No . . . I didn't know." And if that was the case, then who had he been talking to about a story yesterday morning at her apartment?

"His father isn't happy about the fact that one of his first acts in reestablishing himself in the broadcasting community is pulling in favors for a woman suspected of murdering her boyfriend and the wife of a successful Buckhead businessman."

Jolie bit down on the inside of her cheek. "I didn't ask Beck to get involved."

"I know you didn't—that's how Beck is. He sees a wrong and he tries to make it right, even if he hurts himself in the process." Pam wet her lips, and her eyes softened. "Ms. Goodman, I'm not suggesting that you try to stop him—when Beck sets his mind to something, there is no stopping him. But woman to woman, you're in a hell of a pickle here. Don't make things worse by giving the media more gossip for Beck to have to squash."

Jolie pressed her lips together and gave a curt nod. "I understand."

The older woman glanced down, then plucked off a staticky balled-up taupe-colored knee-high that had attached itself to her jacket and handed it to Jolie. "I hope so, for both of your sakes."

Pam turned and strode away, already punching in a number on her cell phone. Face flaming, Jolie walked back into the room, where Beck was ending one cell phone call, punching in another one.

"What was that all about?" he asked.

Jolie folded the knee-high into her hand. "Pam was just giving me some advice."

He nodded absently. "I'm calling the auto service to see if they have a record of servicing that guy's car."

"Beck, how exactly do you know Pam?"

He looked up. "She's my father's mistress." Then he

turned his back and leaned against a sofa table. "Hello, may I speak to the manager, please?"

Jolie studied him, then the rolled up knee-high. Not only had Pam given her advice from one woman to another, she'd given her advice from one woman who loved an Underwood man . . . to another?

She mulled over the revelation, then leaned one hip on the oversized desk that Beck had claimed as a work space. She looked down, frowning when she saw the edge of the group picture she'd asked about sticking out from beneath a newspaper. She looked up to see that Beck still had his back turned. From the sound of his voice, he was not having much luck with the manager of the auto service. Jolie removed the photo and replayed their recent conversation. Why would he have lied about its whereabouts?

This man who had captured her heart in a matter of days had a few secrets. Jolie glanced up to make sure he was still preoccupied, then tucked the picture into her purse. For now, she would keep a few secrets too.

Twenty-three

"Thank you for shopping at Neiman Marcus," Jolie said, handing a shopping bag over the counter with a smile. The woman glanced at the white bandage on Jolie's hand, then returned the smile warily.

"It's nothing contagious," Jolie assured her, instantly assailed by another bout of itchiness, which forced her to scratch her hand through the bandage before the woman looked away. "Really," Jolie said with a smile, still scratching.

The woman hurried away, and Jolie stared down at her hand, irritated. Which wasn't exactly fair since her hand also looked irritated. She made a fist and winced—Beck had made the bandage a little tight this morning when he'd dressed it for her. But after Pam Vanderpool's parting words last night, Jolie had concluded there could be no more hanky-panky between her and Beck. Since getting bandaged would be the extent of him touching her, she could tolerate tight. Tight was good.

To take her mind off her aching hand and off Beck, she

glanced around the nearly deserted shoe department, even willing to tackle an orthopedic-insert customer if necessary, to take her mind off her problems. She was just glad to be back to some kind of normalcy. The afternoon had passed, and she'd only thought of Gary lying in the morgue, oh, a few hundred times. But she knew that number would be much higher if she weren't working.

And then there was the one time that she *hadn't* been thinking about Gary that kept rising in her mind—when she'd climbed on top of Beck Underwood.

She cringed and tried to push aside *that* persistent memory.

She'd come in early to buy a suit for Gary to wear in his casket on her employee discount. Sending him off in style was the least she could do, and although she was a little dismayed when the funeral director had told her bluntly that they wouldn't be needing shoes, she conceded that her credit card couldn't have withstood much more.

The stark efficiency of finalizing the details for his memorial service over the phone had disturbed her. Generic burial plot with footstone? Check. Bargain-basement-priced casket? Check. Floral spray for the casket? Check. Preprogrammed organ music? Check.

To exorcise some of her own grief, she'd stopped at the card shop and written a short note to Leann's sister, and bought a sympathy card to mail to Kyle Coffee's wife later. Loss should never be overlooked, she decided, and although she doubted if anyone would attend, she'd sent a notice of Gary's memorial service to the newspaper.

In truth, though, she was half afraid his creditors might show up.

In the absence of customers, she began to tidy the counter.

"Jolie," Michael said, striding up. "I need to see you in the meeting room, please."

She glanced at her watch. "I still have twenty minutes on my shift."

His face grew stern. "Right away."

"Okay," she murmured, thinking this couldn't be good. Especially since Michael stalked ahead of her the entire way, forcing her to trot. But when they reached the meeting room and Carlotta was there along with Lindy, the store's general manager, she knew they either were getting big raises or were in big trouble . . . She suspected the latter.

Lindy, the redhead with a reedy voice, invited them to sit, which they did. But she and Michael remained standing.

"We received a phone call today," Lindy said. "A tip that the two of you are buying clothes on your employee discount, wearing them, then returning them."

Carlotta looked outraged. "That's ridiculous."

"Carlotta, I must say the high volume of returns that you process for yourself is very suspicious."

Carlotta gave a dismissive wave. "I never try anything on here in the store because I know I can bring it back if it doesn't fit."

Lindy and Michael swung their gazes to Jolie. "Jolie?" Michael prompted.

They weren't going to have to torture her. "There was a jumpsuit—"

"That was my fault," Carlotta cut in. "I talked Jolie into buying the jumpsuit and a great pair of shoes, but she simply couldn't afford them, so she returned them the next day." Carlotta pointed to Michael. "You can attest to that, Michael. The shoes that Jolie returned didn't look worn, did they?"

Michael turned to the manager. "She's right—they were in perfect shape."

Lindy pursed her mouth and looked suspiciously back and forth between the women. "Carlotta, from now on, you'll be limited to one returned item a week, so make sure you try on clothes before you buy them."

"I will," Carlotta said, with just the right amount of contriteness, innocence, and obedience.

"I also read the Sunday paper," the woman said, "so I know that the two of you were questioned in connection with a murder investigation and a robbery during a party over the weekend."

Jolie swallowed hard. Next to her, she could feel Carlotta's nervousness rolling off in waves.

"Both of you are certainly presumed innocent until proven guilty, but I must inform you that if you are arrested, you will be placed on unpaid leave until the matter is resolved."

Carlotta nodded and Jolie joined in.

"That's all," Lindy said. "Ms. Goodman, please accept my condolences on your friend's . . . passing. If you need to arrange time off for a service, we will accommodate you, of course."

"Thank you," Jolie said. "The memorial service is tomorrow evening, so I don't need any time off, but I appreciate the offer."

The woman nodded curtly, dismissing them.

They filed out silently. When they were out of earshot, Carlotta turned on Jolie and glared. "You told!"

"Told what?"

"About the *system*!"

Jolie held up her hands and gave the bandage a scratch.

"I didn't tell. It must have been an employee . . . or what about Hannah?"

"Hannah would never do that to me," Carlotta said.

"Neither would I," Jolie said. "Besides, why on earth would I incriminate myself? So I can add a shoplifting charge to my rap sheet?" She frowned. "And don't act so innocent—I know you took that money from Sammy's purse."

Carlotta's eyes rounded. "I did not!"

Jolie sighed. "Carlotta, I've heard you make comments about what easy pickings a party would be for a thief, and I know you saw the money in Sammy's purse when she paid for her shoes Saturday morning. And," she said more quietly, putting her hand on Carlotta's arm, "I know about the money you owe."

Carlotta frowned. "What?"

"The day I was taking a nap in the dressing room upstairs, I heard voices through the vent—I heard that man threaten you."

Carlotta blanched, looked around, and pulled her aside. "You haven't told anyone about the man, have you?"

"No."

"The police?"

"No."

Her shoulders sagged in obvious relief.

"Who is he? And why do you owe him money?"

"I don't." Carlotta massaged her temples. "My brother owes him."

"Your brother?"

"He had a gambling problem. He's reformed, but he still has a lot of debt. We were able to consolidate some of it and set up payments, but this one guy that he owes ten grand to is breathing down my neck."

"Why *your* neck and not your brother's?"

"Because this guy knows that my brother doesn't care if they rough him up . . . but I do."

"Do you have the money?"

She shook her head. "I scraped together a few hundred dollars and bought another week, but by next Friday I have to have another two grand."

"What are you going to do?"

"As soon as I get my Miata out of the shop, I'm going to sell it. I'd hoped to put the money back into a new car, but right now I need the cash flow."

Her eyes glistened and Jolie's heart went out to her. "Your parents can't help?"

Carlotta gave a little laugh. "My parents are bankrupt upper-class drunks who move around the country staying with any friend who hasn't yet figured them out. I mean, it's no wonder my brother and I are misfits, right?"

"You're not a misfit."

She gave another laugh. "What do you call someone who borrows clothes to crash parties and assume alternate personalities?"

"Creative. It's a shame you can't find a way to make a living at it."

Carlotta looked away. "Look at all the trouble it landed you in."

"I don't believe it—is that a guilty conscience?"

Carlotta looked at Jolie and rolled her shoulders sheepishly. "I have a conscience—just don't tell anyone."

"Carlotta, unless you shot Gary, what happened Saturday night isn't your fault. And crashing the first two parties helped me to get a lot of information I otherwise wouldn't have." *Plus I got to know Beck*, her mind whispered.

"That lady detective told me that Hannah and I made things worse for you because . . . we both have records."

Jolie pressed her lips together.

Carlotta sighed. "Hannah got busted for selling pot when she was in her twenties, and a bookie was trying to get my brother to go off the wagon, so I hit him."

"Oh."

"With a tire iron."

"*Oh.* Well . . . still." Jolie cleared her throat. "But if you did steal Sammy's money, I might be able to talk her into not filing charges."

"You mean *blackmail* her into not filing charges?"

"Well, let's just say I have some dirt on her."

Carlotta smiled, shaking her head. "That would be great, except . . . I didn't take that money. I would tell you if I did, but I didn't!"

"The money was found in the pool filter, and there were only four of us in the pool—you, me, Hannah, and Beck."

"I think we can strike Mr. Moneybags," Carlotta said dryly.

"That leaves Hannah—would she have done it?"

"Only one reason that I could think of—come on, let's go call her. I need to ask her if Russell has that tattoo." They started toward the break room. "So, what's going to happen to you?"

Jolie inhaled deeply, then exhaled. "My attorney seems to think they'll arrest me Wednesday when the D.A. gets back into town."

"Aren't you scared shitless?"

"Well . . . pretty much. The police don't seem to have

the manpower to look into all the leads, at least not right away. But I have a good lawyer, and I hope that some of the leads will pan out before there can be a trial."

"You seem remarkably calm."

Jolie tried to smile. "Give me an alternative."

Carlotta spun the dial on her combination lock and shook her head. "We need to take matters into our own hands, start making phone calls and taking names."

"I'm game."

Carlotta opened her locker and withdrew a pack of cigarettes and a box of matches. "I think I'll go out on the loading dock for a smoke before I call Hannah. Want to join me?"

"No, thanks."

"Oh, Christ!"

Jolie looked up from her own locker to see Carlotta staring at the box of matches. "What is it?"

"I just remembered where I saw that picture on the wall—the pig in the suit that's in your photograph."

"Where?"

She held up the matchbox. "Manuel's Tavern down on North Highland Avenue. It's a hangout for politicians, reporters, cops, attorneys." She grinned. "I've met lots of famous people there—Jimmy Carter." She sighed. "He was in my book."

Jolie nodded absently, aware of a memory stirring just below the surface of her consciousness. "Manuel's," she repeated. "Where have I heard that name . . . word . . . lately?" In the crazy way a person's subconscious teases, she knew it wasn't in association with the bar. It was out of context . . . In a conversation? She shook her head. Maybe on one of the matchbooks in Gary's box of belongings?

No! It was the note he'd scribbled illegibly on the back of a brochure: *hardy manuals*. At the time she had thought it was nonsensical, but maybe there was a connection.

On impulse, she withdrew her cell phone from her bag. "Is there a number on the matchbox?"

Carlotta recited it as Jolie dialed.

The phone was picked up on the second ring. "Manuel's Tavern."

"Yes, is um, Hardy, working tonight?"

"Yeah, he takes over for me at the bar in about an hour."

Jolie's pulse picked up. "Thanks." She disconnected the call. "Want to take a field trip?"

Carlotta shrugged. "Sure. I got my new wheels from the impound lot this morning—that was a degrading experience. Are we going to Manuel's?"

Jolie nodded, more excited than she'd been since . . . last night, with Beck. She pushed the thought from her mind. "Why don't you call Hannah and have her meet us there?"

Manuel's was a neighborhood tavern, full of customers who moved around the bar and the crowded tables with familiarity. The furnishings were old and eclectic: scarred tables, mismatched chairs, a beer can collection, faded photographs. The patrons themselves ran the gamut from suited businessmen shooting pool to dusty laborers ordering from menus. Even so, Hannah stood out, dressed in what could only be described as gothic guerilla. She was sitting at the bar glaring at her cigarette as if she might simply eat it and dispense with the formality of smoking.

"You're going to have to work on looking more approachable," Carlotta commented wryly as she and Jolie slid onto stools on either side of her.

Hannah blew smoke into the air. "I managed to save you seats, didn't I?"

Carlotta winked at Jolie. "Bad day in cooking school, Hannah?"

She ground her cigarette in an ashtray, twisting it until it broke, exposing the fibrous filter. "Russell filed assault charges, the wimp."

Jolie winced.

"I thought that's why you liked him," Carlotta said lightly. "Because he's a wimp."

Hannah gave her a wry smile. "Ha ha."

"You're going to get the last laugh," Carlotta said. "Can't you visualize the courtroom? He'll be in his Brooks Brothers special, and you'll soar in like Elvira and he'll be a big fat laughingstock. The courtroom regulars will crucify him from the gallery."

Hannah managed a little smile. "You're right. That *will* be a rush."

"Hannah," Jolie asked, "does Russell have a tattoo on his wrist?"

She nodded. "Yeah, a tiny thing, four hands or four arms or something. I remember teasing him that it looked like some kind of sissy Boy Scout badge." She looked at Jolie. "Did you bring the picture Carlotta told me about?"

Jolie nodded and withdrew the photo from her purse.

Hannah studied the picture, shaking her head. "Can you believe that your boyfriend and my boyfriend knew each other? Small world, isn't it?" She frowned, then flicked her finger against Russell's wife's face.

Carlotta gave Jolie a sideways glance, lifting her eyebrow.

A plump woman bartender came down to the end of the bar and gave it a swipe with a hand cloth. "What can I get for you ladies?"

"Gin and tonic," Carlotta said.

"Same for me," Jolie said. "I was told that Hardy was working the bar tonight."

The woman looked across the room. "Har-dee!"

A slender middle-aged man serving a tray of drinks looked up.

The bartender pointed to the women. "Fans of yours."

The man tucked the empty tray under his arm and ambled over, sporting a communal grin. "What can I do you for, ladies?"

Jolie leaned forward. "Actually, I was hoping to ask you a few questions."

His eyes narrowed. "You a cop?"

"No. I'm looking for some information about a friend of mine, Gary Hagan."

He nodded, his expression more congenial. "Yeah, Hagan. Likes fancy beer. I haven't seen him around here for a while. How is he?"

"Um, not well," Jolie said ruefully while trying to control her excitement at finding someone who actually knew Gary. She took the photo from Hannah and extended it to him. "I understand that this photo was taken here. I thought you might help me identify some of the people in it."

He squinted at the picture. "Yeah, it was taken here all right. Let's see—that's Hagan, right?"

She nodded.

"This guy's name is Coffee, I think, and that's Russell Island." He looked up. "He's kind of a pansy-ass, always orders a frozen drink."

Carlotta snickered and Hannah gave her a deadly look.

Hardy shook his head. "I've seen these other guys in here, usually with Hagan, but I don't know who they are."

He grinned. "I can remember the drinks people order better than their names."

"Did you happen to overhear any of their conversations?" Jolie asked carefully. "How they might have known each other?"

He drew back a couple of inches, and she sensed his retreat. "You're asking a lot of questions."

"It's for a good cause," Carlotta said, then nonchalantly unbuttoned the top button on her blouse and held the drink the bartender had delivered to her long, slender neck. Because of course, it was so hot in mid-October.

Hardy stared at her cleavage. "Well . . . I don't remember any specific conversation."

Another button came undone. "Do you remember seeing tattoos on their wrists?"

He dragged his gaze up, then pointed his finger. "Yeah. In fact, I think they were all in here celebrating after they got them. I remember thinking they were grown men acting like a bunch of fraternity boys." He laughed. "In fact, I think I might have said something like that, and one of them remarked that they had their own fraternity house."

"What did you think they meant by that?" Carlotta asked, playing with the next button.

Fascinated, Jolie held her breath, wondering what would give first—Hardy, or Carlotta's bra.

Hardy's Adam's apple bobbed. "I'm not sure, but I took it to mean that they had a playhouse, you know, somewhere to take their girlfriends, some place their wives didn't know about. That's pretty common, actually."

Jolie and Carlottta's gaze swung to Hannah.

"Did Russell have a playhouse?" Jolie asked, her heart beating faster.

She nodded. "A condo on West Peachtree. We went there a few times."

Jolie's heart beat faster as a few more pieces of the puzzle fell into place. Gary was a services broker, and he owned a condo on West Peachtree. The four men used it as a playhouse. Hannah could provide the link between the condo and Russell Island, and the tattoos would provide the link between the four men. Hope flowered in her chest. She gave Carlotta a triumphant nod, barely able to contain her excitement.

Carlotta rewarded Hardy with a glimpse of her navel. "Thanks, Hardy."

He grinned, then looked back to the photo, as if hoping to find more details he could expound upon—Carlotta was, after all, wearing a skirt that buttoned up the front.

He pulled the picture closer, squinting.

"What?" Jolie asked, thinking at this point any information would be pure gravy.

Hardy shook his head. "I can't say for sure—this is an old picture, taken before we repainted—but . . ."

"But what?" she prompted.

"I swear this dark-haired lady staring off to the side looks like Della Underwood."

Jolie's heart dropped. "What?"

Carlotta grabbed the photo and jammed it close to her face. Jolie looked over her shoulder and broke into a full-body sweat.

Carlotta nodded. "I think he's right. Della went through a brunette phase in the mid-nineties. Tragic, really."

Jolie fairly buckled under the sense of betrayal—Beck had recognized his sister in the photo. That explained the phone call he'd made from her apartment. "... *you should be thinking of a story. Yes, I got it from her and I have it with me . . . I shouldn't be here much longer."*

He'd called Della to warn her. That was why he was trying to keep the story out of the papers and off television: for Della's sake, not for hers. He hadn't wanted to show the photo to Pam Vanderpool because he knew she would recognize Della.

All this time, Della might have known something about LeMon that would exonerate Jolie . . . or is that what Beck was afraid of? That his sister was somehow involved? He said he'd come back to Atlanta because his sister was going through some things that he wanted to be here for. Had she gotten in over her head with her old lover Roger LeMon?

Her heart shivered in disappointment. She'd imagined the connection between her and Beck, had wanted it to be so. Was she so starved for love that she couldn't recognize the real thing from a come-on? She swallowed hard. No, not a come-on, but worse: *pity.*

She drew in a shaky breath, determined not to cry.

"Do you know Ms. Underwood?" Hardy asked them, handing back the photo.

"Indirectly," Jolie murmured, feeling Carlotta's perceptive gaze all over her. "Excuse me—I need to make a phone call."

"To Beck?" Carlotta asked in a low voice.

"No," Jolie said. She was finished with being gullible. "To Detective Salyers."

Twenty-four

Jolie stood staring down at Gary, glad she'd gone with the blue tie instead of the red one. It seemed more tranquil, and hopefully, more indicative of the resting place he'd made for himself in eternity.

Her eyes filled with sudden tears, and a sob caught in her throat from the guilt over not having cared enough about him. Somewhere there was probably a pretty girl who had been Gary Hagan's first love, who wondered how he had turned out, hoping she would run into him again someday, not knowing that he was dead unless she happened to subscribe to the *Atlanta Journal-Constitution*. Somewhere there was someone who was more qualified to bury him.

At the sound of footsteps behind her, she brushed away tears and turned.

Detective Salyers, wearing her uniform of chinos and jacket came walking toward her.

Jolie tensed. "If you've come to arrest me, can you wait until after the service?"

Salyers gave her a little smile. "I didn't come here to arrest you, Ms. Goodman. I came to pay my respects to Mr. Hagan . . . and to you."

"Oh. Thank you."

Salyers cleared her throat. "Ms. Goodman, I know this isn't exactly the time or the place, but I wanted you to know that I've made this case my top priority—on the clock and off. I truly appreciate all the leads you've sent our way. The information you got from the bartender at Manuel's last night will go a long way toward linking these two murders by way of more than an affair gone bad. We're looking into Kyle Coffee's death, and we're re-examining the West Peachtree condo." Salyers sighed and averted her gaze.

"But?"

Salyers looked back. "But you're still the prime suspect, and my boss is going to recommend to the D.A. tomorrow that an arrest warrant be served."

Panic pumped through her limbs. Jolie massaged her throbbing hand through the bandage. "Okay . . . okay . . . okay."

"I thought this would be better coming from your attorney, but I contacted Pam Vanderpool; she said that you had fired her."

Jolie nodded. Beck had left her a half dozen messages. "I'll find another attorney in the morning."

At the sound of more guests, Jolie turned. Carlotta and Hannah walked in, their footsteps careful and uncertain. Carlotta, always the trendsetter, wore yellow head to toe. Hannah looked surprisingly feminine in a flirty ruffled skirt. Jolie smiled, grateful for their presence. They spotted her and made their way toward the front of the chapel.

"He looks better than the last time I saw him," Carlotta murmured. "Nice suit—everyone should be buried in Prada."

Jolie nodded. She'd paid almost as much for the suit as she had the casket.

Hannah gave Jolie's hand a squeeze. "How are you holding up?"

Her gaze flitted to Detective Salyers, who had taken a seat in a middle pew. "Fine."

Hannah shifted from foot to foot. "Jolie, I stole that money from your boss's purse the night of the party." She puffed out her cheeks. "I was going to plant it on Russell."

Jolie frowned. "Why?"

She shrugged. "To discredit him, to show him that I could. I was trying to get close enough to put it in his jacket pocket when Carlotta grabbed me and we went into the pool."

Jolie bit into her lip. "Hannah . . . have you considered counseling?"

She nodded miserably.

"Omigod," Carlotta whispered. "Jolie, your ex-boss just walked in."

Jolie lifted her head and sure enough, Sammy had arrived, toning down her usual pinkness with a splash of gray.

"Excuse us," Carlotta said. She and Hannah turned and claimed a pew equidistant between Salyers and the back of the room.

God help her, but Jolie looked at Sammy and immediately pondered the woman's motivation. Did she feel obligated to attend because the body had been found in her house? Had she been fooling around with Gary behind

Jolie's back and developed genuine feelings for him? Or was she here simply to give out business cards? (A trick of the trade.)

Sammy stopped in front of Jolie and after an awkward hesitation, leaned forward to give her a stiff one-armed hug. "I'm really sorry about Gary," she said, and she sounded like she meant it.

Jolie felt unexpectedly misty. Was it possible that she and Sammy had simply fallen into a habit of disliking each other? She hadn't exactly behaved well herself, sneaking into the woman's house, ransacking her bathroom, filching a photo frame, then bringing the party to a screeching halt. She was touched that Sammy seemed to be extending an olive branch. "Thank you for coming, Sammy."

Sammy's expression was pinched with compassion. "I wouldn't have missed it." She linked her arm in Jolie's and stared down at Gary. "So young, so handsome, such a tragedy."

Jolie nodded, biting into her lip.

Sammy patted her arm. "Jolie, I have a little confession to make."

At the sound of Sammy's "cajoling" voice, a red flag raised in Jolie's mind. "Confession?"

Sammy looked contrite. "Gary called me at the office a little while after you all started seeing each other and asked me to broker a deal. He wanted to buy a condo that he'd been renting for a couple of years." She gave a little laugh. "He said it was going to be a surprise and he didn't want you to know about it, but he wanted you to get the commission for the sale."

Her stomach gurgled. "So you forged my name on the contract?"

She nodded and winced. "And that was wrong, but

Gary was adamant that he wanted you to have the money." She lifted her manicured hands in the air. "I thought he was getting ready to propose and that the two of you would live there. Since I couldn't cut you a commission check without you knowing the source, I tried to give you the money in little spurts, but you simply wouldn't take it."

Jolie wet her lips. "That's why you were trying to give me money Saturday morning?"

"Yes. I felt terrible that you'd left the agency before I could get you to take it." She laid her ice-cold hand over Jolie's—or maybe it only felt cold because her wounded hand felt feverish. "Jolie, I just wanted you to know the entire story from my point of view."

"In case anyone asks me?"

The woman's smile was poignant. "Yes."

Salyers had been asking questions about the property— was Sammy telling the truth, or covering her tracks? Jolie gave her a noncommittal smile. "I appreciate your concern. And about the money that was taken at the party—"

"It's forgotten," Sammy said emphatically. "It's just money, and it was recovered. This memorial service is a good reminder that life is short, and we can't be consumed by material things."

Said the woman with a room in her home dedicated to crystal dollhouses.

But with her own emotional receptors misfiring, Jolie couldn't decide if the woman was a big fraud, or if kindness was just so foreign to Sammy that she hadn't gotten the knack of it yet.

The funeral director, a pear-shaped, slump-shouldered man with glasses on the tip of his nose, walked into the doorway and signaled that it was time for the service to begin. Sammy patted Jolie's hand, then settled herself in a back pew.

Jolie conjured up a smile for the handful who had gathered for the service and lowered herself to the front pew. The funeral director meandered to the front of the room and flipped a switch. Organ music wafted in from the speakers—a sickly sweet melody meant to wring the emotion out of the most stoic observer.

A cell phone rang, piercing the mood. Jolie pivoted her head to see Detective Salyers reaching into her pocket and ducking out of the pew. She hurried out of the room, and Jolie couldn't be irritated. The woman had come because of her and had other emergencies to attend.

The song finished playing and another song began, this one more mournful than the last. When she looked at Gary's chalky profile, she was overwhelmed with helplessness, assailed with thoughts that things might have ended differently if she'd simply started the car and driven off while he was in the backseat.

Another cell phone rang, and Jolie turned her head to see Sammy jump up and run out, reaching into her purse. Another lead, another sale. Jolie couldn't figure out Sammy, but deep down, she thought the woman was too dim to be truly dangerous. She looked back to the casket and sighed. What-ifs plagued her and she felt torn because she didn't entirely trust Gary. Had he been sleeping with Sammy? Had he been sleeping with Janet LeMon? Selling cocaine to the men who used the condo as their getaway? All of those things were hard to reconcile to the gentle, laughing man she'd known, but what if Gary had only let her see the side of him that he wanted to reveal? Was that why he hadn't wanted her to meet his friends, so she wouldn't see the smarmy side?

At the end of the second song, the funeral director made his way to the front of the chapel to a small podium and began to read the seventy-five-word obituary he'd asked her to write. "Gary Hogan—"

"Hagan," Jolie corrected.

He squinted over the podium at her. "Huh?"

She wet her lips. "It's 'Hagan,' with an 'a.' "

He pointed to the paper. "This says 'Hogan.' "

Another cell phone rang. Jolie turned her head to see Hannah sidling out with her phone to her ear. Jolie turned back with a sigh. "Trust me—it's 'Hagan.' "

"Okay." He cleared his throat, then started again. "Gary Hagan was on this earth thirty-six short years. Born in Germany to a U.S. airman, Gary lived the life of a soldier's son."

Another cell phone rang and Jolie turned to frown at Carlotta, who mouthed, "I'm sorry, I have to get this," and ran out of the room.

The funeral director looked around the room, then looked back to Jolie. "Do you want me to finish?"

"Yes." She'd spent hours on that obituary, hoping to come up with seventy-five words that would have pleased Gary, if he were within earshot. She wanted them to be heard. "And then I'd like another song, please."

He looked over his glasses at her. "You only paid for two songs."

"Bill me."

"Okay." He looked back to the sheet of paper. "Where did I leave off? Let's see, Gary Hagan, blah, blah, blah, soldier's son. Ah, here we are: More than anything, Gary liked to make people laugh. He was known as a person who could make things happen. He loved sports, especially the Braves. He was preceded in death by his beloved parents,

Alvin and Polly Hagan. He is succeeded by an army of friends." The man glanced over his glasses at the empty chapel, then looked back down. "Then it says here 'Magic of thinking big.'" He squinted at Jolie. "Is that supposed to mean something?"

"It was his favorite book," she said wistfully. "And I only had four words left."

The man looked at her as if she were a kook. "Here's your extra song." He flipped the switch, then lumbered back down the aisle.

Jolie sat perfectly still while the song played—it was the first song again, but she didn't care. She sat unmoving until the vibrations of the last note had died, then pushed to her feet and walked to Gary's casket. She broke off one of the white roses from the casket spray and tucked it inside his jacket pocket.

"Gary," she murmured, "I'll bet when you got to the Pearly Gates, you had Braves tickets for St. Peter." She smiled, then bit into her lip. "I want you to know that I'm going to try to figure all this out. I don't know what's going to happen, but I know I was never this brave before, so thank you." She inhaled deeply, bringing the scent of live flowers into her lungs, then exhaled and turned to leave.

A movement in the empty chapel caught her attention. Beck. He was sitting on a rear pew, wearing a suit and tie and a solemn expression.

She stopped, shot through with anger, remorse, shame. Her only solace was in the fact that he didn't know how much he'd trampled her heart—and why would he even guess that he had in such a few short days? It wouldn't make sense, so she was safe from that ultimate humiliation at least.

He stood, shoving his hands in his pockets, and Jolie realized that eventually, she was going to have to move forward. She walked toward him and he stepped out into the aisle.

"I got here a little late," he said, his tone apologetic.

"Thank you for coming anyway," she said. "Detective Salyers was here, and Carlotta and Hannah. Oh, and Sammy."

"She left a stack of business cards by the guest book."

"Sounds like Sammy."

"She's persistent—she called me twice this week trying to get my business."

An awkward pause followed. Beck scratched his temple. "I, uh, was hoping we could talk."

She angled her head. "About the fact that your sister is in the photo I showed to you? And that you deliberately concealed information that might have helped me in some way?"

He nodded, pressing his lips together. "You're right, I did conceal that information from you, and I hope you can forgive me for wanting to protect my sister. But I didn't keep the information from the police."

She blinked. "You didn't?"

He shook his head. "When I left your place Sunday morning, I picked up Della and we went to talk to Detective Salyers. I convinced Della it would be better if the police knew everything."

"What's everything?"

He sighed. "My sister has been in love with Roger LeMon most of her adult life. I don't understand it, but she's blind to the fact that he's not a good guy. They were off and on, off and on. Even after he married, LeMon called Della. She wouldn't have anything to do with him, but I knew she was still crazy about him."

"I feel for your sister," Jolie said, "but wouldn't that make her a suspect in Janet LeMon's murder?"

"It might," he admitted. "Except Della was in a psychiatric clinic in Vermont all summer, up until I got back in town a couple of weeks ago."

"Oh."

"Yeah," he said. "As you can imagine, that's not the kind of thing Della wants everyone to know, especially since she seems to finally be getting back on her feet. So . . ." He gave her a little smile. "I just wanted to apologize and let you know that Pam is willing to take your case again."

She shook her head. "Thanks, but . . . no thanks."

"So . . . you won't accept my help."

Her heart thrashed in her chest like a wounded bird. "No. There are just too many . . . complications—your name, your sister. You're my alibi at the party. How's that going to look to a jury if you're also paying for my attorney and—"

He lifted an eyebrow. "Sleeping with you? Not good. You're right, of course."

Jolie exhaled. The day was catching up with her. "Look, Beck, I've had a long day, and something tells me that tomorrow is going to be even longer. So if you don't mind—"

"Where are you staying?"

"At my neighbor's. She's out of town and said I could use her apartment for a few days."

"Let me get you a hotel room."

With him in it? "No, thank you. Good night."

He reached out to clasp her arm. "Jolie, I can make things easier for you."

Anger blazed through her. "Do you think I'm blind, Beck? I know what I am to you—I'm a project. I'm a 'before.' I'm the damsel in distress that you can swoop in to save and feel good about yourself for a while. Until you get bored and start looking for a new project, or decide to go back to Costa Rica." She pulled away from him. "Go find another charity case."

She sidestepped him, marched out of the funeral chapel, and unlocked her pitiful rental car door. She climbed in and started the engine, then looked heavenward. "God, I'm broke, barely employed, a suspect in two murders, I drive a ramshackle car, and the man I love might as well be living in your galaxy. Please let me know that this is a low point. Send me a sign." She leaned forward, looking for shooting stars, a burning bush, a two-headed goat . . . something.

And she got nothing.

She drove to the apartment complex counting road signs to keep her mind occupied . . . off Gary . . . off Beck . . . off jail. It was just before 8 P.M. when she pulled into the parking lot.

Residents had already decorated for Halloween, putting lighted jack-o'-lanterns in their windows and corn fodder shocks in the common areas. Her hand felt warm and tight beneath the bandage. Maybe Beck was right—maybe it was infected.

Beck.

She worked her mouth from side to side, conceding it would probably take some time to get out of the habit of thinking about him.

She drove past Leann's apartment to check her own mailbox. After a couple of days, it probably would be full.

She parked and walked to the bank of mailboxes, looking right and left, ever aware of her surroundings. Fatigue pulled at her lower back—the shoe department had been much busier than usual today.

The night air was cool—in the forties, she guessed. And so cloudless, the stars took her breath away. A rustling noise behind the boxes also took her breath away, until she realized it was the dry husks of the corn fodder shocks rubbing together. Still, she didn't dawdle checking the mail. As suspected, her box was full—one reason was because Mrs. Janklo's bank checks had been delivered to her by mistake. She looked up at the woman's window and noted that the lights were on. If she knew Mrs. Janklo, she'd be looking for these checks and worried that they hadn't arrived.

Jolie heaved a sigh and opted for the elevator over the stairs. A couple of minutes later, she was ringing Mrs. Janklo's doorbell. She stood in front of the peephole and waved. "It's Jolie, Mrs. Janklo—I have your checks."

The door opened and Mrs. Janklo squinted at her through the chain. "What do you want?"

"Here are your checks," she said cheerfully. "The mail carrier put them in my box by mistake."

The woman's plump hand appeared in the six-inch opening and Jolie gave her the box. "Thank you," her neighbor said begrudgingly.

"You're welcome. Good night."

"Wait, I have something for you." The door closed.

Jolie tried to smile. Mrs. Janklo was famous for her frozen zucchini bread wrapped in layers and layers of aluminum foil. It was god-awful, and Jolie had lost a toenail last year when she'd dropped one on her foot.

The door opened and Mrs. Janklo's disposition seemed much improved. "Here you go—some nice zucchini bread. It'll need to thaw for about three hours."

Jolie juggled her mail and took the icy brick, which actually felt good against her injured hand. "Thank you, Mrs. Janklo."

"And here's something for you that was put in *my* mailbox by mistake . . . a few days ago." She extended a lumpy, padded manila envelope.

Jolie frowned. "When did you say it arrived?"

"One day last week," the woman snapped. "I'm a little forgetful these days." She slammed the door.

But Jolie barely noticed because she recognized the handwriting on the return address: Gary's. Her heart beat wildly. This was the envelope that he'd said "they" had intercepted. He couldn't have known that in this instance, "they" were a nearsighted mail carrier and her nosy, forgetful neighbor.

She raced down the stairs and decided it would be faster to step inside her own apartment to examine the envelope. With a bum left hand and a right hand that shook from excitement, it took her a few seconds longer to unlock the door and the deadbolt. Just as she turned the doorknob, a man's gloved hand clamped over her mouth from behind.

Jolie's cry died against his hand. Terror bolted through her as he shoved his body against her back, his mouth to her ear. "Welcome home."

At the sound of Roger LeMon's voice, she almost lost control of her bladder. His fingers covered her nose too, so she was bucking to breathe. The door opened in front of her and he pushed her inside, sending her sprawling in the darkness against the gray carpet, which was much harder than she'd ever imagined. Everything in her arms scattered and rolled. The front door slammed closed and she heard him fumbling with the deadbolt. Precious time, and she knew her way around in the dark. She pushed herself up and ran for the bedroom. LeMon abandoned the door and lunged after her. He caught her by the arm, pulled her to him, and covered her mouth again.

"Time to die," he growled in her ear, dragging her backward. "After your boyfriend's memorial service, you couldn't live with yourself anymore. You left a note on your computer about the little love triangle between you and Gary and my wife, about how Gary killed my wife, then how you killed him."

She fought him furiously, struggling left, then right.

"It's not going to hurt, you'll be out from the sleeping pills when I slash your wrists."

He released her mouth for a second and when she gasped for air, he shoved capsules into her mouth. She clamped down, refusing to swallow, her screams sounding like mere grunts. Tears streamed down her cheeks. Would anyone question her death? Leann . . . Carlotta . . . Salyers . . . Beck? He had offered her a safe, secure place to sleep and she'd thrown it in his face. She gagged as the bitter powder from the broken capsules began to dissolve in her mouth.

She heard a loud boom, the distant sound of wood splintering. "Jolie! *Jolie!*" a voice shouted.

Beck?

Suddenly LeMon released her. She fell to her knees, gagging, spitting out the capsules, pulling them out with her fingers. Gasping, she dragged herself up a wall and slapped at the light switch. The two men were crashing against walls, floors. Beck had the bulk, but LeMon, to her horror, had a blade. Beck's shirt was cut and he was bleeding. Jolie was terrified at the thought of losing him . . . of him losing his life because of her. She looked around for a weapon. She remembered the fire extinguisher in the bedroom, and then she spied the great frozen zucchini brick at her feet. She hefted it, rushed forward, and brought it down on the back of LeMon's head. The sound of frozen bread connecting with flesh was . . . satisfying, actually.

LeMon dropped like a stone, his knife clattering to the floor.

Beck was at her side in two strides. He cupped his hands around her face. "Are you all right?" he demanded, his voice rasping.

She nodded, then burst into tears. Third time and counting.

Twenty-five

Carlotta's eyes widened. "They were going to do *what*?"

"Murder their wives," Jolie repeated. "Among other things."

"I don't believe it," Carlotta said, setting her bottle of Pellegrino on the table.

Yesterday Jolie had spent most of the day with the police, this morning, she and the girls were at the Crepe House playing catch-up.

"I don't believe that *Russell* would do it," Hannah said.

"Supposedly, his wife was next," Jolie said. "That's why Gary was at Sammy's party—to warn Mrs. Island."

"So that's why he was with Roger LeMon's wife at the river?"

Jolie nodded. "Gary said on the audiotape that after he stumbled onto the fact that the four men were going to get rid of their wives, he told LeMon *he* would do it, then he picked up Janet LeMon under the pretense of taking her to the airport to go on her retreat. He took her to the river to tell her what her husband was planning to do and taped the conversation so she could have a copy for protection. But LeMon had followed them to make sure Gary did it, and when he saw he'd been double-crossed, LeMon shot his wife himself. Took a shot at Gary, too, but it only grazed him. He dove into the water and floated downstream until he thought it was safe to get out, then hiked to my place and took off in my car."

A mistake, he'd said on the tape, because by doing so, he'd gotten her involved. He'd wept, apologizing. That had been the hardest part to listen to. He'd been surprised when Jolie had filed a missing persons report, surprised that she'd cared enough. He hadn't wanted to expose her to his shady friends, hadn't wanted to put her in danger. But when she'd filed that report, she had implicated herself irrevocably. That had tortured him, he'd said.

"He stayed hidden because he wanted LeMon to think he was dead?" Carlotta asked.

"Right."

"So how did Gary get involved with them in the first place?"

"On the tape, he said he met LeMon and started doing little things for him—getting game tickets, that kind of thing. LeMon gave him a lot of referrals, introduced him to Kyle Coffee, Russell Island, and their other pal, Gordon Beaure. After a while, he was working for them almost exclusively. He rented the condo on West Peachtree for their leisure, then handled the sale when they decided to buy the property. He arranged for hookers, bought drugs for them—he even bought a gun for LeMon and taught him how to shoot it."

She swallowed, remembering the desperation in Gary's

voice on the tape. *"I've done some bad things in my life and I've done business with some bad people, but Roger LeMon is a cold-blooded killer, as cold as they come."*

"Who is Gordon Beaure?"

"He owns a liquor distribution company. He wasn't around as much, but Salyers said he had just taken out a multimillion-dollar life insurance policy on his wife."

Carlotta shuddered. "Creepy."

"Yeah," Hannah said. "I wanted Russell to leave his wife; I had no idea he was planning to kill her."

"Or to have her killed, more likely," Jolie said. "Gary said they were all planning accidents. In fact, the police are looking into the possibility that Kyle Coffee might have been killed in the 'accident' that had been previously arranged for his wife. Apparently, he was having second thoughts."

"LeMon will probably get the needle for killing his wife and Gary," Carlotta said.

Jolie pursed her mouth. "And possibly Coffee. Plus he hired the guy who tried to run me off the road. And Gary's tape probably seals LeMon's fate for shooting his wife, but there's still no physical evidence linking him directly to Gary's murder."

"But the creep is going to be charged with attempted murder too, right, for what he did to you at your apartment?"

She nodded solemnly. She could still feel his fingers pressed against her mouth, could still hear his voice in her mind. *"Time to die."* The man's ruthlessness was stunning, even more so considering the fact that he moved comfortably in such polite circles.

"Beck saved your life," Carlotta said pointedly.

Jolie nodded and stared at her hands. Beck.

"So what's going on with you two?"

Twice they'd met to talk, and twice they'd wound up making love instead. Jolie adopted an innocent expression. "Nothing."

"Liar."

She flushed. "I *am* supposed to meet him in a few minutes to show him a house before my afternoon shift, but that's the extent of our relationship—strictly professional."

The fact that he'd had his secretary call that morning to arrange the appointment seemed like a clear indication that he was trying to create distance between them. She knew she should just be grateful for the commission she would earn, but now that she had her life back, her imagination appeared to be running full-throttle with possibilities: a successful business, lively friendships, a love for all time . . .

The girls were staring at her, and for a moment she was afraid she'd said that out loud. "I need to run," she chirped, springing up from her chair. She left cash for her meal and waved, thinking she shouldn't have eaten anything on her nervous stomach. One thing that lifted her spirits was the sight of her Mercury sitting at the curb— Detective Salyers had pulled a few strings. It was nice to have a piece of her old life back, although admittedly, she didn't want *all* of her old life back. She felt as if she'd been given a second chance, and she was going to live life more largely than before.

Minus the party crashing, of course.

At red lights, she reviewed the listing that Beck wanted to see. The house was in the most exclusive neighborhood in Buckhead—Sammy's favorite, in fact. She'd be cross-eyed with jealousy if Jolie managed to sell one of the elite properties. The home was enormous and chock full of amenities, with a price tag to match. Secretly, she was disappointed that Beck had gone the "bigger is better" route, although her inner agent told her to keep her idealistic mouth shut. It wasn't as if he were buying a home for them to share. Besides, a tiny voice inside of her promised, *If he buys a big house, he might stay in Atlanta.* Not that she'd be running into him at the country club.

She pulled up to the house a few minutes early, which would give her time to scout out the uber-structure. From the looks of it, she was going to need a map. She removed the door key from the lockbox device and let herself in the front door.

Huge. Colossal. Gargantuan. She toured the first floor quickly to get a feel for the layout and the yards (plural), then she climbed the stairs and checked the rooms for the best views. She heard the front door open and close, and her heartrate kicked up in anticipation of seeing Beck again. She walked to the landing and looked over, then felt her smile dissolve.

Sammy was frowning up at her.

"What are you doing here?" they asked in unison.

"I'm showing the house to a client," Jolie said.

"Who?" Sammy asked suspiciously.

"Beck Underwood."

Sammy frowned harder and Jolie had the distinct feeling that Sammy wanted to stamp her foot.

Jolie crossed her arms. "What are *you* doing here?" she asked again.

"I just finished showing a house two doors down, and I saw what I *thought* was your car in the driveway."

In other words, it drew attention because it wasn't a

nice-enough car to be in this neighborhood. Jolie checked her watch. "I don't mean to be rude, but my client should be here any minute."

But Sammy walked across the foyer and up the stairs. "While I'm here, I'll just look around."

Jolie glared as the woman sashayed by her on the landing. Her cell phone rang and she pulled it out of her purse, thinking it might be Beck saying he was running late. But when she saw the 904 area code, she smiled—Leann. She had so much to tell her.

"Hello?"

"Is this Jolie Goodman?"

Jolie frowned. "Yes, who's this?"

"This is Rebecca Renaldi, Leann's sister. I'm calling about the card I just received."

Jolie smiled. "You didn't have to call—I hope you're recovering well. I'm so sorry for your loss."

"Jolie, one of us is confused. I didn't lose a baby— Leann did."

Jolie blinked. "What?"

"Leann lost her baby early Sunday morning. Personally, I think it was the long drive."

Gripping the phone tighter, Jolie said, "I thought Leann went to Jacksonville to take care of you."

"No, she came here so I could take care of *her*. Gary was going to join her later."

Starbursts flashed behind Jolie's eyelids. "Did you say 'Gary'?"

"Yeah, Gary—the father of her baby."

Jolie grasped the rail in front of her. Gary and Leann? Bits and pieces of conversations came flooding back to her: Leann telling her to stay away from Gary, exhibiting irritation if Jolie shared personal tidbits.

"I would've thought Leann had told you about the baby and about Gary, but she was probably waiting to see if it would work out this time."

"Th–this time?"

"They dated for about a year, then he broke it off, but she never really got over him. Actually, I was worried about her."

Gary's fatal attraction girlfriend. Leann had moved to the apartment complex within a couple of weeks of when she and Gary had started dating. In the laundry room, Leann had initiated a conversation and fostered a friendship.

"When you see her, you might not mention that I told you all of this."

"When I see her?" Jolie asked, her voice shaky.

"She left this morning to drive back to Atlanta, for good this time."

Jolie's pulse raced. "Earlier, you said something about losing the baby after a long d–drive."

"She drove back to Atlanta last Saturday, against my wishes. But she said she and Gary had some things to talk about."

"I wish you could drive up and crash the party with us. If you left now, you could make it."

Apparently, Leann had made it.

"Jolie, was I right to tell you about the baby?" Rebecca asked.

"Yes," she murmured. "I, um, need to go, though."

"Okay. Nice talking to you."

Jolie disconnected the call, completely numb. She needed to call Salyers. She flipped up the phone.

"Drop the phone, Jolie."

She looked over the rail and her heart stalled at the sight of Leann holding a handgun pointed up at her.

"I said drop it."

Jolie obeyed and the phone bounced down several steps. Leann hadn't told her to, but for some reason, it just felt right to hold her arms up while having a gun trained on her heart.

"That was my sister, wasn't it? I heard the tail end of your conversation. Did you call her?"

Jolie searched for her voice and found it cowering behind her liver. "No. Sh–she called me. I s–sent her a sympathy card. She was confused."

"Ah." Leann laughed. "I'd forgotten how damn polite you are." Her smile was squinty and mean. "It must have been one of the things that Gary loved about you."

"I d–don't think that Gary was in love with me."

"Sure he was," Leann said. "I could tell. Remember the day we all floated down the river? I could tell by the way he was around you."

Oh, God—she had invited them both. Although, in hindsight, Leann had finagled an invitation, no doubt gleeful at being able to torment him all day, reminding him that she could cozy up to any future girlfriend, keep tabs on him.

"The fire at his apartment?" Jolie asked.

"Me," Leann said, proudly.

"The *X* on my face in the photograph?"

"Me."

"The lipstick note to Gary?"

"Me, me, me."

And she'd thought that *Hannah* was scary. "Leann, I don't know how you found me, but my client will be here any minute. Why don't you put down the gun before someone gets hurt."

"You mean Beck Underwood? The man you took up with before Gary was even in the ground? He's not coming."

"The call from his secretary?"

"Me."

Okay, now she was truly terrified. Alone in the house with a crazed gunwoman, and no one around except Realtor Barbie, who was probably lost somewhere in the right wing. And her arms were getting really, really tired. She seriously needed to work on her upper body strength.

"Leann, what do you want?"

"You dead." Quick and to the point.

"What will that accomplish, except to mess up your life?"

Leann smiled. "It will mess up *your* life. Gary and I could have been together if you hadn't come along."

Out of corner of her eye, Jolie saw Sammy walking in front of the house, hands on hips, scowling at the dusty domestic car that Leann had arrived in. She must have found a back staircase and was walking the grounds.

"Leann, can we talk about this? If I had known that you were in love with Gary, I would never—"

"Shut up. I tried to like you, I truly did. Sometimes, I *did* like you. Do you know how many times I could have hurt you? Gary threatened me not to, but he's gone now. Come down here."

"I don't think—"

Leann fired a round into the wall behind Jolie.

"Okay," Jolie said. "I'm coming." She started down the stairs, half relieved, half terrified when she realized that the shot had caught Sammy's attention. The woman scowled at the house and was no doubt thinking about how they could keep out the riffraff agents and lookey-loos.

And she must have thought of something, because she was charging toward the house, a thundercloud on her brow.

Jolie was halfway down the stairs when Sammy pushed open the door like a bad wind, catching Leann between the shoulder blades. The gun went off as Leann went down—Jolie heard the *zwing* of the bullet going past her head.

"Sammy, she has a gun!" Jolie yelled.

But Sammy barely missed a beat as she stepped on Leann's back, reached into her Prada bag, and came out with her own gun, long and blue and a caliber that Clint Eastwood might carry. "Mine's new and it's bigger." She dug the heel of her Manolo Blahnik ankle-tie suede pump into Leann's spine. "I don't know who you are, but move and I'll blow your effing head off."

"She killed Gary," Jolie gasped, reaching for her dropped phone to dial 911.

Sammy glared down at her detainee. "You ruined my Ralph Lauren comforter. You're going to have to pay for that."

Twenty-Six

"It's like, I can't decide between the Ferragamo wedges and the Stuart Weitzman boots, you know?"

Kneeling on carpet-burned knees, Jolie peered at the tortured coed over a mountain of boxes. "Why don't you take both and decide when you get home? You can always return a pair later—if they don't show signs of wear."

The young woman's shoulders fell in relief. "You're *right*. I'll take them both."

"And the Dior sandals?" Jolie encouraged.

"Sure, why not?"

Jolie nodded with approval, scooped up the boxes, and trotted to the checkout counter before the girl could change her mind. Michael eyed the three boxes in her hands with an arched brow. "You're catching on," he murmured. "You just might last after all."

"He says again on my last day."

"Jolie, I understand why you're going back to your old

job, but it's not going to be nearly as exciting around here without you."

"It's not my *old* job," Jolie declared. "I'll be a partner." She smiled at him over her shoulder. "Someday maybe I'll be able to afford to buy a pair of shoes from you."

But Michael's remark rankled Jolie. Returning to the Sanders Agency felt as if she were taking a step backward. Not in pay, of course, but in life experience. Still, she would be secure . . . and alive. That was important, considering that just a few days ago her prognosis for living had not been encouraging.

She rang up the sale and thanked the customer, then glanced around the showroom, a little wistful about leaving after only two weeks.

The most eventful two weeks of her life. Leann had been charged with various and sundry crimes ranging from arson to murder to trespassing, but was already enjoying a nicely padded room at a psychiatric facility just outside of Atlanta. According to her sister Rebecca, Leann had suffered a lifelong history of mental instability, and the pregnancy had only exacerbated matters. Leann had told the police that after Gary disappeared, she was sure he was going to join her in Florida. When she discovered that instead of coming to her in his hour of need, Gary had sought out Jolie, Leann was incensed, and became increasingly distraught after her conversations with Jolie that Gary was not only still alive, but was watching Jolie—protecting her—while Leann waited in Florida, pregnant with his baby.

Suspecting that Gary would follow Jolie to Sammy's party, Leann had made the long drive to Atlanta and had disguised herself as one of the hired help for the evening.

Apparently, after listening to Jolie's party-crashing stories, she had decided to give it a try. Leann had heard Jolie say on numerous occasions that Sammy carried a gun in her purse—finding it had been a cinch, Leann said. She'd skulked around until Gary had appeared. When he sneaked upstairs carrying an armful of coats to the coat check room to follow Jolie, Leann had tailed him and confronted him about the baby. She said that when Gary had refused to accept the fact that the baby was his, she'd shot him through a fur stole to silence the gun and then stuck the gun in Jolie's coat pocket—Leann said she'd have known that shabby coat anywhere.

Ouch.

Jolie touched her temple. Leann was insane, but she wasn't devoid of feelings. The trauma of what she'd done had led to her miscarriage when she returned to Florida. The sadness of it all was so profound, Jolie could scarcely believe it had happened. She decided she might never know why Gary hadn't told her about Leann—had he been afraid it would incite Leann even more? Had he enjoyed taunting the poor woman? Had the baby truly been his? Endless questions had plagued her over the past three days since the incident that had exposed the group of conspirators, which the papers, every bit as slogan-savvy as the Yellow Pages, had dubbed the "Buckhead Brotherhood."

Roger LeMon was being held without bail in the murder of Janet LeMon. Russell Island had wasted no time turning state's evidence and spilling his guts about the foursome's evil plans to inherit their wives' trust funds. The story was a media sensation—part of the reason Jolie was leaving her job at Neiman's was that the security detail had to be increased to keep reporters and assorted weirdos from dogging her.

Strangely, Leann's appearance at the house had been a turning point for Jolie and Sammy. Sammy had admitted that she'd always been jealous of Jolie's relationship with her father. But since the agency's business had been sliding without Jolie's organizational skills to keep things moving, she'd made Jolie an attractive offer to come back. Jolie had held out for a partnership, and Sammy had finally agreed. There had been no hanky-panky between Sammy and Gary, although Sammy had admitted in a rare, sheepish moment that it wasn't for lack of trying on her part.

Beck had called a couple of times. Once they'd talked for a few minutes until the conversation had trailed off awkwardly. The next time, she had listened to his voice message but hadn't returned his call. She knew when to make a graceful exit. Of course, that hadn't kept her from lying awake at night thinking of him. Beck had been her first experience with full-on love, no doubt because her emotions had been running full-tilt since the day she'd met him. But eventually the bewilderment over the mess that Gary had introduced into her life would dissipate, and so would her intense longing for Beck Underwood.

"Hey, short-timer."

Jolie looked up to see Carlotta striding toward her wearing her trademark gapped grin. "Hey yourself."

"I can't believe you're leaving us to go back to Realtor Barbie."

Jolie gave her a wry smile. "Well, she did save my life."

"Is that all?"

"And I'm better at selling houses than I am at selling shoes."

Carlotta nodded. "As long as it's what you truly want."

A little laugh escaped Jolie's throat. "Who gets what they truly want?"

Carlotta studied her for a few seconds. "Are you okay?"

Jolie nodded. "Just a little sad, I suppose, about leaving." About returning to her previous life.

"If it makes you feel any better, I came to tell you that you've inspired me."

Jolie frowned. "How?"

Carlotta's hands fluttered with excitement. "I don't have all the kinks worked out yet, but I want to start a business to place products at high-class functions. I'm calling it Product Impressions. A designer would come to me with, say, a fabulous coat, then I'd hire a model to wear the coat to important places."

Jolie grinned. "And to crash parties?"

A sly smile crawled over Carlotta's face. "Let's just say I would take advantage of any advertising venue that presented itself."

"I'm sure it will be a raging success," Jolie said, then lowered her voice. "How's the other . . . situation?"

Carlotta's smile faded. "Don't worry—my brother and I will work it out." Then she winked. "Call me Monday and we'll have lunch next week, okay?"

Jolie nodded and waved goodbye, glad to have one good relationship to show for her ordeal. She crossed the showroom floor to clean up a few cardboard fillers and stray boxes. Time to clock out and go home.

"Excuse me, ma'am."

"I'm sorry," she said, turning. "My shift . . . just . . . ended." Her mouth went dry. Beck, looking much the same as a few days ago, but so good to her eyes that she was embarrassed for herself.

"Hi," he said.

She swallowed painfully. "Hi."

"How are you?"

"I'm good." Desperate for something to do with her hands, she gestured vaguely toward the showroom. "This is my last day."

He lifted his eyebrows. "Oh?"

"I'm going back to work at the Sanders Agency, except this time it will be Sanders and Goodman."

He grinned. "That's great. I'm . . . happy for you . . . if that's what you want."

Why did everyone keep saying that? She nodded cheerfully, pleased that she at least could share that news before she never saw him again, but wishing she could be as enthusiastic about going back to the agency as she rightfully should be. Jolie manufactured a smile, trying to steel herself against the physical sway he still commanded over her. "Are you shoe shopping?" she asked.

"Actually, yes." He shifted his big body from foot to foot and glanced around at the displays. "I'm going to be needing a couple of pairs of rugged shoes to take back with me."

Her heart jerked sideways. "You're returning to Costa Rica?"

He nodded. "Della is doing great, and she always was much more interested in the family business than I was. I'm just not cut out for Atlanta, at least not at this phase in my life."

She nodded. The not-ready-to-settle-down phase. "Well . . . congratulations." Talking was the best distraction for her stupid heart. She swept her arm out like a game-show hostess. "Perhaps you'd like to see our Gortex boots?"

"Sure . . . how about two pair?"

"Okay."

He captured her hand. "One pair of men's and one pair of women's."

Jolie startled at the bolt of desire that his mere touch summoned. "I don't understand."

His Adam's apple bobbed. "Jolie, I was wondering if you might like to . . . come with me."

Her eyes widened. "To visit Costa Rica?"

"No . . . to live there . . . with me."

She blinked. "Live there . . . with you?"

He nodded, then entwined their fingers. "Oh, I know it's not a partnership in a brokerage company, but I was thinking of a different kind of partnership: Underwood and Goodman."

She was struck mute.

"Jolie," he said softly, "do you remember when you said that people like me don't need anything?"

"I think you're paraphrasing."

"Humor me."

"Yes, I do."

"Well, you were right—partially. I've lived a charmed life, and I've never known what it felt like to need something." He pressed his lips together. "To need . . . someone." A flush rose on his cheeks. "The truth is, you were also right when you accused me of viewing you as a project."

Jolie's heart dipped to her stomach.

He squeezed her hand. "I'm ashamed to say that you were a project to fill a void in my heart. I was selfishly trying to force my affection on you when your life was crazy. Now, I'm being selfish again, but I want to take you away from the bad memories where we can learn everything about each other in a beautiful, exotic land." He lifted her hand and kissed her fingers. "Come with me. Think of what an adventure we'll have."

Her heart vaulted to her throat. "What if I say no?"

"Then I'll have to stay in Atlanta and pester you until you say yes."

"But . . . what would I do in Costa Rica?"

He shrugged. "Sell real estate, sell shoes, sell coffee beans." He pulled her closer. "You can start over . . . *We* can start over. The truth is, Jolie, I'm crazy in love with you."

"You are?"

"Since the day you crashed into me." He lowered his mouth to hers for a slow, sensuous kiss, and Jolie felt herself crumbling, wanting, hoping. Her mind reeled at the possibilities . . . and the risk.

When he pulled back, he squinted. "What's going on in that pretty head of yours?"

"I . . . don't have a passport."

His mouth quirked. "That we can fix. Is that all?"

"I . . . don't have boots."

"Good thing we're in the middle of the shoe department."

Jolie felt engorged with emotion, yet paralyzed with uncertainty. The words were shouting in her heart, but cowering on her tongue. Could she dare say them? Snatches of scenes from the past few days flashed in her mind. Life was so fragile, so random . . . she had nothing to lose, except everything. She could stay in Atlanta and live comfortably and quietly.

Then something Carlotta had said came floating back to her. *"You're too young to be comfortable."*

"Jolie," he said, his eyes questioning. "Is that all?"

"No." She wet her lips. "I . . . I love you too, Beck." She said the words on a long breath that left her lungs empty.

"You do?"

She nodded. "Since the day *you* crashed into *me*."

He whooped and lowered another kiss to her mouth. She poured all her hopes and dreams into the kiss. Beck seemed to understand the leap of faith she was taking and his mouth promised she wouldn't be sorry.

"Get a room!" someone shouted.

Beck lifted his head and grinned at her, his dark eyes shining. "What do you say? My room is five minutes away."

Jolie laughed. "I say . . . let's go crash."

Epilogue

"Take these for sure," Beck said, holding up a pair of miniscule pink lace panties and wagging his eyebrows.

Jolie bounced a rolled-up pair of socks off his arm. "*I'll* sort through my underwear drawer, thank you very much." Then she looked around and sighed. Her bedroom floor was covered with cardboard boxes and crates bound for Goodwill. "Besides, I won't have room in my suitcase for something so impractical."

Beck tucked the panties into the pocket of his T-shirt and gave it a pat. "I got you covered." He grinned and swooped in for a kiss. "In fact, I will personally see to the safe arrival of any sexy underwear you want to take to Costa Rica."

She lifted her arms around his neck and leaned into him for a slow, rocking kiss. She could scarcely wait until they were in Costa Rica together. Long, warm nights lying heart to heart. She couldn't have hoped to be this happy.

"The Goodwill truck will be here soon," he said. "I'm going to start carrying boxes to the curb."

Jolie nodded. "I just have a few more things to sort through." She watched with bittersweet excitement as he hoisted a box of her former life to his shoulder and maneuvered his way through her bedroom door. She turned and caught sight of herself in the mirror of the bureau that was bound for storage. Wild, blonde curls, wide eyes, pink cheeks—she'd never looked or felt so alive.

The past week had been a flurry of packing and planning. Sammy had told Jolie she would have a job at the Sanders Agency if things didn't work out in Costa Rica, and while Jolie was grateful for the offer, she had no doubt that she and Beck would be together always. Since the day he'd come to the department store to ask her to go with him, they had scarcely been apart. After the first couple of days of marathon lovemaking and nonstop talking, she had prepared herself for Beck to take an emotional step back, but instead, to her heart's joy, had discovered that Beck reveled in sharing details of his thoughts and experiences now that he had found someone like-minded. They were two people who had held themselves in check emotionally until each found the person who had the same bone-lonely look in their eyes. Jolie had felt herself unfolding more every day, like a party dress that had been left in a drawer, waiting for the special occasion that had finally arrived.

With a smile on her face, she sorted through her underwear drawer, and, remembering the gleam in Beck's eyes, threw out the sensible in favor of the sensual. Her cheeks warmed at the thought of their physical chemistry, how Beck was able to stir her senses with a look or a murmured word. At first she had to keep reminding herself that she deserved this chance at happiness, but the affirmation seemed to be working, because she had relaxed into the idea of accepting Beck's love.

Having exhausted the drawers in her bureau, Jolie turned to the bookshelf that made up the headboard of her bed. She pulled out *The Magic of Thinking Big* and a rueful smile played over her face at the book that Gary had insisted would change her life. In hindsight, it had: The book had given her confidence to quit the Sanders agency and try her hand at something new, and she wouldn't have met Carlotta or Beck otherwise. On her nightstand lay a padded envelope containing a new pink leather-bound journal that she was going to mail to Carlotta—perhaps she would send her Gary's favorite book as well to encourage her to pursue her idea for a product placement business.

Jolie thumbed through the book, and halfway through the pages stopped to reveal a white envelope simply marked "Jolie." Frowning, she removed the fat envelope and slid her finger beneath the flap. She gasped at the stack of cash inside—all large bills. Folded sheets of notebook paper cradled the money. Jolie withdrew the sheets, hands trembling. It was a handwritten letter from Gary.

Dear Jolie,

I'm leaving this letter in case something terrible happens to me. I'm sorry I got you involved in the mess of my personal life and the mess of my business dealings. Since you didn't get the envelope I sent earlier, these notes explain the crimes that were planned. I'm innocent of murder, but I'm not an innocent man—I figure if I die young, it's payment for other things I've gotten away with in my lifetime.

You see, Jolie, I really loved you . . . or maybe it was the thought of you. You reminded me that there are people in the world who are truly good, and I wanted to feed on your goodness. Unfortunately, I'm in too much trouble to extricate myself. I should have told you that your friend Leann Renaldi is a former girlfriend of mine with obsessive tendencies, although I don't think she'd ever hurt anyone, except maybe me. And if she does, I probably deserve it for the way I dumped her. I can be a real jerk, even though I tried hard not to let you see that part of my personality. You made me want to be a better person, Jolie.

Enclosed is repayment for your car I took the night Janet LeMon was killed, and a little extra for all the trouble I caused you. I hope you can put it to good use. I wish I had met you sooner, Jolie. I hope your life is long and full of happiness.

Gary

Jolie wiped at her eyes, grateful to have some explanation of why Gary had become involved with her in the first place, and what motivated his secretive behavior toward her. He must have entered her apartment and planted the envelope some time after he had talked to her from the backseat of her rental car . . . which explained the finger marks in the dust that she'd found, and the indications that someone had climbed through her bedroom window. She scanned the notes he'd left and decided they would go to Detective Salyers immediately to help fill any holes in the case against Roger LeMon. Then she counted the cash with growing wonder—fifteen thousand dollars.

Since her car had been returned to her, the cash Gary had left seemed extraneous.

Then an idea occurred to her. Jolie picked up the padded envelope containing the leather journal she was sending to Carlotta, and tucked two thousand dollars inside—enough to get the threatening collector off her friend's back. The rest she bundled into another envelope and addressed it to Rebecca Renaldi. A posthumous gift from Gary, Jolie explained, to put toward Leann's treatment. She sealed the envelope with mixed feelings pulling at her—incredulity over the randomness of how people's lives crossed and changed each other, remorse that the same human dramas seemed to play out over and over—greed, ambition, love and hate—with unpredictable results.

"Everything okay in here?" Beck asked from the doorway.

Jolie looked up and felt a rush of love for this amazing man. She set the envelopes aside and crossed the room to slip into his embrace. Tilting her head she smiled up at him. "Yes, everything is okay."

A little scoff escaped him and his eyes darkened with sudden desire before he lowered a kiss to her neck. "We have a few minutes before the truck gets here—what do you say we bypass okay and shoot for spectacular?"

Jolie arched into him and grinned. "Wow me."

What Every
Woman Knows . . .

Let's face it. No one wants to *admit* that they use their feminine wiles to catch a man . . . but the truth is we do! From the first moment he sees you in a sexy pair of high-heeled shoes to the moment he first glimpses you in your wedding gown, a man often doesn't know how much effort we've taken to dress to impress! And while blatantly trying to catch a guy is definitely a "don't," there are little touches that any woman can wear that will make a man take notice.

As for our Avon Romance heroines, they *all* know that a little bit can go a long, long way. And, sometimes, when the going gets tough, it's worth it to pull out all the stops.

Now let's take a peek as four intrepid heroines captivate the interest of the men of their dreams. . . .

Coming May 2004

Party Crashers
by Stephanie Bond

Jolie Goodman's life's a mess. Her boyfriend vanished months ago—with her car! She's broke and working in the Neiman Marcus shoe department, selling tantalizing but financially (for her!) out-of-reach footwear to the women whose credit cards aren't maxed out. And now, the police have come looking for her . . . thinking that she has something to do with her boyfriend's disappearance! But sometimes selling sexy shoes is just as enticing to men as wearing them.

Jolie glanced at the doorway leading back to the showroom, then to the fire exit door leading to a loading dock, weighing her options. She had the most outrageous urge to walk out . . . and keep walking.

Is that what Gary had done? Reached some kind of personal crisis that he couldn't share with her, and simply walked away from everything—his job, his friends, and her? As bad as it sounded, she almost preferred to believe that he had suffered some kind of breakdown rather than consider other possible explanations: he'd met with foul play or she had indeed been scammed by the man who'd professed to care about her.

The exit sign beckoned, but she glanced at the shoe box in her hands and decided that since the man had been kind enough to intercept Sammy, he deserved to be waited on, even if he didn't spend a cent.

Even if people with vulgar money made her nervous.

She fingercombed her hair and tucked it behind her ears, then straightened her clothing as best she could. There was no helping the lack of makeup, so she pasted on her best smile—the one that she thought showed too much gum, but that Gary had assured her made her face light up—and returned to the showroom.

Her smile almost faltered, though, when Mr. Beck Underwood's bemused expression landed on her.

She walked toward him, trying to forget that the man could buy and sell her a thousand times over. "I'm sorry again about running into you. Did you really want to try on this shoe or were you just being nice?"

"Both," he said mildly. "My sister is going to be a while, and I need shoes, so this works for me."

At the twinkle in his eyes, her tongue lodged at the roof of her mouth. Like a mime, she gestured to a nearby chair and made her feet follow him. As he sat she scanned the area for signs of Sammy.

"She's behind the insoles rack," he whispered.

Jolie flushed and made herself not look. The man probably thought she was clumsy *and* paranoid. She busied herself unpacking the expensive shoes. "Will you be needing a dress sock, sir?"

He slipped off his tennis shoe and wiggled bare brown toes. "I suppose so. I'm afraid I've gotten into the habit of not wearing socks." He smiled. "And my dad is 'sir.' I'm just Beck."

She suddenly felt small. And poor. "I . . . know who you are."

"Ah. Well, promise you won't hold it against me."

She smiled and retrieved a pair of tan-colored socks to match the loafers. When she started to slip one of the socks over his foot, he took it from her. "I can do it."

"I don't mind," she said quickly. Customers expected it—to be dressed and undressed and re-dressed if necessary. It was an unwritten rule: *No one leaves the store without being touched.*

"I don't have to be catered to," he said, his tone brittle.

Jolie blinked. "I'm sorry."

He looked contrite and shook his head. "Don't be—it's me." Then he grinned unexpectedly. "Besides, under more private circumstances, I might take you up on your offer."

Heat climbed her neck and cheeks—he was teasing her . . . his good deed for the day. Upon closer scrutiny, his face was even more interesting—his eyes a deep brown, bracketed by untanned lines created from squinting in the sun. Late thirties, she guessed. His skin was ruddy, his strong nose peeling from a recent burn. Despite the pale streaks in his hair, he was about as far from a beach boy as a man could be. When he leaned over to slip on the shoes, she caught a glimpse of his powerful torso beneath the sport coat.

She averted her gaze and concentrated on the stitched design on the vamp of the shoe he was trying on, handing him a shoehorn to protect the heel counter. (This morning Michael had given her an "anatomy of a shoe" lesson, complete with metal pointer and pop quiz.)

The man stood and hefted his weight from foot to foot, then took a couple of steps in one direction and came back. "I'll take them."

A salesperson's favorite words. She smiled. "That was fast."

He laughed. "Men don't have a complicated relationship with shoes."

And the Bride Wore Plaid
by Karen Hawkins

What is to be done with Kat Macdonald? This Scottish miss is deplorably independent, and unweddably wild. But while it's impossible to miss her undeniable beauty, it's also impossible to get Kat to act like a civilized lady. Still, even she cannot resist Devon St. John. A man born to wealth and privilege, he has no intention of ever settling down with one woman . . . until he meets Kat and realizes that his future wife will, indeed, proudly wear plaid.

Devon lifted a finger and traced the curve of her cheek, the touch bemusingly gentle. "You are a lush, tempting woman, my dear. And well you know it."

Kat's defenses trembled just the slightest bit. Bloody hell, how was she to fight her own treacherous body while the bounder—Devon something or another—tossed compliments at her with just enough sincerity to leave her breathless to hear more?

Of course, it was all practiced nonsense, she told herself firmly. She was anything but tempting. She looked well enough when she put some effort into it, but she was large and ungainly, and it was way too early in the morning for her to look anything other than pale. Her eyes were still heavy with sleep and she'd washed her hair last night and it had dried in a most unruly, puffy way that she absolutely detested. One side was definitely fuller than the other and it disturbed her no end. Even worse, she was wearing one of her work gowns of plain gray wool, one that was far too tight about the shoulders and too loose about the waist. Thus, she was able to meet his gaze and say firmly, "I am not tempting."

"I'd call you tempting and more," Devon said with refreshing promptness. "Your eyes shimmer rich and green. Your hair is the color of the morning sky just as the sun touches it, red and gold at the same time. And the rest of you—" His gaze traveled over her until her cheeks burned. "The rest of you is—"

"That's enough of that," she said hastily. "You're full of moonlight and shadows, you are."

"I don't know anything about moonlight and shadows. I only know you are a gorgeous, lush armful."

"In this?" She looked down at her faded gown with incredulity. "You'd call this gorgeous or lush?"

His gaze touched on her gown, lingering on her breasts. "Oh yes. If you want to go unnoticed, you'll have to bind those breasts of yours."

She choked.

He grinned. "And add some padding of some sort in some other areas."

"I don't know what you're talking about, but please let me up—"

"I was talking about padding. Perhaps if you bundled yourself about the hips until you looked plumper, then you wouldn't have to deal with louts such as myself attempting to kiss you at every turn."

She caught the humor sparkling in his eyes and it disarmed her, even as the thought of adding padding to her hips made her chest tickle as a laugh began to form.

"Furthermore," he continued as if he'd never paused, "you will need to hide those eyes of yours and perhaps wear a turban, if you want men like me to stop noticing you."

"Humph. I'll remember that the next time I run into you or any other of Strathmore's lecherous cronies. Now, if you'll let me go, I have things to do."

His eyes twinkled even more. "And if I refuse?"

"Then I will have to deal with you, myself."

"Oh-oh! A woman of spirit. I like that."

"Oh-oh," she returned sharply, "a man who does not prize his appendages."

That comment was meant to wither him on the vine. Instead he chuckled, the sound rich and deep. "Sweet, I prize my appendage, although it should be *your* job to admire it."

"I have no wish for such a job, thank you very much."

"Oh, but if you did, it would then be my job to wield that appendage in such a way as to rouse that admiration to a vocal level." Devon leaned forward and murmured in her ear, "You have a delicious moan, my sweet. I heard it when we kissed."

Her cheeks burned. "The only vocal rousing you're going to get from me is a scream for help."

A bit of the humor left his gaze and he said with apparent seriousness, "I would give my life trying to earn that moan yet again. Would you deny me that?"

Coming July 2004

I'm No Angel
by Patti Berg

Palm Beach's sexiest investigator, Angel Devlin, knows that a tight skirt, a hint of cleavage, and some sky high heels will usually help her get every kind of information out of any type of man. But millionaire bad boy Tom Donovan has something up his custom-made shirt sleeve, and even though Angel is using every trick she knows, it's proving far more difficult than usual to get what she wants.

Tom grinned wickedly. "I caught you."

"But you didn't come after me."

"I hoped you'd come back."

"Why? So you could personally haul me off to jail?"

Tom shook his head. "Because I liked the feel of your hands on my chest and your lips on my cheek. If I hauled you off to jail we'd end up enemies. The fact that you came back means there's a chance for more."

"You know nothing about me but my name." *And the feel of my body,* Angel thought, just barely hanging on to her composure as Tom's hands glided down the curve of her spine, then flared over the sides of her waist and settled on her hips. "Why would you want more?"

"I paid Jorge for a lot more information than just your name," he said. "I know you're a private investigator and that you cater to the ultra-rich. I know that your office-slash-home is right here on Worth Avenue in a building you share with Ma Petite Bow-Wow, the local pamper-your-pooch shop. And if Jorge knows what he's talking about, you're thirty years old, five feet eight inches tall, weigh one thirty-two—"

"Thirty-one dripping wet."

Tom grinned, his laughing gaze locking onto hers. "Should we get naked and dripping wet and weigh each other?"

"Not tonight."

"It's close to midnight. It'll soon be tomorrow."

"Are you always in such a rush to get naked and dripping wet?"

He shrugged lightly. "Depends on the woman."

"Trust me, I'm the wrong woman."

"I disagree."

The music picked up tempo and so did Tom's moves. He spun around with Angel captured in his arms, the heat of his embrace, the closeness of their cheeks, and the scent of his spicy aftershave overwhelming her, making her dizzy.

And then he slowed again. His heart beat against her breasts. Warm breath whispered against her ear. "From what Jorge told me—that you wear Donna Karan's Cashmere Mist and Manolo Blahniks if you can get them on sale—you could easily be the right woman. Of course, there's also the fact that you're soft in all the right places. And going back to your original question, *that*, Angel, is why I want more of you."

Angel laughed lightly. "Jorge was a virtual font of information."

"I figured the soft-in-all-the-right-places part out for myself," Tom said, his hands drifting slowly from her waist to her bottom.

She leaned back slightly and gave him the evil eye. "Excuse me, but we don't know each other well enough for you to touch me where you're touching me."

A grin escaped his perfect lips. It sparkled in his eyes and made the dimple at the side of his mouth deepen as his fingers began to slide again, but not up to her waist. Oh, no, lascivious Tom Donovan's fingers slithered down to her thighs.

That was the first really big mistake he'd made since he'd chosen to follow her.

His fingers stilled, his eyes narrowed, and she knew he'd found the one thing she didn't want anyone to find.

Again his hand began to move, to explore, gliding up and down, over and around the not-so-little-lump on her right thigh. His eyes focused even more as his gaze held hers and locked. "That wouldn't be what I think it is, would it?"

Angel smiled slowly. Wickedly. At last, she again had the upper hand. "If you think it's a slim but extremely sharp stainless steel stiletto that could carve out a man's Adam's apple in the blink of an eye, you've guessed right."

One of Tom's dark, bedeviled eyebrows rose. "I never would have expected a sweet thing like you to carry a stiletto."

"That, Mr. Donovan, just goes to show that you really don't know as much about me as you think you do."

Coming August 2004

A Perfect Bride
by Samantha James

Sometimes expensive clothes and shoes aren't what does the trick . . . occasionally, men simply can't resist the power of a damsel in distress . . . an ugly duckling who unexpectedly turns into a gorgeous swam. When Sebastian Sterling rescues Devon, a wounded tavern maid, he thinks she's a thief—or worse. But underneath her tattered clothes is a woman of astonishing beauty and pride, who he quickly discovers could become his perfect bride.

Jimmy pointed a finger. "My lord, there be a body in the street!"

No doubt whoever it was had had too much to drink. Sebastian very nearly advised his man to simply move it and drive on.

But something stopped him. His gaze narrowed. Perhaps it was the way the "body," as Jimmy called it, lay sprawled against the uneven brick, beneath the folds of the cloak that all but enshrouded what looked to be a surprisingly small form. His booted heels rapped sharply on the brick as he leaped down and strode forward with purposeful steps. Jimmy remained where he was in the seat, looking around with wary eyes, as if he feared they would be set upon by thieves and minions at any moment.

Hardly an unlikely possibility, Sebastian conceded silently.

Sebastian crouched down beside her, his mind working. She was filthy and bedraggled. A whore who'd imbibed too heavily? Or perhaps it was a trick, a ruse to bring him in close, so she could snatch his pocketbook.

Guardedly he shook her, drawing his hand back, quickly. Damn. He'd left his gloves on the seat in the carriage. Ah, well, too late now.

"Mistress!" he said loudly. "Mistress, wake up!"

She remained motionless.

An odd sensation washed over him. His wariness vanished. His gaze slid sharply to his hand. The tips of his fingers were wet, but it was not the wetness of rain, he realized. This was dark and sticky and thick.

He inhaled sharply. "Christ!" he swore. He moved without conscious volition, swiftly easing her to her side so he could see her. "Mistress," he said urgently, "can you hear me?"

She moved a little, groaning as she raised her head. Sebastian's heart leaped. She was groggy but alive!

Between the darkness and the ridiculously oversized covering he supposed must pass for a bonnet, he couldn't see much of her face. Yet he knew the precise moment awareness set in. When her eyes opened and she spied him bending over her, she cringed and gave a great start. "Don't move," he said quickly. "Don't be frightened."

Her lips parted. Her eyes moved over his features in what seemed a never-ending moment. Then she gave a tiny shake of her head. "You're lost," she whispered, sounding almost mournful, "aren't you?"

Sebastian blinked. He didn't know quite what he'd expected her to say—certainly not *that*.

"Of course I'm not lost."

"Then I must be dreaming." To his utter shock, a small hand came out to touch the center of his lip. "Because no man in the world could possibly be as handsome as you."

An unlikely smile curled his mouth. "You haven't seen my brother," he started to say. He didn't finish, however. All at once the girl's eyes fluttered shut. Sebastian caught her head before it hit the uneven brick. In the next instant he surged to his feet and whirled, the girl in his arms.

"Jimmy!" he bellowed.

But Jimmy had already ascertained his needs. "Here, my lord." The steps were down, the carriage door wide open.

Sebastian clambered inside, laying the girl on the seat. Jimmy peered within. "Where to, my lord?"

Sebastian glanced down at the girl's still figure. Christ, she needed a physician. He thought of Dr. Winslow, the family physician, only to recall that Winslow had retired to the country late last week. And there was hardly time to scour the city in search of another . . .

"Home," he ordered grimly. "And hurry, Jimmy."

Carnival Elation

7 Day Exotic Western Caribbean Itinerary

DAY	PORT	ARRIVE	DEPART
Sun	Galveston		4:00 P.M.
Mon	"Fun Day" at Sea		
Tue	Progreso/Merida	8:00 A.M.	4:00 P.M.
Wed	Cozumel	9:00 A.M.	5:00 P.M.
Thu	Belize	8:00 A.M.	6:00 P.M.
Fri	"Fun Day" at Sea		
Sat	"Fun Day" at Sea		
Sun	Galveston	8:00 A.M.	

TERMS AND CONDITIONS

PAYMENT SCHEDULE:
50% due upon booking
Full and final payment due by July 26, 2004

Acceptable forms of payment are Visa, MasterCard, American Express, Discover and checks. The cardholder must be one of the passengers traveling. A fee of $25 will apply for all returned checks. Check payments must be made payable to **Advantage International, LLC and sent to: Advantage International, LLC, 195 North Harbor Drive, Suite 4206, Chicago, IL 60601**

CHANGE/CANCELLATION:
Notice of change/cancellation must be made in writing to Advantage International, LLC.

Change:
Changes in cabin category may be requested and can result in increased rate and penalties. A name change is permitted 60 days or more prior to departure and will incur a penalty of $50 per name change. Deviation from the group schedule and package is a cancellation.

Cancellation:
181 days or more prior to departure	$250 per person
121 - 180 days or more prior to departure	50% of the package price
120 - 61 days prior to departure	75% of the package price
60 days or less prior to departure	100% of the package price (nonrefundable)

US and Canadian citizens are required to present a valid passport or the original birth certificate and state issued photo ID (drivers license). All other nationalities must contact the consulate of the various ports that are visited for verification of documentation.

We strongly recommend trip cancellation insurance!

For further details call 1-877-ADV-NTGE or visit www.GetCaughtReadingatSea.com

----

For booking form and complete information
go to www.getcaughtreadingatsea.com or call 1-877-ADV-NTGE

Complete coupon and booking form and mail both to:
**Advantage International, LLC,
195 North Harbor Drive, Suite 4206, Chicago, IL 60601**